11/20

THE KING OF CROWS

a DIVINERS novel

LIBBA BRAY

ATOM

First published in Great Britain in 2020 by Atom

3 5 7 9 10 8 6 4 2

A CIP catalogue record for this book is available from the British Library.

ISBN: 978-1-907-41046-8

Printed and bound in Great Britain by Clays Ltd, Elcograf S.p.A.

Papers used by Atom are from well-managed forests
and other responsible sources.

Atom
An imprint of
Little, Brown Book Group
Carmelite House
50 Victoria Embankment
London EC4Y 0DZ

An Hachette UK Company
www.hachette.co.uk

www.atombooks.co.uk

For my mother, Nancy Crockett Bray

One need not be a Chamber—to be Haunted....
Ourself, behind ourself, concealed—should startle most.

—Emily Dickinson, "One need not be
a Chamber—to be Haunted"

But I almost think we are all of us ghosts....It is not only
what we have inherited from our father and mother that
"walks" in us. It is all sorts of dead ideas, and lifeless
old beliefs, and so forth. They have no vitality, but they
cling to us all the same, and we cannot shake them off.
Whenever I take up a newspaper, I seem to see ghosts
gliding between the lines. There must be ghosts all the
country over, as thick as the sands of the sea. And then
we are, one and all, so pitifully afraid of the light.

—Henrik Ibsen, *Ghosts*

The question, O me! so sad, recurring—What good
    amid these, O me, O life?

            Answer.
That you are here—that life exists and identity,
That the powerful play goes on, and you may contribute
    a verse.

            —Walt Whitman, "Oh Me! Oh Life!"

IT BEGINS

Somewhere in America

On the last day that the town of Beckettsville would ever know, the weather was so fine you could see all the way to the soft blue skin of the horizon. The land in this part of the country was beautiful. Tall wheat tickled the spring air. Fat maples offered summertime shade. There was a fine-looking Main Street boasting a post office, a hardware store, a filling station with two gasoline pumps out front, a grocery, a pharmacy, a small hotel with a downstairs cafe that served warm apple pie, and a barbershop whose revolving red-white-and-blue pole thrilled the children, a daily magic trick.

A round clock mounted to the front of City Hall's domed tower showed the passage of time, which, in Beckettsville, seemed to move slower than in other places. The people worked hard and tried to be good neighbors. They sang in church choirs and attended Rotary and Elks Club meetings. They played bridge on Friday nights. Held picnics near the bandstand under the July sun. Canned summer peaches for the long winter. Got excited by the arrival of a new Philco radio, electric icebox, or automobile, everybody crowding 'round to see progress unloaded from the back of a truck by grunting, sweaty men. The people lived in neat rows of neat houses with indoor plumbing and electric lights, attended one of the town's four churches (Methodist, Presbyterian, Baptist, and Congregationalist), sent their dead to the Perkins & Son Funeral Parlor over on Poplar Street for embalming, and buried those same dead in the cemetery up on the hill at the edge of town, far from the bustle of Main Street.

As the clock counted down to the horrors awaiting Beckettsville, population four hundred five souls, Pastor Jacobs stepped out of First Methodist Church thinking of that apple pie over at the Blue Moon Cafe—so delicious the way Enola Gaylord served it, with a dollop of cream, and it really was a shame he would not get to enjoy Beckettsville's favorite pie today or any day thereafter. The pastor nodded and said "Afternoon" to sweet Charlie

Banks, who swept the sidewalk free of spring blossoms in front of McNeill's Hardware. Charlie mooned over the approach of pretty schoolteacher Cora Nettles. As Cora marched past him (her own thoughts occupied by a silly but maddening argument she'd had with her mother over the new pink hat Cora now wore—it most certainly was *not* "unbecoming of a serious woman"!), Charlie sighed, thinking that tomorrow, or perhaps the day after, he would finally summon the courage to ask her to the picture show over in Fairview and that she might answer sweetly, *Why, Charlie Banks, I would love to!* so that the world of his heart, which Charlie held so tightly in his fist, would open into the bright, fresh bloom of his long-desired future.

Down that same Main Street, Mikey Piccolo, age ten and with his mind firmly fixed on baseball, tossed the day's *Beckettsville Gazette* over picket fences from a satchel stretched around his neck as if he were Waite Hoyt. He could hear the imaginary crowd roaring inside his head as he narrowly missed Ida Olsen, who played with her rag dolls under the leafy canopy of a sycamore tree at Number Ten Main Street. She stuck her tongue out at the back of Mikey's head but quickly moved to the other side of the giant tree to continue her game, out of sight of the Widow Winters, who had just come onto her front porch. Ida did not care to be pulled into a long conversation about boring things from the past—cotillions, which were dances, apparently, and Times When Neighbors Acted More Neighborly. It was never worth the butterscotch candies the old lady offered from the pocket of her apron, and so Ida kept well hidden. From her perch on the porch, Mrs. Euline Winters soothed herself with the gentle seesawing creak of her rocking chair and a lapful of knitting yarn as she watched the citizenry going about their busy business in the noonday sun. (*What a glorious afternoon it is! So warm and fragrant!*) Her crepe myrtle had blossomed, and the flowers, planted in happier times, reminded Euline of her husband, Wilbur, dead and gone these eight years, and did those people out there, her neighbors, know how lonely she was, sitting alone at her supper table each night, listening to the mocking tick of Wilbur's grandfather clock, with no one to ask, *And how was your day, my dear?*

There were other citizens out and about on this beautiful day. A mailman and the Rotary Club president. A dotting of mothers gathered around the butcher's counter, giving the day's order while scolding their unruly children. The town crank, who complained under his breath about the unruly children and spat his tobacco into the bushes. The young people restless to grow up and leave Beckettsville or restless to stay right there and fall in love, sometimes feeling both in the same moment, as young people do.

This town held many stories. In a few minutes, none of them would matter.

For weeks, some of the town's ghosts had tried to warn the people of Beckettsville. Newly awakened from rest, aware of the terrors to come, the ghosts swept picture frames from mantels. They spilled the milk. They caused the electric lights to flicker until the fragile bulbs exploded with a *pop*. They appeared briefly at windows and in mirrors, their mouths opening in silent screams. The ghosts moaned into the night, but who could hear such alarms over the noise of the radios in every house? The dead of Beckettsville had done what they could, but the people refused to see. Anyway, it was much too late now.

It was Johnny Barton, age twelve, who noticed first. Johnny was upstairs in his bedroom, pretending to be sick again and tending to his model planes, far from the other boys at school who bullied him so mercilessly. ("They're just teasing," his mother would say, as if that was supposed to be a comfort. "Hit 'em back. Be a man," his father would say, which only made Johnny feel bullied twice.) Johnny liked birds and flying things in general, things that suggested you could soar up and away anytime you liked, and so he was zooming his balsa-wood flier past the window when he took note of the curious dark clouds gathering now along that promising horizon. Plenty of storms blew in across the land in spring. But this was something different. These clouds pulled together like filings drawn to a magnet, massing quickly into a living wall. Blue lightning sliced through that thickening dark, as if something terrible was trying to birth itself.

Still gripping his plane, Johnny Barton raced down the stairs. He pushed through the white picket gate of his parents' foursquare and out into the street, not caring about the Model T that beeped its horn angrily as it swerved around him. "Watch out!" the driver, Mr. Tilsen, barked. But that's what Johnny *was* doing, watching out. Every night, he read with relish stories of the Great War. He'd read that, on the battlefields of Flanders and the Somme, fat clouds of smoke and dust announced the arrival of the Germans' monstrous war machines. That's what this strange formation reminded him of now—an invading army.

Others were coming to look at the storm blowing in out of nowhere. Wind whipped the leaves of the maples. A sudden gust blew Cora's fashionable spring hat clean off her head and sent it rolling down the street, where Charlie picked it up, happy to touch something that belonged to her at last. Reluctantly, he handed it back, his fingers grazing hers for one charged moment. Then he, too, turned his head in the direction of those foreboding clouds.

Cora snugged on her cloche and held it in place with the palm of her hand. "Mercy! I hope it's not a twister!"

"Never seen a twister look that way," Charlie answered, his mind more on Cora than the storm.

"Maybe it's the Huns!" Johnny said and scraped his plane through the air. His skin prickled, though he didn't know why.

"Looks like a big old ball of dust," the Rotary Club president said in wonder.

"Should we ring the church bell and get to the storm cellars?" Pastor Jacobs asked.

"Let's wait and see," the president said. He did not like making decisions until he knew what the popular vote would be.

The mothers had left the butcher shop. Their children stopped squabbling and moved close to their mothers' sides. The town crank slowed his chew. The restless young people greeted the arrival of the storm with excitement—finally, *something!* Euline Winters's rocking chair stilled; her knitting needles lay in her lap. "I saw a dust storm like that once when I was a girl. When it was over, little Polly Johansen was missing. They never found her," Euline called, though no one listened.

The clouds had spread out. The citizens of Beckettsville could no longer see the horizon. The high-pitched whine of insects filled the charged air. The birds shrieked and flew away from Beckettsville with a startling suddenness. Ida Olsen left her hiding place and came out of her yard, dragging her dolly behind her. Even though her mother had told her that pointing was rude, she jabbed a finger toward the spot of road still visible. "What's that?" Ida asked.

A lone man emerged from those billowing clouds. He was imposing in stature, with a stovepipe hat atop hair that was kept longer than was the fashion in this part of the country, and an old-fashioned undertaker's coat made of blue-black feathers that fluttered in the gusty wind. The people of this small town were unaccustomed to strangers—there wasn't even a train depot here—and this man was strange, indeed. He walked with a deliberate stride, and that made the people wonder if he might be important. A beautiful crow perched sentinel-straight on the man's left shoulder, cawing like a town crier. To Johnny Barton, it seemed the crow wanted to fly away from its master but stayed as if an invisible chain held it firmly in place.

The man trailing the storm reached the citizens at last. His skin was the patchy, peeling gray of a rotting shroud, and Cora Nettles tried to hide her distaste. She hoped it wasn't catching, some foreign disease. The man tipped his tall hat with easy formality. "Good afternoon."

The president of the Rotary Club stepped forward. "Afternoon. Walter Kurtz, president of the Beckettsville Rotary Club. And who might you be?"

"I might be many things. But you may call me the King of Crows."

The citizens chuckled lightly at this. The Rotary Club president heard and grinned. "Well, we don't get much royalty in these parts," he said, playing to his bemused neighbors, happy to know the popular vote at last. "You on your way through somewheres?"

"In a manner of speaking."

"We don't get many strangers here," Cora Nettles explained.

"I am not a stranger," the man replied, and it left Cora unsettled. She could not place his face.

"You might want to take shelter, sir," Pastor Jacobs said. "There's a storm right behind you."

The King of Crows glanced over his shoulder at the mass of dark clouds hovering on the edge of town, and turned back, untroubled. "Indeed there is." With eyes black and lifeless as a doll's, he surveyed the little town. He inhaled deeply, as if he were not merely taking in air but breathing in the full measure of something unknown. "What a fine claim you have here."

The Rotary Club president beamed. "Why, there's no town finer. You can have your Chicago, your San Francisco and Kansas City. Right here in Beckettsville—this is the good life!"

"We've even got a hotel," Charlie Banks said, and he hoped Cora thought he was clever to mention this.

The corners of the stranger's mouth twitched but did not extend into a smile. "My. And how many souls live here?"

"Four hundred five. Almost six, seeing as Maisy Lipscomb is due any day now," Charlie answered.

"And how many dead have you?"

"I...beg pardon?" Charlie said.

"No matter." The King of Crows smiled at last, though there was no warmth in it. "You've sold me. We'll take it."

"Take what?" the Rotary Club president said.

"Your town, of course. We are hungry."

The citizens laughed again, uneasily this time.

"The pie at the cafe is delicious," Pastor Jacobs said, still trying to make everything seem perfectly normal, though his heart said otherwise.

The Rotary Club president straightened his spine. "Beckettsville is not for sale."

"Who said anything about a sale?" the King of Crows answered. His gray teeth were as sharp and pointed as a shark's.

"I think you'd best move along now," the town crank chimed in. "We don't go for funny business here in Beckettsville."

"Who is we?" Johnny Barton hadn't meant to ask his question aloud, but now he had the attention of the King of Crows, whose stare fell on Johnny, making him squirm.

"What was that, my good man?" he asked.

Johnny had known lots of bullies, and this man struck him as the worst kind of bully. The kind who pretended to be on your side until he led you behind the school for the beating of your life.

"You said *we*. Who is we?" Johnny mumbled. He blinked at the crow on the man's shoulder, because he could swear it now had a woman's face. The bird spoke with a woman's desperate whisper. *"Run. Please, please run."*

"Be still." The King of Crows pulled his hand across the woman's mouth and it became a beak once more, cawing into the wind. The King of Crows's face lit up with a cruel joy. "How smart you are, young man! Who, indeed? How rude of me not to introduce my retinue."

With that, he raised his arms and flexed his long fingers toward the sky as if he would pull it to him. Blue lightning crackled along his dirty fingernails. "Come, my army. The time is now."

A foul smell wafted toward the town: factory smoke and bad meat and stagnant pond water and battlefield dead left untended. Pastor Jacobs put a handkerchief to his nose. Ida Olsen gagged. The crow strained forward with frantic screaming. From inside the dark clouds, a swarm of flies burst forth, as if the town of Beckettsville were a corpse rotting in the waning sun. On that horizon that had seemed so fine moments earlier, the churning clouds parted like the curtain before the start of a picture show, letting out what waited inside.

And though it was far too late for him, or for anyone else in Beckettsville, Johnny Barton heeded the crow's advice; he turned and ran from the horrors at his back.

THE END OF THE WORLD

New York City

The musty tunnel underneath the Museum of American Folklore, Superstition, and the Occult was as dark as the night's shadow, and Isaiah Campbell was afraid. His older brother, Memphis, lifted their lantern. Its light barely cut into the gloom ahead. The air down here was close, like being buried alive. Isaiah's lungs grew tighter with each breath. He wanted out. Up. Aboveground. Memphis was nervous, too. Isaiah could tell by the way his brother kept looking back and then forward again, like he wasn't sure about what to do. Even big Bill Johnson, who didn't seem afraid of anything, moved cautiously, one hand curled into a fist.

"What if this doesn't go nowhere?" Isaiah asked. He had no idea how long they'd been down here. Felt like days.

"Doesn't go anywhere," Memphis corrected, more of a mumble, though, and Isaiah didn't even have it in him to be properly annoyed by his brother's habit of fixing his words, which, to Isaiah's mind, didn't need fixing.

"Don't like it down here." Isaiah glanced over his shoulder. The way back was just as dark as the way ahead. "I'm tired."

"It's a'right, Little Man. Plenty'a slaves got to freedom out this passage. We gonna be fine," Bill said in his deep voice. "Ain't got much choice, anyhow. Not with them Shadow Men after us. Just watch your step."

Isaiah kept his eyes trained on the uneven ground announcing itself in Memphis's lantern light and wondered if the Shadow Men had shown up at Aunt Octavia's house looking for them. The idea that those men might've hurt his auntie made Isaiah's heart beat even harder in his chest. Maybe the Shadow Men had gone straight to the museum, to Will Fitzgerald and Sister Walker. Maybe the Shadow Men had found the secret door under the carpet in the collections room and were down here even now, following quietly, guns drawn.

Isaiah swallowed hard. Sweat itched along his hairline and trickled down between his narrow shoulder blades under his shirt, which was getting filthy.

"How much longer?" he asked for the fourth time. He was thirsty. His feet hurt.

Memphis's lantern illuminated another seemingly endless curve of tunnel. "Maybe we should turn back."

Bill rubbed the sweat from his chin. "Not with those men after us. Trust me, you don't want them to catch ya. Around that curve could be a way out."

"Or another mile of darkness. Or a cave-in. Or a ladder leading up to a freedom house that hasn't been that since before the Civil War," Memphis whispered urgently. "A house that's home to some white family now who might not welcome us."

"Rather take my chances goin' fo'ward."

They pressed on. Around the bend, their tunnel branched into two. A smell like rotten eggs filled the air and Memphis tried not to gag.

Bill coughed. "Look like we just met up with the sewers."

Isaiah pinched his nose shut with his fingers. "Which way should we go?"

"I don't know," Memphis said, and that scared Isaiah, because if there was anything his brother was good at, it was acting like he knew everything. "Bill?"

Bill held up a finger, feeling for air. He shook his head. "Ain't no way to know." He took out a nickel, tossed it, and slapped it down on his arm. "Heads we go left; tails, right." Memphis nodded. Bill took his hand away. "Tails," he said, and they entered the tunnel to their right.

"Maybe those Shadow Men left Harlem and went back to wherever they come from," Memphis said. Water swished over their shoes and trickled down the narrow brick walls. It stank.

"Doubt it," Bill panted. "They never stop. I know 'em."

"I didn't even get to tell Theta good-bye. What if they went to her apartment to find me? What if...what if they hurt her?"

"Only thing we can do is keep going," Bill said. "Soon as we get somewhere safe, you can put in a call to her, and to your auntie."

Memphis snorted. "Somewhere safe. Let me know where that is."

Isaiah chanced another look over his shoulder. Tiny motes of light fluttered in the vast dark. Isaiah blinked, wiped at his eyes. The muscles from his neck to his fingers twitched. Suddenly, his feet wouldn't move. Isaiah felt as if a giant were squeezing him between its palms. The spots of light came faster, and then Isaiah knew.

"Memphis..." was all Isaiah managed before his eyes rolled back and he was falling deeply into space as the vision roared up inside him, fast as a freight train.

Isaiah stood on a ribbon of dirt road leading toward a flat horizon. To his left, a slumped scarecrow guarded over a field of failing corn. To his right sat a farmhouse with a sagging front porch. He saw a weathered red barn. An enormous oak whose tire swing hung lax, as if it hadn't been touched in a good while. Isaiah had seen this place once before in a vision, and he had been afraid of it, and of the girl who lived here.

He heard his name being called like a voice punching through miles of fog. "I, I, I, IsaiAH!" And then, close by his ear: "Isaiah."

Isaiah whirled around. She was *right there*. The same girl as before. A peach satin ribbon clung to a few strands of her pale ringlets. Her eyes were such a light blue-gray they were nearly silver.

Who are you? he thought.

"I'm a seer, a Diviner, like you."

She'd heard his thoughts?

The girl curled in on herself like she'd just stepped into a bracing wind. "Something awful has happened, Isaiah, just now. Like a fire snuffed out, and it's so, so cold. Can you feel it?"

Isaiah couldn't, and that made him jealous of this strange girl. He was fixated on the horizon, where an angry mouth of dark storm clouds gobbled up the blue sky. The clouds cracked like eggshells, letting out a high, sharp whine, a sound so full of pain and fear and need that Isaiah wanted to run away from it. *What is that?*

"The King of Crows and his dead," the girl answered as if Isaiah had spoken. "He's come, like he promised he would. He's come and we're in terrible danger."

Wind snapped the corn on its stalks. Birds darted out from the roiling, dark sea overhead. Their cawing mixed with the gunfire bursts of screaming. The noise stole the breath from Isaiah's lungs. So much hatred lived inside that sky. He could feel the threat trying to gnaw its way out into their world.

The girl reached for Isaiah's hand. Her hands were small and delicate, like a doll's. "He tells lies, so many lies, Isaiah. He's been lying to me this whole time, pretending to be my friend. But I had a vision. A lady named Miriam told me the truth. She told me what he did to Conor Flynn. He wants all of us, Isaiah. He wants the Diviners."

Why?

"Because we're the only ones who can stop him." The girl kept her unearthly eyes on the unholy sky. "I know how to stop the King of Crows, Isaiah."

Where are we? Isaiah asked. He didn't know why he couldn't speak here.

"Bountiful, Nebraska. That's where I live."

Isaiah saw a mailbox bearing the name "Olson" and the number one forty-four. That number came up a lot. He remembered Evie saying it was the number of her brother's unit during the war. But her brother and his whole unit had died, and it had something to do with Will and Sister Walker and Project Buffalo and Diviners.

"Where are you?" she asked.

In the tunnel under the old museum. But we're lost. There's people after us.

"I'm afraid, Isaiah," the girl said. "We're not safe. None of us are. You've got one another, but I'm all alone. I can't fight him and his army by myself. None of us can. We need each other."

The last time Isaiah had seen this vision, his mama had been here, telling him to get out quick. She had fussed at this girl, told her to hush up. He looked for his mother now but did not see her.

"Please. Come to Bountiful," the girl pleaded.

The Shadow Men are after us. We're running from them.

"They don't know about me. They forgot me. Come here. You'll be safe. They won't find you. We must stop the King of Crows before it's too late!"

Wait! What's your name? Isaiah thought.

"Sarah Beth," the girl yelled. The dust billowed behind her pale form. "Sarah Beth Olson. Get to Bountiful, Isaiah! Before it's too late!"

First we gotta get out of this tunnel. Say, can you see a way out?

"You're in a tunnel under a museum, you said?"

Yes! In New York City. Manhattan.

The girl shut her eyes. In a minute, she opened them wide. "Isaiah.

You've got to get out of there right now, you hear? Something's coming. Go back. Take the other tunnel. Oh, Isaiah, you must hurry. Get out now and come to Bountiful before—"

Isaiah came out of his vision, dizzy and disoriented. Memphis's worried face was the first thing he saw, hovering above his own. Isaiah sat up too quickly and caught his brother in the nose.

"Ow."

Bill steadied Isaiah's face in his strong hands. "You all right, Little Man?"

"Y-yes, sir." He tasted blood. He'd bit his tongue. And he was sitting in the fetid water.

Bill helped Isaiah to his feet. "You had a vision?"

Isaiah nodded. His head ached. The sewer smell was making him nauseated.

"What'd you see?" Memphis asked.

"She said…she said to go back. Take the other tunnel," Isaiah said, panicked.

"Who said? Isaiah, you're not making sense," Memphis said.

"Hush. Hush now." Bill held up a hand. "You hear something?"

The boys listened for something under the constant drip of water. Memphis nodded.

"The Shadow Men?" Isaiah whispered. "She said…she said…" The tunnel ahead began to fill with flickering light and deep, guttural growls.

"Not Shadow Men," Memphis said ominously.

The sound was getting closer.

"Back up," Memphis said.

"The hell with that. Run!" Bill said.

Memphis grabbed Isaiah's hand, and they raced back the way they'd come.

"This way!" Memphis said, ducking into the other tunnel, picking up speed as they spied the daylight ahead.

MEMORIES

According to the clock on the bedside table, it was nine fifteen in the morning—
an ungodly hour to flapper Evie O'Neill, who never got up before noon if she
could help it. She'd been having a nightmare, but she couldn't remember a thing
about it now. Evie stifled an exhausted yawn and looked over at her friend, Theta
Knight, who snored lightly. Her sleep mask was slightly askew. Evie nudged
Theta twice before giving her a solid shove. Theta startled awake, hands patting
at the air until they landed on the sleep mask, which she slid up onto her forehead. She blinked at Evie, then at the clock. "What's the big idea, Evil?"

"Darling Theta, did anyone ever tell you that you sleep with your
mouth open?" Evie impersonated a dead-to-the-world, snoring Theta. "I
just didn't want you to choke."

With a groan, Theta pushed herself to a sitting position. "That's called
breathing."

"It's very *loud* breathing." Evie snuggled up next to Theta. For a
moment, she remembered all the times she'd done the same with her best
friend, Mabel. An awful ache ballooned in Evie's throat. She refused to start
the day with tears. "Theta, did you mean what you said last night?"

Theta arched an eyebrow. "I dunno. What'd I say last night?"

"That you'd help me find Sam."

"Yeah, I meant it, kid."

"You're the berries," Evie said and kissed Theta's cheek.

Theta wiped at the spot. "You probably just got a mouthful of cold
cream, y'know."

"Then my lips will be very soft. I want to try his hat again."

"Evil. You've read that hat three times now," Theta said gently.

"Maybe there's something I missed! I could sense how afraid he was,
Theta. You know Sam—he's never afraid. I saw those Shadow Men doing

something to him, and then I could feel Sam's body getting cold and slow and numb."

Theta brought her knees up to her chest and wrapped her arms around them. "You don't suppose he's . . . ?"

"No! He is pos-i-tutely *not* dead!" Evie insisted. She couldn't bear the thought of it. There'd been too much loss already. "Besides, if anybody is going to have the pleasure of murdering Sam Lloyd, it ought to be me."

Theta chuckled and shook her head. "You two. I don't know whether to hope you get married or hope you never do."

"I only want to know that he's okay," Evie said, tearing up at last.

"I know, kid. Here," Theta said, reaching for Sam's hat from the bedside table. "You might as well get started. I'll have the aspirin ready for after. Just don't do a number on yourself."

Evie sat with Sam's hat in her lap. The old Greek fisherman's cap had belonged to him for a long time. With renewed purpose, Evie pressed it between her palms, receiving small glimpses of Sam's past. These memories played across her mind like brief scenes in a motion picture, but all jumbled up: Sam talking to a redheaded lady who was laying out a spread of tarot cards. Sam lifting valuables from unsuspecting rubes on Forty-second Street. The day she and Sam had met, when he'd kissed her and stolen twenty dollars from her pocket. That one made her smile just a bit. There was even a hint of the countless girls he'd charmed into his arms, and it tempted Evie to unlock even more of those memories. Last, she wandered across a moment of the two of them sharing a perfect kiss. And then that gave way to the Shadow Men dragging Sam toward the brown sedan, his body growing cold. But then the hat fell to the sidewalk, and that's where Sam's history with it stopped. If she wanted a deeper read, she was going to need help.

Evie came out of her trance and looked up at Theta with wide eyes. "Theta, darling Theta."

"Uh-oh. I know that tone."

"Please? I only need a boost."

"My power's pretty unpredictable, Evil. What if I accidentally set you on fire?"

"Then I'm glad I'm wearing your pajamas and not my own."

"There's something not right about you, Evil," Theta clucked. "Now, listen: If this goes badly, don't you dare come back and haunt me."

"Your protest is noted."

"Uh, how do we do this? Do I touch you? The hat? Both?"

"Both, I think." Evie glanced at Theta's fingers and thought about them heating up suddenly. "On second thought, the hat."

"Here goes nothin'," Theta said and took hold of the brim with a delicate touch.

Evie shut her eyes and concentrated. A tiny sliver of electricity worked its way up her arm. It tickled like ants, an unpleasant sensation, and Evie tried to breathe through the worry about what might happen if her power and Theta's didn't get along. She hoped that Theta couldn't sense that worry. In a few seconds, the prickling became a surge of energy, as if someone had plugged Evie in to the same electrical socket as Theta, and now their combined wattage was glowing brighter. She could feel Theta's strong heartbeat like her own. With her friend at her side, Evie went deeper, searching for anything about one of the Shadow Men she'd glimpsed. Nothing. Just Sam's memories fighting to get through. What were the limits of memory?

But then, there it was—a small flicker into the Shadow Man who had taken Sam! Adams was the man's name, and the wickedness of his soul was terrifying. This was a man who had killed many times. He said it was out of duty, out of patriotism, but really, he enjoyed it. Power was what moved this man, and this was the man who had Sam. Evie gritted her teeth, going deeper still, grasping for something just out of reach. For just a moment while the Shadow Man held Sam, he was thinking of a place. A destination, perhaps? The contact between Sam's hat and the Shadow Man had been brief. Evie would have to fight to get more, even if it meant a real skull-banger of a headache afterward. Tall trees. A winding drive. And nestled into the thicket, a sprawling manor that Evie recognized. It was a hot day. Strangely hot. A trickle of sweat slipped down Evie's neck as she pushed for more details. Somewhere in the trance of it all, she felt Theta's heartbeat speed up and sensed her panic.

"Jeepers!" Theta yelped, breaking the connection.

Evie's earlier heat was replaced by a sudden cold. She came out of her trance to see an alarmed Theta waving smoke away from Sam's hat. "Oh, Jiminy Christmas!"

"It's out, Theta! It's fine!" The smell of smoke lingered. *That could have been my hands*, Evie thought.

"Good thing I wasn't holding on to you," Theta said, trying to make a joke out of it.

"It would've been a waste of a good manicure," Evie offered. Already, a headache was creeping its way up the back of her neck, threatening to settle behind her eyes, and her stomach churned. That was the price to pay for a deep read.

Theta steadied her. "Easy, champ." She went to the kitchen and fetched Evie a glass of water and two aspirin. After a few sips, Evie's stomach began to settle, though her head still throbbed.

"So? Anything?" Theta asked. Her adopted cat, Archibald, meowed and hopped up onto the bed. Theta stroked his marmalade-colored fur.

"One of the Shadow Men was thinking about Jake Marlowe's estate," Evie said, rubbing her temples. "Now, why would he be doing that?"

"You think those fellas took Sam to Hopeful Harbor?"

"I don't know. But it's the only real clue I've gotten. Do you remember when we visited? Jericho told us he saw two men carrying away a missing Diviner, Anna Provenza. He was going to try to find out more."

"Have you, uh, heard from Jericho at all?" Theta prodded.

"No," Evie said. "Not since...what happened." Add that one to the losses.

"I never figured him to be that kind of fella. I guess you just never know."

The front door opened. A jaunty humming came from the other room and Theta called out, "In here, Henry!" which did nothing to help Evie's headache.

Henry DuBois IV danced in like John Barrymore. He was still wearing what was clearly last night's outfit. In the morning light, he was pale and freckly, his sandy hair sticking up at odd angles along the crown when he removed his ever-present boater hat. Henry was such a contrast to Theta's smoldering looks—soulful dark eyes, enormous high cheekbones, shoeshine-black hair cut into a Shingle bob—that it struck Evie as comical that anyone had ever believed the story that the two of them were brother and sister. But, as Theta had often said, people could be pretty gullible.

"Don't tell me: You're starting a coven." Henry yawned, crawling into bed next to the two girls. "Awfully early for witching hour. And what's that smell? Are you burning toast?"

"It's nothing. Have you even been to bed yet?" Theta asked. She sniffed him. "You smell like a moonshiner's bathtub."

Henry blew a puff of breath into his palm and sniffed it. "Well, you see, there was a second party after the first party, and…" He looked down at his bare neck. "Oh, applesauce. I lost my ascot. Well, it wasn't actually *my* ascot. Anyway, David and I managed about two hours." He paused, looking thoughtful. "Odd dreams."

"Me, too," Evie said. "Can you remember yours?"

Henry shook his head. "You both have on awfully serious faces for"—he squinted at the clock—"nine twenty-three in the morning. You know, I don't believe I've ever even seen nine twenty-three in the morning. Now that I have, I can say with certainty that it looks…early."

"Why are you back so early?" Evie asked.

"David's mother was coming for breakfast, so I thought I'd best make myself scarce."

Theta frowned. "I still haven't heard from Memphis. He didn't call last night, and no call this morning. He's always up early. All this Shadow Men talk has got me spooked now." Theta hugged her knees to her chest. "Evil thinks she mighta found where those creepy Shadow Men took Sam."

"I'm guessing it wasn't the Whoop-Dee-Do Club," Henry said. He kissed the top of Archie's fuzzy head and the cat purred in response.

"I believe they took him to Jake Marlowe's estate," Evie said. "Hen, hand me my stockings, will you?"

Dutifully, Henry lifted the silk stockings from the footboard and offered them to Evie as if she were the Queen of England. Evie swung her legs over the edge of the bed. She rolled one stocking up to her knee and secured it with a garter.

"Where're you going with all that pep in your step?" Henry asked.

"Hopeful Harbor, of course," Evie answered.

Theta threw Henry a look. "She pulling my leg?"

Henry rolled his head toward Evie, who was fixing the other stocking into place, then back to face Theta. "It does not appear so."

Theta scooted to the edge, next to Evie. "Evil. Listen to me: You can't just storm into Jake Marlowe's fancy house. They'll throw you out like a bum."

"I'll use my charm," Evie insisted.

"You're not *that* charming," Theta said.

"I'll have you know that I am."

"*I've* always maintained that you were charming," Henry said, stretching his lanky body across Theta's bed. "Ohhhh. That's it. I'm never getting up again. You'll have to learn to live this way."

"You picked a public fight with Jake Marlowe *that got broadcast over the radio!*" Theta reminded Evie.

"Mmm. That's true. You were…less than charming that evening," Henry said, eyes closed.

"But one hundred percent right!" Evie shot back.

"Jake Marlowe hates you, Evil. He hates Diviners, but he especially hates you."

"Thanks, Theta."

"Don't mention it."

Henry whistled. "The fur doth fly before ten o'clock in the morning, Mercutio."

"I'm just saying, now that there's rumors floating around that Diviners mighta had something to do with the bomb and his fiancée's murder, you can forget about getting into Jake Marlowe's mansion."

"Those rumors are pure bunk!" Evie groused.

"Doesn't matter what's true. It matters what people *think* is true. Besides"— Theta glanced sideways at Evie, weighing how much she could say—"Mabel and the Secret Six planted that bomb. And who was Mabel's best friend?"

Evie stared down at her stockinged feet. "Mabel didn't do that."

"Now who doesn't wanna see the truth?" Theta said gently.

Henry sat up again. "There *is* somebody who might know how to find Sam."

"Who?" Evie said.

Henry cleared his throat. "Somebody you're really close to. You might even be related."

It took Evie a second to understand, but then she frowned. "No. I refuse to speak to him on principle." She crossed the room and ducked behind Theta's painted dressing screen, which had been liberated from a Ziegfeld Follies costume shop. The comment about Mabel had hit home, and Evie was afraid she might cry. She was always a little wobbly after a reading, and this hadn't been any ordinary reading.

"He's still your uncle," Henry said. "And he used to be Jake's best friend."

"If it weren't for Will and Sister Walker and Jake Marlowe, we wouldn't be chasing ghosts and worried about the end of the world," Evie called as she wiggled out of the borrowed pajamas and back into her dress. "If it weren't for Uncle Will, my brother would be alive."

"They're still our best hope," Henry said.

Evie came around the side of the dressing screen. She pushed a wayward curl out of her face.

"Do you suppose…" Evie choked back the lump in her throat, losing her battle. "Do you suppose she's…at peace?"

Theta exchanged a quick glance with Henry. "If anybody's got a right to rest in peace it's Mabel Rose," Theta said quietly.

Mabel did deserve to rest in peace, and Evie knew she was a terrible person, because if there was any ghost she longed to see, even for just a moment, it was Mabel's. The tears threatened again. Evie would not cry before breakfast.

"Fine!" she said, throwing her hands upward. "Let's go see Uncle Will. But don't expect me to be polite."

Henry grinned. "Well, if there's going to be drama, I'm all in. Let me just get changed."

※

Ling Chan doubted that anyone knew the streets of Chinatown like she did. Other people might know the best grocers for bok choy or which fishmonger had the day's freshest catch. But Ling knew where the sidewalks were roughest, which cracks had to be carefully negotiated, and just how long it took to cross Canal Street if you had to be aware of the crush of people around you while also searching for a pebble-free spot on which to land your crutches.

The journey from her parents' restaurant on Doyers Street to Staino's Bakery on Mulberry was only a few blocks, but Ling felt every jolt up her spine. The heavy leather braces she wore chafed against the insides of her knees and her hands were calloused from the grip on her crutches. She was still adjusting to her new life, adjusting to the stares of people who thought that she was someone to be pitied or that she was bad luck. Usually, she kept her focus forward, refusing to look. Other times, though, she'd glare back at the rude ones until finally, red-cheeked, they'd look away. *I'm just like you,* she wanted to yell. *For all your staring, why can't you see that?*

Ling had other things on her mind this morning, and they were all named Alma LaVoy. Alma Rene LaVoy was the most alive person Ling Chan had ever met. The pretty chorus girl was the light in the sky over Chinatown during a New Year's celebration. When she entered a room, the room shifted. It took notice. No one took more notice than Ling. She was in love with Alma, she'd come to realize. *Huh*, she thought, smiling to herself. *This is what love feels like.* But Ling was worried, too. Someone as alive and fizzy as Alma had needs. Physical needs. Needs Ling wasn't certain she could meet. For Ling, love—deep, passionate, intense—was real. But sex? So far, sex was a hypothesis her body didn't seem interested in proving. Alma, on the other hand, seemed very comfortable with sex. And Ling couldn't help wondering how long Alma would want to stick around without getting what every winking Tin Pan Alley or Follies song hinted at between the bars.

At the corner of Mott and Canal, Ling heard her name being called and saw her upstairs neighbor, Mim, hurrying toward her with an urgency that could only suggest the juiciest of neighborhood gossip. For once, Ling was grateful for the distraction. Still, she couldn't help noticing that Mim never once had to look down as she ran.

Mim was breathless when she reached Ling. "Have you heard?"

"Heard what?" Ling said, ignoring her mother's admonition to *Go to the bakery for bread and come right back, no dallying, lass.*

"Ghosts! There were ghosts in Manhattan last night!"

"What? Where?"

"I heard it from Sallie, who heard it from May Wong, whose brother, John, works for a couple on the Upper East Side, the Ashtons. They are so rich, Ling! Four floors—all to themselves! Can you imagine?"

Ling had forgotten that getting coherent gossip out of Mim was like trying to put pajamas on a cat.

"What happened?" Ling said, cutting to the chase. It was her turn to cross, but she would wait for the next go-round.

"They were having a party. They were very drunk. May says they have their very own bootlegger who comes to the house by a secret entrance. Oh, and Mrs. Ashton has *three* mink coats. I'd settle for just one. It wouldn't even have to be all mink." Mim sighed.

"What about the ghosts?" Ling pressed.

"Oh! Well, they decided to bring in a Diviner for a séance."

Ling snorted. "Probably a fake."

"The Ashtons can afford the best," Mim said, a slight dig at Ling. Everybody in Chinatown knew that Ling could walk in dreams and sometimes make contact with the spirit world.

"Anyway, during the séance, she conjured a real, live ghost!" Mim continued.

"Ghosts can't be live. That's why they're ghosts," Ling muttered, but Mim just kept going.

"And John told May, who told Sallie, who told me that Mrs. Ashton could be heard screaming from the library to open the doors right away and to call the police—"

"To *arrest the ghost*? Stupid," Ling grumbled.

"—*aaaand* when they opened the doors, Ling, the chairs were overturned and the Diviner had fainted dead away on the floor. All those rich people came screaming out of the room and left without even taking their coats."

"What did the ghost look like? Was it fresh? Did it say it was hungry?" Ling pressed. The cop on Canal Street looked to Ling but she shook her head. She'd have to wait for the next crossing.

Mim looked at Ling with distaste. "How should I know?"

"Because you seem to know everything else, but not the important things."

Mim's eyes gleamed. "I saved the best for last." She pursed her lips, holding on to the information. She was clearly relishing doling it out in tea-spoonfuls, and now Ling was going to miss her chance to cross Canal Street again. The traffic cop had given up on motioning to her.

"The ghost spoke to them. She said, 'The Diviners did this.'"

All the air left Ling's body. "What?"

"That's what everybody's saying, you know. Harriet Henderson even said in her column that Diviners are responsible for all of this—the ghosts, the sleeping sickness last year, the bombing, and the trouble with all these anarchists, these *foreigners*."

Ling rolled her eyes. "Mim. Your parents are immigrants. So are mine," Ling said. She had very little patience for Mim and her prejudices.

"Those people are different. Not like us," Mim sniffed.

It was almost time to cross again. "I have to go to Staino's for my mother," Ling said. She suddenly wanted away from Mim and this upsetting gossip that didn't feel like gossip, but like a train bearing down on Ling, who had one foot stuck in the ties.

"Say, you know that Evie O'Neill, don't you? The one who was best friends with the bomber?" Mim said, a parting shot.

Mabel. Her name was Mabel, Ling thought, feeling a tightness in her chest.

"You ought to be careful, Ling. You don't want them to come for you."

And Ling could tell there was a hint of glee in the warning.

The spring day had begun to sour. Ling crossed Canal into Little Italy. On Mulberry Street, a crowd had gathered in front of a shop nestled between a pasticceria and a tiny cafe. Several men surrounded a dark-haired woman in a long flowing dress and shawl, preventing her escape. One of the men gripped an ax. Ling could feel the woman's terror as if it were her own. In the street, people looked on, doing nothing.

"Please—this is my shop! My business," the woman pleaded as two men smashed in the front windows with baseball bats, right across the gold-leaf lettering that read FORTUNES TOLD.

Ling froze, unsure of what to do, of what she could do. She'd seen a mob turn before. Not long ago, a man had been openly taunting her on the street in front of witnesses who did nothing to stop it, and if Henry hadn't come along at just that moment, well, she shuddered to think what could have happened to her. Now, though, she was one of those mute witnesses.

"Why are you doing this?" Ling said, sounding every bit as frightened as she felt.

The man with the ax turned to her, his face ruddy with rage. "Stay out of it."

Two big men emerged from the shop carrying a large wooden barrel. "There's at least eight more in there," one of the men grunted. The ruddy man stepped forward and swung the ax. The blade bit into the wood again and again until the barrel broke open and a rush of amber liquid swooshed into the gutters. The pungent smell of whiskey flooded the streets. This woman wasn't even a real Diviner, just a bootlegger using a fortune-telling shop as a front. It didn't seem to matter, though.

"*La strega!*" one of the onlookers shouted and spat at the woman's feet.

Ling knew that word. *La strega.* Witch.

"Oughta lock 'em all up, every last one of those Diviners," someone said as Ling continued up the street, keeping her gaze firmly on the sidewalk as if the only things that could hurt her lived there.

22

FAIRY TALES

Theta, Evie, and Henry strolled arm-in-arm among Central Park's budding trees. Spring had come to the city almost overnight. Pink-and-white blossoms bowed in the breeze. Spring had been Mabel's favorite season, Evie remembered, and she ached not to be able to share it with her. She picked up her pace, eager to question Will about the Shadow Men. It was high time they knew everything about them. Sam's life depended on it.

The three of them passed a governess scolding a little boy in short pants who refused to go home for a nap, but they were too immersed in conversation to hear the child crying, "But I see him when I fall asleep. He's all covered with worms and he says he's going to eat up Mummy and Daddy first and then he's going to come for me!"

"Now, now, that's only a bad dream. Buck up."

A car backfired coming up Central Park West, and Theta jumped.

"Gracious! Just an old flivver breaking wind." Evie giggled.

"Sure. Of course," Theta said, dropping her shoulders. That's what living with Roy had done to her. If you never knew when a smile might turn into a slap or a punch, you stayed on alert. Theta hadn't heard from Roy lately, and that troubled her. She knew she should be relieved, but Roy wasn't the type to let something go. He'd promised he'd get even, and Roy was a man who kept his promises, not out of love but out of spite.

"Oooh, look—a crocus! It truly *is* spring," Evie said, breaking away to admire the new flower.

Henry leaned in to Theta. "It was only a car, darlin'," he said, sensing her worry. "You showed him—that's why he's made himself scarce. What can he do against your power?"

"A lot, Hen. My power's unpredictable. You know that. I almost set Sam's hat on fire this morning. What if Roy goes after the people I love? For the first time in my life, I got something to lose." Why hadn't she heard from Memphis yet?

But Evie was back now, going on about a pair of shoes she'd seen in *exactly that shade of crocus*, and for once, Theta was happy to let Evie prattle on if it meant Theta didn't have to talk.

When they turned onto Sixty-eighth Street, they slowed. Police guarded the entrance to the Museum of American Folklore, Superstition, and the Occult, where a small flock of reporters shouted rapid-fire questions at them.

"Is today 'Win a Free Skeleton Day' at the museum?" Henry joked.

"Hey. There's Woody," Evie said, spying her friend and occasional nemesis, T. S. Woodhouse of the New York *Daily News*, in the scrum. "He'll know the business."

Theta grabbed Evie's sleeve. "Don't call to—"

"Mr. Woodhouse! Oh, Mr. Woodhouse!" Evie bellowed.

"Him," Theta finished as every head swiveled their way.

"It's the Sweetheart Seer!" somebody shouted, alerting the reporters, who now rushed toward Evie and her friends. It had been a while since Evie had enjoyed the bright spotlight of the press's attention, and for just a moment, it felt so good that she quite forgot why she had come to the museum in the first place.

"Golly, is it Win a Free Skeleton Day at the Creepy Crawly?" she quipped, moving quickly ahead of Henry, who complained, "Hey, that was my line."

But when she got closer, she saw the broken windows and the word *Murderers* splashed in red paint across the neat, hand-lettered sign for the museum. Woody was pushing his way toward her, his expression grim. "Evie! Evie!"

"Say, Woody, what's happened?"

"You don't know, Sheba? Didn't anybody telephone you?"

"I was at Theta's last night," Evie said feebly. She didn't like the cold she suddenly felt in her belly. It was the same cold she'd felt when Mr. Smith from the telegram office had come to deliver the telegram about her brother, James, during the war: *We regret to inform you* . . .

"You'd better brace yourself for a shock, kid." Woody reached inside his jacket pocket for his flask. Evie took note of the reporters watching her. She shook her head and he put it back.

"What is it, Woody?"

"Your uncle's dead. He's been murdered."

Will. *Murdered*. The street swam and Evie stumbled a bit. A camera-man's flash went off, capturing her in her shock.

"Who would do that? Who would kill Uncle Will?" was all Evie could seem to say.

"Nobody's said anything yet. Say, uh, you wouldn't have any ideas, would you, Sheba?" Woody lifted his pencil from over his ear and opened a fresh page on his notepad.

Evie glared. "No, I don't, Mr. Woodhouse."

"I'm a reporter, Sheba," Woody said sheepishly but not apologetically.

Will dead. It seemed impossible. Everything about her uncle suggested life. He was never still. *Had* never been still. *Was* still. Now. Another camera flash went off. Evie blinked away spots and put up a hand to block her face. "Please...please don't...."

"You wanna put that flash box away before I break it?" Theta shouted at the photographer.

"Why don't you smile for us instead, beautiful?" a reporter joked.

The others laughed. Theta felt her hands getting warm.

"Ignore them," Henry whispered.

Evie marched forward with grim determination.

"Evie, where are you going?" Henry asked.

"I want to see for myself," she said, muscling her way through the reporters.

Woody chased after her. "They won't let you in, Sheba."

"They have to let me in. I'm his niece." Evie pushed past him and charged toward the museum's steps. "Let me through, please! Let me through! That's my uncle!"

The museum's front doors opened, drawing everyone's attention. Out stepped Detective Terrence Malloy, all one-hundred-eighty-five gruff, Lower East Side–bred pounds of him. His badge shone against his suit lapel and his mouth worked a piece of chewing gum.

"Detective Malloy! Detective—hey, Detective! Over here!" the reporters shouted.

Evie wondered if Detective Malloy liked hearing his name called as much as she had liked hearing hers whenever she stepped out of the radio station. From the look on his face, she decided he did. Reporters clamored for the big man's attention:

"What do you know, Detective?"

"Do you suspect foul play?"

"Say, was it a *ghost*?"

This got a laugh. Evie's cheeks burned. She wanted to slap that reporter. Her uncle was dead and they were making jokes.

"Is it true that anarchists did it?" another asked.

"Is it true that *Diviners* did it?"

"That's ridiculous!" Evie blurted out. "My uncle was a friend to Diviners!"

She had everyone's attention now, including Malloy's. The New York City homicide detective had been her uncle Will's friend once upon a time, before the Pentacle Murders and all that followed destroyed that bond. The look Detective Malloy gave Evie was decidedly less than friendly.

"Well, somebody wasn't a friend to him, Miss O'Neill," a reporter said, oblivious to the silent showdown. "Did your uncle have any enemies?"

"Yeah—was there anything worth stealing in all that junk?" another reporter asked.

"Any dangerous objects?"

The reporters were shouting at her.

"As next of kin, I demand to see my uncle's body," Evie announced over the din.

"That's the stuff, Evie!"

"You tell 'em!"

She had Malloy against the ropes now, and she didn't care that she'd had to use the press to her advantage. If he turned her away, he'd look like a heel. She could see from the way he was grinding that chewing gum against his back molars that Malloy didn't like this one bit.

"All right, Miss O'Neill. I know from experience that saying no to you is a full-time job," he said, getting one in at her expense. "But remember—this is a crime scene. Don't touch anything."

"Say, Detective—couldn't the Sweetheart Seer help crack the case?" The reporter waved his fingers.

"Detective work is what'll crack this case, Johnny. You can print that. Follow me, Miss O'Neill. Your pals have to stay behind, though."

"Evil? You copacetic?" Theta asked, Henry looking on.

"I'm jake. Don't worry."

Broken glass littered the beautiful black-and-white marble floor of the museum's foyer. Evie glanced to her left, at the collections room, with all its rare supernatural and folkloric objects on display. As she followed the detective through the broken museum, Evie could practically hear echoes of a shared past in the walls—there was Jericho taking down a book from a shelf and Sam annoying him by calling him "Freddy." She thought of Ling sitting on the sofa, her crutches beside her, as she scoffed at some corny joke Henry made. She could picture Theta and Memphis making eyes at each other across a library table when they were supposed to be looking for clues about otherworldly occurrences. She could hear Isaiah's laughter and Sister Walker gently admonishing him to concentrate. She could see Will as she had the first day she'd arrived, suitcase in hand, from Ohio. He was standing at a lectern teaching a class of college boys about good and evil, about magic and religion, and about a curious man in a tall hat who seemed to be all those things.

They'd reached the library. Steeling herself, Evie followed Detective Malloy inside. The grand room was a mess. Books lay on the floor with their spines bent. Papers had been strewn about everywhere. Like someone had been searching for something, Evie thought.

"Who's the tomato?" a cop said as Evie walked past.

"Her? She's the stiff's niece," another cop answered.

Evie flinched to hear Will discussed like that.

"You wanna clam up?" Malloy barked and the officers fell silent.

The police photographer's flash blinded Evie. When it cleared, she saw Will's body. He was on his back on the floor, looking up toward the ceiling's painted mural of witches and shamans and vodou priestesses as if he might simply be contemplating America's supernatural past. Except that his blue eyes had gone a milky white, the pupils fixed, and a deep purplish ligature mark encircled his neck above his popped collar. Evie had seen more bodies than she'd cared to in the past several months. But none of them had been Will. *Get up*, she wanted to say. *You're not dead. Get up. Get up.*

Detective Malloy came to stand beside her. "Miss O'Neill, you all right? You feel faint?"

"No," Evie said, and she wasn't sure which question she was answering.

"Do you know anybody who might've wanted to kill your uncle?"

Just me, Evie thought. "No," she said.

"I know this must be a shock."

"Yes," Evie said, her voice barely above a whisper.

"When was the last time the two of youse talked?"

Evie tried not to glance over at Uncle Will and failed. *His eyes.* "Oh.

Um. A few weeks ago, I think." They'd fought. He'd left her a note to come to him before it was too late. She'd thrown it away. Foolish. Foolish.

"And what about the rest of your Diviner pals? Your set used to come to the museum pretty often, didn't you?"

"I suppose."

"Any of them dislike your uncle?"

The full weight of Malloy's questions caught up to Evie. She straightened her spine. "If you've something to say, Detective, I think you'd better come out and say it plainly."

Malloy cleared his throat. "Very well. Miss O'Neill, do you know the whereabouts of Memphis Campbell, his brother, Isaiah, or Margaret Walker?"

It took Evie a few seconds to understand his meaning, and then she was furious. "No, I'm afraid I don't," she said, with radio star crispness. "I know I'm not a famous detective, like you, Mr. Malloy, but did you try going to their homes?" She was baiting the bull, but she didn't care.

Malloy squinted at her. "Yeah. We did, matter of fact. Funny thing is, the three of them are suddenly missing. Not a trace of 'em anywhere."

Now Evie didn't know what to think. Hadn't Theta said she'd not heard from Memphis and was worried? What if the Shadow Men had gotten to them, too?

"Maybe somebody took them," Evie said.

"Took them where?" Malloy asked.

"Well, if you want to investigate another disappearance, Sam Lloyd has gone missing." Evie squared her shoulders. "I have reason to believe he was kidnapped."

Malloy's eyebrows shot up. "Sam Lloyd. *Kidnapped*. Okay."

Evie couldn't miss the snickering of the other officers.

"With all due respect, Miss O'Neill, when Sam Lloyd's around, it's usually people's wallets that go missing."

"But he *was* kidnapped!"

"How do you know this?"

"I read his hat. Swell, you can all have a laugh, har-de-har-har," Evie said to the cops chortling in the corner. "But *I saw*! *I know*! He was taken by two men in suits."

Even Malloy seemed amused. "Men in suits, huh? Haberdashers? Tailors?"

Evie wanted to kick every one of these men. Why couldn't they take her seriously? "Shadow Men," she said, trying to hide how small they were making her feel. As if her intuition wasn't reliable and she was some lunatic.

"Shadow what?" Malloy said.

"That's just what we call them. They wear gray suits—"

"So do lots of fellas."

"And they have these lapel pins, an eye surrounded by the rays of the sun...you know what I'm talking about, don't you?"

Detective Malloy's expression hardened. "Listen, Miss O'Neill, I don't know anything about Shadow Men or object readings or ghosts. What I know is that your uncle is dead—murdered—and you want me to chase after Sam Lloyd, who probably ran off with some chorus girl and is now grifting his way back to Chicago. That seems a bit odd, you ask me."

Evie's eyes welled up. "He didn't run off. He's in trouble. I know it."

Malloy offered his handkerchief. Evie declined it.

"Miss O'Neill," Malloy said in a softer tone. "Memphis Campbell came to see your uncle last night. Did you know that?"

Evie felt a buzzing in her head. "I...n-no."

"And Margaret Walker was seen leaving here not too long afterward. The same Margaret Walker who worked with your uncle—and with all of youse. The same Margaret Walker who once did jail time for sedition during the war."

"Are you saying you suspect Memphis and Miss Walker of murdering Uncle Will? Why? What possible motive would they have?"

"Money, maybe."

"Will didn't have any money! He owed the city a fortune in back taxes."

"Or maybe your uncle had something on 'em both."

"Like what?"

"That's the question I'd like to ask 'em."

The photographer's flash went off. Evie was reminded of the first murder she and Will had investigated, the body of Ruta Badowski. How could Will be dead? And where *were* Memphis and Sister Walker?

"Wait a minute. Detective Malloy, you said someone saw Memphis and Sister Walker here last night?"

"Correct."

"But *nobody* comes to the museum. It was headed for the auction block.

So who was watching it so closely last night? And why did they think to call you?"

"A concerned citizen happened to see."

"That's banana oil!"

One of the other cops whistled. "Temper, temper."

Malloy pointed a finger at the cops. "Pipe down or you're outta here."

The cops quieted quickly. The detective looked down his chin at Evie. He pushed his gum to his back molars with his tongue. "You were friends with Mabel Rose, weren't you, Miss O'Neill?"

"Yes, but I don't see what—"

"Mabel Rose was a member of the Secret Six. When we searched Miss Rose's room after the bombing, we found evidence that she'd been talking to someone we believe might be an accomplice, a Diviner named Maria Provenza."

"Maria wasn't a Diviner—it was her sister, Anna! And those creepy Shadow Men took Anna, too!"

Malloy narrowed his eyes. "And you know this how?"

She'd walked right into his trap like a Dumb Dora.

"See, I've got my own theory about what happened here. I know your uncle from way back. He was…eccentric. But trusting. Innocent. Maybe he knew something about the bombing. About a link between these anarchists and Diviners. Maybe he was gonna spill it and somebody didn't like that."

Detective Malloy had concocted his own fairy tale about Will, Evie could see now. To him, Will was an odd but brilliant ghost chaser in a musty museum who probably had trouble finding matching socks. He was not the man who'd gotten his own nephew killed and unwittingly opened a door for a great evil to come into this world. Will and his friends had been idealistic but reckless, and their recklessness had come at great cost.

"You didn't know my uncle at all."

Malloy's eyes were steely. "Maybe not. I sure didn't know Mabel Rose. Then again, maybe I don't know you so well, either, Miss O'Neill. I heard you refused to sign a loyalty pledge at WGI, and that's why they dismissed you. Maybe I shouldn't just be looking at Memphis Campbell." There was no mistaking the threat in Detective Malloy's words.

"Am I free to go?" Evie challenged.

"Sure. But don't leave town. None of youse."

Evie stormed out and down the front steps, for once ignoring the reporters waving their notebooks in the air, clamoring for a quote.

Woody sidled up to her. "Sheba, hey, Sheba! You okay? Aw, gee, Evie. I'm awfully sorry."

"Thank you."

"Listen. I know that must've been rough." He lowered his voice. "Can you tell your old friend Woody what you saw in there? Is it true there was a five-pointed star drawn on the floor like in the Pentacle Murders?"

Evie didn't know whether to admire the reporter's moxie or spit in his face. "There *was* a message left, Mr. Woodhouse," she said coolly.

Woody poised his pen above the page. "What'd it say, kid?"

"It said, 'No matter what happens to me, T. S. Woodhouse *will always be a rat*!'"

"Was that nice?" Woody yelled after her.

And it was all Evie could do not to give him a very not-nice gesture she'd seen some fellas on the Bowery do.

"Evie! Evie!" Henry waved to her from the corner.

Evie ran and linked arms with her friends, practically dragging them back toward the Bennington.

"Hey, don't pull my arm outta the socket. I got plans for it later," Theta said.

"On the level: Was Will murdered?" Henry asked.

"Yes," Evie said. "And Malloy thinks Memphis and Sister Walker did it."

"Bushwa!" Theta said. Her hands tingled with heat.

"Pos-i-tutely." Evie felt as if she were floating in her body, until a boy bumped headlong into her. "Ow! What's the big idea?"

"'Scuse me, miss. Message for you," he said. He shoved a scrap of paper into Evie's hand and ran off toward Central Park.

Theta peered over Evie's shoulder. "Say, that's a numbers slip. Memphis used to keep those in his socks when he was a runner for Papa Charles."

Something had been scribbled on the other side: *I know who killed him. Meet at Madame Seraphina's shop tonight. Bring everybody.* It was signed *MW.*

MW.

Margaret Walker.

GHOSTS

Evie stood outside the door to Will's apartment in the Bennington for some time. *No one lives here anymore*, she realized, and it sliced through her. Will was dead. Jericho was gone. Sam had been taken. The apartment was now a ghost. She rattled the doorknob. Locked. Evie took the stairwell that led up to the Bennington's roof. When she climbed out onto the tar expanse, she remembered a night in September, when she'd first arrived in the city, excited and hopeful, before the murders, the ghosts, the Shadow Men, and the terrible revelations about what her uncle Will, Sister Walker, and Jake Marlowe had done during Project Buffalo. Before she'd seen firsthand what the King of Crows could do. That night in October—it seemed ages ago now—she and Jericho had gazed out at the skyline, and then they'd kissed for the first time. The memory brought a flush to her skin. She'd liked being with Jericho. Liked his strong arms wrapped around her. He had been Mabel's crush, and she'd kissed him.

Evie couldn't stop herself from thinking that if she hadn't kissed him, if she'd worked harder to make Jericho fall in love with Mabel, maybe Mabel wouldn't have fallen in with Arthur Brown and joined up with anarchists. Maybe she'd still be alive. More than anything, Evie wished she could undo this part of her past. She wished she could stop Mabel from making such a terrible mistake.

And now here Evie was, desperate to find Sam but thinking of Jericho's kiss at the same time. And after what Jericho had done to her at Hopeful Harbor! What was wrong with her?

But how could she both love and hate her uncle Will? They'd fought so bitterly about her Diviner powers. She'd wanted to let the world know— why hide such a talent? Will had insisted it wasn't safe. In the end, Evie had told all those reporters about her object reading. She'd told them because everyone had a right to the truth; she'd told them because she wanted to be famous. Again, both things were true. She loved Will. She hated Will. She was desperate for Sam and she fantasized about Jericho. She wanted Mabel to rest in peace; she'd do anything to talk with Mabel again.

Evie crawled over the roof's edge onto the fire escape, descending till she was level with the window to her former bedroom. She snugged up the sash and angled her body inside. After she and Will had fought and she'd moved into a hotel, Sam had taken over her old room, until he, too, fought with Will and moved in with Henry. The pillows still smelled like him, though. If she wanted to, she could probably get a reading from this pillow and know his secrets, even secrets about her. That wasn't right, she knew. Still, her palms itched with the temptation.

There was a sound at the front door. From Sam's bed, Evie could see the knob rattling. *Uncle Will*, she thought. No. Not Will; of course not. He was dead. Then whom? Sam? Had he found his way back like the Houdini escape artist he was? The knob rattled again, that sound followed by the thud of someone heaving their strength against it. Fear pricked inside Evie. *The Shadow Men*. If they came for her, she'd scream loud enough to shake the building. She grabbed a lamp from the bedside table, grateful that her gloves muted the voices inside it for now, and tiptoed to wait beside the door. Another heave and it splintered open, and Evie brought the lamp down on the intruder's back with all her strength. The intruder stumbled forward and fell to his knees with a groan Evie recognized.

"Jericho?" she said.

"Hi, Evie," Jericho whispered and collapsed on Will's Persian rug.

✺

Evie helped Jericho to the table, then ran to the tap and brought back a cool glass of water, which Jericho gulped greedily. His clothes were filthy and torn, his lips chapped, and he was slightly delirious, as if he'd been wandering for days in some desert.

"Jericho, what's happened? Where've you been?" Evie asked.

"Woods," he gasped between gulps of water.

"What woods? Where?"

"Do you…anything to eat? Please?"

Evie rustled through Will's cupboards, trying not to think about the fact that her uncle was dead; he would never open these cupboards again. She found bread and a tin of peanut butter and made Jericho a sandwich. She took the milk bottle from the icebox, gave it a sniff, and handed that over as well.

"Sorry. This is all there is."

Jericho didn't seem to care; he polished off both like a desperate man. Evie was worried about his weakened state. If Jericho had been in the woods for a long time, it meant he'd been without his lifesaving serum, and she didn't want to think about what that could do to him. But she also remembered vividly the last time they'd been together, and she was wary. She hovered near the door and kept her hand ready to grab the lamp if need be.

Jericho stretched out his arms. Evie startled and reached for the lamp. Jericho saw. He knew why. The misery of it was on his face. The Übermensch serum had turned up some dial inside Jericho, and he'd attacked Evie. If Marlowe's butler hadn't shot several tranquilizer darts into Jericho, he would have been successful. *It wasn't his fault. He was doped up*, one side of Evie's brain said. *But what if it* was *his fault?* said the other. *What if that Mr. Hyde has lived inside Jericho always, and the serum just helped him along?*

"I promise I won't..." Jericho didn't finish. He kept his eyes trained on his hands, which were now wrapped around the empty glass.

Evie blushed but did not leave her place by the door. "I...I know you didn't mean to..."

"If I could take it back, I would."

"I know that," Evie said softly.

"I just keep...reliving that day over and over. I don't remember much of what happened after Marlowe gave me all that serum and I ran into the rose garden and saw you and I..." Jericho gazed intently at the glass. "I'm sorry."

Evie's chest tightened. She wanted to make him feel better. She wanted to keep her distance. "Never mind about that now. Won't you tell me about the woods? Can you tell me now what's happened to you?"

"I...escaped. From Hopeful Harbor."

"Why would you need to escape from Hopeful Harbor? Jericho..."

"I saw it, Evie. I saw the Eye."

The Eye! They'd been searching for clues to its whereabouts for weeks. The King of Crows had told them to hunt down the ghosts and ask them questions if they wanted to know more about the Eye. But it felt as if all they had gotten from the dead were riddles upon riddles.

Evie left her spot by the door and took a seat across the table from Jericho. "You found the Eye? Where is it?"

He nodded, and even this seemed to be an effort for him. "It's not a place.

It's a *machine*. Marlowe's golden machine of the future." Jericho let out a bitter laugh, but then his eyes welled with tears. He wiped at them with his forearm. When he was ready, he continued. "Evie, he's feeding Diviners to it."

"What do you mean?"

"This machine. The Eye. It's…I don't know. Almost like some sort of…telephone line to another dimension beyond this one. And the King of Crows is on the other end of that line!"

Evie's eyes widened. "The King of Crows is talking to Marlowe?"

Jericho nodded. "Yes. Through the machine."

"What's he telling him?"

"That I don't know. But it must have to do with the Eye because that machine is what's keeping the portal between the two worlds open. It's the reason the breach won't close."

"Follow the Eye, heal the breach…." Evie muttered. "That's what Memphis's mother told him to do."

"Marlowe has to charge the machine, though. All that uranium?"

"Ling wondered why Marlowe needed so much uranium, why he was pushing his workers at the mines to produce so much more," Evie said, nodding.

Mabel had been protesting the conditions at Marlowe's uranium mines and defending his striking workers. She'd said that Jake Marlowe wasn't a man to be trusted. Evie wished Mabel could know that she had been right to fight against him. "So it's uranium that makes the Eye work?"

"No. Not entirely."

"What, then?"

Jericho seemed haunted, lost. "Evie…what charges the machine, what makes it possible for him to see into that other world, is Diviner energy. Sam's mother, Miriam, was there. I saw her! Marlowe is keeping her at Hopeful Harbor."

"Sam…" Evie whispered. She was worried anew for him.

"Marlowe was talking to her while she was joined to the Eye. He said, 'You're the only one we've found who can balance the energy from the Diviners and the other side and keep the breach open.' Remember I told you I saw Anna Provenza there?"

"Yes! You said that the Shadow Men were dragging her off somewhere. They said she was a mental patient Jake Marlowe was trying to help."

"All lies. They fastened her to the Eye, and she was seeing into that other world and she was screaming, Evie, she was screaming and screaming...."

Evie wanted to reach out and put her hand on Jericho's arm, but she was afraid the gesture would be misconstrued. In another moment, he calmed. "Miriam knew I was hiding there. She could sense me in the room and she wanted me to know"—Jericho's voice got very quiet—"the truth."

Evie didn't know why her heart was suddenly beating so very fast, or why she had the urge to tell Jericho she didn't want to hear another word. "And what's the truth?"

"She said that what truly powered the heart of the machine, the source of its ferocious energy, were the souls of the soldiers of the One-Forty-Four. They're trapped inside it somehow, caught in some sort of terrible time loop. That one horrible day during the war, when they tore a hole between the two worlds, played over and over again. The Eternal Recurrence."

"James..." Evie said, tears springing to her eyes. That machine was powered by pain—the pain of her brother and of every soldier who'd been in his unit. "What has the King of Crows been telling Jake Marlowe? What has he made him believe?" Evie said, more to herself than to Jericho. "We have to get him to stop this. We have to get him to understand what he's doing."

"If we go up to Hopeful Harbor, he won't even let us in the door. And I-I don't want—I can't go back there."

"He'll be here for Sarah Snow's memorial tomorrow night. We'll go to him. We'll explain—"

"He knows! He doesn't care. He only cares about power. He only cares about winning, no matter the cost."

Jericho was right, Evie knew. She hated Jake Marlowe for what he'd done, for the lives he was still ruining. But she had to get him to try to understand. If Jake Marlowe liked to count himself a winner, she'd have to appeal to the side of him that hated to lose.

"All right," Evie said. "Then let's fight fire with fire. We'll tell Marlowe that we know something important about the King of Crows. Something that will help Marlowe defeat him."

"Like what?"

"That's the bait."

Jericho scoffed. "He'll never go for it."

"He will if we tell him that Isaiah had a vision so vital that we're duty bound to bring it to him."

Jericho pondered this for a moment. "He'll be staying at the Plaza Hotel. He takes a suite there."

"Perfect!" Evie headed for the telephone. "I'll call him—"

"Wait!" Jericho rose, and Evie backed away. Shame burned through Jericho. He would do anything to erase what had been done that day in the woods. He hoped he could earn back Evie's trust in time.

"*I'll* telephone him. No doubt he'll want to reclaim his prize," Jericho said bitterly.

"Well, he can't have you. You're with us now," Evie said.

Jericho was buoyed by a sudden ballooning of new hope. His eyes filled. He wiped them against his dirty shirtsleeve. "I'll go make that call," Jericho said and went into Will's study.

From where she was at the kitchen table, Evie could only hear bits and pieces. Jericho fed Marlowe the story along with one he concocted about the serum causing him to run away. After that, his answers were mostly along the lines of, "Yes, fine," "That will be fine," and "Thank you."

"Well?" Evie asked once he'd returned to the kitchen.

"He's agreed to talk with us."

"Well, that's a start at least. When are we meeting?"

"Tomorrow night. After Sarah Snow's memorial."

"At the Plaza?" Evie said hopefully.

Jericho shook his head. "He's flying to California right after the memorial. He said we're to come to the service and we'll talk there."

Evie groaned. "I can't believe I have to go to Sarah's memorial. Everyone thinks she was a saint, but she was a phony."

"So are lots of folks. Doesn't mean they deserve to be blown up."

"No. No, of course not," Evie said. Mabel, Mabel. What had she been thinking in those final moments under the stage with the bomb? Had she known she was going to die? Was she frightened? In life, they'd shared so much. But Mabel's death was a gnawing mystery.

Jericho was pacing the room, just like Will used to do, and that brought a lump to Evie's throat as well. He didn't seem delirious anymore. In fact, he was as clear-eyed and clearheaded as if he'd just woken from a good sleep.

"Jericho? How do you feel?"

Jericho stopped in his tracks. "Fine," he said, the realization dawning. "I feel...perfectly fine."

"And how long have you been without the serum now?"

He tipped his head back, thinking. "Four, five days at least?" He made a fist, relaxed his hand.

"And you were in the woods all that time, making your way back to the city. On foot. Without stopping to rest?"

"Mm-hmm." Jericho made a fist and flexed his fingers twice more. He really was fine. Better than fine. He felt goddamned immortal, and that confused Jericho: Jake Marlowe was repugnant in so many ways. But that same Jake Marlowe had not only cured Jericho, he'd made him superhuman. He had turned Jericho into his shining example of a superior American, the Übermensch, the Superman.

But did Jericho want to be that Übermensch?

Jericho craned his neck, looking around the empty flat as if truly seeing it for the first time. "Say, where's Will?"

❄

Theta knocked at Adelaide and Lillian Proctor's door. She'd never really had a family of her own, and she'd come to see the elderly sisters as adopted grandmothers. She'd grown especially close to Miss Addie, who had the sight. The Proctor sisters were descended from a long line of witches, and they had been encouraging Theta to become more comfortable working with her own power, though Theta felt no such comfort. Who could, knowing they might start a fire without meaning to? Most of the Diviners had useful powers; Theta saw hers as destructive. Hadn't it only brought pain so far?

She rubbed the silver locket at her neck, a gift from Miss Addie. Bloodstone, for courage. When no answer came at Theta's first knock, she rapped at the door again, and after a moment, a pale and drawn Miss Lillian opened it a sliver. Her face was somber.

"Oh, my dear. Come in. Quickly, quickly!"

Miss Lillian didn't stop to explain, so Theta followed her down the dim hallway, carefully avoiding the menagerie of feral cats at her feet. She wanted to take inventory of them to make sure that none of them had been sacrificed to divination, as she'd made the sisters promise, but there wasn't time for that. Whatever business Miss Lillian was about, it was urgent. At last they came to Miss Addie's bedroom. The curtains had been shut against the day. Miss Addie lay in her bed with her long gray-white hair billowing cloudlike around her face. Her eyes were open and staring straight ahead. She did not speak, and she seemed unaware of either Theta or Miss Lillian.

"I came in this morning and she was like this," Miss Lillian said, her voice breaking.

"Did you call a doctor?" Theta asked, alarmed. She lifted Miss Addie's bony wrist to check her pulse, which was steady.

"Of course I did! I'm not simple!" Miss Lillian snapped. "He said there's nothing physically wrong with her. She just won't wake up."

Miss Addie looked peaceful enough, except for her lips, which quivered as if she needed to say something. "Is it her heart?"

"It's a *curse*!" Miss Lillian shuffled over to Miss Addie's carved vanity. She opened the doors and removed a small jewelry box inlaid with mother-of-pearl. Miss Lillian opened it. There was nothing inside. "This is where Addie kept it all, but it's gone. It was the first thing I checked."

"Kept what? What's gone?"

"His finger. His hair. The *binding*," Miss Lillian whispered urgently.

Theta wanted to scream. Miss Addie was slowly dying, and her sister was talking in riddles.

"Sorry, Miss Lillian, but I'm not on the trolley," Theta said.

"Elijah."

Elijah had been Miss Addie's great love, Theta knew—killed during the Civil War, before they'd had the chance to marry. Even at sixteen, Addie had a strong connection to the world of spirits. She knew there was a trickster spirit who could give her what she wanted, and lost in grief for her dead lover, she went into the woods to bargain with the man in the stovepipe hat. He'd promised that she could have Elijah back if she pledged her loyalty to him. Foolishly, Addie agreed. One moonlit night, Elijah returned, just as the man in the hat had promised, but he was not the Elijah she remembered— young, beautiful, fair-haired, and smiling. He was the Elijah of the dead, with the rot of the grave upon him, and now they were bound for eternity by Addie's promise and the man in the hat's terrible trickery.

"He makes cruel bargains, you know," Miss Lillian said. "Addie was horrified by what she had done. Elijah would never stop coming for her now, she knew, unless she found a way to stop him. At midnight, she dug into his grave, snipped the fourth finger of his left hand, and cut a lock of hair. Then she performed the binding spell, placing it all inside this box for safekeeping. But the man in the hat tricked her again. He got to her in her sleep, she told me. He whispered in her ear to empty the box, to ruin the binding spell. She was left with no protection from Elijah."

"I saw him," Theta said. "That time in the basement." She shuddered at the memory of the rotting ghoul coming after them. There was no stopping him. Just like Roy.

Miss Lillian stroked her sister's hair. "He wants to punish her. To rob her of strength."

"Why?"

"She defied him! He doesn't like that. But I suspect that he wants to keep her from you. So that she can't protect you. Can't teach you. She's trapped like this. There's no telling what he's doing to her." Miss Lillian's eyes moistened again. "I'll do what I can to keep her alive. I have my ways. But I can't hold it off forever. And once she's gone, there's no hope. He will have her for eternity."

Theta wasn't about to let that happen. But how could she free Addie in time? "What can I do?"

Miss Lillian left her sister's bedside and returned after a moment, a slim, well-worn leather book in her hand. "Her diary. Her spells. Go on, take it. She'd want you to have it."

Theta opened it. It was inscribed, *To our Adelaide with love, Mama and Papa. Christmas 1860*. The pages crackled as Theta turned them. Miss Addie's elegant cursive filled each one.

"All she knows of the King of Crows is in that little book. I hope that it can be of help to you," Miss Lillian said. "Please. Please, bring her home, Theta."

ADDIE

Adelaide Proctor's body lay perfectly still, but her feverish mind dreamed of a dew-kissed meadow. Sweet clover as far as the eye could see. And daisies—her favorite. What a glorious morning it was! The sun pushing up fine and warm. The day would burn into a perfect summer beauty. Addie gathered marigolds in her arms, singing "Gentle Annie" as she did:

> *Thou will come no more, gentle Annie*
> *Like a flower thy spirit did depart;*
> *Thou are gone, alas! like the many*
> *That have bloomed in the summer of my heart.*

She stooped to twist a flower from its stalk and add it to her pile. When she raised her head, she was pleasantly surprised to see her lover, Elijah, standing at the edge of the field. The bright sun burnished the top of his blond head to a high gleam. Addie waved and called to him. He did not return the wave but began walking toward her. How she'd missed him! He'd been somewhere....Where was it? Had he traveled to see his cousins in Charlottesville? She couldn't remember, but it seemed he'd been gone for ages. Oh, she was impatient for him to reach her, and so she hurried her steps to meet him, thinking of the evening ahead. They might take her pa's wagon into town. Lillian would have to come, of course. Their mother would insist on a chaperone. No matter. She and Elijah would find a way to steal secret kisses. She loved the press of his lips against hers, a joining of souls. They'd be married soon enough. Yes, he'd asked her to marry him—she remembered now! But they had to wait. Why was that?

A cannon fired, far off. The ground shook a little. Plumes of smoke rose from the distant woods. But never mind that now, for look! Elijah was getting closer. His skin shone clean as a new nickel. He was almost too bright to bear, like an angel fallen to earth. It felt like forever since they'd kissed behind the barn and Elijah had promised they would set up house on a farm down the road from her parents in a cabin he'd built with his brothers.

Addie's steps slowed. Her brothers. Something about her brothers. The sun was a fixed dot in the sky. Again the unseen cannon whistled, and there was a great thumping wheeze, like a steam-powered thresher getting too hot.

Elijah. Yes, Elijah. Go to him.

No, wait. Her brothers. Her brothers were…dead. Some awful fever, wasn't it? A buzzing whine like bees. The machine grew louder, screamed. Where was that hideous sound coming from? She sang over it:

> *We have roamed and loved mid the bowers*
> *When thy downy cheeks were in their bloom…*

Elijah, getting closer. Walking stiff-legged. Strangely.
There was no wind in the meadow. Why was there no wind?

> *Now I stand alone mid the flowers*

Alone.

> *While they mingle their perfumes*
> *o'er*
> *thy*
> *tomb.*

A fly landed on Addie's cheek. She slapped as it bit. Sickly wine-dark blood pooled in her hand. Unnatural. *Unnatural.* The flies were everywhere, and her brothers and mother were all dead, she knew. Had died during the War Between the States. The war…

And Elijah?

Elijah was nearly to her. Nearly to her with his lips that had once kissed her so sweetly. Nearly to her with his sharp teeth bared like a rabid dog's when it growls and, no, that couldn't be right, and mercy, but it was suffocating in the meadow—why was there no wind? The nickel gleam of Elijah's face was no angel's glow but the glare of raw bone peeking through ragged holes in his decomposing skin. Maggots had infested the filthy wool of his gray uniform.

(He'd gone to fight.)

Black flies swarmed the still air around him.

(They would marry after the war, after the war, they would marry....)

The flies crawled across his rotting skin and cold lips because Elijah was dead, was dead, had been dead for sixty years. And just before her dead lover reached out to grab her hair, Addie screamed.

She hitched up her skirts, turned, and ran back toward the white clapboard church in the distance with the black wagon hearse drawn by six white horses out front. Behind her, Elijah was still coming, and there were more dead with him: Spirits who had not been content in death. Some who wanted vengeance. Some who had dealt violence in life and whose bloodlust had never left them. The petty, the empty, the lost, the grudge-holders, the desperately lonely, the weak. Husks of souls who had made bad bargains with the man in the stovepipe hat. Whatever the cause that kept them from eternal rest, these spirits were in thrall to him. Just like Elijah. But Addie had seen to that. She'd made the deal that had cursed her lover. She'd wanted him to rise from the dead, and he had, in his Confederate grays, and now, now she realized the folly of it all. How wrong she'd been. How wrong they had been. Elijah, dying for a bad cause. Addie, resurrecting what needed to stay dead.

Addie ran past the hearse. The skeletal driver tipped his hat. "We've been waiting for you, Adelaide."

With a cry, Addie stumbled back. The church doors opened and she ran inside. But there were no pews, no pulpit. She had glimpsed this place once before, on the night she'd made a deal with the man in the hat. This was *his* land, the land of the dead. A jaundiced moon hung above the twisted fingers of dead trees, stripped of all life. The sky had been emptied of stars.

"Good evening, Adelaide." The King of Crows sat upon a throne of skulls. Beside him stood a sad woman whose dark brown skin erupted in feathers. Her eyelashes twitched—feathers. He had cursed this woman, too, Addie knew. She'd entered into a bargain to save her boys, and he'd made her his shape-shifting messenger between worlds, part woman, part crow. This was Viola Campbell. Mother of Memphis and Isaiah Campbell.

Perhaps they could help each other. Help the Diviners before it was too late. But when Viola tried to speak, it was only a squawk, just before she coughed up a small frayed tuft.

"Adelaide Proctor. Did you think the King of Crows would not come to collect on a bargain?"

The King of Crows. There wasn't enough power in any world for him. His greed was as insatiable as his cruelty.

"Let me go. I'm just an old woman of no use to you."

"But you might be of use to them."

"They'll stop you."

"The Diviners." The King of Crows laughed. "What fun I shall have with them. And with you."

"What do you want?"

The King's dark eyes reflected no light. "Everything."

"You want to remake the world in your image, like a malevolent god?"

"*Your* world created *me*. I am born of your want and greed and neglect. Your death wish. And I shall come to collect. Keep dreaming, Adelaide Proctor. For when you finally wake, you shall be one with the land of the dead. Another hungry spirit in my army."

He gave Addie a push in the center of her chest, and she fell backward into an open grave, sinking down for what felt like forever, and far above, the King of Crows stood at the edge, laughing as he watched her fall.

HISTORY LESSON

At six o'clock, Madame Seraphina, Harlem's number one banker and vodou priestess, opened the door to her basement shop and ushered Evie, Jericho, Henry, and Theta inside. Up and down the block, her loyal runners kept watch from stoops and street corners, ready to alert her with a whistle if it came to that.

"With Papa Charles gone, Dutch Schultz is trying to squeeze in on the Harlem numbers game. His boys roughed up a Diviner, an Obeah man, over on Lenox Avenue a few days ago. I don't go anywhere without protection now," Seraphina said in explanation. "Not after what happened to Papa."

She disappeared into a room hidden behind velvet drapes and reemerged a moment later with Memphis, Isaiah, and Bill in tow.

"Memphis!" Theta ran to Memphis's arms and they held each other tightly. Theta kissed him—mouth, cheeks, nose, mouth again. She didn't care who saw or if they were embarrassed by so much open affection. "Where were you? I was so worried."

"The Shadow Men came after us. We escaped through the tunnel that leads from the museum."

"We got stuck in the sewers! There was a ghost after us!" Isaiah exclaimed.

"A ghost?" Evie said.

"Sewers?" Theta said with a grimace.

"Good thing your auntie dropped off those fresh clothes for you," Seraphina said. She laughed. "Wouldn't bring 'em here, though. She made my runner go to Mother Zion to get 'em. That woman is pious. I will give her that."

Sister Walker emerged from behind a curtained doorway. She appraised Bill coolly. "You promised me you'd look after Memphis and Isaiah, get them out of town."

Bill puffed out his chest. "Wadn't my idea to come back."

"Will Fitzgerald paid with his life so you all could escape," Sister Walker said.

"That's why we came back. I had to know that everybody was okay," Memphis said, holding Theta close.

A whistle came from outside—the prearranged signal from Seraphina's runners. Everyone tensed as someone banged at the door.

"Shadow Men!" Isaiah said.

"Or Bible salesmen," Henry whispered.

"Whatever you do, don't let the Bible salesmen in," Evie whispered back. "They're harder to get rid of than murderers."

Theta smacked Evie's arm. "Stop joking around. This is serious."

Madame Seraphina peeked out through the drawn drapes, then opened the door. Ling Chan stepped inside and took in the sight of everyone huddled together. "What?"

Theta let out her breath in a whoosh. "We thought you might be the Shadow Men."

"I don't think those fellas knock," Jericho said.

"Come. Have a seat," Madame Seraphina said, and Ling eased herself into a chair and rested her crutches against one of its velvet arms.

Henry was grinning at her. Ling exhaled in irritation. *"What?"*

"You're ten minutes late," Henry said, gleeful. "I didn't know you could *be* late."

"I had to ask my cousin Seamus for a ride. Do you know what he does?" Ling didn't wait for an answer. "He eats corned beef for lunch, and then he breaks wind in the car with the windows rolled up. It's a very long ride from Chinatown to Harlem."

"I hope this won't take too long," Henry said apologetically. "I took a new job at the Ambassador Hotel."

"Bellhop?" Bill asked.

Henry looked chagrined. "Playing Chopin waltzes in their lobby."

Evie made a face. "That stodgy place? It's full of dew-droppers and four-flushers looking for some egg to keep 'em in the good life."

Henry sighed. "I know. But I'm very sentimental about the money."

Memphis cleared his throat. "We're all here and accounted for, Sister."

"Almost," Evie said quietly.

Sister Walker crumpled into a chair. She was a tall, broad-shouldered woman, but she seemed suddenly smaller and more fragile.

"Is it true?" Evie asked. "Did those Shadow Men murder Uncle Will?"

Sister Walker nodded, fighting tears. She coughed several times, the cough boiling up from her like tea in a heating pot. She searched in her pocketbook and found a lozenge to soothe her throat. When her emotions and the cough were under control, she spoke slowly, with great effort. "I was upstairs in the stacks when they came in. Will warned me to stay out of sight. All I could do was listen."

Evie pictured her uncle struggling against the two Shadow Men as they strangled him to death. "Why didn't you do something?" she demanded. "Why didn't you scream or...or...he was your *friend*. Why didn't you *stop them*?"

"So they could kill me, too?" Sister Walker held Evie's gaze until Evie looked away. "Will made it quite clear that I should stay hidden. He wanted me to survive, to bear witness. So I could bring this."

From her pocketbook, she removed Will's dusty library edition of *The Federalist Papers* and dropped it on the coffee table.

"The professor wanted us to have a history lesson?" Henry said.

"In a manner of speaking. This is what's left of our files on Project Buffalo," Sister Walker explained. "These files are proof. Proof of our experiments on a vulnerable population of women. Proof of the powerful men who stood to gain from it: The Founders Club. The United States government. Senators and tycoons and generals. Jake Marlowe."

"You," Evie said pointedly.

"If you think they would've let a woman like me benefit from this research, you don't know much. I resisted once and went to prison for it, if you'll recall," Sister Walker answered with cool anger.

Ling opened the book. Official-looking papers had been folded and shoved between the pages. Everything was there—names, dates, progress. There were signatures from two different American presidents, as well as a secretary of war. There was mention of the man in the stovepipe hat in dreams and visions and warnings, all of it ignored. Over Ling's shoulder, Evie read quickly down the page and found what she was looking for: James Xavier O'Neill. Of the U.S. Army. Unit 144. It galled her that she would have to go to Marlowe tomorrow night and try to make peace for the sake of putting an end to the Eye and her brother's misery. To save the world she'd have to compromise with the enemy. "How do we know that's what really happened? How do we know you didn't call those Shadow Men yourself?"

"You'll have to take my word for it," Sister Walker said. Her cough returned.

"Let me pour you some tea," Seraphina said.

Sister Walker put up a hand, then relented. "Thank you."

Ling held up the pages. There were about a dozen of them. "We need to get these documents to the newspapers."

Seraphina snorted. "You think your institutions will save you? They're part of this."

"She's right. I don't think a Big Cheese like Mr. Hearst will publish them. He's pals with the same people who paid for Project Buffalo. Rich, powerful people protect other rich, powerful people. I should know," Henry said bitterly.

Memphis nodded at Evie. "Your friend T. S. Woodhouse might print it."

"That rat at the *Daily News*?" Theta said, an unlit cigarette bobbing against her lower lip. "Why, he'd publish his grandmother's diary if he thought he could get enough column inches for it. At the museum, he was offering Evie a shoulder to cry on and trying to get a quote all at the same time."

"Woody is pos-i-tutely the worst," Evie agreed. "He's unscrupulous and murderously ambitious and, if what I read from his wallet once is true, he has some rather unorthodox habits of a sexual nature—"

Henry raised an eyebrow. "How unorthodox?"

"—which I would prefer not to discuss. Until later. With cocktails. But he's the only one who's believed us about everything so far. He wants the truth as much as we do. And he never quits."

"Then I say we take it to the rat," Memphis said.

"And then what?" Theta said.

"Then they arrest the Shadow Men for Uncle Will's murder," Evie said.

Seraphina shook her head and cackled as she returned with two cups of tea, one for herself and one for Sister Walker. "Those people? They always get away with murder. They got away with killing Papa Charles. Nobody's writing about that in the *Daily News*, I notice."

"You think those Shadow Men killed Papa Charles?" Memphis asked.

Seraphina's expression said everything.

"Fine. I'll take those papers to Mr. Woodhouse myself, then," Memphis said.

"We can't go to Woody just yet," Evie blurted.

Theta eyed her suspiciously. "Yeah? What are we waiting for, Flag Day?"

Evie took a deep breath and let her words out very quickly. "We can't because we have to meet with Jake Marlowe tomorrow night. After we attend Sarah Snow's memorial."

"I beg your pardon?" Sister Walker said.

"The hell we do!" Theta growled.

"Wait just a minute—when did this happen? Who arranged it?" Ling asked.

"Jericho and I did," Evie said.

"Without asking the rest of us?" Ling said. "Who died and made you boss?"

"My uncle Will," Evie said through her teeth.

The conversation turned even more contentious, everyone talking at once, hurling accusations and counteraccusations while Sister Walker tried to calm tempers.

"I've seen the Eye of Providence! I've seen what horrors it can do!" Jericho said at last, raising his voice above the din until everyone quieted. "The Eye and the time loop with Evie's brother and the One-Forty-Four is what's keeping the breach between our world and the land of the dead open. But it's wildly unstable. It's releasing all sorts of strange energy. Marlowe keeps needing to recharge it, and for that, he's using Diviners."

"Using them how?" Ling said nervously.

"He attaches them to the Eye and it sucks the life from them."

"We have to save Sam," Evie declared. "I won't let him be fed to that awful thing."

"The King of Crows is toying with Marlowe, doling out instructions for keeping the breach between worlds open permanently," Jericho continued. "Do you really want to leave that in Jake's hands without telling him what we know?"

"My god. He's still using it," Sister Walker said, disgusted. "He was supposed to destroy it after what happened during the war."

"All the more reason we shouldn't go see that bum Marlowe, you ask me," Theta said.

"If we can't convince Marlowe to destroy the Eye, my brother and the other soldiers will stay trapped in that awful loop, playing out the same agonizing day again and again." Evie's voice broke. She wished Sam were there. She wished Mabel were there. She wished Will were there to tell them what to do. Evie glared at Sister Walker. "And you're responsible for it."

Sister Walker bristled. "That's not true."

"Maybe not fully. But she ain't all wrong, either," Bill challenged. Healed by Memphis's power, he stood tall before Sister Walker. But his youth he could never get back. That had been taken from him by Project Buffalo and the Shadow Men. And Margaret Walker and Will Fitzgerald had let those men do that to him.

Sister Walker started in on Bill while Evie, Memphis, and the others were getting all worked up about Jake Marlowe's machine. Everybody was always talking, and Isaiah never got to speak. Memphis had promised that what Isaiah had to say was important and now, as usual, everybody else was running their mouths, arguing over every little thing. He'd been holding on to his story for as long as he could, but now he felt like he would burst if he didn't talk. "I had a vision while we were in the tunnels!" he blurted. "About another Diviner. She said she was in danger. She said we were all in danger from the King of Crows and his army. And she knows how to stop him! But we gotta get to her. We gotta go to Bountiful."

"Bountiful?" Evie repeated.

"Uh-huh. Bountiful, Nebraska."

"Sarah Beth Olson," Evie said.

"Say, how'd you know her name?" Isaiah was annoyed. Finally, he had something of his own to share that made him feel special, and here Evie had gone and stolen his thunder.

"She was one of the Diviners created by Project Buffalo," Evie said, excited. "I read her chart."

Sister Walker frowned. "I don't remember her. But she could have been one of Rotke's, or someone else's in the department. What else did you get from her chart?"

"She was a little younger than we are. She'd be about fifteen now. Yes, I remember! According to the notes, she had an imaginary friend." Evie's eyes widened. "A man in a stovepipe hat."

"That don't sound like a good thing to me," Bill cautioned.

"Sarah Beth said he lied to her. That somebody named Miriam told her the truth," Isaiah said.

"Sam's mother!" Evie said.

"Gee, how would she know about Sam's mother unless she was on the up-and-up?" Theta asked.

Evie frowned. "There was something written at the bottom of Sarah Beth's chart. A recommendation that they not continue. Why would they say that?"

Sister Walker shook her head. "I don't know. Maybe her powers were too strong. Maybe they frightened someone."

"I thought that's what your bosses wanted—to make us into weapons," Henry said.

"*They* saw you as weapons. But for those of us doing the work in the Department of Paranormal, it was apparent that there was so much more to explore—the potential to create something new. Something that could connect us to the infinite and unseen. Something just outside our grasp."

"We still don't know what we're capable of. We know we can create an energy field and disturb matter, possibly even change its atomic structure," Ling said, ever the scientist. "But is that it? Is there more?"

"There has to be. I think we've barely scratched the surface," Sister Walker said. "Give me a chance to work with you, and we can find out just how strong you are together. We could still unlock wonders."

"But do you know that?" Jericho asked. "I saw what happened to the men of the Daedalus program. *They* got stronger, and then they weakened, went mad. They were on Marlowe's serum—the serum you all developed to make Diviners." The serum that had been flowing through Jericho's body for ten years. The serum he was now without. Jericho shoved his hands in his pockets and squeezed his fingers tight, making fists.

Ling looked concerned. "Will we get weaker over time the more we use our power? Will it make us vulnerable to the King of Crows and his dead? Are there consequences we don't know about?"

"I told you, Sarah Beth can help us!" Isaiah tried again. "She knows how to stop him. And she sure seemed scared of him. She's all alone out there."

"Is there a way to stop the King of Crows that doesn't put us in Nebraska?" Theta asked. "You ever been to Nebraska? It's a real flat tire."

Henry snugged his arm across Theta's shoulders, smiling. "On the bright side, it's all the corn you can eat."

"You're not listening to me!" Isaiah shouted.

"Easy, Little Man," Bill warned.

But Isaiah didn't want to be easy. He wanted to be heard. "Sarah Beth said we're not safe on our own. We're in danger. We need to go to Bountiful!"

"Did she say *how* we can stop the King of Crows?" Ling asked.

"No. She said we have to get to Bountiful first. That we all have to be together for it to work. She saved us from a ghost in the tunnel!"

That got everybody arguing again till the room was like sitting ringside at a boxing match, everybody talking at once, shouting one another down, until Madame Seraphina let loose with a sharp whistle that hurt Isaiah's ears.

"I won't have this bad energy in my house," she said firmly.

"I think we should go to Bountiful," Evie said.

"Evie, you don't know anything about this girl," Sister Walker cautioned.

"Nor do you!"

"Let me work with all of you, strengthen your powers—"

"I'm not going to Bountiful," Ling said. "I have to help my parents with the restaurant. Some of us have responsibilities."

"What's that supposed to mean?" Evie snapped.

"That does seem like a long way to go on just a vision," Henry said.

"She was scared!" Isaiah insisted. He was afraid he would cry, which was what happened when he got angry. "She needs our help. Memphis, Mama always said we should help where we could."

"Well, we cain't help her, Little Man. Got to help ourselves by gettin' outta town," Bill said.

"I vote Bountiful," Evie said, raising her hand.

"Bountiful," Jericho said.

"I say we stay and work with Sister Walker," Henry said.

"I'm with Henry," Ling said.

"Me, too," Theta said, not looking at Isaiah.

"Then we stay here," Memphis said. "We work with Sister Walker and figure out how to stop the King of Crows from doing whatever it is he's got up his sleeve."

Isaiah looked up at Memphis. The betrayal showed in his eyes. Memphis reached out, but Isaiah ran to the other side of the room.

"Isaiah," Memphis called. He felt lousy for making Isaiah feel bad, but his brother would get over it.

"Memphis, how you gonna do that with them Shadow Men after you?" Bill tapped his finger against his temple. "You're not thinkin'."

"I didn't ask you."

"Yeah, well, I'm telling you. Spoke with Miss Seraphina and Octavia. There's a train to New Orleans tomorrow night, and we need to be on it. Got it all sorted with the Brotherhood."

"What are you talking about?"

"The Brotherhood of the Sleeping Car Porters," Seraphina said. "One of them, Mr. Nelson Desir, owes me a favor. The Brotherhood will see you out of town."

"I'm not going," Memphis said.

"The hell you're not."

"I won't warn you again about the bad energy," Seraphina said.

Memphis put his arm around Theta. "We get Marlowe to see reason, he'll call off those Shadow Men. I can stay right here."

"I've known that man more than twenty years," Sister Walker said. "There's no reasoning with him. He believes his way is the only way. He's always right. Dangerously so."

"We have to at least try, don't we?" Evie asked.

"You're still playing by their rules," Seraphina broke in. "You'll never get anywhere that way. Remember: They make the rules to suit themselves. And they change them to suit themselves."

Sister Walker looked at Evie. "I don't like this. What will you do if there are Shadow Men there?"

"If they come for us, we'll show 'em what Diviners can do. We'll give 'em a real lulu of a disturbance," Evie said.

"We create a disturbance and we're playing into everything they believe about Diviners," Theta reminded her.

"I'm not saying we *will* do it. I'm saying we *can* do it. It's good for Jake Marlowe to know that, too," Evie said. "So we're decided: We go talk to Jake Marlowe at the memorial tomorrow night and try to get him to understand how dangerous the Eye is. If he shuts it down, the King of Crows will have no way into our world. Our troubles are solved."

Ling tapped her fingers against the arm of the chair. "Why hasn't the

King of Crows come after us if we're a threat?" The question hung in the air along with Theta's cigarette smoke. "The King of Crows controls the dead. They're loyal to him," Ling continued. "What happens if there are ghosts he *can't* control?"

"I didn't think this situation could get any creepier, but you've managed it," Henry said. "Congratulations."

"If the ghosts come after us, we'll blast them apart until there's not one left," Evie said bitterly.

A triple knock at Seraphina's door put everyone on edge. Sister Walker grabbed a fireplace poker.

"You going to warm them up, Margaret?" Seraphina said, bemused. "At ease. That's my signal."

Seraphina disappeared into the little foyer under the stoop. In a minute she returned, one hand at her hip. "Memphis, did you tell Alma to meet you here?"

"No, ma'am," Memphis said.

"Then who did?"

Alma entered, her chorus girl smile in place. "Hey, everybody."

Henry glanced over his shoulder at Ling. He'd never seen someone blush so hard in all his life.

RING

On the front stoop, Ling and Alma sat together and watched night come to Harlem in deepening shades of blue. Alma looked pretty in her drop-waist champagne-colored dress and matching cloche with a ruby brooch pinned to the ribbon. Ling wished she'd worn something other than the green dress she put on to work at the restaurant. The color washed her out, she thought, but it hid the food stains. There were people returning from work, eager to get back to their homes. Lights blinked on in windows. Down the street, a man took a broom to his sidewalk, brushing away spring blooms.

"Feels nice out here," Alma said after a while.

"Yes. Um. Breezy. But not too breezy," Ling said, a little giddy. Alma made her feel looser, less guarded. But she could tell that Alma was uncomfortable from the way she kept tapping one foot, making her knee shake. "Something on your mind?" Ling asked.

Alma looked down at her shoes. "I've been wanting to tell you."

"Tell me what?" Ling's heart beat faster like it did in her dream walks just before the landscape shifted into something new, something out of her control.

"I've joined up with TOBA," Alma said.

"What's a TOBA?"

Alma managed a half smile. "It's an acronym. Stands for Theater Owners Booking Association, though some folks say it means 'Tough on Black Asses.' It's the outfit that books Negro acts into vaudeville houses on the Chitlin Circuit."

It took a moment for Ling to catch up. "You're leaving?"

Alma looked down at her shoes again. Ling did, too. They were blond satin T-straps of the kind Ling had always liked, the kind she would not be wearing ever again. "If trouble's gonna come calling, it won't find me at home," Alma said. "It'll have to chase me down first."

All the words Ling wanted to say knotted in her throat: *Don't go. I want you to stay. I like you but I'm frightened. Could I love you? Could you love me? Does love even matter in this mess of a world? How can I possibly fight evil without having something worth fighting for?*

"When?"

"Day after tomorrow," Alma answered.

"Day after *tomorrow*?" Ling repeated, barely comprehending.

"A spot came open with a band, the Harlem Haymakers, and I had to jump on it. They have their own bus and everything. I'll be gone about three months. Maybe longer. It's a good way to make money and a name for myself and...Oh, horsefeathers, Ling. I need to leave New York. All these ghosts. And...us."

"Us," Ling repeated.

"I just don't know how we make this work between us," Alma said quietly.

Ling blushed with shame. Sex. It was about sex, or the lack thereof. From the corner of her eye, she watched as Alma laced her beautiful fingers and placed them in her lap. And then Ling forced herself to keep her gaze on the man across the street sweeping his patch of sidewalk. Ling watched the bristles pushing against the wilted flowers and felt as if she, too, were being brushed into the gutter.

"Aren't you...going to say something?" Alma whispered.

What could she possibly say? Ling had allowed herself to imagine a future with Alma while, apparently, Alma had been making other plans without her. The hurt cut so deeply Ling could scarcely catch her breath. "Seems you've already made up your mind."

"Ling...I think you're the bee's knees," Alma said softly after a minute or two had passed. "Honestly, I do. There's nobody quite like you out there."

That's why you're breaking it off with me on a stoop in Harlem. Because I'm so very special.

"I'm sorry that I couldn't...I'm sorry," Alma said. She stood and smoothed the wrinkles from her shiny dress.

The man had finished his sweeping. He headed back toward his house.

"Do you...want me to help you up or...anything?"

Ling cleared her throat. "No. I...no."

"It's chilly. Don't sit out here too long."

There were a hundred things Ling thought to say back: *I'll sit as long as I like. Don't act like my mother. I couldn't feel any colder than I already do.*

"Well," Alma said, still waiting. Ling let her wait another few seconds.

"Well," Ling said coolly. "Break a leg. That's what you say, isn't it? Even though it makes no sense." Nothing made sense. Nothing at all.

Alma gave a nervous little laugh. "Yes. That's what you say. It's supposed to keep away bad luck."

Well, it's not working, Ling thought. She wished she hadn't come uptown. If she'd stayed behind in the restaurant, Alma wouldn't have been able to say good-bye.

Alma walked to the bottom of the steps and looked up at Ling. She had the loveliest face, and Ling's chest squeezed tighter when she thought of never seeing it again.

"You're sure you're jake?" Alma said.

Ling was most decidedly not jake. But when people asked a question, they usually left you clues about how to answer. It didn't take a scientist to know that what Alma was really saying was, *Be okay. I don't want to feel guilty.*

"I have to go work at the restaurant," Ling said in response. She wouldn't give Alma the satisfaction of a clean getaway.

Alma's smile fluttered and her lashes batted away tears. The comment had landed, Ling could see, but she took very little satisfaction from it. "Honey, please, please don't hate me. I couldn't bear it. Clever as you are, you'll find someone. I know you will," Alma said.

Ling's throat burned with all she held back.

"I'll write you. I will! I'll send postcards from all over the country," Alma said, like she was wooing an audience.

"That's too expensive." Ling did not want to cry. Not with Alma there, and with Seraphina's runners keeping watch on the street.

Alma laughed and wiped her eyes with the backs of her hands. "See what I mean? You're always you. Always honest."

But Ling knew that was the biggest lie of all.

Alma pointed a finger at Ling. "You take care of yourself, you hear me? You get Jake Marlowe to stop that machine. I know you can. Do right, Ling Chan."

Do right. It's what Ling's mother would say. But in times like these, how could you know what was right? Ling sat on the steps for a while longer, watching Alma's champagne-colored dress swish down the street. Only when Alma rounded the corner did Ling let out the choking sob.

"Good-bye," she whispered.

Nearby, the bird watched her intently.

※

In the back room of Seraphina's shop, Memphis and Theta kissed until at last, in need of air, Theta leaned her forehead against Memphis's neck.

"I was so worried about you," she whispered.

Memphis stroked a thumb across her cheek. "And here I was worried about you."

She leaned her head back and squinted at Memphis. "You're gonna be on that train tomorrow, right?"

"There's no need."

Theta put a finger to Memphis's lips. "Those Shadow Men are hunting for you and Isaiah."

Memphis kissed Theta's finger and moved it aside. "How 'bout this: If we can't talk sense to Jake Marlowe at the memorial, I will board that train. Scout's honor."

She laughed. "You're no Scout."

"You got that right." Memphis kissed her fully, tasting the chalkiness of her lipstick and not caring. "Hey!" he said, breaking away. "I almost forgot. I sent a poem to the *Crisis*."

"You did?"

"Mm-hmm."

"Aw, Memphis, that's the berries!"

"I s'pose it seems pretty ridiculous what with everything else going on. Not that important."

"It *is* important," Theta insisted. "It can't be all catastrophe all the time."

Memphis smiled, sheepish. He dug into his pocket and pulled out a folded scrap of paper. "I . . . copied it out for you, if you want to read it. Not that you have to!"

"Try 'n' stop me." Theta lifted the folded paper from Memphis's fingers. She opened it. "'The Voice of Tomorrow.' Swell title." She read the first few lines aloud. "'America, America, will you listen to the story of you? You bruised mountains, purpled by majesty. You shining seas that refuse to see. You, haunted by ghosts of dreams…'" She read the rest in silence, then looked up into Memphis's hopeful face. "It's beautiful, Memphis."

"You're beautiful. I just…" He shook his head.

"What?"

"I think about this world. Even without this mess from the King of Crows, it feels broken." He gestured to the other room. "Everybody else, they defeat evil and get to go back to their lives. But you and me?" His body suddenly felt heavier. "What future do we have?"

Seraphina knocked and entered. "Wanted to talk to the both of you," she said, closing the door behind her. "I had a visit from Dutch Schultz's boys today. They said Miss Knight's husb—" She glanced at Memphis. "They said that Mr. Roy Stoughton is looking for you. He's joined up with the Klan to help him."

"He would," Theta growled.

"The Klan is all over this country, in every state of this union, in every small town and at every church picnic. No matter where you go, some man in a white robe will be looking to return you, like property stolen from its rightful owner. You must both be very careful." Seraphina reached into her pocket. "I have something for you, Memphis." In her hand was a simple gold band. "Go on."

Memphis held up the ring so he could read the inscription inside: *To my beloved, Viola. Forever, Marvin.* "This is my mother's wedding ring. She said she lost it. How did you…?"

"She gave it to me. As payment for my services," Seraphina explained.

Memphis closed the ring tightly in his fist. "You might've mentioned that last time I was here."

Seraphina raised one eyebrow, gave a small shrug. "You don't get to be Harlem's number one banker by giving it all away. You and I, we had a quid pro quo, and I didn't know if I might need more information from you. But it's better that you have it." She looked from Memphis to Theta. "At some point, I'm going to need this room back, you know," she said and shut the door.

Memphis examined the ring as if it, too, were a portal to another world.

"There's somebody who could help you with that, you know," Theta said.

"Who?"

"Who? Gloria Swanson, that's who," Theta cracked wise. "I'm talking about Evie."

"Nah. I don't wanna ask her for a favor."

"Why not?"

"I'll feel like I'm in her debt."

"That's dumb." Theta opened the door and stuck her head out. "Hey, Evil!" She motioned Evie over. "Memphis has something to ask you. Go on, Memphis."

"I was wondering if maybe you could read this wedding ring for me. It belonged to my mother. I was hoping…" Hoping what? He settled on a shrug.

Evie seemed to understand. "You bet-ski," she said. She took the ring and cupped it in her fist, squeezing. Evie had read for many strangers. It kept things impersonal. It was quite another matter to read for her friends. Once she knew something about them, it joined her. It made her feel a responsibility toward them that she wasn't always comfortable bearing. But the memories bubbling up from this ring were mostly happy ones.

Evie saw the Campbell family in their comfortable apartment in Harlem. It was as if she had entered the room and stood off to the side, watching but unseen. A ghost. Mr. Campbell was a handsome man, lithe and bedroom-eyed, with a trim mustache above a mouth that always seemed on the verge of a mischievous half smile. He spoke in a Southern drawl—hadn't Memphis said his father's family was from Georgia?—and it gave everything he said a bemused quality. Mrs. Campbell's speech had the lilt of the Caribbean in it. There was music in this house, and laughter and stories.

Mrs. Campbell snuggled up on the bed beside Memphis, telling him stories while baby Isaiah slept in his crib. Memphis giggled—giggled! Though she didn't know it, Evie was smiling as she pressed into the ring.

Another memory: Memphis cuddled a three-year-old Isaiah to himself as if his brother was the thing he loved most. Evie remembered playing hide-and-seek with James, the way he would indulge her as big brothers sometimes do.

"What do you see?" Memphis was asking Evie.

They were happy. This was what a happy family looked like. Even when her own family had been whole, before James went away, it had not been like this. With music and dancing and laughter. Her mother, always anxious and judging. Her love was a corrective love—"Evangeline, stand up straight. Evangeline, don't do that; what will the neighbors say? Evangeline, don't hug quite so fiercely, dear, you'll take my breath away." Her father, always distracted with work, kind enough but needing Evie to be his adoring little girl. Watching Memphis's family now, Evie felt robbed. The sharpness pinched her breath. Her chest ached.

"Evie?" Memphis.

"Oh, um, nothing much yet," she answered and pressed in harder.

Now the ring took on a different feeling. Darker. Like a fairy-tale turn into the woods. Viola stood at a crossroads under a full moon. After a moment, the King of Crows emerged.

Viola was confused. "You are not Baron Samedi."

"I am not many things," the man in the hat answered. He was not yet the King of Crows, but his power was growing. His rumpled coat was thinly feathered. Evie wished she could read something of his, something that would give away his secrets, but this was Viola's ring, after all.

What she saw now came in small bursts, like a radio signal flaring and fading.

"I took bad medicine," Viola said. "I feel it in my body! What if it harms my boys? And... and there are men who would come for them. Bad men."

"You wish protection from this harm for your boys?"

"Yes," Viola said on a whisper. "Please."

"And what will you offer me?"

"I..." Viola removed her pearl ear-bobs. "These were my granmé's."

"Not enough. I would have your pledge. Take my hand."

Viola reached out. In a flash of light, they were in the land of the dead. The sky was the purplish ochre of an approaching storm. The land was as desolate as the pictures she'd seen of the battlefields of Flanders and the Somme. There was a feeling of great emptiness. Even through the distance of an object, that terrible emptiness reached into Evie's very soul like an infection of which she'd never fully be cured.

"Your son is a healer," the man in the hat said, and Evie felt Viola's terror as she peered into those sharklike eyes, now possessed of some new plan.

"Y-yes," Viola said. "And my other son—"

The man in the hat interrupted her with a wave of his hand. "The other boy is of no consequence to me. He has shown no powers. The healer, though. He could prove useful to me. Or dangerous."

"Memphis? He's just a boy. He has no real p-power—"

The man in the hat glared. "Never lie to me."

Viola's heart beat so fast Evie felt her own thumping in sympathy.

"Very well," the man in the hat said with a smile, as if he'd moved on. "I will shield your children for as long as you honor my terms: Upon your death, you will become my servant. You will be under my control."

Viola bristled. She was a proud woman, Evie could sense. But she was also sick and getting sicker. The cancer moved through her blood. She wrote her name inside the man's coat. Quickly, he sealed it shut. A nasty cough seized Viola. She hacked and hacked to expel something caught in her throat, spitting out at last a tiny feather fragment, coated thinly with blood.

"You are mine. Soon enough."

Evie remembered the time she and Memphis had been trapped by ghosts in the subway. She'd thought for sure the ghosts would devour them, but instead they'd sniffed and walked away. Had that been the King of Crows's doing?

"When..." Viola licked her lips. It was a moment before she could speak again. "When does this bargain end?"

"End?" The man in the hat grinned. "The bargains are only null and void if I am no more. Viola Campbell: What is done is done. Your son has no leave to heal you. Should he try, he will violate the terms of this contract. Do you understand?"

"Yes," Viola whispered.

The ring jostled Evie around through time. There was Viola, looking up and down the street in front of Seraphina's shop. *She doesn't want to be seen coming here*, Evie thought, feeling Viola's hesitation. In this memory, Viola Campbell was quite a bit sicker. Her hair had thinned; her previously full face was gaunt. She knew her days were numbered.

"I made a bad bargain. I need protection. Not for me. For my boys."

"You can pay?"

Embarrassment. Fear. Evie felt it all. Viola slid the wedding ring from her bony finger and held it out. "It's real gold."

Seraphina tilted her chin up, appraising the ring before she slipped it into her pocket. The ring was Seraphina's now, and it had her memories fused to it. The perspective changed. That was all.

Evie came out of her trance and handed the ring back to Memphis.

"Well?" Theta asked.

"Memphis," Evie started. "Did you...try to heal your mother?"

Memphis's face showed surprise, followed by pain. "She told me not to do it. Begged me not to." Memphis paused for a moment. "But she was my mother. In the end, I couldn't. I wasn't powerful enough. She died anyway. And I lost my healing."

"But it came back," Theta reminded him.

"I don't think that was your doing," Evie said, rubbing at the back of her neck where the headache was just starting. "She went to him for protection against the Shadow Men, I believe. The King of Crows made your mother promise you couldn't heal her or the deal was off. I think he was trying to trap you."

"Why?"

There was something there. Some reason the King of Crows wanted Memphis.

"I don't know. I know this sounds pos-i-tutely batty, but I almost had the feeling that he's afraid of you. Your mother would've done anything for you, though," Evie said, swallowing down her jealousy. All mothers love their children, it was said. *Not all mothers*, Evie thought bitterly. But Viola Campbell had loved her sons desperately enough to bargain away her soul for them.

Memphis held tight to the ring. "All the more reason why I'm gonna get her back from him."

WITNESS

The street lamps were just winking on as Margaret "Sister" Walker approached her house. She was jittery and exhausted. Will Fitzgerald was dead. She'd heard him struggle for breath as the Shadow Man tightened the wire around his neck. The full weight of the horror hit her, made her bones feel like lead. She remembered meeting Will at the Department of Paranormal in the first years of this new century. They had come from different families, different backgrounds, but in Will she had sensed a kindred spirit when it came to the supernatural. How excited they'd all been by this venture into the unknown, into other dimensions. Through contact with another world, they had hoped to change their own. Naively, Margaret hadn't realized just how different that change looked to each of them, exciting for some, threatening for others. How terribly it had all ended. Of the original members of the Department of Paranormal, only she and Jake Marlowe were left alive. Jake, with his ideas of racial purity and America first; Margaret herself, playing advisor to the ragtag crew of man-made Diviners who could stop him from making a catastrophic mistake if the Shadow Men or the King of Crows and his Army of the Dead didn't get there first.

Margaret willed her tired feet to walk faster. She'd go to T. S. Woodhouse at the *Daily News*, then. The truth would be exposed. Yes, that was the way. The power of the press. She just needed those files. She hadn't been entirely honest with the Diviners. There were also files hidden away in her house. Files that implicated her in Project Buffalo. They were all guilty, Jake most of all, but Margaret knew he would never take the fall for their crimes. She fumbled with her keys in her pocketbook. Almost there. Margaret looked up and clamped a hand over her mouth to stifle her scream.

"Will," she whispered through her trembling fingers.

He stood on her brownstone stoop, wispy as early morning fog. The ligature marks from the piano wire glowed at his neck. The ghost of her murdered friend glanced up at her front door, then back at her. He shook his head slowly. A warning. She found herself nodding. And then he was gone.

Margaret crept into the front yard and pressed herself against the garden-level door, out of sight, hidden by the falling night. Seconds later, she heard the front door open and close. Footsteps on the stairs above. They landed with the arrogant surety of men not used to being questioned about their comings and goings. Margaret pressed herself farther into the deepening shadows. At the gate, one Shadow Man stopped to light his cigarette.

"Guess she's flown the coop," he said to the other, and Margaret scarcely breathed as those sure footsteps carried the men all the way down the block. Margaret made herself count to ten, and then she tore up the stoop and, with shaking hands, let herself in through the front door of the brownstone, into the small foyer. The door to her apartment was ajar. Her sofa and chairs had been slashed to ribbons. Their feathery innards dusted the floor and fell across the ruined furniture. The entire place had been ransacked. They had wanted her to know they were looking.

She raced to the far wall and removed the painting of Paris. She stuck her hand into the hole there, exhaling in relief as she dragged the files from their hiding place. A crow cawed outside her window. Loud. Insistent. Margaret crept to the window. The bird flitted on the ledge. "Viola?" Margaret whispered. The crow squawked something fierce. Too late, Margaret heard the footsteps racing back up to her door. The Shadow Men had returned.

"Margaret Andrews Walker." The man with the small teeth. The one who'd murdered Will. Jefferson was his name. The other, bigger man was called Adams. Looking at them, Margaret felt both hatred and fear.

"You're under arrest," Jefferson said.

They escorted her down the front steps. Her neighbors had come out. Some were just returning from work. They were watching as these men dragged her away. Good. She needed witnesses. Adams pried the files from Sister Walker's hands. She let them go, allowing them to scatter across the front yard.

With a growl, the big Shadow Man reached for one of the Project Buffalo papers.

"Viola!" Sister Walker cried. "Viola, now!"

The crow zoomed down from the window ledge and bit the man's fingers.

"Ow! Goddamned crazy bird!" he said, shaking out his injured hand.

"You'll live. Put some iodine on it," Jefferson scolded as he gathered the fallen files.

"Easy for you to say," Adams said, sullen.

The crow dove down again and snapped up one of the sheets of paper in its beak just before the Shadow Man chased it away with a loud, "Shoo! Or I'll wring your neck." It hopped onto a newel post and blinked at Sister Walker.

"You know what to do," Margaret whispered as Adams retrieved the scattered files. "Keep them safe."

"Talking to birds, Margaret?" Jefferson *tsk*ed.

"It's Miss Walker to you," she said, and then she sat down so that they were forced to drag, then carry her to their waiting sedan. As they did, she looked into the eyes of her neighbors. "Make sure you tell it how you see it. Don't let them murder me and get away with it like they did Will Fitzgerald."

The Shadow Man forced Sister Walker into the backseat of the sedan and locked the door. He turned to the witnesses. "This woman is wanted for the murder of William Fitzgerald, and for treason against the United States of America."

Some on the street looked away, convinced. But others showed doubt.

The bird was also a witness. With a great flapping of its mighty wings, it flew away, the paper still clutched in its beak. It soared above the rooftops of Harlem's Jazz Age magnificence, swooping over Miss A'lelia Walker's mansion, where inside Langston Hughes hobnobbed with the editors of the *Crisis*, who listened to Duke Ellington play and rolled their eyes at Carl Van Vechten. It flew above the neon sky of Times Square, where the city was already preparing for tomorrow night's Sarah Snow memorial, and then all the way downtown to Newspaper Row, near City Hall, where the crow came to rest on the front steps of the New York *Daily News* building. It waited until a door was opened, and then it flew past the startled heads of reporters—"Hey, now!"—who were filing stories for tomorrow's paper. The bird hopped onto the desk of T. S. Woodhouse, where it deposited the file at last.

"You got a visitor, Woody," one of the reporters said with a laugh. "Maybe it's come to collect for your bookie."

Woody tried not to let his reaction to the barb show on his face. And then, as he read through the file on his desk with trembling hands, he tried not to let that show, too.

NIGHT OF THE GHOSTS

Night steals into New York City carefully at first, then falls hard and fast. City neon shows off its shine, hazing the sky with man-made stardust. Street lamps burn. Amber eyes glow in the skyscrapers. Tugboats turn on their navigation lights. And one lady in the harbor hoists a torch. People need light in the dark. They think it will keep them safe from the things hidden there.

✺

In the Russian Baths on East Tenth Street, paunchy old men gather in the basement steam room for a *shvitz*. It is said that gangsters come to the back rooms to trade secrets while deaf masseurs beat their broad backs with oak branches and hear nothing. Eight blocks south is Marble Cemetery, one of the city's oldest graveyards. Records list the reasons for burial: Puerperal fever. Consumption. Dropsy. Aneurism. Hepatitis. Exhaustion. Croup. Broken heart.

So many ways to die.

The basement is a hot cloud. Steam hisses and curls in the corners. Mr. Lubetzky can barely make out the silhouette of his friend Mr. Adleman. Mr. Lubetzky is a million miles away. He's remembering the village he left behind many years ago.

It's too much—the heat and the memory. "Samuel. Let's go for the plunge," Mr. Lubetzky says, easing his aching bones from the wooden seat. He tugs on the door, which will not open. The old man's heart begins to race. He yells for the attendant, first in English, then in Russian. From somewhere in all that steam comes a growl, low and menacing, like a dog gnawing possessively at a bone.

"Samuel?" Mr. Lubetzky calls.

A shape rises in the haze, still growling, and the old man imagines it wearing the Cossack's uniform—some wicked dybbuk who has followed across the great, vast sea to hurt him in this new world. "Hungry," it gurgles and opens its jaw.

❋

A private party. The Casino restaurant in the heart of Central Park. The swells huddle at elegant tables while their chauffeurs stand at the back of the dining room, ready to run out for the bottles of champagne stashed away in parked Studebakers and Duesenbergs. It isn't the dazzling lights of the Casino but the hope of finding stale food in the bins behind the restaurant that draws Oscar Winslow from his sleeping spot on a park bench. Poor Oscar, who fought in the war but came back with a permanent tremor that made factory work impossible. Oscar turned to morphine for the shaking hands and the night terrors, and now he lives in the park, surviving on scraps and the sympathy of strangers.

A rustling draws Oscar's attention away from the stale bread in the rubbish bin. It's coming from the dark thicket across the lawn. Oscar thinks of the eerie calm that would descend on the trenches just before hell came down in cannon fire and mustard gas. "A-anybody th-there?" Oscar is surprised by the sound of his own voice. He hasn't spoken to another soul in days.

On the other side of the bright windows, the bandleader sings a jazzed-up Irving Berlin tune for all he's worth:

"I had a dream, last night,
That filled me full of fright:
I dreamt that I was with the Devil, below."

Everybody laughs. The Devil's their kinda fella. Idealism is for suckers. *"Ain't we got fun?"*

Out back, Oscar is rooted to the spot as he sees the three ghosts moving across the shadowed lawn of Central Park. One wears a filthy hoop skirt. She has cheeks blistered with smallpox. Another, a gray-haired suffragette, gnaws at the still-wriggling body of a squirrel. The third is a young woman, maybe only weeks dead. They are from different eras, different graves, but they have found one another, along with a common enemy—the living. The freshest one trails off into the parking lot, drawn by the lights. She slips into the backseat of a long, sleek Chrysler. "Hungry," she says and waits. The remaining ghosts take notice of Oscar. They smile, as ladies do, and the bright Casino glow catches the razor-sharp edges of their teeth.

"At the Devil's Ball! At the Devil's Ball!"

The bandleader sings. Horns wail. Feet pound the floors with dancing. No one hears Oscar.

※

The Diviners climbed through a back window, letting themselves into the shuttered Museum of American Folklore, Superstition, and the Occult. The beams from their flashlights traveled across what had once been home but now seemed unfamiliar. The glare gave the library's spiral staircase an other-worldly haze and reflected off the stuffed grizzly bear's lifeless glass eyes. *My uncle was murdered in this room*, Evie thought, a shudder passing through her.

"You okay?" Jericho asked.

Evie nodded and stroked the bear's furry paw. "It's just... seeing the museum like this, it's like a body without a soul."

Will had been the museum's soul, and now he was gone, and she was learning more and more that life could turn on a dime like that. People you loved could be gone in a breath. So why didn't knowing that make it any easier to be vulnerable? To tell people that you loved them, that you were hurting, that you were afraid, or that, sometimes, at five in the morning, you were so alone in your skin that you watched the weak light play across the ceiling, willing it toward dawn?

Or perhaps no one else felt that way, and Evie truly was alone.

"See if you can find anything that will help us," Evie whispered. She didn't know why she was whispering. There was no one around to hear them. Not anymore. "And if there's something you want, you should take that, too. It's all marked for the bulldozer anyhow."

They spread out, moving through the museum for the last time. Evie kept an eye on Jericho as he gently picked up each object, saying good-bye to the museum and Will in his silent fashion.

"He really cared about you, you know," Evie said as they made their way across the leaf-and-paper-strewn floor, avoiding the spot by the fireplace where Will's body had been found. Whoever had murdered Will had gone to great lengths to make it look as if someone had been searching for valuables inside the museum.

"Thank you," Jericho said, smoothing the crinkled pages of a damaged book and laying it properly on the table. He spied something shiny underneath one of the long library tables and stooped to retrieve it. Will's silver lighter. How many times had Jericho watched Will flicking the wheel, a nervous tic, as he paced a thinning path into the Persian carpets? Jericho rubbed a thumb across Will's engraved initials.

"You should take it," Evie said softly. "He'd want you to have it."

"I don't smoke."

"You could start."

Jericho grinned. He flicked the wheel, which sparked but did not catch. "Did I ever tell you about the first day I saw this place?"

Evie shook her head.

"After Marlowe…did what he did," Jericho said. He couldn't bring himself to talk about the machinery inside his broken body just now. "Will brought me here first, before the Bennington. Can you imagine being a kid and walking into this place? It was even more of a mess. There were crates stacked up in the butler's pantry, and sawdust and packing hay on the floors. But I loved it from the very first minute I saw it. I don't believe in God, but I believe in history."

Evie gave a small, fond *hmm* of a laugh that threatened to become emotional. "You, um…You really do sound like him."

Jericho inhaled. He wanted the smell of the place in his memories forever. He remembered sunlight streaming through the stained-glass windows. How thrilled he was when Will would give him an absentminded order while he was hunched over some ancient text: *Jericho, up in the stacks, find me J. M. Reginald's* Taxonomy of Spiritual Sensation, *please.* And off Jericho would run, pounding around the spiral stairs, racing from bookcase to bookcase until he found it. The excitement when he and Will would pry open a crate containing some new piece of supernatural ephemera: A weather vane that was said to spin whenever spirits were near. A slate that had been used by a Diviner for automatic writing. A silver spoon for the dispensing of herbs to protect against evil. A velvety seventeenth-century broadsheet proclaiming "wonders and portents"—animals born disfigured and comets streaking across skies. Jericho also remembered the sadness that would shade Will's face toward the end of some afternoons. The witching hour, Jericho had come to call it. How Will would say he needed to be alone to think, and he would go into his study, close the door, and not emerge for hours.

That was why Will paced so much, Jericho had come to realize. Will had thought he could outrun his own grief over both what he had done and what he had allowed to happen during the war. Regrets were like hauntings, Jericho knew, visitations people tried to dispel with busyness or the bottle, with blame heaped on others, or with a relentless urge to reframe and retell their own histories, to make up stories that haunted them less than the truth.

Will had died with all his ghosts intact. And though Jericho did not believe in God, he had seen evidence that there was an afterlife of a sort, a transmutation of energy. He wondered where the newly deceased Will Fitzgerald would fit into a *Taxonomy of Spiritual Sensation*.

The witching hour. He'd seen that same melancholy descend over Evie at times. It was part of what drew him to her as much as her liveliness—that ragged hem of sadness showing. He fantasized about being the balm for her sadness the way Memphis could heal a wound. As if it were a quest and once Jericho had fixed her pain, he would in turn fix his own. He would finally be strong and useful and worthy of love. He wished that he could talk to Will one last time to ask if he had ever felt that way about Rotke.

Jericho remembered something that now, with Will dead, took on great importance. Seized by emotion, he raced into Will's study.

"Jericho? Jericho! Why are we off to the races?" Evie called.

Theta poked her head out of the collections room. "What is it?"

"Leave this to me," Evie whispered back. She followed Jericho into Will's study, shutting the door behind her.

Jericho was pawing through Will's shelves. "Aha!" he said, selecting a book. "This is it." Jericho flipped through the pages, opening the book at last to a soft watercolor of a young man, naked and smiling, with his arms outstretched, as if he wanted to greet the world, then gather it up and hold it to himself. A wheel of light—fiery reds, soft blues, warm gold—shone behind him, and all at once, Evie thought of Mabel's flowery letters describing Jericho as a bright angel. Evie had giggled over Mabel's idealistic view of him. Her heart ached doubly, for the loss of her friend and for Will, murdered here in the museum he loved, which would now be torn down to make room for another anonymous apartment building to house the smart set and their bevy of brats.

But when she looked at the naked man in the painting, she thought of Jericho. She remembered petting with him on the four-poster bed at Hopeful Harbor, the way he'd groaned on top of her with his lips against hers. And she remembered fighting him off in the woods when he'd been in the throes of Marlowe's serum. Was the serum to blame for his behavior? Sam didn't think so. Sam. She'd done more than pet with him. Much more. Why had she come in here alone with Jericho? What knife's edge was she dancing on now?

"What, um, what is this book?" Evie asked, her face hot.

"William Blake poems and paintings. I found them fascinating when I was younger. And a little terrifying. There are a lot of utopian drawings, but a lot of apocalyptic ones, too. Blake would've made a great Diviner," Jericho said with a half smile.

"Perhaps he was," Evie said. "What is this called?"

"*The Dance of Albion.* Looking at it made me envious."

"Envious? Why?"

"Because he was so free. I wanted to be as free as this painting."

Evie moved closer to Jericho in order to see the painting more clearly. Her perfume wafted up, a powdery floral smell. Jericho wanted to cradle his head in the space between her shoulder and neck and kiss the softness there where her pulse thrummed. He wondered if she was sad now, the way he was. He moved an inch closer. With his enhanced hearing, he could hear her heart beating fast and sense her fear even before she took a step back. He couldn't blame her, after what had happened up at Hopeful Harbor. Still, it hurt.

"I used to think death would be like that," he said a bit coolly. "You'd disintegrate into all that light, become joined to it. But now..."

Ling opened the door.

"You know, sometimes people knock first?" Evie said.

Ling made a show of lifting her fist. She banged it against the door once. "We should go. Somebody might see us."

Evie sighed. "Fine. I don't think there's anything in this museum to help us anyway. We're just going to have to figure it out for ourselves." She nodded at the book in Jericho's hands. "You might as well take that, too. They'll just throw it out. Like the rest of it."

They gathered in the library one last time. "Feels like we should have a toast to him," Memphis said.

"You got any hooch?" Evie asked with obvious excitement.

"No."

"Applesauce," Evie mumbled. She was sorry she'd given away her flask.

Memphis lifted his hand. "Everybody raise an imaginary glass to Mr. William Fitzgerald. May he rest in peace."

"To Will," Jericho echoed.

"To Will," everybody said.

"To Will," Evie said quietly. She pretended to drink, then tossed her imaginary glass into the fireplace and shrugged. "Seemed like the time for a grand gesture."

The others pretended to throw their glasses as well, except for Ling.

"Aren't you going to, uh…" Memphis mimed tossing his.

"I pretended to toast," Ling said and left it at that.

Jericho took one last look around. This was the second time he'd had to say good-bye to his home. Maybe that was what growing up was—learning to let go again and again.

"Jericho, are you all right?" Evie asked.

Was anyone ever actually all right? Jericho wondered.

"Sure," he said, turning back toward the way they'd come in. "This place is just another ghost."

⁂

On an Upper East Side street filled with lovely limestones, a supper party is under way. The hosts, a young, devastatingly fashionable couple, have invited all their smart-set friends, whom they've known simply *forever*, don't you know, from their days at the Very Best Schools. The hosts have decided it would be an absolute *hoot* to bring in one of those Diviner types to conduct a proper séance, especially after hearing the gossip that the Ashtons had conjured a proper ghost at *their* last party. *What a riot. What an ab-so-lute riot,* the hostess proclaims between puffs on her cigarette. They sit now, twelve of them, at a round table in the library (*books—who has time to read 'em, but my, how they do jazz up a room!*) while the Diviner (an actress-turned-soothsayer, don't you know) shuts her eyes and advises everyone to hold hands. The lights are dimmed and the candles lit before the servants exit, closing the pocket doors behind them. On the other side of those doors, the servants roll their eyes and move through the huge flat, emptying ashtrays.

"Let us call now upon the spirits," the Diviner intones, using every bit of thespian training she has. She is ready to do her very best work, moaning and writhing. But something is wrong. She can feel something wicked standing right behind her—cold, so cold.

"Turn on the lights!" she screeches. "There is something in the room with us!"

The host leaps up, rushes for the switch. The lights burst their shades with a pop of glass. In the dark, they see him floating there: a man in shimmering waistcoat and riding breeches wearing a severe expression.

"Trespassers…"

The hostess screams to the maid. "Margaret! *Margaret! Open the doors at once!*"

"Trespassers!" the ghost says again.

"Get out of our house—get out!" the host shouts. He is afraid so he shouts very loudly. His voice is brittle.

"You own nothing," the ghost answers. "You live on a false inheritance."

"What do you want?" the hostess screams. She is no longer smug about the Ashtons.

"The Diviners," the ghost answers.

※

As the Diviners came to the end of Sixty-eighth Street, they saw a crowd running toward the park. Evie stopped a trio of young men. "What is it?" she asked.

"Ghosts," they answered, excited. "There's ghosts in Central Park!"

The Diviners raced with the crowd into the park, toward the Casino restaurant. They could hear the screams before they reached the parking lot, which was overrun by people fleeing. Fancy cars swerved out of park, banging into other cars but driving on without a backward glance. Light spasmed behind the Casino's pretty windows.

"Are we going in?" Henry asked.

"Of course!" Evie answered.

"I was afraid you'd say that."

"Wait a minute! What's our plan?" Ling asked. Bloodcurdling screams rang out.

"Same as always," Evie said.

"Same as always?" Jericho asked, confused, but Evie was already charging ahead.

Inside, the beautiful restaurant was a shambles, all overturned tables and palm trees uprooted from their ceramic pots. The orchestra's instruments were strewn about the stage. The people who had not been lucky enough to escape hid behind those tables, trembling with fear. In the center of the room were three ghosts. They shimmered around the edges, but Evie detected a difference from the others they'd faced. These ghosts seemed more corporeal, somehow, and that made them even more frightening.

The ghosts turned to face the Diviners and sniffed.

"Diviners. You've come," the ghosts said in one voice.

The Diviners fell in, formed a line.

"What are we doing?" Jericho asked Memphis. He felt as if he'd arrived to take an exam for which he'd not studied.

"What do you want? Did he send you?" Evie asked the ghosts.

"He grows stronger. We grow stronger. You will be tested." The ghosts drifted closer. They were turning. Dark veins crept up their pallid necks, curving around their cheeks and toward their mouths of jagged teeth.

"Hands," Evie said, joining with the others.

Jericho took hold of Ling's hand, though he still didn't know why.

"You will be tested, Diviner. He will test all of you in time." The ghosts were very close. Their fetid breath was nauseating. Henry feared he might be sick.

"He whispers to us so sweetly in our graves. He asks us why. Why should we have to die? All of that living, only to rot in the end. So unfair. We would have more. More life. And now, because of you, we shall take it. You've made us strong."

"We haven't done anything," Evie said. To the others, she said, "Get ready."

A constant whine, getting louder, as if all the souls in hell were singing.

"What...what are they doing?" Ling asked.

"He will make you see things," the ghosts said.

The sound, louder still. Memphis's body shook from it.

"Memphis?" Isaiah said, scared.

The ghosts seemed bolder. "Chaos is born. The time is now. We are ready. You have made us possible. You did this."

"We gotta do something!" Theta said. Her whole body felt as if it were being squeezed.

"You did this," the ghosts repeated. They made no move to attack the Diviners. "The time is—"

"Now!" Evie called.

The surge traveled through the Diviners and out like a wave. In the seconds before the blast hit them, the ghosts smiled and sighed, as if welcoming their destruction. And then their atoms were scattered into the ether. The light carried on the wind. Fluttered into trees and singed the new leaves. Dusted the rooftops of parked cars whose lights and windshield wipers had gone haywire. Left divots in the lot.

At the first surge, euphoria swept through the Diviners. And then they were on the floor, dazed, waiting for the inevitable crash into sickness that followed the thrilling high from all that death. Jericho's body quivered. He could not get warm. "This is what you do?" he asked, horrified.

"We have to get rid of them," Ling answered, but she could not look him in the eyes.

"It's us or them," Memphis said and spat out blood.

"I suppose you think it would be better to let them rampage through the city?" Evie didn't like being judged, and she especially didn't like being judged by Jericho. "You've got no room to talk. Not after what happened."

The comment landed, Evie could see.

Jericho looked away. "It was the serum."

"Was it?" Evie muttered.

Slowly, the Diviners rose to their feet. There was a fiery hole where the stage had been. The remaining patrons stepped closer, drawn to the spectacle. "You did that," a woman said, eerily echoing the ghosts.

"What if they turn that power on us?" her date asked.

"I want no part of that," Jericho said.

"I don't think we get to be conscientious objectors for this fight, Jericho," Evie said. Her head pounded. The dizzying good feeling had passed. She felt queasy, like her insides were coated in something that would not wash off. She gulped down a few breaths of night air. "Tomorrow night. We meet at the memorial, and we tell Jake Marlowe to shut down that machine." She shouldered past Jericho, stumbling toward the exit, where she knew she would be sick.

MONSTER

Sam Lloyd woke with a headache to beat all headaches and a dry mouth that tasted like day-old sardines. "My kingdom for a toothbrush," he said. "And some aspirin." His eyes hurt as he looked around the unfamiliar room. The place was small and dungeon-like, with very few furnishings apart from the bed where he now lay. He took it in bit by bit: A chair. A table. A toilet and sink. Thick brick walls. In the corner, a radio broadcast a rousing piano concerto that did nothing to help the banging in his head. No windows. The only way in or out of the room was a heavy steel door with a *We're not foolin' around* type of lock.

"It's either the world's worst motel or swankiest jail cell," Sam muttered. He gave his face a small slap. "Stop talking to yourself, Lloyd. That's how they get ya. Dammit. Did it again!"

Sam pushed himself to a sitting position, feeling the ache in his muscles as he did. He was shackled to the bed. He tried pulling against the bindings, but this only brought home how weak he still felt. Whatever juice those creepy fellas had shot into him had really knocked him sideways. He had no idea how long he'd been out. What day was it? What was the last thing he could remember?

Evie. Bits and pieces were coming back now: He had been walking back to see Evie at the hotel. He'd been thinking about her, feeling all goofy, which was why he hadn't seen the two Shadow Men until they ambushed him and stuck a needle into his thigh. His legs had gone numb, and then the rest of him. He remembered being thrown into the back of a car and then . . . he couldn't remember anything after that.

Evie would have no idea what had happened to him. Knowing Evie, she'd be pretty sore about it, too. That thought brought on just the slightest bit of a smile, but then he remembered the night before he'd been kidnapped, everything they'd shared, the soft feel of her body, and he sobered. What if she thought he'd abandoned her, like a real heel? Had the Shadow Men gone after her and the rest of his friends? Were they here now somewhere— wherever this place was? He tried to slip his hand out of the restraints, but it was useless.

Sam's stomach growled. How long had it been since he'd eaten? For the first time, he noticed a silver tray that sat on the nightstand, within reach. Sam was just able to lift the dish's domed cover. They'd left him a sandwich. A *ham* sandwich. Bastards. There was a rattle at the room's steel door. Quickly, Sam lay down, pretending to sleep but keeping his eyelids open a sliver. Through the soft fuzz of his eyelashes, Sam saw the two Shadow Men enter. The skinny one was named Jefferson, Sam remembered; Adams was the taller brute who didn't talk much. Sam wished he could leap off the bed and punch them both. If he could get them to come close enough, he could use his Diviner power to daze them. While they were under his spell, he would find the key, unlock the cuffs, and make a run for it.

Jefferson glanced down at the tray and noticed that its lid was off. "It's no good pretending, you know." He had a voice that sounded as if he'd spent years screaming and was now left with a subdued rasp. "I can assure you that, just as we were able to drug you to sleep, we can do the same to wake you up. The effects are rather unpleasant, I hear."

Resigned, Sam opened his eyes and sat up. "Where the hell am I?"

Mr. Jefferson took a seat while his partner stood watch. "Hello, Sam. Or do you prefer Sergei?"

"I'd prefer that you let me out of here."

"I'm afraid I can't do that just yet."

"Okay. How long do you need? I could wait five minutes."

"Cute." From his pocket, the Shadow Man brought out a paper bag of pistachios, picking through them methodically until he found one he liked. "We need your help, Sergei."

"Why the hell should I help you? And the name is Sam, pal."

"That's not what your mother calls you, though, is it?"

Sam's pulse quickened. He tried to play it cool. "My mother doesn't call me anything. She's dead."

"You help us, we help you." With his thumbs, the Shadow Man split open the pistachio and popped the tiny green nut into his mouth, grinding it between his back teeth while he fixed Sam with a stare.

It was the arrogance of the stare that got to Sam. He summoned up all his anger and called on his power. "Don't see m—*aahhh!*" Sam yelped in pain as his wrists burned beneath the shackles.

Mr. Jefferson smirked. "Did you think I'd trust you?"

"Wh-what did you do to me?"

The Shadow Man clucked and shook his head like a headmaster. "Be a good boy, Sergei, or no dessert."

"I'll kill you. I swear I will," Sam grunted, still in pain.

"I don't think so." Jefferson jerked his head toward the door. Adams opened it and stepped outside. Sam could make out a clank, like a long chain dragging across a floor. The Shadow Man stepped back into the room with a shackled guest, and Sam was suddenly grateful for the bed holding his weight. It had been ten years since he'd last seen her. Ten years since she'd kissed him good-bye and gone to work on Project Buffalo. She seemed smaller to him now that he was older. Gray streaked her black hair. But it was unmistakably Miriam Lubovitch, his mother.

"Mama?" Sam said.

"Sergei!" Miriam tried to move toward her son but her ankles were in irons. Tears shone in her eyes. There were more words, all in their native Russian: Are you hurt? *Nyet*. I love you. *I love you, too, Mama*. And: You got so big! Which made Sam laugh despite the circumstances, because mothers were mothers no matter what. He hadn't been wrong. She was alive. All this time, alive. And these were the sons-of-bitches who'd destroyed their family, who'd kept them apart and *lied* about it, telling Sam's father that Miriam had died of influenza back in 1918.

"Take her outta those chains," Sam growled.

"I'm afraid I can't do that. Thanks to her exposure to Project Buffalo during the war, your mother's Diviner gifts are…substantial. A little iron helps contain them, we've found. A lot of iron makes her docile as a kitten." Jefferson nodded at the shackles around Sam's blistered wrists. "Seems to work like a charm on you, too."

Sam had never felt such blinding rage. He'd always wondered what would happen if he came face-to-face with the men who'd taken his mother. Wondered if he was capable of murder. Now he knew that he was.

"Sorry there's no time for a touching reunion, but Mr. Marlowe requests the pleasure of your company."

With that, Mr. Adams crossed the room, where he unhooked the restraints from the bedpost and used them to bind Sam's hands together in front of him. He yanked Sam to his feet.

"Easy, chump," Sam snarled.

Adams glared at Sam. "Who are you calling a chump?"

"Did I say *chump*? I meant *champ*. I get my vowels mixed up."

Sergei. Be careful.

Sam heard his mother's voice in his head. For ten years, he'd longed to hear that voice. But now that she was reprimanding him, it was, frankly, a little irritating.

I do what I like, he thought, unsure if his mother could hear it.

Don't be a pisher.

Yep. She could hear him.

❋

The Shadow Men escorted Sam and his mother to an elevator that rattled them up four floors to the very top, a button marked only *S*. When the doors opened on the long room, Sam had to blink against the brightness of the day shining through the glass roof. The majesty of it took his breath away for a minute. A solarium, rooms like this were called. Solarium. *S*.

Adams and Jefferson brought Sam and Miriam to an area cordoned off by curtains. "Wait here," Adams said.

Sam snorted. "Oh, *suuure*. Let President Coolidge know I'll be late for lunch, will ya?"

Adams smacked Sam across the face. "Watch your mouth."

"*Ow*," Sam said, genuinely surprised at how much it hurt.

"Mr. Adams. That was unnecessary," Jake Marlowe said. America's favorite millionaire son crossed the room with sure strides. A pair of strange leather goggles, like an aviator's, hung around his neck.

"Yeah. Make him say he's sorry," Sam goaded.

"I'm sure he is," Jake said with paternal disinterest.

Sam glared at Adams, who mouthed, *I'm not sorry.*

Marlowe drew back the curtains and Sam forgot about the Shadow

Men as he took in the sight of an enormous golden sphere of a machine perched on six tall legs like some giant mechanical spider. A dizzying array of tubes and wires sprang from its top and wrapped around antennas that stretched up to a square of open space in the ceiling, reaching toward the sky. A small compartment in the thing's side held a glass tube in which blue electricity crackled, as if Jake Marlowe had managed to capture lightning in a jar. On either side of the machine's gleaming metal belly was a chair attached to a golden helmet full of more wires that looped back into the body of the machine. Sam had never seen anything like it. It was terrifying; it was beautiful.

"Gee, does it lay golden eggs?" Sam joked. He didn't want those bastards to know how scared he was.

Miriam pulled at her chains. "No! Not my son! You promised!"

"We'll keep him safe, Miriam," Marlowe said.

"Safe from what?" Sam asked.

Miriam kept her steely gaze on Marlowe. "Like you did the others?"

"Regrettable," Jefferson said. "But necessary for the good of the nation."

"Safe from what?" Sam repeated.

Miriam shook her head. "I won't do it."

"Miriam…"

"Safe from wh—Hey, is this thing on? Am I broadcasting? Hello!"

Adams and Jefferson took hold of Sam's arms and dragged him to one of the chairs. Adams strapped Sam's arms down against the leather pads. "What's the big idea? Is this an electric chair? Do I get a trial? A last meal? A coupla cookies?"

Sam tugged furiously at the restraints, but they were snug. "Are you gonna at least tell me what this meshuggunah thing is?"

Jake regarded the machine with a fondness Sam had never seen him bestow on another person. "This is the Eye of Providence."

"*This* is the Eye? No offense, Mr. Marlowe, but it doesn't even look like an eye. More like a cuckoo spider or, gee, I dunno, like something a crazed madman with delusions of grandeur would make."

Marlowe ignored Sam as Jefferson and Adams strong-armed a struggling Miriam into the other chair.

"Hey. Hey! Leave my mother alone! Okay, now? *Now* I'm mad. You made me mad. You listening to me, Mr. Heebie-Jeebies Adams and your friend, Jokes Jefferson? When I get up out of this chair, you will be sorry. Very sorry. I'm not kidding. You don't want to fool around with me. I'm really, really mad."

Jake Marlowe fiddled with a control. "Sam. It's going to be fine."

"Fine for me or fine for the chair?"

From inside a drawer, Marlowe withdrew a large syringe filled with a blue liquid. Fear curled around Sam's insides, turning them cold. "Hey. Hey! What's that for?"

"Hold still, please, Sam."

"No, you don't understand. I hate needles. A lot. I—*ahhhh!*"

Marlowe plunged the needle into Sam's arm. Sam could feel the blue liquid rushing into his veins, an oily cold while the site of the shot itched and burned like an ant bite. In his head, he heard his mother: *Sergei, breathe.* Marlowe drew down the golden cap and screwed it into place against Sam's skull. The serum was roaring through his body as if he were the third rail of a subway track taking on current.

"Careful. I just washed my hair," he joked to keep the panic at bay. His heart pounded.

"Relax, Sam." Marlowe.

"Please, Jake…" Miriam pleaded as Jefferson and Adams secured the other cap on her head.

"I promise, Miriam," Jake Marlowe said. "On my honor."

"You have no honor."

"Careful, Miriam," Jake said. His expression slid into something hard and cold, the change so sudden and shocking that Sam was reminded of the way ghosts turned on a dime.

Sam was street smart. He'd grown up on the South Side of Chicago, running from bullies who taunted him for being small and a Jew. He didn't scare easily. But as Jake Marlowe flipped two switches and the Eye of Providence started with a chugging hum that grew deafeningly loud, Sam was animal-afraid. He wanted out of his own body. "Please," he whispered. "Please don't."

Jake Marlowe pulled the goggles up over his eyes. Adams and Jefferson followed suit with their own.

"Where's our goggles, huh?" Sam yelled over the noise. The serum slithered inside him, taking over. His breathing was rapid, shallow. "What's with this stuff you gave me?"

"I need you to see, Sam," Marlowe shouted over the humming. "I need you to tell me everything you see."

The blue lightning flared against the glass tube and shot up the antennas of the Eye, up into the clouds above, making them angry. It reached into Sam's body, too. They were joined. Everything the machine felt, Sam felt. His body shook. Sam strained against the sudden force. He tried to speak but could only grunt: "Nnn-nng-ng." The tear between worlds was stretching wider, birthing pains that rippled through Sam as if he, too, were being stretched open. His skin burned as if a million fire ants crawled underneath. As the pressure increased, he bit his tongue. Blood coated the back of his throat, making him gag. He feared he would choke. He wanted to scream but he could not remember how. All he knew was fear.

"Easy, Sam. Don't fight it. You'll be fine." Jake Marlowe's voice. "Greatness requires some sacrifice."

He was not fine. He was not fine not fine not fine. Tears trickled over his hot cheeks. A burnt-sugar scorch filled his nostrils. He bucked and arched from the current and the serum warring inside him. The dials whirred to a high whine. The life was being sucked from Sam's very bones in order to power Jake Marlowe's monstrous machine.

Sergei. His mother in his head. *Whatever you see, my love, hold fast to yourself. Do not lose yourself to it. Fight, Sergei. Fight.*

Sam could only repeat a mantra in his head: *Don't see me, don't see me, don't see me.* The scream that was torn at last from Sam seemed to echo across forever. And then, in an instant, the pain stopped. He was floating. He was weightless and without form. Around him, the sky exploded into newness, the dawn of all time, and Sam was there for it, joined to it. Every cell in his body yearned for that beautiful dark—no loneliness, no hunger, no fear or grief. Only connection. Belonging. There was the sky and Sam *was* the sky. He waited for a word to be uttered to usher him into being.

"Sam?" Marlowe's voice. It was a universe away. It was an intimate whisper in his ear. "Sam, what do you see?"

A ball of dust spun faster and faster, flattening as it did, and swirled into a gaseous sea of color. Sam felt he was inside the womb of a star and he was the star, watching himself being born. Life inventing itself over and over. Creation, infinite and eternal. How could he possibly report on something so ecstatic? Words were insufficient.

"Sam?" Marlowe.

"It's ... beautiful." Sam.

"What do you see?" Marlowe.

"It's like ... like the beginning of the world." Sam. Was he Sam? He was more than Sam. He was and was not and was again.

The voices of Marlowe and the Shadow Men drifted toward Sam like the conversation was coming through a tinny radio: *Told you ... abundant resources in that world ... King of Crows ... capture him and have it all ... but what does this King of Crows want ... hasn't told us, just wants to keep the breach open, as do we....*

Sam was leaving all that behind like a memory. He was zooming through time, catching tiny slivers of history. Moments unfolded around him, revolutions and rebellions, protests and philosophies, quiet longings and giant leaps of progress, and dreams, dreams, dreams. So many dreams. They were endless, a stardust fuel reborn into the hearts of the people again and again. Also infinite was the quest for power, the capacity for violence.

Dreams. And suffering. And blood.

Sam squirmed against the knowledge of this as it flooded through him, threaded to the dreams until it was impossible to separate them from one another. For every moment Sam witnessed, there were hundreds more passing quietly by. These moments fractured, dividing like cells so that they could be played out to different ends. In one scenario, someone died. In another, they lived. An action brought peace; that same action brought terror. All these moments had millions more living inside them, universes upon universes. Little futures playing out. Fading. Splitting into other futures. Death and rebirth. So much energy. Sam could feel it threaded through him and back out into every one of those futures, those moments. It was dizzying.

"So much energy." Sam didn't know if he'd thought it or said it. He was losing the edges of himself.

"It's you." Miss Addie was framed in the doorway of a white clapboard church. "Tell Theta—the binding spell. Tell her—"

The universe split.

Miss Addie was in an open coffin on its way to the graveyard. She lay perfectly still, like the dead, but Sam could hear her screaming inside his head and he knew she was very much alive.

Split.

Sergei. His mother. *Sergei, I must show you something.*

A moment opened like the petals on a flower: Sam was a boy at Hopeful Harbor and his mother had her hands on either side of his head. She was angry. At him? No. But she was angry. And afraid. Something had happened to make her afraid.

"My love, forget what you know. Do not see," she whispered, and she brushed her thumbs against his temples and it all went away.

Sergei. His mother's voice. Now? Yes, now. Here.

From here on, no more forgetting. Keep awake, my love. Use your gift to stay safe.

Split.

A white buffalo was born. It slithered into weary grass that reached up to welcome its promise. The land held its breath for hope, waiting for the animal to make its first cries.

Breathe, Sam thought. *Breathe!*

Another moment came, followed by another. A woman with red hair and green eyes. He'd seen her once before. At the post office. An Englishwoman. But she was younger here. The redheaded woman pressed her body against a majestic tree. "In some realm, we shall be together," she promised. "I will free you, my love." The world split. The same woman was reaching into the tree and pulling out a dark-haired man like the midwife to a hard birth. He was falling into her arms, gulping for air through all that muck, and she was crying.

Split.

Sam was with Evie, happy in her arms, and she was laughing.

Split.

Evie was just out of reach, and he was screaming at her to stop, to come back. Why?

Sam wanted to follow that future to see where it led because it frightened him.

The universe split again into a fluttering of wings.

There was something familiar about the woman standing before him, her voice a thick rasp. "Listen to me. Quick now. You must break the cycle. Tell Memphis to heal the breach."

Memphis. This was Memphis's mother.

"Break the cycle," Sam repeated. "How?"

"Sam?" Marlowe's voice. "What's that about a circle?"

The cells of time divided again. One moment did not split into other futures, though. It was stuck, like a phonograph needle hiccuping in the same groove, playing the same line of a song over and over. That moment pulled Sam toward it, brightening and expanding, pulsing like a heartbeat. A song punched through the colorful swirl of gases of time and space to reach him now:

"Pack up your troubles in your old kit bag, and smile, smile, smile...."

He was at the edge of a foggy soldiers' camp. The song came from a record spinning around on an old Victrola perched atop a tree stump.

"Sam?" Marlowe's voice again. "Are you inside? What do you see?"

Soldiers in a clearing. Familiar. Something familiar here. A young soldier with twinkling blue eyes and a small pout of a mouth smiled up at Sam, and Sam felt that he knew this man. "It's just about to start," the soldier said.

"Okay," Sam said, though the soldier seemed to take no notice. They were readying for something big, Sam could tell. One soldier danced a little soft-shoe. Another shaved at a mirror affixed to a tree trunk. The soldier with twinkling eyes—*why is he so familiar?*—wrote in his journal.

"Sam?" Marlowe.

"Soldiers. I see soldiers."

Sam focused on the field telephone. Soon that phone would ring. How did he know this? He had the oddest sensation, like knowing that a murder was about to happen and not knowing what to do to stop it.

"Hey, what card am I holding?" one of the soldiers asked the blond twinkly-eyed fella.

"Eight of hearts," the blond soldier answered without missing a beat.

"Son-of-a-bitch, O'Neill. Right again!"

O'Neill. Sam saw the patch on the soldiers' uniforms: 144. He looked again at the blond soldier. Evie's brother. Same bowlike mouth.

"Sam." Marlowe. Insistent. "Leave the soldiers. Tell me what you see around you. Anything about the King of Crows. Concentrate."

Sam walked away from the camp and into the lush winter forest. As he went farther in, the trees became diseased. From the tops of their leafless crowns, foul smoke belched up, blotting out the sky. Ash covered every surface. Sooty flakes fell on Sam's clothes, and where they landed, they bit holes through the fabric. There was some sort of energy field here—Sam could feel it pulling on him, starting to make him uncomfortable, as if all his atoms were being thrown into chaos.

Sergei. Fight it, Little Fox. Do not let it claim you.

"Mama?"

Use your power, my son.

"What else do you see, Sam? We need to know." Marlowe.

"I don't feel so good. I wanna stop."

The pressure of all that energy was squeezing in on Sam. He didn't know how much more he could take.

"Sam. I need you to be brave," Marlowe said.

Sam pushed aside the forest like a curtain. On the other side, as far as Sam's eyes could see, was an army of the dead, hungry and waiting. And sitting on a throne of skulls, the King of Crows. Sam took a step backward. His foot squished into the carcass of some decaying animal.

"Who goes there?" The King of Crows was up and pushing through the dead with his feathered coat flapping and squawking as he moved. "One of Jake Marlowe's little Diviner spies, no doubt."

Use your power.

Don't see me. Don't see me, Sam thought.

The King of Crows sniffed. "Where are you? No matter. Jake Marlowe's hubris will be to my advantage. I will tell him what he wants to hear."

"Pack up your troubles. Pack up your troubles. Pack up your troubles."

Sam was back on the field.

"The time is now!" the sergeant yelled to his men.

"Time to tell the story again," the King of Crows said. "But only for a little while longer." The King of Crows ran a hand across an hourglass. Inside, Sam saw every possible future collapsing into one filled with darkness and horror and death.

"And smile."

The soldiers raced to their positions. Miss Addie stood in the middle of the field. She was an old woman. Her fingernails were bloodied and broken, as if she'd been scratching at something that would not yield. "Sam. I need to tell you about the ghosts. They're not like before. They—"

Split.

There was a young woman in a white dress. "I know you. How do I know you?" she said. A bell tolled. In the distance was a white clapboard church. "I'm to be married there to my Elijah."

Split.

The King of Crows cradled the hourglass. "Soon."

The needle stuck.

"And smile."

Lightning. In the flashes were the dead.

"And smile."

Dust swept across towns.

"And smile."

The dark sky was everywhere.

"All is connected," the King of Crows said.

The Eye was pulling Sam in, drawing his energy like filings to a magnet. The soldiers screamed as the Eye ripped them apart, their limbs and organs fused to its eternally spinning gears. Sam could feel the unholy pull deep in his own body, just one more spark of energy to be fed to the crushing machinery, trapped in its jaws forever.

Sergei! Fight! Do not let it take you!

"D-don't s-see mm-mm-mmeeee!" Sam screamed.

His eyes fluttered open as the Eye powered down. He was back in the solarium. His body hurt as if he'd been beaten, rearranged. Marlowe raced to unbuckle the straps and lift the helmet from Sam's smoking head. There were strange red marks on the skin of his arms. He shook all over and could not stop.

"Just a little radiation burn. Nothing to worry about," Jake said. "I'll have them apply a dressing."

Tears streamed down Sam's face. His nose ran. He couldn't help either. Sam looked over at his mother. Her eyes were closed. She moaned and rolled her head from side to side.

"She'll be fine. Just needs to rest," Marlowe assured Sam.

"You're p-playing with the King of C-Crows. You c-can't trust him."

"Don't you think I know that!" Marlowe snapped. "That's why I need to know what you can see. So I can prepare for it. Be one step ahead of him."

"So the United States government can prepare for it," Jefferson added. "We are paying for these experiments. Don't forget—the King of Crows will become our property."

Sam kept his gaze on Marlowe. "You have no idea who he is. What he is."

"He's the most extraordinary being anyone has ever encountered, Sam. And we—Will, Rotke, Miriam, Margaret, and I—we found him quite by accident."

"That's one way of putting it. You're talking about the tear between worlds," Sam said. He was dizzy and nauseated. It felt as if someone had punched out all his insides and put them back in the wrong order.

"A *door* between worlds!" Marlowe's eyes gleamed. "But we have to stabilize it long enough so that we don't lose our connection to it."

"You can also close doors. I'm just saying, some doors are very good closed."

"That other world is a place of unbounded energy. Of unlimited power. Already, it has given us so much. Why, in just ten short years, Sam, I've been able to provide giant leaps forward in industry and invention thanks to our connection. The power coming from that other dimension and the King of Crows is without limit, Sam! And we, the greatest nation on earth, will control it. It will belong to Marlowe Industries."

"And to the Republic for which it stands," Mr. Jefferson added pointedly.

"What I see is that the King of Crows has got you right where he wants you!"

Sam thought about screaming. There were people who worked here. Servants. Did they know what was going on upstairs in the solarium? Did they care?

"Sir, we have to leave for New York soon. The memorial."

"Yes, yes. I know." Jake sounded irritated by the interruption. And Sam knew that Marlowe would've gone for another round if he hadn't been inconvenienced by his dead fiancée's memorial service in New York City.

"Y-you're a m-monster," Sam whispered through the foamy blood on his lips.

"I hope to change your mind about that, Sam. I truly do," Marlowe whispered. The bastard had the audacity to sound sincere when he said it.

The Shadow Men returned Sam to his cell, locking him in. Sam couldn't do much more than lie in his bed. He felt a hundred years old after what Marlowe's Eye had done to him. And even when he shut his eyes, he could still feel his connection to that other world. He could still hear the screams of the soldiers.

Sam curled up in a ball and cried softly. "Don't see me. Don't see me. Don't see me."

CHAOS

The public memorial for Sarah Snow in Times Square was the biggest ticket since Marlowe's ill-fated exhibition. Two hundred thousand people were expected. Radio microphones lined the stage. Cameras stood at the ready to turn it into a newsreel that would play at every picture palace across the nation. Everyone wanted to be seen and counted at Sarah Snow's memorial. It was all about appearances. And after the bombing, appearances mattered; no one could afford to look unpatriotic. As she moved among the throngs of New Yorkers looking to be counted among the faithful, Evie thought about how Mr. Phillips had asked her to sign a loyalty oath. It was the reason she'd left WGI. From what she'd heard, others were being asked to sign loyalty pledges in businesses all over town. She wondered if any of them had refused. She wondered if she had been stupid to say no.

Newsies pushed into the crowd, hawking the late edition: "Ghosts Take Manhattan! Ghouls in Gotham!" New Yorkers tossed their nickels and crowded around to read about the previous night's hauntings. From downtown to uptown, East Side to West, nowhere was safe. What did the sightings mean? the people asked one another. What did the ghosts want? And most important: Whose fault was it—who should shoulder the blame? The city had the feel of a town awaiting a hurricane.

Evie peered out from under the brim of Sam's Greek fisherman's cap, searching for Jericho in the crowd. She'd been harsh with him last night. It haunted her now. But she was also angry with him for the way he'd judged them when he knew the stakes. Evie and the others were fighting a war, and Jericho thought he could sit it out.

"There's that snake Harriet Henderson," Theta whispered, nodding toward the front of the barricade, where a policeman let the influential gossip columnist pass through and take her seat in the stands next to Jake Marlowe himself. She was wearing a new fur, Evie noted. The gossip business was paying off for Harriet—or the people paying her not to print gossip about them were paying off. Harriet drew a handkerchief from her pocketbook and dabbed at her eyes.

"Impossible," Evie gasped.

Theta tugged her veiled hat down to hide her face. She recognized several Follies girls in the crowd, and she hoped they didn't see her. "What's impossible?"

"Harriet's tears. Why, everybody knows snakes don't cry," Evie said, making Theta giggle.

"Say, Memphis, you copacetic?" Theta asked, concerned.

Memphis nodded. In truth, he was feeling pretty beat up. The previous night's ghost hunting had taken it out of him. Something about it had felt different. Off. He wanted to ask the others if they'd experienced the same unease, but he was afraid of their answers.

Theta waved to Henry and Ling, who were coming through the crowd with Jericho. Evie's heart sped up. What would she say? What would *he* say?

"Hi," Henry said, without his usual bonhomie. "Anyone else have a sleepless night?"

"Yes," Memphis said, and he didn't know if he was relieved not to be alone in that or worried that it meant Henry was also disturbed by their shared experience.

"Evie. Nice hat," Jericho said crisply.

"Thank you. I'm rather fond of it. And the person it belongs to," she responded in kind. Then: "How are you feeling?"

"Fine," Jericho lied.

"Well. I'm awfully glad to hear it."

"Careful, your enunciation is showing," Theta whispered to her.

"What did the ghosts mean last night: *You did this.* Did what? Were they saying what's happening is *our* fault?" Ling asked.

"That's ridiculous! If anything, we're trying to stop this," Evie said, glancing at Jericho, who did not look her way.

"Isaiah, you got a sense about things. What's to come?" Bill asked.

Isaiah shook his head. The visions came when and how they liked. He wondered if it was the same way for Sarah Beth, or if she'd figured out how to master her powers, and if she had, if she'd show him how to do it.

"Where's Sister Walker? I thought she'd be here by now," Theta asked.

"Listen, I know Mr. Marlowe said we was to come up front, but I'd feel a whole heap better if we kept ourselves unseen," Bill said. "There's Shadow Men looking for Memphis and Isaiah."

"I agree," Theta said.

They moved farther into the crowd, away from the main event. Evie couldn't stop thinking about Jericho. Everything between them was strained. But without him, they'd never have gotten through to Marlowe.

"Jericho..." Evie started. "About last night. I didn't mean..." She reached for him just as the conductor played a long note on a xylophone. The Christian Crusaders hummed the pitch together, then began their somber hymn. People's eyes were now on the stage. A wave of shushing rippled through the assembly. Evie retracted her hand.

Memphis gave Theta a sad smile. "I don't think we should be seen together," he whispered.

She nodded. She knew he was right, but she didn't like it.

"Can I stay with Theta up here, so I can see better?" Isaiah pleaded, also in a whisper.

Memphis rubbed his hand across Isaiah's head. "All right, Shrimpy. You can't help being a Shrimpy."

"Hey! Aunt Octavia says I grew an inch! She marked it on the wall."

"Shhh!" a man scolded.

"Still a Shrimpy," Memphis whispered close to Isaiah's ear. "Don't be trouble."

"I won't," Isaiah said, irritated. Why did Memphis always treat him like a baby?

Memphis and Bill moved a few rows back, behind Evie, Theta, Isaiah, and Henry. A few feet away, Ling had found a spot where the ground was a little more even for her crutches.

"You okay?" Jericho asked, coming to Ling's side. He knew it was hard for Ling to stand for long periods of time. And he wanted some distance from Evie.

"Yes, fine," Ling said. It was the pain of Alma leaving that hit hardest tonight. Ling wondered if she would ever find someone who could love her as she was or if she was destined to be alone. She just wanted to get this night over with and go home to dream walk. At least in dreams, she had some control.

The Crusaders finished their hymn and the crowd applauded. It felt as if every person in New York City were packed into Times Square. The city's neon eyes watched from above, remote as any god's. Young girls in white gardenia corsages of the sort Sarah used to wear pushed against the barricades, wailing into their handkerchiefs.

Evie scowled. "That's a bit much, isn't it? Why is everything a performance nowadays?"

Theta raised an eyebrow. "That's rich coming from you, Evil. If you could get somebody to watch you pick up your mail from the mailbox, you would." Theta's grin was short-lived.

"What's the matter?" Evie whispered.

"It's Roy."

Evie and Henry peered around Theta to see Theta's abusive ex-husband, Roy Stoughton, muscling through the crowd in a fine new suit, glad-handing folks as he went, Dutch Schultz's murderous thugs on either side of him. Roy had always hated it when Theta got the attention. He'd wanted to be the important one. As he made his way to the stage, he looked smug, and Theta knew he was lapping it up.

"Why is Roy sitting up there with all the swells?" Theta asked. Under her gloves, her palms began to heat up. For comfort, she patted the pocket of her long cardigan, feeling Miss Addie's slim spell book diary hiding inside, and imagined Miss Addie standing at her side, telling her she was brave.

Some of Dutch's men broke off and moved among the crowd. Theta lowered her head and tugged down her veil again. She wished Sam were there to make her temporarily invisible. She wished he were there with them, period. "Can you see what they're doing?" she asked Evie.

Evie stood on tiptoe, straining. "They're handing something out. But not to everyone. Just some of the men. Oh, no. Here they come. Don't look up!"

Evie and Theta huddled together, pretending to be overcome with grief. Dutch's men moved past them. One of the thugs stopped in front of Jericho and Henry.

"You fellas look like you might want in on this." Dutch Schultz's thug shoved a pamphlet at Henry and Jericho, then moved on, doing more of the same.

"What's it say?" Evie asked as she and the others crowded around Henry and Jericho.

America is in Danger!
From Immigrants! Bootleggers! Negro Agitaters!
Anarchists! Diviners!
The Invisible Empire and the White Knights
of the Ku Klux Klan
invite all White Protestants
to a lecture and rally to discuss the dangers
to America's Great White Race.
Pillar of Fire Church, Zarephath, New Jersey.
April 15, 1927.
Meet at the sign of the fiery cross.
The KKK: Yesterday, Today, and Forever!

"So Roy's in with the Klan now," Jericho said.

"Bullies need other bullies," Theta said bitterly.

"They misspelled *agitators*. Maybe America is in danger from bigots who can't spell," Henry said.

But Theta couldn't laugh. Roy was a threat who'd aligned himself with an even bigger threat.

Up on the stage, pugnacious preacher Billy Sunday delivered a prayer that made God sound like a boxer against sin. Memphis searched the crowd for Sister Walker again. It was odd that she hadn't shown up yet. Now, at last, Jake Marlowe took the stage. The young girls in corsages lifted their arms to him. "We love you, Jake!" they cried.

"Oh, I wish I could comfort him," one tearstained girl sobbed.

"I'll bet you do," Theta grumbled under her breath.

With his sleek hair and blue eyes, Jake Marlowe was the son every mother was proud of, the man every other man wanted to be, the lover every girl desired. He stood now at the microphone and looked out over the crowd, two hundred thousand strong, and paused, gathering his words. His voice echoed over the heads of the people packed into Times Square: "Sarah Snow was the best girl I ever knew. She was a saint. My very own angel."

A collective cheer rose up from the people: "Sarah, Sarah, Sarah!"

"Brother," Evie grumbled.

"We just gotta stick it out and then we get a private audience with Marlowe," Theta whispered.

Jake raised his hands. The crowd quieted, eager to hear whatever the great man would say next.

"An evil deed took her away from me. Took her from all of us. But evil deeds do not arrive in the air like songs on the radio. Evil deeds are perpetrated by evil people. Like those anarchists, the Secret Six. People like Arthur Brown and Mabel Rose."

Evie swallowed down her anger. In her heart, she knew that Mabel had been every bit as good as Sarah Snow—better, even. She did good things just because it was the right thing to do, without expecting any adulation for it. That she had been part of the terrorist group who'd bombed the exhibition was hard for Evie to accept. Her best friend, who had lived her life with a strong moral code, had died violating that code to the worst degree. Evie felt like she was grieving Mabel twice—both the person she loved and the person she thought she knew.

At the microphone, Jake Marlowe was gathering steam. "Or how about this Memphis Campbell? He dares to call himself the Harlem Healer, but at Miss Snow's last revival, he laid hands on a man who died that very same night! Did he also place a curse on Miss Snow?" Jake removed his pocket square and dabbed evenly at his forehead before returning it to its place.

"Or what about the Sweetheart Seer, Evie O'Neill? Did you know that she refused to sign a loyalty pledge with WGI? Now, why would any decent, law-abiding American citizen be afraid of signing such a loyalty oath? Is it, perhaps, because Evie O'Neill was close friends with Mabel Rose, the bomber herself?"

Angry boos erupted in the crowd. Theta squeezed Evie's hand.

"That bum. That lousy bum," Theta muttered.

Evie was frightened. This crowd had once adored her. Now they hated her. And Jake was egging them on. She wanted to leave. But she needed to get Marlowe to see reason about the Eye.

"I'd like you to hear from a man who knows firsthand about the dangers of Diviners," Marlowe said through the microphone. "Mr. Roy Stoughton."

Theta gasped as Roy, in all his awful beauty, took the stage. Around her, women's eyes shone when they looked up at his muscular physique and sensual pout and took no note of the fists that had bloodied Theta so many times.

Roy stepped to the microphone. "Thank you, Mr. Marlowe. Good evening, ladies and gentlemen. I stand before you as a simple man from Kansas. I came to this big city looking not for fame or fortune, but for my wife."

"I stand before you as a man. Who sounds. Like he is reading. From. A. Card," Henry zinged to Theta under his breath.

"Shhh," Theta cautioned.

Roy put a hand over his heart. "You see, she was tempted by the bright lights of Manhattan. She ran away from our happy home. From me. My search took me all the way to the stage of the Ziegfeld Follies. I met Mr. Ziegfeld, by the way. A fine man. Yes, sir, a fine man. And that's where I found my wife—singing and dancing in the Follies. You might know her better as Theta Knight."

An excited murmur rippled through the two hundred thousand people. The heat of gossip. The promise of more to come.

"But to me, she's just good old Betty Sue Stoughton of Topeka, Kansas. Back then, she was my wife. There wasn't any of this running around with flimflam artists and Negro healers. I miss her, and so does her mama. Her mama's not well, you see. This has near broken her heart, she misses her little girl so."

The only thing Theta's adoptive stage mother missed was the money Theta had made for her on the Orpheum Circuit, singing and dancing from the time Theta was three years old till she ran away with Roy at fourteen. The woman had never shown Theta a day's kindness. She was as phony as Roy's story.

Roy had worked a few manly tears into his voice for the crowd. "So if you see her, if you see my Betty Sue, all I ask is that you please, please bring her back to me. Bring her home. I just wanna take her home to Kansas, that's all. Betty Sue—if you're out there, just know that I won't rest until I find you, darlin'. I won't rest a single day."

There it was—the threat in the velvet glove. Roy's specialty. He wanted her to know she was marked. He'd have everybody hunting for her. And the worst part was, the folks in the crowd bought it. They were applauding him like he was a hero. He'd put himself in charge of the story—hers as well as his—and nobody doubted it. Roy took a seat next to Harriet Henderson, who patted his back as if he were a wounded little boy in need of mothering.

Theta could feel the acid in her throat and the heat building inside, seeking a way out.

Jake Marlowe took to the microphone again. "Now, I promise: We're going to dedicate this new church to the memory of Sarah. But before we do, there's something I need to say. These Diviners with their strange powers—it's not natural, I tell you. Can their powers truly be trusted?"

A murmur of doubt moved among the assembled.

"They brought the ghosts on us!" a man shouted.

"Amen! They did, indeed!" Billy Sunday shouted back. "Sorry, Mr. Marlowe."

"Quite all right. Now, I'm a man of industry. Of business," Marlowe continued. "I never went for ghost stories. But people have seen them. They've seen them on the streets. In their very homes. And just last night, in Central Park. Sarah knew there were ghosts," Marlowe continued. "Why, she warned me about them!"

"That isn't true," Evie whispered to Theta. "She didn't believe in them at all."

"I thought this was supposed to be a memorial. Where's he going with this?" Henry said, keeping his voice low.

The air was suddenly electric, a storm building. The klieg lights cast their starry shine upon Jake Marlowe as his voice shook with emotion. "Last night, this city was under attack. It's the Diviners who brought this plague upon us! They are fundamentally un-American. And now, thanks to the tireless efforts of Detective Terrence Malloy, we have proof—proof!—that these so-called Diviners, with their unnatural powers, have aligned themselves with the terrorist bombers who killed innocent people, including my dear Sarah. Last night, tireless federal agents have arrested Margaret Walker, Mr. Fitzgerald's former associate, for his murder and for sedition."

"What's he talking about Sister Walker, Theta?" Isaiah asked as the crowd grew agitated.

"I don't know," Theta said.

"These Diviners—Memphis and Isaiah Campbell, Sam Lubovitch Lloyd, Ling Chan, Evie O'Neill, Theta Knight, Jericho Jones, and their friends..."

"I didn't even *make the bill*?" Henry muttered.

"...are wanted as accomplices in the bombing of the Future of America

Exhibition, in the murder of Dr. William Fitzgerald, and on suspicion of a plot against the United States of America. They were supposed to be here tonight as my guests, but I see that they are not here." Marlowe gestured to the area where the Diviners were to have stood. Evie was grateful for Bill's advice earlier. "I see that, like the cowards they are, they wouldn't dare show their faces at a memorial for a true patriot, Sarah Snow," Marlowe continued.

More boos came from the crowd.

"Evil, we oughta scram," Theta said.

"But we have to talk to Marlowe...."

"Evil, don't you see? He's not gonna talk to us. It's a trap. We gotta go *now*."

But Marlowe was still talking. "And that is why I am offering a five-thousand-dollar reward for each one of them captured alive."

Excited gasps rippled through the crowd: Five thousand dollars—a fortune! And there were at least seven of them to be found!

Detective Malloy stepped up to the microphone. "Anyone harboring these enemies of the state will be charged with treason under the 1918 Sedition Act. Due to their powers, these Diviners are considered highly dangerous. Therefore, we ask that if you do see them, you call the New York City Police Department or the Bureau of Investigation."

"Evil..." Theta said, frightened. Marlowe had betrayed them, put a shiny price tag on their heads. The Diviners had all just become Public Enemy #1. And if anyone recognized them in the crowd, they were done for.

The heat that had been building in Theta's palms could no longer be contained. "Evie, we gotta ankle," she said, wide-eyed. "I-I'm gonna blow."

Theta's face was tight with fear, a sheen of perspiration betraying her struggle. The heat inside her wanted out.

"All right," Evie said, swallowing down her own panic. "Let's try not to make a scene. Isaiah, follow us." Evie pushed against the crowd. "Excuse me, my friend is ill." They were packed in so tightly it was hard to move.

Wisps of smoke curled along Theta's fingertips and a faint orange glow silhouetted her willowy frame. "No," Theta moaned, helpless. "No, no, no."

"There's one!" A matronly white woman in a too-large hat pointed at Memphis. "There he is! That one!"

Memphis put his hands up in a placating gesture. "Me? No, ma'am. You've got the wrong fella."

The woman jabbed her finger excitedly. "That's him! It's him!"

"I saw him first!" another man said, advancing toward the Diviners.

"The devil you did!" another man shouted, pushing through the crowd. Fights erupted among the memorial attendees. They'd gone from sharing grief over Sarah to a frenzy.

Theta rushed toward Memphis, Evie and the others following.

"We need to create a distraction!" Evie said.

"We do that and we prove we're a danger," Jericho said, just as a man made a grab for Evie and Jericho knocked him down.

"Did you see that?" a woman called. "That Diviner hit him!"

"I-I'm sorry," Jericho said, horrified.

"We do nothing and we're going to be trampled by a mob of bounty hunters or shot by police," Evie said.

Detective Malloy bellowed into the microphone. "Hold it right there. Don't move." A line of police pushed into the crowd, guns drawn.

"Shit," Memphis muttered.

"You said a bad word," Isaiah said.

"Come together and get ready," Evie called, reaching out.

"Ready for what?" Ling said.

"I-I don't know yet," Evie said, joining hands with Theta and Henry. "Jericho?" Evie pleaded. "Please?"

"What are we doing?" he asked.

"Nothing like last night," Evie promised, even though she couldn't say for sure what would happen. "Jericho, we need you."

Reluctantly, Jericho reached for Ling's hand. The Diviners made a line facing the crowd, who began backing up.

"What are they doing?"

"Some kinda Diviner mumbo jumbo."

"Get back! Get back!"

"Somebody stop them! We aren't safe!"

"These aren't ghosts, Evie. What are we going to do?" Theta said.

Ling was jostled. She cried out as she nearly lost her balance. If the crowd surged, if they had to run, what would she do? "Make an energy field!" she yelled.

"How?" Henry said. "This isn't the museum. There's no credenza to shape into something else!"

"Just...concentrate. Find something to...to..." But Ling didn't know. She couldn't think. She could feel her friends struggling against one another, fighting their own individual fears. No one could seem to concentrate on any one thing. The connection was elusive.

From the stage, Roy shouted: "There she is! There's my Betty Sue." He nodded, a signal to Dutch's boys. Now they were coming, too. Theta's panic moved through her, along with her fire. Evie gasped and dropped Theta's hand like a hot coal.

"Theta! Theta, you've got to calm down."

"There's my Betty Sue right there. Don't move, Betty. I'm coming." Roy's voice. His men, on the march. The police, getting closer. The crowd on the verge of bloodlust.

"Stop," Theta whispered. She grabbed her friends' hands again, squeezing. "Stop, stop, *stop!*"

The word wrapped itself around the Diviners and shot through them like a burst of energy that pushed several rows of people backward, knocking others down as they flew. They were dazed, and sat, stunned, where they landed in a heap. The energy traveled through the crowd, surrounding them like current along a telephone wire. People were frozen where they stood. The Diviners could see their eyes, wide and afraid. They tried to speak but couldn't. But the people saw. They understood what was happening. Understood how it had happened and who was to blame. Onstage, Jake Marlowe also watched, frozen in place.

"What did we do?" Ling whispered.

"I...I just wanted them to stop," Theta said. She could see the fear and hatred in the eyes of the crowd.

"We've got to get out of here now! Run!" Evie shouted. She let go, barreling around the stage, running toward the sidewalks of Broadway and the throngs of people going about their business like it was any other night in the city. If they were fast enough, they'd be able to lose themselves in that crowd.

"I just wanted them to stop," Theta repeated and took off after Evie.

"Theta!" Henry yelled, giving chase.

"Move, move, move!" Memphis pushed at Jericho's back, trying to catch up to Isaiah, who ran alongside Evie, Theta, and Henry.

The crowd was no longer dazed and fearful. They were angry. Hungry for vengeance.

"There they are!" came a shout.

Theta turned around. Several men rose to their feet from the heap. Mouths set, they pushed toward Memphis.

"Poet—run!" Flames burst from Theta's fingertips and engulfed her hands. Lost to her rage, she glowed like a beacon. "Leave him alone!"

People screamed and leaped back from the heat of her.

"Theta!" Evie said. She doubled back, coming up behind her friend. "Let's go!"

Theta moved her hand quickly. Fire went loose. It caught on the funeral bunting and exploded into sparks. The crowd panicked, running over one another to get away. Police whistles cut across the night. Men in blue thrust into the crowd with nightsticks at the ready. The girls in gardenias shrieked and clung to one another. Onstage, detectives moved Jake Marlowe toward the safety of a waiting touring car.

Right beside Memphis, a policeman clubbed the wrong man, who went limp. Blood trickled down his face. The chaotic crowd surged anew, further separating Memphis from Isaiah.

"Isaiah!" Memphis made a desperate lunge for his brother. "Isaiah!"

"Memphis!" Isaiah called back as he was borne along by the sweeping tide.

The unruly crowd was quickly becoming a mob. Fists swung. Memphis ducked a fight. Isaiah was carried farther away. Memphis screamed his brother's name. Bill snaked his muscular arm around Memphis, dragging him away from the frenzied crowd and toward safety.

In that same crowd, Theta's firepower began to fizzle. That was the moment Evie was most afraid; as soon as the people saw that, they'd come after them. Theta cried out in agony. Strips of molten material adhered to the backs of her hands, stuck there. She'd had no time to remove her gloves before the fire had come upon her. Evie grabbed Theta's wrist, hissing as the last remnants of Theta's heat touched her own glove, and then all of Theta's fire was gone as her rage sucked back up into her body and became blind fear.

"Theta? Theta!" Evie's eyes went wide with horror when she saw the state of Theta's skin, which was deeply blistered.

"H-hurts," Theta cried.

"We'll get you fixed up, but we've got to get out of here, okay?"

Theta nodded, unable to do much else.

Evie saw small Isaiah being buffeted by the throng. "Isaiah!" Evie called. "Over here!" She pushed aside one of the corsage-wearing Sarah Snow girls to get to him. "Where's Memphis?"

"I don't know," Isaiah said tearfully.

Deep in the crowd, Evie locked eyes with Jericho, but there was no way for them to reach each other. "I'm sorry!" she yelled. "I'm sorry for everything."

He was going to try to come for her, she knew. She shook her head. "Bountiful!" she yelled. "Do you understand?"

He nodded, and the crowd overtook the space between them.

"It's you. You're the Sweetheart Seer," said the girl Evie had pushed aside. For the briefest second, Evie was happy to have been recognized, until the girl's face went hard and mean. "You killed Sarah Snow."

"No. No, that isn't true," Evie said.

Henry lodged himself between Evie and the angry girl. "Excuse me, miss," he said. "I'm not from around here, and I'm awfully lost. Can you help me?" With the other hand behind his back, he waved Evie and Theta on.

"C'mon," Evie said, pulling Isaiah in with them. They ran to Broadway and tried to blend in with the theatergoers rushing to make the curtain. At the corner, Theta glanced over her shoulder. She stopped short. "Wait, where's Henry?"

"There he is," Evie said. Talking to the girl had stranded him. He was stuck on the other side of the melee. Citizens-turned-bounty hunters flooded the area between them. Police were on the lookout. Dutch Schultz's men muscled their way through the crowd. When a man didn't move fast enough, one of Dutch's thugs bloodied his nose. It was madness. They were hopelessly separated.

"Henry!" Evie shouted. "Get to Bountiful! Pass it along!"

"Now, wait just a minute—" Henry shouted back.

But already, Evie was moving away. "Sorry—no time to debate it. We meet in Bountiful! Get there any way you can, but go—now!"

"Dammit, Evie," Henry muttered, watching her go. That was the trouble with wanting somebody else to take on making decisions—sometimes they did, and you ended up going to Nebraska.

"Bountiful," Henry repeated, and then he was off and running, wishing that he had Sam alongside him to keep them both invisible.

ESCAPE

A frantic Memphis scoured the crowd for his little brother. "Isaiah! Isaiah!" he screamed till his throat hurt.

Bill pulled at Memphis's arm. "Memphis, we got to move!"

"Not without Isaiah!" Memphis said, shaking the big man off.

Around them, the crowd had gone feral. The night's earlier grief had been discarded, and in its place was a bloodlust for revenge. Back in Louisiana, Bill Johnson had seen a crowd turn. He'd watched, helpless, as men with torches set fire to a black settlement. And the law? Hell, some of those lawmen were the ones who lit the torches. Bill balled Memphis's collar in his fist till they were nose to nose. His voice was low and urgent. "Listen to me. This mob is lookin' for a lynching. Understand?"

Twenty feet away, a man curled up on the ground was taking kicks from Dutch Schultz's thugs while other men cheered them on. Memphis imagined Isaiah on the ground, Isaiah being taken by these furious people.

"I won't leave without my brother," he said again.

"I figured you'd say that," Bill said and sighed, just before he knocked Memphis out and threw him over his shoulder. Memphis would be furious about this when he woke, but he'd be alive to fight another day. Once Bill got him stashed away someplace safe, he'd come back to look for Isaiah.

"Mr. Johnson! Over here!" Henry DuBois shouted as he maneuvered his way against the tide of people like a skinny garter snake. Bill ducked into a doorway on Fortieth Street. There, hidden by an awning, he waited until Henry caught up.

"Hey. What happened to Memphis?" Henry asked, nearly out of breath.

Bill ignored the question. "You seen Isaiah out there?"

Henry nodded. "He's with Theta and Evie."

Bill breathed a little easier. At least the boy was safe. "You see any of the others?"

Henry shook his head and patted the stitch in his side.

"Well, we cain't stay here. Got to move," Bill said.

"Evie said to meet in Bountiful."

"What kind of fool notion is that?"

"It's Evie," Henry said as both explanation and apology. "That's where they're going with Isaiah. That's what we should do. Get out of New York right now."

Bill sucked some air through his teeth, thinking. "There's a train leaving Penn Station for N'awlins in twenty minutes, and we need to be on it. We can make our way from there."

Henry faltered. "Oh. New Orleans?"

"What I said. You got somethin' against N'awlins?"

Henry pictured Belle Reve, his ancestral home in the Garden District of New Orleans, where he was raised. He pictured his cold and distant father reading his evening paper while the household moved around him, making sure he was not disturbed. He pictured his broken mother taking all the silver from the drawers while Flossie, their cook, tried to cajole her away from it and into a warm bath to calm her nerves. He remembered the disappointment on his father's face when he'd discovered that his son was in love with a boy named Louis. He remembered his mother telling him to "fly away, little bird" as Henry slipped out of the house with only his suitcase.

"No," he said at last.

"Good. 'Cause we ain't got much choice in the matter. Anybody asks, this is my brother, Barnabas. He fainted at the memorial because of what them Diviners did. Nobody's lookin' for me and you. That's the advantage we got."

"Is he okay?"

"He'll come around soon enough. Come on. Gotta move with a purpose now. Keep ya head down and don't draw attention."

※

Jericho and Ling had taken refuge in a darkened picture house near Times Square. "The picture's already started," the ticket booth man had told them as they bought two tickets before stealing into the back of the darkened theater. The picture was German. Something called *Metropolis*. For a moment, Jericho was mesmerized by the flickering screen and the sight of a robot transforming into a human woman. Instinctually, he put a hand to his chest where, beneath the skin, a configuration of machinelike parts, fueled by

Marlowe's special serum, kept his broken body functioning. For the first time in ten years, Jericho was without that serum. He took his hand from his pocket and made a fist. It was no trouble, and he breathed a sigh of relief.

"Did you see any of the others?" Ling whispered.

"I lost them in the crowd."

"Where do you think they are? What should we do? Go back to Sister—" Ling stopped as she realized that Sister Walker couldn't help them. No one could. They would have to figure this out for themselves.

"I saw Evie in the crowd. She said we should go to Bountiful," Jericho said.

"Nebraska?" Ling squeaked.

"Shhh!" a man in the back row scolded. Jericho and Ling scooted away from the entrance and back toward the lobby. "Nebraska is over a thousand miles from here. How are we going to get there?" Ling asked.

"Penn Station's not that far."

Ling shook her head. "They'll be watching the train and bus stations."

Jericho nodded, thought some more. "We could go back to the Bennington. Hide out in Will's apartment till tomorrow and see if we can find any of the others."

Ling grunted at him. "The Bennington is the first place the police will think to look."

"Well, I'm sorry that I'm not as clever as you are," Jericho said sarcastically.

"So am I," Ling said, straightforward as ever.

"We just need a place to rest and think," Jericho said.

Ling thought about Doyers Street and her family's restaurant. It had always been the safest place she knew, but now the police would probably be on their way to the Tea House. She hated to imagine her parents' stricken faces or the shame it would bring to them—and the danger. No. They couldn't go there. But where *was* safety and someone they could trust to hide them?

"Alma," Ling said.

"What about Alma?"

"No one knows about her. No one would look for us at her apartment. She's leaving town tomorrow on the TOBA circuit—they book Negro acts into clubs across the country. They've got a bus. We could leave with them."

Jericho raised an eyebrow. "How are we going to explain…? I don't think anyone's going to buy us as an act."

"We'll make up a story. One time I went with Theta to a screen test out in Brooklyn and I had to pretend to be her seamstress to get in the door. I'll say I'm Alma's wardrobe mistress. And you…" Ling scrutinized Jericho's face. "What else do you do besides catalog creepy artifacts?"

"I read a lot of philosophy."

Ling let out a heavy sigh. "Brother."

"And I'm very strong."

"That could come in handy. For now, I'll say you're my cousin."

"I…don't really look like your cousin."

"My cousin Seamus has red hair, freckles, and cheeks that are always pink." Ling shrugged. "But he *is* my cousin."

Jericho didn't seem convinced. Ling grunted in frustration. "Did everyone from your little Hans Christian Andersen village look the same?"

"Hans Christian…?"

"…like you all escaped from a German fairy tale?"

"Shhh!" the same man from the back row scolded. Jericho and Ling moved a little farther into the lobby.

"Hans Christian Andersen was Danish. And no. We did not all look the same. The Jorgensons' daughter, Brigid, had brown hair," Jericho whispered testily. "How do you know that Alma will help us?"

Ling didn't know. She couldn't imagine Alma turning them away. Then again, she couldn't imagine Alma suddenly saying good-bye the way she had, either. Ling had to ask herself if she was suggesting this plan just so she could see Alma one more time.

"Of course she'll help us," Ling insisted.

"And you don't think anybody will notice that we aren't who we say we are?"

"Nobody's who they say they are."

In Times Square, much of the crowd had dispersed. Police rounded up some would-be vigilantes and locked them up in paddy wagons. Firemen sprayed the stage's bunting, putting out the last of Theta's handiwork. As Jericho and Ling approached Broadway, they heard a man pleading for his life. He cowered on the ground, his arms up to fend off the blows and kicks of two men shouting, "Lousy Diviner! Anarchist! Get out of our country!"

"Wait here," Jericho said. Jake Marlowe's serum burned through his veins. He lifted the two men by their suit collars as if each weighed no more than a bag of flour. He liked seeing the fear in the eyes of these bullies. The serum made Jericho's heart pump harder. His act of heroism teetered on the edge of something uglier.

"Jericho?" Ling said. "Jericho. Let go."

Jericho dropped the men on the curb. He unclenched his fists, unsettled by the strong impulses that had seized him.

"Go on. Get out of here," he said to the men.

The bullies stumbled away. When they'd traveled a safe distance, one of them called out, "You're a bum! A bum, you hear?"

Jericho helped the beaten man to his feet.

"They... they just turned on me," the man said. "Thought I was one of those Diviners."

"Go home," Jericho said.

The young man nodded. "Thank you."

Nearby, another fight broke out. Several people rushed in to join, drawn by the possibility of catching a Diviner and meting out "justice." It was getting more dangerous.

"Ling, do you mind if I carry you out of here?" Jericho asked.

Ordinarily, Ling *would* mind, but these were not ordinary circumstances.

"Just don't drop me," she said, clutching tightly to her crutches as Jericho scooped her up into his arms and took off running through the city streets.

Ling had heard girls fantasizing about such scenarios, calling them romantic. Mostly, she found it embarrassing. It was Alma's arms Ling missed. Now that their plan was under way, Ling's worry took over. What if Alma was unhappy to see her? What if Alma *did* say no to taking them along? What would they do then?

What if she was with another girl?

"Am I hurting you?" Jericho asked.

"N-no," Ling said, trying to rid her mind of that last thought. "You're not even winded," she noted. "You're abnormally strong."

"Are you calling me abnormal?" Jericho said, grinning.

They'd reached the symphony of traffic snarling up Broadway. There were people on the street who stared at the sight of Jericho carrying Ling down the street, and she tried not to let it bother her. She was used to stares.

No, that wasn't true.

She had learned to keep her own eyes straight ahead. But she never got used to the looks people gave her in the seconds before they corrected themselves: a combination of pity, nervous gratitude for their own good fortune, and the jolt of fear when they realized—just for a second—that this good fortune was not guaranteed, that anything could happen to them at any time. That they were vulnerable. Those were the people who looked away fastest.

Jericho signaled for a taxi and one swerved to the curb. "Ling, I need you to make a lot of noise."

"What kind of noise? What are you...?"

"Please, my wife's having a baby!" Jericho said as he gentled Ling onto the backseat, shielding her body from the driver's view.

Ling's cheeks burned as she realized what he'd meant by "making noise." She narrowed her green eyes at him. "If we survive this, you are dead to me."

"You told me to be clever," he whispered.

In the rearview mirror, the driver regarded the couple in his backseat with suspicion. "Are you two pulling my leg? Because you can get out right—"

Ling screamed at the top of her lungs. The driver floored it.

"That was impressive," Jericho said as he and Ling walked the two blocks from Harlem Hospital to Alma's apartment building.

"Screaming isn't impressive," Ling said. Her body ached with each step after such a full day, but she was not about to meet Alma cradled in Jericho's arms.

"We're here," she said, stopping in front of a four-story redbrick building with a fire escape dotted with drying laundry. Light bled from the windows of Alma's second-floor apartment. Ling's stomach hurt. She pictured Alma in some other girl's arms. But now Jericho was ringing the bell, and a moment later Alma stuck her scarf-wrapped head out the window and peered down at Ling and Jericho with surprise.

"Ling? Jericho. What on earth?"

"Please, Alma," Ling said. "We need your help."

"Wait there. I'll be right down," Alma said.

❋

At Penn Station, Henry and Bill fell in behind late-straggling passengers scurrying to catch the Crescent Limited to New Orleans before it left the station. Most people hurrying on board now were preoccupied with last-minute things. They were not looking for fugitives.

"What's the matter with him?" one man asked, pointing his cigarette at Memphis, who was still slung over Bill's shoulder.

"He fainted at the Sarah Snow memorial," Henry said. "Terrible scene."

"I heard there was a ruckus. *Diviners*," the man clucked. "Ought to round them all up if you ask me."

"I'll be sure not to ask you," Henry said to the man's back as he boarded the train.

"Now," Bill said. They made their way down the platform to the porter's stand, where a tall man with a pencil-thin mustache was at work directing several porters to the luggage.

"We're looking for Nelson Desir," Bill said to the man in a low voice. "Madame Seraphina sent us? About some important cargo to transport out of the city? You might even say it's *divine* cargo."

"Ohhh." The porter looked around to be sure they were safe. *"I'm* Nelson. Pleased to meet you. Board the last car to the left." He shook their hands. "Welcome to the Brotherhood of Sleeping Car Porters. Don't you worry—the Georges'll see you through and keep you safe."

"The Georges?" Henry said, confused.

"I'll explain later. Right now, you need to board. Train's about to leave the station. You made it just in time."

Behind him, Henry heard a passenger calling for Nelson. "Oh, George, I need this on board, please."

"Yes, ma'am. Right away." He whispered to Bill and Henry, "Go!"

Once they were on board, another porter named Coleman directed them to a private sleeper car at the back of the train. "You should be safe in here," Coleman said.

Henry whistled. It was nicely appointed, with two long seats facing each other, a slim table in between. Above each seat, hidden behind drapes, was a sleeper berth that could be opened up into a bed.

Bill deposited Memphis onto one of the seats.

"He okay?" Coleman asked.

Bill nodded.

"Just sit tight for now," Coleman told them and pulled the door closed.

The train lurched forward. Henry watched the platform receding as the train chugged into the darkened tunnel. In his own seat, Bill breathed heavily and stretched out his arms. He hadn't seen the South in nearly ten years and had vowed never to go back.

"Guess I'm headed home whether I like it or not," Bill said.

"Yeah. I guess we are at that," Henry said.

They looked over at Memphis, who was still out. He'd be powerful mad when he woke, Bill knew. But for now, he was safe. They were all safe. For how much longer, he couldn't say.

✺

Over cups of hot tea with plenty of honey and lemon, Ling and Jericho told Alma about everything that had happened during the memorial.

"We need to get out of New York," Ling explained. "We have to get to Bountiful, Nebraska."

Alma made a face. "Nebraska? Why would anybody wanna go there?"

"There's another Diviner like us, made during Project Buffalo. We need her help to stop the King of Crows. And we have to get to her before the Shadow Men do. We were hoping maybe you could smuggle us out with your band," Ling said meekly.

It took Alma a second to understand, but then her eyes grew wide as she looked first at the six-foot-four-inch Jericho, with a face like a Nordic farm boy's, and then at tiny, half-Chinese, half-Irish Ling, her crutches resting in her lap. "Oh, sure. You'll blend right in with the Harlem Haymakers."

"Please, Alma?"

Alma sighed. "Well, I can't very well leave you here. We've got a bus. It's leaving at nine thirty sharp tomorrow morning. Though Lord knows what to tell the Haymakers. And you can't use your real names. We've got to give you aliases. Something bland and boring."

"Sure. How about Laurel and Hardy?" Jericho said, straight-faced.

Ling frowned. "Was that a joke?"

"Yes. It was supposed to be a joke."

Alma snapped her fingers. "I've got it! Ling, you're now Mary. It's the most common girl's name I can think of."

"Mary...Chang," Ling announced.

"Perfect. And, Jericho, you are now..." Alma bit her lip as she scrutinized Jericho's face.

"Hans Andersen," Jericho shot back, flicking a sideways glance at Ling. Alma put a hand to her hip. "Didn't I just say you needed something bland?"

"Hans is bland. If you're in Denmark."

"Well, we ain't. How about John Smith?" Alma offered.

"Too obvious," Jericho said. "How about…Freddy?"

"Isn't Freddy the annoying nickname Sam gave you?" Ling said.

Jericho smirked. "Indeed."

Alma threw her hands up. "Fine. Freddy Smith it is. Now, it's a big day tomorrow, what with going out on the road and lying to the band about bringing along wanted criminals. I'm going to need all the beauty sleep I can get."

Alma made up the couch for Ling. Jericho took the floor. In the dark, Ling turned her head and watched Alma's door, wishing she were on the other side of it. Ling shut her eyes and pictured her parents' restaurant. She stifled a tiny catch in her chest. That was her home, with two loving parents and a clattering kitchen noisy with neighbors. Doyers Street was the known world. Chinatown offered Ling some measure of comfort and security. But what about the country beyond Doyers Street? Even without malevolent spirits, it was frightening.

But she would get to be with Alma a little while longer. She tried not to feel too guilty about how happy that made her. And just maybe she could get Alma to change her mind.

＊

From their hiding spot in the Ziegfeld Theatre's costume storage room, Theta, Isaiah, and Evie could hear the show going on out front, people laughing and applauding the pretty chorus girls parading across the stage in elaborate costumes as if there were nothing to worry about.

"Hold still," Evie said.

Theta winced as Evie dabbed at her burned hands with witch hazel before applying a balm and two fresh bandages from a kit on the makeup table. "How's that?" Evie asked.

"I wish I had a flask fulla hooch," Theta said.

"You and me both."

"What are we doing here?" Isaiah asked.

"This is how we're getting out of this town. In disguise." Theta dragged out a wardrobe trunk that held a collection of baggy men's trousers, threadbare coats, and beat-up bowler hats. She grabbed a handful of makeup and some sponges. "They're looking for a Follies girl, the Sweetheart Seer, and

113

a Diviner kid. They're not looking for a bunch of hoboes. Here, Evil. Scrub your face clean. Every trace of powder and lipstick, gone."

Evie did as instructed, and by the time Theta had worked her magic, penciling in a mustache and darkening Evie's brows, and the three of them had dressed themselves in rumpled men's clothing, it was certain that no one would suspect that they were the fugitives.

Evie shoved her wavy blond bob under Sam's Greek fisherman's cap and asked, "How do I look?"

"I'd buy a newspaper from you," Theta said.

"I can't tell if that was a compliment or an insult," Evie said.

"Wait here," Theta said and disappeared.

"Where's she going?" Isaiah asked.

Evie shook her head. In a minute, Theta returned.

"What was that all about, Theta?" Evie asked.

"I had to call Miss Lillian and ask her to look after Archie."

"Who's Archie?" Isaiah asked.

"My cat. Didn't you say that Will had a car?" Theta asked. She winced. "Sorry. I didn't mean—"

"Yes. An old Model T. It's the ugliest flivver you've ever seen."

"Nobody'll be looking at it, then. Can you drive?"

Evie batted her lashes. "Like a champ."

Will had parked the car on Sixty-eighth Street. Across the narrow strip of road, the museum sat on its haunches, a wounded animal. The windows were dark. The sign still said MURDERERS.

"Once, he gave me a piece of candy from his drawer," Isaiah said softly. "He said I'd been real brave to work on my powers. And then he showed me how to make shadow rabbits on the wall."

"He did?" Evie said, surprised. She didn't imagine Will being sentimental about children. Funny the things you didn't know about people until it was too late.

Evie waited until she was on Central Park West before turning on the flivver's headlights, just in case anyone was watching. "Let's get to Hopeful Harbor."

"Hey, I thought we were going to Bountiful to find Sarah Beth," Isaiah said.

"We are. But first we're going to rescue Sam," Evie said and pressed the gas so hard that Theta had to hold on to her hat.

NOT ALONE

Vera Mathers hurried to gather her laundry from the backyard clothesline before the rain set in. There'd been so much of it this spring. Every day, the papers reported on the swollen Mississippi River threatening to break through the levees from Cairo, Illinois, all the way down to New Orleans. This morning, there had been a nice April breeze, warm enough that Vera opened all the windows and hung the washing to dry on the line. Now, though, the back of her tongue tasted like a rusty nail. The sky was graying up again. So Vera left her five-year-old daughter, Becky, upstairs in the nursery to play with her dollies while she came outside to tend to the wash.

Vera's husband was a Fuller Brush salesman. He was on the road rather a lot. It was just Vera and Becky most of the time. Becky had been acting so funny lately. Sometimes the girl would stare off into nothing. Just yesterday, Vera had asked her what was so interesting about that spot on the wall and Becky had said "Ghosts," then gone right back to staring until Vera told her to leave the table if she was going to act so silly.

Vera had put in a call to the doctor anyway—a mother couldn't be too careful. He told her it was nerves; it would pass. Vera's mother-in-law, Mrs. Mathers, had died ten months earlier from a broken neck. The old woman had tried to get out of bed in her room up in the attic even though she could barely walk. She'd fallen headfirst down the attic steps and was dead before she hit the bottom. Vera could still see the way her mother-in-law had looked, all broken in a heap. Her eyes open and that little gold cross she wore settled into the hollow of her throat. At the funeral, people said nice things about Mrs. Mathers (wasn't that what you were supposed to do about the dead?). "Why, Vera, you are a saint, an absolute saint to have cared for that bedridden old woman all these years," they told her with a sympathetic pat on the arm. Vera had thanked them and never let on how overjoyed she was to be lowering that witch and her little gold necklace into the ground once and for all. She'd hated her mother-in-law. Hated the way that thankless biddy complained about Vera's housekeeping, hated how she'd wrinkle her nose when Vera brought up the breakfast tray, telling her that the milk tasted sour or the eggs were too soft or the coffee was weak.

Maybe Vera had forgotten to give the woman her heart pills that day. Maybe she'd even forgotten for a few days. Look here, she couldn't be expected to remember everything, could she? What with Becky to raise and a house to run and her husband gone most of the time? Maybe she had taken too long to bring the old woman down to the toilet. Maybe she'd decided, this time, to ignore the woman's grating voice shouting her name. Maybe that was why the old woman had gotten out of bed on her own and tried for the steps. If Vera was supposed to feel shame about it, well, she did not. The past ten months without that criticizing harpy had been some of the best of her life.

With the first crack of lightning, wind lifted the bed linens on the clothesline. Vera jumped back, startled. Somebody was standing out in the tall grass behind the house. With trembling hands, Vera parted the swaying sheets. The field was empty. Nothing but grass bending in the wind. But she could swear she'd seen him in the flash of light—a man in a tall black hat watching her with cold eyes, with *hunger*. Just the glimpse of him had given her the feeling of some unimaginable horror bearing down.

If her husband were home, she'd call for him. But he was in Topeka or Wichita or god only knows where with god only knows whom. She didn't feel safe. Who did anymore? Just that week at bridge club, Mona Miller had said she'd felt a presence—yes, that was it, a presence—and she'd started locking the door and sleeping with a pistol by her bed. "This country's going to the devil," Mona had said, lips pursed. "Anyhow, that's what Reverend Carden says, and I couldn't agree more."

Mona Miller, that little hypocrite. All those visits to the Reverend Carden while his wife was at her sister's over in Lawrence? Did she think no one noticed?

A rumble of thunder brought Vera back to her task. The sky looked like a boxer's face halfway through a fight, bruised and scowling, hinting at more violence. The laundry. Vera moved quickly, removing the clothespins and dropping the sheets into her basket, though her speed had less to do with the angry sky and more to do with some fear crawling up her spine, making her knees a little wobbly, fumbling her fingers. She *had* seen somebody; she was sure of it. She'd seen some*thing*.

Now, why did she think that? Why did she think what she'd seen wasn't entirely human? Her heart was beating very hard. The clouds groaned. She hurried, tearing the clothes from their pins, not caring whether they wrinkled in the basket. Vera had made it to the very last sheet when the back door to the kitchen banged shut. She clutched the last sheet to her chest and watched as, one by one, the first-floor windows slammed closed—kitchen, then powder room, then sunroom. Vera stumbled backward with a cry. Because a gray blot passed behind the last of those windows. A thing so quick it registered to her mind as fog.

"It's nothing," she whispered. "You're seeing things, Vera."

She glanced fearfully at the second-floor windows, which were still open. The filmy white curtains of the nursery fluttered out and sucked back in on a snore of wind. Her little girl was upstairs in that nursery all alone. *Not alone*, Vera's mind screamed. The house slid sideways as Vera fought not to faint. She did not want to go inside. She wanted to leave her child and run down the newly paved road to her neighbor's house a mile away.

No. She was a mother. She had to go inside, had to get her girl.

Vera bolted for the back steps. Thunder growled, coming closer. It sounded like a living thing on the hunt. Vera tugged on the back door. The knob wouldn't turn. *It won't let me in*, she thought. Everything in Vera Mathers's body went tight. She ran into the yard and screamed Becky's name. Oh, where was her girl? The second-floor window in her bedroom squeaked down slowly with a deliberateness that she knew, deep down in the dark place where reason loses its voice, could not be blamed on the storm. It was as if some unseen force had pressed it shut. Vera ran around to the front porch. Before she'd even reached the porch steps, the front door opened with a sigh, as if welcoming her. Vera stared straight into the foyer, at the staircase leading up to the second floor, to the bedrooms out of sight, the nursery all the way up past the shadowy stairwell.

"B-Becky," she said, barely a whisper. Then louder: "Becky! Rebecca Jean Mathers! You come downstairs this instant! Your mother wants to see you!"

The floorboards on the second-floor landing creaked.

"Becky! Becky Jean!"

The girl did not answer. Another sharp crack of thunder broke. Vera raced into the foyer and a gust of wind slammed the door shut behind her. The house was unnaturally still. Sealed like a tomb. Vera had never been so frightened. She wished her husband were home to tell her she was being ridiculous, wished he were going up the stairs instead of her. Her eyes came even with the second-floor landing. She peered around the banister. The door to the nursery was closed. She could hear the girl talking to her dolls. Vera tiptoed toward the nursery. This was the moment she thought she might die of fright. "Please, please," she whispered. Vera burst into the room. The girl looked up, surprised. She had made a tea party for the dolls and was dressing the last one. The floor was littered with her daughter's artwork, another mess to clean up.

"Rebecca Jean, didn't you hear me calling you?" Vera sounded nearly hysterical.

The little girl continued to dress her dolly in its fine blue velveteen dress. "Yes, ma'am. But I needed to get Baby Lucy ready for the tea party."

Vera's fear transformed into anger. She had half a mind to turn Becky over her knee and spank her. Why, she would! The girl would learn to mind, by god. She took a step forward and stopped cold. Muddy streaks marred the clean floor. Clumps of dirt dotted the braided rug. There were worms crawling in all that dirt.

"Did you track all this dirt in on my clean floor, Rebecca Jean?"

"No, ma'am."

Liar. The little liar. Oh, she would get such a whupping! Something shiny showed itself in all that dirt. Vera looked closer and clamped a hand over her mouth to stop the scream. She stumbled backward, away from the gold cross necklace on the rug. In horror, she took in the girl's artwork on the floor: crude pictures of Vera hanging laundry on the line, and in the field beyond, under a sky full of blue lightning, was the man in the tall hat pulling the dead from their graves.

Long shadows climbed the nursery wall like thorny vines growing into something else, something the house could not contain, something Vera did not want to see. A shuffling came from the hallway. Behind them, the door screeched as it began to slowly close, and it seemed to Vera that her heart would explode in her chest as Becky looked over her mother's shoulder and smiled.

"Hi, Grandma."

THE BROTHERHOOD OF SLEEPING CAR PORTERS

Memphis leaned his head against the side of the train and stared out the window at the countryside moving past.

"Where are we?" he croaked. His throat was dry and his neck was sore.

"Just coming into Maryland on the Crescent Limited," Henry said.

"The... Crescent Limited?"

"That train to New Orleans. How are you feeling?"

"Like somebody knocked me out and put me on a train," Memphis said tightly, his gaze still on the shapeless world outside the train window.

"He's worried about his brother," Bill said from the other end of the seat. He had his head leaned back and his eyes shut.

Memphis turned to face Bill. "Damn right I'm worried about my brother. You had no right to do what you did."

Bill kept his eyes closed. "Like I said, live to fight another day."

"I saw Theta and Evie with Isaiah," Henry said. "They'll look after him."

"Not like I will," Memphis grumbled. "New Orleans. That's a long way from Nebraska."

Bill opened his eyes at last. "We couldn't be choosy 'bout which train to catch."

"I've still got some friends in New Orleans. They could get us on a steamboat that'll take us as far as St. Louis," Henry said, trying to mitigate the situation. He hated conflict of any kind.

"You from N'awlins?" Bill said, surprised.

"I suppose I am," Henry answered.

"You got kin there?" Bill asked.

"I suppose I do," Henry said tightly, and Bill knew well enough to leave it alone.

Henry wondered if his parents were still alive. If his mother had gotten any better or if her mind was still broken. He thought of his cold, distant father reading his newspaper at the table as he always did while the servants poured his tea. He wondered when his parents had stopped looking for him.

Or if they had ever started. He could never forgive his father for what had happened to Louis.

"From New Orleans, we can get a steamboat to St. Louis, and then catch a train to Omaha, and from Omaha, we'll get on a train to Bountiful," Henry said. He didn't want to think about his family. There was nothing in New Orleans to hold him but old memories—ghosts it was time to put to rest.

"We can't do that if everybody's out there looking for us." Memphis watched the trees, houses, the tiny lights of the distant cities flying past.

"Isaiah's in good hands," Henry said.

"You don't know that," Memphis grumbled. "What if the police caught up with them? Or those Shadow Men? What if he got separated from Theta and Evie?" Memphis pressed his hands to his temples as if he could squeeze the fear from his mind.

A quick knock at the door. The three of them sat up, alert, only relaxing when Nelson let himself in. "Brought you some sandwiches," he said, sneaking food from his pockets. Memphis, Henry, and Bill dug in, barely taking time to swallow.

"I'll try to get you some pie, too," Nelson said. "If any of us porters come by, we'll give the knock." He rapped five times in a syncopated rhythm—*one, two, three-and-four.* "Otherwise, don't open up."

"How long before we get to New Orleans?" Henry asked.

"Tomorrow evening," Nelson said. "Listen, if you want to keep your mind off of things, you can join the Brotherhood later tonight. Once everybody's sleeping, 'round three or four in the morning, we get a little card game going, shoot some craps. Small bets mostly. But it passes the time when you've got a lot of it weighing down on you."

"Thank you. Much obliged," Bill said.

Henry swallowed a bite of sandwich. "Say, why do they call you George if your name is Nelson?"

Nelson snorted. "Lot of these passengers don't bother to ask our names. They just call us all George, as in Mr. George Pullman, owner of these trains. It's become, you might say, a bit of a rueful joke we all share."

Memphis's jaw tightened. Henry could feel his anger across the table. Though Nelson hadn't said it, he understood that the passengers in question were white like him.

"We take their tips, though. Their money's green enough," Nelson said and winked. "All right now. We'll bring you whatever you need. Just try to stay in here. I'll look in on you later," he said and shut the door behind him.

Memphis and Bill sat on one side, Henry on the other. Henry kept eating his sandwich. He was sensitive enough to know that some private communication had passed between Bill, Memphis, and Nelson, something that wasn't for him. Henry didn't know what to say, only that he felt vaguely guilty about Nelson's comment.

"I've never called anybody George unless it was his name," Henry said, trying to lighten the mood. Memphis crossed his arms and returned to his window gazing.

"Hmph," Bill grunted.

"What's that s'posed to mean?" Henry asked.

"Just that there are lots of ways of calling somebody George." Bill didn't explain further. He finished his sandwich and closed his eyes again.

The only way for Memphis to stay sane was to write. He watched the little houses peeking up between the trees. A poem began to take shape. Within a half hour, it was done. He was proud of the work, but to what end? No magazine would publish a poem by Memphis Campbell, anarchist agitator. He titled the poem "Scenes from a Window" and signed it *The Voice of Tomorrow.*

He had an idea.

There was paper on the train. He wrote out the poem on another sheet. Then he folded it and shoved it between the bed and the wall, where it could be found by a stranger.

❄

The train traveled down the eastern seaboard and into the night. In the wee hours, Memphis, Henry, and Bill played cards with some of the porters. Their sleeping compartment was close quarters and thick with cigarette smoke, but, as Nelson had promised, it passed the time and kept their minds from their troubles for a while. The porters were loose here, Henry noticed. They talked freer. None of that "Yes, sir," "No, sir" radio-soft talk. It was like when the porters stepped outside this room and put on their hats, they'd become themselves once removed, characters in a play. Sometimes you had to become a different version of yourself to move safely through certain spaces in the world. Henry knew something about that.

After the same pot of money had been lost and won and lost again, Nelson dealt a new hand. "Say," he said, tossing down cards with a practiced agility. "Tell me something 'bout being a Diviner. See now, I heard y'all could read a man's thoughts from a mile away. Go on, then. Tell me: What am I thinking now?"

"Probably dirty," Coleman said, laughing through his nose.

"Definitely dirty," one of the other porters, Philippe, said, throwing down a two of diamonds.

"I can't read anybody's thoughts," Memphis said.

"Me, either," Henry chimed in.

Nelson fixed his eyes on Memphis. "You can heal, though, right? The Harlem Healer?"

Memphis nodded.

"Oh, oh! If I cut myself right now, you could fix me up? Is that so?" a porter named Roger said. He was reaching for his pocketknife. Memphis put up a hand.

"I probably could, but I don't believe we should test that," Memphis said, and the man put the knife away.

"Last thing we need is you bleeding all over this carpet," Nelson said, shaking his head. He looked at Henry. "And you? What can you do?"

"I can dream walk," Henry said.

"Dream walk?" Coleman said, making a face. "What on earth is that?"

"I can walk in people's dreams," Henry said, blushing. He felt stupid. His power suited him fine, but compared to Memphis's healing or Theta's fire, it did seem kind of paltry.

Coleman waggled his eyebrows. "Ladies' dreams?" The others snickered at this. Henry blushed again, though this time it had nothing to do with his Diviner ability. "Sorry. We don't mean any harm. Just don't seem like much."

You have no idea how much you can come to know about a person when you see inside their dreams, Henry wanted to say. But it didn't seem like the time or place.

"Y'all see ghosts, though. Am I right?" Coleman said, changing the subject, much to Henry's relief.

"That's right," Bill said, puffing on a cigar clenched between his teeth.

"Well. I got a story for you, then."

"Oh, Lord. Here we go...." Nelson rolled his eyes and shuffled his deck of cards in case anybody wanted to go another round.

"Now, let a man tell a story! It's a good story, too. You'll see," Coleman insisted. "It happened right here on this train. About two weeks ago last Thursday. Now, I had the job of being the porter on duty in the sleeper car. All the curtains were drawn. Folks sleeping off the hooch they snuck on board and were pouring into their ginger ales all night."

"So many orders for ginger ale!" Philippe said on a laugh.

"Coleman'll still be telling this story when we pull into N'awlins," Nelson said to Henry, Memphis, and Bill with a wink. And for a moment, Memphis was entertained enough to put aside his misery.

"We were passing through Alabama, I recall, coming close to Selma. I'm sitting there, feeling a might bit sleepy myself after a long day, when I hear something. I reckon it's one of the customers having a bad dream. But it's real whispery. Like silk rubbed across sandpaper..."

"Silk across sandpaper..." Philippe said dreamily. "Why, Coleman, I didn't know you were a poet."

"You gonna hush up?"

Still laughing, Philippe motioned him on.

"Anyway. The whole corridor started filling up with, well, a smoke, I guess you might say, but to be honest with you? It was more like a strange fog."

Memphis, Bill, and Henry sat forward in their seats, electrified.

"Well, I was afraid it might be a fire, you see. So I got up to check, but there was no fire that I could tell anywhere. I was just about to alert the conductor, and that's when I saw her. She was down at the end of the corridor in that haze. A lady in a long dress and gloves and a flowered hat, like she was going to a church supper. She said, 'Excuse me, porter, is this the stop for Cahawba?' I put my finger to my lips and motioned for her to follow me into the dining car so she wouldn't wake anybody. She just kept waiting by the door. The fog was all around her, and now I really was worried there was a fire. 'I need to get off at Cahawba,' she told me again. I said, 'Miss, I'm sorry, but this train doesn't stop at Cahawba. Selma's the next stop.' 'Oh,' she said. 'But I have an engagement in Cahawba. My brother's in the prison there. I must go to him.' I didn't have the slightest notion what she was talking about, but I needed to let the conductor know about that smoke. So I said, 'Miss, if you'll wait right here a minute, I'll be back to help you.' 'Oh!' she said, and she got the funniest look on her face, like she just remembered something important. 'This is my stop.' And then, as sure as I'm sitting here, she vanished *right in front of my eyes*—the Lord is my Shepherd!—and she took all that mist with her. The corridor was clear as could be. And she was nowhere to be found."

"Or you fell asleep and that was all a dream," Roger said. "Hey, maybe you can ask the dream walker here to find your lady friend tonight."

The other porters busted up laughing.

"Go on, go on, have yourselves a good laugh. But you ain't heard the other half of the story."

Nelson shook his head and spread out the cards in his hand. "Like I said, all the way to N'awlins."

Coleman ignored him. He leaned forward. There was an intensity in his eyes. "When I got to Selma, I asked the stationmaster if he knew of any place called Cahawba, and if so, was there a prison in the town, 'cause I'd had a passenger asking to get off at Cahawba to go see her brother there. Well, I tell you, that man turned pale as an old slug. He said, 'There used to be a prison in Cahawba. It held three thousand Union prisoners during the Civil War, and it hasn't been in use since. Cahawba's abandoned, mister. It's a ghost town, home to nothing but weeds and the dead.'" Coleman straightened his spine with that and raised a hand. "My right hand to God."

For a moment, no one spoke. Then Nelson let out a big, booming laugh. And all the porters joined in once more.

"It happened. I'm telling you it happened," an indignant Coleman insisted.

"I believe you," Memphis said, and the laughter quieted down some. "There's things out there. And they're coming for us. You need to know this."

The mood in the compartment shifted from ease to a charged discomfort.

Nelson held tightly to the deck of cards. "Seraphina mentioned something about a trickster in the crossroads, a King of Crows. What is that?"

Bill blew out a perfect ring of smoke. "The Bogeyman. 'Cept this one ain't somethin' your mama made up to keep you in line. This one is the real McCoy."

"Well, what does he want?"

"Chaos. He wants us good and scared," Henry said.

The train rushed past the clanging bells of a crossing. The sound swam past the windows and faded into nothing.

Nelson shook his head. "There's no order anymore, I tell you. It's like this poem I read by this Irish fella. Something about a falcon not being able to hear the falconer—"

"'Things fall apart; the centre cannot hold; / Mere anarchy is loosed upon the world, / The blood-dimmed tide is loosed, and everywhere / The ceremony of innocence is drowned; / The best lack all conviction, while the worst / Are full of passionate intensity,'" Memphis quoted. "W. B. Yeats. 'The Second Coming.'"

"That's the fella. Yes, sir. No order. No order."

But more and more Memphis had begun to ask himself if there had ever been order, or if order was one more myth people repeated so they didn't have to think too much about the violence lurking just under the surface of every polite exchange, every façade of "civilization." And just whom did "order" serve?

Dawn was sneaking up over the cotton fields. Those first golden stirrings imbued the land with an ethereal beauty. If there were any restless ghosts out there right now, Memphis couldn't see them. He was the only restless thing as far as he could tell.

"This country is haunted. Don't let anybody tell you differently," Coleman said.

As the porters went back to work, Memphis, Henry, and Bill settled into their beds. Exhaustion had found them at last. Memphis could barely keep his eyes open. Already, Henry was snoring.

"Memphis," Bill said from his side. "This place in Bountiful. The farm Isaiah talked about. I seen it before."

"You did?"

"Mm-hmm."

"When?" Memphis said on a yawn.

Bill looked uncomfortable. "When I was taking from the boy."

Taking. That was one way of putting it. Memphis knew that Bill was a changed man, but thinking about who he'd been before, someone who weakened his brother by stealing power from him, made Memphis angry all over again. He flopped onto his back so he wouldn't have to look at Bill. "What about it?"

"I saw into Isaiah's vision. There was a big tree, and dust coming up so thick on the road you couldn't see through it. There was something inside that dust, though. Something that made my neck go cold. And Isaiah was hollering out a warning."

Bill was quiet for so long that Memphis was afraid he'd fallen asleep. "What warning?"

"'Ghosts on the road,'" Bill said.

125

"What do you think it means?"

Bill shook his head slowly, like he was losing an internal argument. "Cain't say. Wherever we're going, though, don't feel like we're heading away from the storm but steering into it."

☀

Memphis couldn't sleep. Every time he'd get close, he'd see Isaiah, lost in the crowd of Times Square, and he'd startle awake. He narrowed the gap in the curtains to close out the light and lay back down. To soothe Isaiah to sleep, Memphis would tell him a story about two brothers who couldn't be separated by anything in this world or the next. Now that story felt like a lie. His eyes were getting heavier, each blink a name—*Theta. Isaiah. Theta.*

A sound pulled Memphis awake, every muscle taut. Bill and Henry were still sleeping, but the train had stopped. Memphis listened. All quiet. He padded barefoot to the door, slid it back, and peeked out. The corridor was dark and empty. Had they slept through till night again? Were they in New Orleans already? Had Nelson forgotten about them?

Memphis wasn't supposed to leave the compartment and risk being seen, but it felt so still, so strangely quiet, and he was worried. As silently as possible, he crept to the end of the corridor. He paused at the entrance to the dining car. Places were set. White linens draped the tables. The car was completely deserted. *Where is everyone?* Memphis wondered. *And why has the train stopped?* At the end of the dining car was an open door leading outside. Moonlight splashed across the steps leading down to the tracks.

"Nelson?" Memphis called.

The steps were cold against Memphis's bare feet. He dropped from the last one onto the ground, then walked backward, peering up to see into the windows. Not a soul. All around him were cotton fields, their white bulbs like a dusting of snow. Had there been an accident? Was someone hurt? Were there injured people somewhere out there? Memphis left the road and stepped into the fields. The cotton plants were as tall as he was; the rows between them narrow. As Memphis pushed his way through, the branches pricked and poked at him. The night sound of feeding insects was loud. Something landed on Memphis's shoulder. With a yelp, he brushed it away. A bug landed on its back in the dirt, legs circling, a boll weevil.

The beetle-like things were everywhere, Memphis saw. They had infested the cotton and were eating it down to nubs. As if sensing him, the insects scuttled down the ruined crop and wriggled fast through the fields, coming together at the end of the claustrophobic row. They crawled toward Memphis in a black-shine wave. Memphis wanted to run but found his feet were stuck fast in the dirt. He glanced behind him. The train seemed a mile away.

The high wail of a trumpet pierced the night. The bugs scattered into the cotton. Far ahead, the tops of the plants swayed violently, then broke with a sickening snap. Something else was coming. Memphis's blood thumped frantically in his ears. The cotton bent again. *Snap. Snap. Snap.* The dead were marching through the fields like soldiers.

Memphis pulled at his legs. They wouldn't budge. The dead were coming. *Snap.* The trumpet sounded again, and the dead stopped, as if at attention. Hoofbeats shook the ground. A phantom-gray horse galloped forward, and on its back was Gabe. His eyes were a dull black. Embalmer's thread hung in broken ends from his bloodied lips.

"Brother," Gabe rasped, making the thread dance. "Heal me. Let me rest."

The dead growled deep in their throats, a hellish chorus.

"Go on, Memphis," Gabe said.

"I…can't…" Memphis whispered.

"Do it! Heal me. Give me final peace. *Please.*"

Gabe was one of the rotting dead. Gabe had been his best friend. Memphis put a hand to Gabe's chest and was answered with a sharp electric shock. He cried out and yanked his smoking fingers away.

Gabe laughed and the dead echoed his laughter. "I don't need your favors, brother. We are powerful now. You'll see. Soon enough." Gabe's voice deepened and warped, as if someone were dragging a finger across the surface of a record to slow it. "How looong will you be aaable to heeeal, brr-roootherrr? Howww much powwwer do you reeeally have?"

He raised his trumpet and blew a long, piercing note. It echoed through the countryside. The sky fractured and filled with unnatural blue light that struck the earth, wounding it. From the wounds, more dead rose, wisps of smoke that took spectral form. So many dead—an unholy crop. Their bodies twitched and fluttered like lightbulbs threatening to short out. But their faces were all the same: powder-pale with snarling mouths hinting at their all-consuming hunger. Their teeth were so much sharper than Memphis remembered.

The field was dying. The trees dropped their leaves. The grass crisped and disappeared.

Gabe lowered his horn. Memphis watched in horror as Gabe's throat ballooned, muscles working to dislodge something trapped inside. His head tilted back. His jaw dropped as if hinged; his lips spread unnaturally wide. Four wriggling insect legs whipped out and embedded their pointed ends into his cheeks. An enormous beetle eased itself from Gabe's ruined mouth and landed in the dirt with a sickening plop. His face and neck bubbled with movement, something eating its way out, and in the next second Gabe's flesh erupted in a spray of dark slime as the bugs burst forth and fell to the earth.

Memphis tried to scream but could not.

The giant beetle rose and stood on two feet like a man. It staggered toward Memphis, evolving.

"You think you're prepared for this fight? You have no idea," Gabe called, his voice joining the swarm. "Strike a bargain with him while you still can, brother!"

Memphis put his hand to the ground and it softened under his touch, greening just enough for him to free his feet. The dead closest to Memphis fell on the new vegetation, screeching and squabbling. In the fields, the dead devoured the dying crop.

"To the King go the spoils," Gabe barked as the sky opened above them. The dead stopped and turned their open mouths upward, and the broken sky pulled the energy from their shaking bodies.

Memphis turned and ran toward the train. He no longer cared if anybody saw him or turned him over to the Shadow Men. He only wanted away from this horror. "Nelson! Coleman!" he called.

Passengers appeared at the windows. Memphis shouted, waving his arms as he ran. The doors were sealed shut; the steps were gone. Memphis slammed into the train and banged his hands against the cold steel. "Let me in! Let me in! Let me in!"

The passengers looked down.

They opened their mouths.

The beetles poured out like dark rain.

Memphis cried out as he came awake to the screech of brakes.

"Wh-what's going on?" Henry asked, dazed. He felt drugged with exhaustion.

Memphis touched a hand to his chest, brushing at bugs that weren't there. Daylight pressed on the other side of the curtains. The car was warm. He was safe in his berth.

Nelson's syncopated knock sounded at the door just before he let himself in. "Get dressed. Hurry," he commanded as he handed Memphis his shoes and shook Bill Johnson awake.

"Are we in New Orleans already?" Henry asked, pulling up his suspenders.

"Not quite. Just came into Sugarland, Mississippi," Nelson said. "We're being boarded by the Pinkertons. They're hunting for Diviners. Somehow, they got a tip some might be on this train. I reckon you were seen getting on in New York."

Henry and Memphis parted the window curtains a sliver. The platform crawled with local police and Pinkerton detectives, gold badges shining on their lapels and guns in their holsters. The conductors were readying the steps for them to climb aboard.

"We're like sitting ducks," Henry said.

Nelson's expression was grim. "That's why we have to get you *off* of this train—now."

WHERE IT ALL STARTED

The drive upstate had taken Evie nearly all night. In the early hours of the morning, when exhaustion had overtaken her, she'd parked Will's car off the road under cover of the woods not far from Jake Marlowe's estate and managed to catch some sleep. Her dreams had been vivid. She'd been running down a busy New York City street after Mabel, but Mabel was always just out of reach. Evie called and called to her, but Mabel did not stop. And then at last, Mabel turned around. In her hands was a bomb inside an hourglass. As Evie watched, helpless, the last of the sand drained away.

"Good-bye, Evie," Mabel said sweetly.

The bomb exploded and Evie woke, breathing heavily, her eyes wet with tears.

Sunlight poured through the windshield. It did nothing to warm her up, though. Her body was stiff and her fingers frozen. She wiped the tears from her face with the back of her hand and nudged Theta with her knee.

"Theta. Theta. Wake up," Evie said, working out the kink in her neck.

"Five more minutes," Theta moaned.

"We have to rescue Sam, remember?"

Theta's groan became a whimper. She sat up and worked her mouth, grimacing. "I taste like I've been licking ashtrays."

"That's because you smoke."

Theta rolled her eyes. "Are you gonna start with that this morning? And by the way, I'd kill for a cigarette."

"How are your hands?" Evie asked.

Theta removed the bandages from her palms. The skin was still red in places. "Better."

"Well, that's something at least." Evie wanted to talk about the dream. She didn't want to talk about the dream. There was a giant hole in her heart named Mabel, and another named Sam. There was only one of those she could do something about at the moment. "How'd you sleep?" she said, trying to redirect her mind away from sorrow.

Theta moved her stiff shoulder in little circles. "Like a pretzel in a cold oven."

In the backseat, Isaiah was curled up under his coat. Theta tugged on his pants leg until he stirred. "Rise and shine, kid."

Isaiah sat up, dazed. "I'm hungry." He rubbed his stomach, which growled.

"We'll eat after we rescue Sam," Evie said. "Promise."

Isaiah regarded Evie warily. "Do you have a plan?"

"I will have," Evie answered, forcing a smile.

"That's a no in Evie-speak," Theta said to Isaiah.

"Isaiah, do you have any…feelings about what's about to happen?" Evie asked hopefully.

Isaiah wanted to be helpful. He wanted to prove how important he was. He shut his eyes, concentrating. *Sarah Beth*, he thought. *Sarah Beth, do you see anything?* When there was no answer, he shook his head. "Sorry," he said, disappointed.

"All right. We'll go with Plan B."

"What's Plan B?" Theta asked.

"The one after Plan A," Evie said. "First things first—we've got to hide this Tin Lizzie."

Evie, Theta, and Isaiah covered Will's Model T with branches. Now they were walking through the woods bordering Marlowe's estate, willfully ignoring the bold-lettered signs that read NO TRESPASSING PRIVATE PROPERTY as birds tweeted in the branches above, sending out the first song of spring.

"How can anyone own the woods?" Evie grumbled. "Only the woods own the woods."

"If you're Jake Marlowe, you can own just about anything you like," Theta said. "Can't believe I'm out here with no smokes."

"Is Memphis gonna be okay?" Isaiah asked. He'd been pretty quiet since they'd left the city.

"Sure he is, kid," Theta answered.

"You're worried," Isaiah said.

"Yeah. I'm worried for all of us," Theta said.

They came to a clearing ringed by tall pines that bordered a large pond gone rancid and overgrown with pine needles. There were no birds here at all. Evie and Theta leaped back, frightened by the sudden appearance of a frog. It was misshapen, its small body covered in sores and a nub where one of its legs

131

should've been. Unable to hop, it stumbled about as if drunk. A few lackluster fish floated beneath the pond murk. One of them had four eyes, Evie noted.

"This is a bad place, isn't it?" Isaiah said, his breath coming out in small wisps of cold.

"Is this it, Evil?" Theta asked.

"Yes," Evie said. "It's a very bad place, Isaiah."

This was where it had all started, where Project Buffalo had turned deadly during the war. The Department of Paranormal had broken through to the dimension of the dead. Evie's brother and his entire unit had been sucked up into Jake's mechanical monstrosity to live out the same day of horror and pain forever. And he would continue that way until they were able to close the breach. If it was the last thing she ever did, Evie would free her brother from that machine.

Sound moved strangely here. Probably the effect of the trees bouncing their voices around, an echo upon echo. The wind seemed to carry distant voices, as if moving them across time. Evie shut her eyes, straining to hear. Finally, she removed her glove and laid a hand on the ground, searching for some trace of her brother. Anything. Anything at all.

Theta touched her shoulder. "You think that's a good idea, Evil?"

Sam was waiting. The present needed her. Evie shoved her hand back into her glove.

They peeked through the trees and saw Hopeful Harbor rising up from spring's first green. It was a breathtaking little fiefdom, all ivy-covered stone and perfectly manicured lawns—a magazine advertisement for the good life. But Evie had been inside its many rooms and had found it oddly cold. It had felt less like a house and more like a beautifully appointed reliquary; it was a place that wanted to preserve the past.

"Look. In the drive," Theta said. She pointed to a brown sedan parked in front of the house. "Shadow Men."

"How we gonna get around 'em?" Isaiah asked.

"I don't suppose you're getting any visions about that, are ya?" Theta asked.

Isaiah shook his head. "Don't work that way." Isaiah looked sad again.

"What is it?"

"If Memphis were here, he'd fuss about the way I talk."

"You can talk any old way you want," Evie said.

The front doors opened. The Shadow Men stepped out, and with them was a woman whose hands were bound by chains. "Come on, Miriam," the smaller of the two Shadow Men said.

"Miriam! That's Sam's mother," Evie whispered to the others.

"Miriam is the one who's been talking to Sarah Beth," Isaiah said.

Miriam's head shot up as if she was listening. Her gaze fell upon the line of trees where Evie, Isaiah, and Theta were hiding, and then her voice was in their heads: *Can you hear me?*

"Yes," Evie whispered. She didn't know if Miriam could hear her like this, but she didn't know what else to do. "I'm Evie. I'm Sam's friend. We're trying to find him. We're here to rescue him."

It is hard for me with so much iron, Miriam said. And Evie could see that even this small exchange was costing her. Smoke rose from her wrists under the chains, and her mouth was set in a tight line. *They hold him below. Third door on right. You must go quickly.*

"What's the holdup?" the bigger Shadow Man said. He came around and took Miriam by the arm, and Evie felt the phantom touch on her own skin. The Shadow Man put Miriam in the backseat and shut the door. The brown sedan prowled in reverse down the long driveway and turned onto the road, driving out of sight.

"Now," Evie said, leading Theta and Isaiah into the rose garden. From her previous visit, she remembered that there was a side entrance into Marlowe's study from there.

"I hope you know where you're going," Theta whispered as they slipped into Marlowe's private office.

"Jericho said there's a secret elevator behind one of these bookshelves."

"Okay. Which one?"

"The one marked 'secret elevator,' I imagine," Evie cracked. "Do I know? Just keep at it till one opens. Wait! I do know."

Evie removed her glove and rested her hand against the books. It would have proved overwhelming had most of the books been read. She could feel small remnants of the past in some, though, and when she came to one that had belonged to Will, she lingered, her eyes stinging with tears. She could see him, young and alive and brimming with hope. He was seated on the sofa with Jake, Sister Walker, and Rotke:

. . . and then she was channeling a spirit from beyond, writing messages dictated from the other side upon the slate. I tell you, we were in the presence of a new frontier!

How had it all gone so wrong? Evie wondered.

"I found it!" Isaiah's happy voice brought Evie back. He'd tugged down two fat volumes of Napoleonic history and the panel had opened to reveal a small elevator.

"Isaiah, you're the cat's pajamas!" Theta exclaimed.

Isaiah gave a goofy smile. "Thanks."

The three of them jammed themselves together in the cramped space. Evie examined the buttons, then selected *B*, and the lift rattled them down to the basement. The doors opened on a long hallway.

"Miriam said third door on the right," Evie said, and she was glad she wouldn't have to read the secrets screaming from any of these other rooms.

"This is it," Theta said. She reached for the knob. Evie grabbed her wrist.

"What's the matter?" Theta asked.

"I just...nothing. Nothing at all." *Please*, Evie thought. *Please let him be alive.*

Theta tried the door. Locked. Of course it would be.

"Theta? Do you think you could burn through it?" Evie asked. She felt terrible asking after last night, but it was the best chance they had of getting into that room.

Theta's hands still hurt, but she wanted to help. "I'll try. But if I burn this house down, you asked me." She pressed her palm against the lock and thought about what those Shadow Men might've done to Sam. The sudden flush of anger frightened Theta. She pulled her hand back quickly.

"What's the matter?" Isaiah asked.

"Nothing. It just...wouldn't come," Theta lied.

Evie slumped against the wall. "Do you suppose there's a key somewhere?"

"It would take us a whole year to find it!" Isaiah said.

"No. I can do it. Just...gimme a minute." Theta placed her hand on the lock again. A second later, she felt Evie's and Isaiah's hands on her arms, giving her strength. Heat flowed into her palm once more, and the lock melted away.

Evie wrapped her coat around the sizzling metal and carefully opened the door.

"Sam?" she whispered into the darkened room.

"Evie? Is that you?" Sam's weak voice nearly wrecked Evie's heart. He sounded sick. Broken. Theta found a light switch and a bare bulb blinked on. Sam lay curled up on a bed against the brick wall. His hands were shackled to the steel railing of the headboard. With effort, he sat up. His eyes were glassy, haunted. He looked like he'd aged ten years. "Evie?"

"Sam! Oh, Sam!" Evie ran over and unlatched the restraints, freeing him. She scooped him up in her arms. He fell against her chest, limp.

"Baby Vamp, is that really you?"

"It's really me," Evie said and kissed him gently on the lips.

He stared into her eyes. "Why do you look like a hobo?"

"I'll explain later. Did he hurt you?"

"Will you kiss me some more if I say yes?"

"I will kiss you as much as you like." And with that, Evie kissed Sam deeply.

"Ew," Isaiah said, embarrassed.

He looked to Theta, who rolled her eyes. "Give 'em a minute, kid."

Sam pulled away. His shoulders shook, and it took Evie a second to realize that he was crying.

"Oh, Sam, Sam." Evie threw her arms around him again.

"I'm afraid this isn't real," he said between hiccuping sobs. "I'm afraid in a minute I'll wake up and I'll be here but you won't be."

"I'm here, Sam, and I promise I will never leave you again." She wiped his cheeks with her scarf. He looked so sad and bruised by life it nearly killed her.

Sam cupped Evie's face between his dry palms. "You're real."

"Yes."

"You're here with me now."

"You bet-ski."

Sam gave Evie a weak smile. "I'm a little disturbed by how much I liked kissing you in that getup."

Evie laughed through tears. "Then I'll wear it all the time!"

Sam's smile died. He was afraid again. "Where are the Shadow Men?"

"They drove off," Theta said, coming to give Sam a hug.

"Theta," Sam said in wonder. He held both of her hands.

"Missed you, too, you little criminal," she said.

"Hi, Sam." Isaiah waved.

"Hey, kid. You got taller," Sam warbled, and Isaiah beamed. "Are the others here, too?" Sam asked.

"We'll talk on the way to the car," Evie said.

"Those Shadow Men'll be back," Sam said grimly. "We have to leave now."

"No kidding," Theta zinged. "And I was hoping to stay for tea. I hear the finger sandwiches here are something else."

"Yeah. Real fingers," Sam said. "Lamb Chop, what's your plan for getting out of here?"

"We don't have a plan," Isaiah said.

"We're…improvising!" Evie added.

"Oh, shit," Sam said and buried his face in his hands.

"Sam Lloyd, don't make me regret coming to rescue you!"

"I'm just saying: A plan. A plan is helpful."

"We didn't have time to make a plan," Evie said. She was starting to feel irritated. "Every bounty hunter and federal agent is out looking for us right now. We drove straight here from New York."

"Will is dead. And Sister Walker got arrested for treason," Isaiah supplied.

"Jake Marlowe declared the Diviners Public Enemy Number One at Sarah Snow's memorial. There's a bounty on our heads."

"And there's a girl in Nebraska, another Diviner. That's where we're headed. To Bountiful," Isaiah added. "And I don't know where Memphis is."

"We got separated in Times Square," Theta said.

Sam's eyes widened.

"So as you can see, we've been rather busy," Evie said coolly. It was amazing how quickly her feelings for Sam could slip from wild love to extreme annoyance and back again. She hadn't quite made it back again. "We have Uncle Will's car hidden in the woods. Do you think you can walk?"

"Yeah," Sam said, wincing as he scooted to the edge of the bed. Evie helped him into his shoes. He grinned. "Hey. My hat."

Evie took it from her head and placed it on his. And just like that, it was wild love again.

"Wait a minute. We've gotta find my mother. I'm not leaving without her," Sam said. "Marlowe's keeping her here. He's using her power to balance the energy of the Eye. He's hurting her."

A wave of hatred rose up in Evie. Ten years. Ten years Marlowe's machine had kept her brother in a state of suffering. "Where is the Eye?"

"On the roof. The solarium."

Evie remembered the button in the elevator marked *S*. It was that easy, then. A quick trip up and she'd end her brother's misery for good. The breach would close. The King of Crows would hold no more power. It would all be over. That she would be the one to smash Jake Marlowe's precious invention was the icing on the cake.

"Marlowe's been making some changes to it," Sam said. "It's much more powerful than before."

"I'm sorry, Sam, but the Shadow Men took your mother in their car," Theta said.

"Where?"

"I don't know. But she told us to find you and go."

"I want to see it," Evie said, jumping to her feet. "I want to see the machine that's trapped my brother. And then I want to destroy it."

"Baby Vamp, you can't," Sam said quietly.

"I can't what?" Evie challenged. If it was the last thing she did, she would destroy that terrible machine.

"Destroy it," Sam said.

"Sure I can. A hammer. A screwdriver. Anything will do," Evie insisted.

"I'm telling you, I know. I've been hooked up to it. It's . . . it's beyond our comprehension, connected to that other world, and more worlds besides. We don't know how that machine works. We don't know what happens to your brother and all those soldiers if you break it. For all we know, it could trap them in that same loop forever."

Evie wanted to scream. "Are you telling me I've made it this far, all the way to Marlowe's house, and I can't even help my brother?"

"I'm sorry, Baby Vamp."

"Why can't just one thing be simple?" Evie said, pressing the backs of her hands to her eyes, which were threatening to erupt again.

"Hey, Evil? We'd better blouse. Those Shadow Men or a creepy butler could find us, and then we're really stuck," Theta said.

"I'm sorry, Baby Vamp." Sam laced his fingers with hers. "I promise we'll figure it out. We'll save your brother and my ma."

Evie nodded. They'd found Sam. It wasn't nothing.

"Alley-oop," she said. Evie and Theta helped Sam to his feet. Isaiah opened the door.

"Hey. You folks are really top drawer. Thanks for coming to my rescue," Sam said. "Honestly? I wouldn't want anybody else to do it."

"Swell. We'll send the bill later," Theta said.

⁂

On their way out, Evie stopped at Marlowe's desk. "Is this where he sits to make all of his terrible decisions?" Evie asked. She let her hand hover above the carefully curated objects there, all of them expensive, she knew. None of them imbued with real meaning.

"Don't do it. You don't want that man's memories in your head," Sam warned.

Evie took Sam's point. She put on her gloves to block sensation, and then she sat in Marlowe's antique wingback chair and scratched out a note. "Dear Mr. Marlowe, What you are doing will have devastating"—Evie sounded the word out, making sure she'd gotten all the letters right—"consequences for the nation. Diviners are your only chance of stopping the Army of the Dead and the King of Crows before it's too late. Sincerely..."

Theta read over her shoulder. "'A concerned citizen'? Evil. He will know you wrote that letter."

"I don't mind if he does," Evie said with a toss of her head. "If he wants to hunt us down, kidnap us off the streets, and feed us to his machine, I want him to know that *I* was in his house. That I touched all of his precious things with my *awful Diviner powers*." Evie wiggled her fingers like a jazz baby. She eyed the pen once more, then put it in her pocket.

"That's stealing," Isaiah said.

Evie patted her pocket. "So it is."

Somewhere in the grand house, the servants were stirring. Voices drifted out from the kitchen. Pots and pans clanked.

"Time to go," Theta whispered.

The four of them slipped out into the rose garden and made their way back to the clearing. Evie shivered as she crossed the spot where her brother's fate had been sealed. She felt like a failure for not destroying the Eye. *We're coming, James*, she thought.

Once they'd cleared the branches from the car and Evie got behind the wheel, she realized she really didn't have a plan beyond "rescue Sam." It occurred to her that driving a dead man's car might get them noticed.

"We need a disguise," Evie said, more to herself than to anyone else.

"I thought that's why we stole—"

"Borrowed," Theta said.

"—*borrowed* these costumes," Isaiah finished.

"I mean a disguise on the road. A way of going to Bountiful without having to look over our shoulders every minute."

From the backseat, Sam said, "Baby Doll's right. I say it's time we run away and join the circus."

"Oh, Sam, be serious," Evie grumbled.

"I *am* serious!"

"Sam! Please."

"Look, we're not too far from Cooperstown. That's where we'll find my old circus buddies. They'll just be getting ready to hit the road for the season. And we'll be going with them."

"Are you pulling my leg?" Theta asked. "Evie, is he pulling my leg?"

"Theta, I honestly haven't the foggiest."

"The circus circus?" Isaiah asked, sounding excited for the first time since they'd left New York.

"The one and only," Sam said, managing a smirk. "Come on, everybody. Didn't you always want to run away and join the circus? What better way to disappear?"

WANTED

Henry chanced another look out the window. The Pinkerton agents were boarding.

"How are we gonna get off this train?" Memphis asked.

"They'll be checking the crew, too, most likely."

"No one's looking for me," Henry said. "Remember? I didn't even get second billing. Here." Henry put a bathrobe on over his clothes and removed his shoes. "Nelson, can you bring a tray of coffee and a covered dish in here?"

"I was just clearing the breakfast trays." He returned with a used one, placing the silver dome back over the messy plate. "It'll be fine as long as nobody lifts that lid."

"Memphis. Into the sleeper. Quickly," Henry directed.

Memphis climbed up. He looked over his shoulder at Henry.

"I hope you're not claustrophobic," Henry said.

"I am."

"Then I'm truly sorry," Henry said, closing him up inside. "Just hold tight for a few minutes," he said from the outside.

Memphis's response was muffled, but it did not sound happy. Henry drew the drapes and settled himself on the seat like a gentleman at leisure.

"What about me?" Bill asked.

"Hold on a minute." Nelson raced out and returned a moment later with another porter's uniform. "Put this on. It's Stephen's. He's the biggest man we have."

The jacket fit snugly across Bill's broad chest and shoulders, and the sleeves were a little short, but it would pass muster if nobody looked too closely. Bill had barely finished fastening the last button when there was a knock at the door.

"Come in," Henry said.

The agent opened the compartment door to find Henry reading

a newspaper, his feet up on the seat while Bill poured coffee and Nelson stood by. Henry looked up from his newspaper with a smile. He stood to greet the detectives. "Mornin', gentlemen. If you're looking for the privy, it's down the hall on your left."

The men flashed their badges. "Pinkertons, sir. We don't see a name registered for this compartment."

Henry forced a smile. "No. I imagine you don't. I'm afraid, gentlemen, that I'm here under false pretenses. You see, I'm William Kissam Vanderbilt III."

"Of the railroad Vanderbilts?" the Pinkerton agent asked.

"The same. I'm here unannounced to see how things are running so that I can make a report for the family. We're looking to make big changes next year, by golly. Big changes! But may I ask what all this is about?"

"Well, sir, we have it on good authority that there're some wanted criminals aboard."

"On *this* train?" Henry said. He wished Theta were here to watch his performance. He hoped he'd have the chance to tell her about it.

"Yes, sir."

"Mercy me. What are they wanted for?"

"Treason. They're some of the anarchists responsible for that tragedy at Mr. Marlowe's Future of America Exhibition, the one that killed Miss Sarah Snow."

"You don't say!" Henry shook his head and clucked his tongue. "What is this world coming to? Why, I was just in New York City seeing to the steel business."

Bill flashed Henry a glance: *Don't push this too far.*

"We're asking everyone on board if they've seen these people."

The detective handed over a large poster with the word WANTED in big letters up top, along with $5,000 REWARD FOR THE CAPTURE OF THE FOLLOWING PERSONS OF INTEREST. There were small pictures of Memphis, Isaiah, Ling, Evie, and Theta. The poster mentioned that the criminals were considered highly dangerous due to their DIVINER POWERS.

"And have you managed to capture any of them yet?" Henry asked without looking up.

"Not as of yet, sir."

Henry concentrated on keeping his hands from shaking. "What can these so-called Diviners do, if you don't mind my asking?"

"All manner of impossible things, Mr. Vanderbilt. They can disrupt radio signals. Communicate with the enemy. They controlled people's minds at a memorial service in New York City. One of them has the ability to start fires with her bare hands. Another of them, Memphis Campbell, murdered the curator of a museum at the urging of his partner, Margaret Walker, a dangerous anarchist agitator. The curator was going to turn them in for treason. Seems these Diviner types are tied in to that group that bombed Mr. Marlowe's exhibit."

Henry marveled at how easy it was for false information to be repeated and spread until everyone just assumed it was fact.

"And you're certain these criminals are on this train?" Henry asked.

"Yes, sir. This was the last train out of New York City last night, and Mr. Campbell and others were spotted by a concerned citizen who reported it to the police. But we'll catch 'em here."

"I certainly hope so." Henry pointed at the picture of Evie. "Now I think of it, I believe I saw this very little lady just last night in the dining car. She was performing some sort of party trick for a couple. Yes, now I remember! She claimed she could read their fortunes in an object. It all seemed rather harmless and silly at the time."

Henry pretended to look at the poster. From the corner of his eye, he saw the agents nodding to each other. "We'd better go to that dining car and ask around. Thank you, Mr. Vanderbilt. You've been a great help. We're sorry to have bothered you."

"The pursuit of justice is no trouble at all, gentlemen. Good day." Henry flicked his newspaper open again and Bill dropped a lump of sugar in the coffee cup.

"I'll show you the way to the dining car, gentlemen," Nelson said, seeing the detectives out. Henry counted to ten under his breath, and then he and Bill scrambled to let Memphis out of his hiding spot in the sleeper compartment. A woozy Memphis let Bill help him down the ladder to the seat and took several settling breaths. He glared at Henry. "Never do that again."

"What? Save your life?"

Nelson gave the secret knock again and slipped into the compartment.

"The Pinkertons are going to ride with us," he whispered. "When we pull into Jackson, they're not going to let anybody leave this train without checking every single person against that poster."

"Then we've really got to get off now, while we can," Memphis said.

Henry pushed the curtains open and looked out at the scrolling landscape. "In the middle of nowhere?"

"Either that or take your chances with the law."

"Middle of nowhere," Henry and Memphis said in unison.

"Can we catch another train at Jackson?" Memphis asked.

"Those men'll be crawling all over the place till they catch somebody. If it was me? I'd go on foot. Stay off the main roads. Best to head north to Greenville or Yazoo City, catch a bus or a train there. But you won't have us to look after you. You'll have to look out for yourselves. I'm gonna ask the engineer for a slowdown. We'll come up with some excuse—reports of branches on the tracks ahead, something. You get to the caboose, and then you jump over the railing and you run."

"What if they see us getting off the train?" Memphis said.

"I'm still stuck on 'jump over the railing,'" Henry said.

"We'll try to keep them busy," Nelson said. "Go on. Get to the back now."

"Boy, I sure wish I had Theta's or Sam's powers right about now," Henry said as he, Memphis, and Bill crept toward the caboose, hoping they weren't spotted by a Pinkerton or an overzealous passenger. "Going invisible or throwing up a wall of fire sure would come in handy."

They slipped out onto the narrow railing and looked down at the ground moving rapidly behind them. The train jerked slightly, then slowed to a fast crawl.

Henry threw one leg over the back railing, straddling it. "Funny how your entire notion of 'slow' changes when you're looking down at some moving railroad tracks and a possible broken ankle or two."

"Do you always talk this much and I never noticed before?" Memphis asked, climbing onto the back railing beside him.

"I don't know. I've never had to escape from federal agents by leaping from a moving train before," Henry snapped back.

"I'd like to shut you both up," Bill said and jumped onto the tracks, landing solidly. He waved at the others to do the same. Memphis dropped down, rolling out into the tall grass running alongside the tracks. Henry positioned himself. The train lurched forward, picking up speed. Memphis gestured to him wildly.

"Here goes my piano career...." Henry said. He let go, landing hard on his side and rolling out of the way. "Ow," he said, wincing as he stood. His left arm smarted from the fall.

"If it's broken, you'll heal it, right?" Henry asked as Memphis ran over.

"Can you move it?" Bill asked.

It hurt, but Henry could, in fact, lift it.

"Ain't broken, then," Bill said. They scurried down the embankment, away from the tracks, hiding in the ticklish grass until the Crescent Limited chugged into the distance under a head of steam and disappeared around a curve. They stood and brushed the fluff and dirt from their clothes. Henry cupped a hand over his eyes to block the hazy daylight beating down on the fertile land of the Mississippi Delta.

"See anything?" Memphis asked.

"Yes. I can confirm, undoubtedly, that we are stuck in the middle of nowhere and a long way from where we need to be," Henry said. "What do we do now?"

"We get to Greenville and catch another train," Memphis said. He slapped a mosquito on his arm and scratched the place where it had bitten him.

"Great stuff!" Henry said. "Which way's Greenville?"

"Beats me," Memphis said. A pair of starlings hopped along the wires stretched between telephone poles. The railroad tracks. The telephone wires. They seemed to go on forever.

"Whole lotta state between here and there," Bill said ominously.

"What's that mean?" Memphis asked.

"I mean you ain't in Harlem no more. You in the Jim Crow South. There are rules about where black folks can and can't be—mostly where we can't be."

"I'm not bowing and scraping for anybody," Memphis grunted.

"Not telling you to bow and scrape. Telling you how not to get yourself killed."

"Lot of ghosts between here and there, too," Henry said.

"I saw Gabe in a dream," Memphis confessed. "At least, I think it was a dream. It was awfully hard to tell. Felt like I was really living it."

"Dreams can be that way sometimes," Henry said. He had been so exhausted he hadn't dreamed at all. "There's an awful lot of mess to work through while we sleep."

"S'pose," Memphis said. He bore a fair amount of guilt over Gabe's death. They'd fought about Theta at Alma's party. Memphis had left him there. And Gabe, drunk, had staggered off and been murdered by the Pentacle Killer. Gabe was stubborn like that. Still, what if? Memphis wondered. What if he'd looked out better for his friend?

And then there was Gabe's troubling warning: *How long will you be able to heal? How much power do you really have?* It had gone right to the heart of it for Memphis. Ever since what had happened with his mother, Memphis had harbored the fear that this gift could be taken from him at any time. After all, so many things had been taken from him already.

Memphis wiped the sheen from his forehead. He felt very small under the pitiless sun. "Gabe said they were getting stronger."

"Who?"

"The dead."

"It was just a bad dream. We got bigger fish to fry, seeing as we've got to walk to Greenville, Mississippi," Bill said. "We go back, we'll be at the depot we just left. We should keep going forward, reckon. Come on. We don't wanna be on these roads after dark," Bill said and set out to follow the ribbon of tracks, wherever it led.

"You think there might be cemeteries along here? Some of the King of Crows's ghosts?" Henry asked, falling in behind.

"There's some things in this world that's scarier'n ghosts. You just do what I do, understand?" Bill said without looking back. "And keep up. We still got a long way to go."

Memphis waited until they came to the first mailbox. He opened it and left the poem from the Voice of Tomorrow inside.

CIRCUS

When Evie had first met Sam, he'd told her that he'd made his way from Chicago to New York as an acrobat. Evie was never quite certain when Sam was telling a tall tale, and she'd always figured the circus story to be just that. Now, as they rode in the back of a kind farmer's truck toward Cooperstown, Sam regaled them with stories about the Great Zarilda herself—fortune-teller and experienced con artist who managed to mix both arts; her boyfriend, Arnold the Painted Man, who was covered in tattoos from forehead to the tips of his toes; sweet-natured Johnny the Wolf Boy; Bella the Strong Man, who could lift two grown men above his head; Polly the Bearded Lady; "Doc" Hamilton and his Traveling Medicine Show; and Mr. Sarkassian, the cheery ringmaster. He told them about the acrobats and roustabouts, about the clowns and lion tamers, about the animals themselves. It sounded like a fantastical traveling city.

"Do they have real lions?" Isaiah asked, excited.

"Real lions, and elephants, horses, dogs, a goat, and a tiger."

Isaiah's eyes widened. "A tiger?"

"Uh-huh. There's a Russian fella who can put his whole head inside the tiger's mouth. Unless the tiger's eaten him already."

"Can I pet the tiger?"

"Sure you can. I wouldn't recommend it, though."

The farmer let them off outside a gate bearing a painted sign that read, HOME OF THE GREAT ZARILDA'S WONDROUS TRAVELING CIRCUS EXTRAVAGANZA. MARVELS AND MIRACLES AWAIT WITHIN!

"This way," Sam said, opening the gate.

A grass-striped gravel road led them past an algae-furred pond. A small city of beautifully painted wagons sat in the field. Simple cabins perched up on the hill across from one another like ladies and gentlemen waiting to start a dance. About one hundred yards behind the houses, in a dirt clearing, were a corral and a paddock where men with pitchforks speared hay, which the elephants lifted with their trunks and stuffed into their mouths. A couple of sleek white horses galloped behind a fence. A lioness relaxed on the floor of a cage while her mate paced, letting out a lazy roar that showed off an impressive mouthful of teeth, nonetheless.

"Can we send that lion to the Shadow Men?" Evie joked.

"I'd hate to give the fella indigestion," Sam shot back.

"Sam? Sam Lloyd! Is that really you?"

A big, bold woman marched down the hill, her arms swinging forward and back in time with the flow of her gold satin dress and leopard-print shawl-collar coat. A red, permanent-waved bob puffed out from under a brown cowboy hat. On her feet were a pair of cowboy boots, and in her mouth was a long cigarette holder clenched between very white teeth ringed by crimson lips. Just behind her walked a lanky man with more facial hair than Evie had ever seen. The sleeves of his white shirt had been rolled to the elbows. His forearms and the backs of his hands were covered in soft brown fur.

Sam waved. "Hiya, Zarilda! Hey-o, Johnny! Remember me?"

Zarilda squinted, then her eyes went wide. She let out a whoop and threw open her arms. "It *is* you, you little cuss! Come on over here and give your Aunt Zarilda a proper hello!" A blushing Sam walked forward like a schoolboy and let Zarilda wrap him in an enormous hug. She was a tall woman, nearly six feet, and probably close to three hundred pounds, Evie figured, with a square jaw and a face that could be described as handsome. She kissed both of Sam's cheeks, leaving red lipstick prints there. "Look at you!" she said, cupping his chin. "Why, you're a man now!"

"Yeah. I suppose I am," Sam said proudly.

Evie rolled her eyes. "Oh, brother."

Sam gestured to the others. "Zarilda—these are my pals: The smart aleck with a heart of pure gold-plated tin is Evie O'Neill. The one who looks like she wants to make sure you're not selling her a fake Rembrandt is Theta Knight. And this kid here, well, this is the Amazing Isaiah Campbell, seer of futures, the real McCoy."

Isaiah grinned goofily to hear himself so described.

Zarilda squinted at the three of them and puffed on the cigarette sticking out from its pearled holder. "Y'all starting your own circus? I don't need the competition, Sam."

"We surely don't," the young man with the facial hair echoed in a gentle voice. Up close, Isaiah could see that his hair was more like a pelt of thick brown fur, and he was covered in it except for his nose, lips, and big brown

147

eyes. "How d'you do? Name's Johnny Mendez. But you can call me Johnny the Wolf Boy."

"To what do we owe this sudden pleasure, Sam?" Zarilda asked.

"You mean you haven't heard?" Evie said. Theta elbowed her.

"Heard what? To be honest, we've been busier than a tick at a dog convention. We've got a show to get ready for. Advance men are already out drumming up business—we hope."

"Zarilda, on the level: I'm coming here hat in hand"—quickly, Sam removed his cap—"to ask for help. We're on the lam, Z. We need cover."

"Did ya finally rob that bank, Sam?"

"If I had, we'd be on our way to Mexico with the loot."

"For all I know, you *are* on your way ta Mexico. You always did have a rotten sense of direction."

"Say, I like her," Theta said.

"There's bad people after us, Z. Those same fellas that took my mom."

Zarilda and Johnny exchanged a quick glance. "Aw, Sam," she said in her thick Texas drawl. "Honey, I a'ready knew you were in trouble. The cards told me so."

"We're just glad you're here," Johnny said.

"I don't want to get *you* into any trouble," Sam said.

"I'm a circus girl. I live for trouble."

"We've got to get to Bountiful, Nebraska," Evie said.

"We figured we could travel with you without anybody knowing," Sam said.

"What's in Nebraska?" Zarilda asked on a thin stream of cigarette smoke.

"Another Diviner. We think she's in trouble. Listen here, Z, I can tell you all about it later. Just believe me when I say we need to disappear and that we're trying to stop something terrible from happening."

"It's a matter of life and death," Evie added.

"Do you really have a tiger?" Isaiah asked.

Zarilda smiled, charmed by Isaiah. "We surely do, honey. A real corker of a tiger." She tilted her head and took in the motley crew. Sam was nervous. If she said no, then they were really in a pickle.

"I know you have the circus to look after," Sam said. "And I know the circus is a family, and you're the head of that family."

"That's true. And I have to look out for my family. But that family includes you and yours, Sam Lloyd."

Theta exhaled audibly. Evie had the overwhelming desire to hug Zarilda.

"Well, I cain't promise Bountiful, but your timing is good. We're heading out for the season first thing in the morning, headed west. You're more'n welcome to ride with us. Come on up to the camp proper, why don't ya? We'll scrounge up some bunks and something to eat."

"You're an angel, Zarilda," Sam said, following Zarilda and Johnny up the path.

Zarilda laughed. "I'm a medium and a fortune-teller and a lifelong carny. I'm also practical. I expect y'all to work for your passage. Norma Jane got in the family way and ran off with one of my best new tumblers two days ago. I could use another acrobat. You weren't half-bad as I recall, Sam."

Sam stuck out his hand for a shake. "It's a deal. I'm a little outta practice, but I'll get it back. Or kill myself."

"Well, if you die, I can charge double for the next show." Zarilda winked. "We'll keep it to the ground for now, Sam."

"Sam, are you sure you should be doing that?" Evie whispered. "After all you've been through?"

"Everything's jake, Baby Vamp," Sam said, but there were dark shadows under his eyes, and Evie was afraid that whatever Sam had seen during his time in the Eye haunted him still.

"I'll be the judge of that," Zarilda said. "You remember how to do the tricks I taught ya?"

Sam tapped the side of his head with a finger. "Like an elephant."

"Show me. Hasan!" Zarilda shouted to one of the acrobats, a wiry, dark-haired man with the bearing of a professional dancer. "Let's do the lift."

Evie held her breath as Sam straightened into a perfect handstand balancing atop Hasan's palms, raised high above his head, and held the position longer than she thought possible. Then, with perfect grace, Sam flipped backward in a somersault and landed on his feet.

"Like riding a bicycle," Sam said.

Theta applauded. "That was the berries, Sam! And here I thought I was the elephant's eyebrows 'cause I can tap-dance."

"You are the elephant's eyebrows, Theta," Sam said, rotating his shoulders.

"What about me?" Evie asked, throwing her arms around Sam's neck.

"You're the full elephant."

Evie wrinkled her nose. "That was a compliment?"

"And how," Sam said and kissed her cheek, while Theta looked on, missing Memphis something terrible.

Zarilda jerked a thumb at Evie, Theta, and Isaiah. "What about your friends? They do anything I can use?"

"Isaiah here can see the future. Theta is a bit of a firebug. And Baby Doll here can read objects."

Zarilda raised both eyebrows. "Lands' sakes! I meant could you muck a stall or sew a spangle. I didn't know you'd brought me an entire side-show, Sam."

"Trouble is, that'll get us noticed, and not in a good way, Z. We need to stay hidden."

Zarilda pursed her lips, thinking. She nodded at Theta. "Well, you sure are a beautiful one. And you can dance?"

"I hope so. I was in the Follies."

"A real, live Follies girl? All right, then. We'll get you fitted for some tap shoes. You can dance between acts as Lady Liberty. Isaiah..." Zarilda patted his cheek. "Can you really see the future, sugar?"

"Yes, ma'am. Sometimes. But..."

"But?"

"I can't always control it. And the future I see, it isn't always so nice."

Zarilda brought her face close to Isaiah's. He could smell her perfume. She smelled nice. Like honeysuckle. "Well, then. Let's find something else for you to do. You like animals?"

Isaiah nodded.

"You can help Giacomo and Johnny take care of the beasties," she said, and Isaiah grinned to think about getting to feed the elephants and brush the horses. He wished he could tell Memphis that he'd been chosen for this very special job, and he tried not to worry that he didn't know where in the world his brother was, whether he was safe from cops or mean people or ghosts.

Zarilda moved on to Evie. "You're cuter'n a june bug."

It bothered Evie to be called cute instead of beautiful. Even so, she smiled her charming best. "Why, thank you ever so much," she said, using every bit of the elocution lessons she'd had for the radio.

Zarilda hooted, a big, cracking laugh that rang over the road. She hooked a thumb at Evie. "Where'd ya pick her up, Sam?"

"Would you believe a museum of the occult?"

"I'd believe just about anything. Listen, honey, you can drop the debutante act. Just speak plain and honest."

Evie blushed. She wanted to protest, but she knew it would only make her sound more like a princess. "I really can read objects," she said.

"Well, now. That might come in real handy. But first, we got to get you a proper disguise. Follow me."

Zarilda led them through the camp, which was alive with excitement. A whole family of acrobats practiced together, leaping onto one another's shoulders and grabbing for hands to form a human pyramid, all of it happening so fast it was like a magic trick. A trainer coaxed a trio of elephants onto three different round steps, where they balanced on their rear legs, front legs resting on the back end of the elephant in front of them to form a chain. A girl vaulted onto the back of a horse like it was nothing.

"This way," Zarilda said, taking them into a room filled with traveling trunks open to reveal all manner of costumes.

"Holy Moses," Theta said, holding up an ornate jeweled headpiece for one of the horseback riders. "It's like a whole traveling Follies show."

"Let's see. Theta, try this on." Zarilda handed Theta a green toga-style gown, and Theta disappeared behind a dressing screen. Evie looked lovingly at the sparkly sequined numbers with their plumes of feathers at the shoulders.

"Just like a diamond," she said, stroking one.

"Yeah. Diamonds get noticed," Zarilda said, closing the trunk. "Come with me." From another trunk, she selected a pair of baggy pants with suspenders, a puffy shirt, and a plaid jacket. Two big brown shoes and a red straw wig completed the outfit.

"A...clown?" Evie said, her heart sinking.

"Best way I can think of to disappear," Zarilda said.

"It had to be clowns," Evie said and sighed.

Fifteen minutes later, Evie emerged from the costume cabin in the ridiculous getup. Her face had been coated in greasepaint, with an elongated, sideways red mouth painted over her own Cupid's bow lips.

Sam grinned and elbowed Theta, who tried not to laugh. "How 'bout that? Your outside finally matches your insides, Baby Doll," Sam said.

Evie ignored the jibe and admired herself in a funhouse mirror. Nobody would recognize her. The glamorous Sweetheart Seer from New York City was gone. It thrilled her, and it made her a little sad, too. She was perfectly anonymous, the very thing she'd fought becoming her whole life.

"This is pos-i-tutely the worst moment of my life."

"Look here, Baby Vamp—Zarilda is giving us safe passage as far as Kansas. We all gotta give something back."

"I know, but"—Evie shuddered—"*clowns*."

Sam came up behind Evie and hugged her. "Aw, I think you're just about the cutest clown I've ever known."

Evie raised an eyebrow. "How many clowns *have* you known?"

Sam mimed zipping his lips. "I promised not to talk about that. I'm a gentleman."

Evie turned side to side, examining the costume. "I sure hope these clown pants don't start talking to me. I don't think I wanna know their history."

"I'll second that," Theta said. She was dressed in the sparkly green toga-style gown, complete with shiny crown and tap shoes. "Behold, Lady Liberty, minus the torch."

"Hey! How come Theta gets to look good?" Evie grumped.

Theta shrugged. "Wigs make my head itch."

"Don't worry, once we put the green face paint on her, she won't be quite so stunning. Or noticeable, if you catch my drift," Zarilda said with a wink.

Isaiah bounded over with Johnny the Wolf Boy on his heels. "I got to pet the elephants and watch them feed the tiger and there's a poodle who can balance on a ball!"

"*I* can't even balance on a ball," Evie said.

Zarilda appraised Evie. "Say, that clown outfit looks pretty good on you."

"I can't tell if I'm supposed to say thank you," Evie said.

"Way I fig'er it, while you're playing clown, you can sneak a read of somethin' belongin' to somebody, feed me the lowdown on 'em before the show. It'll be fortune-telling like they ain't seen before. Good for business."

"You want me to snooker them?" Evie said.

"Aw, hell. These folks wanna be snookered. That's why they're in the fortune-teller's tent. Look here, I got mouths to feed all winter, honey. This feeds 'em. I help you, you help me."

"One summer, I had to help at my father's office," Evie said. "As long as I don't have to put anything in a file cabinet, I'll do whatever you need."

"Attagirl! Congratulations, everybody. You have now officially run away and joined the circus."

Over a delicious lunch of rabbit with roasted potatoes, carrots, gravy, and biscuits, everybody ate their fill, except for Johnny the Wolf Boy, who refused to eat anything but the vegetables. "I feel a kinship with the animals I take care of."

Isaiah ate and ate until his stomach felt close to bursting.

Zarilda passed him more biscuits and winked. "That's one of the best reasons to join the circus—three squares a day from the lunch and dinner tent."

While they ate, Zarilda explained to the Diviners how things worked. Circus life was as organized as any military operation. Already, the advance men had gone ahead from town to town to post the bills, make the necessary arrangements, and drum up excitement. Tomorrow morning, the circus train would roll out before dawn. By noon, they'd unload at their first stop. People would travel from all over just to catch a glimpse of the circus wagons and performers as they paraded down Main Street, entertaining the cheering throngs and enticing them to the fairgrounds and the Big Top show itself. Those same crowds would pack the food stalls that popped up outside the circus, eager to fill their bellies with fried fish, hot ham, fresh buttered biscuits, popcorn, and cake.

"Why, I tell you, the smell is a carnival unto itself," Zarilda said, and even though Isaiah was full, his mouth watered. "The children'll clamor for nickel candy and red balloons to lord over their friends. Everybody turns out in their best glad rags. The pious folks won't come in the Big Top—they think the circus is sinful. But they'll hover around to get as close as they can to all that 'sin'!" Zarilda let out a honking laugh and slapped her leg, and Evie decided she was mad for the Great Zarilda.

"Where we headed?" Sam asked, savoring a slice of apple pie.

"Pennsylvania, West Virginia, Ohio, Kentucky, Indiana, Illinois, Kansas, Iowa, Nebraska."

"Ohio," Evie said with scorn.

"Baby Vamp here's from Ohio. She just *loves* her hometown," Sam singsonged.

"If I never see that place again, it'll be too soon," Evie said.

"Well. Everybody's gotta be from somewhere. I'm from Texas myself. But, big as that state is, it wasn't big enough to hold me. I guess I'm just a born traveler. There's nothing like the thrill of bein' in a different town every week. Meetin' all those people. Realizing we've all got dreams and a need for a few hours of shared wonder. Guess I'm a circus woman, through and through. Oh, I also enjoy taking their money. Sure beats working the family farm. Lots of folks don't have much going on. The circus brings a little magic to town, and everybody wants magic in their lives," Zarilda said, finishing up the last few bites of her lemon cake.

"Unless that magic comes from Diviners," Theta added dryly.

The room got very quiet.

"All right. Time to level with us, Sam. You know I don't keep secrets from my circus family," Zarilda demanded.

Sam confessed everything—from Project Buffalo to the King of Crows, Jake Marlowe's Eye, the restless dead, and their hope that reuniting with Sarah Beth Olson in Bountiful would provide the answers the Diviners needed in order to defeat the King of Crows and close the hole between dimensions. When he had finished, the tent was pin-drop quiet.

Polly the Bearded Lady leaned against Bella the Strong Man for comfort. "Are there really ghosts out there? Bad ghosts?" she asked.

"I'm afraid so," Evie said.

"I've communed with the spirits some before," Zarilda said. "They never bothered me none."

"This is different," Evie said. "These ghosts are joined to the King of Crows. It's his Army of the Dead."

"Well, what's he training his army to do?"

"That's just it—we don't exactly know. We're hoping Sarah Beth will be the ticket. She seems to have the answers we need."

Zarilda whistled. "Well, I will do ever'thang in my power to git you where you need to be."

"Hey! Would ya look at that?" Sam grinned, tapping the list of towns they'd be visiting. "Looks like we'll be heading straight for your hometown after all, Evie."

Evie's eyes widened in horror. "What?" She ripped the list from Sam's hands and read through. There it was, right after Morgantown, West Virginia: Zenith, Ohio.

"It isn't funny," Evie fumed as Sam chuckled.

"Oh, come on—can I help it if I'm dying to see the town that spawned you, Baby Vamp?"

"Spawned is about right. It's an oozy swamp of a place, all vipers and crocodiles. It's so inbred, it's a miracle people have their own teeth. Besides, what if people recognize me?"

"In your clown getup? Sister, if they do, you've got a whole secret life you never told me about."

"Zenith," Evie groused. "I'd almost rather have the Shadow Men take me."

Sam got quiet. "Don't say that."

"Sam…" Evie said. He left the table and walked down the hill toward the pond.

"Sam!" Evie called out, following him. "Oh, Sam. I didn't mean it. I'm sorry."

She threw her arms around his neck and covered his face with kisses.

"Say," Sam said, coming up for air, "I like the way you apologize."

"Don't get used to it," Evie said with a laugh. "I'm very rarely wrong, don't you know. Oh, Sam. Won't you tell me what's eating you?"

They walked down near the elephants.

"I saw things when I was hooked up to the Eye. Things I couldn't understand. It was like time was all around me, and the past and present and future were all mixed up, with different outcomes each time."

There had been a future without her. And that had frightened him the most. But how could he tell her that?

"I don't understand."

"Ling and Jericho are the Einsteins, not me, Baby Doll. All I know is, I saw lotsa different futures playing out. But then I saw the King of Crows. He had this hourglass. He said all those stories would just become one. The one he's in charge of—death and horror, everywhere."

Evie rubbed her arms against the sudden goose bumps. "Well, we simply can't allow that to happen. We'll have to stop it. That's all there is to it."

"It's got something to do with the changes Marlowe's making to the Eye. The King of Crows is whispering in Marlowe's ear. And those bums have still got my mother."

"We're going to get her back. I promise. And we're going to kick those Shadow Men in the shins."

"Sounds like you're drunk when you say that."

"I wish I were," Evie grumbled. "I suppose I could always get sizzled on Doc's homemade hooch."

"Only if you want to grow hair on your chest. Say, Evie?"

"Yes, Sam?"

"Would you mind apologizing to me again?"

Evie smiled and wrapped her arms around his neck once more. "I'm sorry, Sam." She leaned forward inch by inch, parting her lips seductively, getting Sam hot under the collar. At the last minute, she dodged and kissed him playfully on the cheek. That was Evie. She had a way of making even ordinary moments into fizzy affairs, and he was grateful for the distraction.

He smirked. "See, I don't believe you're sorry."

"How about now?" Evie said, kissing him so passionately that Sam's head went as buzzy as if he'd fallen from a great height.

"The question is, how sorry?" He wanted to hold her all day and all night.

"Very, very sorry," Evie said.

She pressed herself against Sam, and he was overcome both with desire and gratitude. Kissing her pushed away his pain and made him feel, for the moment, that all their futures would be all right. He drew her in closer. He wanted more than just a kiss, and from the way Evie's lips traveled his neck, Sam thought she did, too. Eyes closed, he moaned. "Whaddaya doin' to my head, Baby Vamp?" He laughed and opened his eyes. "Say, that tickles!"

"Jeepers!" Evie jumped back as an elephant's curious trunk explored Sam's ear.

"Hey, what's the big idea?" Sam said, whirling around. "Hattie? Aww, it's Hattie! I guess she remembers me."

"Doubtful," Evie said, laughing.

"Yeah? How you figure that?"

"Hattie is a woman. If she remembered you, Sam, I'm sure she'd slap your face with that trunk," Evie said. She looked up at him through her lashes. "Well. I suppose I'd better go cool off. Don't want to cause a scandal on my first day with the circus." She turned and walked back toward Theta and their cabin.

He didn't want her to go. Ever. "Wait! You gonna apologize for that comment about Hattie?" Sam pointed to his lips.

Evie grinned and kept walking. "Not on your life, Sam Lloyd. You still owe me twenty clams."

Sam watched her go, fighting the urge to run after her and beg her to stay with him all night. With a sigh, he turned to Hattie. "I think she might be part elephant, too, the way she never forgets."

※

Jake Marlowe crumpled the note Evie had left on his desk for him. He was furious, Miriam Lubovitch knew, and this pleased her.

"How did she get in here?" Jake demanded of Jefferson and Adams, who had the audacity to act unperturbed. "This will not be appreciated by your employers."

"You asked us to bring you the Russian. If you'd wanted two Russians, you should've said so," Jefferson said and bit into a pistachio.

"My son is American," Miriam corrected. "And he is missing?" A cruel mirth lit up Miriam's eyes. "How is it people are always leaving you, Jake?"

Jake glared and Miriam sobered. He'd never hit her himself. But she could feel he was on the verge. Marlowe paced the length of the room, and Miriam wondered if he knew he was doing exactly what Will Fitzgerald used to do.

"Well," he said, running his fingers through his slicked-back hair. "We'll just have to get him back. Along with all of his friends. You'll help us with that, won't you, Miriam?"

"Why should I do this? Why would a mother work against her son?"

"We could force you," Adams said.

Miriam stared straight ahead and would not meet his eyes. "When I am free of these chains, I will break your mind into pieces."

"Enough, Miriam," Jake said. "You'll help us because there's a price on

Sam's head. Isn't it better that we find him and the others and bring them in safely?"

Miriam scoffed. "Safe? This is safe?" She lifted her chin and spoke with pride. "I know my Sergei. He is clever. I will—what is it you say? Place my bets on him." She nodded at the crumpled note. "And his friends."

"The Eye is unstable, Miriam! You know this."

"The Eye *you built* is unstable," she said pointedly. "Maybe you should not have built it to begin with."

Jake changed his tone. He smiled. "Miriam. Miriam. Think of all we've been through. All we've done toward this moment."

"All *you've* done!"

"You were part of the department, Miriam. Don't forget that. You were there, too."

Miriam couldn't deny this. She'd not wanted to come when they'd asked, but once she'd been recruited, she had felt a fierce pride that she, a Jewish immigrant from a Russian shtetl, a fortune-teller, might prove an American hero. If only she'd known then how disastrous it would be, how she would lose years with her son, and for what? She'd tried to warn them. No one had listened.

"I know it's been difficult, Miriam. We've all sacrificed so much— you most of all. Do you want that sacrifice to be in vain? We are so very close to marching into that other dimension and making it ours. We could have dominion over death! We can claim that land and control the King of Crows! We only need to keep it open a little while longer, until I can finish the modifications. But without Diviners, we can't charge the machine to its full power."

"You make it all sound so reasonable."

"We are creating the future, Miriam. Just like we did seventeen years ago. But without our babies, our Diviners, our *weapons*, we lose."

He smiled as he patted her hand. And in that moment, Miriam knew she hated Jake Marlowe more than she had ever hated anyone, even the Tsar, and that was saying something.

Miriam yanked her hand free. "Then you lose."

A furious Jake Marlowe nodded to the Shadow Men. "Take her back. Chain the door to within an inch of its life. And then go find me some Diviners."

THE HARLEM HAYMAKERS

As Alma had promised, the bus for the Harlem Haymakers' barnstorming tour of the country showed up promptly at nine thirty AM.

"Do you know what a miracle that is? A bunch of musicians showing up on time?" Alma laughed.

Henry would love that joke, Ling thought. She hoped Henry was okay, that he'd gotten away all right last night. She'd asked Alma to grab some newspapers. Every one of the papers was a special edition, with screaming, giant headlines:

TERROR IN TIMES SQUARE! MANHUNT ON FOR DIVINERS!

PUBLIC ENEMIES! MARLOWE OFFERS BOUNTY!

MEMORIAL MAYHEM! DANGEROUS DIVINERS WANTED FOR TREASON!

"Anything about the others?" Jericho asked as Ling scoured each one.

Ling shook her head. "If they'd been caught, the papers would be talking about it."

"I guess that's good, then," Jericho said. "We all managed to get away."

"Not Sister Walker," Ling said. "If they try her and she's found guilty, she'll face the electric chair. She didn't kill Will Fitzgerald. I know she didn't."

"How are we going to prove that she didn't?" Jericho asked.

"All finished," Alma said, snapping her suitcase shut. She'd let Ling pack some of her clothes to wear on the road.

"Sorry I didn't have anything for you," Alma said playfully to Jericho. "We can pick up something for you on our travels."

"I'll be all right," Jericho said.

Alma made a stink face. "If I have to ride that bus with you, friend, you're going to need a change of underwear."

"Oh." Jericho blushed so hard, Ling was afraid he'd burst.

Outside by the bus at the curb, a skinny dark-skinned man wearing a tan fedora and a red bow tie shouted up the steps. "Shake a leg, Alma!"

"I'm shaking, aren't I?" she called back.

Jericho carried down the two suitcases and tied them to the roof of the bus alongside the instruments already piled there. The skinny man eyed Jericho. "How do?"

Jericho extended his hand. "Freddy Smith."

The other man gave it a solid shake. "Heywood T. Holliday. But everybody calls me Doc."

"Doc...Holliday?"

Doc grinned. "It gets me some funny looks sometimes. But it's memorable! You, uh, a friend of Miss Alma's?"

"Yes. I think."

"Which one is it?"

"I think," Jericho said. "Excuse me."

Jericho fell in beside Ling. "Need anything?"

"Yes. Not to be wanted for murder. And to figure out how to stop the King of Crows," Ling said.

"I mean more along the lines of getting on the bus."

"I can manage," Ling said.

Alma jogged along right behind them, full of good cheer, a slash of red lipstick livening up her mouth and making her smile even brighter. At her neck was a pretty pink silk scarf tied into a lopsided bow. "Doc! These are my dear friends, Mr. Freddy Smith and Miss Mary Chang. They're...cousins. They're headed west to visit a sick aunt. I told them they could ride with us, seeing as we're going that way."

Doc folded his arms at his chest and motioned Alma to the side with a jerk of his head. "Miss LaVoy," he said evenly. "You know I'm not running no taxi service. Who are these people you're putting on my tour bus? *And one of 'em is a man!*"

"Yes, I can tell. I had anatomy in school."

"Alma."

"I *told* you, Doc, they're friends of mine. Friends *in need*."

"Do I look like a charity? Who said I got two empty seats?"

"If you don't want Leah to know about Martha, and Martha to know about Shirley, I suggest you bring them along," Alma said, fluffing and straightening the bow at her neck as if that were her only real concern.

"Now, that's just doing a fella dirty," Doc complained.

"Now, see here, the big fella's strong. He can unload all the instruments and haul 'em back up again. And he can be our muscle on the road. Or help us get food or whatnot when we can't find colored accommodations," Alma said.

"And the lady?"

Alma winked. "Honey, she's with me."

Doc's eyebrows shot up. "Oh. That's how it is?"

"Yep. That's how it is."

As Ling boarded the Ford AA bus, she was stunned to discover that the Harlem Haymakers were women. "Mary Chang, Freddy Smith, may I introduce Harlem's finest all-girl orchestra!" Alma proclaimed. "Everybody, these are my friends Mary and Freddy."

The girls, some of whom looked to be as young as Ling, said their hellos. Seeing Ling's crutches, a big-boned girl with reddish hair got up to offer Ling her seat up front. Ling thanked her and moved to the back, where she wouldn't have to talk to strangers. She didn't like small talk and wasn't good at it, and she had no intention of starting to learn now. When Jericho got on, he felt the women's eyes on him, scrutinizing.

"Hmph," one girl in a blue cloche said and raised her eyebrows to the girl sitting next to her. A girl in a fur-trimmed shawl-collar coat fluttered her lashes at Alma. "You bringing along your sweet man, Alma?"

"Mr. Smith is here to help us with the equipment on this trip, and to be our muscle," Alma said, head held high, as if she dared any girl to dispute her story.

"I got some equipment he could help with," one of the women whispered to her friend, and they burst into cackles.

"*Laaadiess, please*," Alma trilled.

A girl checking her lipstick in a compact mirror laughed. "Don't play auntie, Alma!"

"Comport yourselves with dignity," Doc growled from the driver's seat, earning *boo*s and hoots, calls of "Pardon *me*, Daddy!" and plenty of rolled eyes from the girls.

"I must've been plumb out of my mind to take this gig," Doc muttered. He pushed the electric starter and the bus purred to life. "Next stop, Philadelphia, P-A! Look out, America—here we come!"

Ling and Jericho learned everyone's names. The girl in the fur-trimmed coat was Guadalupe—Lupe to her friends—and she was the drummer. Doc was the promoter and bus driver. The blue cloche girl was Eloise; she played clarinet. The kind girl up front who'd offered Ling a seat was Babe: "I play the saxophone." The girl checking her lipstick was Dorothy, who played piano. There were the twins, Sadie and Sally Mae, both on trumpet, and Emmaline, a pixie of a girl with a dusting of freckles across her nose who informed Ling and Jericho that she played "banjo, guitar, and poker, but not in that order."

"And I sing and dance and lead the band," Alma said, stretching out her long legs on the seat.

"Here come the Harlem Haymakers!" Lupe called and whistled.

At a stoplight on 125th Street, several police wagons blocked the street. Police officers fanned out, going door to door, stopping in all the businesses.

"Who're they looking for?" Babe asked.

"Bootleggers, I'll bet," Alma said quickly as Ling shrank down in her seat and pulled her coat collar up.

"Must be somebody big," Doc said from behind the wheel. "Guess I'll have to go around."

"Say, who knows all the words to 'California Rose'?" Alma started up a song to distract everyone, and soon the bus was full of Harlem's all-girl orchestra singing every blues and jazz number they knew. The bus ride took them downtown to Canal Street. As they rattled past Chinatown, Ling got a catch in her chest. The news would be hitting her street, too. Ling worried about how much shame this would bring to her parents. All the gossip flying around the neighborhood: "Did you see about Ling Chan?" "Yes! An anarchist!" She worried that people would stop going to their restaurant or—worse—that people would show up to harass her family. Ling loved her parents deeply. They were good parents, and she had tried to be a good daughter. It was astonishing how quickly your life could be upended. One day, Ling could walk, and then, after her sickness, she couldn't. Yesterday morning, she had been a good citizen; today, she was a wanted criminal with a price on her head.

"You okay?" Jericho whispered.

Ling was surprised that he noticed. "Just tired."

"You'll see them again," he promised.

And all Ling could do was nod again so she wouldn't cry. Alma and the others were still singing. She hoped they weren't going to sing the whole way. She bunched up her sweater to use as a pillow, placed it where the seat met the window, leaned her head against it, and closed her eyes.

She woke inside a dream. As always, she marveled at the freedom she had when dream walking. She could walk. Run. Dance. Paralysis had no reach here. She hoped she might be able to communicate with Henry.

"Henry?" she called.

She stepped through a doorway and found herself on the evening streets of a Cubist Chinatown. It was like looking into her little part of the world from many different angles. Long blocks of light for windows; soft blobs of red swaying between steeply angled fire escapes. Lanterns. The tenements stretched into points until they were joined to the night, and it was impossible to tell where building began and sky left off. People moved about like shades, quivering shapes with eyes set at odd angles, seeing nothing. Was Henry among these many shapes?

"Henry?" she called again, moving among the faceless crowd.

It wasn't Henry but Mr. Levi who appeared. He had been their neighbor for many years, but he'd died a month earlier, and Ling had thought it sad to watch them carry out his possessions to the junk man. He looked just as he had the last time she'd seen him, in his white shirt and long tweed coat, a hat on his bald head. His face was thin and gray.

"He'll test every one of you in time," Mr. Levi said, then melted like paint.

Whispers bounced through the canyon between tenements, a pressure building inside Ling's body: *We're coming, we're coming, we are coming.* Around the blind curve of Doyers Street, a monstrous shadow clawed up the fronts of the buildings, reaching over the fire escapes toward the lighted windows and the precious life inside. It swirled around the ghostly figure of Will Fitzgerald. He looked haunted. He raised his hand as if trying to hail her from far away.

"Change…" was all Will managed before the shadow rose up behind him like a wave, blotting out everything.

Ling woke. The bus was noisy with chatter and the hum of the road.

"You were dream walking," Jericho said quietly.

Ling nodded.

"Anything?"

"I didn't find Henry, or any of the others," she said. "But I saw Will."

"And?"

She shook her head. "It was like he wanted to warn me, but, I don't know, I don't know. I keep thinking about what those ghosts said to us in Central Park. *You did this.* Did what?"

EVERYWHERE

The Museum of American Folklore, Superstition, and the Occult was locked, naturally, but that didn't stop a good reporter like T. S. Woodhouse. Woody wrapped a rock inside his jacket to muffle the sound, then smashed it against the stained-glass window, picking out enough of the shards to climb inside without impaling himself. The police would be back soon. He didn't have long. Footprints showed in the dust. Lots of footprints. Police, no doubt. But there were women's footprints, too. Woody smirked. They'd been here, and he was sure it was Evie leading the charge. Good for her.

Woody had been to the museum a few times. He'd always found it musty and sad. Now he looked for anything that could help him with what he'd seen on the report the bird had brought him. A secret government project to make Diviners was a pretty big story. And Woody intended to break that story.

A bird darted into the museum with a great squawking and flapping of wings. It fluttered up near the painted ceiling, then hovered near the door into the hallway. Could it possibly be the same bird? That was crackers. Then again, strange things were happening.

"Okay," Woody said. "Okay, I'm on the trolley."

He followed it into Will's study. The bird settled on Will's desk and hopped onto a stack of newspaper clippings, some of them yellowed with age. The bird tapped its beak against the stack and hopped off. Woody skimmed the first four articles, his skin prickling. This wasn't just a story; this was a terrifying warning.

Woody read through the stories, noting the one thing they all had in common: "Reported seeing a man in a tall hat"; "Saw a man in a stove-pipe hat"; "Claims he was visited in dreams by a man in a stovepipe hat just before he saw the world burn." Woody's alarm grew when he realized that the clippings went back some ten years. Whatever had been happening had been going on for some time. Building. Woody shoved two handfuls of the clippings into his pockets.

The bird cawed and cawed. It flew out and back into the library.

"You sure keep a guy hopping. What is it that…" Woody's words died on his lips.

The hazy form of Will Fitzgerald stood beside a chalkboard in the corner. Woody's mind reached for the comfort of a rational explanation and found none. His reporter's cynicism deserted him. Woody shut his eyes tightly. When he opened them again, Will's ghost was still there. Woody's knees buckled. He grabbed the back of a chair to steady himself.

"W-Will…" he croaked.

The ghost nodded slowly and raised a hand. What if it came after him? Woody had to fight the strong urge to run as words slowly chalked themselves onto the slate:

They need you.

Tell the truth.

Talk to Margaret.

And then, in a flash, it was all gone—Will's ghost, the words, the bird. Woody stood alone, trembling in the museum with the clippings still in his pockets. He let out the yelp he'd been holding back, and then he ran to the window where he'd broken in, hissing as he nicked his hand on a sharp edge in his hurry to get out.

An hour later, he was camped outside the Tombs in Lower Manhattan along with most of Park Row's reporters, waiting for a statement from Detective Terrence Malloy on the incident in Times Square, the arrest of Margaret Walker, and the continuing manhunt for the missing Diviners.

"What happened to your hand, Woodhouse?" A reporter in an ill-fitting hat motioned with his pencil at the bandage Woody had hastily wrapped around the cut from the window glass. "Your bookie come for a finger at last?"

Woody didn't take the bait. He'd spent the last hour reading through all of Will Fitzgerald's newspaper clippings. Ghosts. They were everywhere. And who was the man in the hat? *What* was he?

Detective Malloy sauntered from the jail accompanied by six of his men to face the reporters, who immediately began barraging him with questions. Malloy assured everyone that Jake Marlowe had been taken to safety and that the New York bulls, along with the Federal Bureau of Investigation, were doing everything in their combined power to bring the fugitives to justice. The manhunt had gone nationwide.

"We believe some of these anarchists boarded a train at Penn Station last night. Our agents across the country are working to apprehend them," Malloy announced. "We'll get 'em, and that's a promise."

A reporter chewing gum noisily raised his pencil. "Where was that train headed, Detective?"

"That's confidential."

"Hey, Detective! Has Margaret Walker 'fessed up yet?"

"No comment."

"You gonna let us talk to that Walker woman?" another reporter asked.

"No," Malloy said.

"Is that your final word?"

"Sounds like the final word," the first reporter said around his gum.

Woody raised his hand. "Detective Malloy! T. S. Woodhouse of the *Daily News*."

"I know who you are, Mr. Woodhouse," Malloy sneered.

"What if Diviners aren't a menace? What if they're trying to protect us from a much greater danger?"

Malloy folded his arms across his chest. "Yeah? What danger is that, Mr. Woodhouse?"

"Danger from another world."

"You mean like Canada?" the reporter in the bad hat asked.

"Yeah, Charlie. Canada." The gum-chewing reporter laughed.

Woody cleared his throat. "My, ah, *sources* tell me there was a secret project during the war that opened up a portal into another dimension. The entity from that world, the man in the stovepipe hat, is behind all this unrest."

It took approximately five seconds before the entire assembly broke into wild laughter.

"Hey, Woody, who's your source on this—Crazy Al, who talks to the pigeons in the park?"

Another reporter tapped the side of his head. "I think his bootlegger is cutting his whiskey with gasoline and it's gone to his brain."

Woody ignored them. "You never did solve the Naughty John case," he reminded Malloy.

"Sure we did. Officer Lyga was a hero."

"C'mon, Detective. We all know that's bunk and you and the boys are covering up what really happened up at Knowles' End," Woody pressed.

"Yeah? And what's that, pray tell?"

"What if it's like Will Fitzgerald said, and it was ghosts? There *are* ghosts. They're here. You can't deny that."

"I haven't seen any ghosts," Malloy said.

"It's true. The folks at the Casino were pretty splifficated that night," a reporter with a ruddy face and a gruff voice posited. "For all we know, the Diviners paid some actors to show up and make 'em look important just to throw us off the scent."

"Anarchists," the reporter in the hat said, shaking his head, and Woody wanted to take him by his lapels. This was how it happened if you weren't careful. Somebody tried to redirect the story, and if nobody challenged it, that story became what everybody considered the truth.

"What about that night on Wall Street a few weeks back? The police were there when the Diviners faced off with—"

"*Actors.* Stage magic," the reporter insisted. "C'mon, Woody. Why're you falling for this bogus, fake medium bunk?"

"Seems like the *Daily News*'ll print anything these days," Malloy echoed with a chuckle, earning a few laughs from the reporters.

"It isn't bunk!" From his pocket, Woody grabbed a stack of newspaper clippings he'd taken from the museum. "These tell a different story. The professor was cataloging these. Ghost sightings and disturbances. Warnings. They're from all over the country. And guess what? These started showing up just after the war. A lot of 'em mention that man in the hat."

Malloy glowered. "Where'd you get those?"

Woody shoved them back into his pocket. "An interested party." He didn't need to tell Malloy that *he* was the interested party.

Malloy spread his arms wide. "Now, listen to me: There are no ghosts. There's no secret project that opened up a door to some other dimension. That's just plain crackers. But there is a threat to our national security in these Diviners with their unnatural powers palling around with anarchists who bomb innocent citizens and try to destroy this country. This is the greatest nation on earth. We aim to keep it that way. With law and order. So help me god."

A reporter nodded. "Pretty speech, Detective. Say, you running for governor?"

Malloy puffed up, pleased with himself. "That's all for today, gentlemen."

The ruddy-faced man laughed. "Gentlemen? We're reporters."

"Hey, Woody! You need a ride to the cemetery to talk to your sources?"

the gum-chewing reporter called out, earning another round of chuckles. It burned Woody up.

"I'm gonna blow this story wide open. And when I do, we'll see who's laughing."

"Aw, faith and begorrah, Seamus," the reporter said, mocking him. "You're all wet, Woody. Go see your bookie and leave the reporting to the real boys, why don'tcha?"

"Go to hell," Woody said back. He needed to talk to Margaret Walker and find out what was happening across the country. There was a threat coming, he knew. While everybody was dancing in nightclubs and reading Harriet Henderson's gossip pages and arguing about evolution and Prohibition and how short women's skirts had gotten. While people were letting themselves get distracted by the latest John Barrymore picture or Mae West sex scandal and telling themselves that everything was the berries because men like Jake Marlowe were making the stock market soar. Woody was twenty-one and as ambitious as they came. That was true. But even more than making a name for himself like his hero, H. L. Mencken, Woody wanted to report the truth. Because he was afraid of what he was learning. Yes, he was afraid.

Woody gazed up at the looming stone fortress that was the Manhattan jail.

How was he going to get in to see Margaret Walker?

As Woody turned the corner, he saw Roy Stoughton, Theta Knight's supposed husband, talking to some of Dutch Schultz's henchmen. Woody pretended to be taking notes, but he was listening.

"What do you mean you lost her?" Roy said. He was angry.

"She disappeared, Boss."

"Did you put out the word with the Empire?"

"Talked to the Grand Dragon myself. They're telephoning every klavern and asking them to pass along the word. No matter where she goes, she'll have our boys looking for her."

Roy Stoughton was in with the KKK. As the son of Irish immigrants, Woody had no love for those cowards with their white sheets and burning crosses. But the Diviners were in a heap of trouble if the Klan was looking for them, too.

Woody reached into his pocket and took out one of the clippings, reading it once more with dread. "They're everywhere," he muttered and hurried back to his office.

THE GHOSTS INSIDE THEM

It was lunchtime, and the breaker boys were headed home from their first long shift at the mines. All morning they'd climbed up the noisy, constantly moving chutes, sorting through the day's haul to separate useless rock from valuable coal.

They'd just come over the ridge and were taking their favorite shortcut through the holler down toward the company town where they all lived. The walk was steep through the trees. The smoke from the coke ovens cooking down the coal hung along the pipe-cleaner tops of the mountains, erasing the sky. The dark seemed to come earlier here. Some said the mountains were haunted by the ghosts of dead miners. There were moonshiners up there, too, and they kept watch over their stills with rifles.

The four of them had been laughing about something that had happened earlier in the day. One of the younger boys, Giuseppe, had picked up two pieces of rock and stuck them in his cheeks like a squirrel gathering nuts. Well, they'd all fallen out over that one, laughing until the foreman barked at them to get back to work. That shared laugh had broken up the long day, though, and they enjoyed reliving it now on their walk.

"Naw, Jakub. It weren't like that," Buster said, trying to catch his breath. "It were more like 'is." Buster dropped to his haunches and hopped around, scratching under his armpits and mewling.

"Buster, you plumb crazy. That ain't no squirrel—'at's a dadgum kitty cat!" Buster's brother, Junior Lee, said, coughing along 'with his laugh. He was thirteen, and next month, he'd graduate from working the chutes to going down into the mines proper with his daddy and his uncle Joe.

"Do it more!" Gabor said. He was only ten, and his English was tinged with the soft rhythm of his parents' native Hungarian.

Jakub hopped around, trying to make his pals laugh again, but Junior

Lee had stopped short in the blue-gray woods. He held up a hand. "You hear sump'in'?"

Buster's ears still rang from the constant agitation of the mine's machinery. "Like what?"

Junior Lee smiled mischievously. "I'll bet it's some o' the other boys playing a trick on us. Let's hide here and wait for 'em!"

Delighted, the boys grabbed pebbles and pine cones, stuffing them into their trouser pockets, then picked their hiding places—Junior Lee cloaked by a hemlock tree, Buster and Gabor crouched behind a large rock, and Jakub, the smallest, on his haunches in a thicket of bushes. They waited with coiled glee. What a good time this would be! Those pranksters sure would be surprised when they got hit with rocks and pine cones. But the other boys were taking their sweet time.

Junior Lee was the first to feel that something wasn't right. In a matter of seconds, the woods had gotten very cold. "Feels right airish all of a sudden," he said.

They abandoned their hiding places. The mist that had been side-stepping up the mountain had swooshed into the holler and filled up the gaps between the trees. They knew these woods well, and yet, which way was home?

The sound was back, and this time, it was plain that it wasn't coming from boys playing tricks. There was a high whine like mad hornets escaping a nest and coming to sting. A deep, low growl echoed off the mountains. The boys hunted some, but this didn't sound like any animal they'd ever aimed for with their daddy's guns. Whatever it was, it seemed to be everywhere.

The sky had gone dark as a bucket of coal dust. The trees were nothing but skeletons in the gray wool fog. Buster had heard his daddy talking about the time he'd narrowly avoided being trapped by a cave-in, how seconds before, the canary had started screeching; it had made his whole body go tight as a wire. Buster was tight now. The birds flapped up from the trees in one giant wave. There was something here with them in the mist. The boys felt it deep in their bodies, lighting up the parts of their brains that hadn't changed for humankind since their cave ancestors had hidden from predators in the dark.

"Mama be expectin' me," Buster said feebly. It was easier than saying, *I'm afeared of these woods*.

The mist had come up so hard and fast they could hardly get their bearings. And that hornet sound. Sweet Lord, but it put the hair on the back of Junior Lee's neck to standing on end.

"Junior! Buster! Gabor!"

That was Little Jakub. Where had his voice come from? The mist si-goggled it something fierce. Nothing was straight. Which way was the road? Should they go home? Home was where their mamas were. They wanted their mamas, though they'd never say so.

Junior Lee saw the glow first. It was off to the right, and he was sure it was the porch light of the company store in the miner camp. "Home's just over yonder," he said. "Come on. Hurry!" He didn't want to be in the woods anymore, and he set off toward the comforting glow. It was so chilly. Junior Lee's breath came out in puffs. The other boys were behind him. He could hear their footfalls back a ways. The crack of a branch.

"Keep up!" Junior Lee said and kept walking. But the woods didn't look right. He was confused. The glow had moved off to his left some. And to his right. It was in two places at once. Three. "You see that?" he said.

No answer.

Junior Lee turned back. The boys were not behind him. "Jakub? Buster!" His voice echoed and was swallowed. "Gabor?" Another crack of a branch. Junior Lee whirled around. There was no need to call for the boys. They were there, carried in the arms of the ghosts streaming out of the woods. Jakub's eyes were still open but unseeing. His head hung at a funny angle from his neck. What was left of Gabor and Buster made Junior Lee vomit into the leaves.

The ghosts kept coming, more and more. Some of the ghosts were ladies in very old black dresses and with white bonnets on their heads. Some were miners rotted through with the black lung. The glow had been from their headlamps, that third eye pulsing into the gloom. All of them were hungry. Their eyes, ringed in darkness, burned with it.

They opened their mouths and a liquid coursed from their ruined lips, black and thick, like they'd been chewing tobacco without stopping.

The ghosts spoke in one voice. "This world will be ours. But first, let us pay tribute."

Junior Lee would never have to worry about a mine cave-in, never have to listen for the shrill warning of the canary. He would never work deep underground with his daddy, never wake in the night with a burbling cough, never turn fourteen. The ghosts would make sure of it.

Junior Lee fell down on his back.

"Please. Don't," the boy whimpered. His lips moved silently, praying to the god his ma and pa told him lived up in the sky. But that sky was infected now, bruised and angry. The birds screeched away from the swirling, seemingly endless hole at its center, and if Junior Lee hadn't been so terrified, he might've marveled at this new sight—the soulless cloud eye shedding tears of blue light into a world that didn't know it existed.

The ghosts surrounded Junior Lee.

They growled and bared their teeth: "All praise the King of Crows."

The mountains swallowed up his screams.

※

Boley, Oklahoma

The town of Boley had been founded in 1903 in Creek Nation Indian Territory by descendants of African and Creek Freedmen, and in the subsequent years, it had grown to become a very prosperous town. That was why Mr. S. S. Jones had come to town with his film camera to document Boley's success, to show others of his brethren that a dream was alive in Oklahoma. His guide, Mr. James Powell, proudly showed off the local bank and the oil derrick that produced more than two thousand barrels of crude per day. Yes, sir, things were very good in Boley.

It was mid-afternoon now and unseasonably warm on the dusty plains of frontier country. The two men perspired in their suits, ties, and hats, and so they took refuge on the front porch of the general store and sipped glasses of lemonade made cold with ice from Boley's own ice plant. The two men removed their hats and let the gritty wind cool the sweat beaded along their neatly trimmed hairlines, compliments of Boley's own, very busy barbershop. The men tipped their heads back and took in all that sky—so much sky it seemed like nothing could ever stop its reach.

"The land's been very good to us," Mr. Powell said proudly.

"I see that," Mr. Jones said.

Mr. Powell couldn't help noticing that Mr. Jones seemed miles away.

"Mr. Jones, I don't mean to pry, but is something on your mind? Are you not enjoying your time here in Boley?"

"Oh, I'm enjoying my time tremendously. I was just thinking about something peculiar that happened on the trip out here. I guess it's got me spooked. You ever hear of a town called Edna?"

Mr. Powell shook his head slowly. "Can't say as it's familiar to me. Is it nearby?"

"Farther east. About forty miles, maybe, on the railroad line."

"What about it?"

"Well, I passed by it on my way to Stillwater last week. Saw it from the train window, you see. Looked like a nice little town. The train stopped for a few minutes to let some folks on. There were even some children who'd come down to the tracks to wave at us and hear the engineer toot the whistle. A week later, I passed by it again on my way back and..." He shook his head.

"What is it?"

Mr. Jones gave Mr. Powell a sideways glance. "Well. It wasn't there anymore."

Mr. Powell smiled with polite confusion. "I'm afraid I don't understand."

"Neither do I." Mr. Jones stared into his nearly empty glass. "What I mean is, just one week earlier, from my seat on the train, Edna had looked like a nice, thriving little place with wildflowers growing in the tall grass down near the tracks—an explosion of color, pink and orange and purple. But now it looked dead. A ghost town."

Mr. Powell didn't like the word *ghost*. The residents of Boley were descendants of former slaves. They carried their ghosts inside them. When Mr. Powell looked around at the town of Boley, four thousand souls and counting, he saw the future. He imagined more Boleys in a nation that would finally live up to the ideals it espoused. "Could you have been on a different route, maybe?" he said, trying to be helpful.

Mr. Jones was resolute. "No, sir. It was the same route. I saw the sign: Edna. But this time? Two big fat vultures circled above the town square. And those wildflowers that had been budding up nice and pretty? Well, Mr. Powell, they were dead as could be. Not a thing growing there, from what I could see."

Mr. Powell had grown up in the church. The filmmaker's story sounded biblical to him, like Sodom or Admah. Still: "Maybe it had to do with the angle of the sun, or maybe there had just been a flood and folks had been forced to evacuate." He was grasping for answers. The story of the dead town crawled under his skin. He wanted to be rid of the feeling.

"I even asked one of the porters if he'd noticed the change. But he just said he'd been busy with passengers and hadn't paid any mind to it," Mr. Jones continued. "But that town looked...*haunted* to me, sir."

"Goodness. That is something." Mr. Powell cleared his throat. "Fine day today, isn't it?"

Mr. Jones took the polite cue. He swallowed the last of his drink. "Indeed. And that lemonade was mighty refreshing, thank you. I do believe you promised to show me that bank."

"Yes, sir. Coming right up!" Mr. Powell left the porch and walked ahead, proudly talking about Boley's status as one of the nation's wealthiest towns run by and for black folks. Mr. Jones nodded along. But he remembered something else glimpsed from the train window. Something he was too afraid to mention. The sun had just sunk below the horizon; evening swooped down over the plains. He'd watched the vultures as they'd flown a figure eight, going tighter and lower, until they hovered above a scarecrow-like figure of a man in a coat and a tall hat standing alone on that flat, ashen land. Electricity arced about this man until he, himself, glowed with its energy. The man punched his hands up toward the sky as if he might rip the guts from it. The clouds roiled and groaned as if in pain, like it was giving birth to some new horror, and the man in the hat laughed and laughed, as though nothing at all mattered and soon, nothing ever would.

SOME WOUNDS

Memphis had been out of New York City only once, when he was around six, and he and his mother had gone to Baltimore to see the cousins. It dawned on him now that it was probably during that trip that his mother had taken him to a Project Buffalo office to be evaluated. Memphis had no memory of going to an office and answering questions about any powers he might have. All he recalled was running barefoot with his cousins and gobbling up spoonfuls of rice and *sòs pwa* while fireflies blinked against the dusk. It was funny what you chose to remember and what you chose to forget.

After Harlem, the wide-open space of the South was a shock to Memphis. Everything was so spread out. You could walk for ages and pass nothing at all but some kudzu or an old man rocking on his front porch, a spittoon at his feet. Everywhere he looked, though, Memphis saw something he wished he could tell Isaiah or Theta about. He never realized quite how much of his day he saved up to share with his little brother, or what tiny stories he tucked into a pocket to tell Theta about later, when they were lying in each other's arms. If you didn't get to share what you saw, what you experienced, it was almost like it didn't happen.

Now that the immediate danger had passed, he took a moment to marvel at how different this part of the country looked from New York City. It was such a big country. A fella could forget that walking the same streets all the time. And each place was different from the last. From the train, he'd seen the tiny mountain towns of West Virginia, the leafy green tobacco fields of North Carolina, and the red earth of Georgia, where his father's people were from. When this was all over, he hoped to take another train with Isaiah and show him how big it all was. *Look it there*, he pictured himself saying to his wide-eyed brother. *You know why the dirt is red like that? 'Cause it's wounded and needs a healing.*

"How long you think before we get to Bountiful?" Memphis asked. They'd been walking for some time, and his shirt stuck to his back with a damp sweat.

"Depends on the trains," Bill said.

"My feet are blistered balloons," Henry complained. "*Buh-listered buh-looooons, buh-listered b-b-b-uh-loons*," he sang, drifting into a hum.

"We haven't seen anything but railroad tracks and that river for miles now," Memphis said.

"That's not just a river. That's the Mighty Mississippi," Henry said.

"Okay," Memphis said, annoyed. He wasn't looking for a geography lesson. All he wanted was to get back to Theta and Isaiah and put things right.

"The Mississippi is more than two thousand miles long! It goes from Minnesota all the way to the Gulf of Mexico, like a big scar down the middle of the country."

"Mmm."

"It's looking awfully high, though. It's been eight months of rain. If the levees break…" Henry whistled. "You don't want to be anywhere near it."

"But the levees'll hold, right?" Memphis cast a nervous glance at the swollen river.

Henry shrugged. "The levees are man-made. The river's the river. It's got a rebellious, unpredictable spirit."

"Swell," Memphis said under his breath.

The rich black earth of the Mississippi Delta was fertile and promising and flat. Sun beat down on the bent backs of workers planting seed, some singing to one another as they did, a call-and-response that put Memphis in mind of his days as the Harlem Healer in the storefront church, with his mother looking on proudly in her Sunday hat. The singing was a way to break up the monotony of the labor, Memphis knew, and a way to feel less alone out there under all that sky. Memphis was struck by the lush beauty of Mississippi, and by what he knew it had cost families like his to create it. He'd had ancestors on his father's side who'd worked the cotton and tobacco fields, who had harvested sugar and rice. Men and women whose labor had made other men and women rich. Looked to him like it was still that way. The anger of the injustice, the beauty of the land, the resilience of the people raised new passion within him. He tried to commit what he saw and felt to memory so that he could write about it later. He no longer felt that he wanted to write; he felt *compelled* to write. All of it. Whenever they stopped to rest, he hurriedly scribbled down the words that had been playing in his head, and as they traveled the roads, Memphis left copies of these poems here and there, in the hope that they would be found. He thought of them like little seeds. "Like Johnny Appleseed," he told himself.

"What's that about apples?" Henry called over his shoulder.

"Nothing," Memphis said.

The Delta revealed itself like a dream, in wind-stripped wooden shacks and children running after a dog that had treed a squirrel, in migrant workers selling food from the back of a truck, in billboards full of smiling white faces drinking Coca-Cola, and overhead, in clouds so fat with pink-gold light they seemed as if they'd been painted by a heavenly brush. At a crossroads, they waited while a procession of black churchgoers dressed in crisp white crossed in front of them, the ladies with their protective umbrellas held high against the sun, singing on their way to a pond for a mass baptism. "Heard the floods might come like Noah," a woman at the end of the line explained from under the shade of her parasol. "Don't wanna be caught unprepared."

Back a ways from the road, a mansion rose up, white-columned and black-shuttered. Its many windows stared out, keeping watch over the land like a double row of eyes. "Plantation," Bill said, frowning. A little farther on, they passed a lean-to where a grizzled man sat on the front porch picking out a blues song about the Devil and the moonlight that did nothing to put them at ease.

They'd been walking along the railroad tracks for some time when they finally came to a tiny town out in the middle of nowhere with a filling station that doubled as a general store and post office. Memphis started toward the door.

"Hold up a minute," Bill said.

"Why?" Memphis said. He was exhausted and thirsty and impatient.

"Got to make sure it's safe to go in," Bill said. A dark brown man came out of the garage, wiping his fingers on a bandanna, and Bill exhaled in relief. "Afternoon," he said and gave a courteous nod.

"Afternoon," the gentleman returned with a pinch to the brim of his hat and that same dip of the head.

"Nice day," Bill said.

"Yes, sir. That it is."

"Feels like rain's coming, though," Henry said.

"Yes, sir. Been rainin' for months. Just keeps coming down on us. They say the levees gettin' washed away all up and down the Mississippi. Folks are worried way down to New Orleans. Heard they might even hafta blow up the levees in Plaquemines Parish."

Bill shook his head sadly. "Ain't that something? Cain't fight Mother Nature."

"No, sir. You surely cain't."

Memphis wanted to scream in the face of all this Southern politeness. Why couldn't they just ask about a ride to Greenville and be done with it?

"What can I do you for?" the man finally asked.

"Well, sir, we're lookin' to get to Greenville. Got some kinfolk there. Don't suppose you know anybody headed that way? We'd be mighty grateful for any help," Bill said.

"You almost there. 'Nuther thirty mile, give or take, but I hear the river's washed out parts 'tween here and yon. My cousin, Jesse, has a truck. He's going thataway and can take you far as Yazoo City."

"Much obliged," Henry and Bill said at the same time.

"Happy to help. We got to look out for one another, don't we?"

"We surely do," Henry said.

"I'd like to mail this letter, please. And buy some stamps." Memphis handed over his latest poem. He fished in his pocket for change. "How much for that?"

The man blinked at Memphis, taken aback. Henry bristled. In his head, he translated New York City speak into Southern speak: *If it wouldn't be too much trouble, could I get you to mail this letter for me?* Memphis's way was more direct, and Henry preferred it. But it was funny how the things you learned growing up had a way of sticking with you. Memphis had been straight-forward; Henry had heard rude.

"New York City, huh? Never been there." The man examined the envelope slowly, carefully. It made Henry nervous.

"We ain't never been there, neither," Bill said quickly, cutting Memphis off. "It's one of them sweepstakes, you see."

"Yes," Henry added. "We hope to win a prize."

"That so? What kinda prize?"

"A jar of Ovaltine," Henry lied.

"Huh. Ovaltine. Well, I'll be sure and post this for you with tomorrow's mail. That'll be two cents for postage, and a dime for the stamps."

"Maybe you should let Henry and me do all the talking," Bill said as they waited on the steps of the filling station for Cousin Jesse to arrive.

"Why?"

"You talk like a city boy."

"People around here pride themselves on their hospitality," Henry added.

"You're saying I was rude?"

"I didn't say that," Henry mumbled.

"Hmm." Memphis couldn't wait to get back to New York City.

The screen door creaked open. The man came out with a bucket of blue paint and a brush. He leaned a ladder up against the store, then dipped the brush into the paint and swiped it across the porch ceiling, turning it a pale robin's-egg blue.

"Looks real nice," Memphis said. He flashed Henry a look. The look said, *Look how polite I am!*

"Haint Blue. To keep the ghosts away," the man grunted. "Been having some troubles 'round here. Folks say the nights are haunted. Like the past is rising up out its grave to make itself known. You best be careful after dark, now. Don't go camping in these woods." He pointed the brush at a truck coming up the path, its tires kicking up dirt. In the back were cages packed with squalling chickens. "That would be Cousin Jesse."

In the back of Cousin Jesse's truck, Memphis, Bill, and Henry were nestled among wire-strung cages full of agitated chickens. Their wings flicked Memphis's and Henry's cheeks, making them flinch. It was noisy and smelly.

"Damn," Memphis said, waving away the smell.

"Man didn't have to give us a ride, but he did," Bill said.

"Don't need a sermon," Memphis grumbled.

"When a man's been the beneficiary of a miracle, it changes the way he sees things," Bill said. "How you gonna fight the King of Crows if you don't believe there's any goodness in this world worth saving?"

They rode in silence for some time until the truck began to slow.

"I'd take you farther, but I got business this way," Jesse told them as he let them out on the road about ten miles from Greenville. "Y'all watch out for that river. And stay out of the woods at night."

"We heard about the ghosts," Henry said.

"Ghosts, nothing. It's the Klan you got to worry about."

It was getting toward dusk. The sun slipped down and swaddled the horizon in softer blues. Memphis was tired. At his side, Henry, too, was lagging.

"Can we find a place to sit down?" Memphis asked.

"I'm glad you said it first," Henry said, grinning. "Hey. There's a sign for a town, looks like." Henry hurried toward the black-and-white marker. But when he reached it, he froze.

"'N—'" Memphis refused to repeat the insult. "'Don't let the sun catch you in this town after sundown.'"

"What I tell ya?" Bill said, walking down the railroad embankment and into the cover of the impartial trees.

They camped in a copse of woods. Bill found some branches and piled them up. The wood was damp, and it smoked something awful, but at last it caught fire. They warmed their hands and Bill took out some bread and oranges they'd managed at a little stand on the road.

"Thought we weren't supposed to stay in the woods," Memphis said quietly.

"Don't see that we got much choice," Bill said.

"I've heard about towns like that," Henry said.

"Sundown towns." Bill practically spat the words. "Towns that don't want black folks, so they post a warning sign, letting you know they'll be coming for you if you're there after dark."

"Charming," Henry said bitterly.

Memphis stared into the fire. "Why are we trying to save this country? What's it ever done for us?" In his mind, he could still see those words on that hateful sign. "Maybe we should just let it burn. Maybe we should let the King of Crows have it all."

Bill let the question sit for a long time. "It's the only country we got, I reckon."

"That's a bullshit answer," Memphis grumbled.

"Only answer *I* got, too."

"I can't walk down the street with my girl. Can't even go into some towns." Memphis flicked a glance Henry's way. "You can't walk down the street free, either."

Henry's cheeks burned with embarrassment that Bill knew this about him now, that he liked boys. Bill seemed like a man's man, like his father. And Henry hated that he could punish himself with shame like this. He was who he was, and he had no intention of not being who he was. So why was he letting shame call the shots?

"Usedta think I could make a difference," Bill said. "'At's how I ended up workin' for them Shadow Men. Found out real quick they jus' wanted to use me up and spit me out when my sight was gone and my body weak. But when I look at Isaiah, you and your friends, well…then I git to thinkin', maybe y'all be the ones to fix it."

Memphis found Bill's answer unsatisfying, though. "Tired of healing things." Right then, there was only one place for that anger to find release. While Henry lay on the ground and sang a song to keep himself from feeling too lonely and Bill patted the sides of a stump like a drum for accompaniment, Memphis took out his notebook and started to write.

> The earth of Georgia is red
> Red like a wound that's bled
> And scabbed over
> Bleed again, bleed again,
> And again
> Some wounds just won't heal

He wrote until he could barely keep his eyes open and a new poem had been born on the page, one that told of their walk through the Delta with all its ghosts. He was planting his own seeds. When he had finished, he signed it *The Voice of Tomorrow*.

"What're you doing?" Henry asked on a yawn.

"Starting a revolution," Memphis joked.

"You don't have to tell me," Henry said.

"Just telling my story," Memphis said.

❋

Bill couldn't say what it was that woke him, only that he'd come out of sleep alert and uneasy. The fire was out, but there was a glow coming from deeper in the trees. He remembered that they were not too far from a sundown town, and that made him very nervous. That glow could be a cross burning. There might be a whole klavern of white-hooded thugs nearby, just waiting for a chance to egg one another on, to prove to one another that they were men in charge, men who would do whatever it took to stay in charge.

And here he was with two boys they might use to make their point.

An owl hooted from some unseen spot. Except for that glow in the distance and the small sliver of new moonlight, it was pitch-dark. Anything could be hiding in those woods. Bill knew he needed to see for himself what was there among the trees. Leaving the boys behind, he moved as stealthily as he could toward the strange phosphorescence and wished for the comfort of New York City's bright lights. The April chilliness mixed with the damp had brought up a light fog. Bill heard voices. It was impossible to say where they were coming from, how far or near. They seemed to bounce around in the fog. The voices faded, and in their place, Bill heard weeping, a deep, mournful lament. The crying, too, came and went. It changed in tone and timbre, but the pain was always the same.

Something brushed across his shoulder. Bill whirled around. "Who's there?" he demanded. He fumbled in the dirt for a rock, just in case. If it came to it, he had his hands. Places had an energy. As a Diviner, Bill knew this. This place was drenched in sorrow and hate and horror. His arms began to shake. He needed to get away. To get back to Memphis and Henry. Didn't matter that it was still dark; they'd go, walk down the center of the railroad tracks if need be. Safer than here.

A deep, guttural moaning surrounded him. It gained power, getting louder. Louder still. Bill dropped the rock and put his hands over his ears. The brush—one, two—across his shoulder again. He whirled around and looked up, his mouth opening in a soundless scream.

Ghostly bodies hanging from the trees.

Puckered skin where eyes should be.

Bloated, fingerless hands.

The keening poured from the ghosts' mouths on thin ribbons of fog. And in that fog, under this collective hymn of rage and witness screamed into the woods long after death, there were dogs barking and men laughing, there was pleading to no avail, the sound of the land refusing to stay silent.

It brought Bill to his knees. He struggled to stand. He backed away. As one, the men's heads snapped up. They spoke with one hissing voice: "Ghosts on the road, ghosts on the road, ghosts on the road!"

With a cry, Bill turned and ran back toward the camp.

※

The next morning, Memphis had to shake Bill out of a deep sleep. The big man woke with a start. He sat straight up, gasping for as much air as he could fit into his lungs. He put his hands to his throat.

"You all right?" Memphis asked.

Bill glanced over his shoulder at the perfectly ordinary woods. He looked out at the distant railroad tracks and the sundown town sign looming over them. *Who could be all right knowing the things I know?*

"Let's just keep moving," Bill said.

They passed through a small town that had a tiny post office. Memphis tucked the new poem inside one of the Crescent Limited envelopes he'd kept and marked the front: Care of Mr. T. S. Woodhouse, the *Daily News*. For the return address, he wrote simply, *The Voice of Tomorrow, Somewhere in America.*

BARNSTORMING

The Harlem Haymakers' bus kept going past Philadelphia proper and out an unpaved road that led to a muddy parking lot across from an old barn-turned-dance hall. The whole place looked like it might fall down in a stiff wind. The Haymakers peered out through the dirty bus windows.

"This is the Centurion?" Ling asked.

"What on earth? That's just a shack!" Lupe said.

"I suppose this is why they call it barnstorming," Alma said. "Come on, ladies. Shake a tail feather. We've got paying customers to entertain."

"Didn't know we'd be playing real barns," Babe said with a shake of her head.

"Jericho, let's start unloading this bus," Doc called.

The Philadelphia Centurion—which was, as Babe kept pointing out to anyone who'd listen, *not* really in Philadelphia: "They just flat-out lied!"—hosted a clientele happy on moonshine and illegal whiskey. At the tables, women pulled flasks from secret pockets sewn into their slips; men took them from hat ribbons and hollowed-out books. But the joint was jumping and eager for more. There were several acts on the bill—comics, dancers, singers, and various orchestras. The Harlem Haymakers were listed fifth.

"We probably won't even get onstage before midnight," Sally Mae griped as they slipped into their uniforms in a makeshift dressing room made from a curtain clipped to a clothesline. They could hear two comics telling blue jokes to a room that loved every one of them.

"At least we get to play," Lupe said, rotating her wrists to warm them up.

Ling was still a little rattled from her cryptic dream walk. What had Will meant by "change"? Change what? One thing she wished she could change was Evie's crazy decision to go to Nebraska. It made her sore that, in typical fashion, Evie had made a choice without considering its effect on anybody else. She was selfish. And yet...

And yet, her rash decision had allowed Ling this time on the road with Alma. In her own selfish way, Ling was greedy for it. And for the hope that she might get Alma to change her mind about the two of them. Ling thought Alma looked so beautiful in her silver sequined dress with the fringed hem, a thick rhinestone headband resting across her forehead just like royalty. She ached to hold her hand, to sit together somewhere, just the two of them. She couldn't bear the idea that they might never sit side by side like that ever again.

The Harlem Haymakers watched from the wings as the Thompson Brothers finished a jaw-dropping tap-dance number that saw them hopping from table to table, never once losing a single syncopated step. The crowd roared their approval, stomped the floor for more.

"Lord, we have to follow *that*?" Alma said and bit her lip.

"You'll be swell," Ling said.

"You really think so?" Alma asked.

"No. I only said that so you'd be quiet," Ling teased. Teasing was good. It was something people did to show their affection, she'd heard. But what if Alma didn't think it was funny?

"That was a joke," Ling said, cheeks burning.

"I do know a joke when I hear one," Alma said, and Ling couldn't tell if she'd liked it or not. "Oh, golly Moses! I completely forgot—I need a name!"

"You have a name—Alma LaVoy," Ling said.

"A stage name. Something like Queen of the Blues."

"Mamie Smith is Queen of the Blues," Babe whispered as she fit a new reed into her saxophone.

"See what I mean? All the good names are taken!"

"You could be the Empress," Emmaline said.

"You could be Miss High-Hat," Lupe said with a roll of her eyes. "That's accurate."

"I am not going to dignify that with a response, *Guadalupe*," Alma sniffed.

Everybody threw out names then, some dirty, most silly, none of them right. After an encore, the Thompson Brothers were taking their last bows. It was almost time.

"What about the Countess?" Jericho offered.

Lupe reared back slightly and put a hand to her chest in mock-surprise. "He speaks."

"Don't be mean, Lupe," Alma chided.

"Who's being mean? I like the sound of his voice very much."

"The Countess," Alma said, mulling it over. "I like it. It's high-class. The Countess is mysterious." Alma threw a hand across her forehead like a silent film star. "She is the blues. She is . . ."

"Talking about herself in the third person," Jericho said, making Alma giggle and Ling jealous. She wanted to be the one to make Alma laugh.

"Do you have a name for *me*, Big Six?" Lupe brushed up near Jericho and poked at him playfully with one of her drumsticks.

"Mm-hmm," Jericho said.

"Well, what is it?"

"Lupe," Jericho said. "Have a good show. I'll be in the back if you need me."

Lupe fanned herself. "Whoo!"

Alma shook her head. "Don't start, Lupe. You remember Billy?"

"And Marvin. And José," Babe said, rolling her eyes.

"Charlie. Jenks. Salvatore," Eloise added.

"Jealous?" Lupe said, fluttering her long lashes.

"Save that eyelash batting for the paying customers," Alma said. "We're on."

The Harlem Haymakers marched onstage single file and took their seats.

"Ladies and gentlemen, what a treat we have for you tonight. An all-lady orchestra, all the way from New York City! And I hear they play almost as good as they look," the emcee said and laughed. The audience laughed, too. Ling could see that Alma was irritated. Behind the drum kit, Lupe began to play a beat, drowning out the emcee, who didn't care to be so rudely dismissed.

"Let a man finish!" he barked into the microphone, making it squeal with noise.

"I try, but they never do," Lupe said, giving herself a rim shot. The women in the barn-turned-nightclub cheered at this, and there was nothing for him to do but turn it over to Alma.

"Please welcome the Harlem Haymakers, led by Miss . . . uh . . ." He looked over to Alma.

"The Countess!" Alma said, curtsying. Ling felt nervous for all of them. She'd freeze in the glare of all those lights.

But Alma shone. "Good evening to you all. We are the Harlem Haymakers, so I hope you're ready to make some noise out there tonight! This is a song we brought all the way from New York City. It's called 'Sweet-Talk Me, Daddy, Like You Used to Do.' Let it fly, ladies!"

The Harlem Haymakers launched into a swinging jazz number. They were good. *Really* good. Ling enjoyed seeing the doubt on people's faces turn to surprise, followed by delight. Alma sold it for all she was worth, and when she broke into her dance, she was every bit as talented as the Thompson Brothers, who watched her from the back of the club, shouting, "Whoo! Get hot! Stomp it, Countess!"

Ling had lived her whole life in the roughly six blocks of Chinatown. She loved those streets and the people on them. But being here in the Centurion with Sally Mae and Sadie's trumpets blowing loud and Lupe grinning while she kept wild time, with Alma's shoes tapping out a beat on the rough-hewn wood stage and the whole barn shaking from unrestrained joy, made Ling feel alive in new ways. There was a whole world out there she didn't know about. It was high time she did.

But first, she and the Diviners would have to save it.

✳

Folks at the Centurion told them about a boardinghouse out on an old farm road that welcomed TOBA performers, and once they'd secured lodgings, with the girls taking up two rooms and Doc and Jericho taking up another, everybody stumbled toward bed, half-dead but still vibrating from the night's success.

"Good night, Farm Boy," Lupe said and blew Jericho a kiss.

"Good night," Jericho said, blushing.

In his room, he dropped to the floor and did one hundred push-ups without stopping.

"Damn. You're not even breathing heavy, brother," Doc said. "You some kind of super man?"

"I eat my spinach," Jericho said, shaking out his arms. His body felt good. Strong.

"Good thing. There's a lot of road to cover between here and—Where'd you say you and your *cousin* were headed?"

"Nebraska. To see our sick aunt," Jericho repeated.

"Sick aunt. Riiiight," Doc said. He shook his head as he lowered it to his pillow.

Jericho lay in his own bed and stared at the ceiling. He wondered if the others had made it out of New York okay. If they'd found one another and were now on their way to Bountiful. He wondered about Evie. If she missed him. If she was thinking about him the way he was about her. She'd been pretty insistent on rescuing Sam. After what Jericho had told Evie about Marlowe's operation, he figured she'd head straight to Hopeful Harbor, and that had him worried. If Sam *was* there, that meant Shadow Men. The thought of those Shadow Men capturing Evie and Marlowe attaching her to the Eye was unbearable to him. In his memory, he saw Anna Provenza strapped into the machine as she peered into some other dimension, moving from ecstasy to terror. He heard her desperate final screams as the Eye pulled the life from her.

He was getting riled up, and his serum-enhanced body began to respond with a faster heartbeat and heightened senses. He could hear the girls in the next room—*"Anyone seen my Madame Walker's Tetter Salve?" "Here. Just use mine."* He could sense their heartbeats somehow. It frightened him. He felt trapped in his own body. He needed to get rid of some of this wildness inside. Jericho bolted out of bed, down the stairs, and outside, breathing in lungfuls of cool, crisp air. And then he was running off toward the wooded field out back. Under the huff of his own breath, Jericho could hear everything hiding in the night. The slithering of small creatures in the brittle grass. The pecking of birds in the nest. The groaning of spring-hungry trees as their new growth stretched against the confines of the chilly April ground. It was all beautiful to him. His body began to calm. He felt at one with the creatures and the trees and the night.

Light poured through the gaps in the trees. Jericho went a little farther in and saw that there was a log cabin perched on a small bit of hill. The cabin's two windows glowed yellow, like the eyes of a wolf. Smoke poured from an old stone chimney. It had a strange odor. A garter snake slithered across Jericho's bare foot, startling him as it ribboned past into the brush. Jericho drew closer. Against the side of the house, rabbit skins hung from nails to dry. The skins still had the heads attached. The dead eyes seemed to follow Jericho.

Jericho couldn't see into the windows. The glow was far too strong.

There was an ax stuck into a tree stump, and a cauldron that he knew from his farm days was used to make lye soap like the kind his mother would sell at market. Jericho remembered accompanying his mother and father a few times in the back of their horse-drawn wagon as they made the journey from their farm in Pennsylvania Dutch Country to Philadelphia. How Jericho had gawked at the buildings and the people in their fine city clothes. How happy he was to return to the farm again.

The cabin door creaked open slowly, but no one emerged. It was as if the cabin were issuing an invitation. Jericho edged closer. Through the narrow opening, he could make out a hearth and the last of a fire burning there. He should go back to the boardinghouse. He should not be out here alone in unknown woods. But he had to know. His acute hearing picked up the splintering of the twigs as the fire consumed them for fuel. The scraping of branches against the windows. And a slurping, like a hungry man finishing his soup.

Jericho stretched out his hand and pressed the door back. His mind took in the room bit by bit: Braided rug. Tall chair, tattered covering. Beside the chair, a man crouched, curved back to the door. He was eating something from the floor. Jericho took a step forward. Behind the chair. Near the cabin wall. The body of a deer, still twitching. Its chest torn open. Flesh peeled back. The man. The man dipping his hands into the cavity. Hands coated in wine-dark blood. Hands pulling up entrails like weeds. The man stopped. Turned his head slowly to face Jericho. His eyes were black as endless night.

"Poor boy," he said and smiled, and that was when Jericho felt the room swim. He feared that he would faint at the sight of that bloodied mouth. The animal flesh hanging from pointed teeth, draped across the fouled chin.

"Poor boy," the man said again, in a voice thick with blood. "With no home to call your own. Orphaned again. Who will ever want you?"

If Jericho had been able to speak, he might have said, *Stop.*

The man hopped forward on his haunches. "He is coming. It is his time now."

He straightened and Jericho saw that he was tall and muscular, with veiny arms. Blood spilled from his sharp mouth and down the front of his bare chest. "He will come and this nation will tremble and welcome him like a god!" The man's laugh burbled up from deep in his chest, like some swallowed animal desperate to get out. On the floor, the deer's legs twitched.

"Come. I will give you a home, poor boy. I will tear the flesh from your bones and break those between my teeth."

The man swiped at Jericho with filthy hands.

Jericho ducked from his grasp. He stumbled backward out of the cabin. And then he turned and ran faster than he ever thought possible into the woods. A fog had come up, turning the woods unfamiliar. Where was the boardinghouse? Where was he? Behind him, the night was alive with every sound imaginable. Birds screamed and lifted from their nests with a great flapping of wings. It hit his ears like a deafening punch. He slipped, fell, and staggered into a run once more.

"Poor boy! Poor boy! Poor boy!" The sound bounced from tree to tree. Jericho could no longer tell if it was only one voice or many. "Poor boy!"

Someone waited at the edge of the foggy woods. The serum punched through Jericho's veins. If it came to it, he could throw a right hook. His arms ached to do it. The waiting man wore a soldier's uniform. Jericho slowed with relief. The man turned. Jericho stopped, unable to take another step.

"Hey, kid. How've you been?" Sergeant Leonard said. His face was death-mask white. Bruised shadows showed beneath his deep-set eyes.

"You're dead," Jericho whispered.

"I'm sorry about what I made you do. I never shoulda made you do it," Sergeant Leonard said.

Jericho sank to his knees. "You're not here. I'm dreaming." Jericho made a fist over and over.

The night sounds had nearly found them.

Sergeant Leonard parted the soupy mist like a curtain. Beyond it was the road, and next to it, the boardinghouse. He was almost there.

"Don't wander around in the woods, okay, Jericho?"

"You're not here," Jericho croaked. Fist. Fist. Fist. Fist.

Sergeant Leonard's eyes were immeasurably sad. "Sorry, kid. It's about to get rough," he said and disappeared into the screeching night.

IF THAT ISN'T MAGIC

The next morning, the circus readied to move out of Cooperstown. Elephants and horses pulled the beautifully painted circus wagons up a ramp and onto the special railcars. The acrobats, wire walkers, animal act trainers, sideshow performers, and clowns alike scurried aboard with their traveling trunks, filled with everything they'd need on their tour of the country—greasepaint, makeup, costumes, shoes, and props. To Evie, it was as if a small city were being transported on the spine of a lumbering beast that floated from town to town.

"All aboard that's coming aboard," Zarilda called.

"You ready, Baby Vamp?" Sam said, sneaking a kiss from Evie.

"Do I have a choice?"

"Not really. Come on." Sam helped Evie onto the train and led her down the corridor through the performers getting themselves situated. He escorted her into an empty compartment and shut the door. Then he pulled her into his arms and buried his face in her hair.

"Missed you last night," he murmured, and kissed a trail down Evie's neck to her collarbone. When her eyes fluttered open, he smiled mischievously at her. "I admit, I was kinda hoping for a little midnight visit."

"I was dead to the world last night," Evie said.

Sam's wolfish grin disappeared. "Don't say that."

"Just an expression."

"Kinehora, poo, poo, poo," Sam said and spit.

Evie raised an eyebrow. "Why did you do that?"

"Keeping away the evil eye," Sam explained.

Evie stroked a hand down Sam's cheek. "You look beat, Sam. Are you sure you're copacetic?" She'd been worried about him since his trials with the Eye. There were definitely things he wasn't telling her.

"Sure," Sam said. But he wasn't convincing.

The Diviners sat in their train compartment watching the countryside roll by. They'd wave back to the people who'd wandered down to the tracks, excited to see the circus train zooming past. It *was* exciting, and Evie wished they could enjoy it without having to worry about Shadow Men or Jake Marlowe's machine or facing ghosts or whatever the King of Crows was up to now.

"Say, Isaiah, you want to try to talk to Sarah Beth, see if she can tell us anything more?" Theta asked once they'd had their breakfast and settled in for the ride.

"Okay," Isaiah said. He shut his eyes and tried to let himself relax. But he felt funny with the others watching him. "Sarah Beth," he said. "Sarah Beth, it's me, Isaiah. Can you hear me?" He waited, but when nothing came, he shook his head. "Sometimes I gotta have something that belongs to the person. Or I gotta be touching 'em, like when I held Sister Walker's hand." He frowned. "Is Sister gonna be okay?"

"We're gonna make sure she is," Sam said.

"Did she really kill the professor?"

"Naw. 'Course not. That's bunk," Sam promised.

"You sure going to Bountiful's the right decision?" Theta asked once Isaiah had gotten up to wander the train. "We haven't even heard from this girl since that first time."

"I just hope the Shadow Men haven't gotten to her. If Jake Marlowe finds out she knows how to stop the King of Crows, he's gonna want her," Sam said.

Evie watched the day brightening over the sweet green hills. "I just hope we can get there in time."

The train crossed the state line into Pennsylvania. The conductor tooted the whistle as the circus's first stop came into view. Like turning the crank on a well-oiled machine, the performers hurried into their costumes while the roustabouts began unloading. Everything was taken from the trains and put onto the wagons for the trip through town. It was quite something to see the caravan parade down Main Street. First came six dapple-gray horses in plumed harnesses pulling a bandwagon of drum, banjo, and trumpet players, and in the wagon behind that one, an organist playing a rousing tune on the calliope. Stilt-walkers lumbered down the street, towering over the spectators lining the roadway. Acrobats followed in their wake, turning somersaults that defied gravity. Equestriennes in jeweled headdresses waved from the backs of cantering show horses whose manes had been braided with colorful ribbons. From behind bars, the lions and tiger roared at the crowds, pacing the limited length of their cages. The elephants' thudding footsteps sent up clouds of road dust and made the fringe on their red satin capes sway to and fro. On a practiced cue from Giacomo, the elephants lifted their mighty trunks and let loose a trumpeting bellow that thrilled the children watching from the sidelines. The throngs of spectators roared their own approval in return and waved their tiny American flags.

"Doc" Hamilton spoke through a megaphone from the back of his Traveling Medicine Show: "Folks, there is absolutely no charge for this show—it is that important! You must try the curative powers of this patented vitamin vitality tonic, guaranteed to smooth your skin, grow you a full head of hair, put some pep in your step, and keep you forever young. You owe it to your health! Just a sip of this elixir will fix what ails you!"

In the sideshow wagon, Johnny the Wolf Boy howled and beat his chest while Arnold flexed his muscles, showing off his many tattoos. Bella the Strong Man lifted Polly onto his right shoulder so she could wave to the crowds with one hand while stroking her beard with the other. Isaiah walked beside Billy, the goat, grinning at his good fortune. Sam performed several impressive backflips in a row. He looked back, pleased with himself, and winked at Evie, and she laughed in delight.

The clowns were up next. With three others, Evie jumped from their wagon and ran up to the children, who were squirming for a view of the parade. She pulled a long line of colorful scarves from up her sleeve and used it to skip rope, pretending to stumble. The children laughed, and Evie thought it was a wonderful sound. It was a far cry from the glamour she'd enjoyed as the Sweetheart Seer, and, if she were honest, she would hate for anybody to know how far she'd fallen, from radio star to traveling circus clown, but Zarilda was saving their lives and getting them closer to Bountiful. Besides, being a clown was still attention-getting, and Evie loved few things more than that.

Decked out as Miss Liberty, Theta kept pace with Isaiah as they walked side by side, waving to the crowds. Isaiah's grin was one hundred percent real—he was clearly having the time of his life. Theta's was pasted on. She couldn't help looking out into those crowds of people and wondering if anybody recognized them. Was the magic of the circus enough to hide them, or was there somebody out there right now, rushing off to make a telephone call to the authorities? Were there Shadow Men watching from under the brims of their gray hats, just waiting for nightfall and a chance to pounce? Could Roy be here somehow?

Theta's hands heated up beneath her white satin gloves.

"Isn't this the berries?" Isaiah said, feeding a treat to Billy from the flat of his palm. The view ahead was an agitated frenzy of people and flags and color.

"Yeah. The cat's pajamas," Theta answered and kept waving.

※

Once they'd reached the fairgrounds, the roustabouts got to work, pounding stakes into the ground, spreading out the canvas tents and ropes. Up went the Big Top, the ticket booth, the sideshow tents and medicine wagon, the nickelodeon stargazer—"Peer into the Infinite and See Your Fate!" Enterprising local folks set up the many food stalls that bordered the long road into the circus grounds. It was a symphony of intoxicating smells—popcorn and caramel apples, cotton candy and fried chicken to make the mouth water. People had lined up ten deep, money in hand and eyes wide, eager for every bit of the culinary splendor. Out by itself on the edge of the fairgrounds was Zarilda's fortune-telling wagon. "I like to give it that air of mystery so's when folks come in, they feel like they're entering another world," she explained with a wink.

Evie gagged as she and Sam passed the elephants' cage, where the boys were busy mucking out mounds of manure. "When you imagine the glamour of the circus, you never think about the potency of the elephant dung."

Sam shrugged. "You get accustomed to the smell."

Evie waved her hand in front of her nose. "I never want to get accustomed to this smell. If I do, my life has taken a terrible turn."

"You got me, didn't ya? Couldn't'a gone too wrong," Sam said and kissed her.

Evie laughed. "Now you've got greasepaint on your mouth."

"I've had worse."

"Wish I'd known that before I kissed you."

❋

People streamed into the fairgrounds by the thousands with their Cracker Jack and souvenir flags and programs, and Evie started to believe that Zarilda's sign about marvels and miracles wasn't just a line. It was true that everybody was looking for just a little bit of magic to believe in. So why was it so hard to believe in Diviners?

In the Big Top, Evie felt just as wowed by the circus as did the paying customers. She and Isaiah watched as the ringmaster, Mr. Sarkassian, held up a succession of rings and trained dogs jumped through them, then balanced on their hind legs like ballerinas. Between acts, Theta came out and danced the Charleston and some soft-shoe with a couple of other dancers, and even though it wasn't the Follies stage, Theta still shone brightly. When it was time for the trapeze, Evie held her breath as Hasan swung by his knees and caught Flora, the elegant trapeze artist who just happened to have the mouth of a longshoreman. On the ride out from Cooperstown, Evie had learned a lot of new words from Flora that she could never say in polite company. The tumblers were on next. Sam executed three flips in a row before locking hands with Hasan and leaping into a handstand position above the other man's shoulders. Evie was amazed by his surefootedness and agility. Sam was sensitive about being small, she knew, but here, that was to his advantage.

She looked out into the stands at the faces. They all wore the same expression of awe. But Evie knew from reading objects that some of those people were sad. Or they felt that nothing good would ever happen again. They worried about their children, or about the cost of heating the house. They tried not to think about what that cough they couldn't get rid of meant, if it meant anything at all. Some of them were in love with people they could never have. Some of them had to hide who they really were from the people who were supposed to love them the most. But you wouldn't know that just from watching them now, or from passing them on the fairgrounds. Once you did know it, though, you saw them differently. No longer as separate from you. Some of them had big dreams, and these were the people Evie felt the greatest kinship with—those, and the ones who were lonesome for something they couldn't quite put their fingers on. Something just out of reach that kept them restless and a little scared that they would always feel this way.

The people watched the circus and Evie watched the people. *Can't you see?* she thought. *You* are *the whole circus.*

Johnny rushed over to Evie. "Zarilda sent me! She said to get a wiggle on."

"Here goes nothing," Evie said, securing her ratty clown hat on her red wig.

A line of eager hopefuls had formed outside Zarilda's fortune-telling wagon. "Step right up, folks! Don't be shy. What you desire to know will be known. The spirits will see to it!" Zarilda said. She looked the part for sure, in her emerald-green satin dress topped by a flowing flower-print silk coat of purple and gold, a rhinestone headband sitting pretty on top of her red hair. She was a carnival queen.

Evie went inside Zarilda's wagon. "You ready for our act?" Zarilda asked Evie as she set up her table with tarot cards and a crystal ball that cast prisms around the wagon.

"What do you do with that?" Evie asked.

"Talk to the spirits, of course."

"You can communicate with the dead?"

"Mm-hmm. Sometimes, yes. I ain't sayin' I'm a real Diviner. I'm what you might call more of an Interpreter. But I do all right. And what I don't know I fake."

"Well, how do you do it?" Evie pressed.

"Darlin', I'd love to talk about the dead all day long, but we got a show to do, and paying customers. You know what you need to do?"

Evie nodded. "I clown around with somebody's scarf or hat, get a read, then come back and feed you the information."

"That's the ticket!"

Outside, Evie waddled up to a man and offered her paper flower for him to sniff. While he did, she stole his hat and placed it on her wigged head. It was tricky having to grab information so quickly, but she didn't have much choice. She pressed into the hatband. Bingo! The man's name was Donald. He was a schoolteacher from Erie, and he was hoping to buy a small house for his family back home on Poplar Street. Evie returned the hat and helped herself to a few more trinkets—a glove, another hat, an umbrella—all of them carrying memories and emotions and wants. At last, Evie threaded a woman's scarf around her neck and pranced about like royalty, making everyone laugh. The woman's name was Emily, and she was lonely. Evie blushed to know this. It felt wrong. Emily had come to the circus as a last outing. She planned to drink poison when she got home.

Evie hurried back to Zarilda. "You have to stop the woman in the scarf. She plans to kill herself."

"What on earth!"

"Tell her...tell her not to do it. Tell her there's so much to live for."

Evie waited nervously for an hour for Zarilda to finish her fortune-telling.

"Well?" she asked when Zarilda emerged for a cigarette.

"You were right, kid. It all came pouring out of her. But when she left my wagon, she seemed lighter. I read her palm."

"I didn't know you could read palms."

Zarilda wiggled her hand and shrugged. "Let's say I *interpret* palms. Anyhow, I told her that soon her luck would change, and something new and exciting would come into her life."

"Is that true?"

"It is if you believe it's true."

Evie frowned and Zarilda lit a cigarette. "Oh, look, kid, who can say where hope comes from, huh? Maybe it's a fella who tells you your dress is pretty. Maybe it's a picture show you see on a Saturday afternoon. Or the first flower you spy coming up, letting you know there's spring right around the corner if you just hold on. And sometimes, it might just be a coupla misfit gals working the carny, pulling the con but for good. Folks can think this"—she waved her plump hand with a flourish—"is all smoke and mirrors, but today we gave a woman hope who didn't have but a lick of it left. Shootfire if that isn't magic."

✳

Sam wiped the resin from his hands and went out to look for Evie.

He passed by the stargazer tent. The contraption was really just a glorified kaleidoscope. Sam had always loved those. The line was short and he had a nickel. "What the hell," he said and waited his turn.

He stepped up onto the orange crate, feeling a little embarrassed to need it, wishing he were taller, and dropped his nickel into the slot. He draped the curtain over his head and peered into the viewing holes. The mechanism clicked. Stars appeared, rotating like clockworks across a night sky. Sam concentrated on making out the various constellations. The stargazer picked up speed. Faster and faster still. Sam had the sensation of zooming into that starry sky, of being pulled deeper into space, of not being able to stop his velocity. His body was melting away. He was losing himself, becoming porous. Tears stung at his eyes but he could not blink, could not look away from all that space, so much like Marlowe's Eye. Something was in there with him. He could sense its presence. Whispers whizzed past on comet tails. *You will forget. The living always do.* Stars flattened into points of light, whooshed past like bullets. *This land is haunted. All haunted. All are haunted.* A scream was building inside Sam, but so was the pressure. It trapped his scream inside him. His mother's voice: *Do not lose yourself to what you see.* The thing in there with him was closing in. It was evil. He could feel it. It wanted him. Wanted him with a hunger that frightened Sam. The voices grew louder. *We see you.* He felt it all around him, nearly touching. He could not let it catch him. *Don't see me, don't see me, don't see me,* Sam thought, just as the flattening stars on the horizon exploded into a blinding flash of white. A giant mushroom-fat cloud burst up, and everything burned around the edges of the film. Sam gasped and reeled back, rubbing his eyes.

"You okay, mister?" The man behind him in line steadied Sam as he stumbled.

Sam blinked and saw light. He didn't answer. He staggered out of the stargazer tent, still blinking. On the other side of the Big Top, he thought he saw the King of Crows, his feathered coat fluttering in the wind, and he was laughing. Sam wiped at his streaming eyes. When he looked again, it was only the ringmaster, Mr. Sarkassian, in his top hat and tails, smoking a quick cigarette before heading back inside the Big Top. A minute later, the man who'd steadied Sam came out of the stargazer tent. Sam approached him. "Say, mister—what did you see when you looked into that thing?"

The man smirked. "Just a bunch of stars. Waste of a nickel, you ask me." Sam felt wrong. The encounter had slithered under his skin, and he felt that he would infect anybody he touched. Isaiah was running toward him, full of excitement. Sam didn't want the kid to see him like this.

"Sam! Hey, Sam! I saw the poodle roll the ball all the way across the ring, and then! Then Billy, that's the goat, he jumped over three rings in a row, and then—"

"That's swell, kid. Go see the lions. They're the cat's pajamas, too," Sam said, patting Isaiah's back and brushing past, leaving the kid outside the stargazer tent.

Isaiah was hurt. He'd been excited to share his news, and here Sam had gone and treated him like he was just some kid! The older ones never took him seriously. He was almost eleven! Back home, there were kids his age who were numbers runners and newsies. Why, some of 'em even *smoked*. He was tired of being treated like a baby.

If he could control his power more, then they'd have to see him as being just as good as they were. But his visions just seemed to show up whenever they wanted to. How did you call down a vision? How did you make it pay attention to you?

Sarah Beth was a seer, like him. Maybe she would know.

Isaiah made his way through the bustling circus. Behind a tent, two clowns practiced a juggling trick. Isaiah peeked into the sideshow wagon and caught a glimpse of Johnny in his cage, teeth bared as he howled at an imaginary moon, making a lady scream. Isaiah needed a place where he could be alone. He snuck into the acrobats' changing tent and hid behind a trunk.

"Sarah Beth?" Isaiah whispered. He shut his eyes and tried to picture her. *Sarah Beth, can you hear me? Sarah Beth… Sarah Beth…*

A tingle traveled from his neck to his arms, which stiffened, then relaxed. It felt good, as if he were floating in a warm bath. All he saw was darkness. That part scared him a bit. He didn't like the idea that there could so much nothing. But then veins of blue light spasmed in the dark, and tiny clouds of jittery, colored light. It reminded Isaiah of shutting his eyes after bright sun and still seeing that light on the backs of his eyelids. Something was coming toward him within the dark. The girl!

"Sarah Beth! I was tryna find you and I did it! I did it!"

"That's 'cause our powers work real good together." Sarah Beth smiled. Her teeth were small for her mouth, and Isaiah felt sorry that she didn't have much of a smile.

"Does that mean our powers will get stronger?"

Sarah Beth nodded vigorously. "Once you get to Bountiful. We'll work on 'em all the time. Why, we'll be so strong everybody will be amazed!"

This thrilled Isaiah. He imagined the surprise on Memphis's face when he showed him what he could do—whatever that was. He imagined his big brother saying something like, *Isaiah, today you become a man.* Already, he liked that Sarah Beth thought of the two of them as a team. It would be like when the Yankees came from behind and wowed everybody.

"At least they're not afraid of you. My mama and daddy are afraid of me," Sarah Beth said. Isaiah thought that was really sad, but he couldn't tell if Sarah Beth felt sad or mad about it.

"Why?"

"They don't understand my gifts. They don't like it none, either. I'm not…normal. Like other girls." Now Sarah Beth *did* seem sad to Isaiah. He wished he knew what to say to make her not be so sad.

"Do you really know how to stop the King of Crows?"

She nodded. "I think so. I can't do it by myself, though."

"Can you tell me?"

"When you get to Bountiful. It needs to be all of us. He'll try to keep us apart so we can't get strong and defeat him. You know what he did to Conor."

Isaiah did know. Conor was dead, and it was the King's army that did it.

"Don't worry, Isaiah," the girl said.

"I'm not."

"Yes, you are. I can tell. Where are you? Why aren't you here?"

"We're traveling with the circus," Isaiah said.

"The circus?"

"Uh-huh. They're helping us get to Bountiful."

"Oh. I'll bet the circus is something. I've always wanted to see it, but Mama says we can't spare the time away from the farm. And she's worried it'll be too much excitement and I'll have a fit. I never get to go anywhere," Sarah Beth said, sounding both mad and sad again.

"I'll bring you a souvenir!" Isaiah said. He was excited that he'd have something to tell her about that was special.

Sarah Beth's whole face lit up then. "Well, that's real nice, Isaiah. Real nice. It'll sure be good to have a friend. You will be my friend, won't you, Isaiah?"

"I will," he said.

She put out her hand, palm up, and Isaiah understood that she wanted to touch their hands together. Softly, he touched his skin to hers. She gasped, and her eyes rolled back in their sockets just like Memphis said Isaiah's did during a fit. And then Isaiah felt like somebody was squeezing him from all sides, like a tube of toothpaste. He saw so many things, coming hard and fast: A golden machine surrounded by the rays of the sun. Soldiers falling from the sky. The King of Crows opening his coat with the too-bright lining. And Isaiah wanted to see what was there for him. What was waiting inside that coat. But then he was somewhere else. Dust-covered towns still as death. Bone-white bodies glinting in dust. The sharp curve of teeth. Ghosts on the road. An army of hungry dead as far as Isaiah could see, and they were running.

Sarah Beth's blank face, looking at him. "Are you my friend?"

The sound of water. Water all around. Rising, rising, pulling him down…

When Isaiah came to in the acrobats' wagon, he was sweated wet. But he was okay, too. Not woozy the way he sometimes was after a vision. He had a new friend, and together they were going to do great things. They would stop the King of Crows.

He couldn't wait to get to Bountiful.

FLOOD

"This is it! Greenville, Mississippi," Henry said with relief.

"Remember what I told you now," Bill warned.

"Mmm," Memphis said, committing to nothing. He'd already had enough of the South. He wished he were back in Harlem, at the 135th Street Library, talking to Mrs. Andrews, his favorite librarian, or listening to the rumble of the elevated train running the length of Eighth Avenue. The lack of city noise here unnerved Memphis, especially after his bizarre dream on the train. All those insects and nature sounds. He needed the hustle and clamor, the streetside jazz of New York.

"I hope there's something to eat in Greenville," Henry said, rubbing his stomach, which growled loudly.

"Then walk faster," Bill said.

When they reached Greenville, the town was frantic with activity. Crowds swarmed the platform of the train depot. Big men heaped over-burdened suitcases and household belongings—mattresses, linens, crates of china—onto trucks. At the banks of the swollen river, other men rolled more of those belongings onto waiting steamers and boats of all kinds. They'd staked their hopes on catching a train heading west out of Green-ville. But the sight of that packed depot didn't fill Henry with hope.

"Pardon me, ma'am," Henry asked a woman in her Sunday best holding the hands of two well-dressed children. "When's the next train headed north?

"There are none. This is the last one out of Greenville, and it's headed to Vicksburg," the woman answered.

"The last one for how long?" Henry looked down the platform at the sea of anxious people waiting to board.

"Who can say? The river's already busted clean through at Cairo, and they say Greenville might be next. The water's rising up near Mounds Land-ing. If that goes, we'll flood. Plenty of folks say it'll be all right. They're stay-ing put. But, young man, if you don't already have a ticket for this train, you won't be getting out. You'll have to take your chances here."

"Looks like we're stuck here for a while," Henry reported to Memphis and Bill.

"Hey, you. Y'all need to be working." A National Guardsman with a rifle on his back pointed at Memphis and Bill. "What're you standing around for? Mr. Percy said every man should be working on the levee. Get over there and start hauling those sandbags," he ordered and motioned with his gun. "Go on, now."

Memphis balled his fists. Bill whispered: "We're wanted men. Remember?" Bill hoisted one of the heavy burlap sacks on his shoulder with a grunt and fell into the line of other men wading through the current to shore up the spots that had been weakened by the deluge. With a grunt, Memphis hoisted his own, struggling under the strain of it. It had to weigh fifty pounds, easy. When Henry reached for one, the Guardsman stopped him. "That's all right, sir. You don't have to do it."

Henry glared. He wanted to punch this man. "If it's all the same, I'll work beside my friends."

He reached down again to lift the sandbag, but he was skinny. His legs buckled from the weight of it.

"Hold it like this. Use your knees," a tall man in a brown felt hat said. The man was sturdy, with broad shoulders and deep, soulful brown eyes that put Henry in mind of the great actor Paul Robeson. He helped Henry shoulder the weight properly.

"Thank you," Henry said in a pinched voice. He staggered after the man through the ankle-deep water to the levee.

"Well. That oughta do it," Henry said, securing the bag in place.

The man who'd been so kind gave him a baleful look. "We're just getting started. My name's Nate Timmons."

"Henry…Smith," Henry lied. He put out his hand, and after a nervous second, Nate gave it a quick shake.

"Nice to meet you, Mr. Smith. You don't mind my asking, why're you doing this? You could get on a train or a steamboat."

"Can you, Mr. Timmons?"

"Nope. They won't let us go nowhere."

"Then I'm not going, either."

Nate regarded Henry curiously, as a man he didn't quite know how to classify just yet. "Well, Mr. Smith, I surely hope you know how to swim if it comes to it," Nate said.

"You really think the flood's gonna come?" Henry asked.

"I surely hope not. But there's no telling," Nate said.

All afternoon, Memphis, Henry, and Bill worked to shore up the weak spots along the protective levee. It was hard work filling the burlap sacks with pounds of sand and then carrying those sandbags, pushing them into place. On the other side of that wall, the mighty Mississippi groaned and shoved its weight at their work. Henry had grown up in New Orleans. He knew about floods that threatened Plaquemines Parish and other low-lying areas, but he'd never seen the Mississippi so high, so angry.

"Haven't seen you before," Nate Timmons said to Memphis and Bill as they delivered another back-bending load. "Nate Timmons."

"I'm Bill Johnson. And this here's my cousin, Floyd," he said, nodding at Memphis. "And this is . . ."

"Henry *Smith*," Henry said pointedly. "We've already met."

"Real nice to meet you," Nate said. "You work for Mr. LeRoy?"

"Who?" Henry said, and Memphis flashed him a look that said *Don't give us away.*

"Senator LeRoy Percy? He owns most of this Delta. We all work for him. Hear tell, he and his son, Mr. Will, are the ones who won't let us evacuate."

"How come?" Memphis asked as he scooped more sand into a burlap potato sack.

"They're afraid we won't come back. They call Greenville the 'Queen of the Mississippi Delta.' Why, Mr. Al Jolson himself played the opera house. But the money comes from the fields we work. And all the money goes right back to landowners like Mr. LeRoy."

Memphis listened to Nate's story and felt his anger boiling up again. He wondered where Isaiah was just now. If he was safe or had found enough to eat. If somebody with a rifle was making him work on a levee. If that man with the gun had an itchy trigger finger. He felt that the worry would drive him mad.

"We're from New Orleans. Musicians," Henry said, answering Nate's question at last, and Memphis was glad Henry would provide the cover for them.

"Really, now? What do you play?"

"Piano," Henry said.

"Guitar," Bill said.

Memphis wiped his brow. "I just came along with my *cousin* to see the country."

Nate grunted as he shoved a sandbag into place. "Well. You don't mind my saying, you sure picked a sorry time to come to Greenville."

❊

At the end of the day, the men were exhausted and muddy.

"I'm so worn out I can't even feel my face," Henry said. "I still have one?"

"You still talking, ain't you?" Bill jibed.

Nate Timmons invited them to stay with his family in their two-room house out on the edge of town, near where Nate and several other families worked the land. They walked past the railroad tracks and into town to Washington Avenue and Main Street. Nate pointed out the various points of interest—a jewelry store and the printing shop where his friend Gibson worked. There was a grocery store, Joe Now New, run by a Chinese family, and Henry made a note to tell Ling about it later. Memphis's heart leaped when he saw a bookshop.

"That's Mr. Granville Carter's shop. First black man to own a bookshop in Greenville. Fine man. Over there's the hotel, and there's Main Street, which goes on for a good long while, all the way out to the white folks' cemetery."

"The cemetery," Memphis repeated with a look to Henry and Bill.

"Yes. Cemetery. Don't they bury folks where you're from?" Nate joked.

"Yes. But sometimes they don't stay buried," Henry said.

Bill coughed loudly in warning. But Nate just laughed. "Oh, that's a mighty good one! Here now. We're coming up on our neighborhood," Nate said.

To Henry, it felt as if they had crossed an imaginary border, from white spaces to black. From a certain freedom Henry took for granted to a newfound awareness of just how that freedom was assumed or refused.

The Timmons house was small—two rooms with a covered front porch and an outhouse 'round the back where they also kept chickens in a coop. Around a modest supper, Nate and Bessie told their guests about their life working the land in Greenville, about their desire to migrate north—"Got kin in Chicago and St. Louis. There's good work there."—and about their fears of a flood.

"Steamboats come yesterday, took the white women and children to

Vicksburg and other parts, to their people. No steamboats coming for us," Bessie said, nursing her baby girl, Loree. "Some folks got on a big old barge, but it was so full I was afraid it'd tip over out there in all that river. Good thing we got Remy's houseboat. Remy's a Cajun, came up from Louisiana and stayed."

Henry thought of Louis, his drawl peppered with bayou French. Every time he figured he'd healed that wound, something would come along to pop the stitches of it again. It was what David always feared, that Henry was still in love with another man—a ghost. David. Henry hadn't spoken to him since they'd made their big escape. Was David worried about him? Was he spending his nights down in the Village with other boys? That thought made Henry jealous, which surprised him. Henry hadn't felt jealous in a very long time. He usually kept things light, flitting from fella to fella, never committing to just one. But now, suddenly, he wanted David.

"…Anyhow, Remy's got a houseboat he built himself. He's real nice to our boys," Bessie finished, pulling Henry back to the present.

"Anyway, Mr. Will made it so's we couldn't leave. So now here we are. Got the National Guard and their rifles to keep us here, make us work for free."

"And if you refused?" Memphis asked.

"Kind of hard to argue with a rifle in your face," Nate said. "And if you're looking for the law to be on your side, well, the Greenville County Prosecutor's the Exalted Cyclops of the local Klan."

"Exalted Cyclops. Grand Wizard. Why do all of those Klan titles sound like terrible fantasy novels?" Henry said.

"Nate and I've been talking," Bessie said. "Flood or no flood, we're heading north. I've been taking in wash for Mrs. Stein and saving every cent for train tickets to St. Louis."

The Timmons boys, Tobias, age seven, and Moses, age ten, clamored for attention, and Memphis got a lump in his throat watching Nate and Bessie with their sons. It reminded him of evenings with his mother and father, when there was music and laughter in their house on 145th Street. Long before Memphis had ever heard of Project Buffalo or the King of Crows or Diviners. He longed for that time again, but you couldn't go backward. There was only forward.

"Mama, can we go play with Buddy?" Moses asked, and Memphis saw that there was an old yellow hound dog sniffing around the front porch.

"Go on," Nate said.

"Don't feed that dog my soup bone, hear?" Bessie called as the boys barreled out the front door. She shook her head. "Those boys dote on that dog like he was their third brother."

"You, uh, heard any unusual stories around here?" Memphis ventured once the boys were out of earshot. "Stories about strange goings-on?"

"What kind of strange?" Bessie asked, shifting her baby to the other breast.

"Ghosts," Henry said with a glance to Memphis.

Nate laughed. "This whole country's fulla ghosts. They don't bother us none." Nate wiped his mouth and fingers clean. "But why you want to know about that?"

"Oh, just something we heard. You know how people talk," Henry said and left it at that.

"I haven't heard about any ghosts. But my friend Lorena told me something funny just this afternoon," Bessie said. "She said she overheard Mr. LeRoy telling somebody about these Fitter Families tents been springing up everywhere, at every fair and carnival and circus across the state. Heard tell they're looking for people. *Special people.* Diviners."

"That a fact?" Bill said blandly, flicking a warning glance to Memphis and Henry.

"Heard Mr. LeRoy say that those Diviners are ruining the country. That they blew up that big exhibition in New York City, and there's a bounty on their heads now. Five thousand dollars for each one captured. It was in the papers just today."

"New York City. Might as well be on Mars," Nate said, grinning.

"Where'd y'all say you're from, again?" Bessie asked.

"N'awlins," Henry drawled.

"Oh, that's a fine place, I hear."

"Yes, ma'am. It surely is."

They slept on the porch. Bessie wanted to give them the boys' bed, but Memphis wouldn't hear of it. "We'll be fine out here, ma'am."

"I didn't expect the news to show up in a place like Greenville so soon,"

Henry said as he lay on the front porch and stared out at all those stars. "You think the Shadow Men will find us before we can get to Bountiful?"

"We'll move on in the morning, maybe see if we can catch us a train at Vicksburg," Bill said.

"Feels like we should've warned them about the dead," Memphis said, pulling the quilt up around his ears.

"We do that, we call attention to ourselves. I don't think we should say nothing at all 'bout ghosts," Bill scolded.

But Memphis wasn't so sure. Didn't they have a responsibility? People had to look out for one another, didn't they? Beyond rules and electric lights and tea dances, wasn't that, at the very bottom of it all, what made for civilization?

❋

In the cemetery at the far end of Main Street, the cool April breeze caressed the headstones. *Here lies. Here lies.*

Lies.

The dead rose up from the dirt like wisps of pale smoke. Restless. Hungry. Why were they here? Who had called them into service after so many weeks, months, years, a generation or more moldering below?

They walked for miles. To Mounds Landing, where the levee was weak.

Hungry, they bit into the sandbags.

❋

When Memphis fell asleep at last, he dreamed of the Hotsy Totsy. Gabe was there, still alive and playing his trumpet so sweet that a man from Okeh Records walked right up onstage and offered him a contract. But when Memphis looked again, it was the King of Crows, and Gabe was signing his name. Gabe fixed his burning, empty eyes on Memphis. "You're next, brother," he said. And then he raised his trumpet, blowing for all he was worth, holding that one sweet high note for so long that the whole club was going wild, stomping feet and shouting.

"Memphis! Get up! Now!" Bill jerked Memphis awake.

Memphis was awake, but Gabe was still holding that sweet high note.

Memphis rubbed sleep from his eyes, tried to focus. It was the fire whistle, not Gabe's horn. And the church bells were ringing, too.

"What time is it?"

"'Round three AM."

"What's going on?"

Nate Timmons burst onto the porch, panic in his eyes. "The levee broke up at Mounds Landing! The Mississippi's coming to drown us all. We got to get to high ground right away!"

One of Nate's friends raced along the dirt path in front of the houses giving a warning: "Pack up! Time to get to the levee! Get to the boats!"

"We got to get to the levee," Nate said.

Henry tied his shoes. "You ever been through a flood?"

"No," Memphis said.

Bill grunted. "He ain't from the South. You and me, we know."

"Boys! Take the family pictures down and put 'em on the boat. Be careful with 'em now!" Bessie Timmons ordered, the babbling baby perched on one hip. The boys scooped up the framed photographs of their grandparents and ran toward their adopted uncle Remy's waiting shantyboat.

"Mama! I can't find Buddy," Tobias cried. "I called and called but he won't come."

"We can't wait for no dog," Nate warned.

"We can't leave without him, Daddy," Moses pleaded.

"Buddy, Buddy!" Tobias yelled and burst into tears. "Buddy..."

"He'll be all right, boys. He's a smart dog. He'll swim to high ground. But we got to go."

Fat tears rolled down the boys' faces. They wiped them away angrily. Memphis's heart ached for them. How often had Isaiah cried like that?

"Hey. Hey, you boys want to hear a story? I know a good one. A real good one," Memphis said. "But it's a story I can only tell on the boat."

"Why?" Moses asked.

"'Cause that's the kind of story it is. Come on."

"I hear she's coming t'rough!" Remy called from his shantyboat. He was a stout man with black hair and twinkling blue eyes. "*Allons!*" Remy had built his boat by hand, Bessie had told them, with whatever scrap he could find—discarded timber, tin, chicken wire. It was a little floating house on a barge in the middle of Greenville's rapidly flooding streets. Rain hit the tin roof, making an awful racket. While Remy, Bill, and Nate steered the boat toward the high ground of the levee and Henry helped keep Bessie Timmons comfortable while she nursed her baby girl, Memphis spun a story to keep Tobias and Moses from missing their dog too much—and to keep them from realizing the danger.

"You like spooky stories?" Memphis asked.

"Yes," the boys said and sat forward. Memphis cast a wary eye toward the fast current eddying at street corners, buffeting the boat. He hoped Remy and Nate were as experienced as they seemed. Church bells clanged out a warning. People flocked into the streets, which were taking on water. Several were trying to save what they could, throwing everything into pillowcases they balanced on their backs. People were desperate for boats. A neighbor waved frantically. "It's my momma. She cain't walk too far," the man explained, and Nate and Henry pulled them both aboard.

There was a sudden crack, followed by a large roar, like a wounded giant going down hard.

"Water's coming!" Remy yelled.

Memphis and Henry felt true fear then, watching as the full force of the Mississippi rumbled into Greenville fast as a freight train. The river crashed against telephone poles, snapping wires and knocking them into the raging water. Hundred-year-old trees buckled and fainted like tired debutantes. Now the water was electrified and weaponized with debris.

"Remy, you steer straight!" Bessie called, clutching her baby in one arm and gathering her two boys with the other and holding fast. She kept herself tight but Memphis could sense just how scared she was, how scared they all were. The shantyboat hit a current and spun around.

"Hold on! Hold on!" Nate called, gripping the side of the boat.

They could hear the livestock screaming as the water rose up and swept them away. A mule cried out, front legs pedaling against an unbeatable tide. It went under and was lost to the churning flood. Desperate citizens climbed up onto their roofs to escape the wrath. Some of Greenville's elite, the ones who'd chosen to stay behind, had abandoned their fancy houses and plantations and sought shelter downtown in banks and the top floors of hotels.

The levee, when they made it, teemed with people streaming in from the flood. Carrying little more than the clothes on their backs, they trudged up the muddy embankment. Others arrived in boats carrying what little of their possessions they'd managed to salvage. Nate helped his wife down from the boat. She looked forlornly at the narrow eight-foot-wide earthen dam heaped for miles with refugees and what had been saved from the flood. Memphis, Bill, and Henry dragged pillowcases filled with the Timmonses' few precious memories from home and dropped them gently onto the cold, wet ground.

As dawn broke, they could see the damage. The devastation was shocking. It was as if they were adrift in a new sea, cut off from civilization. In the camp, babies cried, and some adults wept softly. Others stared, mute.

"Isaiah. Theta," Memphis said, his heart sinking.

"Yeah," Henry said, his heart sinking, too. "We're not getting to Bountiful anytime soon."

*

Within days, the Red Cross had arrived and set up A-frame tents. But there were no beds to be had yet, and inside those tents, people were sleeping on the cold, muddy ground.

"I hear there might be as many as five thousand folks here," Remy said.

On one side of the levee was the flooded Mississippi, drowning everything till all that could be seen were the tops of spindly trees, a few leaning telephone poles, and the pitch of roofs. On the other side of the levee, the National Guard patrolled, walking up and down the bank with their rifles at their shoulders.

"I hear they make us work on the levee and in the camp. Make us do the hard work," Nate said, following Memphis's gaze to the soldiers. "If we don't, they get the Red Cross to hold back our rations until we do. Can't win."

Anger coiled in Memphis's belly, and he vowed to himself that later, he would spit that howl up as a poem. He would document what was happening in Greenville, and he would figure out how to send that poem back to Woody at the *Daily News*. He would use his voice to give the people of the levee a voice.

By the end of the week, Memphis had sent five new poems to Woodhouse, five dispatches from an America not everybody got to see. But he was worried, too. What if the others had already reached Bountiful while Memphis and Henry and Bill were stuck in Greenville, Mississippi?

Refugees from all over the flooded Delta were coming to the eight-mile-long levee. It was a tent city as far as one could see. They'd gotten to work putting up lights and building a mess hall and a tent where relief workers handed out dry clothing. Barges with latrines floated beside the levee. And every day, supply boats arrived. It was the job of the colored refugees to unload the food, water, medical supplies, piping for plumbing, and clothing and haul it into the camp if they wanted their Red Cross rations. Anyone who refused was denied food and water or threatened with the end of a rifle. Worst of all, they were trapped; the National Guard issued the passes for leaving the camp. The powerful men of Greenville—politicians and the men who owned the land, the mills, the factories—had made certain that only white people were given those passes to come and go.

"They won't let us leave. They won't let us eat unless we work night and day till we can't work no more. And if we refuse, they might shoot us," Nate said, his jaw tight.

"They don't want us leaving Greenville. They don't want to lose their workers," a skinny man said.

"There's not gonna be a crop next year. Too much water. The river seen to that," Remy said.

"I just want to wipe the slate clean, start over up north," Nate said.

The skinny man shook his head. "They know it, too. That's why they won't give us no passes. Every time we try 'n' step up, they push us back down."

That evening, after the work was finished and a meager supper consumed, Bessie Timmons called excitedly, "Hey! Come look at this!"

Someone in the camp had managed to save an upright piano. It sat on a couple of two-by-fours. People crowded around, testing the keys. It wasn't in tune, but it wasn't badly out of tune, either. After all the kids had given it a go, Henry asked, "Say, do you mind if I play a little bit?"

A woman sorting through a sack of clothes obtained from the relief tent shrugged. "Belongs to everybody in the camp, far as I can tell."

With that, Henry sat down to play. He'd missed the piano, and music poured out of him. Everyone gathered 'round to hear. They had need of distraction from the misery of the flood and the conditions in the camp, the fears of sickness and the worry about what was next.

"Say, that's pretty good. What's that called?" Bessie asked.

"It's one of my songs," Henry said, blushing a bit with pride. "It's called 'Because You're Mine.'"

More people drifted over. While Henry played softly, Memphis regaled everyone with a story.

"You ever heard about the Voice of Tomorrow?" Memphis asked.

"What's that?" Tobias said, scrunching up his face.

"More like, who's that?" Memphis said.

"Who's that?" Moses echoed. "Is he here? What's he look like?"

"Who said it was a he?"

"It's a girl?"

"Didn't say that, neither." If Isaiah were here, he'd tease Memphis for not talking "proper," the way Memphis always fussed at Isaiah for it. But why? Why shouldn't they talk any way they wanted? Memphis had seen it all his life—men talking free and loose in the barbershop then talking "white" on the streets. He'd fallen right in, hadn't he? Even in his own poems, he'd laced up his language tight. No more. He didn't care what they thought. He would please himself first.

"The Voice of Tomorrow can be anybody. That's the point, see. You never know. Could be right here in this camp. Could be you." Memphis pointed at a little girl in braids. "Or you." He pointed to her brother. "Or skinny Moses over there, scratching at that mosquito bite on his knee."

The children giggled at this and teased Moses, who rolled his eyes. But from his lopsided grin, it was easy to see he was pleased to be called out by Memphis. The adults had come over to hear the story now. Looking at these good people Memphis had come to know, he thought about the danger they were in, not just from the flood. He didn't want to scare them. But he did want to warn them so they wouldn't be caught unawares if the dead came calling. They deserved to know.

"See, the Voice of Tomorrow has to fight the evils of the world. There's a man in a tall hat, goes by the name the King of Crows."

One of the kids cawed, and this set off a round of cawing until Nate told everybody to "hush up now and listen to the man's story."

"How come he's called the King of Crows?" Moses asked, giggling. "That's a funny name."

"Crows are messengers from the land of the dead. They can bring messages from spirits, from the ancestors. The land of the dead is where the King of Crows works his magic to unleash it on us out here."

A little girl pursed her lips. "There's no such thing as a land of the dead."

"Yes, there is, too. And it's a place you don't want to be. That's why you should never make a deal with the man in the hat."

Some of the children looked a little scared, and Memphis wondered how honest he should be here. Wasn't that how fairy tales worked? You told just enough of the terrible truth—*There are cruel people. Not all parents love you. The world isn't fair by a long shot.*—and you dressed it up in ogres and brave princesses and giants. Mostly, you reminded people that the evils of the world had to be fought. Even if you weren't sure you'd win. You still had to go into the monster's den. You had to face your fears. You still had to stand up to the monster. So he told the children sitting outside the tents in the mud of the Mississippi about that trickster god, the King of Crows, who would stop at nothing till he ate up the country, and then the whole world, unless he was stopped by people being brave.

"The ghosts are here. Walking around this country. You got to be looking for 'em, all right? Look for the little things—birds that fly up and take off real sudden. A sound that makes the back of your neck prickle up, or a cold fog that rises out of nowhere."

The children had gone stone quiet. Memphis was struck anew by the power of story. Before he had wanted to write himself, before his weekly visits to the 135th Street Library, there had been his mother telling him about François Mackandal and the Maroons up in the hills, plotting rebellion. All those stories about her homeland, a place Memphis had never seen but felt he had because of her stories. She'd instilled a resistance in him with every word.

"Would you bargain with the King of Crows?" Memphis asked.

"No!" the children answered, a thunderous cry.

"Well, now. I don't think the King of Crows is gonna get a lick of sleep tonight. I think he heard that cry all the way in the land of the dead. And he knows that the Voice of Tomorrow is coming for him."

"You need to be careful with that Voice of Tomorrow stuff," Bill scolded later as they lay on the cold, damp ground and tried to get some sleep.

"Why? Why shouldn't they know? They need to be able to protect themselves. Can't do that if they don't know the truth."

"Because the wrong person might hear."

Sometimes, Bill got under Memphis's skin with his nagging. "Who'd be looking for us in a refugee camp on a levee in Greenville, Mississippi?"

"These Shadow Men, they got eyes ever'where. The Red Cross. National Guard. The police and the Klan. Those Fitter Families folks hunting for Diviners. Yeah, they looking for us all right. Jake Marlowe needs us. The King of Crows wants us."

"Why hasn't the King of Crows just taken us, then?" Henry wondered.

"Don't know. He's got some plan at work. Toying with us for fun," Bill said.

"Maybe he's afraid of us and what we can do," Memphis said.

"I wouldn't bet money on that," Bill said.

Memphis couldn't sleep. He left the tent and sat with a view of the mighty Mississippi and the other overflowing river—the tent city stretching out for miles. He wondered what difficulties Isaiah and Theta and the others were facing, wherever they were.

"I just wanna see my brother and my girl again. I just want them to be safe. That's all I'm asking," Memphis said, praying to a god he wasn't sure he believed in anymore. A god he wasn't sure believed in him, either.

SPELLS

When all the people had gone home and the fairground lights were dimmed, the circus folk gathered in the cook tent for their supper. Soon, the roustabouts would yank up the pegs and bring the Big Top down in a puddle of canvas. Then everything would be loaded onto the trains for transport to the next town.

Doc Hamilton was enjoying generous swigs from his bottle of "Gentlemen's Elixir" and was on his way to being quite drunk. Polly looked on disapprovingly.

"Want some?"

"Some of us have to keep our wits about us," she said in English that carried a Romanian accent. Bella rested his bald head on her shoulder. "I can't perform tricks if I'm not in best shape. If I'm not—what is it you say, Samuel?"

"Pushing on all sixes," Sam said.

"Yes. On the sixes," Polly echoed.

"Suit yourself," Doc Hamilton said, upending the flask.

At the table, Johnny finished counting the money. He smiled, his bright teeth shining out from all that fur. "One thousand dollars. Not bad."

Everyone applauded. Some banged the table in celebration.

Johnny dropped the fat green stack into Zarilda's open cigar box and she held it aloft for a moment, triumphant. "They said vaudeville would bury us. Then they said it was the picture shows. Now everybody and his dog's got a radio—Ma and Pa and kiddies gathered around the old squawk box ever' night. But they still come out to see us. When the circus rolls into town, folks line up and down the roadways, cheering and clapping. You know why?"

Zarilda took a moment to look around the table with a showman's instinct for suspense.

"Because *we are the dream makers*!" she said, rippling her fingers through the air as if spreading fairy dust. "We show 'em wonders! No matter what troubles they carry from home, no matter what heartbreaks hide inside their rib cages, for a time under our tent, they can have wonder again. They can

believe that all things are possible. *We*"—and here Zarilda paused again—
"we make the impossible possible."

The moon rose like the answer to a forgotten prayer. Stars glittered in a velvety sky. It had been a long day, and a good one. Everyone drifted toward bed and sleep and dreams. Theta tucked Isaiah into his berth on the train.

Isaiah worried the edge of his blanket. "Do you suppose Memphis misses me?"

Theta carefully lifted the blanket free of Isaiah's fingers and pulled it up to his quivering chin. "I'm sure of it."

"You think he's all right, wherever he is?"

"I'm sure of that, too," she lied. On impulse, she kissed Isaiah's forehead. "Get some sleep, Ice Man."

Isaiah turned on his side and shut his eyes. "Only Memphis calls me that."

"Well, now I call you that, too. Just until he gets back."

Theta stepped off the train and into the night. The fairgrounds clanged with the noise of the circus coming apart. Already the Big Top, the cook tent, and all of the seating had been disassembled and loaded onto the first line of railroad cars to make the trip to the next town ahead of the performers. They were a dreamlike city rolling through the dark of night past slumbering towns full of people with jobs and houses and ordinary lives. People who had no notion of the danger awaiting them. Was Memphis in one of those towns they passed by? Could he be lost in the throngs of happy, flag-waving spectators gathered along the sides of the roads as the circus paraded through? And where was Henry? Theta missed them both so much. Tonight, it weighed heavily on her.

How could so much change happen in such a short amount of time? It didn't even feel like the same world. Now Henry was somewhere out there in this vast country, and maybe he was safe, but maybe he was facing somebody who'd figured him to be a boy who liked other boys and who didn't like it one bit. Somebody who thought he had the right to teach Henry a lesson. Maybe that person would feel like he had to prove to himself or his friends that he wasn't as small and powerless as he felt inside. Theta shuddered thinking about what harm could come to the two boys she loved the most. She wondered if she would be able to cultivate her own power in time to do whatever was required to stop catastrophe.

Theta wandered past the darkened sideshow wagons painted with the image of a snake-draped, scaly woman with a forked tongue. Near the animal cages, she bumped into Johnny the Wolf Boy. "Just making sure my friends are all right," he said, nodding toward the tiger, lions, elephants, and horses.

"What's the word? I thought we were getting out of here?" she asked.

"The flood's really causing trouble. The railroad fellas are taking us on a different route, but it looks like we're here till dawn at least. I don't know if I can even sleep without the feel of the rails under me," Johnny said, grinning. "Good night to you, Miss Theta."

"'Night, Johnny."

Back in her compartment, Theta took out Miss Addie's spell book, hoping it would be of help. There were long lists of plants and their uses, most of it folk medicine, which Theta found very interesting. There were instructions for calling the corners, with an underlined note to "know your intent. Search your heart." And there were spells, of course.

But the book was also Miss Addie's diary. Theta skimmed the first page, then turned to the very last entry, a quirk of hers that used to drive Henry crazy. "How can you read the last page of a book first?" he'd say in mock-outrage. "I hate suspense," she'd answer. Miss Addie's last entry had been dated July 1864: *It is finished.*

The door to the compartment blew open. Theta yelped.

"Sorry! Didn't mean to scare you," Evie said, traipsing in.

"Were you with Sam?" Theta asked.

Evie smiled. "Mm-hmm." Her hair was a mess and her lips were chapped.

Theta stroked her thumb across her own lips, wishing Memphis were there to bruise them with fevered kissing. She ached with missing him.

Evie slipped out of her dress, leaving it in a heap on the floor. She was such a slob. If Theta had ever left her things out of order, Mrs. Bowers or Roy would've hit her for it.

"You just gonna leave that there for the maid?" Theta said pointedly.

Evie picked up the dress with two fingers and laid it across her trunk. Stifling a yawn, she crawled into bed, burrowing under the covers. She nodded at the book on Theta's bed. "Whatcha doing?"

Theta sighed. "Trying to make sense outta Miss Addie's spell book and diary."

"Anything useful, like how to turn men into frogs?"

Theta flipped onto her side to face Evie, resting her face on her fist. "Mostly there's *beaucoup* about plants and herbs-*avous*."

"Well," Evie said, facing Theta. "I suppose you could always make a witchy meat loaf." They shared a giggle. Evie lost her fizz. "That seems like a joke Mabel would've made."

"Yeah," Theta said sadly.

Evie propped herself up. "I was thinking—"

"Always dangerous."

"Zarilda says she can talk to spirits. What if…"

"Don't, Evil. Let it alone."

"But what if she's not okay, Theta?"

"If something weren't jake, don't you think she'd appear to you first?"

Evie played with the edge of her quilt. What she didn't tell Theta was that after Mabel had died, Evie had stolen Mabel's coat from her closet. It was an impulsive act. Evie had been desperate for a physical remembrance of her best friend, and Mabel would never wear the coat again. The first night, Evie had curled up with the coat, crying. But she couldn't resist leaning into its secrets for long. As the coat's memories performed their striptease of moments small and fleeting, of feelings that seemed outsized comparatively, Evie searched for the moment that would absolve her. Here was Mabel's passion for the labor fight. Here was her unrequited crush on Jericho. Here was her irritation over having to attend a strike with her parents when there was something wonderful on the radio. It had made Evie smile to know that even Mabel could tire of doing good. But other glimpses of Mabel's private life had needled under Evie's skin: Mabel turning her face this way and that, up and down, trying to find the angle that suited her best, the one that allowed her to believe for just a moment that she was a narrow idea of beautiful. Something bitter and surprising had crept in: Mabel's envy. She had often felt left out. She'd wanted to have Diviner powers like the others, something of her own to make her feel special. She had both loved and resented Evie—and she was angry with Evie for interfering in her life by talking to Arthur. There had been no time to make up. As far as Evie knew, Mabel had died still angry with her, and that ghost haunted Evie more than any of the others.

What happened after that day was lost. Mabel had not worn this coat to the exhibition. Her motivations and feelings on that day were not available for anyone to know. In life, she'd been an open book. In death, she'd become a painful mystery.

"We fought, you know. About Arthur," Evie said at last.

"You were right about him."

"Our last words to each other were cross. It haunts me, Theta. I wish I could undo it."

"Aw, Evil. Why're you doing this to yourself? Mabel loved you. She knew you loved her."

Evie didn't want to talk about it anymore. It was making her unbearably sad. "Did Miss Addie really raise Elijah from the dead?" she asked, changing the subject.

"Yeah. And it didn't go so well," Theta said firmly.

Evie put her hands up in innocence. "I'm no necromancer. I swear."

"I saw him, you know."

Evie made a face. "How did he…look?"

"Not…good."

"Well. That was very descriptive, Miss Knight. Thank you."

"I ain't the poet. I leave that to Memphis." Theta thought back to being trapped in the basement with Miss Addie. The slow shuffle of Elijah's dead feet against the floor. It made her shudder still. "The way he kept coming after her…it reminded me of Roy."

Evie heard the worry lurking there. "Theta…" she began, searching for a delicate way to phrase what she needed to say. "I know how much you love Miss Addie. But what if she isn't under the King of Crows's power? What if she's just lost inside her mind because she's very old?"

"No. He's got her. I'm sure of it."

"But the doctor said—"

"To hell with what the doctor said! Sometimes a girl just knows. My gut says that rat in the hat has Miss Addie."

"You made a rhyme."

"Wasn't intentional. Or the point."

"Theta. I don't know much about witches. But I believe in you. And your gut."

Theta was touched by this. She'd never really had a close girlfriend before—Roy had been too jealous. And she felt a little guilty that it took

221

Mabel's death for her to get closer to Evie. She knew how broken up Evie was about losing Mabel.

Theta held up her pinkie and reached across the narrow space between their beds. "Hey. Pals-ski?"

The last time Evie had done a pinkie swear was with Mabel. "Pals-ski," Evie said quietly. She hooked her little finger through Theta's and pulled. "I'll leave you to it. But if you do happen to come across a spell for turning men into frogs"—Evie yawned—"do let me know. Never know when it might come in handy."

"'Night, Evil," Theta said, and she could swear Evie was already out.

Theta picked up Miss Addie's diary again, flipping to a random page.

> *June 2, 1864*
>
> *I ache for Elijah so much it is as if someone had taken an ax and cleaved me in two. Mother says if I do not eat, she'll force the porridge into my mouth. She may try all she likes. I will not have it.*
>
> *"Dear Sister," Lillian said. "You must live on. What would Elijah say if he could see you thus? Let us work the spell of forgetting to ease your pain."*
>
> *But I do not want to forget. I do not want to lose what little I have left of him. My Elijah. My one true love.*

Theta teared up. Miss Addie had put into words her own feelings exactly. Being away from Memphis was like losing half of herself. Missing Henry was an ache deep in the heart. Not knowing if they were alive or dead or in danger made it that much worse.

She decided to go back and start at the beginning. As she read, she found that the diary was a small window into history, both the country's and Miss Addie's. Theta learned that Miss Addie had been from a modestly well-to-do family. In addition to her sister, Lillian, she'd had two brothers, a mother, and a father. They lived in a fine redbrick house named Rose Manor for its prized roses. There were stables and tobacco fields, and there had been servants.

No.

There had been *slaves*.

Theta loved Miss Addie, but this new knowledge was deeply upsetting. The Miss Addie she knew was kind and concerned for the well-being of others. She was descended from ancestors who had, themselves, been persecuted and hung during the Salem Witch Trials. How could that be the same person speaking so casually of owning other human beings? Someone like Miss Addie might've owned Memphis's grandparents. And Elijah, Addie's great love, had been fighting for the Confederacy when he was killed. Theta had seen him herself. He'd come up out of the grave, out of the stinking past, rotting inside that uniform—dead, but still he kept coming. Theta closed the diary, feeling troubled and unsure. Beside her sat Miss Addie's spell book, which was full of information that could help in the fight against the dead. But should she follow the advice of a person who had taken part in something she found so awful?

Adelaide Proctor had lived a long life after the war. She'd left her home and moved to New York City. She'd done missionary work for those in need. Maybe she had come to see how wrong she and her family had been. Or maybe, deep down, Miss Addie still held fast to those terrible beliefs. Theta didn't know, because they'd never talked about it. And now she knew this. She wished she didn't, but she did.

Theta was resolved to save Miss Addie from the King of Crows. Once she did, though, they would need to have a talk. She forced herself to keep reading:

June 28, 1864
The old cunning folk talk of the man in the tall hat. They say he can grant wishes if you are willing to seek him and offer a bargain.

July 1, 1864
I am resolved. I shall leave my wish for him in the hollow of the old elm and seal it with a thumbprint of my blood. I will make a pact.

Theta's heart beat faster. For the next few pages, there was talk of the war raging on and the names of men killed, but nothing of Elijah or the man in the hat. And then, finally:

> July 7, 1864
>   Tonight. So mote it be.

Theta's hands trembled as she turned the page.

> I have met the man in the hat. I fear to commit to words what transpired. In truth, I am uncertain, myself. It all seems as a dream. He has promised me the return of my love. And in return, I have pledged myself to him. I have forfeited my power and, I fear, my mortal soul. Yet, Elijah shall live again. We shall live out our lives together forever, nevermore to be divided. I shall be his wife and we will be happy.

Theta knew the end of the story, but a sense of dread filled her anyway as she turned the pages, reading quickly:

> There were petals on the doorstep again. Lillian was cross with me. But I am beside myself. It is a sign, just as the man in the hat promised. Elijah is coming for me. . . .

> . . . What have I conjured?

> . . . Father and Teddy are gone. Dead from the fever. This is my doing. I cannot meet Mother's or Lillian's eyes. I have brought about an abomination. Or perhaps it is I who is the abomination. He will never let me be. "Till death do us part." That was the bargain I made, and the man in the hat means to keep me to it until I am driven mad by my sins

or taken by my dead lover, to what terrible fate, I cannot say, I dare not imagine....

———

...Tonight, I shall go to Elijah's grave to perform the binding spell. To the devil with the man in the hat.

An entry later that same night said simply, *It is finished.*

And then Addie's entries stopped altogether, as if she wanted no further record. No proof of what she'd done.

"How do you bind somebody?" Theta wondered aloud. If the spell had been done before, then it could be performed again.

Theta returned to the spell book. There were spells reaching back generations, but the language was stiff and formal and very hard to understand. Was *shew* the same thing as *show*? But at last, she found the spell she wanted. From what she could gather, you had to set your intention. You had to weave yourself into the spell you cast so that you could not escape your part in it.

"What does that mean?" Theta whispered. She wished Addie had written out exactly what she'd done—and in plain English. Theta shut the book. "This is crackers," she said to no one. "I don't know the first thing about being a witch."

But she was tired of doing nothing while Miss Addie wasted away. Binding Elijah's angry, possessive ghost from doing any harm to Addie was the best she could do. She read through the spell and gathered what she needed. Then she left the compartment.

In the pale moonlight, the darkened wagons were ghosts of the day that had been. A gentle breeze ruffled the Big Top as it lay on the railroad car.

For her spell, Miss Addie had taken a lock of Elijah's hair and cut off a finger bone. Theta's stomach turned at that. Theta had nothing of Elijah's to use. The spell book said you could write the name of the person you wanted to bind from doing harm on a piece of paper, tie it up with string, and burn it.

"'What you do shall return threefold,'" Theta read aloud. "Gee, thanks, creepy book. What does that mean?" She was really flying blind here.

She wrote Elijah's name on a piece of paper. She had no string with which to tie it up. Miss Addie had used Elijah's hair, so Theta yanked out a strand of her own hair and wrapped it tightly around the folded-up paper. "I bind you from doing harm, Elijah. Go back to your grave and harm no more." She felt silly saying it, but she had to do it for Miss Addie's sake—for all of their sakes. She couldn't bind every single one of the Army of the Dead, but she could take out this one lousy bum.

Theta lit a candle and cupped the flame with her other hand. She dripped the wax down onto the offering. "I bind you from doing harm, Elijah. I bind you from doing harm. I bind you from doing harm." She touched the flame to the paper. The flame mesmerized Theta, as if she could feel it within her. As if she could feel a generation of women who'd been cast out, hung, stoned to death, and burned alive taking root now. She could swear she saw Miss Addie's face in the flame. The fire and its vision exploded in a bright flare. With a yelp, Theta dropped it. Out in the night, a hawk called three times. Theta let the hair-and-paper bundle burn until it was a charred mess. Then she buried it in the earth and tamped it down with her foot. Was she supposed to feel different now? Well, she didn't. How did you know when a spell had worked?

"Buncha bushwa," Theta said on a sigh. She gathered everything into her pockets, thinking of all the times she'd seen Miss Addie wandering the halls of the Bennington, sprinkling salt from her own pockets, intoning some spell of protection while the residents shook their heads and called her crazy. "Now *I'm* the crazy lady," Theta said.

On her way back to her compartment, the breeze shifted. In it, Theta thought she heard a faint shuffling. The crack of a branch. She surveyed the deserted fairgrounds. It was pretty quiet except for Billy, the world's loudest goat. Theta went to his stall to check on him. She found him standing in the corner, bleating.

"You're gonna wake everybody up," Theta said. She tossed him a little bit of feed. He stopped making noise long enough to eat it. "Get some sleep, pal. Big day tomorrow."

As a bone-tired Theta nestled her head against the pillow, she thought she heard that same shuffling sound. She held her breath, listening.

"Just the wind," she whispered and shut her eyes.

☀

Isaiah spoke into the dark, careful not to wake Sam. "Sarah Beth? You out there?" He closed his eyes, willing her to appear, and in a moment his arms tickled. His body trembled. And he was in the dark space.

She was standing with the storm at her back. "Isaiah! How long before you're in Bountiful?"

"Dunno. Still with the circus. Sure does take a long time to cross this country."

"The King of Crows is up to something bad. I can feel it. Can you?"

Isaiah couldn't feel it, and that upset him. He'd always been able to sense danger. Why not now? "Mm-hmm," he said. He didn't want to admit this to Sarah Beth. What if she didn't think he was special? What if she didn't want to be a team? "What do *you* see?" Isaiah asked, fishing.

"There's something in the towns. Places nobody else sees," she said. "I don't know what, precisely, but I've got a pain in my belly over it. Oh, you've got to hurry, Isaiah! I don't know how much longer we've got."

"I promise we're coming, Sarah Beth," Isaiah said.

"I can't wait to meet proper," she said.

"Likewise."

The moon kept watch over the sleeping circus. Over the painted wagons. Over the long snake of railroad cars waiting for morning. Over the empty food stalls and the muddy fields trampled by thousands of footprints. The moon kept watch over the sleeping circus and the deep, dark shadow passing over it.

※

The next morning, as Sam was getting dressed, he saw Zarilda marching toward the animal cages in a determined way with her hair still in rollers and her robe on. Johnny the Wolf Boy trailed her, crying inconsolably. Sam hurried out after them barefoot, his suspenders loose and *thwapp*ing against his trouser legs.

"What's the matter?" Sam asked, catching up.

"It's…Billy," Johnny said between hiccuping gulps of tears. "He's… dead."

The performers, still in their robes and pajamas, came out of their compartments and gathered around the animals' cages on the open train car. The goat lay in the straw. His neck had been torn out. There was a jagged slice down his belly, and his intestines had been dragged out through the hole. His heart was missing. Elsie the equestrienne turned and vomited into the mud while one of the acrobats patted her back. Sam felt a little green himself.

Johnny wiped his nose on his furred arm. "Who would do such a terrible thing?"

"What is it?" Theta asked, coming up behind Sam. She gasped when she saw the mutilated goat.

"I'll get a shovel," Johnny said. "I'll bury him out yonder." He walked away, still saying, "Who would do such a terrible thing?"

"I fed him last night," Theta was saying to Sam and Evie as the train finally got under way. "He was kind of agitated. I think there was somebody in the camp. I kept hearing noises. Last night I'd have said it was just some drunkard, but not after this."

"Shadow Men?" Evie asked.

"Why would Shadow Men go after a goat and not take us?" Sam said. "I've spent time with those fellas. And while I'm sure they'd kill anything, I'm also sure they'd come for us over a goat."

Heavy-hearted, Theta returned to the compartment she shared with Evie. Dry leaves littered the floor. "For Pete's sake, Evil, you are the biggest slob," Theta said. She swept up the debris, opened the train window a sliver, and dumped it out.

※

Evie found she enjoyed circus life. She was particularly enamored with the circus's grande dame, the flamboyant Zarilda. When Zarilda laughed, her whole face laughed. It was a cackle that started low and deep, then rumbled up through her lungs and out of her mouth bright and sharp as machine-gun fire. Sam had told Evie he loved Zarilda's laugh so much he would tell jokes just to hear it. She dressed in flowing, jewel-toned dresses and capes that swished and swayed as she moved among her circus family, giving a cheek a pat of encouragement or delivering cups of strong Turkish coffee served in delicate china cups that she swore had been carried to this country in a basket strapped to the strong back of her Roma great-grandmother. It was hard to know if anything Zarilda said was true, but when it was so much fun, who cared? Zarilda's caravan traveled in style.

She absolutely refused to wear a girdle. "Don't like 'em. They pinch in all the wrong places. Listen here, I'm fat. I know it. I'm fine with it." She winked. "So's Arnold."

Arnold the Painted Man was Zarilda's great love. Every inch of him—from his toes to his bald head—had been inked. There were even two thick blue-black curlicues around his eyes like Tutankhamun, the boy pharaoh. Evie had found the sight of Arnold terrifying at first. But soon she came to see him as a walking story. Every tattoo had a tale to tell. "The whale and anchor are for his days as a sailor," Johnny the Wolf Boy explained. He spoke for Arnold most of the time, Arnold himself being mute. "That one there, the shamrock, is for an old Irish lover, and that"—Johnny pointed to the inked heart just above Arnold's own—"is for Zarilda."

"Arnold saw something he shouldn't have when he was a kid," Zarilda told Evie later. "Whatever it was, it shut him up for good. But there are other ways of talking. Arnold makes his point clear."

Just like Arnold's tattoos, every person in the circus had a story, too. Polly's parents and the townspeople had seen her beard as a manifestation of something evil. When she was seven, her parents sold her to a traveling carnival, where the owner beat her regularly. She'd had a baby by the time she was fourteen. The baby didn't live. Finally, Polly saw her chance. They were in Ireland when she stowed away on a ship bound for America. She met Zarilda the first month.

Theta's palms heated up as she listened to Polly's tale. She felt the abuse as her own. "I know what it's like having somebody parade you on a stage every night," Theta said, nodding at Polly.

"My fur started when I was nine," Johnny said. "My mother tried shaving it off. I'd be covered in nicks for a few days, and then it would just grow back. Finally she took me to the priest to see if they could exorcise it from me. They said it was a demon. But it was just hair," Johnny said. "That's when I ran away and joined up with the circus. I figured this was the one place they could love me like this." He gave a small dismissive laugh that was completely undone by a hopeful sideways glance.

Mr. Sarkassian had escaped from the Armenian genocide. His entire family had been shot by the Turks. Elsie, an equestrienne, had left her Boston Brahmin family when her marriage to a wealthy playboy became too much to bear. Flora's family in Brooklyn was so poor, she said, "I never seen soap till I joined the fuckin' circus!"

"Flora. Language?" Zarilda said with a nod toward Isaiah.

"Aw, shit. Sorry, kid."

"Everybody's running from something," Zarilda said. "But here, everybody's got a place."

Theta had bought a newspaper as they'd left their last town, and she and Evie sat side by side eating stale popcorn and scouring its pages for any mention of their friends. Mostly, the local papers reported on local things, which was a relief. On page three, though, was a slim column about the New York *Daily News* publishing poems and reports sent to reporter T. S. Woodhouse from some possible anarchist collective called the Voice of Tomorrow.

"The Voice of Tomorrow. That's Memphis. I know it," Theta said, grinning. She told Evie about the poem Memphis had shared with her back in Harlem. "He's alive."

The article went on to say that the Bureau of Investigation was tracing the postmarks of the letters. The last several had been posted from Greenville, Mississippi, the site of the terrible flood. So Memphis was alive, but he was in danger. Theta knew the Shadow Men would be on their way to Greenville now, and she hoped he had moved on.

"Please be safe, Memphis," Theta said.

☀

The train was passing through Kentucky, which, Mr. Sarkassian had told Isaiah, was a name derived from an Iroquois word that meant "land of tomorrow." Isaiah liked the way that sounded. Land of Tomorrow. Sometimes he could see tomorrow, though it wasn't always happy when he did. The train came around a hilly curve of thick green trees. Morning fog poured down the hillside and settled into the valley below. They were coming up on one of those small depots where the people often came out to wave. The driver blew the whistle to let folks who had a mind to come see the circus passing through do that. The train slowed as it neared the depot.

"Where is everybody?" Isaiah asked. He opened his window and stuck his face out. The air felt wrong somehow, and it smelled bad.

"Whew!" Evie said, waving a hand in front of her nose. "Is there a sulfur stream nearby?"

"Looks like coal mining," Sam said. He put a hand over his nose.

"Where are all the people? Johnny, did we just chug into a ghost town?" Zarilda asked.

"Bells Junction," Theta said, reading the sign next to the depot. The fog thinned to a smoky haze. The houses dotting the hillside looked as if they'd been deserted for a hundred years. Ash settled over the rooftops and trees. It was as if a giant dust cloud had come through and wiped the place clear of every living thing.

"I wonder what happened to it," Theta said.

"One of those boomtowns-gone-bust, I'll bet," Zarilda said, snugging the sash up on the train window again. She wiped her hands free of some of the dust that had drifted down the hill. "I once saw a boomtown spring up in the Texas panhandle after they discovered oil there. Shoot, within three months that town went from one thousand to twenty thousand people. And when the oil dried up a few months later, the town dried up with it. There and gone in under a year."

"Huh," Sam said. But to him, Bells Junction didn't look like it had been left behind.

It looked like it had been eaten alive.

As Isaiah watched Bells Junction disappearing from view, he thought about Sarah Beth's strange warning: *There's something in the towns.*

FACE THE FUTURE

"I want you to tell me everything you can about the Eye," Ling said to Jericho. They were driving west from Knoxville to an Elks Lodge outside Nashville. She and Jericho sat at the back of the bus, feeling the hum of the road under them while Doc drove and the Haymakers caught a much-needed nap.

"It's a monster. Just like him," Jericho said.

"But how does it work?"

"Only Marlowe knows how it works."

"Can you remember any details?" Ling asked.

Jericho searched his memory. He'd been so horrified by what he'd seen that he'd tried to forget. "In the center is the heart of the thing. I hesitate to use that word because that machine is utterly heartless. The souls of the soldiers are inside."

"And they're caught in a time loop, living out that same terrible day the rift was opened?"

"Yes. Somehow, that loop, their suffering, powers the machine and keeps the portal between our worlds open. But it needs an extra boost of energy from time to time to keep it open, to stabilize it."

"That's where the other Diviners come in."

"Yes. Marlowe has a control—Sam's mother. Her energy is a balance between the heart of the machine and the other Diviner, somehow."

"What is it about her?"

"I don't know. Hence my use of the word *somehow*."

"You don't have to get sore. Or use *hence*."

"The other Diviner's energy is sent up into the rift," Jericho continued. "But in the process, the Eye drains that Diviner's life force. I think some Diviners are able to withstand the draining for longer than others. And no, I don't know why or how. It seems to be completely individual."

Ling shuddered to think that she'd once considered Jake Marlowe a hero. "Seems like he needs to do it more often now." She tapped her finger against her chin while she thought. "The rift is in danger of collapsing. Or the King of Crows wants Marlowe to think it is. Either way, that uranium-and Diviner-enhanced energy is going straight to him. He's building up this enormous, possibly catastrophic power, and Marlowe and the Shadow Men are too dumb to see that."

"But why? What does the King of Crows want?" Jericho asked.

Ling stopped tapping her finger. She sighed. "Good question. He's raising an army, but for what? What can an army of the dead do?"

"He wants to take over the country, maybe the world," Jericho offered.

"So does Jake Marlowe," Ling said pointedly. "But for what reason?"

"What if there *is* no reason?" Jericho said after a moment.

And Ling found that answer the most chilling of all the possibilities.

"I think tonight during the show, you and I should experiment by trying to combine our powers," Ling said.

"What kind of experiment?"

"I don't know. Hence my use of the word *experiment*."

"Touché. But I'm not truly a Diviner," Jericho said.

"I'm not so sure about that. Your strength—that comes from Marlowe's serum?"

"I suppose it does," Jericho said. "I didn't have it before."

"So he made you into a Diviner. Like all of us. You *are* a Diviner."

A Diviner. A robot. An experiment. That's what Jericho felt like. Marlowe's science project. As if Marlowe were a god making something from clay in his image, or the image he desired. A golden son. Only Jericho was no golden boy. He was a mess, all balled up about his Jekyll-and-Hyde nature. He was afraid of his impulses and desires. It made him think of the German film he and Ling had wandered into back in Times Square, with the mad scientist transferring the soul of a woman into a machine.

"I suppose so," Jericho said quietly.

"You are. I'm sure of it. The night we fought the ghosts, and on the night of the memorial—both times, I could feel you in there with us."

"You could?" Jericho said. He didn't know why this made him feel so hopeful all of a sudden.

Ling nodded. "Could you feel us?"

"A little."

"Well. A little is something. It's a start," Ling said.

She granted him a real smile that made him feel, for just a moment, like he was not alone. He wished he could tell Ling about what he'd seen in the woods, but he was afraid. If he didn't say it aloud, it was like it didn't happen. He knew Ling. She would want to know everything. She would want to make sense of it. He'd have to tell her about the Daedalus program. He'd have to tell her that every single one of the men who were involved began to deteriorate over time. They went mad, lost their strength, died. Every single one of them, except Jericho. That was why Marlowe had wanted him as his Übermensch. What was it Marlowe had said? Something about Jericho's makeup that was exceptional. Something Marlowe coveted for his lousy eugenics program. Jericho didn't want to be his experiment. He also didn't want to end up like those other fellas. Like Sergeant Leonard.

He knew the question she'd ask: *You haven't had anything strange happening to you, have you?* No. He would not tell Ling. And then it wouldn't be true.

"Tonight, then," Ling said.

"Tonight," Jericho agreed.

They stopped for gasoline and sandwiches at a little shack near the Clinch River in a pretty valley protected by hills blooming with dogwood. They were huddled over their lunches at two picnic tables, everybody talking about how swinging the Chester B. Mosely Orchestra had been the night before, and Ling liked hearing how the acts would pick up little things from one another, urging one another on toward excellence. She knew that during the next performance, the girls would try something new and daring they'd learned, and maybe it would work and maybe it wouldn't, but it was all about the risk. A light fog spilled over the tops of the hills. It was pretty, but it gave Ling the heebie-jeebies.

"Something feels strange about this place," Ling said, biting into her bologna sandwich. She missed her parents' cooking.

Alma peeled back the bread to remove a slimy pickle. "The only strangeness is this sandwich. Ugh," she said out of earshot of the girl who worked the gas station and who was bringing out a pitcher of iced tea.

"You mean, like it's haunted," Jericho said. He polished off half of his roast beef with nary a complaint.

"Or will be." Now, why had she said that? Such an odd thing to say. "Is there a graveyard near here?" Ling asked the girl with the tea.

"You really know how to make an impression," Alma muttered and tried to hunch down lower to hide her embarrassment.

The girl shook her head. "Not that I know of. Why do you ask?"

"This land—feels like there's some power in it. Something bad," Ling said.

"You'll have to excuse Miss Chang," Alma said. "She's got a delicate condition."

"No, I don't," Ling protested.

The girl from the gas station laughed. "You sound like Old Man Hendrix!"

Jericho's blond brows furrowed. "Who?"

"An old coot usedta live 'round here. A soothsayer, I reckon you might call him. He got religion after his little girl died. Shame about that."

"The daughter or the religion," Jericho muttered, and Alma nudged him quiet with her elbow.

"Golly Moses, the two of you!" she hissed.

"Mr. John Hendrix spent forty nights in the woods and came out with all manner of visions about this land."

Goosepimples rose on Ling's arms. "What kind of visions?"

"He said there'd be a town built on Black Oak Ridge with a heap of factories and whatnot, all to fight a great war."

"We've already had a great war," Jericho said bitterly. "Wasn't that enough?"

"He said whatever was built in those factories would make the earth shake with a terrible noise. Don't know what to make of it, but folks around here seem to believe he was a true prophet."

Ling couldn't help but think about Jake Marlowe.

"Say, y'all heard about this Voice of Tomorrow?" Babe asked.

"What's that? Is it a new kind of radio?" Eloise said.

"No. Somebody's been leaving these poems and stories all around and mailing them to the *Daily News* back in New York. Whoever it is calls themselves the Voice of Tomorrow."

"Roses are red, violets are blue, I sent my love to the *Daily Neeews*," Sally Mae said, cracking herself and Sadie up.

"Not like that. These are serious poems. About hauntings and ghosts and America. Oh, and somebody called the King of Crows."

"The what?" Jericho said, choking slightly on his sandwich. Ling elbowed him.

"The King of Crows."

"Who's that? He got a territory band?" Lupe asked.

"Do I look like I know?" Babe said. "Anyhow. It's got folks pretty riled up. It's got 'em talking about how things are in this country. And how they should be. About darn time, you ask me."

"Memphis?" Ling whispered to Jericho.

Jericho nodded. "Memphis."

OPPORTUNITY

New York City

The letter, addressed to T. S. Woodhouse, the *Daily News*, had no return address, but Woody had come to know that handwriting by now. Eagerly, he sliced open the top of the envelope and tugged out the poem inside. The Voice of Tomorrow had sent him another one.

He checked the postmark—Greenville, Mississippi. Wasn't that where the flood was? Woody hid the envelope under a stack of racing forms at the back of his drawer. He put the letter to one side and started typing.

Exclusive to *The Daily News*
by T. S. Woodhouse

Another poetic missive has arrived from the mysterious town crier named the Voice of Tomorrow. Many have wondered, Who is this unknown everyman delving into the state of the nation and into the heart of America's eternal struggle: Who, exactly, gets to be called an American? Is it America only for a select bunch of swells whose ancestors came over on the *Mayflower* or the *Maine*? (And weren't those same folks fleeing from persecution themselves? I ask you.) What about the Iroquois or the Chippewa, who were here first? As long as we're asking, shouldn't they have first say in the matter?

Well, the Voice of Tomorrow seems to say, if that's the case, you're gonna have a mighty small America, in size, in stature, and in that most American of concepts—heart. If the Constitution put down by our Founding Fathers is to be believed and all people are created equal, why is it that one hundred fifty years later, our mysterious scribe seems to say, we still haven't made good on that promise? Now, some folks call the Voice of Tomorrow a radical. Well, then, so were the fellows who dumped tea in Boston Harbor. For that matter, so were the same folks who gave us that Constitution the politicians like to beat their gums defending when it's convenient for them and chip away at when it's not.

Another reporter named Charlie slapped the morning edition of the paper, open to Woody's column, down onto Woody's desk beside his agitating Underwood. "Woody, how come you keep publishing these radical poems?"

Woody continued typing. "Why, Charlie! When did you learn to read?"

"Wise guy. C'mon. Who's this fella sending you this stuff?"

"The Voice of Tomorrow. Says so right there. Charlie, you might need to fire that reading teacher you hired after all."

Charlie leaned forward, hands on the edge of the desk. A shock of his brilliantined hair came loose. "They say he's some kind of dangerous criminal. A Bolshevik. Or one of those Secret Six types. Or worse! It might even be a whole slew of 'em. A fella's gotta be careful nowadays."

"That's true, Woody," another reporter, Ellis, called from two desks over. "Why, you might open up a letter and get your hands blown clean off, like what happened to Mr. Rockefeller's maid during the Wall Street bombings."

Woody made a show of digging out and holding up the paper-thin envelope. "It'd have to be a mighty small bomb."

"What if it's one of those Diviner types? I hear they can do all sorts of magic—disrupt radio signals or read your mind! Even put thoughts in your head—like they did in Times Square! I wouldn't put it past them to make a bomb. Like that Evie O'Neill. She was friends with Mabel Rose."

Woody dropped his amused smile. "Evie O'Neill is no anarchist."

The typing reporter laughed. "Aw, look at that. The rat is soft on the Sweetheart Seer."

"Excuse me, gentlemen. I must be in the wrong place. I thought this was a news joint fulla reporters, not a bunch of gullible yes men."

The other reporter held Woody's gaze. "Just sayin'. Watch your step, Woodhouse."

"That a threat, Charlie?"

The man's cheeks pinked up. He shrugged, then turned back to his doughnut, hardening on the plate.

"Woodhouse!" the news editor barked and jerked his head toward his office.

Charlie chuckled. "So long, Woody. Been nice knowing ya."

"Close the door behind you and take a seat," the editor grumbled at Woody, who complied. "Who are these letters coming from?"

"How should I know?"

"But they come addressed to you."

"Lots of stuff comes addressed to me. I'm a reporter."

The editor tapped his pencil against the desk, weighing his next words. "Some fellas wanna talk to you. I told them you were out on a story."

A prickle of adrenalized dread poked at Woody. He was a reporter, so it was often hard to separate fear from excitement. "What fellas?"

"Don't know. Government types, maybe. Not the sort of men you say no to."

"You know how you say no to men like that?" Woody paused. "You say, 'No.' Try it sometime."

"Don't push your luck with me, Woodhouse, or you'll be out of a job." His editor softened. "Just be careful, okay?"

Woody grinned. "Since when is the American press careful?"

Woody went back to his typewriter.

"Hey, Woody. We're taking bets," Charlie called.

"On what?"

"Margaret Walker. You think they'll fry her in the chair, or will it be execution by firing squad?"

"I think you're dripping mustard onto your page there."

"What? Ah, horsefeathers!"

Woody handed his latest column to the secretary and grabbed his hat. "Sue? Could you be a dear and bring that to the copy boys for the late edition? Thanks."

"Sure, Woody. Where ya headed so fast?"

"Confession."

It had taken all of Woody's gambling pot to get in to see Sister Walker. He'd had to bribe one of the cops he knew was on the take. And he'd had to borrow his cousin Michael's priestly raiment with a promise he'd come back later to confess his sins and say his Hail Marys.

Now, with the clerical collar pinching his neck, Woody sat across a table from Margaret Walker. He was allowed only fifteen minutes. He had to make it good.

"I know about Project Buffalo," Woody whispered. "I saw the file. A little bird told me. That's usually a figure of speech, but in this case, it's not."

"I know," Sister Walker said.

"Why aren't you telling them the truth, Miss Walker?"

She looked at Woody with a mixture of contempt and irritation. "Who listens to women?"

"I believe Memphis Campbell has been sending me stories. I've been printing them in the paper."

Sister Walker allowed a small smile at this. It was short-lived. "We have to stop Jake Marlowe from using the Eye."

"The Eye?" Woody said, jotting it down in the notebook he'd stashed inside his priestly frock. "Is that the machine Jake Marlowe was building during the war? The one that could supposedly break into another dimension?"

"He did build it," Sister Walker said. She leaned forward and lowered her voice to almost a whisper, telling Woody quickly about the Eye, what it had done, what it was still doing.

Woody's hands shook as he took his notes.

"I need you to get the proof, Mr. Woodhouse. Before it's too late. The Shadow Men—"

"Shadow Men?"

"Rogue government agents. They work outside the law. Wherever there's a coup to protect American interests, you can be sure the Shadow Men were part of it. And they are very invested in this machine of Marlowe's. In eugenics and in Diviners and in the King of Crows."

Woody felt dizzy trying to keep up.

"They ransacked my apartment. They stole my files. I'm sure they've destroyed them by now. I saw the ghost of Will Fitzgerald. He warned me not to go in. I should have listened."

"His…ghost?" Woody felt a chill, remembering his own encounter with Will's ghost.

"Never mind that. We have to keep Evie and Memphis and the rest of the Diviners safe. This witch hunt is a ruse. They need the Diviners for malevolent purposes." She leaned close. "For Jake Marlowe."

"Marlowe? But he hates Diviners," Woody said, playing devil's advocate one more time. No reporter could afford to look too gullible.

"He helped *make* Diviners. We all did."

"Jake Marlowe? Surely not."

Sister Walker scoffed. "Like I said, who listens to women?"

"I believe you, Miss Walker," Woody said. Jake Marlowe was the most famous anti-Diviner in the nation. If it turned out that he'd not only made his own stock of Diviners but had been killing them off, well, that was front-page news. Hell, that was career-making news. "What can I do?"

"Investigate Project Buffalo and the tie to Jake Marlowe and the Founders Club. You've got to expose the truth before Marlowe can find our Diviners. Before he can use their power to open the portal between worlds permanently. Before there's no hope left."

Again, Woody felt dizzy. He didn't understand half of what Miss Walker was saying to him. Woody's hero, the reporter H. L. Mencken, had made his name in Dayton, Tennessee, reporting on the Scopes Trial—the Trial of the Century. America, with its stated separation of church and state, had been torn asunder over the teaching of evolution and the larger questions it asked: Was humankind descended from apes? Was God a collective delusion? And what was happening to America? The Trial of the Century, though, was really about the soul of the country. The divide between young and old, traditional and modern, past and future. For a nation that believed itself ordained by God, this was a reckoning. For what else might they have to question about themselves, then? What might they have to question about false inheritances? What Margaret Walker was whispering to him now made that story seem nearly insignificant.

Footsteps sounded in the corridor. Their time was nearly up.

"Where should I look first?" Woody asked.

"There's an old Department of Paranormal archive in Washington, D.C. In the basement of a building not far from Capitol Hill. Don't write this down." She whispered the address and Woody nodded.

The bribed cop poked his head in. "Time's up, *Father*."

"They say they're going to try you for treason," Woody said as two guards came to take Miss Walker back to her cell.

"Funny who gets to define *treason*," she answered. "If that little bird comes back? Pay attention."

Woody pushed through the protestors gathered outside the prison. Some shouted "Death to traitors!" Others cried "Free Sister Walker!"

When he returned to the *Daily News* offices on Park Row, there was another letter waiting for him. It was postmarked from Mississippi. There was no return address.

✲

Marlowe Industries laboratory
Northern California

The eager young man apprenticing in Jake Marlowe's laboratory stood behind Marlowe, waiting for the great man to notice him. When he did not, the young man cleared his throat. "Mr. Marlowe, sir?"

"Yes? What is it?" Marlowe said, barely glancing up.

"Mr. Petrovich just...expired, sir."

Jake placed a paternal hand on the young man's shoulder. "Just call him the Diviner. No names. Makes it easier. Less personal." He patted the young man's shoulder exactly twice and then peered through the lens at the lightning crackling inside the chamber. It would do for now. The Diviners they were bringing in simply weren't powerful enough, not even with the extra boost of serum Jake was pumping into them. Some couldn't take it at all; they convulsed, went mad, left this world burning up from the inside. Others managed a wild boost of Diviner insight into the supernatural realm, but it cost them. No matter what, Jake had to do whatever was necessary to keep the portal from closing until the modifications to the Eye were complete. Once the Eye was rebuilt according to the King of Crows's specifications, once they got it to Death Valley, it would all be worth it.

He couldn't kid himself, though. What he would need to make it happen was the formidable energy of Evie O'Neill, Memphis Campbell, and all their friends. What they had was something special. Something unprecedented. Revolutionary. He was still furious that Sam had managed to escape, and that it had been Evie O'Neill who'd helped him *right there in Jake's own house*!

I built them, Marlowe thought with a touch of pride. He was disappointed to think of all his prototypes being destroyed in order to stabilize the breach so that they could capture the King of Crows and harness the power inside the land of the dead for American interests. But in order to build something extraordinary, you often had to make sacrifices.

He could hear Margaret Walker in his head now: *You talk all the time about making sacrifices, Jake. But why is it always other people having to put their comfort and lives on the line? What sacrifices have you been willing to make?*

Margaret Walker. She never liked him. She never really understood his great plan. Margaret was very smart, but there was only so far she could go. The bloodline, of course. It limited her.

The lightning in the glass dazzled Jake, but there wasn't enough of it.

More. He needed more.

"Bring in the next Diviner," Jake said.

The young employee of Marlowe Industries turned a bit green. "Another one, sir?"

"That's what I said."

"If you don't mind my saying, sir…"

"I'm sure I will."

"It's just…they scream so much. I-I've never heard such screaming."

"This is unprecedented territory we're entering. Imagine if you had been driving your wagon across the vast plains to stake a claim that would allow you to establish yourself in this country for generations to come. Well, this is our new frontier. And we must drive our wagons forward, damn the cost." Marlowe's enthusiastic smile hardened. "Of course, if you're unable to complete simple tasks, I can always ask someone else. Many would welcome this opportunity."

"No, sir. That won't be necessary." The employee grabbed the keys for the holding cells. After all, this was a great opportunity in a land that wasn't quite as full of them as people thought. He wanted to make a name and a fortune for himself. He'd better do as he was told and stop asking questions. At the door, though, the employee looked over his shoulder at his boss.

"Mr. Marlowe?"

"Yes?"

"Do you know *my* name?"

Jake Marlowe stared. "It's Mitchell, isn't it?"

"Martin," the young man said.

"Yes. Martin." Marlowe smiled. "I see great things for your future, Martin."

The young man smiled in return, happy to be seen, to be thought worthy. It was a start. He, too, wanted more in the land of more.

"Thank you, sir. I won't disappoint you," Martin said.

"Swell. Then bring me the next Diviner."

HEALING

Outside his family's tent, Nate Timmons was sitting on the ground with his face buried in his hands. Beside him, Moses and Tobias were uncharacteristically quiet. Tobias had started sucking his thumb.

"What's wrong?" Memphis asked Remy.

"It's Bessie. She's got the typhoid, they say. Floyd, she's bad off."

"The Red Cross will help."

"The Red Cross is taking care of the white people, *bon ami*," Remy said.

"I lost everythin' else. Can't lose my wife to this flood. Please, Lord, please." Nate broke down and wept quietly, and the other men turned away out of respect. Moses and Tobias started to cry, too.

"I wanna see Mama," Tobias said.

One of the other women picked Tobias up like he was her own. "Not just yet, baby. Come. Come play with Maxine."

Memphis remembered his own mother lying on her bed, dying of cancer. He knew what grief was coming for these boys if their mother passed. He started toward the tent. Bill took hold of his arm. "We have to keep low," he reminded Memphis sadly.

"She'll die if I don't," Memphis said.

"Sometimes it's hard to understand the way of things," Bill said.

Memphis had had enough of *the way of things*. He shook free of Bill's grasp. He spoke firmly, clearly: "I can do it. I can heal your wife, Mr. Timmons."

Nate looked up at Memphis, red-eyed and bewildered. "You ain't no doctor."

"I'm telling you I can do it. Just take me to her, all right? Take me now."

The tent where Bessie Timmons lay was rancid with sweat and sick. Thick breath wheezed in and out of her lungs. She had waded through a flood to come live in a dank tent on top of an eight-mile-long levee with thousands of other refugees. Sometimes, sickness came on like the flood itself, with no way to hold it back. But other times, sickness came about because of the carelessness and unfairness of the world.

"Don't you worry, Mrs. Timmons. I'm gonna do right by you." Memphis whispered it like a prayer. Memphis had been afraid of being found out as a Diviner with a bounty on his head. Now he had another fear: What if he couldn't heal this woman after all?

He placed his right palm atop her damp, feverish brow; the other hand he pressed to her rigid belly. The healing power came on so much stronger than before. It reached out and pulled him like a crocodile's jaws. There was a tight squeezing in his chest, and then the sickness traveled back and forth like a current, from Bessie to Memphis, thinning out each time until it was nothing but a low hum between them. A second jolt shot through Memphis. His whole body felt electric. He was a bird soaring high above the country before it was a country, when it was a quilt of tribes. Down below, majestic buffalo stampeded across the plains, and it was a sight to behold. He felt Bessie's body healing, growing stronger, could sense that body taking her forward, bearing another child, lifting grandchildren into her arms— even great-grands. Bessie Timmons was going to be all right. More than all right. A third jolt came, and Memphis fell to his knees beside Bessie. His hands shook. The muscles of his arms ached as if he'd been doing push-ups for days.

"Water," Bessie Timmons said. She sat up. She was drenched in sweat. "Please. Can I have some water?" A bowl of it was fetched and she drank greedily. Outside the tent, families gathered, looking in on the scene: Memphis Campbell, on his knees in the dirt beside the bed of Bessie Timmons, who seemed right as rain. Completely healed.

Moses crept forward. "Mama?"

"That my Moses? Come give your momma a hug now."

Memphis felt Bessie's pulse. Where it had been weak it was now steady and strong. She rolled her head toward Memphis. "I...I felt you. Must've been a dream. But I could've sworn you were with me. But in that place, you had a different name."

"Fever dreams are funny that way. How you feeling, Mrs. Timmons?" Memphis asked. Lord, but he was tired.

"Fine, thank you. A might bit hungry. But just fine, thank you."

Bessie smiled at Memphis, and for just a minute he could pretend it was his mother, and that he had healed her and kept her from the clutches of the King of Crows.

"Well. I'm just glad you're feeling better, ma'am. I would appreciate it if we could keep this a little secret between us."

"All right. Memphis," Bessie said, making Memphis go cold. "That was the name I heard."

"Like I said, fever dreams are funny."

Bessie chuckled weakly. "Well, you surely are a miracle man. I thank the Good Lord for bringing you to me."

That night, to celebrate the saving of Bessie Timmons, the refugees gathered around a small campfire to share what food they had. Somehow they'd managed to make a feast of Red Cross rations, and it fed everyone. "Gonna have us a true *fais-dodo*," Remy said, and Henry smiled to hear a phrase he knew so far from the home where he'd first heard it. He sat at the rescued piano and banged out all the songs he knew, and then Nate Timmons sat down and showed off his stride piano chops. They sang and danced, and Memphis took note of all of it, how no matter what miseries life threw at people, they managed to make the best of it. But they needed one another for that. Maybe he and the other Diviners—his friends—didn't know what they were doing just yet. But they would figure it out. Because they had no choice and because they were joined. He watched a grinning Henry banging out a song on the piano, adding haunting little flourishes and chord changes. He'd never realized what a beautiful musician Henry was, and Memphis felt a joy that his friend was so full of happiness just now. To share a joy was to make it last longer. The women danced and clapped hands. Someone who worked the food tent had managed a pot of coffee somehow. It was tepid, but that didn't matter. The smell alone was a welcome respite. Strong and chocolaty, it blotted out the stench from miles of fetid floodwater. Bill and Henry passed around cups until all who wanted it had some. It was nearly time for the children to go to bed, though they insisted through their yawns that they weren't sleepy at all.

"Can't we have just one more story?" Moses begged. "Floyd! Tell us a story, please?"

"A story, huh?" Memphis said. "All right. All right, then. I got one for you. Who here has heard about Diviners? Okay. All right. Quite a few folks. The rest of you I'm guessing don't have no interest in hearing about magic and ghosts and whatnot. Maybe I should tell a Bible story instead...."

The children screamed in protest. They demanded the other story.

Memphis held them in suspense for a little longer, fighting a grin. When he looked up, the eyes of all the children were on him. Hopeful. Eager. Something shifted inside Memphis, and the story, his story, began to come out as if it had been waiting patiently for him to tell it. "Once upon a time, there were some friends called the Diviners. They were object-readers and fire-makers, dream walkers and invisible men, future-seers and, yes, healers...." Memphis told the story of this band of heroes battling evil in the land, trying to right a wrong that had been done many years ago, and of their great foe, the King of Crows, and his Army of the Dead. There was nothing but the night and the fire and the ancient, lasting story of good versus evil, of life and death hanging in the balance. It was a thread woven through all of humankind: this need for story to explain the unexplainable, to comfort the hurting, to promise that no one was alone. Evie's uncle Will had said there was no greater power on earth than story. And in this shared moment, Memphis knew that it was so.

"And that concludes this episode of... the Voice of Tomorrow!" Memphis said.

The children protested, wanting more.

"Wait just a minute! But what happens after they face the King of Crows? How does the story end?" a boy named Jeremiah asked.

"I suppose that depends on us," Memphis answered. "We've got to be the heroes of our own stories. Sometimes that means reading the past for clues. Sometimes that means peering as much as you can into the future to light the way. Sometimes you got to work where no one can see you until you're ready to be seen. Sometimes you got to walk in dreams so you know what a dream feels like, so you know the shape of your own longings. Other times, you got to bring the fire of your anger and righteousness! And sometimes, you've got to heal the things that are broken or sick. Even when it scares you. Even when you feel like walking away and pretending you never saw the sickness. Don't need special powers to do any of that. The truth is, the story never ends. It's always happening. But whether it tips toward evil"—and here Memphis held out a fist—"or good," he said, offering the other, "well, now. That's up to all of us. We are all storytellers telling the story, adding our piece."

Memphis caught Bill's eye. He expected him to be angry. To rebuke Memphis with a look for telling that story. Instead, the big man seemed moved.

"I'm scared of the King of Crows." Jeremiah burrowed into his mama's side.

Memphis looked the boy in the eyes. "You know what heroes do? They pay attention. You be on the lookout for trouble, now. Things you might tell yourself are nothing to worry about. Just your mind making too much of it. It's like the flood coming through—it gathers strength fast, and then it's too late."

"What kinds of things?" Moses asked.

"You wake up in the night because you feel like there's something near. If you're out walking and a crow caws nearby three times, like a warning, or sudden mist comes up, making it hard to see, or the sky shudders with lightning the color of a dead man's eyes. If the hair on the back of your neck stands up and tells you to get moving quick, well, go and get your friends real quick. And if you see an ash-gray man in a tall, tall hat and a coat made of birds, a coat he's starting to open up to mesmerize you, just...run!" With that, Memphis reached out and tickled Tobias. All the children squealed, then collapsed with laughter.

"Come. Time for bed," Mrs. Timmons said. She and the other mothers corralled the children toward the tents. The adults thanked one another for the food and Memphis for the story. Old Mrs. Jessup nodded at Memphis. "You know about the man in the hat, do you?"

"Yes, ma'am," Memphis said, surprised.

"Then you know the danger. Don't let him trap you with the lies inside his coat."

Memphis, Henry, and Bill retired to their own tent. Before he ducked inside, Memphis took one last look at the sky.

But it was only sky.

"If I'm not mistaken, I could swear you shed a tear over my story tonight, Bill," Memphis said as he entered the tent and stretched out. He could hear Henry snoring softly.

"You was mistaken," Bill said. "Go to sleep. Long day tomorrow."

Memphis turned onto his side, grinning.

❋

Word got around, as word always does, about what Memphis had done for Bessie Timmons. Others began asking for his help, and Memphis obliged: an infected cut here, a feverish child there, a barking cough or some other waterborne illness. What the Red Cross held back, Memphis gave. Day after day, he brought ease to those in need of it. When he returned to his tent later, a handkerchief-wrapped bundle would be left on his doorstep—a ration of bread. A jar of water. A piece of meat. Small thank-yous from the kin of those he'd helped.

The children followed Memphis now wherever he went, especially Moses and Tobias, who saw him as their hero. It made Memphis miss Isaiah all the more.

"Can you show me how to do it?" Moses asked one evening as Memphis, Henry, and Bill shared a supper of beans and bread at a long table with many others in the food tent.

"Don't work that way." Isaiah would have a fit making fun of Memphis for not speaking "proper" English. But who got to decide what was proper and not? Tying his words up with "proper" strings made it hard for Memphis to think, hard for him to express himself. The words had to come however the words came, on a tide of feeling.

"You got kids?" Tobias asked, bringing Memphis back to the moment.

Memphis laughed. "How old do you think I am, Shrimpy?"

Moses and Tobias burst into giggles, and Memphis thought about Isaiah's laugh, which was just about the best sound in the world.

"We gotta get off this levee and on to Bountiful," he said to Bill and Henry on the way back from dinner.

When they reached their tent, Nate Timmons was sitting in front of it, whittling a stick. He looked very serious.

"How's your wife feeling?" Memphis asked.

"Better." Nate kept whittling. He dropped a curl of wood onto the ground. "You're the one they looking for. Memphis Campbell. The Harlem Healer. The Diviner."

Memphis's stomach went cold. Five thousand dollars was a lot of money. Enough to get a sharecropper and his family off this levee and headed up north.

"Don't worry. I won't tell." Nate looked up at Memphis not with suspicion or greed, but with a soft pleading. "But you got to be careful, you hear? Word gets back to these white planters like Mr. LeRoy or those National Guard boys, they'll turn you in quick as a snakebite turns bad."

That night, as Memphis lay on his blanket on the ground inside the tent he shared with Bill and Henry, he could tell Bill was mad about something. He could hear Henry outside the tent playing that piano and singing, keeping everybody entertained. It was just Memphis and Bill.

Memphis propped himself up on his elbows. "What is it?" he asked at last.

"You don't know nothing 'bout your powers, really. None of y'all do."

"So?"

"So you don't know if what you got...how long it lasts."

"I'm fine," Memphis growled.

"Yeah, you fine, now. Enjoying being the big man on the levee. Memphis, if you use it all up here, what you gonna do when it counts—when you got to heal the breach?"

Memphis had worried before that his power might be finite. He did feel awfully tired after a healing, and that worried him a bit. During the initial phase of a healing, the sickness in the person transferred to Memphis. He could feel it invading his body, and that was often the moment that scared him most: What if he got stuck with that sickness? When Papa Charles had made him heal Dutch Schultz's boys, Memphis had even gotten rashes and sores.

Back when he was the Harlem Healer, his mother used to say there was no sense hiding your light under a bushel: *Whatever gifts you've been blessed with, you must share them. There will always be enough. Think of Jesus and the fishes and the loaves.* But now Memphis was concerned. What if he needed the healing at some point and it wouldn't come? Maybe he should hoard the power and use it only for the people closest to him.

So the next day, when word came that the Robinson family would sure appreciate a healing, Memphis said he wasn't able. It was only a cough; a cough was nothing. No reason to think it wouldn't get better on its own. He felt lousy about it, though. Because the thought had also occurred to him: What if the secret to his power was in using it? What if, rather than a battery being drained, it was like a muscle being trained, and the more he used it, the better he'd get?

"Henry," Memphis whispered into the dark of the tent later that night. *"Henry."*

"I'm awake." Henry rolled over to face Memphis. "Can't sleep, either?"

"No," Memphis whispered. "I wanted to ask you something."

"Sure. Just don't ask me state capitals."

"You think, maybe, we could look for Theta in dreams? What I mean is, is there a way I could be awake with you in that world? I promise to heal you up afterward, take the edge off of what it does to you."

"It's Ling who usually has luck finding people. But we could try. If we're together, we might boost each other's powers."

"All right, then. What do I need to do?"

"Well, Ling always says that we need something that belongs to the person. A ring, a comb, anything, really."

Memphis's heart sank. Then he remembered: "Wait! I got this book of poems she gave me. Does that count?"

"Don't see why not."

Memphis got up and dug his waterlogged copy of *Leaves of Grass* from his knapsack and handed it to Henry. "What now?"

"We'll need to be close to each other. We need to be touching."

Memphis flinched just slightly. Not enough to be obvious. But Henry had been trained all his life to spot these reactions. It was a matter of survival. Henry had learned to change his walk, his manner of speaking, anything that might "give him away" and make some fella uncomfortable, perhaps even uncomfortable enough to do Henry harm. But he hadn't thought he needed to hide himself from a friend.

Henry remembered one time going with his father to the barbershop. He might've been four or five years old. Young. He'd been walking in the French Quarter with his handsome father, taking note as his father stopped and said hello to the other men on the street, all of whom seemed to look up to him. Henry had been so happy and proud, he'd wanted to give his daddy a kiss. When he tried, his father got angry, pushed him away. "What are you doing?" he'd reprimanded, keeping his voice low, and Henry understood he'd done something wrong, but he didn't know what or why. "Men don't kiss other men," his father said briskly. They'd walked on as before, but Henry's happiness had been stolen, replaced by shame.

A knot formed in Henry's throat. The familiar swallowed howl of shame. He was afraid he might cry, though he'd been told his whole life that men didn't do that, either. "You know, on second thought, I'm bushed. I should probably get some rest," Henry said, saving face.

But then Memphis put his hand on Henry's arm. "I'm sorry. I never… I…I don't know how to do this right."

"Does anybody?" Henry asked. "Here." He handed back *Leaves of Grass*. "You hold on to that. I'll do the rest." They lay down on their mildewy Red Cross blankets. Henry edged a foot over, touching Memphis's foot. They waited.

"Now what?" Memphis said.

"Now you become my lover man." Henry cracked up laughing. Like alchemy, he'd transformed his shame into wit. Laughter was power.

Memphis laughed, too. "Okay. All right. I see you."

"Do you?"

Memphis quieted. "Trying."

"Yeah. Me, too." Henry took a deep, cleansing breath. "Sweet dreams, Memphis. Good luck."

It took some time for sleep to come. When Henry woke at last in the dreamscape, he was surrounded by waving stalks of golden wheat, and there was Theta, wearing a silver gown that Henry recognized as being her favorite among her Follies costumes. Henry was overjoyed to see her. They'd never been apart so long.

"Theta? Theta, darlin'. It's me, your old pal, Hen."

"Hey, Hen," Theta said, twirling slowly.

Henry looked around for Memphis and was disappointed not to see him. Perhaps their powers didn't work together after all. He could at least try to get some information.

"Theta, darlin'. Are you in Bountiful?"

"Bountiful?" Theta said, and Henry couldn't tell if that was an answer or not.

"Can you tell me where you are?"

"I'm here," Theta said dreamily. She watched a line of Cherokee women as they danced. Henry was struck by how much she favored these women. Almost by instinct, Theta began to move as they did.

"But where is here, honey?" Henry pressed.

"The circus."

A drop of rain fell slowly, growing bigger as it descended, spreading out like a new universe straining at the borders of its raindrop womb until it popped. Out sprang a boldly striped circus tent. The tent wrapped its arms around them until they were all cradled inside its expanse. In the center of the ring, Theta lifted her arms, like a ballerina before a performance. And then, to Henry's astonishment, Memphis entered the ring. Neither seemed to recognize the other directly, but each wore a vague smile. Memphis took Theta's hand. The top of the tent became a silvery moon, and then they were moving together in a beautiful dream ballet. Memphis lifted Theta into the air. She arched her back and spread her arms like a bird flying. People reached for meaning inside dreams. Their yearning found expression in endless ways. Everything was possible here. Futures were born. For how could anything start without a dream first?

Memphis cradled Theta gently in his arms, twirling around until they became a bright ball of energy that soared up, up, up. And then everything was gone. Henry was alone.

"Always the bridesmaid, never the bride," Henry said.

"Henry? Henry!"

"Ling!" Henry shouted.

She was on the other side of a river.

"I found you," she called.

"How do you know it wasn't me who found you?"

"Don't annoy me so soon," she said. "How do I get across this thing?"

Henry had brought his own unconscious here. The river, separating them.

"Where are you?" they each blurted at the same time.

"I'm with Alma and Jericho on the Chitlin Circuit."

"You're pulling my leg."

"No, I'm not. I'm nowhere near your leg."

"Figure of speech."

"You and your strange figures of speech," Ling tutted. "We're somewhere in Tennessee, on our way to Arkansas."

"Are Isaiah and Theta with you?"

"No," Ling called back.

"Any sign of them in your dream walks?"

Ling shook her head. Henry's heart sank. He'd so hoped to give Memphis some good news. Something solid to ease his mind.

"Where are *you*?" Ling asked. "Did you make it to Bountiful?"

"Not yet. We're stuck on a levee in the middle of the Mississippi flood, darlin'."

"That's not a song of yours, is it? Or another figure of speech?"

"Sadly, darlin', it is all too true. The Pinkertons boarded our train and we had to jump off—and I do mean jump. So that makes the Shadow Men, the police, and now the Pinkertons. I've never felt so wanted by so many men but so unhappy about it. If only Gary Cooper were looking for me."

"You really could make a joke of anything, couldn't you?"

"Not that unfortunate nightgown. That's a tragedy."

Ling and Henry yelped as the landscape shifted under their feet, unbalancing them both. The ground cracked and broke apart like an earthquake. The river geysered up between them, turning Ling into a watery reflection.

"Henry!" Ling shot out a hand, but it was no good. The ground shifted again, and then Ling vanished from the dream.

"No, wait! Ling! *Ling!*" Henry cried.

The wall of water rose higher and transformed into a giant rattlesnake that loomed above him, its tongue flicking menacingly. Where it struck the ground, lightning crackled. Henry scrambled backward only to see that he was at the edge of a cliff. Before him, the snake liquefied, taking on yet another, more frightening shape.

"Do you like to walk in dreams?" the King of Crows said, walking toward Henry. "How about nightmares?"

The King of Crows stretched out his hand, and a paralyzing cold seeped into Henry's legs. "Maybe you'll need your friend the healer to help you? Let's give him a real challenge, shall we? Something to slow him down a bit, hmm? A taste of what's to come."

The King of Crows waved his arm as if conducting. The field of wheat reappeared. Memphis and Theta were there, still dancing. "What do you think? Will he help you? Or perhaps he's so happy in this world, dancing his cares away, that he won't even want to wake up."

The icy cold immobilizing Henry's legs crawled up into his lungs, making it hard to breathe. "Memphis," Henry choked out. "Wake. Up."

"Yes. Wake up, Dream Walker," the King of Crows said and laughed.

Henry's eyes snapped open. He was on his back in the refugee camp struggling for breath. He couldn't move. All he could do was lie there, knowing that he was slowly dying. Beside him, Memphis slept on, lost to his happy dream. To break the spell, Henry needed to wake him up. But after every dream walk, there were a few minutes when Henry was completely paralyzed.

"Memphis..." he rasped. The air in front of his eyes became black dots. His foot was still nestled close to Memphis's. He concentrated on moving just his foot. If he could just kick Memphis...He strained. Nothing. His vision swam. Soon, he would lose consciousness. Henry thought of never seeing Theta or Ling ever again. His foot twitched and brushed against

Memphis's ankle. And again. Memphis stirred. *Come on*, Henry begged. *Wake. Up.* The reserves in his lungs were nearly gone.

His foot kicked out suddenly, like an angry mule. Memphis bolted awake, still a bit sleep-dazed. He looked over and saw Henry struggling.

"H-help," Henry eked out on the last of his air.

"Hold on, hold on!" Memphis was saying, putting his hands against Henry's chest. And then, all at once, Henry could feel Memphis drawing the sickness from his trembling body. They were joined, and it wasn't much different from a dream walk. Henry heard both of their heartbeats, at first out of sync, and then in the same rhythm. The cold grip on his lungs loosened. Henry's breathing returned to normal. He sat up, coughing and sputtering.

"Better?" Memphis asked.

Henry nodded. Tears streamed down his face. His nose ran. It had been like drowning inside his own body. He drew in more air, not even caring about the pungent smell that hung over the camp. "Th-thanks."

"What happened?" Memphis asked, once he was sure that Henry was all right.

"The King of Crows," Henry said. "He did this. He wanted you to heal me. To use your power."

"You mean use it up?" Memphis was nervous now.

Henry drew in several deep lungfuls of air. "I don't know. He said he wanted to give you a real challenge. A taste of what's to come."

"A taste of what's to come. What does that mean?"

"Dunno, but I don't like the sound of it." Henry wiped his nose on his sleeve.

"Do you think he would've . . . killed you?" Memphis said.

Henry wasn't sure. It seemed more like a challenge than a murder attempt. "It's like he wanted to use our powers against us. To let us know that he could do it. That bastard came for me in a dream walk. He used the dream against me. I had just found Ling, too."

"Ling! Did he . . . ?"

"No. She vanished before he got to me."

"Did she say where they were?" Memphis asked.

"She and Jericho are on the Chitlin Circuit with Alma."

Memphis couldn't help it. He burst out laughing. "Now, *that* I'd like to see."

And despite his near-death experience, Henry had to admit it was funny.

"Did she say anything about the others?" Memphis asked.

Henry shook his head. He could see how disappointed Memphis was by this. "Sorry, Memphis," he said, and Memphis patted Henry on the back the way fellas did when they didn't have words.

When Henry and Ling had confronted the ghost of Wai-Mae in the dream world, it had been terrifying. But to a certain degree, Henry had understood her motivations. The dream world had belonged to Wai-Mae as well; it had been the only escape for the angry, abused, scared girl who had died so tragically. This was different. It was like having someone break into your house and intimidate you into leaving it. The King of Crows was not lost or scared. He was cruel and power-mad and he needed to be stopped. Henry grasped this with new urgency.

Somewhere close by in the camp, a baby was crying. A mother soothed it, cooing softly. Everywhere was the sound of the river.

"Do you remember anything from your dream walk?" Henry asked after a moment.

"Only a little. I dreamed about holding Theta," Memphis said. "But it felt like she was really in my arms."

"She was, Memphis."

"You think she'll remember when she wakes up?"

"I hope so."

The following night, while the Haymakers played their set, Ling and Jericho finally seized their chance to experiment with combining their powers. As they walked toward the woods, away from the dance hall on the edge of town and the cars parked every which way in the dirt lot, Ling was telling Jericho about her encounter with Henry in the dream world.

"...and then the river rose up like a wall and I lost him. Very odd."

"Why odd? That happens in dream walks, doesn't it?"

"Yes. I suppose it does." Ling shook her head. "It's probably nothing, but I had the strangest feeling that something was working to keep us apart."

"We don't have to do this if you don't want to," Jericho said. They'd reached a stopping place where they could still hear the music but were far enough away from the hall that Ling thought it would be safe.

"No. We should try," Ling said. "We have to start figuring these things out for ourselves."

She balanced on her crutches and took Jericho's hands in hers.

"It feels like we're about to square dance," Jericho said. "Just so we're clear, I don't dance."

"Neither do I."

"Well. I'm glad that's settled. Now what?"

Ling bit her lip, thinking. "Your power is strength. Mine is dream walking. I honestly don't know how our powers combine."

"Maybe I can make your dream walking stronger?"

"That's what Henry and I seem to be able to do together," Ling said. She looked around, buying time while she thought. "Let's concentrate on one thing, a transference of energy."

Jericho's lips quirked. "If you want me to carry you somewhere, you only have to ask."

"That was a joke?"

"Yes."

"So you're getting funnier."

"Thank you."

"That wasn't a compliment. Henry's the funny one when he should be serious, and I mostly find it annoying."

Jericho found Ling's irritation with him hilarious, like having a younger sister to torment. "What if I'm more than just Jericho the Serious?"

"But you are serious. You're a brooder."

Jericho scoffed. "I am *not* a brooder."

Ling's expression didn't change. "Did anyone ever make you read *Wuthering Heights*?"

"No," Jericho said, unsure of where this conversation was headed.

"Count yourself lucky. It's full of annoying people. There is a man named Heathcliff. He is the biggest brooder of them all."

It took Jericho a minute to catch up. He laughed. "Are you...are you calling me a Heathcliff?"

"If the shoe fits."

"The shoe does not."

Ling exhaled noisily. "Do you see that light pole over there?"

Jericho looked over his shoulder at the pole strung with a fat yellowish light. "Yes."

"What if we tried to make it disappear?"

"You really think we could? Isn't that more of Sam's territory?"

"There's only one way to find out."

"What if something goes wrong and we end up making the dance hall disappear instead?"

"Hopefully that won't happen."

Jericho raised both eyebrows. "That's the best you've got?"

"Science requires experimentation. And danger."

"At least we won't have to listen to any more of Doc's long-winded stories," Jericho said, making Ling smile at last.

"Here goes," Ling said. She and Jericho squeezed their hands together and stared out at the light pole. Sweat beaded on Jericho's forehead. *I'm not a real Diviner,* he thought. But Ling held fast to his hands. He could hear her heart beating in perfect time, could sense her excitement and her fear. He could just make out the silhouette of her thoughts, bits and pieces and vague hopes. It was as if they were one person, almost. Jericho had never experienced such an intimate encounter before. It was so much deeper than something physical. It frightened him; he wanted more. *Can you feel me?* he wondered.

To his great surprise, he heard Ling's voice. *Yes.*

He almost let go. The shock was so great.

Ling?

Jericho.

He was giddy with the sensation. *Hey. Do you smell something?*

Yes.

Sulfur. Like a match being struck. He heard a discordant, mechanical hum. Pressure began to build inside him. So much pressure. He feared it would rip him in two.

Ling?

I feel it.

What is that?

I don't know.

Should we stop?

Not yet.

The hum getting louder, becoming a clang. A scream. Something was taking shape. A dark wood. All bare trees and sickly pale bark. High above, a yellow moon hid its shine behind thin gray clouds.

Where are we?

Ling did not let go of Jericho's hands. *I think we're in the land of the dead.*

And then as suddenly as the sensation had come, it was gone. Jericho and Ling stood near the dance hall, still holding hands and panting for breath.

"Wh-what just happened?" Jericho said.

"I'm not sure, but I believe somehow we managed to open up a door into that other dimension—*his* dimension," Ling said, clearly excited.

"But we don't know how we did it," Jericho said.

"Doesn't matter," Ling said. "The important thing is, we know we *can* do it."

"There you are!" Lupe called, coming out of the lodge with her snare drum. Only now did Jericho and Ling realize that the Haymakers' set had ended.

"Mr. Smith, could you be a lamb and help me with this?" Lupe asked.

"Of course," Jericho said, moving to help Lupe even though it was obvious to everyone else she didn't need it. She was just inventing ways to be around him.

"You are just the sweetest," Lupe said, smiling.

"It's no trouble," Jericho said, oblivious, and Ling could see the disappointment on Lupe's face as he carried the drum to the bus without so much as a backward glance.

＊

"Why are you sweet on Evie?" Ling asked the next night when it was just the two of them backstage.

Jericho looked up from his book. "Who said I was—"

"You're nothing alike. Nothing."

"You're the scientist. Isn't it 'opposites attract'?" Jericho challenged and turned the page.

"Sometimes forces repel, too."

"You don't think much of Evie, do you?"

"I don't always feel that she's a serious person."

"Neither is Henry. And you seem to like him just fine."

"I'm not jealous, if that's what you're thinking."

"I didn't say that. You judge her differently because she's a girl."

"*I'm* a girl!" Ling protested.

"Henry goes to parties. Henry comes home late. Or stays out all night. He makes jokes all the time. But it doesn't seem to bother you. Why can't Evie do the same?"

"I…" Ling started, but there was nothing else to add.

Jericho shrugged and went back to reading.

Ling did judge Evie differently. And part of it *was* that Evie was a girl, Ling realized with great discomfort. She also didn't like Evie all that much. The two of them had little in common. If not for this mission, they would not have known each other, or ever spent time together. Ling thought of Evie as frivolous and a little reckless. Also brave and daring. And selfish.

"Evie couldn't see that Mabel was ripe for joining up with anarchists. I just don't understand how a person who reads objects and collects so much about people and who they are could choose to be so blind," Ling said.

"If you knew all those things about people, wouldn't you want to be blind sometimes? Going to parties and living fast is Evie's revenge on a cruel world. She looks it in the eye and says, 'You will not break me.'" Jericho let out a long exhale. "And then she usually gets drunk."

"So she's pretending all the time."

"Not all the time."

"Did she pretend with you?"

Jericho's jaw tightened. "Now, see here—you aren't invited to comment on everything in my life."

"She's never going to be with you. She loves Sam. Stop pining for her, *Heathcliff*!" Ling clapped a hand over her mouth, embarrassed by her sudden outburst. "I'm sorry," she said from behind her fingers. "I didn't mean to be so…"

"Honest?" Jericho finished.

Ling dropped her hand, letting it rest on her crutch again. "I want better for you. You deserve happiness."

"No one's ever said that to me before."

"Well. Now someone has."

Jericho had not experienced much happiness since he was a kid working his parents' farm. That was one of the reasons he'd clung to Evie. Being with her was such a big ride that it didn't leave room for all the feelings Jericho pushed down. What did happiness look like when you didn't know?

"What makes you happy?" Jericho asked.

"Oh," Ling said, surprised by the question. "Um, science. The beauty of it, especially physics. My father's soup dumplings—taking that first bite and the soup squirts into your mouth, hot and savory. Chinese New Year. This one dress my mother sewed for me that's my favorite color of blue. Thinking." *Alma, Alma, Alma.* "You?"

Jericho thought long and hard. "Reading, especially philosophy. Also thinking." He let out a long breath. What he wanted to add to his list was the time he and Evie had been up at the top of the Ferris wheel, when he realized for the first time that he might be in love with her. "Ferris wheels," he said. "The farm."

"Which farm?"

"My family's farm in Pennsylvania. It's—it was—really beautiful. And there's a satisfaction you get from planting a seed or a cutting deep in the ground and watching it grow. Knowing you had a hand in it."

"Oh. Then why did you leave?"

"I caught infantile paralysis."

Their shared affliction. But Jericho had escaped its ravages, it seemed.

"After that, I became a ward of the state. I spent a long time in one of Marlowe's inventions, something he called an iron lung. It breathed for me. All I could do was stare up at the ceiling or look out the window at the changing seasons. I thought about what my family would be doing, whether it was planting or harvesting time. If there'd been a wedding or a barn raising. If my mother was pickling or canning. It was Marlowe who saved me."

"This must be hard for you, then."

"Not really," Jericho said. "I wasn't a real person to him."

Ling could scarcely catch her breath. There were layers to Jericho she had not considered. "I didn't know. I'm sorry."

Jericho shrugged it off. "You've had your share of hard luck, too."

Ling cleared her throat. "Lupe likes you, you know."

Jericho's brow furrowed into a V. "Lupe who plays the drums?"

262

"No. Lupe the Pope. Yes. That Lupe."

"Oh," Jericho said. Then: "Ohhh. How can you tell?"

Ling wanted to resist making another sarcastic comment, because she was pretty sure that Jericho was sincere about not being able to tell. "I know through a magical radio wave only girls can hear and understand. I'm breaking my oath to tell you. I'll probably be excommunicated," she said, losing her battle against sarcasm. "Honestly, Jericho, anyone with eyes can tell."

Lupe liked him. Jericho rolled it over in his mind as he watched her tapping out a steady rhythm on the high hat from his spot in the wings. She was smiling like she was having the time of her life. Guadalupe de la Rosa. Even her name sounded like music. Like Evie, she was outgoing. But Lupe wasn't Evie, and that, Jericho knew, was Ling's point.

His palms got a little sweaty thinking about it all. Jericho didn't have a lot of experience with women. Not like Sam. He didn't want to be like Sam, going from girl to girl. Then again, Sam had won over Evie. But Jericho knew he could never be something he wasn't. He would never be Sam.

Guadalupe de la Rosa wasn't afraid to travel the country and make her own way. That was very brave, Jericho thought. And she played the drums. What if she thought he was boring—a *brooder*? And what would she think if she knew about all he'd been through? If she knew about the things Marlowe had done to him, about the machinery keeping him alive?

"What do I do?" Jericho asked.

"You're asking me for romantic advice?" Ling said.

"I suppose I am."

"Just talk to her," Ling said.

"What should I say?"

"You read a lot. You'll think of something," Ling said.

Jericho spent the next two songs, the band's last, watching Lupe and working up the courage to approach her. What if Ling was wrong about Lupe being interested in him? Maybe she was just friendly to everyone.

The set ended.

"Thank you so much! You've been the berries!" Alma said and blew kisses to the audience.

Jericho licked his hand and smoothed back his hair. He looked to Ling, whose lips turned down in distaste. "Did you just spit into your hair?"

The band was headed for the wings. They were full of high spirits and beautiful noise.

"Lupe!" Jericho said, a little louder than he'd intended, as she came offstage.

"Yes?"

"You were really good tonight," Jericho said. *I shouldn't have spit in my hair*, he thought. He handed her a towel so she could mop her brow and then looked quickly to Ling, who pinched her lips shut and tried to pretend she was interested in the state of her nails.

"Why, thank you, Mr. Smith," Lupe said with exaggerated politeness.

"Just Freddy," he said. She didn't even know his real name. Was it doomed?

Lupe smiled. "Okay, *Just Freddy.*"

"Fred!" Doc called. "You gotta clear the stage so Snub Wilson and his Troubadours can go on!"

"Be right there," Jericho answered.

"No time for flirting. We got a schedule to keep!" Doc snapped.

Jericho blushed so hard he was afraid he'd turned purple. "I, ah, I'd better do as the man says."

"Well, you know where to find me," Lupe said coyly, and played a tiny riff against a wood beam.

Lupe watched Jericho march onto the stage and pick up the bass drum with one hand as if it weighed nothing. "Whoo! He is really strong. And handsome. Don't you think he's handsome?" She nudged Ling.

Ling regarded Jericho briefly. It was like trying to get excited about her cousin. "I suppose he's all right." She remembered she was supposed to be helping Jericho. "That is, I've heard *lots* of girls say so."

"Oh, are you and he ...?" Lupe motioned between Jericho and Ling.

"No! No," Ling said.

"Definitely not," Alma muttered under her breath.

Lupe leaned her head against the side of the stage and heaved a tiny sigh. "Yes, ma'am. Verrry handsome."

"For a brooder," Ling said under her breath.

Alma looped an arm across Lupe's shoulder, singing: "*I feel so blue, can't get over you...*"

Lupe slapped at her arm. "Would you quit it, Countess Cut-Up?"

"Every day I cry, why, Daddy, oh why," Alma sang, louder, and even Ling couldn't help giggling.

"To hell with you!" Lupe said.

Alma put a hand to her chest in mock-umbrage. "How unladylike!"

"Level with me, Alma—does the Big Six have a sweetheart?"

"Don't ask me, ask Li—that is, ask Miss Chang."

Lupe looked hopefully to Ling. "How's about it, Mary?"

Ling watched Jericho packing up the Harlem Haymakers' instruments. She thought about his tragic start in life, and about his unrequited love for a girl he'd never have. Maybe Ling couldn't make up for what he'd been through. But she could help that stubborn boy face the future.

"Well?" Lupe asked and bit her lip.

Ling let loose one of her rare, goofy grins. "No, Lupe. He does not."

※

Night after night, Jericho and Ling watched the Harlem Haymakers turn the clubs, barns, lodges, and dance halls of America's black vaudeville circuit into a sweaty, happy, stomping-and-clapping party. Some of the male territory bands and promoters wouldn't take the all-girl orchestra seriously—until the Haymakers started to wail. And boy, could they wail! Lupe would keep perfect, can't-stay-in-your-seat time while Dorothy let loose on the keys and Emmaline strummed the banjo. By the time Babe stood to take her sax solo and Sadie and Sally Mae joined in on trumpet, the whole place would be shaking. And, of course, there was Alma, who burned so brightly onstage. She was the perfect bandleader, singing and dancing and working the crowd into a joyful frenzy.

In the wings, Jericho tapped his foot in time to the music. He was a little off-beat, Ling noted, but he was so serious all the time that it was nice to see him loosen up. She found she was starting to warm to him. Being on the road together brought a forced intimacy. When you had to ride for hours on a bus together through all sorts of weather, experiences good and bad, when you had to share uncomfortable accommodations or withstand the stares of strangers, when there was time to notice the small things about a person, like how they came alive when passing a sun-drenched stretch of pastureland and you realized they saw that same beauty you did—these things opened that person for you. It made you see them.

On the dance floor of a barn-turned-nightclub on the outskirts of Yet-Another-Town, Arkansas, the Saturday-night patrons shimmied and Charlestoned and Black Bottomed, trying to shake off the cares of the week and the everyday blues of a nation that couldn't ever seem to hold up its end of the bargain. Ling was jealous of the dancing. There was rarely a moment when she wasn't having to work around the limitations of her body. Discomfort was a daily fact of life. Sometimes the ache was a nuisance. Other times, it was a storm that clawed and pulled and made it hard to concentrate on anything else. Mostly, Ling resented pain because it kept her from thinking, and thinking was what Ling did best.

And she needed to think just now. How were they going to stop the King of Crows? She and Jericho hadn't been able to enter the land of the dead again after that one surprise night in Tennessee. Nor had she been able to find Henry in a dream since the last time. She wondered if he and Memphis had made it off the levee. She wished she could talk to Henry. He always made her feel better somehow with his corny jokes and spontaneous musical numbers.

I miss you, Henry, you annoying boy, she thought.

Nearby, Jericho watched Lupe, who, between numbers, would glance in his direction, a playful smile on her lips when she caught his eye. Jericho hadn't said anything to Ling—nor did she want to know the details—but it was obvious to anyone with eyes that their romance was under way. Just that morning, Jericho had entered the bus whistling. Jericho. Whistling. It was as unfathomable as a talking giraffe. But she was glad that he had stopped moping and found some happiness at last.

Now if only Ling could figure out her own love life.

She'd thought being on the road with Alma would bring them closer together. Instead, they'd never seemed farther apart. Alma was polite enough, but that was just it—she was cordial to Ling in the same way she would be to any stranger. It hurt deeply. And who did she have to ask about it? Of the Haymakers, only Sally Mae liked girls, as far as Ling could tell, and she only knew that because she'd accidentally walked in on Sally Mae petting hotsy-totsy with a half-dressed chorine on the bus behind the Royal Theatre in Baltimore. "Knock next time," was all Sally Mae said later.

And anyway, Sally Mae clearly had no trouble with sex.

Ling loved Alma, but when she thought of making that love sexual, it was like a wire that didn't quite connect to a battery. It was more theoretical than actual. She liked kissing and cuddling, but she knew that alone wasn't sufficient for Alma.

From the church Ling had received the message that sex was shameful. Over time and with much thought, Ling had come to see this indoctrination as unscientific and not in keeping with nature. It wasn't shame Ling felt with Alma; it was frustration. Ling was alive in her mind and in her heart and even inside the multiple, swirling universes of dreams. Why wasn't that enough?

Onstage, Alma crooned a heartfelt torch song about a woman who just couldn't get over her man, no matter what he did. She sang the number with such conviction that it made Ling a little dizzy. She wasn't the only one. A few women in the audience looked up at Alma with stars in their eyes. Ling tried not to be jealous but, just like the woman in the song, it was no use. How on earth was she going to help stop the King of Crows when she couldn't even fathom her own heart?

After the show, the girls and Jericho boarded the bus. Doc had secured the Haymakers a night's lodging at a motel friendly to folks on the circuit, according to word of mouth. The show had gone well and the Haymakers were in good spirits as they rehashed the evening's best moments, with Alma leading the charge. Jericho sat with Lupe and Babe, smiling as he listened. Ling sat alone, staring out at all that dark.

As they exited the bus, Alma called Ling over. She held up a motel key. "I don't know how to say this, so I'm just gonna come out with it. Got us our own room. If you want to share it with me," she said. "But you don't have to."

Ling's stomach knotted. She knew what that meant. "No. I want to."

Alma's face brightened. "Okay, then."

They lay in the small bed in the anonymous motel. It was the first chance they'd had since they'd been on the road to really be alone. Most nights, they shared a room with all the girls.

"Did you like tonight's show?" Alma said, facing Ling.

"Yes. You were swell," Ling said, happy to be beside Alma.

Alma brushed a strand of hair from Ling's forehead. "I've missed you. I've missed us."

"Me, too," Ling whispered.

Alma draped a muscular arm across Ling's belly. She kissed Ling's neck. Ling tensed. She wanted to be held by Alma, only held, and Alma's kiss was an announcement of wanting more. Alma's mouth moved to Ling's shoulder.

Ling stared up at the ceiling, trying to figure out how to get back to the moment they'd just shared. With a finger, Alma turned Ling's face toward her own and kissed her with real passion. Ling liked the kiss very much, but she was afraid of what more might be expected. How could she make herself feel something she didn't?

"I-I'm... I'm awfully tired," Ling lied.

Ling saw the light dim in Alma's eyes, and then Alma flopped onto her back and let out a sigh. Disappointment lived in the new space between them. Two hot tears leaked down Ling's face and tickled her ears.

"I can't b-be what you w-want," Ling said, struggling to find the words. "I can't be something that I'm not."

"Well, neither can I," Alma said tearfully.

Ling shut her eyes tightly and wondered why the world, with all of its glorious possibilities, had decided to narrow itself so rigidly: this way or that way, yes or no, feminine or masculine. Where were the maybes, the strange and beautiful variants, the deeply personal in-betweens? As a scientist, Ling had to keep an open and curious mind, to explore all sorts of permutations. It seemed to her that there were endless variations for love, too, if only people would allow their minds to consider them.

Ling opened her eyes again. "Why...?" Ling stopped, afraid to say this aloud. "Why can't we be something new?"

"What do you mean by that?"

"What if our love is like a new species, something with no classification yet? What if what we have together doesn't fit neatly into any labeled drawer? That doesn't mean it isn't real."

Alma turned her head toward the open window, through which shone a buttery spring moon.

"There might need to be compromises," she said at last.

With effort, Ling curled herself toward Alma, the window, the moon. "I understand."

Alma shifted onto her side, facing Ling once more. She stroked the backs of her fingers against Ling's soft, full cheeks. She kissed Ling, once on the lips, then on the forehead. It was very nice, Ling thought. It was enough, though she knew it wasn't enough for Alma. "Whatever you do, will you come back to me?"

"Yes," Alma said. "Always."

That same buttery moon bleeding through the motel's thin curtains kept Jericho awake. Doc was gone. No sooner had they settled into the room than he'd slapped on some aftershave and headed out again, saying, "Don't wait up for me, Freddy. I got friends in this town." Jericho got out of bed and performed a set of one hundred push-ups, then he stepped outside for some fresh air. He was pleasantly surprised to see Lupe standing by the railing, looking up at the moon.

"Couldn't sleep either?" he said.

"Not with the way Babe and Dorothy snore. Sounds like the roof's about to come off," Lupe said, making Jericho laugh. He tended to do that a lot around her. "How come *you* can't sleep?"

Jericho pointed at the night sky. "Who could sleep with that moon?"

Lupe grinned. "That there is a dancing moon."

"I was going to suggest taking a walk."

"Dancing is like walking, only faster."

"I don't dance."

Lupe made a face. "*Pffft*, Freddy."

Jericho wished he'd used an alias that didn't remind him of Sam's teasing now that it was coming out of the mouth of a girl he was falling for.

"I truly do not," Jericho said.

Lupe's bright smile drooped. "What's the matter? Don't you like me, Freddy?"

Jericho's breath caught. "I like you very, very much," he admitted.

Lupe broke into a satisfied smile.

"But, um, I have another name, a middle name, that only my family and closest friends call me."

"Yeah? What's that?" Lupe teased.

"Jericho."

Lupe's eyebrows shot up. "Like the Bible?"

"My parents were religious."

"Like my abuela."

"Your what?"

"My grandmother," Lupe explained. She pursed her lips. "Jericho... Jer-i-cho..." she said, and he loved the way she made it sound. Like he was someone else. Someone who deserved happiness.

"Follow me." She took Jericho's hand and guided him through the parking lot into the flat field behind the motel. Jericho tensed, thinking of the last time he'd gone wandering off from an inn. But he would not allow Sergeant Leonard and his dire warnings to intrude on this moment.

"Hold me right here," Lupe instructed, moving Jericho's hand to the middle of her back. She placed her hand on his shoulder. Their other hands were joined in the air. "Now: one, two, three, four," Lupe intoned, pushing and pulling Jericho into each movement.

The only other time Jericho had danced with a girl, it had been on a disastrous date with Mabel. They'd ended up salvaging the night in the end, but Jericho never felt a spark with Mabel. Not like he had with Evie. And nothing like what he felt standing so close to Guadalupe de la Rosa. He wished he were more graceful and experienced. Mostly, Lupe moved around him, leading him through a series of steps that seemed complicated and confusing. When he got them wrong, which was most of the time, Lupe would break into snorts of laughter. Jericho was not offended. He found it all pretty funny, too.

"Okay, okay. Be serious now," Lupe said, still fighting the giggles. They resumed their positions. Jericho moved in closer. Lupe raised her chin and looked into his eyes, and all at once and completely, Jericho fell hard for her as they moved seamlessly together, one, two, back and forth and sideways. He even finished by dipping her low, his mouth near her neck. When he lifted her body back to standing, her face was flushed.

"You have that whole room to yourself?" she asked.

"Yes," Jericho said.

"Seems a lonely shame," she said and bit her lip.

This time, Jericho led the way.

Jericho had read many books in his eighteen years. Thousands of pages full of words, but none of them were adequate to describe what transpired between Lupe and him in that room with only a golden moon as witness. There was nothing he had ever experienced that could match the profound sympathy of their bodies learning this new dance, nothing that had prepared him for how incredible it was to be that close to another person. If he were doomed to repeat his life endlessly, at least there would always be this moment.

They lay together, his arm around Lupe, her head resting on his chest, which had never felt more human. The sky was brightening toward morning. His right hand tingled, half-asleep. For a moment, the old panic resurfaced. Jericho made a fist, just to be sure, and sighed in relief when it was easy to do.

As easy as falling in love with Guadalupe de la Rosa.

※

Everywhere they traveled, the ghosts followed. After the music and the dancing, when folks let down their guard, it was the ghosts they wanted to talk about. Sometimes, when they went out back to pee in a field behind the dance halls, lodges, and nightclubs, the spaces they'd had to carve out for themselves on the edges of white towns, they got a shiver up the neck and a need to race back toward the lights of those clubs, to the sweat of the dance, to the human press of communion. Sometimes they spoke of things glimpsed from a bus window late at night when most everyone else was sleeping and it felt as if the country's loneliness had crawled out of its graves to stand along the split-rail fences and beside the red barns and Burma-Shave signs, on the high ridges of desert canyons and Civil War battlefields, out where the buffalo had once been plentiful. Ghosts? They saw these winking reminders and quickly told themselves they had not. They did not want to believe in ghosts.

"I've got a ghost story for you—it really happened to my sister," Babe said as the Ford rolled into another night on its way to the next town. "My people are from South Carolina. That's where my sister, Doreen, lives, and all my cousins, too. Doreen's a nurse. She went to deliver a baby out near Pickens. A fine boy," Babe said.

Alma wrinkled her nose. "Pickens! What kind of a name is that?"

"Shh, Alma, let her tell it," Emmaline chided.

"It is a funny name," Alma whispered to Ling, and held her fingers where no one could see, like a secret they shared.

"He took his sweet time coming, though. Doreen had to drive back home in the dark. She said her little headlamps were the only light, and she couldn't see farther than the little bit of road in front of her. All of a sudden, those headlamps fell on a white lady waiting by the shoulder with her suitcase. She was dressed real nice, and Doreen stopped and asked her what she was doing out there in the dark—she was likely to get run over! Well, the lady said her name was Reecie Cowan and she was going to Spartanburg and would be much obliged for the ride. They rode together for a few miles. Doreen asked the lady all about herself. She said Reecie told her she was going to Spartanburg to meet her fiancé, who'd run off after getting her in the family way. His name was Milton Swinton, and after she'd threatened to report him for desertion, he told her to meet him at the Calvary Baptist Church outside town and they'd get married there. Doreen figured that was why she was dressed so nice. Sure enough, about a mile from town, they were coming up on Calvary. The lady started acting strange. 'This is where it happened,' she told Doreen. 'Where what happened?' Doreen said. 'This is where Milton Swinton bashed my brains in,' the lady told Doreen. And then, right in front of Doreen's eyes, Reecie started to bleed from her head. Blood pouring down all over her pretty dress. 'I'm dead. I keep forgetting as long as there's no justice.'"

Two seats up, Lupe jumped at this and Jericho put an arm around her shoulder, holding her close. She gazed up at him, happy, and Ling looked away, embarrassed.

"My sister stopped that car on a dime and got out, screaming. She said she looked over and Reecie was on the side of the road again with her suitcase. The blood was drying up, pulling up into the air like rain in reverse. 'Tell the police to look for my locket. He kept it. And don't pick up anybody else on this road,' Reecie told her. 'It won't be safe after I'm gone. There's bad ghosts these days. Ghosts that belong to the man in the hat.'"

"What did she mean by that?" Sally Mae asked. She'd been resting her eyes, not really interested till now.

"Beats me. Doreen didn't know, either."

Alma squeezed Ling's hand, and Ling nodded without looking. Up front, Jericho leaned forward, suddenly tense. *Say something*, Ling thought. *Say something, Ling.* But then Eloise was asking what happened next and Babe was talking again.

"Then? Then Reecie Cowan *disappeared*." Babe snapped her fingers. "Well, Doreen liked to nearly die from fright. She hopped back in that car quick and drove with her hands so tight on that wheel and didn't stop till she got to Spartanburg! The next day, she asked around and heard that there'd been a girl named Reecie Cowan found out on the road near Calvary Baptist Church. She'd been murdered, her skull bashed in with a rock. They never found her murderer. She'd been dead eight years. Doreen told them she thought it was Milton Swinton who'd done it, but Milton Swinton was friends with the mayor. He was married to a Lassiter girl, who came from money. He said he didn't do it, and they believed him, and Doreen said she felt so bad for Reecie, wandering that road, just waiting for justice."

"When did this happen?" Ling asked.

"She told me this story about two years ago October, and it had happened the spring before."

"That's a long time. It's been going on a lot longer than we thought," Ling said.

Lupe turned around to look at Ling. "*Dios mío*, Mary!" she laughed. "You sound as creepy as that ghost lady."

"What's been going on a lot longer?" Eloise asked.

"Nothing," Ling said. Jericho glanced over his shoulder and caught Ling's eye. She shook her head.

"I've got one for you," Eloise said, in between bursts of blowing on her nail varnish. Ling was amazed that she could paint her nails on a moving bus. "I heard from my friend Joe, who heard it from his friend Jorge, who got it from his girl, Fatima, and she got it from her cousin Johnny, who plays with a territory band on the circuit."

"Lord, Eloise, we don't need the whole begat'n Bible. Just tell the story," Alma said.

"Just letting you know where I heard it. Anyhow, two weeks ago, they went to play a little town in the Piney Woods of Louisiana." Eloise pronounced it *Loose-ee-ana*. "But when they got there, they said that town was just plain gone."

"What do you mean, gone?" Jericho asked.

Eloise shrugged. "Gone. Nobody there anymore. They said it looked picked over, like a big old vulture had got to it. A ghost town. It was like Judgment Day had come to call. And when they were leaving, Johnny said he swore he could see strange storms passing through, tearing up the sky." She winked. "But Johnny likes to exaggerate. Probably they just didn't want to play that town 'cause the booze was no good, and they needed to make up a story for the promoter."

"Seems like there's a lot of ghost stories these days," Lupe said, burrowing into Jericho's side again.

"There've always been ghosts," Dorothy said.

"You think it's true, that the Diviners are making it happen?" Sadie asked.

"No, I don't," Alma said decisively. "That's bunk!"

"Don't get hot, Alma. Nobody accused you of being a Diviner," Sally Mae said.

"What if I were?" Alma challenged.

"Then we'd all be five thousand dollars richer!" Doc called from behind the wheel.

And everybody laughed, grateful for the break in the tension. Everybody except for Ling, Jericho, and Alma.

"I think one of those Diviners even has the same last name as you, Mary," Sally Mae called. "Better watch out they don't confuse you two!"

Ling stiffened.

"That Diviner's name is Chan, not Chang," Lupe said with annoyance.

"Mary's no Diviner," Babe tutted. "That girl can't even sing. If she had some kinda powers, wouldn't she at least be able to sing?"

"It's all right," Alma whispered to Ling. "Nobody would turn you in."

Ling nodded, but something about Babe's and Eloise's stories unnerved her more than usual. A sense of something bearing down that was far too big and coming much too fast for them to handle on their own.

ZENITH, OHIO

"Zenith, Ohio! Coming in to Zenith, Ohio!" the conductor called as he walked through the train car. Evie's heart began to beat faster. She snugged down the window and stuck her head out as they approached. There it was—her hometown, just as she'd left it.

"They should've named it Nadir, Ohio," Evie grumbled.

Sam put an arm around her and rested his chin in the space between her neck and shoulder. She liked the weight of him there. "Where should we go first, Baby Vamp? Can I see your room? I'll bet it's very frilly."

"We are not going anywhere. Did you forget that I can't show my face in that town?"

"Shame. It's such a nice face."

"Aw, you're all wet."

Evie was going home. When she'd left in infamy as "that troublemaking O'Neill girl," she'd vowed to come back as a star. For months, she'd harbored fantasies of returning, decked out in her New York finery—the latest fashion from Bendel's or Bonwit Teller, maybe something that had come all the way from Paris. It brought her great satisfaction to imagine sashaying into the town's swankiest hotel, stockings rolled down, hem shortened to a scandalous length, and being escorted to the very best table, where she would hold court. She'd look those Blue Noses and Mrs. Grundys who constantly judged her square in the eyes and give them her brightest smile, but they would know that she hated them.

Now those phonies thought she was a disgraced radio star guilty of treason. Instead of coming home a glamorous It Girl, she was returning as an anonymous circus clown.

Swell.

Safe in her greasepaint and wig, Evie galumphed through the heart of the town, waving to the crowd. It was still all there, unchanged: the churches, the shops, the country club where Evie had gone to luncheons with her mother's fancy friends and had to keep her back and her smile straight, knowing she was being scrutinized on her manners and found wanting. She felt a surge of anger when she passed the Zenith Hotel, where she'd read Harold Brodie's ring and gotten exiled to New York City for it. She'd told the truth about that louse Harold, and everyone, including her parents, had believed the boy over her.

All of it seemed banal to Evie now. These little people with their little lives. Their petty concerns—whether Mrs. Berg's toast points had been soggy at the bridge club or if Mr. Tufts had made a fool of himself putting on airs around Evelyn Miller, who was half his age. Their mothers would suck the misery marrow from those bones of contention for a month. No matter what those people did going forward, they would forever be known and judged by their all-too-human mistakes. And for what? So those petty folks doing the judging would have something to feel superior about? So they wouldn't have to think about their own emptiness?

It won't keep you from dying, Evie thought as she waved to the faces both familiar and strange lining the roadway. But they were dying already in so many ways. Trapped in their little cages of loneliness and desperation and bitterness.

Once upon a time, Evie had cared about such things, too. She'd wanted that easy life of never-ending parties and handsome beaus driving her around town in their new autos where she could be seen by all. She'd wanted desperately to be liked. That girl and her wants seemed to belong to a different lifetime. It was astonishing to Evie that she'd ever wanted any of that life at all. She didn't know what she wanted next, but she hoped it would feel truer. She wasn't even sure there would be a something next. Not if they couldn't stop Jake Marlowe and the King of Crows. Not if they couldn't stop evil from destroying it all, even the stupid country club luncheons Evie loathed.

Right now, though, she wished more than anything that she had one of those flower buttons that squirted water so she could spray Norma Wallingford square in the face.

She'd work on being a better person tomorrow.

As the caravan continued down Main Street, Evie was chilled to the bone to see new signs posted: DIVINERS ARE A THREAT TO OUR NATION. REPORT YOUR SUSPICIONS TO THE AUTHORITIES. KEEP AMERICA SAFE! KEEP AMERICA FIRST! She tried to catch Theta's and Sam's eyes, but they were too far ahead. The Blue Noses of Zenith had gone from being phonies to being dangerous phonies.

Evie's breath caught as she spied her mother and father in the crowd. They looked small and spent, like they were watching the circus but seeing none of it.

Mama. Daddy. I love you, Evie thought rather suddenly, and then they were moving away from her.

※

While Zarilda's crew set up the tents and wagons and stalls all over again on the Zenith fairgrounds, Evie sneaked back into town, still in her clown getup. She wanted to see her parents again, and remember James. But every front yard she passed, every corner she turned, made her uneasy. Inside Mr. Beaton's five-and-dime, where Evie had spent many an afternoon lusting after the penny candy on display, a couple of kids she didn't know giggled at her in her getup, and she responded by dancing the Charleston. The bell over the door tinkled and Evie went still as her mother entered the shop with her head lowered. She seemed so much smaller and more drawn than before. The presence of her mother, so close, brought a small lump to Evie's throat.

"Good afternoon, Mr. Beaton. May I get an ammonia Coke, please?"

"Yes, Mrs. O'Neill. Coming right up."

The bell sounded again. It was Harold Brodie's mother, along with two of her country club friends. As she spied Evie's mother, a terrible delight showed in her eyes. "Why, hello, Mary. How are you feeling, dear? Must be such a shock to hear about Evangeline. And after all you did for her," she tutted with fake concern.

Evie's mother looked stricken. "Yes. Well. I-I'm afraid I'm not feeling well. Mr. Beaton, I believe you'd better forget about that ammonia Coke. I'd best go home and rest."

"Of course, Mrs. O'Neill." Mr. Beaton took note of Evie for the first time. "Can I help you?" he asked tersely.

Evie shook her head and strutted a funny strut, and Mr. Beaton snorted and went back to stocking the shelves. "Circus people."

Evie's heart ached to see her mother having to leave the shop with her pride in tatters. She knew how much her mother enjoyed being seen as a good, pious woman with a sterling reputation—a pillar of the community. Evie hadn't made it easy for her, she knew, and she wished she could take back some of her antics. Not all of them, just the really stupid stuff. Mostly,

277

she wished she could ease her mother's shame over it all. She wondered if her mother finally understood that these Blue Noses she'd been trying to impress all these years weren't worth impressing. They were just scared little people letting fear dictate their lives and the lives of others.

"Scared little mice with their twitching mice noses," she whispered to herself as she narrowed her eyes.

With Evie's mother gone, Mrs. Brodie and her cohorts dug in on their gossip. "I always knew something wasn't right about that family. That daughter! An anarchist! Good luck removing *that* stain from their reputation, I say. You know she accused my son publicly of doing something unspeakable to a chambermaid at our hotel? Why, when I think of the way he suffered from that indignity. She was always a bad egg, if you ask me."

"Loose and wild. And that comes from a mother not having a firm hand," said pinch-faced Mrs. Wylie. "I've never had a day's trouble from my Isabel."

That's because Isabel can scarcely think for herself enough to order an ice cream, Evie thought. She was glad that her makeup hid the heat in her cheeks. On her way out of the shop, Evie swiped her palm along her grease-painted jaw and pressed her messy hand against Mrs. Brodie's beautiful camel coat, leaving an indelible mark. It was juvenile, of course. Horrible, really. And very, very satisfying.

Out on the street again, she smiled for the first time. "Good luck getting *that* stain out of your coat, you old witch."

At the corner of Elm and Poplar, Evie saw her mother heading up the hill toward home. Evie followed from a safe distance. When her mother reached the front steps of their house—their house!—Evie stepped through the gate and into the yard. Her mother turned around, brow furrowed above her cheaters in a disapproving look Evie had come to know well over the years. "May I help you?"

Evie took a few steps closer. "Mama. It's me."

And if Mrs. O'Neill hadn't been holding on to the railing, Evie was fairly sure she would've fainted dead away.

☀

The house smelled like her childhood, a combination of coffee, the morning's bacon, bleach, and a mustiness the bleach could never touch. Nothing had changed. There was her father's chair by the fireplace, just like always. There was her mother's chair across from his, a knitting basket on the floor beside it. A tiny museum of middle-class domesticity. Everything preserved as if to move even one thing might upend the fragile order and send the whole house crumbling to dust.

They sat at the kitchen table. Evie's mother had offered her tea, which Evie did not drink. Touching the cup would overwhelm her with memories she could not bear.

"Did you do those terrible things they're accusing you of, Evangeline?" her mother said.

"No, Mama. I promise."

"That isn't what they're saying in the newspapers and on the radio. In town."

"We didn't cause the trouble, Mama. We're trying to stop the trouble!"

"Then why don't you turn yourself in to the authorities and explain it to them? They'll help you."

Evie shook her head. "That's what you want to believe, because you've never been on the wrong side of the law."

"I should say not!"

"The law works for the powerful."

"Well." Her mother pressed her lips tightly together, cutting off whatever she had been about to say next. She peered into her tea. "You don't know what this has done to your father."

"I'm sorry."

"I've given up garden and bridge club. I can't show my face in town."

Oh, why couldn't her mother just once believe in her? Why couldn't she listen? "The people who are after us are the people who killed James!"

Her mother's eyes narrowed. "You're being deliberately cruel, Evangeline. You know that James was killed in the war."

"He was, yes. But not in the way you think. Not in the way they told you. I need to tell you something about James. And Uncle Will."

Her mother's lips quivered. "Poor Will. Poor, poor Will."

Evie swallowed hard. "Do you remember those vitamins Uncle Will gave you when you were expecting James?"

Her mother's expression suggested she was searching her memory. "Yes, I do. What of them?"

There was nothing but the truth now. Evie told her mother everything about Project Buffalo, and Will's part in it, and her mother's unwitting part as well. How those vitamins had turned her children into Diviners experiments, how James had died during a top secret military operation at Jake Marlowe's estate during the war. She spared her the grisly details of Marlowe's Eye. No mother should have to hear that.

When Evie had finished, her mother looked worn out from the force of so much truth all at once. She shook her head and waved her hands as if pushing that truth away. "Will would never do such a thing!"

"But he did, Mother. He did."

"No. He wasn't that sort of person."

"He was a lot of things. Most people are." How easy it was to absolve yourself. "We all are," Evie corrected.

"You're telling me that my brother had something to do with James's death?"

"Yes," Evie said, so softly it was almost as if she hadn't spoken at all.

"I just can't believe it," her mother said, shaking her head again. And Evie wondered if that was an affirmation or a denial. Her mother's face crumpled. "Why did you come?"

The lump in Evie's throat hurt as she swallowed. "I wanted you to know that I'm not a criminal. I...I wanted you to know that you were a good mother, and that...I love you."

Her mother's eyes filled with tears, which she blinked away quickly. She folded the hem of her napkin over twice. "Well. I appreciate that."

The disappointment stung. Deep down, Evie had known her mother was who she was. She was never going to sweep Evie into a warm, motherly hug and tell her daughter that she loved her no matter what. But knowing this didn't stop Evie from wanting that elusive affection. Hoping for it. *This time.*

She'd come home, she told herself, so that she might tell her mother that she loved her. Now she realized that she'd lied to herself. She'd come home because she'd hoped at last to feel loved.

"I must be getting back," Evie said numbly. "I have a show to do."

"Evangeline!"

"Yes, Mother?" Evie said, letting the hope back in.

"You might use the cellar door. So no one sees."

Evie passed through the house one last time, stopping next to a side table that held a picture of James in his uniform. He was so beautiful, and so young. Evie renewed her determination to save him from the Eye's awful torments. There were bare spots on the wall, and Evie realized that those were the places where pictures of her had once been displayed. They were all gone. She had been erased from the family story.

Evie cried the whole way back to the circus camp. When she arrived, Sam was sitting on the steps of Zarilda's wagon in an undershirt and trousers. "Hail, hail, the conquering Zenith hero!" he called. "Did they give you the key to the city? Better yet, did your folks give you any rubes for the road?"

Evie kept walking.

"Aw, c'mon, Pork Chop. I was only teasing. Hey, Baby Vamp?"

Evie did not break stride. The circus went blurry. She blinked but it only happened again. She didn't know where she was going. The fields were loud with barkers enticing folks into tents. All these people. Did any of them feel truly loved?

"Baby Vamp?" Sam had caught up to her outside the empty elephant cage. "Aw, Sheba. You're crying."

"You're very observant," she shot back, and then she couldn't stop herself from sobbing. Sam pulled her to him and wrapped her in a hug.

"It's okay, Doll. It's okay," he murmured and kissed the top of her head.

"What's the matter?" Theta's voice.

Evie was still crying and so didn't know what Sam whispered to Theta over the top of her head. She only knew that now there were two sets of arms around her, holding her close, holding her up. She only knew that she had family after all.

ONE OF THEM

The towns began to blur together. Evie read so many objects she lost count. Time and again, she was struck not by the specifics of the object itself—bought on a whim at a department store, inherited from a beloved grandfather, given in love, given begrudgingly, stolen from an enemy, stolen from a complete stranger—but by what the objects meant to those who held them. How the objects revealed the yearning of those people who were so much more alike than they ever realized. If they had, Evie wondered, would it have made them kinder to one another?

Sometimes, though, reading objects had the opposite effect. Artie Wilson's pocket watch was just such an example. Evie had lifted it as part of her act with Zarilda; making a show of pretending not to understand how a pocket watch worked, she swung it in front of her face, pretending to hypnotize herself, much to the amusement of the audience. The entire time, she read for information she could pass along to Zarilda. Artie Wilson was a loan officer at a bank in Marion, Indiana. He was also a Grand Exchequer for the Marion KKK. There'd been a meeting recently, and at that meeting, they'd discussed the manhunt for the Diviners. She could see Artie Wilson palming that pocket watch as he talked with the other men. "One of our brotherhood is looking for his wife. Seems she fell in with those Diviners on that manhunt list. He wants her back—wants to clear her name and help her get right again. Theta Knight. Pretty. Be on the lookout."

Evie came out of her trance. Artie Wilson was laughing at her antics along with everybody else. She forced herself to look deep into his eyes and found that the most terrifying thing of all was just how completely ordinary he looked.

Evie grabbed Theta as she was on her way into the Big Top. "There's a fella here. I read his watch. He's with the Klan." Evie took in a couple of steadying breaths. "Roy's put out the word to the Klan everywhere. They're looking for you. They're looking for you *here*!"

Fear flooded through Theta, making her want to curl up in a ball like a frightened child.

"If they try to touch one hair on your head," Evie was saying, "I will... I will... pos-i-tutely do something they will not like!"

"You're in a clown suit," was all Theta could say.

"I will do something, Theta. I don't know what, yet. But mark my words, I'll do it."

Petite Evie looked so thoroughly ridiculous in her baggy clown costume with the painted face and straw hat that it sideswiped Theta's fear for a moment. More than that, though, she was struck by the love and fierceness of her friend. She knew Evie meant it. Evie would fight by her side to the death. Theta hoped it wouldn't come to that.

"I love you, Evil," she said.

Evie grinned and squeezed Theta's hand. "Oh, mercy! I'm almost on! My big entrance!" Evie said and ran off to take her place inside the tent.

"Ya know, you're supposed to say 'I love you, too,'" Theta called after her.

Roy was hunting her. It made Theta's palms catch like kindling. She couldn't possibly go into the Big Top just yet. Not like this. A quick walk would calm her down. She marched toward the animal cages when she heard a woman cry out.

"Please, Billy. Don't. Please!"

The woman's pleading, frightened voice lit a fuse inside Theta. She'd said those words, in that tone, enough to Roy to know that this woman was in trouble. Theta came around the side of the tent. The woman wasn't much older than Theta. She was on the small side, and already a bright red splotch marked her face where he'd slapped her. The man, bigger, older, still had his hand raised. With the other, he held the woman tightly by the arm.

"Please," the woman whimpered.

"You'll do as I say, Wilma!" the man said through his teeth.

Theta could practically feel the sting of his grip; she'd felt such a grip on her own arm plenty enough. Her heart raced in sympathy. "Let her go."

"This is none of your business," the man growled at Theta.

The heat moved through Theta. If she used it, she might get all of her friends in trouble. If she didn't, this woman... well, Theta had a very good idea of what would happen to her when they got home, if this bastard even waited that long.

"I said, let her go," Theta said, more forcefully.

The man prowled toward Theta like one of the circus lions spying a pigeon outside its cage. "Who asked you?"

Beads of sweat pimpled Theta's upper lip and along her brow. The fire was coming. If she ran, she might be able to stop it. She didn't want to stop it. He was almost to her when it tore through her body, engulfing her hands in orange-blue flames. The man fell back, afraid. The voice coming out of Theta crackled with fire as well. "If you ever touch her, I will come for you. I will find you. I will burn you for every woman who has ever been hurt by men like you."

Theta lifted her hands in front of her, mesmerized by the sight. Her rage was intoxicating; she felt as if she might let the fire blaze until it consumed every bit of her.

The man turned and ran across the fairgrounds, screaming for help from "a crazy woman!"

The slapped wife fell to the ground, also afraid. "Please. Please don't."

"I won't hurt you," Theta promised. Already, her fire was ebbing. She trembled from the might of all that anger as if she had run for miles. The skin along the backs of her hands had begun to hurt. She raced to a bucket of water sitting outside the lions' cage and stuck her hands inside, sighing with relief.

"You need to leave him. He's a bad man," she said, removing her hands, which hurt, and helping the woman to her feet.

"He isn't bad all the time," the woman said. There was an old bruise below her eye.

"That's what I used to tell myself, too," Theta said.

The woman's face crumpled. "What choice do I have?" she said. She straightened her dress and smoothed her hair. "Billy! Billy, wait!" the woman called and ran after him.

❉

"I shouldn't-a done it, Evil," Theta said later. Evie had found a nail file, which she was calling a "blessed miracle," and she was shaping Theta's ragged fingernails after having doctored Theta's hands, which looked sunburned. "I put us in danger of being found out. And for what? She just went right back to him."

Evie paused. "Round or pointy?"

"Surprise me," Theta said.

"Pointy it is," Evie said and scraped the file against the side of Theta's index fingernail. "Oh, Theta, honey, it isn't as if you *meant* to hurt him—"

"That's just it, Evil: I *did* want to hurt him. I wanted to hurt him real bad. I wanted to see him scared, and when I saw that fear, it felt so good I wanted to do it some more. I wanted him to be scared the way I was scared all those times before." Theta stared at her hands as Evie worked some cream into her cuticles. "I don't know if I should be trusted with this power. I-I couldn't stop and it bit me back."

"Well, it *is* your power. It lives in you, and it isn't going away. We're just going to have to figure out how to control it some, I suppose. Though I don't mind if certain terrible men are afraid of you," Evie said.

"Boy, do I know how to make an entrance," Sam said, barging into the room. "What's this about terrible men?"

"Nothing," Evie said, then added, "Don't be one."

"Wasn't planning on it." He pulled up a chair and sat down.

Evie batted her lashes. "Scram, Sam Lloyd. This is a private conversation."

Sam got up and put the chair back. "Fortunately, I also know when to make an exit."

☀

Isaiah wandered the fairgrounds. He bought himself some Cracker Jack and fished out the prize, a little toy soldier he put in his pocket for later. Isaiah frowned as he passed a Fitter Families tent. He'd been to one of those at the Future of America Exhibition, and he hadn't liked it. The people weren't nice. They had mean ideas about who mattered and who didn't. Isaiah looked at all the pamphlets they had stacked on the table. One of them was a WANTED poster with pictures of him and his friends: HAVE YOU SEEN THESE ANARCHISTS? Isaiah didn't know what an "anarchist" was, but he understood the five-thousand-dollar reward.

"Please don't touch that," a white man in a brown suit and wire spectacles said to Isaiah. He was balding a bit.

Quickly, Isaiah put the WANTED poster back down. The man didn't seem to recognize Isaiah. For that, he was glad. Unsatisfied with Isaiah simply putting the poster back, the man came over to escort him away from the tent. But no sooner had he taken hold of Isaiah's hand than a vision came down over Isaiah, and there was no stopping it. He could see this man's future playing out on the picture screen in his head.

"What's the matter with you? Are you playing games?" the man said as Isaiah shook.

The words poured out of Isaiah. "Your bank is gonna fail, mister. You're going to lose all your money. Every cent. You'll jump from the roof of a high building and smash yourself down below."

The man yanked his hand free. Isaiah felt dizzy. Theta was running toward him. The man's face was scared and angry. "Are you one of them?"

"Come on, Isaiah. Let's go," Theta said, cursing herself for using Isaiah's real name.

"I couldn't help it, Theta," Isaiah was saying. Theta had pulled him into the dressing tent, where she sponged his face with cool water.

"Don't worry," Theta said. "I can't always control mine, either."

Theta wrung out the sponge and returned to her compartment. Once again, there were dried leaves and flower petals all over the floor. Furious, Theta swept up a handful of the crumbling petals and marched off the train, straight over to Evie, who was still decked out in her clown costume and talking to Sam. "Okay. The first coupla times were mildly funny, Evil. Not anymore," Theta fumed. She shoved the handful of dead flowers into Evie's hand. "If you're going to drag half the forest into our compartment, can you clean up after yourself? I'm not your maid."

"Theta, what's eating you?" Sam asked.

"Stay outta this, Lloyd. This is between me and Evil."

"Honestly, Theta. I haven't the foggiest."

"You didn't put those in our compartment as some kinda prank?" Theta said.

"On the level, no," Evie said.

"Well, then who did?"

SERMON

Viola Campbell strode through the land of the dead in her blue-black coat of many feathers. All were sleeping here, having given up their bounty of electric life to keep the breach open and the King of Crows free to move between worlds as he wished. It all went to him, save for the smallest dregs, just enough to keep the dead hungry and mindless and in thrall to him. Viola did not see him. Under the jaundiced moon, she raised her arms. In life, her elegant hands had been the envy of many as they rested upon her Bible, her eyes closed in prayer. Small, downy feathers sprouted from the backs of them now, and her nails were the sharp, curved claws of a bird. Her voice had become raspy, given to squawks and caws. She did not know how much longer she would have the faculty of speech, and she meant to use it while she still could.

"I would speak," she said to the diseased elms, to the slugs and maggots riddling the threadbare clothing of the dead, to the dead themselves.

"Speak…" the dead echoed, one voice.

"Yes," Viola said. "I would tell you a story."

"Only he tells the stories," the dead intoned. "Only the King of Crows."

"Not this story. This is a story of the river." Viola smiled. A smile was reassuring. The dead settled. "A story of the river. Hear the word."

The moon shed its cold light on Viola's shoulders. "The river is a watery sword that cuts the nation in two."

"The river, the river, the river is a sword," the dead answered.

"Yes," Viola said. "Call-and-response."

"Call. And response."

※

CALL: The river is a ghost, a legacy in sediment, in silt, in sorrow.

RESPONSE: The river is a ghost.

CALL: The river flows and swirls, cuts and gouges. It shapes the land. The river is an outlaw. It will not be subdued. It will not be colonized.

RESPONSE: The river is an outlaw; it will not be subdued.

CALL: The river bears the history. What is past is also current.

RESPONSE: The river bears the history.

CALL: The river is a witness.

RESPONSE: Witness!

CALL: Yes. Witness. The river remembers the Spaniard lusting for gold, proclaiming himself a god to those who came first. He cut off their hands and infected them with the pox of violence. The river heard their cries. It does not forget. *Beware false gods*, the river sang from its depths, and waited. That lustful man died of fever, and his men slipped his body into its watery shroud. The river has the last laugh. Hear the truth of the river!

RESPONSE: Hear the truth of the river!

CALL: Two men in a canoe thought they'd discovered this river. Huh. They didn't discover nothing. The river is and has been.

RESPONSE: The river is a witness.

CALL: The missionaries and traders. The pioneers and trappers. The politicians and myth-makers. The settlers staking their claims through the hearts of those who honored this land first.

RESPONSE: The river is a witness.

CALL: The army builds its levees, claims victory over the river, but they will never control the great spirit of the waters. *Nothing belongs to you*, it whispers. The river changes course, digs in. It shapes the land the whole time. The river is not a line but a circle. The river is change, and change cannot be stopped. *Change*, it sings. *Change or be lost*.

RESPONSE: The river is a witness.

CALL: The river is a watery sword. It cuts the nation in two. But the nation is already divided. It must be healed. We must heal. Change or drown. Unify.

RESPONSE: Wade in the water.

Viola stopped. Tears sprang to her eyes. "Yes," she said. "Yes."

CALL: The ghosts of the river are awake and angry. They gnaw dirt from their man-made graves. They vomit it up, expose the bones. Too much history to swallow. The river roars with pain, with release. It asserts itself: *No more. I will rise up, I will rise up, I will rise up.* Hear the word of the river.

RESPONSE: Rise up. Rise up. Rise up. Rise up.

"Rise up," Viola intoned. "Rise up. Rise up."

In her clapboard church tomb with the stench of rotting daisies in her nostrils, Adelaide Proctor's mind stops wandering its labyrinthine halls for just a moment. "Rise up," she whispers.

Aboard Jake Marlowe's silver dirigible high in the clouds, Miriam Lubovitch stirs, feeling the itch under the iron shackles at her wrists. "*Podnimat'sya*," she says softly, again and again, a phrase carried over rough seas from the old country, a prayer, a battle cry.

Outside the jail where Sister Walker lies on her cot, the protestors shout for justice. "Rise up," Margaret says into the darkness of her cell.

"Quiet in there," a guard barks.

In the cell next door, a woman picks up the call: "Rise up. Rise up."

The King of Crows walks among the graveyards where the dead do not rest easily. "Rise up," he purrs. "Rise up and join me."

The ground shakes as the dead obey.

The river rolls on, listening, taking down the history, burbling up its warning as it goes. Not far from that great river, in a small-town church equidistant from a Temperance office and a secret moonshiner's still, the pews are half-full with parishioners, arms raised, eyes closed, fingers stretching up, searching for a signal from an absent god. The ghosts wander inside, drawn by the light. They take their seats in the back row, waiting.

"Ride on, King Jesus!" the preacher shouts to the rafters. "He is risen! Hallelujah!"

"Hell-elujah," the ghosts whisper. Unseen, they move among the fervid faithful, touching galvanic hands to foreheads, pulling out life while the people fall to their knees and tremble with this new belief, the sudden, terrible knowledge of what awaits.

"Rise up," the ghosts groan as the life flows through them and up into the broken sky.

A country road. Men swaddled in white call themselves knights, protectors of the empire. The ghosts of the Confederacy pass the torch, and the men set fire to the night.

On the reservations, the land cries like a refugee for the lost country. The land is choir; it sings a song of truth. In the company towns by the mines, the factories, the mills, the canneries. In the sharecropper shacks out from the plantations. In the small immigrant neighborhoods of the shining cities on the hill. In the watch factories where radium girls lick the ends of their brushes and glow like dying stars. Near the factories, the mills, the canneries, the river struggles for breath under the grime. The King of Crows touches staticky fingers to the struggling current. "Rise up." From fouled waters crawl all manner of misshapen things: Four-eyed frogs with three legs, tumorous tadpoles. Birds, feathers heavy with oil, drown themselves in the shallows. Sickly fish swim past, seeing nothing.

In a dark alley dogs snap at each other over a single bone. They fall upon each other, tearing until both are too injured to eat it.

The river is a witness.

The Eye of Providence stretches a golden hand into Sam as he sleeps. If he were to ask, Henry and Ling could tell him that what we do not face in the light comes for us in the dark. Sam tosses. Turns. He dreams of the white buffalo calf. Its mother mewls into a dark and fractured night, staggering across scorched earth, searching for a safe place to rest among so much death. She is heavy with the weight of life inside her: the bones, fluid, blood; the three hundred days of dreams. So much weight; she can go no farther. Moaning, she lowers herself into a patch of diseased flowers, thrashing, until, with a final push, she expels her child from its gestational dreaming. The white buffalo calf slithers out into this world on a tide of blood. Breath stirs in its new lungs. The mouth parts, ready to make a sound. The calf opens its eyes and sees the bared teeth of the world and the power of the night behind it. It opens its mouth to cry, and the world descends. Sam does not know it, but he is crying. Crying for what is lost. He would cry a river.

The river unifies. The river divides. East and West. North and South. Rich and poor. Black and white. Have and have not. Down to the river and leave your sins behind. Shall we gather at the river?

The hour grows later. Supper dishes have been washed and dried and placed in cupboards. Everything put to order.

"There is no order, no order," the ghosts cry.

Children with mint-fresh mouths promised in magazine advertisements don pajamas and sit at their parents' feet. Mama with her needlepoint. Papa with his pipe, a gift for ten years' service at his good job. Papa turns on the radio. Everywhere in this nation, its eyes and ears on the radios and the amusements it offers: the peppy orchestras, the romantic crooners, the comedy duos, the thrilling serials. It is the national pastime. (It passes the time. So much time and past.) Under the amusements is the thin static of insects, and just under that, the King of Crows whispers like an infection into those eager ears: "We are not strangers, you and I. Search your hearts. I am here, have always been here. You know me."

"We know you," the people repeat.

"I am in you."

"You are in us."

"Let it rise up."

"Rise up."

Papa rises. He descends into his lair, the basement, past the neatly lined-up jars of pickled okra and the tools placed just-so in their metal box. Past the fishing tackle hung upon the wall, to the drawer where he keeps his grandfather's pistol and the bullets, fitting their gold weight neatly into each snug hole and spinning the chamber, watching the revolutions. The gun is a circle. He rises and enters the parlor, where the radio plays a jaunty tune. The fresh-mint children regard him and the gun curiously. "Papa?" Mama drops her needlepoint and screams. Four bullets later, it's quiet, except for the blood-spattered radio.

The river is a witness.

America's favorite son sleeps on. A four-poster bed with beautiful linens. He is far from the river.

"Sleep. Sleep and follow me," the King of Crows whispers.

Jake Marlowe rises and follows the King of Crows into the desert strobed by harsh white light, as if the sky is a giant camera taking evidence. Atoms dance along the mountaintops, which catch fire. Black smoke curdles the view. The mountains undulate, rise and fall, one wide as a fat man, the next skinny as a little boy.

"Do you know me?" the King of Crows calls.

"Yes," Jake Marlowe responds.

"I am what you seek," the King of Crows calls. "I am where you lead."

"Yes," Marlowe responds.

In the serrated light, Jake sees a field of ragged, haunted people, mouths open in a scream like a factory whistle. Shadow. Light. Shadow. Light.

Smoke pours from their mouths and nostrils. "This keeps happening," they say.

White-hot light violates the sky.

Shadow. Light.

They crumble into ash.

Light. Shadow.

Bodies piled in mass graves. "This keeps happening."

Shadow.

Shadow.

Where is the river? Who will witness?

Jake Marlowe walks out of the desert but he does not leave it.

Theta finishes her last cigarette and stomps it into the ground. She shivers for no reason and boards the sleeping train. Roy and his men drive in the dark, tires circling against the rise of the road. Someone thinks they saw her in Kentucky with a circus, so Roy is going to Kentucky. Roy's daddy was from Kentucky. He used to beat Roy with a belt buckle. Roy can still hear the clang of metal under the humming tires. His daddy was beat by his own pappy, and his pappy by his father before him. Roy used to joke that their family tree was just a big old belt passing from hand to hand. A circle. Roy thinks of Theta. Thinks of the belt. Presses the gas.

Theta sleeps. Something else is awake. Elijah shuffles up the steps of the train, trailing dead leaves. He finds her cabin. He can always find her. They are bound together now, forever. But not yet. First, a gift. A proper courting. He lays the daisies upon her pillow. They brown and curl under his touch. Worms wiggle under the covers, make a home in the future. Theta sleeps. Elijah strokes a filthy finger down her hair and is gone.

The sky crackles with light. The dead are in the woods. Along the quiet roads. Near the edges of towns. They ask for rides to see a brother in a prison that hasn't been in use since the Civil War. Or to a town where they plan to be married. These cars will be found later, abandoned. Doors open. Headlamps still on. Perhaps a strange pattern burned into the seats. Scratch marks. Dust everywhere.

The ghosts reach the edges of the towns. The husband rouses from slumber and a dream of sun-stippled valleys for just a moment. "Did you hear that?" he asks his young wife. "Come to me, lover," she says, taking him in her arms, and the warning is forgotten. There is lightning in the sky. The ghosts step into the streets.

The dead of Greenville float in the river. ("The river, the river is a witness.")

Here and there, a bloated arm catches on a half-submerged telephone pole. Shirttails snag against a section of severed fence. The dead are caught in riptides, swirl around and around, becoming a circle. The call is passed from mind to mind: "Rise up," they say from the watery depths and float toward the levee.

Rise up, Memphis thinks, his pencil making its own swirls and loops upon the page, forming words. The hands of the ancestors guide his strokes. Witness. Witness. The river travels on, telling the story to any who will listen. It knows the people are unreliable narrators. They do not know themselves.

The radio ends its broadcast. A little music to play it out, burbling through speakers, sweet as a river. *This is your radio announcer, wishing you all a pleasant evening. Good night. Good. Night.*

Good night to the oil fields smelling of sulfur and profit. And to the miners' shacks leering lovesick into streams shining up with fool's gold. Good night to the boomtowns, built in fever dreams, jilted when spent. Good night to Alma's arm across Ling's body, the birth of something new. Good night to the railroads carving scars across the land. Good night to the atoms impatient for more, eager to rise up in new horror. Good night to the husband and wife, young lovers, as the dead watch from the foot of their bed. "Hungry," they whisper. Good night to all. All the asleep with the dead on their doorsteps. All are sleeping.

Only the river is awake. And it is screaming.

RIVER

Memphis woke to Nate Timmons shaking him.

"Memphis," he said in an urgent voice. "I heard something you need to know. My cousin say he heard some guards talking. Say there's some men on their way in from Washington to search the camp. Said they heard some poems from the Voice of Tomorrow had been mailed to a newspaper in New York, and those letters was stamped *Greenville*. And then they heard about healings taking place on the levee. Those Shadow Men you told me about? They coming for you and your friends, Memphis. You got to go. We got to get you out of here."

"How we gonna do that?" Bill said, throwing off the thin blanket and pulling up his suspenders. "We need passes to get out."

"Nate, you were wanting to go north, weren't you?" Memphis said.

Nate rubbed a hand down his face, thinking. "Remy's boat would do, I reckon. But we got to go past the guard to get it."

"The Shadow Men aren't here yet. And the camp's eight miles long," Memphis said.

Bill hurried into his boots. "Better hope they start at the other end."

Quickly and quietly, Memphis, Bill, and Henry gathered their things. Nate Timmons had Bessie stuff what she could into a pillowcase. She was tearful about having to leave behind even more of what little they had.

Moses and Tobias were worried sick about their dog, Buddy. It had been several days since the levees had washed away, stranding them all in the refugee camps.

"Please, Daddy. Can we go looking for him?"

There was the issue of the passes—the National Guard wasn't handing them out, except to white people. But two young boys desperate to find their lost dog pulled at the heartstrings of one of the guards.

"I can't let you go, sir. But I can let the boys out," explained the sympathetic guard to Nate Timmons. He handed over half his sandwich to the boys. "I got a dog back home, too. Here. He'll be hungry. Give him this, compliments of me and my Rover."

Bessie was beside herself with worry. "There's all manner of things in that water—telephone wires and snakes! They can't go alone!"

"I'm sorry, ma'am. Orders are orders."

Henry wanted to say to him, *You know this isn't right, so why are you playing along?* But he knew the answer: *Rules.* That was always the answer: *Because this is the way of things.* But the way of things was wrong.

"I'll go with 'em," Henry said, staring down the guard, who, with a nod, allowed it.

"Thank you," Nate said to Henry.

Bill clapped a hand on Henry's shoulder. "Best be quick about it. Go and come back fast as you can. We got to pack up and slip out tonight."

☀

With Henry on board, Moses and Tobias took a pirogue from its mooring, paddling back toward the town they'd had to abandon when the flood set in. The sky had grown ominous again, and Henry feared rain would pour down before they could get back. Moses steered the boat through Greenville's mostly sunken streets. The flood had been a capricious god: some houses had taken on water up to the roofline; others had come out relatively unscathed. Likewise, there were streets passable by car, while some streets lay under a good five or six feet of flood. They passed a grocery store where the water reached to the bottom of a sign advertising ice-cold Coca-Cola for a nickel. Henry thought about how good that soda would feel sliding down his parched throat. At each corner, the boys called Buddy's name and listened for his bark, their little shoulders sagging when there was no reply. To keep their minds off their dread, they scavenged for useful scrap—some timber or tin, maybe a lantern, if they got really lucky.

Henry watched snapped branches and twigs float by helplessly in the current. He was a lot like those sticks, he thought. He'd been drifting along in life, allowing himself to be pushed by tides, telling himself he was helpless against it all. That was a convenient lie. He might *feel* powerless at times, but he was not. This realization struck him with such great force it was almost as if a hand had reached into his chest and thumped a finger against his heart, making it beat with new urgency.

If they survived this journey, if they put a stop to the King of Crows,

Henry meant to make something of his life. He meant to be someone worthy. No more of this frittering his time and talent away because he was scared to put himself out there, and that included with David. He didn't know if he and David were a true match, but he would never know as long as he kept his guard up in order not to be hurt again. That's what he always did, tell a joke or find someone else when things began to feel like something genuine. Well, he was tired of feeling haunted—by Louis, by his father's disappointment, and his mother's illness. He'd let himself fill up with ghosts of shame until there was no room for love. No more. No more.

A song was beginning to take shape in Henry's head. It was a song with the silt and sway of the river in it. It was a love song to the country and its people; it was an elegy for the country and its people. It was a song for himself.

The boat pulled on, past houses where rich landowners lived, houses with grand front porches that were completely underwater now.

Tobias leaped up suddenly, rocking the boat. "There he is!"

"Hey now!" Henry yelped, pulled from his reverie.

"Land a'mighty, Toby! You wanna turn us over?" Moses fussed.

But Tobias was waving his arms. "Buddy! Buddy!"

A loud barking came from the porch of one of those grand houses where the water was only up to the porch steps. A bedraggled yellow hound dog paced back and forth on that porch, wagging its tail excitedly, making little rolling jumps.

"All right, Buddy. Here comes the cavalry," Henry said. Thinking about David and seizing life had given him new strength. He grabbed Tobias's abandoned paddle and steered them even with the porch. Buddy jumped into the water, splashing everyone.

"Thanks, Buddy," Henry said, shaking the water from his sodden sleeves. Moses pulled the sopping dog into the boat. Buddy repaid both him and Tobias with vigorous face licks. Moses fed the hungry dog the half a sandwich, and Buddy gobbled it down greedily.

"All righty, then. We've singlehandedly saved Greenville's muddiest dog. Let's head back," Henry said.

A mighty crack of thunder sounded.

"Not more rain! Come on, now!" Tobias grunted and slapped a hand to his forehead with the dramatic flair particular to children.

But Henry felt the same unease he did when a dream walk began to edge into nightmare. The strange clouds were bunching together in a familiar, threatening way. Blue-tinged lightning bit at their dark bellies.

"What's *that*?" Moses asked, looking up.

Henry's heart, which had only moments ago felt renewed, began to beat very fast.

"We need to get back," he said and pushed the paddle against the side of the porch to turn the pirogue around.

Buddy backed up in the boat, growling low.

"Buddy, shush!" Moses said into the dog's fur, but Buddy wouldn't be calmed. He growled low in his throat and kept his eyes on whatever lay ahead in the foul water. Henry froze, paddle lifted, muscles tense. Alert. The boys, too, had stilled.

"You hear something?" Moses asked quietly.

"Yeah. Buddy's growling," Tobias said.

"Uh-uh. Something else."

"Quit it, Mose!"

"No foolin'!"

The birds cried out to one another all at once, then fluttered up from their refuge in the trees and took off fast, huddled together in a protective swarm. There was another, louder peal of thunder. Henry lifted his eyes to the sky, which was breaking apart. Buddy barked furiously. He bared his teeth and pawed at the side of the boat. The water, ten feet deep and murky, could be hiding anything.

The muddy surface rippled.

Something was rising up from underneath.

"Boys," Henry said firmly. "Get in the house. *Now*."

❄

Back on the levee, Bill cupped a hand over his eyes and looked up at the storm rolling in. "Don't like the looks of that sky."

"That's some kinda *canaillerie*," Remy said. "*Mon dieu*, we sure don't need more rain."

Bill kept his eyes trained on the thick dark clouds fighting with one another. Lightning, blue and sharp, struck out over the wide river. It was followed by a clap of thunder that shook the ground underneath the tents. Whispers floated in its wake. Like the sky had exhaled.

297

"Never seen a storm quite like that one," Nate said.

"Naw. I 'magine you ain't," Bill said grimly. "Memphis?"

"Yeah. I see." Memphis turned to Nate and the others. "You need to gather everybody, quick. We've got to move out now. We can't wait."

Bill came to stand beside Memphis. "What's comin' you don't wanna be here for."

And something about the big man's warning seemed to hit home with Nate Timmons, whose grandmother, touched with the sight, had known which mushrooms to avoid and which could be made into a tea to weaken a cruel master—and when the Angel of Death was nearby. A Diviner, through and through.

"Mose and Toby ain't back yet," Nate said.

Memphis could picture the boys playing in the knee-high floodwaters, fooling around when they weren't supposed to, as boys who can make a carnival out of catastrophe will do. He could picture Henry playing the easygoing uncle, splashing along with them, hearing only the whoosh of the river as the dead descended.

It had grown dark suddenly, as if a switch had been thrown.

Some of the women poked their heads out of their tents and looked up. "More rain? Lord, I hope not."

"We have to go get them. Right now," Memphis said.

"How we gonna get off this levee?" Nate asked.

"Remy's boat," Memphis said.

"We got a boat but *no pass*," Nate shot back.

"We're gonna have to make a stand here," Bill said solemnly.

"If they're looking for us, we need to take the fight away from all these people," Memphis said. He wished Henry were there. At least they could try to join their powers together.

"Memphis." Bill nodded in the direction of the submerged railroad tracks, where the bloated dead of Greenville crawled up out of the water and onto the levee. They glowed like some kind of rare underwater sea creatures who'd ventured too close to the surface. They flickered as if they might disappear, but as they moved toward the others, they solidified into a more corporeal state. These ghosts were a new threat.

"What is that?" Nate whispered.

"That's what we're trying to stop," Memphis said. "How many you count?"

"Maybe a dozen," Bill said.

"You think the two of us...?"

"Can't guarantee it," Bill answered.

"We have to try."

Memphis reached out and took Bill's hand.

At the end of the levee, the ghosts did the same.

"What are they doing?" Memphis whispered.

"You ever seen 'em do that before?" Bill asked.

"No. It's like...like they're imitating us."

With their hands joined, the dead raised their arms, drawing the lightning to them. It crackled around their flickering, rotting bodies. They opened their mouths, jaws unhinging. An unholy shriek shot across the levee.

"Ahhhh!" Memphis shouted. He dropped Bill's hand to cover his ears.

It was a chaos of sound inside his head, like the world ending. Barks. Growls. Screams. A radio scrolling through stations so quickly it became cacophony. A fist of noise punching through him. Memphis was brought to his knees. Beside him, Bill staggered, his face contorted in pain. The refugees on this part of the levee were affected, too. Voices swirled through the din:

> *You did this.*
>
> *Hunted us down. Annihilated.*
>
> *We feel you.*   *You are in us now.*
>
> *We have your power.*

The air wobbled and warped. The high-pitched sound pricked a hole in the wall of sandbags protecting the levee. Water gurgled in the cracks, pushing to be let in. If the sandbags gave way, the swollen Mississippi would wash over the levee. National Guardsmen were running into the camp. "Here now! Stop that! Stop that screaming!"

The sound stopped. Memphis wiped drool from his mouth. Gasped for breath. The dead were gone. He saw them slipping back into the water, facing the city. One of the Guardsmen shot his rifle into the air. There was chaos in the camp, too, as they confronted the refugees who pushed back. More Guardsmen were coming.

"Memphis, we got to go now," Nate said. "My boys."

It seemed to Memphis that his heart might burst as they raced down to where Remy's boat was tied to a stump. Quickly, Remy untied the boat and pushed off into the overflowing Mississippi. They watched as the tent city on the levee grew smaller in the distance.

"You think da ghosts out here?" Remy asked, face grim as his eyes darted left and right, watching.

"Yes," Memphis said. He didn't know what these new, powerful ghosts were capable of, and he hoped they'd be in time to save Moses, Toby, and Henry.

Remy steered the boat through the flooded town, toward the silent edges. Shadows deepened the spaces between the abandoned, half-drowned houses. Any one of those houses could be hiding the dead.

"No birds," Bill said ominously.

Memphis could feel the stillness pressing in.

"This would go a whole lot faster if we could use the motor," Remy said.

"Don't want to call too much attention to ourselves," Memphis said. "Trust me."

"I think you better tell me the truth now, Memphis," Nate said. "My boys are out there."

"He's coming," Memphis said, and he took no pleasure in being right. "The King of Crows is sending his dead."

An iridescent figure appeared at a dark upstairs window. Even from that distance, Memphis could feel the ghoul's dead eyes trained on them. In the boat, they were completely exposed. The ghoul's lips peeled back to show its teeth. It beat its hands against the window, *thwack*.

"Just keep going," Bill said. "Don't look back."

"*Allons*," Remy said and paddled faster.

Just like in Memphis's dream, the dead were rising up, this time out of the water, and crawling onto the roofs and porches of Greenville. There were two more on a sleeping porch, gnawing on the carcass of some animal that had been left behind when the flood hit. Did these dead have powers? Would they open their mouths and drown the boat? Nate's eyes were wide, wild. Memphis knew what he was thinking: *My boys. I've got to get to my boys before they do.*

When Memphis was running numbers for Papa Charles, he'd met a man who'd been a soldier in the Great War, part of Harlem's 369th Regiment. He talked about what he'd seen over there: Men being blown apart by machine guns. Dying of mustard gas. Climbing into trenches and stabbing each other to death with bayonets until all humanity was extinguished.

"What it was, we were fighting a war with no rules," the man had said, staring at his cards and placing his bet. "It was as if all the rules had gone right out the window."

Memphis and his friends were fighting a war with no rules, too.

"There's two," Bill said.

"I see 'em," Memphis said.

A splash as one of the dead slipped into the water and went under. Where it entered, the water was electrified for a moment.

"Remy, can't you make this thing go faster?" Bessie said urgently.

Memphis grabbed a paddle and kept his gaze on the murk, alert for movement.

"There! That's our boat!" Bessie cried, pointing to the empty pirogue out in front of the plantation. "Where are they?"

Upstairs in the big house, Henry guided Moses and Tobias over water-logged carpets, past gilt-framed oil paintings of plantation owners and their wives going back generations. Henry knew their kind, men like his father. Whether it was land or people, they enjoyed owning. Henry could see it in their expressions: These were people who *expected*.

It smelled overwhelmingly of mildew and rot. The stench burned at Henry's nose. There was no electricity due to the flood. The house was thick with shadows. The only illumination came from the bursts of lightning at the windows. It had a disorienting effect, coming in quick flashes that reflected off a silver candlestick or the edge of a mirror, revealing an open doorway that had been hidden in the gloom. The house had many rooms. The dead could be waiting in any of them. Near the top of the grand, wide staircase, Buddy growled.

"Don't move," Henry whispered to the boys.

A familiar voice rang out: "Moses? Toby? You in here?"

"Daddy!" the boys shouted. Nate Timmons bounded up the stairs in three seconds flat and crushed his boys to him in a fierce hug. Memphis and Bill, Bessie and Remy were right behind them, wading through the water.

Loree burbled inside the cradling sling across Bessie's chest. "It's all right, little one," she cooed.

Memphis wanted to tell Henry about the levee and the ghosts they'd seen, but it would have to wait. They needed to get out of Greenville right away. A heartbeat of lightning illuminated the gloom for two seconds. Buddy growled, teeth bared again. His fur stood on end.

"Memphis..." Henry whispered.

They were at the far end of the hall. A man with side whiskers and a woman in a hoop skirt. Their eyes were black shine, their pale skin iridescent as a bucket of silvery minnows. Henry recognized them from the oil paintings he'd seen.

"My house," the whiskered man said. "My. House."

Even in death, these people gave off a desire for domination, as if they could rot for a thousand years and the violence still wouldn't leave their bodies. They had no conscious thought beyond their rapacious greed. They spoke as one, their voices crackling and hissing like a scratched phonograph record through a megaphone.

"Boys, get behind me," Nate said, guiding them gently with his arm. Beside her husband, Bessie held tightly to her baby. She grabbed a candlestick from the drenched mantel and raised it high.

"What do you want?" Memphis asked.

"All that we are owed and then some. This world belongs to us. My house." The ghostly couple hissed.

"If you hurt us, the King of Crows will be angry. He needs us," Henry said.

"We do as we please. We answer to no one. My house. My house. My house."

The police had called the Diviners anarchists, but these ghosts were the true anarchy, Henry thought. People who made the rules only to break them at will.

"Trespassers," the man said. "My house."

With that, the couple lunged. Nate yanked the boys out of reach. Undeterred, the ghosts grabbed Remy, who screamed as they bit into his arms with their teeth. His eyes rolled back in his head. They were sucking the life from him, wavering between flickering illusion and something more corporeal and much more dangerous. Memphis and Henry had never seen anything like it, and they were afraid of these new ghosts.

"Remy! Remy!" Nate shouted.

Bessie Timmons brought the candlestick down against the head of the ghostly mistress of the house. The ghost put a hand to her head, staggering. She vomited black bile down the front of her high-collared, frilly gown. Her eyes burned with both hunger and hatred.

"Move!" Bessie screamed and tore down the wide staircase of the ruined house with Tobias's hand in hers, Moses quick on her heels. Bill threw Remy across his broad shoulders and followed after. Remy twitched like a caught fish.

"Hold on, hold on," Bill grunted.

They raced to the boat, still hearing the cries of the ghosts: "My house!"

Greenville's unsettled dead were coming up out of the flood now. Their hunger spilled off them along with the water.

"We're like sitting ducks out here," Henry said.

Clutching her baby to her, Bessie Timmons ran over to the outboard motor and pulled the string. "Tired of this nonsense," she said and steered a path out toward the swollen expanse of the Mississippi River, leaving the dead behind.

"Is Remy hurt real bad?" Moses asked.

Remy's muscles contracted involuntarily, reminding Memphis of the worst of Isaiah's fits. Remy's face was a mask of fear. His eyes were wide and he was pale, nearly gray. Puncture wounds marred his arms where the ghosts had bitten him. Thick dark veins crawled up the man's arms.

"What is that?" Henry asked.

"I don't know," Memphis said. "But it's moving fast. He'll be gone in minutes if we don't do something."

Memphis moved toward Remy, but Bill grabbed hold of his arm. "That ain't no ordinary healing, Memphis. You don't know what that is. Best to let me lay him down gentle."

Memphis was afraid. He didn't know this otherworldly infection that was taking over Remy's body. He was afraid to touch his hands to it. Maybe Bill was right. He didn't have to take it on, even though Remy had been very brave. Even though he had saved them twice with his boat. In the corner Moses was crying softly. "Nonk Remy," he said.

Memphis shook off Bill's hold. "I can do it. I've got to try."

Memphis kneeled beside Remy. Under those spreading, twisting veins of rot, Remy's flesh had gone gray. The wounds seemed to be choking him from the inside. Memphis could see clear through to the bones under the man's skin. Remy was trying to talk, his voice no more than a whisper. "I... see... everything... Too... much... too... much."

Memphis placed his hands on Remy's chest. "I'm gonna help you, Remy. Just let me—"

"N-no. D-don't," Remy whispered.

Don't try to heal me, son.

But already, Memphis was drawing the sickness into his own body. It curdled inside him, rot and decay and hunger. His eyes turned the black of the dead. And then he was falling down into an endless grave. He saw Marlowe's golden Eye taking the screaming soldiers up into its mechanical heart to play out the same pain endlessly. He saw Adelaide Proctor nearly swallowed up by a giant oak that imprisoned her. He saw a dying town of dried rivers and topsoil gone to dust and a half-starved child pawing at the ground for the last turnip. The King of Crows's disembodied face loomed, moving closer and closer. Vines of the grave slithered through his eye sockets and still the King of Crows laughed, and in the next flash, it was Memphis's own face he saw atop the King of Crows's stiff collar. The snakes encircled his head like a scaly crown. A skittering disturbed the fine white linen of his sleeves. Something moved fast under it, and then beetles peeked out from the lace-trimmed cuffs, pouring out in streams of black-backed shine, swarming his body. He walked across a carpet of ash. Bony hands reached up from that carpet, scrabbling for Memphis's ankles, tearing at his trouser cuffs. He yelped and kicked them away. He opened a door and saw the hungry dead descending on town after town until there was nothing left. The pain was suffocating. As if Memphis were absorbing hundreds of years of it. It lashed him. He was breaking. He cried out in agony. The voices swirled inside him: *You'll never heal this. You cannot heal. Never. Never heal this. We will pull you under with us. With us.* Memphis was losing his strength. Remy had been cursed. He was dying and taking Memphis down with him.

"Memphis, let go!" Bill Johnson yanked Memphis free seconds before the rot overtook Remy, turning him into a petrified man. The boat was silent with horror. There was only the sluice of water, the purr of the motor.

"Memphis," Henry said.

Memphis shook all over. He bent over the side of the boat and vomited.

He had never experienced a healing like that. Nothing he could have done would stop the rot.

Bill Johnson let Remy slip into the flood. His body crumbled into the churning water and was gone. They hung their heads and said a prayer for their dead friend. The boat sailed up the Mississippi, headed north. Nate took over the steering so Bessie could nurse the baby and get some rest. The boys, exhausted, slept inside the little house.

"What was that that got Remy?" Nate asked once he knew the boys were sleeping.

"I don't know," Memphis said. "I never felt anything like it." He'd seen and felt terrible things. Still saw them. "I'm sorry I couldn't save him."

Nate was quiet for a long time. "Nothing to be done."

The sky had begun to clear. The sun was poking through clouds.

"Won't be no crop. Water took it all," Nate said, breaking the silence. "Me and my family moving north. Gonna start over, start clean. We'd be proud to take you far as we can."

"Thank you," Memphis said.

Nate put a hand on Memphis's shoulder, looking from him to Henry and Bill and back again. "You get in there and fight this wickedness. Know that we're with you, you hear?"

"We know," Henry said.

The river carried them forward. It was a thing of destruction and a thing of awe, a proud spirit winding through the country.

"That wasn't an ordinary ghost," Henry said. "Usually the ghosts have a deal with the King of Crows—they suck up some power and give most of it over to him. But these ghosts didn't seem aware of those rules. Or they didn't care. They just wanted to take as much life as they could. They wanted to hurt us."

"I know," Memphis said, and it made him anxious about what might lie ahead.

Nate steered the boat straight, chasing sun for as long as they could.

YOU WILL BE SORRY

"On the level: Can you really communicate with spirits, Zarilda?" Evie asked late one night as she and some of the other circus folk gathered in the circus train's dining car.

Zarilda snapped down cards in a game of solitaire. "Only if the spirits wanna communicate," she said around the cigarette holder between her lips.

"And how much do you charge for your services?" Evie asked.

"As much as I think I can get."

Evie rose from her seat. She fished a dollar from her coin purse and laid it on the table beside Zarilda's deck. "I'd like to speak with a friend."

Sam looked up from his Zane Grey adventure novel. "Baby Vamp..." he warned.

"Evil. You think that's a good idea?" Theta chimed in from where she was playing checkers with Johnny.

"What in the hell's the matter with just playing cards and reading magazines?" Elsie said in her honking Brooklynese. "It was a long day!"

"Maybe she can tell us something about what's happening, something we need to know. Oh, look, I just want to know that she's jake," Evie pleaded.

Zarilda regarded Evie through the smoke of her cigarette. "You know, sugar, I've done this a thousand times. Mostly, folks want to be reassured that everything's fine. So that's what I tell 'em. But if I read for you, I won't lie. Now. You sure you want the full truth?"

"She was my best friend. I need to know." Evie placed a black jack on a red queen that Zarilda had overlooked. "Please?"

Zarilda pocketed the dollar with deliberateness. Then she swiped the abandoned solitaire game back into the deck and put the cards aside. "What's your friend's full name?" she asked.

Mabesie. Pie Face. "Mabel. Mabel Devorah Rose."

"Devorah," Sam repeated. "Her Hebrew name."

Mabel had been Jewish, like him. But unlike him, she'd been a believer.

She'd even converted, because her mother wasn't Jewish. He wondered now if it had ever bothered her that Sam took his Jewishness for granted. Her parents were modern. Socialists. New Yorkers. But Sam's parents had immigrated from Russia during a pogrom. They had run for their lives, leaving behind their possessions but not their superstitions. Growing up in New York's Lower East Side and Chicago's South Side, Sam had been steeped in tales brought over straight from the shtetls of the old country, tales of golems and dybbuks and mazikim. It was meant to keep them in line, to make them do right. It was to remind them where they came from, how good they had it here. Remind them that no matter where they settled in this world, they were Jews first. But to Sam, none of those stories of demons and restless spirits ever seemed as frightening as what the real world cooked up: Czars who murdered peasants because they could; people who went along with it. Governments who could experiment on innocent citizens. Or Shadow Men who could take a mother away from her son with a threat of deportation, who could hook that same son up to a soul-breaking machine in the name of patriotism and progress and profit.

He knew now, of course, that there were restless, demonic spirits who meant harm. And still he was more afraid of what people could do.

Sam put down his book and came to stand beside Evie. "You sure you wanna do this, Doll Face?" It didn't sit well with him, this raising of the dead, disturbing their rest. Especially Mabel's rest.

"Yes," Evie said, headstrong as ever.

"All right, then," Zarilda said on a sigh. She stubbed out her cigarette. "Gather 'round, ever'body. Seems we got some séance-ing to do."

"Aw, Jesus Christ, Z!" Elsie grumbled, slamming down her *Photoplay*.

"The more people, the stronger the signal," Zarilda responded. "Now, then, place your hands on the table, please, like so." Zarilda pressed her palms against the small table. The others pulled up chairs and followed suit. Evie sat across from Zarilda, flanked by Theta and Sam.

"I speak now to the one in the spirit world called Mabel Devorah Rose," Zarilda intoned. All trace of her carefree spirit was gone. She was deadly serious. "Speak to us now, Mabel."

"Yeah, hurry it up, Mabel," Elsie grumbled.

"Do you mind?" Evie snapped.

Zarilda's eyes fluttered closed as her head bent forward and lolled left to right, from shoulder to shoulder, a turbaned pendulum. She lifted her head with snakelike movements, as if searching for a signal. "Mabel...Mabel... speak..."

Goosepimples dotted Evie's arms. The room had grown noticeably colder, and hazy.

"She's at peace. I can sense it. A place of deep rest of—"

Whip-fast, Zarilda's head snapped back with an inhalation of breath so sharp it seemed to bring pain. Her chest bowed out as her arms shot straight to her sides, then stiffly back, like someone or something had them pinned behind her. Zarilda spoke gibberish. Her warm brown eyes rolled back in their sockets. For the first time, Evie was afraid.

Wisps of pale gray smoke wafted out of Zarilda's throat, and with it, whispers. Like several voices talking at once. Just under the whispers were demonic cackles and moans that made Evie shudder. Whatever Zarilda had come into contact with, it was not Mabel. Evie didn't want to know these spirits.

We have the old witch. Adelaide Proctor. She is here. She will be ours!

Theta squeezed Evie's hand harder. "Miss Addie? It's Theta! Where are you?"

Another small voice broke through, like a radio signal fighting static. "Evie?"

"Mabel," Evie whispered. "Mabel—I'm here! Oh, please, please talk to me! I miss you so, Mabesie."

But Mabel's voice was gone. In its place was the unholy din:

You will be sorry.

You will be sorry.

You will be sorry.

Zarilda's head flopped forward on a mighty groan. The fog dissipated. The voices were gone. Zarilda came to, her mascaraed lashes fluttering open. Arnold raced to the small sink, returning to his lover's side with a wet rag to cool her face. He nodded emphatically at Johnny, who said, "She'll need to rest now."

Elsie still sat at the table, her eyes big as quarters. "What in the hell was *that?*"

"That was Miss Addie," Theta said on their walk back to their compartments.

"I'm just saying, we can't be sure of what's what anymore. That coulda been, I don't know, some ventriloquist spirit," Sam said.

"Do you trust Zarilda?" Evie asked him.

Sam nodded. "She's the real McCoy, all right."

"I'm sorry, Evil," Theta said.

"Don't be. I only wish I'd been able to talk to Mabel."

Sam slipped his arm around Evie's waist. "Maybe Zarilda is right and she's at peace, Baby Vamp."

But Evie wasn't so sure.

※

A sleeping circus was like a dream waiting to take flight. The tiger paced in its wagon. It stuck its black nose between the bars, sniffing for freedom, until it gave up at last and settled down in the sawdust. The elephants, too, slept. Evie was envious of their rest. It was her own restlessness driving her now; no matter how far she traveled, she'd never be able to outrun it. Evie pulled Mabel's favorite ornamental comb from her coverall pockets. Carefully at first, then with abandon, she removed her gloves. The comb was cool between Evie's palms. It jolted her back in time—just an ordinary day, the two of them walking Manhattan's congested sidewalks after going to the picture show, past the men selling roasted nuts from a cart, past the Automat with its revolving trays of food for a nickel, past the grand Art Deco façade of Bonwit Teller, where they stopped to swoon over an evening gown of peach perfection. Nothing special at all, really. But here under the stars, with Mabel dead and gone, dead in her grave forever—*forever*, that terrible word—the memory was like touching a hot stove. Evie could scarcely bear to relive it.

Mabel had loved Evie. Mabel had envied Evie's daring, and Evie had envied Mabel's goodness. Sometimes it was a bridge between them; sometimes it was a wedge. If only Evie had tried harder to understand that. Would it have mattered? Or were people just who they were, no matter how much they tried to be something or someone else? How many times had people scolded Evie or offered "helpful" advice designed to fit her into a smaller world that would make them less uncomfortable but that would never make her happy? People had to be who they were. The challenge was to love them for it. And to be honest when they'd hurt you. To apologize when you'd hurt them. It seemed pretty simple on the face of it. So why was it always so hard?

Evie left the train and walked out into the cool, clear night, wandering far from the empty circus camp. There in the tall spring grass of Illinois, she lay on the ground and let herself cry until she was emptied. Then she stared up at the moon for a long time, wondering why she couldn't seem to make a real connection to Mabel. Maybe it was as Sam said and she was at peace. But Evie was not. It ate her up to know that the last encounter she'd ever had with her best friend had been an argument. If only she could talk to Mabel just one more time. If only she could know.

Wind whistled through the leaves. A frog croaked nearby. And another sound, faint but very present. Like the low growl of some injured, hungry animal. Evie sat up quickly. Her arms prickled with gooseflesh. Far behind her at the sleeping fairgrounds, the two lanterns hanging from Zarilda's wagon were like the eyes of a dragon. Thinking of those awful voices coming out of Zarilda's mouth made Evie shiver. She shouldn't have come so far all alone.

"Okay," she said, smoothing down her dress with a trembling hand. "I'll simply walk back. *'Pucker up and whistle / till the clouds roll by / have a happy little twinkle in your eye....'*"

Evie stopped short. There in the fields: a shimmering ghost, keeping pace with her. Even from this distance, she could see that the eyes were shiny black buttons, soulless. No. Not completely. This ghost seemed to be wavering between states. She looked confused, as if she did not quite know how she'd come to be here. The ghost appeared to be traveling alone, but so was Evie. If she called out to Sam or Theta, the thing could be on her before help arrived. Evie hastened her steps. So did the ghost. It watched her closely, mimicking her movements. It was *studying* her, she realized, unnerved. She could sense its quickness. The confusion was temporary, Evie felt. Underneath, there was a fast, feral quality to this one.

Calm, keep calm, Evie thought. She just had to get close enough to call for Sam and Theta. Together, they could annihilate this filthy thing before it turned. *You'll be sorry, you'll be sorry, you'll be sorry.*

"Sorry, sorry," the ghost echoed in its strangled whisper.

Evie stopped cold.

"Sorry. So sorry. Sorry," it said.

Had the ghost...read her mind? Evie turned slowly toward the thing.

No matter how many dead she'd faced, it never stopped being terrifying. *That's what happens to every one of us in the end*, Evie thought. Who wouldn't want to fight it?

"I want to talk to you," Evie said. "I want to ask you some questions."

"Questions?" the ghost echoed.

"Yes. I know you must answer truthfully."

"Yes," the ghost answered. Her tongue caressed the edges of her teeth. They weren't sharp yet, Evie saw, but they would be soon.

"How can we win against the King of Crows?"

"Only the dead can defeat him."

"What does that mean? Why do you always talk in riddles?"

The ghost clutched at her stomach. "We aren't meant to come back. It makes us hungry. A great sickness deep in the belly. We must feed from the living to stay. That is why we join with the King of Crows. He promises power. He gives us just enough. And he takes the rest."

"So why not go back to your graves?"

"Once we are awake again, we cannot rest."

"Why not?" Evie glanced toward the dark train. Her muscles tensed, ready for flight.

"It's the Eye. It joins us as one. Its golden energy keeps us here. But it also keeps us hungry. We can never give it enough. Never give him enough."

All the ghosts were connected. *All* of the dead. "Have you seen a girl named Mabel—"

"Rose," the ghost finished.

Tears sprang to Evie's eyes. "Yes!"

The ghost seemed to truly see Evie for the first time. "She is important to you?"

"Yes. Very important. She was my best friend."

"What will you give me to know?"

Evie was newly afraid. This was daring. This ghost was a step up from the others she'd met. She was not obedient. Evie could tell that the ghost was *thinking.*

"What do you want?" Evie asked.

The thing ran its dark tongue across the edges of its teeth again. "I hunger."

Evie took a step back. "There are animals in the woods."

"No. Not enough. Not like the living. And you are a Diviner. Yours is the sweetest honey of all. Give me some of your life and I will connect you to the Eye. You may find your friend."

"I can't do that. You'll hurt me."

"Not if you offer it. If you place your hand upon my heart."

"How do I know you're not lying?"

"I cannot lie. I am the dead."

Evie knew she should scream for Sam and Theta now. But if she did that, she'd never know about Mabel. She was sure it was Mabel's voice she'd heard tonight.

"All right," Evie said. "But you have to help me talk to my friend first. Can you do that?"

"The Eye joins us. I will ask. Ask for your Mabel Rose." The ghost closed her eyes. Evie took this moment to really look at the woman and was surprised to see that she wasn't much more than a girl. More like Evie's age. Her dress was somewhat modern—a dress that had been fashionable right after the war—and Evie found herself suddenly wondering about this spirit in front of her. How had she died? Was it sickness? An accident? A broken heart? Had she lost someone she loved in the war, too? There was a brooch fastened to a ribbon at her hip. It was unexpected and stylish and Evie wondered if they might have been friends had they known each other before the girl's unfortunate death. That was dangerous. This girl—no, this ghost, this *dead thing*—was the enemy. Wasn't she?

The ghost opened her eyes, and they were as black as eternity. The blank unknown of those eyes startled Evie into taking another step backward. She was afraid again. Out here in this field alone, surrounded by stars and the dead. What had she been thinking? *What had she promised?*

The ghost locked her bottomless gaze on Evie. "I have heard from your friend. From Mabel." There was a moment's hesitation, as if the ghost were weighing whether to speak further.

"What did she say?"

The ghost did not answer. Evie grew impatient.

"Please. Please tell me!"

"You should not disturb her rest."

Evie blinked back tears. For as long as Evie could remember, Mabel had been there, her North Star. They'd traded letters furiously, Evie less frequently as she got interested in boys and petting parties. She regretted that now, regretted not paying more attention. How she wished she could race down the stairs to Mabel's apartment and tell her everything. She just wanted the chance to apologize for all the wrongs.

"Could you give her a message from me?"

"If she wished to speak with you, she would. She is at rest."

Evie was angry at this ghost. "Mabel would never say that. I was her best friend."

"It is not the dead who are so restless, but the living. You must let her go. Your promise now."

"Well, I can't! I won't." Tears raced down Evie's cheeks, hot against the cool of her skin. She brushed them away angrily. Why wasn't Mabel speaking to her? Was she still mad at Evie for telling her that Arthur was a bad influence? "Mabel? Mabesie! It's me, Evie!" Evie cried. She was met with silence. "Mabel! Talk to me. Talk to me!"

"Your promise now," the ghost said, getting closer.

"I need to know—"

"Your promise now!"

"Why won't you talk to me!" Evie screamed. Furious, she pushed the ghost. Her hand went inside the dead girl's chest as if passing into a wall of jelly and stuck fast. The ghost let out a tiny sigh. Evie could feel the raw hunger that gnawed inside the girl, a constant, sharp pain that was nearly alive in its driving need. Evie would do anything to make it stop.

"Let go…" Evie rasped. "Let…go…."

The ghost had her tight. Evie could feel herself joined to so many dead.

There it was. A brief glimpse. Mabel. Mabel. The name swam inside Evie's head. *Mabel, it's me. It's Evie. I'm here. Talk to me. Talk to me!*

She thought she could feel it, a slight stirring. Mabel's lips parted in a gasp, as if she might speak.

The ghost had its mouth open. Its teeth had come in, razor sharp. Evie screamed as she saw those teeth coming for her neck. With her free hand, Evie grabbed hold of the stylish brooch, and its memories, undimmed by the grave, rushed into her.

She could see this girl when she was alive, and oh, how alive she had been! There she was laughing and smiling with her friends. Marching with the suffragettes, a banner, VOTES FOR WOMEN, shining across her chest. She was proud, this one. Defiant. The brooch had been given to her by her sister. No. A friend. Her *best* friend. One she'd loved as dearly as Evie had Mabel. They were not so different, Evie and this ghost. It was the pills. The girl had swallowed them all. There it was, under all that life, the dreadful loneliness. *I am drowning in emptiness. No one sees. I will go out without a sound.* But now the girl was in her head. They were connected. *You understand loneliness, don't you? I know you. I see you. You court death all the time. Sometimes, you wish you'd gone instead of him. Instead of her.*

Yes, Evie thought. *Yes, I do.*

Let go. So easy to do.

"Yes," Evie whispered.

Give me what you have and I will bring you over. Over to Mabel. And James.

"Evie! Evie!"

Theta was running toward her, with Sam close behind. It startled Evie from her dreamy state. She let go of the brooch, severing the connection, and pulled her hand from the ghost's chest, wiping it furiously against her dress.

Theta pulled Evie back to safety. The ghost pointed a bony finger at Evie. "You'll be sorry. You'll be sorry."

"You're the one who'll be sorry," Sam barked. He joined hands with Theta and Evie.

"Wait! Just another minute, I—" Evie said.

"We can't wait, Baby Vamp! Quick—before she comes for us," Sam said.

But the ghost made no move. She stood perfectly still. "You'll be sorry," she repeated.

Within seconds, Sam, Evie, and Theta had annihilated the dead girl. Evie felt the familiar surge of overwhelming energy coursing through them all, the temporary euphoria making them feel invincible, as the ghost's atoms were scattered to the winds.

"Ohhhh," Evie said, falling into the grass. Somewhere inside she still felt the ghost's terrible hunger. She let the bloodlust run through her. When it left, she shivered from the lack of it. She felt awful now. She knew Sam and Theta felt the same. That was the price.

"What were you thinking? Were you trying to be dumb?" Theta said when she could speak again. She coughed something up into the grass and wiped her mouth with the back of her hand.

"I heard Mabel's voice! I did, I swear. I had to know if she was okay," Evie said.

314

Theta softened. "And is she?"

"I don't know."

※

She dreamed of Mabel's funeral. The mourners dressed in black, crying at the graveside. And her brother was there in his war uniform. He came to sit beside her. "It's going to get rough, old girl," he said. A crow cawed from a headstone across the way. It had a woman's face. When Evie looked away, her brother was gone. In his place was the dead girl with the brooch. She pointed that bony finger at Evie. "You'll be sorry," she said.

The mourners gathered around the gravesite and tossed in their handfuls of dirt. But the coffin was open. "What are you doing?" Evie said to them. "You're getting her dirty!" She jumped down into the grave. It was wider than it looked. Up close, she could see the worms wiggling from the tall earthen sides. She pushed a hand against the grave wall to steady herself and it gave way. There was a hole now, and when Evie peered into it, she could see into another universe, a place of dead trees and, far off, the Eye, shining gold, creating death.

Evie turned back to Mabel. She brushed the dirt away from Mabel's serene face, from her pretty yellow dress. She brushed dirt from Mabel's hands and the skin slipped off like rumpled paper. Underneath was a mangled hand, the work of the bomb. Evie saw that the other sleeve was empty, the arm simply gone. And Mabel's face was not serene at all. Explosion burns marred her cheeks. A chunk of her neck was missing.

"No," Evie said. "No."

She covered Mabel with dirt to keep her safe and whole. Other things were slithering out of the grave now. Two tiny green snakes plopped down and twined around Evie's shoes. With a cry, she stepped on them. Fingers pushed their way through the packed dirt surrounding her. The grave walls were growing. Higher and higher. She would never get out if she didn't start. "I have to go, Mabesie. I'm sorry," Evie said.

She kissed Mabel's cheek and started to climb.

Mabel opened her eyes.

SECOND SON

Jacob Ennis Marlowe was a second son. His older brother, John Edwin "Ned" Marlowe, Jr., had been the favorite, as first sons so often are. Ned was also delicate. A hemophiliac, he'd been only fifteen when he'd suffered a fall and bled to death. Jake had been lucky. The "royal disease" had not been passed to him.

The morning following Ned's death, the staff swabbed and mopped Hopeful Harbor until it gleamed. But his mother could never bear to live in the house after that. Too many memories. Was that Ned bounding down the stairs now? Was that his laugh outside by the rose garden? The house was full of ghosts, and Martha Marlowe spent a fortune on spirit mediums in an effort to make contact with her son on the other side, a practice Jake both resented and found fascinating. One night, his mother held a séance in the library. Jake hid in the closet to watch through a crack in the door. As the medium begged for a sign from the world beyond, the crystal chandeliers winked. A cup that had been Ned's favorite shot to the floor and broke. Had it been coincidence? Or was it evidence of a world beyond this one?

In that moment, Jake Marlowe became determined to find the answer.

The Marlowes moved to an apartment along the East River in Manhattan. But Jake longed for the simple pleasures of Hopeful Harbor. The lush grounds. The servants bustling through the corridors. The elaborate dinners his parents had hosted for important, elegant people who were not mediums and fortune-tellers. It had all seemed to belong to a time untouched by loss and calamity. Jake Marlowe, the great inventor and industrialist, the trumpeter of progress, was actually building blindly toward the future in the hope of recapturing an idyllic past that had never truly existed in the first place.

The servants could have told Jake this if he'd ever been willing to listen. Downstairs, their hard work hidden from sight, they worried they'd be let go for some small infraction—a meal that hadn't been quite enough; the silver not polished sufficiently; the time Maisie asked for a few days to see to a sick sister but was told she couldn't be spared from her chores, so she'd not been there when her only sister died. That idyllic past Jake glorified had not been so idyllic for them.

The ghosts could have told Jake this, too.

Jake Marlowe went on to a prestigious boarding school and then to Yale, as wealthy sons do. He joined a secret society there, but it bored him. Those boys drank port and indulged in symbolic rituals, putting on the trappings of magic when there was real magic out there somewhere, to be found and conquered, Jake was certain.

Meeting Will Fitzgerald had seemed like fate stepping in. Will was wildly intelligent, if lacking in social good fortune. His Irish last name and Midwestern bluntness had made him a bit of an outcast among most of Yale's elite. Will had never been chosen to join Skull and Bones or any other fraternity, but his brilliance, curiosity, and tenacity commanded respect. Jake had never noticed the slim, bespectacled boy until, during a dreadfully dull lecture on *Hamlet*, Will had raised his hand and made an argument that William Shakespeare might have himself been a witch. He held forth with such dizzying argument that the professor had ordered him from the class for disorderly conduct. On his way out, Will had retorted, "There are more things in heaven and earth, Horatio, than are dreamt of in your philosophy," a line he would use time and again.

Jake had chased after him on the snowy lawn.

"Have you ever heard of Diviners?" Will had asked him as they warmed their hands on cups of weak coffee.

From that moment on, Jake Marlowe and Will Fitzgerald had been the best of friends, with a shared mission: to reach into the supernatural realm and decode its mysteries. That passion would take them to the Department of Paranormal, and to Diviners. For Will, this study meant crossing the nation to collect their stories. For Jake, it was about collecting their blood.

For years, he'd been reading about heredity and bloodlines. Eugenics was the science, and it promised that selective breeding was the answer to all social ills. Blood was the problem and blood would prove the cure.

Will disagreed. He believed eugenics was bigoted nonsense. Margaret Walker called it an abomination and the seeds of genocide—one had only to believe a race or ethnicity inferior in order to justify murdering them.

While Jake was busy working for the Department of Paranormal, his parents nursed their wounds with a tour of Europe. In April, they cabled that they would return to New York from Southampton via an elite ocean liner, and expected Jake to meet them when they docked. They'd catch up over luncheon at the Plaza.

It was Miriam Lubovitch who warned Jake. The Russian fortune-teller, a Diviner of great skill, had brought her young son, Sergei, up to Hopeful Harbor for his assessment. During the meeting, Miriam went rigid, her face contorted with fear. "Your mother and father, they travel by sea?"

"Yes."

"This they must not do," Miriam had said in her broken English. "Is bad voyage."

Jake had chuckled at this. "It's an unsinkable ship, Mrs. Lubovitch."

Miriam shook her head sadly. "No such thing."

Four days later, the *Titanic* struck an iceberg in the North Atlantic, four hundred miles off the coast of Newfoundland. Of the more than two thousand, two hundred passengers aboard, more than half were killed, including John and Martha Marlowe.

Jake was now alone in the world. Some said the Marlowes were cursed. Jake pushed back against such superstition: What if he could keep disaster from befalling the nation? What if he could ensure the safety of others and promote their well-being through medicine, inventions, or machines? What if Diviners and their connection to the unseen world were the key to these wonders? What made a Diviner, was the question. For Jake, it came back to blood.

But the more he worked with these fascinating Diviners, the more he became unsettled. How could you ever fully trust a person who might be able to read your history in an object or see the future before it happened? And what about all these immigrant Diviners? Were they loyal to the United States or to the countries of their birth? Diviners were useful, but they were also dangerous, and their powers had to be carefully monitored and controlled. Only the right sort of person should be entrusted with such gifts. If a new breed of Diviner was going to be developed in the laboratory, that Diviner must be of superior stock. The future should belong to people just like Jake Marlowe.

Of course, Jake had experimented on himself first. He'd wanted to be the Adam of this new genus. The injection had burned in his veins, and a deep purple bruising had bloomed immediately at the injection site, frightening his fiancée, Rotke. "I'm a pioneer on the new frontier," he had said, and then he waited through the shakes and sweats that raged through him for hours. The next day, when Margaret had him guess at a series of cards, Jake got only one right, as anyone might.

"Don't take it on the chin," Will had said. "I didn't fare much better."

"You are not me," Jake had snapped.

He changed the formula and tried again. And again. It had never taken. Not once. Jake Marlowe could not become a Diviner. He'd never been denied anything but this. The unfairness of it enraged him.

The war had come on, and the government had pushed for more experimentation with Diviners. With funding from the elite Founders Club, Jake had perfected his serum, he felt sure. He was ready to prove it with Unit 144. Jake had built a prototype for the Eye of Providence when he began receiving messages from the mythical being of which all Diviners spoke, the man in the stovepipe hat, about whom Cornelius Rathbone had told them. The King of Crows. He was sending messages only through Diviners, however. Once again, Jake Marlowe, the golden son, had been denied. The King of Crows, it seemed, only wanted to bargain with Diviners. For once in his life, Jake had no power, no influence.

But things had changed. The King of Crows was communicating with Jake now, through the Eye. And once Jake Marlowe burst through to that other world and stabilized the breach, he would march into the land of the dead with the world's mightiest army and take what had been denied him. Jake Marlowe would own the most powerful Diviner of all.

But only if he could find Evie O'Neill, Memphis Campbell, and the others.

The Shadow Men had returned yesterday afternoon with a girl they'd procured via one of the Fitter Families tents, at a county fair somewhere in Pennsylvania. The girl didn't have much Diviner in her, but Jake couldn't afford to be picky. The Eye needed her energy to keep the portal open. They were running out of prospects. They were so close. Nothing could be allowed to jeopardize the mission. Most of the subjects brought to Hopeful Harbor were awed by the grandeur of the mansion—for a time, at least. But this girl had not stopped crying. When Marlowe instructed the bigger Shadow Man to strap her down, he'd hesitated.

"Mr. Marlowe, she's only eleven. I've got a niece who's eleven."

Marlowe had done the job himself, placing the cap on the frightened child's head, assuring her that she was being very brave, that she was making a great contribution to her country. Miriam had refused. Even in her chains, she'd resisted fiercely, bucking and scratching and spitting Russian curses at Marlowe and the Shadow Men as they forced her into the chair.

The girl had delivered a brief message from the other side: *Death Valley. May 27. All shall be ready for you.* She'd screamed as her head caught fire.

The hour was late now, half past eleven. Jake wandered through the dark, empty house. He'd be leaving for California soon and did not plan on coming back for some time. The servants had covered the furniture in sheets. It was a house full of ghosts. When he reached the ballroom, he had the strangest feeling he was not alone, even though he'd sent the servants home.

He nearly dropped his glass of milk.

"Will..." Jake said no louder than a whisper.

The ghost of his former friend was a pale reflection in the gilt mirror.

Words appeared on the glass.

Destroy the machine.

Break the cycle.

Heal the breach.

Jake's terror gave way to anger. Will was a ghost. Even in death, Will Fitzgerald had managed to best him.

"Go away, Will!" Marlowe screamed. He threw the glass, and it shattered against the empty mirror.

Jake raced for his telephone. Though it was nearly midnight, he rang Harriet Henderson.

"Mrs. Henderson? It's Jake Marlowe. I'm terribly sorry to call you so late, but it's rather important. I wondered if you might be able to write a column for me tomorrow. Ah, you're too kind. You see, it's about this new machine I'm working on, something beyond anything we've imagined. Oh, I'm afraid I can't say too much more than that. The military is involved, you see, but don't print that. When the time comes, you'll have an exclusive on it, I promise. Yes, just say that you've got a well-placed source and you've heard that it's more than just a machine, it's a revolution. Yes, that's it—a new American Revolution. And it's going to make America the jewel of nations for generations to come. Why, I can promise you that's true, Mrs. Henderson. Harriet. The name? Yes, indeed.

"It's called the Eye of Providence."

ASHES TO ASHES

The Harlem Haymakers had been driving across Illinois for hours. "Gonna need to get more gasoline if we want to make it to Chicago," Doc announced over the noisy engine. "Keep your eyes peeled for a filling station."

A haze hung on the day; the sun was formless. The land was hillier here. Spring had come up fine and fair. Another five miles down the road, though, the green gave way to patchy, drought-stricken grass that blew across the cracked road in broken tufts. It should have been full spring here. Instead, brittle leaves drooped from ash-pale branches. The grass and shrubs by the road were coated in a fine gray dust. It was like being in a petrified forest, Ling thought. A white sign with black lettering announced that they were now entering the town of Beckettsville.

Lupe wiped gray flecks from Jericho's shirtsleeve. "Is there a smelting plant nearby?"

"Don't see one," Jericho said.

Lupe gave him a flirtatious grin, and Jericho smiled back. He hoped they'd have some private time tonight after the show. Chicago, Illinois, would be better seen with her.

"Gonna take you dancing," Lupe whispered.

"Well, you know how much I enjoy dancing now," Jericho said with a wink.

"Lord, the two of you gonna be like this the whole way?" Alma muttered.

Doc turned down another street. It, too, was empty.

"Where *is* everybody?" he said.

Small clouds of flies were everywhere. Two leering vultures perched on the wires of a telephone pole that had gone white with disease. Newspapers skittered down a sidewalk covered in dead leaves. The street came out on a downtown square surrounding a town hall with a clock mounted to its tower. The clock had stopped. There were plenty of automobiles and trucks parked here, but no people. The town square seemed as deserted as everything else.

Doc parked in an empty spot. "I'll go ask where we can find a service station. Don't want to waste too much gasoline. If you're stretching your legs, be quick about it."

Most of the girls elected to stay on the bus. "Gotta sleep while we can," Babe said, shutting her eyes. "And there's sure nothing here to see."

Ling grabbed her crutches.

Alma made a pleading face, with her hands pressed together, prayer-style. "Oh, come on, honey. Let's stay on the bus. We can grab forty winks. Even twenty winks," she begged.

"You can stay on the bus. I want to see what's going on," Ling said and headed for the bus steps, maneuvering them with care.

Lupe shot Alma a *Hey, you picked her* look. "Curiosity killed the cat," Lupe said, shutting her eyes.

"*Somebody's* curiosity is a pain in Alma's rear end," Alma grumbled and exited the bus after Ling and Doc.

Jericho kissed Lupe's forehead. "I better go with them. I won't be a minute."

With her eyes still shut, Lupe waved good-bye.

In the deserted street, Ling covered her nose with the scarf Alma had lent her. "Smells bad. Like something's gone rotten." Gnats garlanded Ling's head. She batted them away. "Shoo!"

"This is farm country. Maybe it's manure?" Alma said.

"Doesn't smell like farmland to me," Jericho said, coming to stand beside them. "More like a slaughterhouse."

Alma crossed the quiet street to a bank. "Gotta be people in here," she said, jogging up the marble steps. A deep gray residue was baked into the limestone façade in varying shapes, almost as if someone had tried to paint a dull mural and abandoned it midway through. The smell was strong here. Alma had to breathe through her mouth. She tried the doors.

"Anybody?" Ling called from the sidewalk.

"They're locked. Hold on." Alma came around the side. She cupped her hands over her eyes and stood on tiptoe so she could peek through the bottom of a long, barred window.

"Well?" Ling asked.

Alma stepped back and jogged across the street to rejoin her friends.

"I couldn't see anything in there. Too dark. Looks like some sort of wicked storm came through here."

"Could be a flood, I reckon, what with all this bad rain and the levees breaking," Doc said.

"No watermarks on the buildings," Jericho said. In fact, the land was drought-dry and cracked. Jericho couldn't imagine anything taking root in that ruined soil ever again.

"Dust storm?" Ling offered.

"If so, it was mighty powerful," Doc said.

Alma snapped her fingers. "We could check the storm cellars!"

They walked farther on Main Street, past a yard where crepe myrtles, leeched of their bright pink, had dried to a powdery gray. Ling touched one and it crumbled between her fingers like old chalk. The house was a white colonial with black shutters open to the gloomy day. "Hello?" Jericho called as they crept up the long brick walkway that led to the grand front porch, which held a ceiling fan whose blades were stilled. A ball of yarn and one knitting needle lay splayed beside a rocking chair. The screen door was askew, one of the hinges popped.

"Anybody home?" Jericho called and knocked. There was no answer.

"Storm cellar?" Alma reminded him.

They left the porch and came around the side of the house to a tidy back garden gone to seed, every living thing the same powdery gray as up front. A storm cellar was off to one side. Jericho knocked. No response. "Should I...?"

Ling nodded. Jericho and Doc opened the storm cellar doors and peered into the deep, musty dark. "Hello?" Jericho called. "Is anyone in there?"

An eerie quiet wafted out with the dust.

"Are those...claw marks in the door?" Alma asked, holding fast to Ling's arm.

Jericho looked on the outside of the door. "Where?"

"No," Alma said. "On the *inside*."

In a spot near the handle, the wood had been scratched to splinters.

"I'm going in," Jericho said.

"Careful," Ling said.

Jericho let himself down into the inky dark. A kerosene lantern hung from a hook on the wall beside a box of matches. He turned the knob, letting out the fuel, struck a match, and brought up the flame inside the glass. He lifted the lantern out in front of him, letting its glow illuminate the dark space by degrees. The dust was everywhere. Several broken mason jars glittered up from the dirt, their contents strewn and rotted, giving off faint traces of tomato and summer peach. There was a woman's shoe turned on its side, and a dusty teddy bear missing an eye and an arm. Some kind of stain marked the floor. Jericho crouched down and put his hand to it. It was hard and gritty, like a burn. He stood back and held the lantern up high to get a better view. He thought he could almost make out the silhouette of a hand, fingers splayed.

"Hey, kid. Maybe you shouldn't hang around in this place. Whaddaya think?"

Jericho cried out and nearly dropped the lantern.

"What is it?" Ling yelled down.

With a shaking hand, Jericho lifted the lantern, peering into the darkness where, seconds before, he'd heard Sergeant Leonard's voice issuing a warning. There was nothing there.

"Jericho?" Ling's called down. "Are you all right? Answer me!"

"Who's Jericho?" Doc asked Alma.

"You're dead," Jericho whispered to the empty dark. "You've been dead for years."

"Freddy?" Ling said, more careful this time.

Jericho made a fist and it was no trouble. He was fine. Completely fine. "I'm not going crazy," he said to reassure himself. "I'm not."

Quickly, he climbed back up and slammed the heavy wooden doors on the empty cellar.

"What's the matter?" Ling said. She never missed a trick.

"N-nothing," Jericho stammered. "Just got spooked down there in the dark is all. It's empty. Let's move on."

"Wherever this town went, it sure went in a hurry," Alma said as they walked through empty streets, passing vacant houses and abandoned storefronts. "It's giving me the heebie-jeebies." She coughed. "So much dust. Say, do you think there was some kind of explosion?"

"If there'd been an explosion, seems like it would've taken out some of the buildings, or the windows at least," Doc said.

Ling was reminded of Eloise's ghost story. She pushed the thought from her mind.

They passed by a library and a Methodist church. Jericho hopped up onto the sidewalk and approached McNeill's Hardware. He cupped his hands around his eyes as he peered through the dirty window. There were shadows inside, but when he pushed open the door, the shadows fell away. There was nothing inside but shelves of untouched dry goods and piles of that same ashy dust.

"Nobody there, either," Jericho said, coming out to the street again.

The small town looked to have been vibrant once, and not that long ago. The dust was everywhere now, though. Ling transferred her crutches to her left hand and bent as low as her braces and pain would allow. She scooped up a handful of the everywhere-dust. It was heavier and grittier than sand.

"Ashes to ashes, dust to dust," she said, spooking herself.

Cradling both crutches under her left armpit to hold herself up, she brought the palmed dust to her stomach, peering at it as she rubbed her thumb through. Her thumb caught on a sharper bit. She dusted away the excess to examine it. There. Hidden inside. A sharp sliver of bone. She showed it to the others.

"Looks like a dog's tooth," Jericho said, holding it up.

"What killed the dog?" Alma asked. Then: "Doc, can you please find some damn gasoline?"

Under a little hill of dust, Ling spied a smashed model airplane. The wings were sheared off; it was mostly a mess of balsa wood.

"Feels...haunted," Ling said. "Like a graveyard." But graveyards were full of the dead. This felt slightly alive, as if the dead were part of the bricks and mortar and husks of trees, as if, were she to expel a mouthful of air, all of it would crumble and she would see what was behind it. She got a sudden chill. When she turned around, she saw Will Fitzgerald in the middle of the street. He shook his head slowly. And then, in a wink, he was gone.

"What is it? What's the matter?" Alma said.

"We should go," Ling said, trembling. "We're trespassing here."

Jericho looked around at the empty storefronts, cracked sidewalks, and weedy brown lawns. "Trespassing on what? There's not a soul here."

"I don't think that's true," Ling whispered.

"We can't go anywhere. Gotta find some gasoline first. Here. Let's go this way," Doc said.

It had gotten colder. The messy sun had been swallowed up by bleak clouds that seemed to be keeping watch like sentinels as Ling and the others wandered past pleasant, preserved houses behind white picket fences guarding neatly trimmed, very dead hedges. For all of Ling's belief in science and evidence and fact, she also had a Diviner's sense of the otherworldly. There were mysteries that could not be quantified. There was instinct, and intuition, and Ling's were screaming at her now.

"Hey, look!" Doc called, rounding a corner.

At the end of Poplar Street, yellow light seeped out from a large house whose front door hung open. As they got close enough to see, Alma stopped short. "Perkins and Son Funeral Home." She stepped back, hands up. "Oh, no. Uh-uh. No, no, no, sir."

Jericho started up the walk.

"Are you out of your *mind*?" Alma planted her feet firmly and folded her arms. "The United States Treasury doesn't *mint* enough money to make me go in there."

"Suit yourself," Jericho said. The front steps creaked under the weight of his feet. Ling followed behind.

"Ling…" Alma glanced at Doc and back. "*Mary Chang!* Don't you do it."

"If there's somebody inside, I want to ask them what happened," Ling explained.

Doc shrugged and followed, his hands in his pockets. "Don't wanna be a coward."

"Am I the only one here with a lick of common sense?" Alma complained, but she hurried after. She wasn't about to stay behind alone.

"Look." Ling noted the stripes etched into the funeral home's wooden door, an echo of the screen's patterning. "Looks almost like a burn."

"It's like what I saw on the side of the bank," Alma whispered.

"And in the storm cellar," Jericho said.

"You didn't say anything about that," Ling said.

Sergeant Leonard. In the cellar. Sergeant Leonard, making Jericho feel crazy. "It might've just been a stain," he said.

Inside, the foyer was the soft dark of perpetual dusk. A bereavement book lay open on a marble-topped chest. A white ribbon dangled from the book's center crease. Halfway down the page, the names stopped.

"There's nothing since this date three weeks ago," Ling said.

"So…nobody's died since then?" Alma said hopefully.

The light they'd seen from the street bled through the inset windows of the closed chapel doors and onto the burgundy rug of the foyer. The windows were stained glass, impossible to see through.

"I'll go in first," Jericho said.

"I'm not going to give you an argument," Ling said.

Jericho pushed through the doors. The chapel was heavy with shadows. The light was coming from a room in the back and off to the right. Up front, a casket bedecked in rotted floral wreaths rested on a bench.

Alma whispered to Ling, "I don't care if we have to walk all the way to our next show, I am not passing that."

"I'm with Alma," Doc said. "This doesn't feel right."

Jericho marched forward. He rested his hand on the lid of the closed casket, then licked his lips, nervous. "Okay. On the count of three."

Alma whispered. "Don't you dare!"

"One…"

Ling nodded. If something awful lurked inside, how would she get away? "Two," she said, fighting her fear.

"Three!"

Ling thought her heart might stop as Jericho threw back the lid. Empty.

"Oh, my Lord," Alma said, one hand on her heart, the other seeking support from the back of a pew.

Doc pointed to the lighted room off to the right. "I believe that's the mortuary proper over there. Hey, now, wait a minute! That was not meant as an invitation to go in!" Doc called after Jericho, who had started toward it. He turned to Alma and Ling. "That white boy is strange. Creepy. He's just plain creepy."

The acrid smell hit them before they even entered the room. "Somebody making pickles?" Ling asked, wrinkling her nose.

"That's formaldehyde," Doc said, putting his handkerchief to his nose. "For preserving the corpse."

Alma gagged and cupped a hand over her mouth and nose. "That's formaldehyde?"

"Nope. *That* is the corpse," Doc said, nodding at the bloated body laid out on a table.

"How come you know so much about this?" Alma asked, pinching her nostrils.

"My uncle Ray is an undertaker."

On a tiny table, Doc found an open tin of Vicks VapoRub. He swiped a fingerful beneath his nose and handed it to the others so they could do the same. Ling shut her eyes for a few seconds and waited for the nausea to pass.

"This here's a cooling table," Doc continued. "It's got holes in it. You've got to drain the fluids so gases don't build up inside the body. I'm guessing the embalmer was just getting started when whatever happened happened. That's why the body's all blown up like that."

Alma gagged and spat. "I will never eat again."

"Definitely not aspic," Jericho muttered.

"Ugh. Aspic? It's like stiff jelly." Ling picked up a pair of scissors.

"You had to say *stiff*?" Alma growled. "No! Li—*Mary!* Don't you dare—"

Ling poked the swollen corpse with the tip of the scissors. The skin split open.

"Why did you do that?" Alma cried.

"I don't know. I just...had to." Blushing, Ling dropped the scissors in a bowl. "I was...curious."

Alma shook her head. "Lord Almighty."

"Folks left in a hurry. That body's been there for weeks," Doc said. "Who would run off and leave a dead body on the table?"

"So far, it's the only person we've seen in this town," Jericho said.

"Yeah. Don't that seem mighty odd to you?"

"This whole town feels like it's been embalmed, too," Alma said, spritzing herself and the room with an atomizer of perfume she'd taken from her purse.

"Yes. Preserved," Ling said. She wanted to look away from the dead body but found herself oddly fascinated. The man was naked, and that alone caused her to blush. Her true fascination, though, was for the man's ravaged state. In the end, this was what happened to everyone. One minute, you were gloriously alive. A sentient creature. Making plans. Full of purpose. The next, you were a cadaver on a cooling table in a funeral parlor with purpled fingertips and yellowed, engorged skin ready to burst. You were stiff and cold and just plain *gone*. Ling had seen the dead before. Cleaned up. Prepared. She'd even talked to spirits in dreams. But this sudden encounter with the cold reality of death was so startling and violent in its erasure of any illusion that one could escape it. The absence of life was palpable in the room. It made her desperate to prove how alive she was. She wanted to kiss Alma. To eat her father's soup dumplings. To get out of this town. She wanted to *think*, because thinking made her feel so very alive, but right now, she was having trouble doing even that. The town was wrong. And had she seen Will back on the street? Or had she imagined it, a manifestation of her fear?

Flies swarmed around the lightbulbs and flitted past a tin of Bickmore Mortician's Powder and tubs of paints and waxes, and then over a magazine, *The Embalmer's Monthly*, open to an advertisement.

"'Clark's Hard Rubber Embalming Pump and Bulb Syringe *and Extras*.' I don't believe I want to know about the extras," Alma said, her mouth turned downward in utter distaste. She threw her hands in the air. "I've had enough. There's bound to be a filling station down the road. But I am not staying one more doggone minute in this tomb of a town."

They left the funeral home and stepped back out into the street. The sky overhead was unsettled, announcing an approaching storm. Doc sneezed twice and pulled a handkerchief from his pocket. "This dust is getting to me."

Across the street was a diner. The blinds were drawn at all of the windows except for one, where it was halfway up. Through the narrow space at the bottom, Ling could swear she saw people inside.

"Hey, I think I found them!" She moved her crutches forward, going faster than she should, feeling the ache in her hips. She'd need a long soak and some aspirin tonight if she hoped to get any sleep. Gold lettering across a front window identified the diner as the Blue Moon Cafe. Jericho pushed open the door to let Ling in.

"Hello?" Ling called into the semidarkness. On the luncheonette counter, cups of congealed coffee sat next to plates of rotting food being scavenged by clumps of flies. The stale air carried the punch of sour milk and rotting meat. More of those indeterminate shadows had been burned into the walls of the diner. It was still and quiet. No one was working behind the counter or in the kitchen, that Ling could see. But in the very back of the diner, a half dozen people were huddled around the same table—not eating. Not talking. Just sitting.

"Pardon me, do you have a filling station in town?" Alma called from the front door.

No one answered.

"We're down to our last little bit," Alma said nervously.

She was met with silence. Ling's earlier apprehension became anger. It was like they were purposefully ignoring Alma, and Ling had a good idea as to why.

"The lady asked a simple question," she said with an edge to her voice.

"Let's just go," Alma said in a stage whisper.

"Not yet," Ling said and moved forward, maneuvering around tables on her way to the townspeople who were being so rude. She was almost to them when she noticed that the man on the end was covered in that same fine gray powder as the rest of Beckettsville. His hand rested on the table, and though the room was dark, Ling thought that his hand looked... unwell. Ling came to a stop. "Alma..." she started.

"So much... *dust*." Doc said and sneezed hard.

The gray man on the end caved in on himself, turning into a pile of ash. Alma's scream was like a fist.

One by one, the remaining customers shriveled into dust. With horror, Ling and Jericho realized that what they'd seen in the town, what coated their hands and shoes and clothes, were the remains of every man, woman, and child of Beckettsville.

"Doc! Get the bus!" Alma screamed. "Go! Go!"

Doc wasted no time. He pushed out the door and raced down the street. Giant storm clouds were massing in a strange pattern at the edge of town.

"Jericho..." Alma said. "What's that?"

"Nothing we want to be here for," Jericho said grimly.

"Ling!" Alma shouted. "Ling!"

Ling didn't move. Instead, she stared at the people who were now piles of ash and at the ash that had spattered the front of her dress. She pawed frantically at it, but all it did was ink itself in deeper, a tattoo of death.

"Ling," Jericho said, coming to her side. "We have to go."

"I can't run," she said through gritted teeth.

"You don't have to," Jericho said and lifted Ling and her crutches into his arms because he was her friend, and right now Ling needed him to be the kind of friend who could help carry her to safety.

Outside, the sky had gone from hazy to angry. Blue lightning fractured the ominous clouds. Carrying Ling, Jericho ran back toward the courthouse with Alma on his heels. They were relieved to see the Ford bus rounding the corner, Doc blasting the horn as he drove toward them. He yanked open the door.

"Get in! Get in!" Doc called. Jericho helped Ling and Alma inside. They plopped into their seats, breathing hard.

"Is anybody gonna tell us what's going on?" Babe asked, wiping sleep from her eyes.

Doc gunned the Ford's motor once more and careened down the abandoned street, driving among piles of ash.

"Hey! What about the filling station?" Eloise asked.

The bus bounced, coming down hard, sending the girls into screams.

"What in the Sam Hill!" Lupe said, bracing herself between two seat backs.

"Doc, go, go, GO!" Alma shouted.

"I *am* going!"

Lightning struck the land and bit into the rooftops. The energy of it danced on Ling's and Jericho's back molars. This was no ordinary lightning, they knew. Doc had steered the bus back toward the town boundary.

"Ling," Jericho said, and she looked over her shoulder. She saw the first one shuffling out of a house. The next two came down a side street on the left. Two more. Three. As the bus came even with the church, Ling saw the disturbed graves on the hillside. Saw the dead streaming down toward the town with the angry storm growling around them. *His* dead. The hungry kind.

"Sweet Jesus in heaven, what is that?" Eloise shouted.

"Doc, don't you stop driving," Alma commanded.

"Wasn't planning on it, Miss LaVoy!"

The little girl came out of nowhere, into the center of the road.

"Lord Almighty!" Doc said and slammed the brakes hard. Everyone screamed as the Ford fishtailed wildly, before coming to a stop. In the road, the little girl hadn't moved. She had the soulless eyes of the dead. Her lips spread into a smile, exposing the gleaming points of her teeth. The other dead swarmed the street, coming to stand beside her.

"How many of them are there, you reckon?" Doc said, reaching for the sawed-off shotgun he kept hidden under the dashboard.

"That won't help," Ling said, and Doc clutched the gun to his chest, not sure what to do.

"I count twelve," Jericho said.

"Fifteen," Lupe whispered.

"They planned this," Ling said. "They're...*thinking*. How did they start thinking?"

The dead joined hands.

"What are they doing?" Jericho asked Ling.

"I-I don't know."

All at once, they opened their dark mouths. A piercing shriek rent the stillness and sent the vultures flying. Everyone on the bus clapped their hands over their ears. Jericho dropped to his knees, howling in pain. As one, the dead lifted their arms. The road buckled. The air around the bus warped visibly. The force of it spun the bus around like a toy until Ling feared she might vomit, if she didn't pass out first. The girls screamed and slammed from one side to the other. Ling gripped the back of the driver's seat, grateful for the strength she'd built in her arms. The bus rocked back and forth, threatening to tip over, then settled. The engine cut out. The windshield wipers swished of their own accord.

Jericho pushed himself up from the floor. He checked on Lupe. "I'm jake," she said.

"Nobody's jake," a frightened Babe corrected.

Jericho ran up and sat next to Ling. "How did they do that?" he asked as quietly as possible.

Ling's eyes were wide. "I think...I think they're combining their powers, like we do."

Jericho shook his head, as if it might do some good. "How is that possible?"

"Doc, get us out of here," Alma said. More dead were streaming down from the graveyard.

"Trying, ain't I?" The Ford made a strangled-duck sound as Doc pumped the gas pedal.

"No, wait! You'll flood the…engine," Jericho warned as the bus died.

"Doggone it!" Babe said.

"I don't wanna get turned into dust," Alma said, fighting tears.

"Jericho. I need your help."

"You mean destroy them," Jericho said. "Blast their atoms apart. Be a weapon."

"What choice do we have right now?" Ling asked.

"We could use our powers to fix the bus, get away," Jericho suggested.

"You think they're going to let us out of here?" Ling said.

"We can't take them all on."

"We can't leave them behind to go after the next people who wander through here."

It's a real conundrum, ain't it, kid? Sergeant Leonard said. He was seated at the back of the bus. *I'm sorry I asked you to help me kill myself. That was a terrible thing to do to a kid.*

Tears sprang to Jericho's eyes. He could hear his blood thrumming. "No. You're not here."

"Jericho! What are you talking about?" Ling said.

"Who's Jericho?" Doc said.

Jericho kept his eyes trained on the dead soldier sitting at the back of the bus.

You're the only one who made it. Impressive. Sergeant Leonard's expression darkened. *But for how long?*

"You go to hell!" Jericho screeched at the empty seat.

"Who's he talking to?" Babe whispered.

Everyone was looking at him. Lupe was looking at him. He wanted to tell her to run as far away from him as she could get. He wanted her to hold him close and promise everything would be all right. Jericho's fingers twitched. *Make a fist*, he thought. He was too afraid.

"Jericho, what's the matter with you?" Ling.

"Why you keep calling him Jericho?" Doc demanded.

"It's his middle name," Lupe said.

Jericho's heart beat strangely. *What's the matter what's the matter what's the matter with me?*

"There's more coming!" Alma yelled, panicked.

"Jericho. Please," Ling said.

With a growl, Jericho pushed himself out of the seat, bending it slightly as he did. "Open the door, Doc," he said.

"Don't go out there," Lupe begged. Jericho looked at the dead gathering in the road like a flock of predator birds. He imagined them coming for her and the rest of the Haymakers.

"Doc. Open the door or I'll tear it off," Jericho said.

Doc opened the door.

Jericho helped Ling down. The two of them stood in front of the bus, facing the dead of Beckettsville. "We could still fix the engine and run," he said.

"We have to eliminate the threat," she said.

"What if it doesn't work?"

"We can't think about that." Ling reached out. Jericho accepted her hand. "Now!" Ling said. She squeezed Jericho's hand tightly, thinking only of destroying every last ghost in Beckettsville. She could feel the first inklings of their gifts coming together, signals seeking each other. Out of the corner of her eye, Ling saw Will Fitzgerald up on the hill, barely a glimmer, his eyes wide and his mouth open, his splayed hand reaching toward the two Diviners as their bodies jerked with the strength of their joining. Ling and Jericho weaponized their power, sending it toward the line of dead in the road. The dead shut their eyes. They smiled, as if welcoming the destruction. And then their atoms blasted apart, knocking Jericho and Ling backward.

Ling grimaced as she hit the ground. The usual high that accompanied a "kill" was absent, and in its place was nausea and the taste of blood in the back of her mouth. The storm clouds had cleared. Ash swirled in the air like gray snow.

Behind them, the bus roared to life. "Get on this bus now!" Doc shouted.

The bus doors flew open and Alma rushed to Ling's side, helping her up, half carrying her onto the bus. "Jericho! Get her crutches!"

Jericho staggered to his feet. Across the street, Sergeant Leonard stood with his hands in his pockets, his expression grim. *That's how they get you, kid. It's a slippery slope.*

Jericho grabbed Ling's crutches and limped onto the bus.

"I don't know what you did, but it feels like this baby's running on pure electricity," Doc said appreciatively. He gunned the motor and swung into reverse and finally they were speeding away from the town of Beckettsville. In their seats, the girls clutched one another, eyes wide.

Jericho stared at his shaking hands. And then Lupe was beside him, her hands covering his till they quieted.

"I'm guessing you're some of those Diviners they're looking for," Doc said at last.

Ling nodded.

"Well, I'll be.... You're that same Diviner after all?" Babe said.

"Are you going to turn us in?" Ling asked.

"Nobody here will do that. Am I right?" Alma looked around the bus for confirmation and got it in nods and *amen*s.

"What's your power?" Lupe asked Jericho.

"Super strength."

"Ohhhh," the girls said in unison.

Lupe threaded her arm through Jericho's. "He's taken, ladies."

"We didn't mean to put you in harm's way by keeping secrets," Jericho said to the others. "We just needed help."

Lupe rested her head on Jericho's shoulder. "Doesn't everybody?"

Ten miles down the road, they found a service station. As the attendant filled the tank, Lupe asked if he'd heard anything about a town called Beckettsville. "I don't keep up with the news," the man said. "If it doesn't concern me, I don't concern myself."

"You might want to think twice about that," she said, handing him the money.

They drove toward Chicago. It was getting dark. After the earlier excitement, the girls had gone to sleep. Jericho relieved Doc at the wheel so he could get some rest, too. Ling came to sit in the seat behind him.

"You jake?" she asked.

"No. You?"

"No."

"Why didn't they fight back?"

"I don't know," Ling said. "It was almost as if..."

"They were waiting for us to do it?" Jericho finished.

"Yes." Ling felt queasy. Something was fighting to take shape inside her head.

"You said that energy can't be created or destroyed, right?" Jericho said.

"Right," Ling said. "But it can be transferred."

"Transferred," Jericho repeated.

"Maybe our energy went to them," Ling said, thinking aloud. "Maybe every time we obliterated one of them, they absorbed our power, and it only made the whole stronger. Jericho, I think the dead are starting to develop Diviner powers."

Jericho thought back to the night of the Casino restaurant and the ghosts' peculiar words: *You did this.* "Ling, where did you get the idea to annihilate the ghosts in the first place?"

It was the first time they met the King of Crows at the asylum. He'd told them to destroy the ghosts, Ling remembered. No. That wasn't precisely what he'd said. Words mattered, she knew. What he'd said to them was that power lay in information—both in what was told and in what was held back. Will and Sister Walker had kept the truth from them, and it had carried a price.

But what else? Ling concentrated, trying to bring up more. The King of Crows had asked if they'd felt a surge of power when they dispatched the dead. Ling had been the first to answer honestly: Yes. It was intoxicating to blast apart the dead, nearly primal. She shut her eyes, trying to recall his exact words. She could see him preening before them. His smudged, tattered cuffs peeking out from his coat. Memphis's sad mother standing behind him. The rain. Conor Flynn and Luther Clayton moments before the King and his dead claimed them.

His words. His words. Words were important.

"'Did they not tell you that with each wraith you destroy, your powers grow?'" she repeated now. And only as she said it aloud did she realize what a twisty bit of word gaming it was. *Did they not tell you.* No, Will and Sister Walker had not told them that. Because, she realized just now, it wasn't true. In fact, after their initial intoxication, the Diviners felt weakened and sick... and vulnerable. And when Theta wanted to know if the King of Crows was actually asking them to destroy his ghosts in a bid to get information from them, he'd given a trickster's smile and said, "I ask nothing. Your choices are yours alone."

You did this.

Your fault.

This is your doing.

How could they have been so foolish? He'd baited them to give up their power to him and his dead, and they'd fallen into his trap so easily.

"Ling?" Jericho prompted. "Did you hear what I said?"

"Yes." Ling stared out the window at the night coming toward them like a flock of angry birds. "We got the idea from him. From the King of Crows."

THE ENGINE OF THE NATION

The Timmonses' shantyboat had made it on the Mississippi as far as the Arkansas-Tennessee border. From there, the family was heading north and east, toward St. Louis first and possibly on to Chicago. Memphis, Henry, and Bill needed to head west, to Nebraska and Bountiful. Moses and Tobias threw their arms around Memphis and Henry for tearful good-byes and gave Bill's hand a solid shake.

Memphis crouched down to look the boys in the eyes. "You remember what I told you about telling your stories, won't you?"

They nodded.

"All right, then."

"Will we see you again?" Moses asked.

"I surely hope so," Memphis said.

The three men hopped a freight train headed to Oklahoma. Through the spaces between the slats, they watched the country run past like a picture show. There was so much country, and it was all so different. You could practically feel the young nation searching for itself, Memphis thought: In the small towns. The steel bridges spanning the rivers. The railroads stretching out and laying claim to more and more land. The cowboys riding high in the saddle. The reservations pushed to the edges. The triangular oil derricks looming over the distance, great wooden giants announcing themselves with a breath of fire and smoke. The train ticked across a stretch of track slowly enough for Memphis to watch as two men worked to break a horse. They held fast to ropes looped around the wild thing's neck. It bucked and struggled and kicked, keeping up the fight. Memphis wrote it all down.

They hopped off the train and slept for a night near tribal lands. Henry's dream walks were filled with the land's memories. Bullets passed through the air, spinning circles into the ghostly forms of murdered Osage, then pierced the ground, which bled oil from its wounds. When Henry woke, just before dawn, he could swear he saw the faint figure of a man cradling a handful of earth like a newborn and telling it the history so it would never forget. The sun pierced him through with holes till he was filled with light and absorbed into the day.

The Diviners walked under sun, through rain, a diaspora of dust carried upon their soles. They made it to the thriving boomtown of Borger, Texas. Its unpaved streets were congested with cars coated in panhandle mud and parked every which way. Bill didn't know how anybody could travel on streets so crowded with cars. The clang-and-wheeze of the pumps hung in the air, and for a moment, Henry thought of the Eye's incessant whine. Everywhere were men burning with the fuel of dreams and get-rich-quick schemes.

"Oil, folks! That's what runs the engines of the nation—oil!" a prospector called from a soapbox. "Three months ago, this town had four hundred people and some tumbleweeds. Now? Why, there's thirty thousand here, all of 'em looking to get rich quick. Black gold!"

Though he'd protested mightily, Bessie Timmons had pressed five dollars into Memphis's hand back in Arkansas—"We got to look out for each other, and that's that." They used it now to buy coffee and chicken from a stall, listening to the gossip in line:

"Heard about these Diviners they're searching for?"

"Yessir. Worth about five thousand clams apiece, they say."

"Gotta catch 'em alive, though."

"Aw, now, where's the sport in that?"

"I heard they can find oil by smell."

"And take out telephone lines and radio signals if'n they've a mind to."

"That ain't nothing. I heard they can kill ya just by looking at ya!"

This was how information spread, person to person, rumor to rumor, picking up embellishment, fear, and justification along the way, carrying a little something from each of its tellers until it had a life of its own. Until it became either sickness or legend.

"Hell, I say let 'em alone. If they snaked one over on the gum'ment boys, then they're proper outlaws, like Frank and Jesse James!"

"You hear that? We're outlaws," Henry whispered as they walked away, heads kept low.

"Don't wanna be an outlaw," Memphis said. He'd thought a lot about the thin line between villains and heroes, the way the needle moved back and forth, sewing between those two things till they were forever linked. He only wanted to be free to be himself, whatever that was, and to love

Theta. He wanted to be reunited with his brother. And he wanted to take down the King of Crows.

There was other gossip in town.

"You hear about that funny business out in New Mexico?"

"How's that?"

"Oh, some kinda lightning storm, real odd-like. Was a fella passing through said he saw it. Said it done tore up the whole sky near where the oil comp'nies been drilling. Said it was like the sky had caught fire, like it might rip in two. And there was ghosts streaming toward it."

"Ghosts?"

"Yes, sir. Ghosts. Just drawn to it like bees to honey."

"Aw, hell. That fool was prob'ly drunk. Don't pay it no mind."

"Well. That's what he said, anyway."

Bill swiped a newspaper from a bench, and they pored over its pages. The manhunt was still on. And there were rumors that Jake Marlowe was putting the finishing touches on a machine that would change everything. ANOTHER AMERICAN REVOLUTION! the headline promised.

"We've got to get to Bountiful," Henry said.

"How?" Memphis asked.

Henry looked out at the sea of automobiles. "I've got an idea."

In the lobby of a small hotel, Henry found a telephone booth. He placed a collect call to David. He felt lousy about it, but it was the only way.

"Whom shall I say is calling, sir?" the operator asked.

"Mr. Henry."

The operator placed the call. In a moment, David's voice came over the line, all the way from New York, and Henry hadn't realized how desperately he'd needed to hear it until now. It was as if he'd been carrying a heavy load for miles and had only just put it down.

"*Mister* Henry?"

Henry wanted to rush in. To say everything. To profess his love in a hundred ways. But anybody could be listening. The operator, the folks just outside the booth. Privacy was a myth. And there was a bounty, if not on his head, then on the heads of his friends.

"Is this Mr. David Cohn? I have a message to relay to him from a Miss Vanessi," Henry said, using their private code name, an old joke.

"Ah, yes. I was very worried about Miss Vanessi. I hoped she hadn't fallen into the shadows, or something worse."

"Not yet. Though she has had her share of frightening adventures during her travels. It seems that Miss Vanessi is in need of a small transfer of funds. In particular, the money marked 'piano fund.' She wondered if you might be able to send it to her Western Union? The office is in Borger, Texas." Henry gave the information.

"My. Miss Vanessi sure does get around," David said, writing down Henry's instructions.

"She's a real swell, that girl. Loves the grit of the land beneath her nails."

"Does she?"

"No. Not one bit. But here she is."

"I'll see to that wire immediately," David promised.

"She thanks you, sir. And she hopes that you're keeping your wits about you."

"I am keeping alert, yes."

"Good. Good. Miss Vanessi would be bereft if harm were to come to you. As a matter of fact, she wanted me to express to you how very much she misses you, and to let you know that the thought of seeing you once more keeps her from giving up when all seems lost."

David's voice was full of emotion. "Well. Please do let Miss Vanessi know that I think of her and only her night and day."

"I'm sure she knows and feels likewise, though she might not be able to tell you so very often given the difficulty of her present circumstances. Speaking of, what is the news in New York these days?"

"Oh, you know, this and that. I did read that this nosy reporter, Mr. Wood-something-or-other, has been printing the most inflammatory articles about Fitter Families tents being fronts for some devious eugenics program responsible for the mysterious disappearance of several Diviners. He's also been publishing poems from some outfit named the Voice of Tomorrow. Oh, and there's been quite a lot of rain."

"Ah, rain in New York. Unavoidable. I do thank you for the weather report."

"Don't mention it."

Henry gripped the receiver to his ear, loath to let go. "Well. This must be costing you a small fortune, sir."

"I'll rob a bank."

"No need. Miss Vanessi refuses to marry a pauper."

"Tell Miss Vanessi 'I do.'"

"I will tell her, sir. I most certainly will tell her."

By the next afternoon, Henry had the money he'd asked for, along with fifty dollars more that David had thrown in from his own pocket. Henry held the bills to his chest as if they were David himself.

"We have enough to buy a car now," Henry announced.

They found someone eager to sell a 1925 Model T Roadster Pickup, and Henry arranged to meet the seller—a heavyset, balding man whose nose was peeling from a terrible sunburn—in front of Western Union.

"She's a real beaut," the man said in a thick drawl.

Henry kicked the tires and frowned slightly. "I'd be willing to take this one off your hands for fifty dollars."

"Now, see here! This cost me nearly two-hun'erd eighty-five new!"

"Oh, come now. That's nothing now that you're rolling in oil money. Besides, an important fella like you can't be seen driving this old heap," Henry said.

The man removed his fedora to scratch his head. "I'll let her go for one-fifty."

"Eighty-five."

"Ninety-five!"

"Sold!"

"I would've gone as high as a hundred twenty," Henry told Memphis and Bill after the sale was final. "But now we've got twenty-five dollars left over. That should see us to Nebraska, with a motel room to boot."

The ground gave a deep rumble. Whoops and hollers erupted in the fields.

"What is it?" Memphis asked.

"The future," a man answered.

A derrick had hit its payload. The earth belched up its hidden riches a hundred feet into the air, blocking the blue sky. New crude showered down like rain on the rejoicing roughnecks who bathed in it, smearing one another's faces with its promise.

Memphis's pen hovered above the page in his notebook. And then he wrote.

America, America, God shed his grace on
  thee.
A hundred feet high and climbing, a
  geysering
A misering of liberty
Deep in the soil,
the oil of us
lies
blood of the nation, black as
night
over the winter prairies and small towns
black as silt
along the riverbanks
Wade in the water
Wade in the water, people, black
As me.
Oh, my brothers,
And where is this crown for the good
of our brotherhood
For what is brotherhood
From sea to shining, when will you see?
Which America will it be?

Memphis mailed the poem to Woody.

Then he wrote out three more copies and left them around town for anyone who had a mind to listen.

WHERE WE WILL MEET

Dreams are gateways to the other worlds.

Worlds we perceive just out of sight, in a bar of music or a stranger's face.

Dreams are where daring is born. "However did you get the courage to do that?" "Why, it came to me in a dream...."

Dreams are the shadow self let loose. You could murder in a dream, just pick up an ax and split anyone you like right through the skull, then rise the next day, safe in your bed, with nothing more than a vague feeling of slight unease that's gone—*poof!*—the minute you walk out your door. Dreams take the unconscious desires you let loose inside their houses off to the cleaners so you don't have to see the mess.

Dreams are where we will meet again. In love. In yearning. In fear.

Dreams, like countries, are ideas; all reality gestates first inside a dream.

Dreams are information for those who will read their tea leaves come morning. They are tiny little maps of the soul. Of every secret we push aside while we are awake. Of each tiny red-balloon hope whose dangling string we might reach for. Dreams connect us to every living thing, from the tiniest pea shoot to the rocks hurtling through space.

Dreams are miracles.

Dreams are portents.

Dreams know you better than you know yourself. They know everything.

Pay attention.

Henry DuBois IV walked through this dream's mirrored rooms, passing every one of his selves but not really seeing, and when he opened the door at the end of that long glass hallway, there was a giant map in front of him. The map took up the whole of the sky. Where there might be constellations there were road lines and tiny black dots of towns, squiggly red river markers and embossed mountain ranges. A globe come to life all around him. But what seemed static at first was not; every bit of the map moved just slightly as Henry looked at it, till it seemed he was seeing the echoes of the land it was before and possibly the direction it would take in the future. Dreams are not static. Neither are maps. *Listen*, this map seemed to whisper. *All of time and space exists at once. Dimensions fold upon themselves. Borders are arbitrary. Empires rise and fall. Towns come, towns go. The river is never the same from second to second. Ephemeral—great word, look it up.*

"Where's Ling?" Henry said, ignoring the voice.

"Henry!" Just like that, it was Ling Chan calling his name. They'd found each other. Dreams let that happen sometimes.

"Ling! Ling!" Henry waved his arms wildly.

She ran to him, and he wrapped her in a big hug until she broke away, embarrassed, saying, "That's enough."

Henry grinned. Ling was still Ling. "How are you? *Where* are you?" He was overjoyed to see her again.

"I'm still with Alma and Jericho. We've been everywhere, Henry— Philadelphia, Baltimore, and about twenty little towns in between. And Henry, I saw Chicago! Al Capone came to the show. Have you ever been to Chicago?"

"No."

"Well, their pizza is just awful. Too thick—like a sandwich. Now we're in Missouri. There's nothing good to eat. So much mayonnaise." Ling curled her lip in distaste. "I miss the soup dumplings at the Tea House."

Henry laughed. God, he was glad to see her.

"How are you?" she asked.

Henry sobered quickly. "We've seen some things, too, Ling. Some terrible things."

"Ghosts?"

"Not just ghosts," Henry said, leaving it at that for now. Ling was here. He was so grateful. He tipped his head back to look at the map. "Whose dream do you suppose brought us here?"

"Pins. Just like the one Sam and I found." Evie was in the dream now. It was a big dream, big enough for everybody. She was staring at the map, at a thumbtack that had appeared right in the center.

"Evie," Henry said. "Hey, darlin'." He knew she was sleeping and wasn't aware of him, but oh, how he'd missed her. Isaiah arrived and stood next to Evie. His eyes were glazed. One by one, the Diviners appeared, like the dream was birthing them. And still, there was room.

"Why are we here?" Evie asked.

Ling pointed to the center of the map. "What is that?"

There was a pinprick red dot. A town. But the dot was growing larger. Larger still. Its borders elongated until Mabel Rose stood against the unfurled map. She wore the yellow dress she'd been buried in, the one Evie had bought for her. The map moved across Mabel's face like a picture show. Her face was electric with tiny lines, as if she were a destination herself.

Even in sleep, the sight of Mabel tugged at everyone. Henry could see Evie breathing faster. Henry felt it, too. He missed her. But was she just a figment created from their collective yearning? Or was she something more?

"Ling, is she... real?" Henry asked.

"I don't know. I can't tell."

Mabel held something tightly in her hand. A glow seeped out between her clenched fingers. She opened them and the glow flew up and pinned itself to the map. There was a name printed there.

"'Gideon, Kansas,'" Ling read aloud.

"That is where you will understand," Mabel said. "That is where we will meet."

Vines grew up from the ground and wound around Mabel's legs and arms, crisscrossing rapidly until she was consumed by them, eaten up by the map of the earth.

Gideon, Kansas. The letters grew larger. The glow surrounding them was so bright that Henry had to put up a hand to block it. Its brightness was an assault.

"Stop!" Henry shouted.

He was pulled from the dream state with a sudden violence that left his body hurting and shaking with chills. Once again, he hadn't been able to say good-bye to Ling.

In the neighboring bed at their cheap motel in Texas, Memphis woke, trembling. "I dreamed about Mabel," he said.

"M-me, t-too," Henry said, fighting the effects. Memphis reached over and lay a hand on Henry's arm, and in a moment, he was better. "I was dream walking. Ling was there. Memphis, we were all there. We were all together in that dream."

"That has to mean something, doesn't it?" Memphis asked.

Dreams are miracles. Dreams are portents. Where had Henry heard that?

"Yeah. Yeah," Henry said, thinking of that bright glow. "I think it means we're going to Kansas."

※

In her bed on board the rolling circus train, Theta woke with a start. Dawn showed at the window. They'd reach their next destination soon. Beside her, Evie tossed and turned, moaning: "Don't go, Mabesie...."

"Evie." Theta shook her awake.

"What? What? I...I was dreaming. Deeply dreaming," Evie panted. She put a hand to her heart.

"Of Mabel?"

"Yes," Evie said, surprised. "There was a place on a map—"

"Gideon, Kansas," Theta said.

Evie was too stunned to do much more than nod. There was a knock at their door. When Evie opened up, she was surprised to see Sam standing there in the corridor, shirtless and barefoot, wearing a dazed expression.

"Hey. I hope I didn't wake you. I had the strangest dream...."

"A map. Gideon, Kansas. Mabel?" Evie asked.

"Okay. We might be spending too much time together," Sam said.

Isaiah wandered down out of his compartment. "I saw Mabel," he said on a yawn.

"Start packing," Evie said, opening up her trunk and taking out the few things she'd need. She'd pay Zarilda for them out of her check.

"Packing for what? We got two days of shows in Jefferson City," Sam called.

"Not anymore," Evie called back. "We're going to Gideon."

By eight o'clock, they'd packed their things. Sam broke the news to Zarilda.

"I surely hate to see you go," Zarilda said. They'd pulled into the depot. The whole circus had come to see them off. Johnny the Wolf Boy had tears in his eyes. "Aw, come on over here and give your Auntie Z some sugar." Isaiah fell into Zarilda's embrace. He hated to say good-bye. She kissed the top of his head and tucked a Hershey bar into his knapsack. "If you get hungry."

The entire company lined the roadway to wave the Diviners off. Arnold had lent them a truck the circus used to move supplies. It was a big, lumbering thing, but it would drive them where they needed to go. He also provided a road map.

"You be careful now. What with those Shadow Men and that terrible Roy out looking for you. Not to mention the ghosts," Zarilda said.

"Gee, Zarilda, when you put it that way, sounds like we don't have a chance in hell," Sam said.

"I'm serious, Sam Lloyd. Be careful who you trust. Stick to the back roads. And keep your head down—you tend to get a li'l cocky, my friend."

Sam spread his arms wide while walking backward. "I'm not cocky. Can I help it if I'm just that good?"

Evie batted her lashes. "You could always try."

Theta had opened the map.

"Lemme look," Sam said.

"You can't read a map," Theta said without moving.

"It's true. I hate maps. And directions. And rules."

Theta hadn't been back to Kansas since she'd run away after her power first came in. Kansas was the place where she'd been abandoned by her parents. Kansas was Roy and pain. She did not want to go to Kansas. But sometimes you had to do things you didn't want to do, things that frightened you, if they were the right things. With her finger, she followed the squiggly line through Missouri and into Kansas. Gideon was a tiny town in the northwestern part of the state. She whistled. "That's a long way."

"Then we'd better get started," Evie said. Mabel had reached out at last. Mabel would be there waiting. Mabel needed her.

"If you ever decide the circus life is for you, well, you know where to find us come November," Zarilda said.

There will be a November for you, Evie thought as they waved good-bye to the circus. *We'll make sure of it.*

❄

While Ling waited for Jericho to buy their train tickets, she thought about the dream and fought the uneasy feeling in her gut. She had spoken to spirits in dreams plenty of times. What she'd seen last night had been indeterminate. Had that been Mabel's ghost? Was she issuing an invitation, or a warning? And if Mabel Rose was no longer at rest, what did that mean?

Alma wasn't happy about Ling and Jericho leaving for Gideon. She stood on the train platform in the early morning light. There was still a bit of sleep crusted in the inner corners of her eyes where she hadn't managed to get all of the previous night's makeup off. "Can't you at least stay on till Detroit? You don't even know anything about this town."

"Jericho and I had exactly the same dream, Alma. And Henry was there, too. I can't explain it, but I know we have to go," Ling said. "It's a sign."

"What if it's a bad sign?" Alma asked.

"That's the trouble with signs," Ling said. "You don't know till you get there."

While Ling said her good-byes to Alma, Lupe lay on the backseat of the Ford with Jericho. "I can't believe you're leaving me," she said, wrapping her arms around his waist.

"Just for a little while," Jericho said. He stroked her hair away from her face.

"You're gonna find you some other girl out there. I just know it," Lupe said.

"Not one who can play drums like you can." Jericho kissed Lupe on her perfect mouth. He thought about Evie less and less. "You are my *ranita*."

Lupe burst out laughing. "Do you mean *mi reina*?"

"Does that mean 'my queen'?"

"Yes."

"That's what I meant. What was the other thing I said?"

"You called me your little frog."

"You're that, too."

"And you are *mi amado*," Lupe purred into Jericho's ear and kissed his neck.

"What is that?"

"My love." She sat up and buttoned her blouse. "Gideon, Kansas, eh? I'm pretty sure the only thing to date there are cows."

"I won't ask the word for that."

They held each other for another minute. "You be careful. I'm scared of those ghosts, Jericho."

He kissed the top of her head. *Me, too*, he thought.

Jericho waved to Ling as he headed toward the platform.

"I guess this is it," Ling said. She and Alma hugged, and Ling breathed in Alma's scent, trying to memorize it. Ling could hear the chugging of the train and see puffs of black smoke coming around the bend.

"I've been thinking about what you said. About us being something new. Something we don't know the name for yet," Alma said.

Ling prepared herself for bad news. "And?"

"I was thinking, I like new."

Ling let sail one of her biggest smiles.

"So do good, all right?" Alma said.

"All right."

"You ready?" Jericho asked Ling.

"No."

"Good. Me, neither."

Ling and Jericho boarded the Atchison & Topeka headed to Gideon. Whatever was waiting for them there, they'd meet it head-on.

GIDEON

Gideon, Kansas, was a small, pleasant-enough-seeming spot on the western edge of the state. Down the long stretch of Main Street, there were the usual suspects: A hardware store. A barbershop. A cafeteria with gold lettering on its windows advertising that it served BREAKFAST, LUNCH, AND SUPPER, and a garage with two round-topped gasoline pumps out front alongside a pillar of stacked tires. In front of the bank, the Stars and Stripes fluttered at the top of a flagpole. A row of houses with deep front porches so much the better for sitting out on a fine summer's evening with a pitcher of lemonade shared among neighbors while children ran up and down the street after fireflies with mason jars. And in front of those houses were the rows of telephone poles to keep people connected. Birds hopped along the wires, curious about what was going on down below. At the end of the block sat a white-steepled Presbyterian church with a sign out front listing the worship time: Sunday morning, ten o'clock. And at the other end sat a small train depot bordering railroad tracks that disappeared into the distance on either end. It was the sort of town, Henry thought, that appeared on postcards representing America.

They had parked the roadster pickup on a side street where the three of them watched the citizens of Gideon through the dirty windshield.

"Seems friendly enough," Memphis said, nervous.

"Sure. Friendly town. Friendly people. Friendly crosses burning in the night," Henry said under his breath.

Bill opened the door. "Come on. Let's see if the others made it."

The citizens of Gideon seemed fairly ordinary. They shopped and stopped in for a shave at the barbershop or visited the bank teller. And if they glanced toward the newcomers in their midst, it was momentary. They had stories in their heads, and they went about their business.

"Why did Mabel tell us to come here?" Henry said.

"Beats me," Memphis answered.

Henry slowed, squinted, then grinned. "Hey!" he shouted, waving. He nudged Memphis and Bill. "Look!"

Just ahead, in front of Frederickson Masonry Store, stood Theta, Evie, Sam, and Isaiah, looking just as lost.

"Isaiah," Memphis said, choked up. Then: "Isaiah! Isaiah!"

Memphis was running toward his brother as fast as he could and narrowly missed being hit by an auto motoring down the street. Memphis scooped his brother up in his arms. When he saw Theta coming up behind Isaiah, he wished he could do the same with her, but he didn't dare out here on a street in western Kansas. He looked into her eyes, and she returned the gaze of affection.

"Hey, Poet."

"Princess," he said.

And if it could be said that two people could embrace inside a gaze, then it was true for them. Henry kissed Theta's cheek and she kissed his and then they were hugging, the unlikely brother-sister act.

Isaiah talked a mile a minute, trying to tell Memphis the entirety of his journey out on the sidewalk of Gideon. "…and they had lions, Memphis, real lions, and I got to feed 'em. Me. I did it. Well, with a li'l help from Arnold…."

Memphis held his brother close and didn't let him go, wouldn't let him go ever again.

"See, I told you they'd meet us here." Ling's voice, reprimanding Jericho. They were down at the bottom of the street, just up from Gideon's train depot.

Evie waved her arm like a window washer. "Ling! Jericho! Over here!"

"Baby Vamp, we gotta work on your quiet voice," Sam said, sticking his hands in his pockets and looking down at his shoes. "What happened to 'let's not call attention to ourselves'?"

"You made it," Evie said as Jericho and Ling drew near. "Oh, I've missed you both. Hello, Jericho!"

"Hello, Evie. You changed your hair."

"Yes," she laughed, running a hand through it.

Henry barged in and dropped his boater hat on Ling's head. "Take it off," she said.

Henry did as he was told. "You're happy to see me, though, aren't you?"

"Yes," Ling said with absolute sincerity. "Yes. I am very happy to see you."

"Well, gee. Now I'm…what is that word you use, Sam? To mean overcome with emotion?"

"*Verklempt*?"

"I am *verklempt*," Henry said.

"Gesundheit," Evie chimed in. Being reunited with her friends made her giddy. She'd missed them so.

"I might remind you that you're all wanted by every Pinkerton, every sheriff, every Shadow Man in this country. Might be better if we broke up this li'l reunion," Bill warned.

But none of them could stand to be separated again. It was true, though, that they needed a safe place to congregate. The local library had a little sitting garden off to the side. They met there to catch up while life in the town went on around them. Men piled out of trucks and ambled into the feed store. A quartet of boys started a stickball game down one of the streets, and Isaiah ached to join it.

"We were with the circus," Isaiah announced to everyone else.

"My pals from before New York," Sam said. "They—"

Henry grinned. "Don't tell me—you were the high-wire act, Sam, and Evie, you were the high wire."

"Hysterical," Evie said and rolled her eyes. "Where were you?"

"Stuck on a levee in Greenville, Mississippi," Memphis said. "We got caught in the flood."

"I'm glad you're safe," Theta said.

"Where were you?" Evie asked Jericho and Ling.

"With the Harlem Haymakers," Jericho said.

"What is that, some kinda farm league?" Sam asked.

"Harlem's all-girl orchestra," Ling said proudly. "Alma helped us get away on the TOBA circuit."

"An all-girl orchestra?" Evie said. "That must account for it. Jericho, you look pos-i-tutely different—I can't quite put my finger on it."

"It's because Jericho has a girlfriend named Lupe now," Ling said. She was not about to watch the Jericho and Evie sideshow start up again.

"Oh?" Evie said with a smile that Theta and Henry had come to know as her radio smile—bright and fake.

"Well, gee. That's swell, Freddy. Just swell," Sam said.

Jericho looked embarrassed. "Thank you, Ling."

"You're welcome."

Jericho stole a glance at Evie, who was doing her level best not to look at him, he knew. He still had some feelings for her. He couldn't deny it. But his time with her had always been fraught, colored by John Hobbes and Will, Sam and Mabel and Hopeful Harbor. With Lupe, he'd started something fresh. Something that had no past. He liked that. A tiny, petty slice of his heart was glad Ling had blurted out the truth. He wanted Evie to know that he could get along just fine without her.

"So why are we here?" Ling asked.

"Did you dream of Mabel? Was it Mabel who told you to come?" Evie asked.

Everyone nodded.

"But why Gideon, Kansas? Doesn't seem like anyplace special," Jericho said.

Down the street, the boys' stickball game had become contentious. They argued until someone's mother yelled out the front window at them to stop squabbling.

"Something feels strange to me," Ling said.

"We're fighting ghosts and trying to figure out how to repair a hole between dimensions. You might have to be more specific," Sam said.

"Why Gideon? It's just an ordinary town," Ling said.

Jericho folded his arms. "I just said that."

"No, you didn't. You said it didn't seem like anyplace special."

"That is quite literally the same thing."

"Maybe because it's so ordinary, it was a safe place to meet," Henry speculated. "Mabel said, 'That is where we will meet.'"

"She also said, 'That is where you will understand,'" Ling said.

"Understand what?" Sam said.

"There's something I need to tell you," Ling started. "It's about us and the ghosts…"

Isaiah…

The voices of Memphis and his friends faded to a murmur. It was Sarah Beth he heard now.

Isaiah, talk to me.…

His eyes rolled up in their sockets and his body went rigid as the vision

354

swept through him like a brushfire, pulling him into their shared space of the dark room. There, Sarah Beth kneeled and brushed the pale yellow hair of her porcelain doll. She glanced up and smiled. "Isaiah! Where are you? When are you getting to Bountiful?"

"We're on our way, but we had to stop in another town first."

"What do you mean?" Brush. Brush. Brush.

"Our friend Mabel, she came to us in a dream and told us to meet in Gideon, Kansas."

Sarah Beth stopped brushing the doll's hair. "Who?"

"Mabel Rose. She's passed on, but—"

"Why did you listen?" Sarah Beth said. She seemed angry.

"She's our friend."

"Why did you listen?" Sarah Beth repeated. No, not angry. Scared.

Behind Sarah Beth, the dark was not a nothing. It was full of terrors. It dropped away, and Isaiah began to shake as if the world were tilting off its axis. He saw himself back at Jake Marlowe's Future of America Exhibition, in the Fitter Families tent, holding fast to the bronze medal he'd wanted but that they wouldn't let him have, the one that read, YEA, I HAVE A GOODLY HERITAGE. All the things he'd seen with that medal in his grip came rushing over him in their horror now: Visions of bone-thin prisoners behind barbed-wire fences. Tall smokestacks belching a foul pollution into the air. Boxcars with hands reaching out of the slats. Now there was more coming: Gray skies choked with smoke. Humans struggling for survival among shriveled crops and polluted streams. Piles of dead bodies, so many that it made it hard to weep. As if people were no more than stones and there was no point in crying anymore because there was nothing to be done. The horror rolled over everything, unstoppable. Behind it all, Jake Marlowe's golden machine churned eternally. The Eye symbol beamed out from the forehead of the King of Crows. Isaiah could see him lurking inside its golden body, like he was part of the machine, and he was grinning, and his eyes, his eyes were a forever night that nobody could wake up from no matter how hard they tried.

Isaiah came out of his vision. He was lying on the ground with his head in Memphis's lap and all his friends crowded around him.

"Is that boy all right?" some lady was asking, and Bill was telling her that the boy was fine, just having a fit that would settle in a minute, no need to worry none, and it all sounded like a conversation underwater. Isaiah needed to warn them that Gideon wasn't safe. But he couldn't seem to speak.

The low rumble of thunder reverberated through the town. Jericho squinted up at the sun. "Doesn't *look* like rain."

But the thunder answered differently.

"Gracious," a woman on the street said. "Sounds like we're about to get a storm, Frank. You'll want to pull in the rugs."

"Oh, it's just some clouds squabbling, Florence. It'll pass."

The thunder came again, heavy and pounding, as if some wild thing had broken free of its cage. The people of Gideon came out of their shops and filling stations and pretty houses with nice front porches. They gathered in the street. Dark clouds were swirling above the town. A red pulse beat behind them, like a fire ready to break out.

"What *is* that?"

"Never seen anything quite like it."

"It was pure blue a minute ago!"

"Theta…?" Evie said.

Isaiah fought his wooziness. He clawed at Memphis to get his attention.

"Me-mem…phis…" Isaiah spat out the words on a hoarse whisper: "Th-th-they're…c-c-com-ming."

When the sky cracked open over Gideon, the people were too startled to scream. They had no reference for what they were seeing, and so they were simply stunned into silence. The Diviners knew better.

"Do you see…?" Evie said.

"Yeah," Sam said. "We're about to have company."

"He's f-f-found us," Isaiah said, struggling to his feet. "They're c-coming."

Angry lightning shot down from the clouds and arced around the town like the talons of a feral bird intent on making Gideon its prey. The lightning made contact with a distant grain silo and a farm. They wavered for a moment, an X-ray image, and then they were simply gone. Nothing but smoke and fire and rubble. A locust smashed against the windshield of a shiny Chrysler. Its bug guts spread out jellylike against the glass. Another hit, and then another, locusts falling from the sky like raindrops. The birds pushed off from the telephone wires. The citizens ducked as the birds swooped through the town, crying. The people crowded together. Fear had picked up along with the storm. A great shadow moved across the land like fingers reaching toward Gideon. Down the road, a giant billowing wall of dust gobbled up everything in its path. And out of the dust emerged a man.

A farmer in coveralls and a brown hat elbowed his neighbor. "What in the name of heaven? How's he doing that?"

"Dunno." The other man called to his wife, who was coming out of the dry-goods store, "Myrtle! Is the circus come to town?"

"Not that I know about," the wife answered, holding fast to her hat. "Mercy! What on earth?"

Behind her, the shop boy carrying her bags of flour, sugar, and salt slowed and gaped, slack-jawed, at the angry sky and the ominous, stormy dust cloud that roiled behind the King of Crows, who moved with some secret purpose toward the good citizens of Gideon. The shop boy's mother had told him that staring was rude, but who wouldn't stare at this man? Blue lightning sparked along his feather-caped shoulders and danced atop his tall hat. His shadow stretched out before him, reaching the town first. And as he walked down the center of Main Street, seemingly oblivious to the destruction in his wake, he tipped his hat.

"Good afternoon. How do you do? I am the King of Crows."

There were a good many people gathered on Main Street now.

"Must be one of those circus fellas. Maybe even something with the Elks or Booster Club," a man whispered to his wife, his brain still trying to make sense of the senseless, to banish fear with any form of reason.

"We all need a good boost now and then, don't we?" The King of Crows raised a hand. The electricity along his fingers grew fainter, shorting out.

"A magic trick!" a young girl in pigtails said in wonder.

"I have more magic tricks up my sleeve. Would you like to see?"

"Don't listen to him. Don't let him get inside your head," Sam said to the people of Gideon.

"Ah. At last. Welcome, Diviners." The King of Crows rested his thumbs against the lapels of his shine-slick feathered coat and faced the Diviners, drawing the attention of Gideon's townspeople.

"You know this fella?" the farmer asked just as a woman in a simple cloche squinted at the Diviners and asked, "Who are you?"

"Don't you recognize these criminals in your midst? These are the Diviners. That radical sort wanted by the authorities across the nation for the bombings at Mr. Marlowe's exhibition. For the murder of Sarah Snow."

The buzz of gossip filled the streets: "I heard about it on the radio." "Lands' sake! How'd they get to Gideon?" "This is a safe place."

"We're not going to hurt you," Theta promised.

"How do we know that?" "You killed Sarah Snow!" "Ralph, grab the rifles and get the sheriff."

"We didn't. I promise you," Henry chimed in.

Sam put up his hands in a peaceful gesture. "It isn't true."

"Which part isn't true? Are you them?"

"We're Diviners, yes, but we didn't do those things. I promise," Evie added. "We're innocent."

"No one is ever truly innocent. As you'll soon see," the King of Crows tutted.

The street teemed with people. The citizens streamed out of their pretty houses and shops to gawp at the strangers in their midst. A man with a napkin stuffed into the neck of his shirt arrived. He didn't remove it. He was accustomed to handling any small squabble in the town easily, and he hoped to go back to his early supper. "Afternoon. I'm the mayor here," he said without offering his hand.

"What a fine town you have here, sir," the King of Crows said.

"Towns don't come much finer than Gideon," the mayor agreed. "You can have your Kansas City or New York. Why, this is the good life right here. In Gideon. And now we'll be known as the town that caught America's Most Wanted."

"Indeed, a fine town," the King of Crows said, ignoring the mayor. "We'll take it."

"Beg your pardon?"

"I said we'll take it."

"Gideon isn't for sale, mister."

"Ah, yes. Like the Louisiana Purchase, or Manhattan. I see. Should I have come with a purse full of beads and a wagon of diseased blankets?"

"Mister, I think you should leave. We'll take care of things from here."

"Will you? I rather doubt it." He breathed in deeply, and if he exhaled, it was hard to tell. "Can't you smell the history in the air? No doubt their grandfathers rushed across these prairies in their wagons, knocking down the natives, smashing in their brains in their zeal to stake their claim. That pioneer spirit. My, what a land! What a people! I've learned so much from you."

He turned to Memphis and Ling, to Isaiah just behind. "They'll never let you in, you know. Not without constant vigilance and revolution. And even then, they'll do it begrudgingly. This land bleeds with its wounds still. Wouldn't you like to see justice served? Maybe even revenge for the generations destroyed?"

Memphis could feel the "yes" crawling up to sit angry and hurting on his tongue. Beside him, Theta whispered, "I would."

Several of the men from Gideon had loaded their rifles. They took aim at the King of Crows.

"Look how small and scared they live. Reaching for their guns at the slightest provocation." The King of Crows *tsk*ed and shook his head. "They don't want to hear what you have to say. This is what they want: blood."

The sheriff cocked his gun. "Mister, we don't want any trouble here."

"And yet." The King of Crows inhaled deeply. Exhaled. "So be it. Behold! Feast upon the story of yourselves."

With that, the King of Crows opened his coat, and the citizens of Gideon were mesmerized by what it held inside: A history that shifted to suit whatever the viewer wanted to see. One that let them be the heroes of their stories, with a right to whatever they held, whatever they had taken, whatever they wanted next. One that granted them permission for their greed. "Who wants to etch their names into this story?"

A gleam dawned in the sheriff's eye. "I do."

"Me! I want it."

"So be it. But first, let us call forth your dead. Come. Come out."

One by one, the dead of Gideon appeared, faint wisps between houses, a handful of phantoms standing beside the headstones that marked their lives with a few etched words. A boy with brown hair and freckles walked from the cemetery and into the street.

"Harry? Is that my Harry?" a tearful woman cried. "Harry, it's Mama." She started toward the boy. Evie and Theta tried to hold her back.

"You mustn't go," Evie said.

"But that's my boy!" the woman said with great longing.

"No. Not the way you remember," Evie said.

"Your dead are here," the King of Crows said. "Look. There they are. All nicely arrayed. They watch you. They know what secrets beat inside your hearts. It pulls them from their graves. They, too, see a new frontier."

The ghost boy, Harry, snapped at his mother like a rabid dog. She cried out and fell back. The ghosts of Gideon showed their sharp teeth. Fear shot through the townspeople. They'd heard old-timers talk of having to massacre the Kiowa, Cheyenne, and Comanches who stood in the way of settling this land. But they, themselves, had never faced such a threat.

"What's going on here, mister?" the mayor asked. With a shaking hand, he pulled the napkin free from his collar at last, as if that might make a difference. "What is this?"

"An accounting," the King of Crows said. "Do they frighten you, your dead?"

"Sheriff, get them out of here!" someone shouted.

"I will take these dead from your town," the King of Crows promised. "Think of me as a vigilante spirit from a nation that loves its law and order conducted by outlaws. But first, ask yourselves, good citizens: Would this be happening if there was not rot within Gideon? Would your dead rise from their graves and come for a reckoning if all were well?"

"What's he doing?" Sam whispered to the others.

"What do we need to do?" a man in suspenders asked.

"You can't trust his promises," Ling warned. "They're riddles. They'll tie you up."

"Hush up! You're wanted by the law," the sheriff said.

"I require payment for my services. Who among your neighbors will it be? Will it be the widow Merriwether, so young and fair? And rich now, too. Her husband is among your dead. Did he really die of a bad heart?"

"He *was* awfully young," another woman in a pale blue dress said, holding tightly to her little girl, who clung to her mother's skirts, too frightened for tears.

"Why, Sue Ellen," the young widow Merriwether said. "I mourned my George! I could scarcely stop crying. You remember—all of you remember!"

"He wasn't in the ground three months before you took up with Ernie Porter!" a large man in a sweat-stained white shirt called out.

"You're only sore she didn't take up with you, Virgil!" an old woman with a lined face shot back. "Stop this nonsense at once. This is not who we are in Gideon."

"If you're looking to take somebody, why not make it Esther there!" the big man said, pointing to the old woman who'd called him out. "The old busybody. Thinks herself better'n the rest of us."

"Stop it!" Evie shouted. "Can't you see he wants you to turn against one another?"

The dead moved closer. Black drool dripped from cracked lips as they sniffed the air, hungry. The people stepped back, terrified. New accusations flew:

"The druggist makes moonshine in his basement! I've heard about the still!"

"Now, see here, Parker…" a man, presumably the druggist, said.

"What about the janitor, Quinn? You know how the Irish are."

"And what's that supposed to mean?" a grizzled man with a brogue answered.

"I knew there'd be trouble when we let the Polish in to work the mills. What with their foreign ways, and Catholics to boot!"

"Here! Take the parson's wife! She's so high and mighty!"

They pushed the parson's wife forward as she wailed, "I've been to your homes! I've sat with you in your weakest hours."

"And judged us for it."

Isaiah had been stepping closer to the King of Crows, trying to get close enough to grab his mother in her crow form from the King's shoulder. With a grunt, he reached for his mother and missed, coming up with only a feather yanked from the King's voluminous coat. The King of Crows whirled around. His eyes were a soulless deep, and Isaiah found he could not look away. "Did you steal from me, boy?"

"Get away from my brother!" Memphis spat through tight teeth, fists at the ready. He wrapped his arms protectively around Isaiah.

The King of Crows looked from brother to brother, some terrible thought twisting his lips into a cruel half smile. "You'll beg for a bargain one day, Healer. I will deal with you both in time," the King said. "But now, to the business at hand. Why should I be satisfied with a paltry offering when I could have everything?

There was a high, piercing shriek, followed by the skin-crawling insect drone the Diviners knew all too well. The wind blew harder, sending hats pinwheeling down Main Street. Bright blue lightning showed in the billowing dust wall, blocking any escape from Gideon. The cloud mass groaned as if it needed to unleash something from within its gut.

The King of Crows raised his arms, and with it, his voice. "Can you hear our humble wagons rumbling across this great nation? I will call them forth—a Manifest Destiny of the Dead."

The dust and clouds peeled back, forming a hole, as if the world itself were splitting open into a giant mouth ready to devour everything in its path. All they could see was a stretch of darkness, and inside a glimmering: an army of dead, thousands of them, coiled and ready.

A woman burrowed into her husband's side. "What in the name of heaven…?"

"Hey. Hey, you promised to keep us safe," the mayor said.

"I promised no such thing. I promised to take your dead from you. And I will. They will join my army. But first, they must feed. How about a little cheer to get us started, hmm?"

The King of Crows pounded his walking stick against the street. "Jamestown. Salem. Sand Creek. Omaha. Monticello. Andrew Jackson. Lorem Ipsum. Rah. Rah. Rah."

He repeated it, beating the stick faster and faster in time with his words: "Jamestown.Salem.SandCreek.Omaha.Monticello.AndrewJackson.LoremIpsum.Rah.Rah.Rah."

As a girl, Evie had once spun a shadow lamp faster and faster until the paper-cut images blurred against the light and became one undulating line of shadow. She thought of that now, watching the great wall of dead pouring out of the tear in the clouds. It was as if the dead had slipped off the lamp of the world and were moving with an awful quickness. Driven by an insatiable hunger, they hit the small town of Gideon like unleashed floodwater. They'd been emptied of any moral sense or shared humanity. There was only a burning need to consume and destroy. The ghosts moved with the force and power of a great machine, one consciousness ruling all.

Their noses twitched, or, where there were no noses, their mouths hung slightly open. They were breathing in life, sniffing for prey.

The King of Crows stood in the center of the street with lightning crackling all around him, a conductor directing a discordant symphony.

A man, half-devoured, twitched on the ground, his eyes beginning to lose focus. In horror, Evie watched as a charcoal veining crawled across his body, until he was a dried-out husk. She screamed, and what was left of the man caved in on itself and became a pile of dust. Already, a gray pall climbed up the sides of the houses with their pretty front porches. No one would sit there on a summer's evening again. The ground cracked open. Broken. Dead. The flowers wilted on their stems. The dead sucked the life force from a mother who still clutched her little boy. But three more of the ghouls descended and ripped the crying child from his dying mother's arms. Teeth sank into flesh, the sound like a seam ripped viciously apart. The victims screamed when the teeth bit in, when they still thought they had a chance, but once they realized the battle was useless, the shock of that violence—the utter hopelessness—turned their screams to a whimpering gurgle of resignation, and then a terrible empty silence.

"We have to get together!" Evie shouted from the library steps. "We have to fight back!"

"We can't!" Ling said. "That's what he wants—if we fight back, we'll give them our power!"

"We can't just let them destroy the town!" Sam said.

"Let's try to form some sort of barrier, then. A shield!" Ling shouted.

"That one! He has defied me long enough." The King of Crows pointed a yellowed fingernail at Bill. Two ghouls rushed for him. Bill snaked a hand around the throat of one of them and it fell to dust. Jericho ripped a fence post from a yard and swung it with all the force of his serum-enhanced body. It came down on the soft head of a ghost of a girl, no more than twelve, and her bashed skull skittered across the road and came to rest at the base of a white picket fence. Jericho stared in bewildered horror. He had wanted to be a philosopher. A scholar. The dead girl's body twitched. The ghostly hands reached up to find an empty neck, and then her atoms blasted apart.

More were coming. Again, he swung. *Like a brute*. And again. Was this all the world really understood? A creature opened its mouth. Rage. Hunger.

A reflex even after death. Jericho hit the dead man until there was nothing left to hit.

"There's too many of them! We'll exhaust ourselves," Evie said. She'd never felt so helpless. "What do we do?"

Theta wished she had salt in her pockets like Miss Addie, and then she wanted to laugh at the idea that salt could protect them from this.

"We have to try something!" Memphis shouted. "Get together!"

The Diviners linked hands and faced the Army of the Dead.

"What now?" Henry asked. "Ling?"

"I don't know! Why are you asking me?"

"Because you're the smart one!"

"Think…think of, um, think of, of, of a wave—push them back!" Ling yelled.

Their molecules fused together. Ling could feel their fear combining, too, making it difficult to concentrate. It was like a gas hose come loose, spraying fuel everywhere. They sent a wave of energy buckling fast down the street, bending the buildings inward as if they were made of water instead of brick. The first fifty ghouls flew backward and then apart. The filling station burst into flames.

"We can't stop them without destroying the town," Ling said.

"Go again," Sam said, squeezing Henry's and Evie's hands. He pushed his energy down the line before everyone was ready.

"Ahhh!" Ling fell forward, breaking the chain. Radiation burns striped down her left arm. Their power felt unstable. Wrong. A row of houses to their right wobbled.

"We have to do it," Sam said. "We have to take 'em out."

"No. No, we can't," Ling insisted.

"Ling, we don't have a choice," Theta said.

You did this. This is your fault. The choice is yours.

Six ghosts advanced on a yard where four men stood emptying their guns into the dead, to no avail.

"Go!" Sam said. The Diviners stiffened as they connected and blasted the ghosts apart. For just a moment, there was the familiar euphoria of victory. And then, something new.

"Oh, no…" Evie said.

In horror, they felt themselves connected to every ghost rampaging

364

through the streets of Gideon. The pain of their attack rippled through them, knocking them back. *What you do shall return threefold.*

"I tried to tell you," Ling said through her pain. "We've joined our power to theirs. All those ghosts we've been destroying? It's only made them stronger!"

"Yes. Yes," a voice hissed. "I've come for you, my love." Elijah shuffled toward Theta. She screamed and searched for a safe place to run. The streets were overrun with the ravenous dead.

"I am not your love. And neither is Adelaide. I worked the spell. I bound you from doing harm." Theta fell against the side of a truck.

Elijah took a step closer. He was the same gray as his moldering uniform. "You bound me to yourself. She will die soon. You will be my new love."

"The hell I will." Theta's fear ignited her rage. There had been so many who'd tried to lay claim to her, promising her safety only to prove they were the monsters all along. "Stop!" Theta said. "Stop it!"

She pushed him away. Her hand went through his chest as if he were made of mud. He was far more solid than any ghost she'd encountered before. Theta screamed as his chest caught fire. Elijah looked down, furious. Theta backed away. The flames engulfed him, and she cried out. Deep inside she could feel the pain as if she, too, were burning.

"Theta! Theta!" Memphis had her, had his hands on her, cooling the burn. Together, they ran from the screeching Elijah.

"Do not harm the Diviners," the King of Crows growled in warning to his dead. "Every piece of history needs its witnesses."

The dead sniffed anyway.

"Obey me!" the King of Crows commanded, and reluctantly, the dead slunk away to attack the townspeople.

"What do we do?" Isaiah asked. "Memphis, what do we do?"

"I don't know, Little Man."

If they tried to destroy the ghosts, it would destroy them as well. If they did nothing, Gideon and its people would be lost.

"Did you hear that?" Evie asked suddenly.

"Hear what?" Ling asked. She was leaning on one crutch and using the other to protect two little girls cowering behind her.

"Someone's calling me...." There it was again—her name being called in the sweetest voice. Evie felt as if all her molecules were being drawn to something across the street. She took a step back from the melee to see what it was. There. Over the heads of running townspeople and hungry spirits. Over the abandoned toys, the lost shoe in the road, the screaming, the smoke. There, shimmering in front of the church. There, in the yellow dress. There.

"Mabesie?" Evie had feared that if Mabel ever did appear to her, it would be as a ghost mangled by death. But this Mabel was whole, with an unearthly presence her best friend had never known in life. It was the same red-gold hair curved into a soft, wavy bob. The same pale skin, made paler. Just as in the dreams, she wore the dress she'd been buried in, the yellow-sun confection Evie had bought for Mabel at Gimbels with her very first big radio check. Evie couldn't look away.

Through the din and the screams, Mabel's voice reached out to her: "Evie. There you are."

"Mabel, oh Mabel!" Evie cried. Mabel was like a dream that Evie was afraid would evaporate before she could reach the friend she so ached to see once more. Like James, Mabel had become Evie's obsession: If only she could change the past. If only she could right the wrongs. If only she could bring back what had been lost. If only. This tangle of love and remorse, hope and need drew Evie forward, toward the phantom that shimmered so promisingly in the road.

"Evie! Stop!" Ling yelled, but Evie no longer heard her. Behind Evie, her friends were locked in battle. The townspeople screamed in terror. She was vaguely aware of Theta shouting her name, as if Evie herself were a precious thing in danger of being lost.

Mabel. Dear Mabel. Evie had to see her. Had to touch her.

Mabel extended an arm toward Evie. "You came. I knew you would."

"Yes. Yes, of course," Evie said, walking toward her. It was really Mabel. "Of course I would."

"I said you would understand. And do you understand?"

Evie wanted to be closer to Mabel. She was still afraid Mabel would disappear.

"I don't think you do," Mabel said. Her voice took on a harder edge. "I told you to let me rest. I was having the most beautiful dream. I was…happy."

Evie slowed her steps. Mabel's eyes. Those eyes that had shown sympathy. Irritation. Wariness. Joy. Those eyes were as blank and black as a pair of dull coat buttons.

"Mabesie?" Evie came to a sudden stop. Her skin prickled.

Mabel lifted her chin. Her lips twitched, revealing pointed teeth. And then, like the others, she *sniffed*. She was breathing in Evie's scent, tracking her. Evie tried to speak Mabel's name again, but fear reached up from her gut and strangled the sound. Mabel closed her black eyes for a few seconds, inhaling deeply, her body spasming, desperate. Hungry. Whip-quick, she opened her eyes and faced Evie. She lurched forward like a foal testing its legs, suddenly realizing their strength and speed. "I told you. I told you. But you never did listen to me, did you?"

Instinctually, Evie took a step back. Her mind struggled to make sense of the moment: Mabel was the kindest person Evie had ever known. Her best friend. Mabel would never try to hurt her. Would she? Mabel's gait was uneven, but she was closing the distance. It was only now that the spell was broken that Evie realized the terrible danger she was in. She had allowed herself to be separated from her friends when they needed her and she needed them. Together, they were stronger. Evie knew this.

"Evie! Watch out!"

Theta never called Evie by her actual name, and that was what made her turn her head to the right. She sucked in a terrified breath. The ghoul was *right there*. Grave dirt matted its hair; its face was skeletal. It let out a long hiss of desire. Death had not dulled its burning need to take. Even in death, it still wanted.

"No—" Evie started. She put a hand to the thing's decaying dress, stiff with rot. Maggots pushed out from the holes in the fabric and crawled across the back of her hand and Evie screamed and screamed. Theta was coming. She was shouting to Henry, whose blue eyes widened in alarm. Theta and Henry were too far away. They were trapped on the other side of Main Street with a wall of hungry spirits between them.

"Mabel…" Evie whispered.

Mabel, her best friend, who had also been the best of them. Mabel, in her yellow dress, bright as sun. Mabel watched and did nothing to stop this. In that moment, Evie didn't care to live. Who would want to live in a world where you could find no good?

The ghoul was face-to-face with Evie. She could smell its stench, like the water in a vase of rotting flowers. It grabbed her around the neck. Evie clawed at the thing. It tightened its grip and her head went buzzy-light. Mabel was still watching.

The thing's voice slithered into her ear. "I would have all the life you possess...."

Razor-like fingernails pierced her right side and reached inside her. The pain was enormous. Evie wanted to scream but had no breath for it. That cold hand was digging under her skin. The ghoul positioned its mouth above hers.

Evie could feel her life force being sucked from her body. Her bones felt close to snapping. This would not be a peaceful death. She struggled against the ghoul's hold, and even in this terrible death grip, she could still get a sense of the life it had lived before: A house in town. Ruffled dresses and elegant, candlelit balls. Piano lessons. A husband. Four children, two of them dead—measles, a fall from a horse. All of that humanness that should have joined them.

The pain was unbearable. It hurt too much to cry.

"Give up, Evie." Mabel's dry voice. "Why don't you ever give up?"

"I...I..." Evie coughed out. She was losing her strength. *Let go*, she thought. *Just let go.* If she did, the pain would stop. She would see James. And Will. It would be someone else's trouble to stop this terrible plague on the world. It would no longer be Evie's responsibility but Theta's and Henry's. Ling's and Jericho's. Memphis's and Isaiah's and Sam's. Her friends.

"I...can't," Evie said, barely a whisper.

Evie heard the lurching mechanical heartbeat of the Eye. The screams of the soldiers. Her brother. Screaming into eternity. She was screaming inside, too. They were being ripped apart with a machinelike violence, all their screams lost under its constant clanging. Evie felt herself slipping under, one more Diviner fed to the Eye to keep open the tear between the worlds. She saw the future under the King of Crows. He and his dead would eat through this world until all that was left were bones and ash, lies and corruption. She knew that they would never stop coming unless somebody stopped them. And who would be left to do that?

"I. Won't. Give. Up," Evie whispered.

She cried out in fresh pain as something bright and hot exploded near her. The ghoul feasting on her shrieked and let go. Evie crumpled, but from the ground she saw Theta, bright as a phoenix. The ghoul had been lit up like a bonfire. Theta, her face twisted with pain and rage, took out two more. And then Theta turned toward Mabel.

"Th...Theta. D-don't," Evie croaked. "It's M-Mabel."

"No, it's not." Theta raised her fiery hand to strike.

But the King of Crows was calling all his dead to him. "Enough! I would have your tribute now," he commanded. The spirits moved toward him in blind obedience, Mabel included. The King of Crows opened his mouth and the life the ghouls had taken flowed into him, leaving them with that slight ache in the belly that told them to feed and keep feeding. That nothing would ever be enough to sate their endless need. The King of Crows shone like a terrible beacon against the dark dust settling over every inch of Gideon. He had been recharged by the carnage. He and his dead would move on. Take another town. And another. And another. A death cult on the move until there was nothing left to take.

"Thank you for bearing witness, Diviners," the newly restored King of Crows trumpeted. "Not that anyone will believe you."

With that, he turned toward the widening hole in the dust, back toward the land of the dead, with his army, with Mabel, following.

"Theta?" Evie croaked. Because something wasn't right. She'd never been so cold before. What was happening? Where her dress had been torn open, Evie saw that the wound in her side was turning sour and spreading. Tiny branches of gray rot inched across her stomach and up toward her heart.

"Th-Theta?" Evie struggled for breath.

Theta's fire left her all at once. She looked panicked. Now Evie was truly scared. Theta. Calling for Memphis. Screaming for him: *Now, now!* Memphis racing to her side. His worried face. Talking: *Too much. Fall back. Storm cellar.* Sam. Poor Sam. Lifting her up so all she could see was smoke and sky.

And she could feel what the ghoul had left behind in her. Could feel the pain and anguish of Marlowe's careless machine, the Eye, tearing apart whatever it wanted. She could feel the dead, too. Was joined to them, to the mindless horde. The dark sky was shot through with cold blue flashes of light that announced themselves but illuminated nothing. She was dying, she knew. She might become one of those hungry things. Just like the one that had bitten her. Just like Mabel.

That is where we will meet. That is where you will understand.

GRAVE ROT

Jericho helped lower Ling into the storm cellar, then slammed the doors shut and threaded a shovel through the handles just to be sure. Henry and Theta cleared off a worktable, and Memphis and Sam laid Evie down on top. Bill pulled the chain on the bulb. In its weak light, Evie was a pale fish thrown from the sea, gasping for breath.

Sam was frantic. "Memphis. Tell me you can heal her, pal. Please, please, tell me you can."

"Poet? Can you?" Theta wiped away a tear.

"That's a wound from the dead. Doesn't work the same. It's...it's beyond me." What he didn't say: *I'm afraid. Afraid of what might meet me on the other side of that healing.*

Ling marched over and took Evie's wrist. "Her pulse is weak."

Sam fell to his knees. There were tears in his eyes. "Memphis, I'm begging you."

"I'm trying to tell you—that's not just any wound. It's grave rot," Memphis said as gently as he could.

"What are you talking about? Grave rot, what is that?" Ling asked.

"They're getting powerful, like us. They're teaming up, like us. You just saw what they can do," Memphis said.

"Whatever's happening with the Eye that's making the connection unstable between our worlds is also doing something to the ghosts," Henry said.

"I don't think it's just that," Memphis said solemnly.

"We did this," Ling said.

Memphis nodded. "Yeah."

"What are you talking about? She's dying!" Sam shouted.

"Every time we blasted apart one of those ghosts, we sent our power into that other world. To him. To his dead. Energy is neither created nor destroyed. Everything is connected," Ling explained.

"I tried to heal a man in Greenville who got attacked by these new dead. When I put my hands on him, I could feel my power being sucked out of me. Grave rot turns its victims directly into that," Memphis said, pointing to what lay beyond the cellar doors. "And it nearly killed me. I don't have any protection against it."

Theta looked from Memphis to Evie. If Memphis did nothing, Evie would surely die and become one of the King's dead, or dust. But if he did heal her, he could meet the same fate. "What are we gonna do?"

"We can't go on without Evie. We need all of us," Jericho said.

"She's not looking too good," Henry said.

Evie's breathing was a wet, labored wheeze. When Memphis looked down, he saw Remy lying on the boat. He remembered the horrors he'd faced while under. He didn't want to go back there. He'd do anything not to go back there.

"Evie pulled me outta that mess in Times Square. One night, my stomach hurt and she brought me some soup on a tray," Isaiah said. "She helped take care of me, Memphis."

"All right," Memphis said. He couldn't let his friend die. "All right, but it's gonna take all of us to fight this. Theta! Gonna need you to cauterize that wound when I'm through, burn out the rot."

"Whatever we're doing, we need to do it fast." Henry nodded at Evie. The rot was spreading across her belly, an inky stain.

"Henry and I can try to create a dreamscape to protect us, a bubble of safe passage for us to occupy," Ling offered.

"What can I do?" Sam asked.

"Try to keep the dead from seeing us. For as long as you can," Memphis said.

"What about me, Memphis?" Isaiah asked.

"Just . . . stay by my side," Memphis said. "Stay close."

"I wanna help."

"That is how you can help."

" 'S all right, Little Man. You ain't less for it," Bill said.

But it felt like it. Hadn't Isaiah made it all the way here from New York? That he'd gone under before the fight in Gideon wasn't his fault. Once again, Isaiah had been pushed aside, and he was mad about it.

"All right. Let's go. Everybody put your hands on Evie," Memphis said. He took off his shoes and socks and squished the earth of the storm cellar between his toes. He poured the dirt from Seraphina's gris gris bag into his palms and wiped them with it. He couldn't say why, only that he needed something to ground him, something from home. He looked into Evie's fluttering eyes. "Listen here: Don't let go till I say. Then get the hell out."

With that, Memphis placed his hands above Evie's slowing heart. He could feel the land of the dead pulling at him. Voices calling, *He is here with us. The Healer. Get him. Take his power.* He could feel the sickness slithering inside Evie, trying to take her under. He was frightened. It was too much for him.

"Memphis?" Henry's voice. "Why don't you think just about healing."

Instantly, Memphis began to relax. With his friends beside him, giving him their strength, he concentrated only on healing Evie. But the infection was insidious. No sooner would he cure it in one place than it would try to take root in another. He knew he had to keep it from her heart.

The voices were back. Memphis saw terrifying things from the corners of his eyes. And then he heard Sam: "Don't see us." The voices receded. Sam's voice: "Go on, Memphis." Memphis worked as fast as he could. He could feel the sickness trying to invade him. His lungs hurt. His breathing was labored. He had to get out. Whatever he'd done would have to be enough.

"Get out," Memphis said, straining, and the trance was broken. "Theta. Now."

Theta's hand glowed red. She pressed it against Evie's side, wincing as Evie moaned, forcing herself to keep it there for a count of ten to sterilize the wound as best she could. The skin along Evie's right side above her hip was red and weepy. Ling found a tin of bandages among the storm cellar's supplies. Together, she and Sam wrapped the bandage around Evie's middle to cover the injury.

"Now what?" Ling asked.

"We've stopped it from spreading," Memphis said, brushing an arm across his sweating brow.

"Will she be okay?" Isaiah asked.

"I don't know, Ice Man."

Sam held Evie's hand and tried to rub warmth back into her cold fingers. She had dainty hands, and it surprised him that he'd never quite noticed this before, and he wished everything were normal so that he could tease her about it, call her some stupid nickname that she would pretend annoyed her when they both knew she liked the attention.

Sam swallowed around the lump in his throat. "You gotta get better, okay, Lamb Chop? I still owe you twenty clams. The Evie O'Neill I know would never let me get away with that."

Jericho looked on and tried to pretend it didn't bother him. No matter how he tried, he couldn't quite erase his feelings for Evie. He came around the other side of her and rubbed her left hand. Sam glared. Jericho ignored him. He caught Ling's eye. She shook her head, angry with him. That was harder to ignore.

"How far are we from Bountiful?" Jericho asked.

"A full day's drive, reckon," Bill said.

"Listen," Henry said.

"What?" Ling asked.

"That's just it. It's quiet."

Carefully, Jericho opened the storm cellar doors, and they emerged into a ruined world. Gideon's sidewalks were empty, its windows broken. A bicycle lay overturned in the street beside a doll with its arm missing. The wheat fields had gone to chaff. The pond was dry. So were the oil pumps. Gideon had been leeched of anything that had value. Gritty ash blew through the abandoned streets. The town was dead and gray.

A town fit only for ghosts.

BOUNTIFUL

"Go this way," Isaiah said, pointing to a dirt road off to the right that carved through seemingly endless fields of old, dead corn without even a Burma-Shave sign to break it up. They'd been driving for hours and seen nothing but sky, wheat, cows, and corn.

"That way? You're sure, kid?" Sam asked from behind the wheel.

Isaiah wasn't entirely sure of anything. But it felt right, and Evie was sick. They had to get to Sarah Beth. "Yes."

"All right. I trust you," Sam said grimly and banked a sharp right.

In the back of the truck, Evie was pale and sweaty. Theta and Henry watched her nervously. The truck careened across some railroad tracks, and up front, Ling told Sam to be careful. Corn leaves slapped the sides of the roadster. Memphis worried they'd be lost in that leafy maze. And then they reached the end of the field, and there it was, just as Isaiah had seen it in his visions: The weathered farmhouse with its sagging porch and the red barn. The old oak tree and the tire swing hanging on a rope from one of its massive branches. There was a tall silo, and a windmill, and land for as far as a body could see. And when they got closer, a rusty mailbox with the name Olson and a number on the side: 144.

Isaiah looked up at the drawn curtains of the second-story windows. "We're here."

Theta stepped out of the truck and rubbed the feeling back into her legs. "Hello? Can anyone help us?" she called.

No one seemed to be home. Out here on the plains, the air was sticky with rain that wouldn't come, and Henry thought about all that water drowning Mississippi while this part of the country looked to be in a drought. The crops drooped on their stalks, their leaves eaten through by bugs.

Sam rushed up the steps of the porch and knocked at the door. "Hello? Is anybody home? We need a doctor!"

A sandy-haired man in coveralls came out from the barn, mopping his neck and brow with a bandanna. The front of his shirt was sweated through. "You folks lost?"

Memphis looked around at the lot of them: Dirty. Scared. Half-crazed, with a very sick girl lying dead to the world in the back of their truck. He wondered if that farmer would reach for a gun soon. Once he knew who they were, Memphis couldn't imagine he wouldn't.

"Our friend is hurt, mister," Theta said. "She needs help."

"There's no doctor here. You'd be better off driving into town. It's about five miles thataway," the farmer said and pointed right, toward a seemingly endless road bordered by fields of yellow-brown grass.

"She won't make it," Sam said, his voice breaking.

"Well, son, I'm real sorry, but we can't help you."

"Are you Sarah Beth's daddy?" Isaiah asked.

The farmer's eyebrows shot up. "How do you know my Sarah Beth?"

"She comes to me in visions," Isaiah said. "That's why we're here. To keep her safe. We're the Diviners."

The farmer's surprise slid into suspicion. His mouth turned down at the corners. "I'm gonna have to ask you to leave. You're trespassing on private property."

"Please," Ling said. "We've come all the way from New York City. Your daughter called us here."

"My daughter can't call nobody. Don't make me go for my gun," the farmer said.

The screen door creaked open and snapped shut behind a small, barefoot girl with startling gray eyes. Her pale blond hair hung down her back in two slim braids already coming loose from their peach ribbons. One half of her face drooped as if from palsy.

"Sarah Beth. Go on back inside," her father commanded.

Sarah Beth ignored him. She leaned against the peeling porch railing and stared out at the Diviners until her eyes found Isaiah.

She smiled with one side of her face and waved. "Hey, Isaiah. You made it."

Isaiah gave a small wave back. "Hey, Sarah Beth. We came. Just like you asked."

※

Jericho carried a shivering Evie upstairs and placed her on a bed in a shaded room. She was pale as new milk. Sam covered her with a wedding-ring quilt, tucking it carefully around her. The farmer's wife, Mrs. Olson, touched the back of her hand to Evie's forehead and frowned. "Lands' sakes, she's burning up." Mrs. Olson hurried away and returned with an enamelware bowl half filled with water. She soaked a cotton rag, wrung it out, and pressed it against Evie's flushed cheeks. In the doorway, Sarah Beth watched, sucking on the end of her braid.

"What happened to her?" Mrs. Olson asked.

"The dead got to her, didn't they?" Sarah Beth said from the doorway.

"Sarah Beth!" Mrs. Olson scolded.

"That's right," Jericho confirmed.

Sarah Beth stared at her dumbfounded mother. "I tried to tell you, but you never listen to me."

"We'll explain everything later," Theta said to Mrs. Olson.

Finished with her ministrations, Mrs. Olson stood, cradling the bowl under her arm. "We were about to sit for supper. Pump's out in the yard if you care to wash up first."

Sam didn't want to leave Evie's side. "Somebody should stay with her."

"You gotta eat, Sam," Theta said, but Sam didn't move.

"We can take turns," Jericho said, squeezing Sam's shoulder.

In the little yard next to the house, Jericho pumped the red handle. Ice-cold water trickled over Ling's dusty hands.

"Reminds me of home." Jericho surveyed the vast expanse of half-tended farmland. It was planting time. If things weren't set right, the Olsons would lose their farm pretty quickly, he knew.

Theta and Ling helped Mrs. Olson set the dining room table. Sarah Beth sat in a chair, staring out the window. She didn't offer to help, and Mrs. Olson didn't fuss at her for it, Ling noticed. Ling's own mother would never tolerate that. Everybody had to pitch in at the restaurant. Ling wondered what damage the Diviners serum might've caused to the girl. She seemed a bit frail and childlike.

They gathered around the table, and Mrs. Olson, a raw-boned woman with freckled cheeks and eyes the blue of sun-faded cornflowers, had them bow their heads and say grace before serving up a supper of corn fritters along with heaping bowls of sauerkraut and apple butter. The Diviners ate hungrily. Isaiah felt Memphis's knee pressing against his own under the table, and he knew it meant to be careful, to watch and not talk too much. It got Isaiah's back up some. He was not a baby. Across the table, Sarah Beth dug into her applesauce. She gave Isaiah a furtive smile, which put him a little more at ease, like their friendship was a room, already prepared, and he could step right into it. The other Diviners told the Olsons about Isaiah's visions of Sarah Beth and about the town of Gideon and what had happened there with the dead and the King of Crows and Evie.

"I tried to warn you not to go. Didn't I try, Isaiah?" Sarah Beth said.

Isaiah wanted to answer, but he was mindful of Memphis's knee warning, so he just nodded.

"All this time Sarah Beth's been telling us these stories, well, we just assumed that's all they were—stories. Her imagination run wild. She has such a wonderful imagination," Mrs. Olson said, stroking her daughter's hair. "But you're telling us they're true?"

"Yes, ma'am," Jericho said.

"Sarah Beth and me, we can see the future some. That's how I knew you were here. She told me to come," Isaiah said.

"Don't talk with your mouth full, Isaiah," Memphis said.

Isaiah chewed the bite in his mouth and glowered at his brother. Here he'd been gone for weeks, surviving without him, and now Memphis was treating him like a little kid again.

"We wanna stop him. But we have to get our friend well first," Theta said.

"You can stay here till she's better. Can't they, Papa?" Sarah Beth said.

Mrs. Olson cast a worried glance at her husband, who took his time considering. "The papers say you're wanted for treason. We're a law-abiding family. Never courted any trouble. Tell me why I shouldn't turn you in and collect the reward money?"

"Jim..." Mrs. Olson said with a note of soft pleading.

"I want to hear it from them," the farmer said.

"You can do that, sir," Jericho said. "But I suspect you believe what we're telling you, or else you would've already placed that call."

"Your daughter told you about the man in the hat, didn't she? She's been telling you her whole life," Henry said. He thought of his own mother, ignored and institutionalized.

Mrs. Olson glanced furtively at her husband. Mr. Olson gave a terse nod.

"If we don't put a stop to this, the world as we know it will end," Henry said.

"How will you do that?" Mrs. Olson asked.

"That's what we're here to find out," Henry said.

Mr. Olson grunted.

"Jim. We can't let that poor girl go in her condition. It wouldn't be Christian," Mrs. Olson said quietly.

Mr. Olson sopped up his applesauce with the broken edge of a fritter and said nothing.

"I grew up on a farm. Looks like you could use some help," Jericho said at last. "If you'd allow us time for our friend to heal, and to speak with your daughter about how to stop the King of Crows, we'd be happy to work around the farm."

"You know how to work a thresher? A plow? Can you milk a cow?" Mr. Olson challenged.

"Yes to all three," Jericho answered. "Do you have any hired hands?"

"Used to," Mr. Olson said and didn't comment further.

"They left 'cause they were scared of me," Sarah Beth blurted.

Mrs. Olson put down her fork. "Now, Sarah Beth, that isn't true, dear."

"Yes, it is," Sarah Beth answered. If it was true, she didn't seem bothered by it.

Mr. Olson chewed thoughtfully. "All right, then," he said at last. "Anybody comes around asking, you're just hired help. Anything happens to my Sarah Beth, though, and you'll answer to the law. Or to me."

"Much obliged, sir," Bill said evenly, but Henry could feel the big man's discomfort.

Mrs. Olson smiled with relief. "I'll make up some beds after supper."

"I'll help," Theta said.

Sarah Beth put her napkin on the table. "May Isaiah and I be excused, Mother? I want to show him the kittens."

Mrs. Olson sighed. "You be careful under the porch. And don't get too close to the mama. She'll scratch."

"We won't. Come on, Isaiah!"

"Isaiah," Memphis prompted.

Before Isaiah followed Sarah Beth outside, he dutifully carried his plate to the kitchen sink. "Thank you for supper, ma'am."

"Why, you're very welcome, Isaiah."

The screen door creaked open and Sarah Beth's voice drifted after her: "...the little calico is mine. She's the prettiest one...."

Ling tried not to stare at Sarah Beth's plate, still on the table. "Is your daughter very ill?"

Mrs. Olson scooted food around on her plate with her fork. "She has these fits. The doctors can't do anything for her. They say a bad one could... well, I ask the Lord to watch over her."

"It's because of Project Buffalo," Ling said.

Mrs. Olson's brow furrowed. "Project Buffalo?"

"A government experiment. We were all part of it," Ling continued. "Did you have trouble having a baby?"

Henry spat up his milk. "You'll have to pardon Ling, ma'am," he said when he recovered. "She had her manners removed with her tonsils as a child."

Ling blushed. "I'm sorry if that was rude."

"That's all right, dear. Just a surprise is all," Mrs. Olson said. "I kept losing them. After the third time, Dr. McCormick came around and said he'd heard about a cure for troubles like mine. I went to Omaha, and they had me take a test."

"Guessing at cards to see how many you got right?" Sam said, taking his place at the table. "She's finally sleeping a little easier," he said to the others.

"Yes, that was it," Mrs. Olson said, passing down a plate to Sam. "I must've done all right, I suppose. They took me on. Gave me—"

"Vitamins," Sam and Ling interjected.

"That's right!"

"What in the Sam Hill is Project Buffalo?" Mr. Olson asked.

The Diviners explained Project Buffalo to Mr. and Mrs. Olson, how the Department of the Paranormal had instigated a eugenics project aimed at raising a generation of enhanced humans, a so-called super race of powerful Americans they might use to defend the nation someday.

"Mostly they experimented on immigrants, Jews, Negroes, Catholics, Chinese," Sam said. "People they thought of as expendable."

"We're just Americans," Mrs. Olson said.

Ling bristled. *We're all Americans*, she wanted to say. She cleared her throat. "After everything that went wrong during the war, they decided that letting us have those powers was too great a risk. They started experimenting on us. Or killing us. Those who hadn't died from the effects of the serum already."

"Killing?" Mrs. Olson repeated.

"Yes," Theta said.

"Oh my word. They told us it was just about having healthy babies." Mrs. Olson teared up. "Do you suppose that's what happened to our Sarah Beth? That she was...hurt...somehow by what they did?"

"We don't know that," Theta said. "But it sounds like they abandoned you."

"They sure did," Mr. Olson said bitterly. "We wrote to 'em, told 'em about Sarah Beth's fits and visions and whatnot. They were no help at all. Finally, we got a letter saying the whole department had been shut down. And that was that."

"For a while, she didn't seem troubled all that often. A fit here or there. But they started up again last year," Mrs. Olson said.

"We took her to see Dr. McCormick. He told us there wasn't anything that could be done except put her in an institution. So we just brought her home. We do the best we can."

Project Buffalo seemed to have saved its cruelties for Sarah Beth Olson, who, it seemed, might not make it to her next birthday.

Mrs. Olson's eyes filled with tears. "I'll get the cake," she said, hurrying to the kitchen and leaving the others to eat in silence.

✳

"They're down here." Sarah Beth took off her shoes and scooted under the broken latticework of the aging porch. Isaiah could hear the kittens mewling, and it excited him. He'd always wanted a pet of his own, but Aunt Octavia had forbidden it. "The last thing I need around here is one more thing to look after," she'd say, not mean, just sounding tired. Isaiah hoped he might get to keep one of these kittens, if he showed he could take good care of them.

There, in the soft dirt beneath the porch, Isaiah fell in love for the first time. A gray-and-orange mama cat, fluffy as could be, nursed seven babies. They were so tiny, Isaiah thought they looked more like big mice than cats. They were working hard to open their eyes, which were blue.

"Can I hold one?" he asked.

Sarah Beth nodded.

Carefully, Isaiah scooped up one of the kittens and nestled it close to his chest. It was mostly gray with some orange spots. The kitten mewled weakly, the softest little cry, and nuzzled close to Isaiah. "It likes me!" Isaiah said, and it seemed to him he'd never felt so much joy over something so small. "See?"

But Sarah Beth didn't seem impressed. "Come on," she said, getting on her hands and knees to scoot back under the break in the porch. "I want to show you my favorite place on the farm."

Isaiah was sad to leave the kittens so soon. "I'll come back and see you every day," he promised as he placed his new friend near its mother. He crawled back out from under the porch and brushed himself off.

Sarah Beth was marching over to the old oak with its tire swing. Isaiah marveled at the gigantic tree. It was even more majestic than it had appeared in his visions. Sarah Beth lifted her skirt and stuck her legs in through the tire. "Push me? Then I'll push you."

Isaiah gave Sarah Beth a push. "Higher," she called, and Isaiah obliged.

"What do you call your power?" Sarah Beth asked Isaiah as she swung gently back and forth, kicking her legs.

"Call it?" Isaiah made a face. "It doesn't have a name."

"I call mine moon glow, 'cause it's like sharing a secret with the dark."

Isaiah liked the way she said this. It sounded pretty, like the way Memphis talked.

"Push," Sarah Beth instructed. Isaiah shoved with both hands. "We can share moon glow, you know. It'll make our powers stronger. I'll show you."

Abruptly, Sarah Beth stuck her feet down and skidded to a stop in the dirt. She climbed out of the swing and motioned for Isaiah to follow her into an old cornfield. The plants were taller than Sarah Beth and Isaiah, but the corn had been left to rot. It was brittle and yellowed, and bugs had eaten holes in the husks. Sarah Beth led him deep into the ruined field, and Isaiah cast a worried glance over his shoulder. He wanted to make sure he could still see the house. In the distance, the farmhouse's pitched roof peeked out above the dried cornstalks.

"That's far enough," Isaiah said.

"Fine," Sarah Beth said with a toss of her braids. "Here. Give me your hand."

Isaiah balked. "Why?"

Sarah Beth put her hands on her skinny hips. "Well, if you're only going to be silly, then I won't show you."

Isaiah was torn. He didn't like being called silly, but he was nervous about offering Sarah Beth his hand. "Will it hurt?"

Sarah Beth smiled. "Not at all! It feels awfully good."

"Wait a minute. How do you know that?" After all, Sarah Beth had lived out on the farm her whole life without other Diviners around.

"I know it the way you and I know things. Because we're special. We need to start joining our powers together and making 'em stronger or we won't ever be able to beat the King of Crows."

That was true. And coming together was what Sister Walker told them they were supposed to do. Henry and Ling went dream walking together all the time. Isaiah reckoned this wasn't much different from that.

He offered his hand. "All right. Show me how."

Sarah Beth smiled, showing the tips of her small, grayish teeth. She took hold of Isaiah's hand. "Let's moon glow together."

His body stiffened. He felt a tug, as if his heart were being pulled into Sarah Beth's orbit, and then his body went warm and relaxed, a very pleasant sensation.

Isaiah?

He could hear her inside his own thoughts. "Mm-hmm."

What can you see?

Isaiah told her what he saw: a strange, golden machine humming and glowing with life. The machine was terrifying, though. Screams came from inside it.

It's scary, Sarah Beth said.

"It's changing again," Isaiah said.

What Isaiah saw next frightened him far more. It was like Gideon everywhere. Cold and empty, with the dead, so many dead, scavenging for whatever they could find, snapping at one another over the picked-over remains of a dead animal.

Do you see him? Do you see the King of Crows?

"Yes, I see him." In the midst of this barren landscape, the King of Crows sat on a high-backed chair inside a ruined mansion. He was demanding his tribute from the dead even though Isaiah could tell he didn't need it anymore and there wasn't much left to give him.

Is he alone? I can't tell from here.

"Yes."

There's nobody with him. Are you sure?

Isaiah couldn't be sure, because he was feeling tired.

"Just the dead, I think," he answered.

Don't let him see us! Sarah Beth warned. *Is this the future?*

Isaiah hoped not. Just as quickly as it came on, the vision wobbled, and then it was gone. When they came out of it, Isaiah was tired and a little cold.

"Whoo, that sure made me tired."

"Me, too," Sarah Beth said. "We're going to have to get our strength up," she said, patting his shoulder. "We'll make our moon glow so bright!"

Isaiah liked that they had shared the same experience, the same feelings. It was a special bond between them. Everybody else was always so busy, but she had time for him. She was his friend.

He was starting to like Sarah Beth. She understood how hard it was to be a kid. He liked that they had their own special power apart from the other Diviners—a secret. Memphis was always fussing at Isaiah to grow up. What Isaiah just did with Sarah Beth, wasn't that being his own man? Yes. He decided it was so.

"Come on. I'll give you that push on the swing I promised."

"Are you okay to push me? You won't faint or nothing?" Isaiah said. At dinner, he'd gotten the idea from Mrs. Olson that Sarah Beth wasn't well.

Sarah Beth narrowed her eyes. "I can push just fine, thank you very much."

"I didn't mean nothing by it," Isaiah said, embarrassed.

"Go on. Climb in," she said when they had reached the oak tree.

Isaiah put his hands on the rope. He was flooded with memory. Hadn't he seen this very tree in his visions before? There had been something bad about it, something that had frightened him.

"Are you getting in?" Sarah Beth said, impatient.

Isaiah climbed in. Sarah Beth grunted and shoved. After the third push, Isaiah gained some air, reveling in the freedom of his body and the lightness of late spring bending toward summertime. The sun hadn't gone to bed yet; it was sitting low on the land, getting sleepier. Isaiah thought about the kittens under the porch. He couldn't wait to see them again.

The swing slowed. Sarah Beth had stopped pushing. She stood watching him with her skinny arms dangling at her sides, and she looked as sad as Isaiah had ever seen a person look. Sad and mad at the same time.

"I hate it here. I'm lonely. Ma and Pa don't really love me. I don't have any friends. Everybody's scared of me."

"How come they're scared of you?"

"'Cause I'm different. Just like you. I can see things like ghosts and the future, and it makes people nervous. Even the pastor gets nervous around me. And I'm not pretty in the way the other girls are," she said softly. "I don't belong anywhere in this world, Isaiah. Not a blessed place."

"That sounds real sad," Isaiah said. He was afraid Sarah Beth might cry, and he wouldn't know what to do then. "I'm not scared of you."

This seemed to be the right thing to say, because Sarah Beth brightened. "You're brave, Isaiah. I knew you would be."

Isaiah puffed out his chest. "One time, Barney's baseball went under the fence, and I was the only one who went after it!"

"The older ones ignore you, don't they? I can see it."

Isaiah shrugged it off. "Used to it by now."

"It isn't fair. Why, you have the most special power of all! They should treat you with respect. You can see into the future. And you can see him, too, can't you?"

Him. The King of Crows.

Isaiah nodded.

"Well. We just have to stick together, I suppose," Sarah Beth said and giggled, and Isaiah laughed, too. He felt lighter than he had in some time.

"Will you be my friend, Isaiah?"

Isaiah smiled. "You bet."

❋

It was after supper, and Theta and Memphis were hiding in the hayloft. They'd been frantic to be together after so long apart. Their reunion had been quick and fevered, nearly desperate. Now, they huddled together for comfort, listening to the cooing of night birds and the insistent buzz of cicadas. Memphis had his arm around Theta as she leaned her head against his chest.

"Do you think Evie will be all right?" she asked softly.

Memphis kissed the top of her head. "We've done all we can."

"I've been reading Miss Addie's spell book. There's *beaucoup* folk medicine in it. I might be able to mix up a poultice for her."

"All right. But I don't think you'd better tell Mrs. Olson it's witchcraft. Doesn't seem she'd take kindly to that."

"Gee, and here I was gonna go and ask for her broom," Theta joked, then went solemn. "She has to be all right, Memphis. She just has to."

"I know." What they'd faced in Gideon had been worse than any of them could've imagined. Like David facing Goliath without even a slingshot. Memphis kissed Theta again and again, as if to reassure himself that she was in his arms at last, and not a dream. "I was afraid I'd never see you again," he said, looking into her big dark-brown eyes. She was the most beautiful woman he'd ever known. Theta kissed him back and burrowed into his side, her nose against his shirt so that she could smell the musky tang of the day on him. She didn't care that they were both still dirty from the road and sweaty from what they'd done earlier.

"What happened in Gideon…what happened to all those people and the town," Theta said. "Will that happen everywhere?"

"From what Ling and Jericho told us about Beckettsville, it sure sounds that way."

"How come nobody's taking notice?"

"Well, boomtowns come and go. Or the railroad bypasses a town and that town is forgotten, I s'pose. There's a new scandal in the papers every day to keep everybody entertained, or people are so busy paying attention to what's right in front of 'em they don't see what's going on with their neighbors," Memphis said. After all, they'd been the only witnesses to the attacks in Gideon. But there was more to it than that: People had to want to see. Memphis thought about the porter's story on the train from New York, and Ling and Jericho's account of Beckettsville, told to them on the furious drive to Bountiful. He thought back to those newspaper clippings Will Fitzgerald used to keep, all those stories printed in small columns in back pages, written in a sneering tone that said it was so much nonsense and people didn't need to pay it any mind. And he thought about all he'd experienced since leaving New York City—the refugees on the levee, the National Guard, sundown towns, the great big mansions sitting like kings on the land not far from the small shacks where folks didn't even have running water or shoes. The way people could look at you like you weren't the same as them, like you didn't belong on their side of the street. Or the way their eyes could glance off you, like you were a ghost in your own country. Again and again, it came back to what Will had said—that stories, not borders, made nations. Ghosts were stories.

He inhaled deeply and let his breath out slowly with his words. "It's hard enough to get people to pay attention to the monsters we live with in plain sight every day. The ones in the mirror. How we gonna get people to see ghosts they don't want to believe in?"

Theta knew they should be getting back. They couldn't risk being found here. "At least Elijah won't be bothering Miss Addie any longer," she said, moving toward the ladder. She'd go inside first. Memphis would count to fifty and follow.

"Hey." Memphis laced his fingers in hers.

"Hey."

"I love you, Theta."

They kissed, and Theta felt as if that kiss was the only thing that made sense.

As the sun set, Theta gathered salt, garlic, and honey to make a thick paste. She applied the mixture to Evie's angry skin and covered it with a cloth she'd soaked in a tub of water with silverware in it. Sam wanted to stay all night by Evie's bedside, but Mrs. Olson insisted it wasn't proper for a young man to spend the night in a young lady's room. She allowed everyone to look in one last time on Evie, who slept fitfully, her hair damp with sweat as she shivered under her quilt. "I'll pray for her," Mrs. Olson said. She handed the men an oil lamp and directed them to the farmhands' sleeping quarters near the barn while she led Ling and Theta to a narrow room off the kitchen before heading upstairs to her own bed.

Wind rattled the bones of the old farmhouse. The early dark pressed its curious face against the windows of Evie's room as she dreamed.

❋

Her eyes fluttered open to a narrow strip of gray high, high above. It flashed with light and shadow. Dirt walls surrounded her. Cold tickled the inside of her veins, making her flesh ache. Her body felt weighted with invisible stones.

Did she have a name? She could not recall.

With difficulty, she sat up, shifting the dirt. It tumbled down in a deluge, splattering her legs, hands, and face. Her heart was sluggish. Her lungs were heavy and tight. She opened her mouth for more air and coughed up tiny clumps of wet dirt. What was inside her? Above, the gray sky cycled swiftly—*lightdarklightdark*. A pale girl in a yellow dress appeared. She looked down. Both the girl and the dress were familiar.

"I tried to tell you," the girl said sadly.

Lightdarklightdark.

There was the drone of an approaching insect swarm, and the high, mechanical whine of some engine lurching toward disaster. A choir of screams rising like an angry river. Her earlier sleep had dissipated. In its place was a growing dread.

Where am I? Help me!

The girl shook her red curls. "I told you that you'd be sorry. Oh, why wouldn't you ever listen, Evie?"

Mabel. Mabel. Mabel.

And she was Evie.

And they had been in Gideon with the King of Crows and *oh god oh god oh god!* Evie scrabbled desperately at the earthen walls till her fingernails broke off. That was the heaviness inside her. The dead were a part of her. She could hear their voices all at once, thousands strong. She could feel them; she knew their pain and hunger. She, too, was hungry. A panicky nausea gripped her guts. She heaved and heaved. Four pale pink maggots fell from her lips and into her filthy lap.

"I told you. I told you!"

The machinelike shriek was everywhere.

The King of Crows's face loomed before her in the grave. "I told you we'd only just begun our dance." He stroked Mabel's hair.

Evie tried to scream and vomited a stream of black bile. The oily ooze poured out of her. It coursed over her chin and down her neck, just like every ghost they had ever annihilated.

As if she were one of them now.

PLAYING WITH FIRE

New York City

A palpable tension pulled through the newsroom as two men in gray suits and hats and overcoats walked purposefully between the rows of reporters and stopped in front of Woody's desk.

"Mr. T. S. Woodhouse?"

"Sorry, boys. I already gave to the Girl Scouts this year."

"Cute. I'm Mr. Adams. This is my associate, Mr. Jefferson."

The Shadow Men. Woody tried to remain calm.

"We'll need to see these letters, if you please, Mr. Woodhouse."

"Why? They've already been printed in the paper."

"But you're going to stop printing them in the paper."

Woody smirked. "I don't know how well you boys can read, but the Bill of Rights guarantees a free press. You don't even have to read very far. It's the First Amendment. I could print my laundry list, as long as it was factual."

"It's a matter of national security. You understand."

"I understand that you're asking me to divulge my sources." Woody kept up his reporter's bravado, but inside he was afraid, and he hoped the Shadow Men didn't see him swallow hard just a moment after he spoke.

One Shadow Man leaned so close that Woody could see the first hint of a five o'clock shadow on his jaw. "We are at war, sir. War from within. There are those who would tear apart the very fabric of freedom, and they must be stopped."

"You and I might not be in agreement on just who those usurpers of freedom are," Woody answered. "One person's treason is another's patriotism."

"Careful, Mr. Woodhouse. You sound a bit like an anarchist yourself." The Shadow Man leaned back. "We already know this is the work"—he stacked one quarter, then another on the edge of Woody's desk—"of a dangerous Negro agitator." He added a third, straightening the edges with clean fingers. "Worse than Marcus Garvey." A fourth quarter. A fifth. "And we got rid of Mr. Garvey just fine." Six pieces of silver. "So I'll ask you again, Mr. Woodhouse: Where is Memphis Campbell hiding?"

Woody kept very still. "How do you know it's Memphis Campbell?"

The Shadow Man's mouth tightened into a semblance of a smile. "He sent a poem to the *Crisis*. The poem was called 'The Voice of Tomorrow.'"

"That doesn't prove anything. Just like I'm sure there's no connection between Luther Clayton shooting at Evie O'Neill and *Project Buffalo*."

The Shadow Man stopped smiling. "It would be a shame if you ended up a story yourself, Mr. Woodhouse. Like poor Dr. Fitzgerald, dead in his museum, more than likely killed by his coldhearted Diviner niece and her Diviner friends, under the tutelage of Margaret Walker. That's what we're up against. Anarchists with special powers. Enemies of the state with the means to destroy this great nation. What happens if such power goes unchecked?"

Woody looked up at the Shadow Man and found that his eyes were the same gray as his suit. "An excellent question: What happens if power goes unchecked and unbalanced?"

"You be careful now, Mr. Woodhouse. When you play with fire, or with people who can make fire, well, you might get burned." Quick as a rattler strike, Mr. Adams swept the quarters into his palm and shoved them in a pocket, out of sight.

※

Woody tapped his foot nervously. This was the sixth house he'd been to in three days. Each one had the same story: A daughter or brother or cousin had gone to a county fair or carnival and into the Fitter Families tent, where they'd taken a test. The daughter or brother or cousin had something special about them—they got premonitions about cards, fires, twisters, or even when somebody was going to die. Two had mentioned visions that had left them feeling unsettled for days—a man in a tall hat walking just ahead of a great big storm. These daughters, brothers, and cousins would come home from the fair with a bronze medal that read, YEA, I HAVE A GOODLY HERITAGE. And soon after, they'd disappear. Like Annabelle Carter did.

"You said your sister went missing two days after the carnival came to town, Mrs. Plunkett?"

"Yes," the woman said, pouring tea into two china cups.

"And she'd visited the Fitter Families tent?"

"Yes. She came home with a bronze medal! She was so proud of it. It's on the mantel there, beside her picture."

The woman pointed to the offensive medal resting above the fireplace. Woody offered a fleeting smile and sipped his tea. "You mentioned that Annabelle thought she'd been followed the next day?"

"Yes. She told my husband and me that the same brown car had been shadowing her around town."

Nice choice of words, Woody thought. "Did she get a look at the two men driving it?"

Mrs. Plunkett's cup halted halfway to her mouth. "How did you know it was two men?"

※

Bob Bateman had been a guest on Evie's "Pears Soap Hour with the Sweetheart Seer." He'd brought a comb as his object and told her it had belonged to a war buddy of his. Except that Evie swore it was her brother's comb. It had been the start of Evie's fall, Woody remembered. She'd gotten upset and accused him of lying while on the air, then she'd chased him down the street, demanding answers. It had been scandalous, and the advertisers had not been happy about it.

The question remained: Who had given Bob Bateman that comb and arranged for him to go on her show?

Bob Bateman wasn't answering Woody's telephone calls, but, Woody discovered, he had a brother who'd done prison time. That fella worked at a scrapyard in New Jersey.

Woody dodged his way through piles of metal odds and ends, careful not to cut himself on anything sharp. He found Albert Bateman smoking a cigarette while taking a busted-up two-seater down to parts.

"Albert Bateman?"

"Who wants to know?" the man said around his cigarette.

"I'm T. S. Woodhouse. Of the *Daily News*? I had some questions about your brother?"

"Oh. You boys finally paying attention?"

Woody didn't follow, but a good reporter never let on. "That's right. I am. Can you tell me what happened?"

"It's like I told everybody—he was bumped off."

Bob Bateman was dead? "You know who did it?"

"Prob'ly those same fellas who paid him to go on the radio."

"What fellas would that be?"

"Bums in gray suits."

"You know their names?"

"No." Albert Bateman took the cigarette out of his mouth and ground it under his boot. "And I don't wanna end up like Bob, neither."

"Just to confirm, how did Bob end up?"

"Buried in an ash heap in Corona with his throat slit."

Just like Ben Arnold, Sam's informant, had been.

※

Woody had one last name on his list.

Mr. Paul Peterson was a resident of the Derryville Home for the Aged. He was also a Diviner. Woody had come across his story in the *Daily News* archives, filed under people who had predicted tragedy or disaster. Paul Peterson had foretold a fire that decimated a mill in a nearby town, and he had premonitions of the 1900 hurricane that killed six thousand in Galveston, Texas. That had brought him to the attention of the Department of the Paranormal and a young Jake Marlowe and Will Fitzgerald. Now Mr. Peterson was seventy-five years old, with liver-spotted hands and a rocking chair. Woody had told the nurse he was Peterson's nephew. He bribed the old man with a secreted cigar.

"You worked for the department for a time?"

"That I did. Here and there."

"Did they take your blood?"

"No. They did not," Mr. Peterson said on a puff of spicy smoke. "Mr. Marlowe didn't want me for his little eugenics project."

"Oh. Why's that?" Woody asked.

"On account of the blindness."

Only now did Woody realize that Mr. Peterson could not see.

"Of course, I wasn't fully blind then. But I was losing my sight, sure enough. Nothing they could do to stop it. My hearing was just fine, though. I heard Mr. Marlowe and that other fella—oh, what was his name...?"

"Mr. Fitzgerald?"

"That's the one. They argued. Mr. Marlowe said he couldn't take a chance with my blood. It was tainted. He said the Founders Club wouldn't like it."

Woody made a note. The Founders Club. All these wealthy, important men who believed in eugenics. Hadn't Evie mentioned them at one point? It was all coming together, piece by piece. It would be a real lulu of a story.

"What were you being recruited for?"

"Oh, some experiment. Magic, don't you know. Marlowe was building a machine that ran on Diviners energy. There were these kids around. All of 'em guessing cards and reading objects. One of 'em got a terrible nosebleed. The army took everything over at one point. I remember that."

"The United States Army?"

"That's the one we've got, isn't it? Anyhow, I left for a time. My wife was dying."

"I'm sorry to hear that."

"Happens to us all in the end, Mr. Woodhouse. Nothing to be done."

Woody was coming to like Mr. Peterson's dry humor. "How's that cigar?"

"Wonderful. Thank you. I went back to see Mr. Marlowe, though, during the war. I'd had a premonition that something catastrophic was going to happen up at Hopeful Harbor. That's his family estate, you know."

"What sort of premonition?"

"Oh, couldn't make much sense of it at the time. Something about a big hole torn in the sky and another world on the other side of it. A terrifying world, Mr. Woodhouse. Full of dead, hungry things."

Woody could tell that this memory still had the power to unsettle the old man.

"What happened when you told Mr. Marlowe?"

Mr. Peterson's jaw tightened. "He clearly thought I was an old fool, even then. He told me I was mistaken. That something wonderful was about to happen there. Something that would change the course of the nation." Mr. Peterson sighed. "Well, there must've been truth to what he said, because I never heard boo about it. The war ended. Mr. Marlowe went on to give us all sorts of wonders—medicine and all manner of inventions. And here we are. Except..."

"Except?"

"Well, sir. The spirits have been talking to me again lately. Showing me terrible things, Mr. Woodhouse. I know I'm not long for this world. They've told me that, too. My heart, you see. It doesn't work right. My lungs are filling up."

"What have the spirits been telling you?"

"That that hole I saw back in 'seventeen did come to pass, and those dead, hungry things have been coming into this world all these years, getting stronger, all because of him."

"Him?"

"A tall man in a hat and a coat made of crows. The spirits who tell me these things, they're mostly good. They're afraid, Mr. Woodhouse. Of what might come to pass if this King of Crows gets his way."

"And what's that?"

"Pestilence. Violence. Death everywhere. An army of dead eating the living down to ash."

Woody took it all down, writing so fast he could hardly keep up. The information was explosive. He couldn't wait to get back to New York and start his report. But first he had to go to Washington, D.C. He had to search for the office Margaret Walker had told him about. He had to find whatever records he could in the archives to support his story. Then and only then would he report.

"Thank you for your time, Mr. Peterson."

"Thank you for the cigar, Mr. Woodhouse."

They shook hands, and Mr. Peterson stiffened. His mouth parted as he let out a long, strangled sigh. "The spirits have a message for you, Mr. Woodhouse…." Mr. Peterson's grip tightened. His voice was a strained whisper. "You…must be careful…now." His speech slowed as if he were reading words appearing one by one across the sky. "Careful in the rain. On the marble. The angels…of our…better nature. The cleaning woman. Such a sacrifice." Mr. Peterson put up a hand. He winced as if someone had thrown a hot light across his face quite suddenly. "In the dark. Something is coming! Coming after you—so sharp!"

The Diviner sagged and loosened his grip. Woody snapped his hand back as if it had been fouled.

"Be careful, Mr. Woodhouse," Mr. Peterson whispered. "Oh, please be careful."

SHADOW AND LIGHT

At the first cock crow, Jericho pulled on his trousers and boots and shook Sam and Henry awake.

"Wh-what is it? What's the matter?" Henry said.

"Time to get to our chores. Rise and shine."

"I will rise," Henry muttered, half-dead. "But I pos-i-tutely refuse to shine."

"C'mon, Little Man. Time to get up," Bill said and nudged Isaiah from bed, steering the sleepy boy to his clothes and shoes.

"Things sure do happen early on a farm. Even earlier than the circus," Isaiah said on a yawn.

Jericho peered out the window. The horizon blushed a golden pink, a sunrise he could practically feel inside his cells, as if his body had never forgotten those days of getting up in the dark to gather eggs and milk cows. As Henry and Sam groaned and fumbled for their clothes, Jericho thought about the hard work that awaited them and how much they would hate it.

"You're smiling. How come you're smiling?" Sam asked.

"No reason," Jericho said and grinned wider.

They filed out into the side yard and waited for Mr. Olson. Upstairs in the house, a light shone in Evie's room. Framed in the window, Mrs. Olson wrung out a cloth and bent down, out of sight. Jericho's earlier levity sank to the bottom of his stomach.

"She gonna be okay?" Isaiah asked.

"'Course she will," Bill said.

Memphis patted Sam's shoulder. "She'll pull through. She's strong."

The back door swung open. Mr. Olson seemed surprised to see everybody lined up and ready to work.

"Mornin', Mr. Olson," Jericho said.

"Mornin'," Mr. Olson said. "Looks to be a fine day."

"Yes, sir," Bill said.

In their coop, the chickens squawked and clucked.

"Think you can collect the eggs?" Mr. Olson asked Isaiah.

"I can get him started," Bill said. "Then Memphis and I can come join you in the field."

"All right, then." Mr. Olson handed two pails to Jericho. "You know what to do with these?"

"Yes, sir."

"Well. Let's get to it, then," Mr. Olson said and headed toward the pasture.

"What are those for?" Sam asked as Jericho led him toward the barn.

"You're about to get a real education, Sam," Jericho said, sliding open the barn door. The smell—hay, sawdust, manure, the earthy sweetness of leather—greeted Jericho like a long-lost friend. The cows lowed mournfully in their stalls.

"What's the matter with 'em?" Sam asked, stepping back. "They don't sound happy."

"They're full of milk. If you were full of milk, you'd make that noise, too. They need to be relieved." Jericho swung open the stall door and entered. He positioned a low stool beside one of the restless cows and patted the seat.

Sam balked. "You're pulling my leg, Freddy."

"Nope. But you, my friend, are about to be pulling something." Jericho motioned Sam over to the stool.

"I don't usually like to be this close to my food," Sam said.

Jericho ignored him and reached under the cow. "Grab hold. Like this."

"Do I take her to dinner first?"

"Sam."

"I never…you know. On a cow, at least. What if she doesn't like it? What if she kicks me?"

"I wouldn't blame her."

Jericho guided Sam's fingers, pulling down. The milk hit the pail in a splattering stream. "It hit my eye!" Sam squeaked, blinking hard.

"Congratulations. You can tell everybody about this back home."

"I'm never telling anybody about this. And you're not gonna, either."

"Just keep it up. One, two, one, two. Like a dance step." Jericho was overcome by the memory of Lupe teaching him to dance behind the motel and was filled with longing for her. He wondered where the Haymakers were now and if she was also thinking of him and how long it might be before they were together again.

"Sure. Just like a dance step…in the world's worst nightclub," Sam said, fully extending his arms to keep as much distance as possible between himself and the cow. He gripped the cow's udders like he was learning to drive.

Jericho patted Sam's shoulder on his way out of the pen.

"Wait a minute! Just where do you think you're going, Freddy?"

"There's three more cows to go. And don't call me Freddy." Jericho closed the stall door behind him, grinning as he heard Sam squeal, "Wait a minute! Hey, don't…don't move! Stay still!"

The day came up in dazzling blue—a good omen for planting. Jericho hooked a team of draft horses to a wooden plow and grabbed hold, walking behind them as he guided the blade through the earth. With his enhanced strength, breaking up the ground was no trouble at all. He worked for hours without getting tired. The soil was awfully dry, though. Jericho crouched down and grabbed a palmful. It crumbled between his fingers. "Not looking so good," he announced to Mr. Olson, who'd come to admire his handiwork in the field.

"Drought. Don't it figure—there's folks down south getting drowned by floods. Sure wish we could take the burden of rain from them and bring it to our crops. Hate to think what'll happen if this dry spell lasts much longer. The topsoil could blow clean away." Mr. Olson slipped off his hat and wiped a sleeved arm across his damp brow. "During the war, there was plenty for us. Corn fetched a dollar twenty-one a bushel. Now I'm lucky to clear forty-one cents for that same corn. Whole place is mortgaged to the hilt. It's like they plumb forgot about us out here. Jake Marlowe eats the food we raise. Doesn't mean he wants to pay for it. Those men in the boardrooms don't have dirt under their fingernails. They don't know what it takes to work the land."

Jericho looked up. Not a rain cloud in sight.

"You think you could put a little touch of healing on these crops?" Jericho asked Memphis later as they gathered around the pump. They dunked their rags in the cold water and wiped the sweat from the backs of their necks.

"Does it work on plants, Memphis?" Isaiah asked. He had a cup of seeds. Bill had told him he could follow behind the plow and plant them deep in the earth and beautiful things would grow.

"I don't know. I think it only works on people," Memphis said. "And there's a lot of land. Truth is, it really beat me up to help Evie. If we're gonna fight the King of Crows and heal that breach, I need to build up some strength again."

Jericho nodded. That was their priority. But his heart sank for the Olsons. They were close to losing the farm, he knew, and he hoped that whatever he and the others did here would be enough to turn the tide for them.

"What these crops need is rain," Bill said. "And none of us has a power for that."

Memphis cupped a hand above his eyes to block the sun's glare. "Never thought I'd say this after what we went through in Mississippi, but come on, rain."

※

The first chance he got, Isaiah was under the porch with Sarah Beth, holding the kittens. He nuzzled his favorite against his cheek and told Sarah Beth what he'd heard about the drought hurting the earth and making the crops fail. "You think we could bring on rain with our moon glow?"

"I don't know. But there's no reason we can't try. Maybe we'll discover a whole new power!"

This got Isaiah excited. Why not? Maybe together, he and Sarah Beth would turn out to be more powerful than any of the others. Maybe they would be the key to saving the world. They might even get a parade out of it! Isaiah quite liked the idea of that. He pictured riding in the back of a touring car down Fifth Avenue under a snow of paper streamers, the crowd cheering his name as if he had won the World Series.

"Come on," Isaiah said, gentling the kitten next to its mother again.

He and Sarah Beth sneaked into their special place in the dried-up cornfield.

"Here," she said, holding out her hands.

Isaiah looked around nervously. It was daylight now. Somebody might see him. He would be in trouble.

"Isaiah!" Sarah Beth stomped her foot.

Nervously, he took hold of her hands.

"Rain, rain, rain…" Sarah Beth chanted.

Isaiah joined in. "Rain, rain…"

They turned their faces up toward the sun and waited for a wet kiss of hope across their noses. Waited for proof of their magic.

"Try again," Sarah Beth said.

"Rain, rain, rain!"

But it was no use. On the fifth try, Isaiah accidentally burped. They broke into a fit of giggles and couldn't get serious again. Their mission abandoned, Sarah Beth said, "Come on. I want to show you the river."

Isaiah dutifully followed Sarah Beth until the river was in sight.

"Sometimes I can catch a frog or some tadpoles here," Sarah Beth called out over the burbling of the water as they neared the tributary that bordered the far edge of the farm. She took off her shoes and stockings and walked to the snaking water's edge. The embankment sloped down to slick rocks and a slow-moving, white-gray current. "It's down some 'cause there hasn't been any rain."

It looked plenty deep enough to Isaiah. He hadn't learned to swim yet, so he kept a respectful distance. But he could see the marks on the sides of the bank where the water had been and knew that Sarah Beth spoke the truth.

"Mother won't let me in the water. She's afraid I'll catch my death of something. But I get as close as I can anyway," she said, giving a naughty smile.

Isaiah liked that they had yet another secret, but he was also afraid of getting in trouble with Mrs. Olson. His mama and Aunt Octavia had raised him to be respectful of rules, and he was envious of the way Sarah Beth didn't seem to worry too much about that. Sarah Beth showed him where she kept an old tin pail tied to a branch with a twist of rope. He helped her lift it up out of the shallows. A school of minnows scurried back and forth along the pail's flat bottom. "We'll feed these to the mama cat so she can make milk for the kittens," Sarah Beth said, and it made Isaiah happy to think about that.

They spent some time playing along the river's edge. Sarah Beth showed Isaiah how to skip stones properly, advising him on how to angle his throw to make the most jumps possible before the stone sank out of sight.

"Your friend is really sick, isn't she?" Sarah Beth asked as she skipped a pebble across the rippled back of the river.

"Yeah. I s'pose she is," Isaiah said.

"Let's moon glow," Sarah Beth said abruptly.

"But we couldn't bring on rain."

"No. Let's moon glow to see if we can find out anything about your friend."

Isaiah agreed that this was a good plan. But he didn't want to hold her hands out here where anybody could see them, so they curved around out on a jetty that Sarah Beth said was usually underwater.

"Not too close," Isaiah said, mindful of the river.

"Let's really go all in," Sarah Beth said. "Let's see what we can do together when we truly put our minds to it."

"All in," Isaiah agreed.

They joined hands. The pleasant, warm sensation enveloped Isaiah. He was in that dark place he was coming to know as the in-between space where he and Sarah Beth would meet.

Sarah Beth?

"I'm here, Isaiah."

He saw her outlined by shadow. She held out her hand here, too. He reached for it, concentrating for all he was worth. Suddenly, they were in a forest of barren, broken trees, and it was night but there were no stars, only fat birds with many eyes watching them from sickly branches.

"Isaiah? Where are you? I can't see you! Come find me."

Isaiah wound his way through the dark wood until he came to a desolate clearing and a golden, spiderlike machine rising up to a sky churning with electricity. He still couldn't find Sarah Beth. The machine gave Isaiah a funny feeling, though, like a slumbering giant in a fairy tale who might wake and bring his foot down to crush Isaiah. *Like Jack and the Beanstalk*, he thought.

I think that's the Eye, the machine that's causing all the trouble.

"Ohh. Do you see him anywhere?"

Isaiah pushed deeper into this vision. It felt as if he were flying across fields of death, until at last he spied the King of Crows sitting upon a high throne made from skulls and bones. Rats poked their twitching noses from eyeholes before scampering back inside with a flick of their long pink tails. The dead surrounded the throne, staring up at him with worshipful eyes.

"Where are you? I-I can't find you. I'm scared, Isaiah!" Sarah Beth said.

"I hunger," the King of Crows said.

"We hunger," the dead responded.

"I would have more."

"More."

"They are keeping it from us."

"They are keeping it from us."

"Let us take back what is rightfully ours. The time is now."

"The time is now."

Isaiah's mother was there in the crowd, but she was not looking up at the King of Crows. She was looking at him, and her eyes were wide. Isaiah started to call to her, and she put a finger to her lips and shook her head desperately. Around her, a ripple passed through the dead. They sniffed and growled.

"Who goes there?" the King of Crows demanded.

Isaiah was frightened. He wanted out of there. *Sarah Beth? Sarah Beth!*

He didn't know enough about how their moon glow worked. What if he ran and she was left behind? The dead were moving, sniffing for him.

"Isaiah? Isaiah! Where are you?" Sarah Beth called.

Sarah Beth, we gotta go now!

The starless night was alive with birdlike shrieks and growls. He felt the touch of Sarah Beth's fingers inside his vision. And then he was being pulled from the land of the dead into a different vision. What Isaiah saw now was the river at the edge of the Olsons' farm. Swollen to twice its size, it moved with terrifying swiftness. Sarah Beth's socks and shoes lay in the grass beside a rock covered in blood. He did not see her. Where was she?

The vision expelled Isaiah. He came out of it, gasping and trying to get his bearings. He was back by the thinning stripe of river, which gurgled tamely, and there was no blood on the rocks that he could see.

"Isaiah?" Sarah Beth was breathing heavily, too. "Did you see him?"

"Uh-huh."

"He's planning something, isn't he?"

"Sure seems like it," Isaiah said, but as with all his visions, he couldn't say when this would take place.

"I hope your friend heals up quick. We need to get to work before it's too late," Sarah Beth said. She frowned. "What is it? Your face has gone all funny."

"Did, um, did you see anything else?"

"No. Did you?"

Isaiah felt guilty about the river vision. What if what he'd seen had been some warning about Sarah Beth? She wouldn't see her own future coming for her, probably. He didn't know for sure, and he didn't want to scare her. What if she didn't want to be his friend anymore?

Sarah Beth stamped her foot. "Isaiah!"

"You, uh, you said your mama doesn't let you go in the water?"

Sarah Beth growled low in her throat and twirled around. "She won't let me do a *doggone* thing!"

"What if your mama's right about that river being dangerous?"

Sarah Beth rolled her eyes. She put her hands to her hips. "Don't tell me you're gonna fuss at me, too! Never you mind about Mother. Tell me what else you saw!"

"I saw his throne in the forest. All made of bones!"

Sarah Beth nodded. "Me, too. But how come I didn't see you there?"

"Dunno." He thought for a moment. "Maybe we can only talk to each other."

"Maybe. Well, no matter. Now we know where he keeps himself. That's something, isn't it?" She wiped a hand across her brow. "Whew. Moon glowing sure does make you tired, though. Doesn't it?"

"Sure does."

There had been a rock covered in blood. Her shoes. Her socks. Isaiah's stomach hurt from keeping this secret. He wished he knew what to do. He lay back in the grass and stared up at the clouds changing shapes in an effort to calm his racing mind.

"At least we're learning how to control it some. Neither one of us has had a fit since you've been here. I reckon if we keep at it, we'll get so strong we'll never be tired at all." Sarah Beth lay down next to Isaiah. He could feel the heat of her small body. It made him nervous, though he couldn't say why.

Isaiah got quickly to his feet. "Let's go feed the mama cat."

They walked back to the house, carrying the pail of minnows between them. Isaiah resolved to keep Sarah Beth safe. He'd make sure she didn't get hurt in the river. He'd keep her away from it, if necessary. As they walked, Isaiah told Sarah Beth all the "Who's this?" jokes he knew, and was delighted when she laughed and asked for more, and soon, his earlier worry eased.

His smile vanished, though, as they rounded the barn. Bill Johnson was drinking from a cup of water. A memory flooded Isaiah. In a vision months ago, he'd seen a man like this, tall and broad-shouldered and mighty as an African prince, and there had been a warning in it. *Ghosts on the road.* Isaiah hadn't thought of Bill at the time because the man in his vision had been young and strong and Bill was still Blind Bill Johnson and he was old and worn out. Isaiah had seen a fat wall of dust billowing up in the distance with something mean and white glinting inside it. Ghosts on the road.

"What's the matter?" Sarah Beth asked.

There was no scary wall of dust out there now that Isaiah could see, only a plain dirt road leading nowhere for miles. The day was sunny and fine, and Bill Johnson was fine, too.

"Nothing," Isaiah answered and let that go, too.

※

Sam couldn't remember ever being so exhausted. "Even my tongue is tired," he said as Mrs. Olson rang the bell for supper.

"Not tired enough," Jericho said.

The Diviners washed up and joined the Olsons at the table, where they tucked eagerly into a hearty dinner of roast beef and potatoes. Theta asked Sarah Beth about the vision that had brought them to Bountiful in the first place. "You said you know how to stop the King of Crows?"

Sarah Beth nodded, beaming.

"She waiting for an invitation?" Sam muttered to Memphis, who elbowed him to keep quiet. "Fine, no hurry," Sam grumbled. "It's only the end of the world we're worried about here."

Sarah Beth glared at Sam. "I don't have to tell you if you're not going to be a gentleman. I only like gentlemen."

Memphis flashed Sam a *Didn't I try to tell you?* look. "Apologize," he whispered to Sam.

"I'm sorry, Sarah Beth. Go on," Sam said, chastened.

"We have to work on our powers," she said. "We have to work on our powers *together.* We weren't all together before. And we won't be till your friend wakes up and gets stronger."

"Her name is Evie," Ling said.

"When Evie gets stronger," Sarah Beth said. "You said your powers were like wild horses you can't control. I'm the reins. I can keep everything controlled. Like your mother does, right, Sam?"

What his mother did was beyond what anyone should be asked to do. Sam hoped Sarah Beth wouldn't have to absorb the pain his mother did. "Sure. Right, kid," Sam said.

Sarah Beth tossed her hair over her shoulder. "I am not a kid."

"Goodness. All this talk of powers makes me feel unsettled. It isn't good for Mr. Olson's digestion. Why don't we discuss something more pleasant over supper?" Mrs. Olson suggested.

But no one could think of much to say, and they passed the rest of the meal in silence.

Just before turning in, Sam went upstairs to see Evie, where he found Sarah Beth sitting on Evie's bed, holding her hand. Sarah Beth's eyes were closed and her lips were moving.

"Whatcha doing?" Sam asked.

Sarah Beth jumped. "Lands' sake! You like to stop my heart!"

"I'll bet your heart's too strong to stop just from the sound of my voice, though it has had that effect on lots of girls older than you," Sam said.

Sarah Beth didn't laugh. She was a little humorless, Sam had noticed, which put him at a disadvantage in trying to make friends. "Whatcha doing with Evie?"

"Praying. Mother said I should."

"Oh," Sam said. "Well. That's real nice."

"Will she get better?" Sarah Beth asked.

"Sure. Sure, she will."

"What's the matter with your voice?"

"Nothing. Just, I ate some bread and, uh, it...it scratched my throat is all."

"You sounded like you were gonna cry."

"No. Naw. I don't cry, kid."

Sarah Beth bristled. "I keep telling you! I'm *not* a kid. I'm a lady."

"Sure. Of course you are." He bowed to her in a courtly way.

This made Sarah Beth smile and blush just a little, Sam saw. He felt sorry for her. Thanks to Project Buffalo, Sarah Beth Olson *was* still a kid in so many ways, but she clearly didn't want to be. Like anybody, she wanted to be loved and adored, desired, even, and here she was all alone on this farm for so long she'd had to invent a different version of herself just to feel okay.

"Thank you for sitting with Evie. I'll take over now, my lady," Sam said. He bowed.

Sarah Beth giggled. She jumped up and half curtsied. "I hope she gets better," she said and closed the door behind her.

Sam dragged a chair to Evie's bedside. He checked the dressing Theta had put on Evie that afternoon. The wound was smaller, the edges no longer a bruised black. Her lips were still pale gray, though. Sam rubbed warmth into Evie's cold hands.

"Hey. Hey, Baby Vamp. It's Sam. You remember me? The fella who's goofy for you? I was just thinking about that first time I saw you in Penn Station. You were looking at yourself in the shop window, making sure your hat was on straight. I could see your reflection. You weren't sure if you looked like a city girl or some rube from Ohio. My first thought seeing you...well, my first thought was, *That there is a bona fide mark, Sam Lloyd.* Gonna level with you, Baby Vamp. Street smarts you did not yet have. But watching you bite your kisser and fix your hat, I thought, *Why does a tomato like that doubt herself?* Even then, I knew you were like the Fourth of July inside a person. And then I stole twenty bucks from you like a lousy bum. But that twenty bucks brought me back to you, so maybe I'm also a real smart bum."

Gently, Sam brushed a curl back from Evie's cool forehead. He was relieved that at least she was no longer feverish.

"I know I got a reputation as a cake-eater and a con. I can't keep you in pearls, and the only joint I can afford is a hash house. I never wanted my name in lights the way you did. Me? You know I operate like a shell game, *don't see me* and all that jazz. But if that's what you wanted, well, by golly, I'd be in the front row, cheering you on." Sam cleared his throat, but his voice stayed thick. "I'm cheering you on right now, Baby Doll. I'm in that front row telling you you can do this, you can get stronger and stronger, and then you're gonna rise up outta that bed and show us all that Evie O'Neill moxie. You got to, okay, honey? Because I can face just about anything the King of Crows throws at us. But I can't do it without you. *Ikh hob dikh lib.* I love you, Evie. I love you."

Mrs. Olson knocked and opened the door, carrying an oil lamp that blazed the edges of her white. "Time to let her rest, young man."

Sam wiped his eyes quickly so Mrs. Olson couldn't see. He kissed Evie's forehead and tucked the blanket up under her chin. He watched her for a few seconds more. Her eyelids twitched. She was sleeping, but her mind was active.

"I wish I knew what she was dreaming," he said.

☀

Shadow.

And light.

She was in the desert under a bloodred moon.

"It is going to happen soon," Memphis's mother said.

The King of Crows sat upon a tall throne fashioned from all manner of bones. Twisted inside this dreadful reliquary was Mabel. Her hands pushed out from between two rows of skulls as if reaching through the bars of a cage.

Miss Addie on the steps of a church. Her eyes widened. "There's a fox in the henhouse."

The Eye churned gold. The noise of it was like a dying man trying to breathe and scream at the same time.

James. His eyes were haunted, weary, as if he had lived a thousand lifetimes in a matter of seconds and saw nothing but that for an eternity.

Stop. This. Please. We are trapped inside a loop of time we are trapped we are trapped we are trapped!

Inky clouds snake-whipped the red sky. The mountaintops caught fire. The dead dotted the wasteland. They opened their mouths like radios and the song poured out:

"Pack up your troubles.

Pack up your troubles.

Pack up your troubles.

And smile

Smile

Smile."

The song was warped and it was everywhere.

"This keeps happening," they said, and crumbled to ash.

Evie felt their deaths inside. She screamed in pain.

The soldiers' faces twisted in fresh agony.

James.

"There's a fox in the henhouse!" Miss Addie shouted. "Everything is connected."

The dead spoke their lament: "This keeps happening."

The circle turned. She saw it happening again and again. Each time, the soldiers were sucked up through the portal and into the Eye.

Mabel crouched among the rotting leaves. "The world is a terrible place. It never learns."

That isn't true, Evie wanted to say, but her mouth was full of dirt.

The song started again. The phonograph a circle.

Pack up your troubles.

This keeps happening.

Pack up your troubles.

Smile, smile.

This keeps happening.

Smile.

"They're playing our song," the King of Crows said and smiled. "Come. Let's dance."

Purplish veins pulsed under Evie's pale skin. Something trying to be born.

No. No, I won't let you. I won't!

She tore at her skin as if she could pull out the sickness.

Evie screamed as the ground began to swallow her whole.

WIRELESS

The next morning, as the Diviners shared breakfast in the Olsons' kitchen after their early chores, Evie shuffled in, pale and weak, and leaned against the doorjamb. "Am I dead?"

Mrs. Olson screamed and dropped the cup in her hand, which Jericho reached out and caught.

"Are we all dead?" Evie mumbled. She inhaled, breathed out. "Death smells like bacon."

"Evil? Evil!" Theta was up and running, guiding her friend to a seat at the table just as Evie crumpled from exhaustion. Mrs. Olson hurried to bring Evie a tin mug of cool water.

"How're you feeling?" Jericho asked, smiling at her.

With the morning sun on his face, he put Evie in mind of the Blake painting he'd shown her back at the museum. "Like I just lost a fight with Jack Johnson," Evie managed. "How long have I...?"

"Three days," Ling said.

"...eight hours and forty-two minutes," Sam finished. Sam was there, kneeling beside her. How happy she was to see him. He looked as if he hadn't slept in days.

Evie touched a hand to her side and doubled over. "That smarts."

"So don't touch it," Ling said.

"What is this?" Evie noticed the bandage around her middle, the dressing Theta had made.

"Just some folk remedy," Theta said. "Courtesy of the Proctor sisters, if you're on the trolley."

"Ah," Evie said. "I am now."

"We were worried sick about you, Baby Doll." Sam held her hand. His was warm, and she was grateful for it just now.

"I had the strangest dreams," Evie said. "But I can't remember them now."

They'd felt important, though. Like clues. Or warnings.

"Memphis healed you!" Isaiah said.

"Tried to, at least. I kept it from getting any worse, I s'pose."

"Memphis. Darling Memphis. How can I ever thank you?" Evie said.

"You can get well," Memphis said. "We've still got a fight ahead of us."

"Yes," Evie said. The memory of Gideon flooded in. Mabel. It made her dizzy. She wanted to run away from what she'd seen. Evie tried to stand, swayed, and fell back into the chair.

"Back to bed with you, Sheba," Sam insisted.

Theta and Sam helped Evie upstairs to her room and into bed. Theta shooed Sam away. "Scram, Lloyd."

"But—"

"No *if*s, *and*s, or *but*s to it. I need to see to her. You can bump your gums at her later," Theta said, shutting the door over his protests. "Let's take a look at you, Evil."

Theta helped Evie out of her filthy dress. Evie wrinkled up her nose. "Something smells pos-i-tutely putrefied."

"That's you. Three days, no bath?"

"You might want to burn that dress."

Theta made a face as she tossed it to the floor. "Mm-hmm." She peeled back the dressing she'd made the night before. "Well, it looks better than it did. I've been reading Miss Addie's spell book about herbal remedies and poultices. I applied fresh ones morning and night," Theta said.

"Like a proper witch," Evie said, peering down at the serrated injury. The puncture marks. The feathery charcoal veining mixed with a puckered pinkness and fading bruises. It would leave a substantial scar, she knew.

"Does it hurt bad?"

Evie winced and nodded. It was the wound to her heart from Mabel's betrayal that hurt the most. "Theta, do you think that was really Mabel in Gideon?"

Theta sat next to Evie on the narrow bed. "It sure looked like her."

"I wanted to see her again so desperately. I couldn't bear the thought that she had left me. I couldn't let go." Evie took in a shuddering breath. "I suppose I was always a little jealous of her. She was smart and good. I wanted her to need me. If someone so good could need me, then I couldn't be all bad."

"Would you stop with that?"

409

Evie ignored Theta. "The truth was, I needed her. Desperately. Enough that I disturbed her rest."

"I don't know, kid," Theta said gently. "Ling always says that when you walk in dreams, you find out that people are much more than one thing. Maybe you were wrong to disturb her rest, but maybe some part of Mabel wasn't completely at peace."

Evie took this in. What did it really matter now? The Mabel Evie had known and loved was gone. The real Mabel had been so much more complicated than Evie wanted to admit. Simplifying people was a way of not having to think too much about them, to make them fit into your own story. People were inconvenient, though. Behind the idea of a person you constructed to suit yourself, the people you loved had their own stories—whole worlds going on inside—and you ignored them at your peril.

"It's funny. I used to feel that I wouldn't care if I died. I just kept throwing myself at life, hoping I'd hit a bull's-eye eventually. I thought death would be a relief from all that feeling. A relief not to have all that pain. Not to care so much," Evie said. "I'm sorry. I'm probably shocking you. Blame it on my sickness."

Theta let out a little *ha*. "You think you're the only one who ever feels that way? For an object-reader, you miss a lot about people."

"You, too?"

"Sure. Sometimes. It's like being swallowed up by Loneliness, capital *L*."

"That's it." Evie was so grateful to hear another person voice her feelings that she was afraid she would cry. She wanted Theta to stay right there on the side of the bed forever.

"I used to think nobody felt that way. Now? I figure everybody feels that way here and there," Theta continued.

Evie swallowed against the lump in her throat. Her voice was husky. "How do you go on...with all that loneliness inside you?"

Theta held Evie's hand and looked her straight in the eyes. "You gotta make that son-of-a-bitch spit you back out again."

Evie laughed. Laughter was good. It was a step toward life.

"There's things out there that wanna kill us. We can't kill ourselves," Theta said.

Evie's eyes welled with tears, but she didn't want to cry. She'd been lost in darkness for days. There was sun outside her window, and her friend was beside her.

"Here. Bend down. You've got hay in your hair," Evie said.

Theta blushed, and Evie suppressed a grin imagining just how it had gotten there. Theta leaned forward and Evie brushed it free.

"Swell. I'm glad to know we've reached the grooming stage of our friendship."

Evie's smile was short-lived. "Theta."

"What is it?" Theta patted at her coveralls. "Do I have a live chicken on me somewhere, too?"

"I have to put things right with Mabel. It's my fault, and I've got to fix it."

"Evil…"

"I've got to, Theta!"

"Okay," Theta said. "But don't fall into the same trap."

"What do you mean?"

"You can't do everything. Mabel has to want to fix it, too."

"There's one thing we can fix right now," Evie said. "Darling Theta, can you help me get a bath?"

Theta wrinkled her nose and offered her hand. "I was afraid you'd never ask."

※

After another day in bed, Evie begged to get up and be useful. She sat out on the front porch enjoying the May sunshine while she cut up potatoes for planting. Sarah Beth came to sit at Evie's feet.

"Do you remember anything?" she asked.

"No. Not really," Evie said.

"Me, either," Sarah Beth said, and Evie didn't know what she meant. With a giggle, Sarah Beth reached her fingers into the bowl of water, fished out a hunk of raw potato and popped it into her mouth, and then ran away, clearly gleeful to have gotten away with her potato theft.

Henry and Sam came by.

Sam leaned against the porch railing and grinned at Evie. "I heard the prettiest girl in the world was sitting on this porch in Nebraska."

Henry batted his lashes. "Oh, gee. Thanks, Sam."

Evie laughed. "I look pos-i-tutely a fright, Sam."

"How would you know? You can't see and you won't wear cheaters," Sam shot back.

"When are we going to start working on strengthening our powers?" Evie asked.

"Baby Vamp, you're not well enough."

"I'll be fine."

"You got winded walking to this porch."

"I was just excited about the cows. I heard they give gin. Oh, look, we've lost too much time already, and it's all my fault!"

"A few more days, okay? I won't almost lose you twice," Sam said with such love that Evie was too undone to argue.

"All right, Sam. You win. A few more days. But I'm going to have to come up with a hobby to keep from losing my mind out here on the prairie."

"When you're ready to take up horseshoes or yodeling, let me know. So I can go the other way," Henry said, making Evie laugh all over again.

Later, while Evie was resting in her room, she was surprised by a visit from Isaiah.

"I have something for you. Been saving it," he said shyly. He offered Evie the blue-black feather.

"Where'd you get this?" she asked, sitting up in bed.

"In Gideon. I stole it from the King of Crows."

Evie trembled, excited. "This comes from his coat?"

Isaiah nodded. "He didn't like that I took it."

"No. I imagine he didn't. That was very brave of you, Isaiah."

Isaiah beamed. He'd done a good thing. Somebody saw. "I thought maybe you could read it."

Evie knew she should rest. But the temptation was too great.

"All right. I'll give it a try. Isaiah? If something…should happen to me, run for the others, all right?"

"All right."

"Here goes," she said, going under. A moment later, she came out of her trance. "Huh. That's odd."

"What's odd?"

Evie twirled the feather slowly by its shaft. "I couldn't get anything from it. There was a great amount of squawking. And whispers. And then when I pressed into it further…" She shook her head, as if she couldn't quite believe it herself. "Nothing. Pos-i-tutely nothing."

❄

Evie rested. She did not remember her dreams. When she woke, the sun was high in the sky. She challenged herself to a walk to the barn, determination in every step. There was no choice; she simply had to build up her strength. There was too much at stake. She nodded at Mr. Olson and Jericho, who were inside working on a piece of machinery.

"Evie! What are you doing out of bed?" Jericho asked.

"I'm perfectly fine. The cat's pajamas," she lied.

"Jericho, hand me them pliers there, will ya?" Mr. Olson said.

Jericho went back to his repairs. He had been remote with her in Gideon before the attack. Evie wondered about what Ling had said, that Jericho had a sweetheart. Had it been a fling, or something more serious? Traveling with an all-girl orchestra sounded quite glamorous. His sweetheart probably was, too. Evie thought about her own looks just now. She was pale and thin with drab hair that hadn't seen a beautician's comb in ages. Oh, why should it bother her? But it did. It wasn't so much that Evie wanted Jericho as she wanted him to keep wanting her. It was utterly selfish, she knew. More about her vanity than anything else.

The old Evie would've flirted with Jericho. She would've reached for all her feminine wiles to pull his desire back to her. She was not the old Evie. Instead, her interest was piqued by a ham radio taking up space on a table against the wall.

"You have a wireless!" she said excitedly.

"Belonged to my brother, Joe," Mr. Olson said, glancing over his shoulder. "He was a radio operator in the navy during the war and took a real liking to it. He built that crystal set himself. After he died, the radio came to me."

Mr. Olson didn't seem to want to elaborate on his dead brother, and Evie didn't press. "Does it still work?"

"Sure does." The farmer put down his pliers. He wiped his hands with a bandanna as he made his way to her. "Why, I've heard news from as far away

413

as Topeka. It can get you the news faster than the papers can sometimes." He shook his head and scratched the back of it simultaneously. "Seems like everything moves fast these days—motor cars, radios, and bad luck. Joe was real handy—could build or fix anything. He built him an iron windmill tower and attached an antenna to the top along with a—whatchamacallit— a transmitter! That's it over there in the corner."

Evie knew how it all worked, but she wasn't about to let on. Who would suspect a girl of knowing such things? Who would suspect a girl of using that knowledge to help counter the story Jake Marlowe, the Founders Club, the Shadow Men, and all the powerful men behind them were putting out about Diviners? She patted the radio's side and smiled coyly. "Oh, my. I surely do love *Captain Nighthawk*. It's my favorite program. Gee, Mr. Olson, would you mind terribly if I came out here to listen at night? I promise not to play it too loud."

"Be my guest." Mr. Olson chuckled. "That radio'll probably be grateful somebody's taking an interest in it. I never was much for it."

"Oh, glory hallelujah!" Evie whispered excitedly to the others later. "Now we can keep up with the news. We can stay one step ahead of trouble. If there are ghosts out there, or towns in trouble, we'll hear about it from the amateur radio operators. But more than that, we can tell others about what we know. We can warn them. Get them to join us in the fight. We can tell them what to look for."

"What's the range on that thing?" Sam asked.

He tapped a finger against a dial and Evie removed his hand.

"Sorry," he said.

"Ling's smiling," Henry said. "It's like a Santa Claus sighting. Shhh, now. Don't disturb it."

"Don't you see?" Ling said.

"Not yet," Henry said in a singsong voice.

"Radio transmits and receives electromagnetic waves. We can amplify the signal. Using our powers together. We can make this radio signal go as far as we like. Or far enough, at least," Ling said. "That should be our first test."

"Do you think *they'll* know?" Evie said.

The dead. It was unclear to what extent the dead's powers were still linked with theirs.

Ling thought. "Sam, can you make us invisible long enough to put some magic into this thing?"

"Yeah. I think I can do that."

As they got back to their chores, Evie took Memphis aside. "Can you meet me in the barn tonight after Ma and Pa Olson go to bed?"

Memphis gave her a funny look. She grinned. "Trust me: I've got a pos-i-tutely brilliant idea."

THE VOICE OF TOMORROW

Bedtime came early for the Olsons, as it did for most farm people. Evie watched for the light under their door to go out. She counted silently to two hundred, then she tiptoed downstairs and out into the cool Nebraska night under a mantle of stars. She came around back to the farmhands' sleeping quarters and tapped on the window. Memphis snugged it up. "Meet me in the barn," she whispered.

The Olsons' barn was a far cry from the pristine studios of WGI. Hay covered the floor. Milk pails and tackle hung from hooks. Instead of New York City swells, her audience was made up of horses, cows, and pigs sleeping in their pens, giving off the occasional whinny, moo, and snort. But it would do. She dragged two stools up to the worktable with the ham radio, listening to the hum as it warmed up, and readying the receiver and microphone.

The barn door slid open as Memphis let himself in.

"What's this clever plan you've got?" he asked.

Evie patted the stool next to her and Memphis took a seat.

"You know how you've been sending those letters from the Voice of Tomorrow?"

"*Was* sending," Memphis said, his face clouding over.

"Exactly my point. Welcome to the new Voice of Tomorrow." She slid the microphone closer to Memphis.

He stared at it. "You...want me to talk on the radio?"

"Pos-i-tutely."

"I don't know how."

"You do what you always do—you tell your story! But you tell it into the microphone, and it'll reach thousands all at once. You don't have to worry about the Shadow Men scaring the *Daily News* into not publishing your stories. You can go directly to the people. We need to tell people what's happening in this country, and this is a pos-i-tutely brilliant way to do that."

In the Bible of Memphis's youth, the Word was the beginning. God spoke the universe into being. For Memphis, poetry was not just words on a page; poetry was life. Speeches led men into battle. Fairy tales had the power to frighten or explain. Story was creation. It was the promise of a true more.

Evie flipped a switch and the radio hummed.

"Don't we need Sam to..." Memphis wiggled his fingers.

Evie laughed. "Just a trial run," she whispered. "Ready?"

He exhaled a nervous breath, shook out his hands, and nodded.

Evie got up on the microphone. "Good evening, defenders of democracy. This...radio program could be coming to you from an underground storm shelter in the heartland of America. Or from a reservation in the Black Hills of South Dakota. Perhaps we are broadcasting from a ship anchored off the coast of California, or from a tenement on the Lower East Side of Manhattan. We are everywhere, just like the radio waves reaching you in your living rooms at this very moment. Perhaps you've heard of us in the newspapers—the Voice of Tomorrow. Perhaps you've heard that we are radicals. Well, if the honest truth about what is going on in this country is radical, then so be it. There are ghosts in this land, ladies and gentlemen. Whether you want to believe it or not, they're here. And we're going to have to face up to it if we want to survive." Evie paused. She looked over at Memphis, who nodded. Evie turned back to the microphone. "And now, a message from the Voice. Of. Tomorrow!"

Evie shifted and Memphis took his place in front of the microphone. His heart sped up as it always did when he had to speak in public, even if he couldn't see that public, and it amazed him to think that once upon a time, when he was the Harlem Healer, it had been no trouble at all for him to stand up in front of the congregation and heal the sick. But those had been his people, his church, with his mama standing by, smiling at him to show that it was all right. It had been three years ago, and it was forever ago, and he was no longer that young man who knew everything. At this particular moment, he wasn't trying to convince anybody of anything. He only wanted talk to them, human being to human being. He only hoped he could be heard.

From his pocket, he retrieved the poem he'd written that morning and tried to get the words to sit just right in his mouth.

"America, America,
Who are we?

> *brothers and sisters, sons and daughters*
> *I've seen the best of us, braving floodwaters*
> *on eight miles of drowning earth.*
> *Refugees, refugees*
> *I've seen the hopeful, bathed in the torchlight of*
> *Liberty, that harboring girl.*
> *I've seen the worst of us, torches in the night*
> *A mockery of the torch in the harbor.*
> *Oh, America, America,*
> *God shed his grace on thee,*
> *Now He asks from His nightclub in neon*
> *   heaven—*
> *Think upon four score and seven*
> *And ask yourselves, Is this who we are?*
> *Is this who will we be?*
> *Who will we be?"*

Moved, Evie nodded at him to continue. Memphis held up the paper and shook his head. *There's no more*, he mouthed.

"That concludes this inaugural program of the Voice! Of! Tomorrow! Stay tuned, America."

Evie powered down the radio. "How do you feel?" she asked Memphis.

"Aahhhhh!" Memphis leaped up, laughing as he shook out his hands to release his nerves. He beamed. "I feel for all the world like a lamp somebody finally figured out how to plug in."

The next day, Memphis wrote whenever he could. During a break when baling the hay. After planting corn. While Sam, Henry, Bill, and Jericho cooled off on the porch with tall glasses of lemonade before they started in on the rest of their chores. He'd always worried that he didn't really have anything to say. But the last few weeks and last night had shown him that he did. He'd just finally stopped trying to say it like other people. As himself, he had plenty to say.

For the next few nights, after the Olsons had gone to bed, Evie and Memphis stole out to the barn. It gave Evie a sense of pride that she knew how to get the radio up and running. Those months at WGI had made her a star, then they'd been witness to her spectacular fall. Now they were giving her a sense of purpose beyond fun or fame. It wasn't just Evie anymore; it was all of them.

They were still afraid to use their powers as a group, though. Instead, they paired up in different configurations, concentrating on sending the signal farther, hoping it worked. True to his word, Sam gave them cover while they touched the radio. One night, Evie asked the others to join in for a little radio play she'd written with Memphis's help. Theta, Sam, Henry, and Isaiah played their parts. Even Jericho agreed to read one line.

Only Ling refused. "It's like a hideous school play."

The Diviners crowded around the one microphone, taking turns and trying not to bump heads as they did.

Evie: Once upon a time, in a country much like our own, a terrible evil stalks the land.... The King of Crows and his Army of the Dead approach, as the good citizens of the nation sleep soundly in their beds, oblivious to the danger that awaits them....

Theta: There's wickedness in the land. Don't you see? The King of Crows and his dead are coming. They're here! Look! I see them glimmering in the corn and on Main Sleet.

"Street!" Evie whispered.

"Work on your handwriting," Theta whispered back.

Sam: I hear there's towns being turned into whole ghost towns. Why, didn't you hear about Gideon, Kansas?

Jericho: No. How come we haven't heard anything about it, then?

Sam made a face at Jericho's wooden delivery. Jericho shrugged.

Henry: Maybe they don't want you to hear about that. They'd rather you think the Diviners are wicked, when they're simply trying to stop catastrophe!

Evie nudged Isaiah and he strummed his thumb against a saw, making an otherworldly sound.

Isaiah: Gosh Almighty!

Isaiah looked very pleased with himself.

Ling rolled her eyes and whispered to Theta, "This is so corny. I am embarrassed for all of you."

Evie: Citizens of this land, never fear, for the Diviners are here. But all citizens must do their parts. Beware! Be aware! And now, a message from the Voice! Of! Tomorrow!

They paused for Memphis's nightly poem. He was getting more comfortable in front of the microphone, adding touches of all he carried with him—the storefront preachers, the rapid-fire cadence of the barbershop, Walt Whitman and Langston Hughes and Bessie Smith, the wild improvisation of jazz. When he spoke, it was like listening to something exciting and new, and Evie hoped they were reaching people out there in the dark. She hoped somebody somewhere was listening.

Someone *was* listening.

Several schoolteachers in Lincoln crowded around their boarding room radio. An elderly couple in a little brick house in Iowa. The Timmons family, in the front parlor of a cousin's house in St. Louis, the first stop in their great migration north.

"Daddy, is that...?" Moses asked, eyes alight.

"I'd bet my last nickel it is," Nate answered, feeling the same hopeful fire.

Someone was listening.

In her cell, Miriam Lubovitch heard and did what she could to boost the signal further. It was reaching into homes in Idaho. The migrant camps of California. The mills of New England. The oil fields of Texas. In his newsroom, T. S. Woodhouse listened; he threaded fresh paper into his typewriter. In one of the many empty rooms of his California mansion nestled among the redwoods, Jake Marlowe heard. He telephoned the Shadow Men, but they were in their brown sedan, also listening.

Someone else was listening.

The dead under the earth.

The dead crawling out of the earth.

The dead streaming into the countryside.

The dead were listening.

※

"'Who is the Voice of Tomorrow?'" Evie read from the *Omaha Morning World Herald*. It seemed that several newspapers had picked up the story about the unusual radio broadcasts being heard all over the nation. No one could tell where this Voice of Tomorrow radio show originated. Where were these people? *Who* were they? Were they connected in any way with the mysterious poems and letters that had been published by the New York *Daily News*? Or was this a new outfit who'd been influenced by those poems? Were these folks patriots or traitors?

Evie thought back to Mrs. Withers teaching American History at Zenith High School. Truthfully, she'd paid very little attention in class; she'd been much more concerned with getting Edward Schultz to notice her or daydreaming about being famous one day. Mrs. Withers was telling the story of some American Indian battle and how the Dutch had managed to "subdue them." Evie had only been listening because Edward was out with mumps, and she'd had nothing better to do. But she had thought at the time, very briefly, about that word, *subdue*. And she'd wondered, what would the Indians have said about that same battle? Now, reading about herself and her friends, she realized how much it mattered who got to tell the stories that ended up in the newspapers and the history books.

"There is no greater power on this earth than story...." she muttered.

It was something that Will said once. He'd said that people thought borders and lines on a map made nations, but that in truth it was stories that did. In her memory, she could see Uncle Will pacing the floor in the dusty, wonderful museum. (Oh, how she missed it! Why had she not appreciated it then?) How passionate he had been. How long ago that seemed.

Stories *were* power. And whoever controlled the story controlled everything. A story could bring people together, or it could tear them apart. It could spread like a sickness, infecting people. It could lead them into battle or shake them into seeing what they had refused to see before. The Shadow Men. Jake Marlowe. Harriet Henderson. Roy and the KKK—they were all trying to get people to buy into the story they were telling. The Voice of Tomorrow was a story, too. And like many stories, it had grown bigger. It was no longer a person. It was a movement.

In New York City, people were beginning to ask questions: Why weren't they allowed to hear Margaret Walker speak for herself? She had been the last person to see Will Fitzgerald alive—perhaps she had valuable information! Some in the city weren't willing to accept what Detective Malloy and Mayor Jimmy were telling them about her. They wanted to hear her story told from *her* lips. Outside the jail, a growing number of protestors gathered, shouting for justice. From her cell, Margaret Walker listened to the swell of voices. She hoped by the time she got to speak, it would not be too late.

In his tiny apartment a few blocks from Tin Pan Alley, David Cohn kept his radio on. He'd read about the broadcasts in the *Daily News*. The sound of his lover's voice coming through the speakers had brought him to tears. He missed Henry like nobody's business. When this was all said and done, he intended to kiss Henry DuBois IV as he'd never been kissed before—enough to knock the doubt and the ghosts from that boy's mind. David sat at his desk writing lyrics for a melody he couldn't quite hear, but one that he knew Henry would. It was a love song. It was *their* love song. He prayed they would all survive long enough for Henry to sing it.

"Come home to me, Henry," he whispered.

In her shop, Harlem's number one banker, Madame Seraphina, listened, laughing softly, like a cat. "Well, well, well," she said. "Fight on, Baby Oungan."

Backstage at a Masonic lodge in Louisiana, Alma and Lupe heard the gossip from others who'd been listening. Territory bands spreading the news as they went. "I tell you what, it's really got me thinking about how things are—and how they could be," somebody said. "How they should be," Alma corrected.

Harriet Henderson also heard. Her fingers tapped against her type-writer keys, pecking out words of doubt and accusation.

Men in white hoods listened. They passed the word along to other men, who passed it along to Roy, who drove into the mythic West with a fire in his belly, Manifest Destiny come calling with both fists on the wheel.

The news reached Jake Marlowe in his laboratory deep in the majestic redwoods. "What do you mean you can't tell where it's coming from?"

"They're doing some kind of Diviner hoodoo on it," the Shadow Man explained. "Impossible to get a fix."

"Nothing is impossible," Jake said. He said that so often it had become his slogan. And as if to prove his point, at that moment the Eye began trans-mitting to him from the other dimension, delivering a message from the King of Crows himself.

"They're coordinates," Jake said. "He wants us to go to the desert. Death Valley."

"When?" the Shadow Man asked. There were people in Washington who'd want answers, not questions.

"He didn't say when. He has some new specifications for the Eye."

Excitedly, Jake watched the instructions roll off.

Someone else had been listening, too.

❁

One day followed the next. The bright blue mornings pushed up from the land like a barn raising, a promise of something solid and good. Sometimes, when Theta rubbed the washing against the scrub board in the steel tub and looked out at the waving wheat, she could swear she heard the ghostly thunder of buffalo running across the plains. She shut her eyes and let that sound rumble through her soul. Memphis wrote by lantern light every evening. Isaiah tended to the kittens, feeding them milk from an eyedropper, feeling like a proud father when they'd take a few toddling steps. Henry gave Mrs. Olson lessons on the family pump organ in the parlor so that she could play whenever the church organist went to visit her daughter's family in Lincoln. Ling taught her how to make beans the way her father did in the restaurant, and Mrs. Olson, in turn, introduced Ling to her family's recipe for apple butter, which Ling found so delicious she wanted to spread it on everything. She couldn't wait to share it with her parents, back in their apartment on Doyers Street. And with Alma, wherever she might be. Ling hoped she was safe. Out here, surrounded by so much peaceful beauty and far from danger, it was easy to forget how great that danger actually was. But all they had to do was watch Evie fighting to regain her strength to be reminded.

Bill hadn't worked the land in more than a decade, but it came back to him quickly. It felt good to use his hands, to remember the ways of the earth. But this time, it felt good because he was doing it for somebody who was not Mr. Burneside. At the thought of his name, Bill spat into the dirt. He'd tried, but he still couldn't forgive the man for what had happened to Samson. Bill had cared for that powerful horse every day for five years. Theirs was a special bond. And Samson had died all because of an arrogant man's pride. Bill had warned his boss not to take the horse out in that flood, but that pompous fool couldn't let himself be wrong. In the end, Samson broke his leg, and it was Bill who'd had to ease the great animal's passing. He'd cried the whole time. He'd loved that horse as he'd loved no other. Yes, it felt good to work the land on his own terms. The honesty of his body clearing and planting. He liked it out here under the big sky. Maybe he would have some land of his own yet. Maybe even a wife, a family.

Still. Late at night, he was unsettled. It was Isaiah's vision about the ghosts on the road that continued to haunt him. Which road? When? The boy's prophecies weren't all easy to decipher, and this one kept Bill on edge. He vowed to stay sharp, looking out for any hint of danger. This he could do. Everybody had a part to play. These young bloods were the future. Bill's part, as he saw it, was to do whatever he could to keep them safe.

PROPOSAL

Mrs. Olson had insisted that Evie sit on the porch steps and soak up the sun.

"It'll do you good," she said, patting Evie's shoulder, then going inside to make a rhubarb pie that Evie could practically taste.

Sam entered the yard. He took off his cap and bowed. "Pardon me, aren't you the Sweetheart Seer of Cowtown?"

"I'm terribly sorry," Evie said, rolling down her stockings and stretching out her legs. "But I'm not supposed to listen to a thing Sam Lloyd says. Doctor's orders."

"Speaking of doctor's orders, when this is all over, I'm gonna take you to Goldberg's Delicatessen on Fifth Avenue."

"What's so special about Goldberg's Deli?"

"Doll, you have never had pastrami like this."

"You know, I really thought this was going to be a much more romantic conversation."

"What could be more romantic than sharing the world's best pastrami sandwich?"

"I could think of a few things," Evie said flirtatiously.

"Oh, yeah?" Sam bent low so he could peek through the screen door into the house. When he was satisfied that no one was watching, he sneaked over and kissed Evie deeply.

Evie broke away and craned her neck, looking for the Olsons. "Sam, don't. You'll get us in trouble."

"I invented trouble. I know how it works. But hold on a minute. I want privacy for this next part anyhow." Sam held Evie's hand. "Don't see us," he intoned, rendering them invisible to everyone but each other. They were sitting on the porch steps with a view of the long road, the greening fields, and all that blue sky above. The kind of sky that made you feel infinite. Sam kept stealing glances at Evie. He rolled a tractor nut between his grease-stained fingers. "Ever seen one of these?"

Evie glanced at it. "Sure. In a picture of the crown jewels once."

"Ha!" Sam laughed.

"What is it?"

"It's a nut."

"A … nut?"

"Yeah. See, it, ah, it slips over a bolt like … say, hold out your fingers for a second, I'll show you."

Evie gave Sam a dubious look and put out her hand. "Sam Lloyd, don't you get that stuck on my finger!"

"Don't worry. Plenty of grease on it," Sam said. He slipped it easily over her ring finger. It was too big. "Like that."

"And what does this nut do?"

"It joins two things together. And that makes things work. In union. Like, you know. A marriage." Sam kept turning the nut around Evie's finger slowly.

"Well. Now I know all about how nuts and bolts work. I'm practically an expert." Evie went to remove the nut, and Sam covered her hand with his.

"Don't take it off just yet, will ya?"

"Sam?"

It seemed to Sam that he had never in his entire life been as nervous as he was just now. Or as sure. "Evie O'Neill, would you marry me?"

Evie raised an eyebrow. "Didn't we play these roles already? A few months ago?"

"That was pretend. I mean on the level. Evie O'Neill, would you do me the honor of becoming Mrs. Lamb Chop?"

Evie could scarcely catch her breath. "If you're pulling my leg, Sam Lloyd, I swear on all things holy …"

But his face didn't have even a trace of a smirk.

Evie beamed. "Well, I'm telling you right now that you'll have to find me a better ring. I am pos-i-tutely *not* wearing this one."

"Does that mean … ?"

Evie laughed and threw her arms around Sam's neck. "Yes! Yes, Sam Lloyd. I will marry you!"

"Hot dog!" Sam lifted Evie up and twirled her around.

"Ow!" she said and grabbed her side. "War wound."

"Sorry, Baby Vamp," he said, putting her down gently.

But then they were kissing and Sam felt just like that blue sky shining over the newly tilled soil of the Nebraska prairie. Limitless. He cupped Evie's face between his palms and stared into her twinkling eyes. "Listen, I'll need to keep that twenty dollars I stole from you. For the ring."

"Sam!" Evie rolled her eyes and laughed. "Oh, who cares?" she said and kissed him again.

＊

The air was oppressive, and still the rains would not come. Jericho feared that all their work would be for naught without it.

"The crops need rain," Isaiah said to Sarah Beth as they sat in the corn, hidden from view. "You think we can try again?"

Sarah Beth grabbed his hands. "All right. Let's bring on the rain."

"Rain, rain, rain," they intoned, louder and louder till it was nearly a shout, and then Isaiah felt them joining, the vision coming on. In it, rain clouds rolled over the countryside. He could practically smell the iron of a deluge. When he came out of it a minute later, though, the sky was still blue, and Isaiah was disappointed that their gifts were not sparking as he'd imagined they would.

They abandoned the corn for the river, where they took off their shoes and stuck their toes in the water. Sarah Beth showed Isaiah the fish sidewinding between the rocks. They took turns tossing sticks and pebbles into the water and watched them float downstream. That morning, Isaiah had noticed a fine peach fuzz budding along his upper lip. In a few days, he'd be eleven, not quite a man but no longer a boy. He stroked his upper lip, hoping Sarah Beth would notice. Instead, she palmed a rock and raised it overhead. "I'm strong," she said and slipped in the grass, nearly tumbling into the river.

Isaiah pulled her back from the brink, remembering the vision—the river, the rock, the blood. "You got to be careful, Sarah Beth."

"I will. Thank you, Isaiah." She looked down at his arm, the ropey muscle trying to come into being.

Isaiah felt proud. "Getting a mustache," he said.

"That so?"

"Mm-hmm."

Sarah Beth grinned with mischief. "Duck!" she shouted.

Isaiah dipped just as Sarah Beth tossed the rock. It sailed over his head and hit the water with a splash.

She started to go after it. Isaiah stopped her. "We ought to be getting back now or I'll hear about it."

They tromped back toward the farm through the tall grass, the two of them giggling over some private joke. But when they reached the edge of the yard, Memphis was there, and he looked unhappy. He took Isaiah by the arm and pulled him behind the barn.

"Where've you been?" Memphis demanded.

"Fishing," Isaiah said sulkily. "I was hoping to catch something for supper." It was his first lie to his brother, and it was surprising to him how easily it came.

Memphis let out a long exhale. "All right, Shrimpy. But you've got chores to do. We're guests here, remember? You can't just go running off whenever you feel like it."

"Look!" Sarah Beth shouted.

Memphis and Isaiah came around the barn. Sarah Beth was pointing to the sky.

Overhead, storm clouds were rolling in above the prairie wheat. The wind had picked up. Isaiah could taste the wet in it. In the field, Mr. Olson stopped the tractor and took off his hat. Two fat drops hit his upturned face. "Rain," Mr. Olson said, as if on a prayer. Two drops became two more until it was a downpour. Rain had come at last to Bountiful.

"Grab the buckets!" Mr. Olson ordered.

Sam, Memphis, and Henry hauled out every tin pail and wooden bucket they could find. Bill and Jericho helped lead the animals back into their pens. Isaiah and Sarah Beth ran in tight circles, whooping and hollering. Theta stretched out her arms like a scarecrow and let the rain soak her. Ling and Mrs. Olson came out from the kitchen to see.

"Have you gone crazy?" Ling asked.

"Yes! We are rain-struck!" Theta called back. Drenched to the skin, she Charlestoned in the softening earth.

Mrs. Olson put out her hand. "I'll be! Rain at last!"

The crops bent with gratitude under the weight of the water. It was a proper blessing of rain.

"I reckon you all are good luck," the farmer said. "First real rain we've seen in ages."

"Sarah Beth! Come in out of it, honey. You'll catch cold," Mrs. Olson called.

Sarah Beth rolled her eyes so that only Isaiah could see. "What did I say? Always bossing us around."

Isaiah grinned. Before she left, Sarah Beth looked right into Isaiah's eyes. "We brought down the rain, Isaiah. You and me. We did that. By sharing our moon glow. I always believed you and me would be special together, but now I know it's true."

And Isaiah had no reason not to believe her.

※

The rains lasted two full days and put everyone in a fine mood.

"That'll help the crops for sure," Mrs. Olson said. She opened the kitchen window so that they could listen to the patter of it collecting in tin pails and, farther on, to the roar of the river coming to life with new water. To celebrate the little miracle, she'd baked a lemon cake with a sweet icing that was so good Isaiah ate two pieces.

Isaiah liked being on the farm. It was so different from his life in Harlem, but he enjoyed both. Feeding the piglets was one of his favorite chores, and he would let the squealing runts sniff at his fingers, laughing at the tickle of their noses and tongues against his skin. His absolute favorite thing, though, was caring for the kittens. He would pick them up one by one and hold them to his chest. Sarah Beth didn't seem to care about them one way or the other. Mostly, she liked playing with her dolls or sharing moon glow. But every chance Isaiah got, he'd scrabble under the porch and care for the babies, watching as their fur came in, noticing the personalities that were emerging.

"The orange one? I call her Mopsy. She's gonna be the troublemaker. I can tell already by the way she scoots the others out of the way to get to the mama," Isaiah said to the others as they set about their work on the farm, painting and planting, milking and baling hay. He loved talking about the kittens. *His* kittens, as he'd come to think of them.

"That a fact?" Bill said, half listening.

It bothered Isaiah some that nobody really paid attention to him. Nobody except Sarah Beth.

Mr. Olson walked through then, a real serious look on his face.

"Something troubling you, Mr. Olson?" Bill asked.

"Anybody leave the door to the henhouse open?"

"Isaiah?" Bill asked.

Why did everybody always want to blame him? "No, sir. I latched it up good, just like you showed me."

Mr. Olson shook his head. "Well, a fox must've got in there somehow. There's four dead chickens, by my count. A real mess. They've been eaten right down to the bones."

Over lunch, Evie and Sam finally shared their good news with the others.

"Well, this calls for a celebration!" Mrs. Olson said. "I've got some homemade grape juice."

"Oh, glory be!" Evie said.

"Uh, Lamb Chop? I think it really is grape juice," Sam whispered.

Evie caught Jericho's gaze once, across the table. It was impossible to read what he was thinking. She wished she'd had a chance to tell him privately first, but Sam had been so excited he'd blurted it out immediately. And anyway, Jericho had a sweetheart. She decided not to let it worry her.

"*I've* had lots of suitors over the years," Sarah Beth announced suddenly as her mother poured everyone small glasses of deep purple juice. "Very important men. They bring me all manner of fancy things from their travels. Lace handkerchiefs and ruby ear bobs. Every last one of 'em wants to marry me when *I'm* old enough."

Not one soul had set foot on the farm since they'd been there, and Mr. Olson had said Sarah Beth had no friends. It was as if she lived in her own fantasy world, and Memphis wondered how on earth they'd be able to use her gifts with their own in order to fight the King of Crows when the girl seemed to have a hard time facing reality.

"Our Sarah Beth is very popular," Mrs. Olson said, playing right along.

"I'm sure she is," Sam said, flicking a glance Evie's way. "Which one you gonna marry, then, Sarah Beth?"

Sarah Beth pushed a fuzzy ringlet over her shoulder. "The one who promises to make me his queen."

"Well, that'll be one lucky fella," Sam said and winked, to Sarah Beth's delight.

"Eat your carrots, dear," Mrs. Olson said.

"How old is your daughter?" Henry asked Mrs. Olson after their lunch. He and Theta washed dishes while Evie and Ling sat at the kitchen table drying.

"Fifteen. But her mind is like that of a child of ten or eleven. The doctors don't think she'll ever mature much beyond that." Mrs. Olson inhaled as if she hadn't breathed so deeply in years and needed to remind herself that she could. "She's a little girl in so many ways, and always will be."

"I tell you, you've brought good luck to this farm," Mr. Olson said, barging into the kitchen and dropping the day's newspaper on the table for Ling, who liked to pore over its pages every day. He grabbed one of the clean glasses and filled it with milk, which he guzzled down, leaving the glass on the counter for his wife, who dutifully dunked it into the tub of water for a washing. "Got the planting done and brought the rain. And I never seen Sarah Beth so happy. She almost seems normal."

Evie was shocked by the casual insensitivity of Mr. Olson's remark. She saw Ling stiffen, too. No wonder Sarah Beth seemed odd and lonely and a bit sour. Evie felt sorry for Sarah Beth, and she resolved to treat her with kindness.

"Oh no," Ling said. She had opened up the Bountiful *Daily Bee*. "Listen to this: 'Jake Marlowe to Test New Machine,'" she read. "'Promises the Eye of Providence will supply the nation with energy for generations to come. Already, the United States military is securing a portion of Death Valley, making it a restricted zone for the inventor's latest experiment.'"

"Isn't making things a restricted zone Mr. Marlowe's specialty?" Henry said with a sneer.

"Death Valley? That's a long way from Hopeful Harbor. Why Death Valley?" Sam asked.

"More importantly, it means he's nearly ready to go again. And once he does…" Evie didn't finish, but everyone understood the stakes. "Does it say when, Ling?"

Ling skimmed the article and shook her head. "It only says later this month."

"That could be three days or two weeks from now," Theta said.

"He can't do it without us, though, can he?" Henry asked.

"Unless the King of Crows has shown him a way," Ling said.

"What's this?" Jericho tapped an article on the opposite page. "'Mysterious ghost towns reported,'" he read. "'Authorities are perplexed by recent stories of vanishing towns. Gideon, Kansas, once a thriving little spot known for its charming Main Street, is now only home to piles of dust and debris, its people mysteriously gone, much like the famous lost colony of Roanoke, Virginia. Other towns seem to have dried up as well, including two here in the Cornhuskers State—Singing Springs and Pine Bluff—with no word as to the whereabouts of the inhabitants, though in all three places, the graveyards had been desecrated.'"

"We have to get to work right away!" Evie said, standing quickly. She grew dizzy and nearly fell over.

Sam helped her back to her seat. "We're not doing anything till you're well enough."

"Maybe the rest of us can work while you get stronger," Ling said.

"Sarah Beth said it has to be all of us," Henry reminded them.

"I can do it," Evie said, wincing from the pain in her side.

"Lamb Chop. We just got engaged. I won't lose you," Sam said.

Evie caught Jericho's eye for just a second and blushed. "Okay," she said. "But I won't sit it out much longer. We can't afford to wait."

"Nebraska. Do you suppose he's making his way here to find us?" Theta asked.

"Don't know, but he's collecting an awful lot of dead along the way," Sam said.

※

Evie asked Jericho to meet her on the porch. Now he was standing in front of her, and she felt as nervous as if she were facing an entire army of ghosts.

"Jericho," she started. "I'm sorry. I should have told you before...."

"Yes. Probably. Congratulations, by the way."

"Thank you. I don't suppose you could be happy for me, could you?"

"I'm not *not*-happy for you," Jericho said. After a pause, he added, "I will always regret what happened...what I did...at Hopeful Harbor."

"I know," Evie said. "Your sweetheart—"

"Guadalupe," Jericho said and smiled.

"Guadalupe," Evie repeated. How was it possible to feel relief, happiness, and jealousy all in one go? "Do you love her?"

Jericho blushed. "I'd prefer to keep that to myself."

"Right. Of course. Pos-i-tutely. Say, do you remember that Ferris wheel ride up in Brethren?" Evie blurted out.

Remembering that night had kept Jericho going at times—and held him back at others. A ghost of a memory. "Yes. It was a great view from up there."

"Yes. A truly spectacular view," Evie agreed.

"Really clear night, as I recall."

"Yes. Lots of stars."

"A very…nice evening. Well, before we were chased by a murderous religious cult and nearly killed."

Evie laughed and Jericho laughed and there they were again, all the things that kept them tethered still firmly between them. But perhaps the tethering had grown looser.

"If Sam's right and there are all those other universes out there, perhaps in one, you and I have settled down with a pack of smart, unruly children," Evie said after a moment.

Jericho only smiled. He looked out at the unbroken line of rural Nebraska. "This is the only universe I really know anything about, Evie. And you are marrying Sam. And I have a sweetheart named Lupe. And we have a mighty big fight ahead of us, something more important than this." He took a deep breath. "You and I weren't meant to be."

"Except as friends?" Evie asked hopefully.

Jericho shook his head, gave a little laugh. And then he smiled at her. A real smile. He stuck out his hand. "Sure."

Evie gave it a solid shake. It felt like a prelude to good-bye, somehow.

Like putting away old things to make room for the new.

❋

While the others returned to the farmwork, Evie sat reading a dull article in the *Saturday Evening Post* while Mrs. Olson worked on a piece of embroidery.

It was just the two of them in the parlor. Evie figured this was her best chance to ask Mrs. Olson more about Sarah Beth. "Mrs. Olson, I hope you don't mind if I ask you about Project Buffalo."

"No, that's fine," Mrs. Olson said. But Evie could tell by the way the woman straightened her spine and stared at her needlework that she did mind.

"It's only that I saw Sarah Beth's chart. It said they didn't recommend proceeding. Do you know why?"

"I suppose you'd have to ask them," Mrs. Olson said, a bit defensively, and pulled the needle through her sampler.

"I wish I could," Evie said as kindly as possible.

Mrs. Olson kept at her embroidery. "At first, Sarah Beth's visions weren't all that peculiar," she said a moment later. "She might know precisely when it was going to rain, or when someone would be coming for a visit. She said she heard spirit voices."

Like she'd heard Isaiah, Evie thought. Perhaps Sarah Beth had been hearing other Diviners, much like Sam's mother did.

"But then it all changed," Mrs. Olson said.

"Changed how?"

"Sarah Beth told us she had an imaginary friend, a man in a stovepipe hat. That's when she started having the upsetting visions."

Evie tried to keep her voice calm. "Upsetting how?"

"We had a handyman named Jack. One day, Sarah Beth told Jack that he was going to die. A fall from a horse that would snap his neck. That's what she said, 'You're going to snap your neck.' Well, I made Sarah Beth apologize! But she insisted she'd seen it 'in a dream.' That's what she called her visions. Three days later, a snake spooked the horse Jack was riding. The horse bolted. Jack fell off. He died of a broken neck. Well, after that, most of the farmhands left. Some because the farm was failing and the money was gone, others because they feared Sarah Beth. Then she started having more of her fits. It frightened us. We're just ordinary people. We didn't understand a lick of what she was saying, talking about soldiers being sucked up into the sky and a land of the dead. 'The dead are coming.' That's what she'd say. Until a few weeks ago. Then she said, 'The dead are here.'"

Sarah Beth Olson had been seeing glimpses of the future for a long time, but no one had been listening to her. Could she see what lay ahead for the Diviners?

"You love her very much, don't you?" Evie said.

"A mother always loves her children," Mrs. Olson replied.

Evie had heard her mother say the same thing, but it wasn't true. Evie's mother had loved James beyond imagining. He brought her joy. Her love for Evie was an obligation and an open wound, and Evie was the salt. But she believed that Mrs. Olson loved her daughter—and that she was frightened of her, too.

Mrs. Olson dropped her embroidery into her lap and turned to Evie. "Oh, please promise me you'll look after my Sarah Beth. The doctor said a bad fit could kill her. She's all we have."

Evie held Mrs. Olson's hands and looked into her eyes. "She's one of us. I promise we'll look after her, Mrs. Olson."

"Thank you." Mrs. Olson smiled like she had a naughty secret to share. "I don't suppose I could interest you in a little more pie?"

Evie grinned. "You most certainly could."

She followed a suddenly chatty Mrs. Olson into the kitchen.

"Lands' sakes!" Mrs. Olson exclaimed, stopping short in the doorway. "How did this mess get all over the floor? I just swept it right after lunch!"

"If it's mud, I blame Sam. He's an absolute slob," Evie said, coming up behind her.

"Not mud," Mrs. Olson said, reaching for the broom. "Daisies, of all things! Bunches and bunches of rotted daisies."

ALL OF US TOGETHER

"It's time. We can't put it off any longer," Evie announced the following day over Sam's objections. It was Sunday afternoon. Their chores were finished. Mr. and Mrs. Olson had gone to a neighbor's farm a few miles away for the men to play horseshoes while the women quilted. The Diviners had the farm to themselves. "Marlowe and the King of Crows are already steps ahead of us. We can't afford to wait."

"All right. But what do we do?" Henry asked. "All we've learned how to do is destroy ghosts."

"What if we feel them, the dead, inside us again?" Ling asked. To think there'd been a time when she hadn't feared spirits at all. But after Gideon, she was terribly afraid.

"Now we're all together, it'll be different," Sarah Beth said. "Isaiah and I've already been working on our powers. Isn't that right, Isaiah?"

"Isaiah? Is that true?" Memphis asked. He did not sound happy.

Isaiah shrugged and avoided Memphis's gaze.

"You're all scared on account of what happened in Gideon," Sarah Beth said. "That's what he wants, is to get you good and scared. So you'll doubt your gifts. So you won't fight back. You can't trust what he says."

"The last few times we used our powers, we weren't thinking; we were reacting, out of fear," Ling agreed.

"How do you know all of this?" Jericho said to Sarah Beth.

"Because I used to talk to him," Sarah Beth answered. "I know how he thinks. I know how he tricks and lies. We have to get our powers good and strong so we can take him out. If he goes, the dead go with him."

"You're sure about that?" Jericho said.

Sarah Beth stared him down. "Yes."

"All is connected…." Sam said.

"What's that?" Evie asked.

"Something I heard when I was in Marlowe's Eye. All is connected. Us. Them. The dead and the living. All of it."

"And we're connected to the dead and the King of Crows," Ling said. "So how will we defeat them without also destroying ourselves?"

No one had an answer for that. They were, they knew, flying blind.

"I keep telling you," Sarah Beth said, exasperated, "if we share our moon glow—"

"Our *what*?" Sam said.

"It's what we call our gifts," Isaiah explained, registering the dirty look Memphis was throwing his way.

"Sounds like a perfumed soap," Sam said.

Evie elbowed him. "Behave."

"Well. It does," Sam muttered.

"What were you saying, Sarah Beth, before you were so *rudely* interrupted?" Evie asked.

"We hafta strengthen each other. Get used to sharing our powers."

"Well," Evie said, yanking up her sleeves and putting out her hand, "I suppose there's only one way to find out."

For the past few months, whenever the Diviners had used their powers together, it had been mostly with one aim: obliterating the ghosts. It was harder than they thought to switch gears. What shape should their powers take? How could they make that happen? They might feel the spark of something, but in the next second, they could sense one another's fear and indecision, and then, just as quickly as it had come on, the spark would disappear. The Diviners tried again and again, but nothing worked very well or for long. They might make the air around them wobble slightly, and once, for a moment, they could hear voices swirling down the telephone lines, but they were gone in seconds. They weren't discovering anything new or significant. Nothing that could help them defeat the King of Crows. It was as if, when they joined hands, each one was lost in a fog, unable to access the others. As one hour became two, the Diviners began to feel desperate and exhausted. Tensions flared. Accusations followed.

"You shouldn't have made a joke before we started, Henry. It ruined our concentration," Ling snapped.

"I don't think one joke will be the end of us," Henry answered in kind.

"My bones ache," Ling said. Standing for so long was murder on her spine. Memphis helped her sit.

"Something is wrong," Evie said. "Don't you feel it?" The sun beat down on the back of her neck. The wound in her side throbbed.

The Diviners sprawled out in the prairie grass, feeling frustrated and out of ideas.

"Maybe what we did in the past with the ghosts took away some of our gifts," Memphis said.

"When we killed them, you mean?" Henry said.

"For the last time, you can't kill a ghost. They're already dead," Ling snapped. When Henry flashed her an annoyed look, she muttered, "I'm simply being factual."

"When we destroyed the ghosts. Is that more factual?" Sam said.

"Don't yell at Ling," Evie chided.

Sam spread out his arms. "Who's yelling? I'm not yelling. I'm just… nudging."

"Words and accuracy count," Ling said.

"So you've said. A lot," Henry grumbled.

Theta held up her hands. "Fine. Everybody's had their say. In her spell book, Miss Addie talks about intent. About knowing what's in your heart. Maybe that's the way to go."

"What's in my heart is wanting to end this thing so we can go back to normal," Sam said.

"Yeah? Define normal," Memphis said.

"Whaddaya mean?" Sam asked.

"I'm not so sure I want to go back to how things have been," Memphis challenged.

"I don't understand, are we fighting the King of Crows or aren't we?" Isaiah asked.

"I'm just saying that not everything is jake for all of us," Memphis said, looking at Henry and Ling and Isaiah.

"It seems so impossible," Evie said. "Who are we? Not even a dozen people going up against… all of that?"

"What if not all of us make it back?" Theta said quietly. "What if none of us do?"

"Well, I'm awfully glad I'm broke, then. Makes it easier to face certain death knowing I won't be giving up an apartment on Fifth Avenue," Henry said. When no one even cracked a smile, he added, "That was a joke."

"Haha," Theta said without mirth.

"Told you: We've got to build up our strength so we can destroy the man in the hat," Sarah Beth said. "He's tied to that machine and the dead. If he goes, it all goes."

The next day and the day after that, the Diviners got together in the evenings to work. They were already exhausted by the demands of the farm, though. The strain was beginning to show in their bodies. Tiny sores appeared on Memphis's forearms, and he didn't know why. Ling pulled out strands of loose hair. Evie was still weak and needed frequent breaks. And more than once, Theta's uncontrolled firepower had forced them to drop hands quickly as it traveled through and singed them.

By the third night, they were aching and injured and no closer to a breakthrough.

"Here goes nothing," Theta said, grinding her cigarette beneath her heel and joining the circle.

"Theta, we've got to at least try," Evie said.

"What if I burn you again?" she said, embarrassed.

"You've got Miss Addie to think about. And I've got Mabel," Evie reminded her, and Theta came and took her place beside Evie.

"Just imagine the King of Crows's face when he sees us standing up to him," Sarah Beth said and grabbed Evie's other hand. Evie made contact with a signet ring Sarah Beth wore and was flooded with a rush of memories, and just as suddenly, the memory was snatched away. Evie broke away, gasping.

"Baby Vamp! You all right?" Sam asked, approaching Evie and Sarah Beth.

"I-I'm jake. Just...got spooked, I suppose."

Once Evie got her bearings, she noticed that Sarah Beth had wandered away and was chattering to Isaiah about the kittens. She seemed perfectly fine. But Evie knew: Something truly terrifying had happened to Sarah Beth Olson.

Evie waited until she and Mrs. Olson were washing dishes before she found the courage to ask about what she'd felt. "I don't mean to pry, Mrs. Olson, but did something happen to Sarah Beth, perhaps during one of her fits?"

Mrs. Olson busied herself scrubbing a sink that was already sparkling clean. "Yes. Sarah Beth had a very bad episode. Last year. Summer."

"What happened?"

"She died."

"She...died?" Evie said.

"Just for a little while. She had no pulse. Her eyes were...fixed." Mrs. Olson blinked away tears. "But then she came back! God returned her to us. And after that, I knew the Lord had to have a plan for my Sarah Beth. And now here you are. Well, I can't help but think this was what the Almighty intended. For Sarah Beth to join with you on your mission."

A short time later, as Evie rested on the porch, she watched Sarah Beth heading to the barn with a rag doll in each hand.

"You feeling all right, Sarah Beth?" Evie asked, worried about the girl's constitution. She hoped they weren't harming her in any way.

"Mercy me, you sound like my mother!" Sarah Beth said with enough umbrage to amuse Evie.

"What's that all about?" Henry asked. He was just coming up with Ling. Evie shared Mrs. Olson's story.

Henry whistled.

"Mmm," Ling said, her brow furrowing.

"The definitive Ling Chan *mmm*," Henry said. "All right. I'll bite. What does that *mmm* mean?"

"What if it wasn't God who returned her?" Ling asked.

☀

Isaiah had been in the barn visiting the new calf. He heard Sarah Beth and decided to sneak up on her and give her a proper scare. She was over by the thresher, playing with two of her rag dolls. It was strange for Isaiah to know that Sarah Beth was nearly the same age that Memphis, Theta, and the others were. She seemed so much younger, as if she were only a year or two older than Isaiah himself. He sometimes thought of her as being like a doll, too. One of those fancy porcelain kind that were kept on a high shelf so they wouldn't get soiled. Hidden by three tall hay bales, Isaiah watched Sarah Beth. He couldn't make out what she was saying very well. That garbled voice of hers was soft and babyish and hard to hear. He could only catch little bits here and there as she pressed the two dolls against each other, making them kiss.

"...forever and ever...you're the most beautiful girl in the world...."

Isaiah wondered if she was thinking about Sam or Jericho or Memphis, or even Isaiah himself. That made him blush something fierce. Sarah Beth stopped mashing the dolls together. Absently, she ran a hand across her small breasts and closed her eyes, lost to some other private thought. Isaiah's shock turned quickly to embarrassment. He coughed so Sarah Beth would know he was there and bent over his shoe, pretending to tie it.

Her shadow loomed across the pale straw as she towered over him. "You shouldn't go sneaking up on a person like that."

Isaiah finished tying his shoe. "Didn't know you was here," he said, hoping she couldn't read his embarrassment. But Sarah Beth never seemed to be embarrassed about anything. "Whatcha doin'?"

Sarah Beth's expression softened. She held up a doll made from a flour sack. "This one is the lady. And this one is the gentleman." The gentleman was made of burlap, with red stitches for eyes. "They've been courting. They're in love, but they can't get married yet. They will, though."

"Can we go see the kittens now?" Isaiah asked.

Sarah Beth and Isaiah crawled under the porch so Isaiah could cuddle Mopsy and the others. He liked the feel of their fuzzy heads brushing against his cheek. He kissed Mopsy and put her back with her mother.

"They'll be weaned soon," Sarah Beth said.

"What's that mean again?" Isaiah asked.

"They won't be going to their mama for food. They'll have to find it themselves."

"Won't you feed 'em?"

"Not much to feed 'em with. Daddy said they gotta go. We can't afford 'em."

It crushed Isaiah to think of the farm without the kittens. Maybe he could convince Mr. Olson to let him keep Mopsy. Of course, first he'd have to convince Memphis.

"Come on," Sarah Beth said. "Let's go play in the corn."

Isaiah had come to like the old, dried cornfield. It was their private shelter, like a secret kingdom right outside the farmhouse. Deep in the corn, there was a bed of brittle, yellowed husks ready for the spring burning. Isaiah and Sarah Beth lay on top of them and looked up through the swaying stalks at the blue sky, talking about all the places they'd like to see someday.

"Tell me about New York City!" Sarah Beth said.

"It's pretty nice," Isaiah said, thankful to be talking about something he knew.

"I want to see it. I want to see London and Paris and the Nile. All the places that only exist on my little globe."

"Me, too."

"But I want to go with my husband one day," Sarah Beth said and giggled. She cupped her hands around her mouth to protect her secret as she whispered, "One day I will."

Isaiah blushed. He didn't know if she was trying to tell him that she liked him the way Memphis liked Theta. Isaiah didn't feel that way about Sarah Beth, but he didn't want to hurt her feelings or make her mad, so he just said, "The Nile's in Egypt. That's where the Pharaohs lived. I read about them in the Bible."

Sarah turned on her side and rested her head on her elbow. "Do you have a special sweetheart?"

Isaiah glanced sideways very quickly but did not turn to meet her face, which was too close for his comfort. "Nah," Isaiah said, embarrassed. He'd thought Alma was the prettiest girl he knew. Sometimes, he wondered what it would be like to kiss her. He wondered how you kissed. At the picture show, fellas like Rudolph Valentino mashed their mouths against the girl's mouth, but Isaiah couldn't really figure out what they did once their lips were pressed up against each other's like that. It didn't look particularly romantic, but people sure did get hot under the collar watching it.

Sarah Beth was looking at him peekaboo from under her curtain of hair. She smiled her tiny smile. "I could show you how to kiss proper. My gentleman won't mind."

Isaiah's heartbeat quickened. Most fellas he knew minded when you kissed their sweethearts. They minded quite a bit. "I don't believe I better," he said and felt the heat rise in his cheeks.

"Oh, Isaiah," she giggled. "It's like sharing moon glow. That's all."

Sarah Beth pressed her lips to his and held them there. It felt like kissing something with no give, a rock or a tree. Isaiah sat up and pulled away. Sarah Beth's face was hard to read. Had she liked the kiss? (He had not.) Did she want another one? (He hoped not.)

"How was that?" she asked and bit her bottom lip.

"Fine, I suppose."

"You suppose?"

"I ain't got nothing to judge it by. That was my first time."

Sarah Beth lay back on the corn silk again. "When my gentleman makes me his queen and we are in Paris or Egypt, I shall kiss him all the time." Sarah Beth wrapped her arms around herself and made kissing noises.

"How did you know about the King of Crows and how to stop him?" Isaiah blurted. He wanted to know, but he also wanted her to stop making those embarrassing noises.

"Hmm, should I tell you?" Sarah Beth said coquettishly and giggled. "Seeing as you are my very best friend, I reckon I can. It was during one of my bad fits. My heart stopped beating for a full hour!"

Isaiah didn't think that could be true, but he said only, "Golly, Moses! That's a long time!"

"I was there, in the land of the dead. I had a vision." She cupped her hands and whispered, tickling Isaiah's ear. "There's something about his coat and all those stories inside the lining. It's all there. Every single story. All the history. But he lets the people choose. They see what they want to see. They hear what they wanna hear. They tell what they wanna tell."

"What's that got to do with stopping him?" Isaiah asked. He was getting tired of her games.

"*His* story's in there, too. You have to be able to stare through all of it to see what's really there."

"Have you seen it?" Isaiah wanted to know.

"Maybe," Sarah Beth said, all high-hat. "Ladies are allowed to have secrets. It's part of their charm."

"I have a secret, too," Isaiah said. Because suddenly, he wanted to share something with her the way she had with him. And maybe he wanted to one-up her, too. "I plucked a feather from his coat. In Gideon."

Sarah Beth's mouth fell open. "Where is it? Can I see it?"

"I gave it to Evie."

Sarah Beth pouted. "You gave it to her instead of me?"

"So she could read it!"

Sarah Beth seemed to mull this over. "Well. What did she say?"

"She couldn't get anything from it."

"I can't believe you didn't tell me till now. You must never lie to me like that again. Not if we're to be friends. Don't you see? We got these powers because we're special. We're the chosen."

"We got these powers because they gave our mamas some kind of vitamins called eugenics. We're experiments."

Sarah Beth tossed her hair over her shoulder. "Maybe for you. Mine's natural."

"No. No, it ain't."

"Mine is natural!" Sarah Beth barked, but like a quick summer storm, she calmed. "I'll bet yours is, too. We came after them. Like I said, we're special. We brought down the rain!"

That made some kind of sense to Isaiah. His auntie always tutted that pride goeth before a fall, but Isaiah liked feeling a little apart from the others. He liked feeling special.

"Where'd Evie put the feather?" she asked.

"Beats me."

"She really couldn't get anything from it?"

"That's what she said."

"She's probably lying."

"She wouldn't do that."

"My mama and daddy lie to me all the time," Sarah Beth said, quiet-like. "They don't want me to know how sick I am. Or that they're afraid of me. They act like they ain't, but they are."

"How come they're afraid of you?" Isaiah's parents had never been afraid of him that he could recall.

"'Cause I'm not like them. They wanted an ordinary, pretty girl who'd help around the farm and not be any trouble. I'm a burden. They say I'm not but I know I am. I can feel it. Just like you can feel the truth behind what folks say."

"Like I said, I ain't afraid of you."

Sarah Beth smiled real big, and that made Isaiah happy. "I know. Friends?"

"Friends."

She scrabbled to her feet and set off at an uneven run. "Last one to the tire swing's a rotten egg!"

From a short distance away, Bill watched the two of them taking turns on the swing. "Don't like the way Sarah Beth plays with Isaiah," he said to Memphis. They were mending a break in the fence near the road. "Don't seem natural."

"Nothing about any of this is natural," Memphis said. "That girl can't help the way she is."

"Ain't that."

"What is it, then?"

"Her parents baby her too much, for one."

Memphis couldn't disagree with that. The Olsons loved their daughter, but they'd let that love keep them from disciplining the girl. They treated her like a fragile little bird who might break. Memphis didn't think she was fragile and believed that her parents should give her a chance to show how resilient she could be. But it wasn't his place to say so.

"What else?" Memphis asked.

"Don't know. Sometime, they run off together into the corn or down by the river, and when they come back, Isaiah seems...different. Not himself. I think the boy might be getting sweet on her."

Now Memphis was worried for a whole different set of reasons. All the time Memphis had told Isaiah he needed to start growing up and become a man, maybe Isaiah really was becoming a man. But he hoped Isaiah wasn't foolish enough to practice on the Olsons' daughter.

That night before bed, Memphis took Isaiah aside. "Isaiah, I don't think you should play with Sarah Beth so much."

"But she's my friend!"

"She's the Olsons' daughter."

"What's that supposed to mean?"

Memphis bit down on all the worry and anger climbing up into his mouth: *Because you never know if the farmer who seems friendly suddenly reaches for his gun because he has the gun and the power and you don't have either one.*

"We don't know these people," he said,

"Sure, we do."

"No. We don't. They're letting us stay on till Evie's better, and we need to show them we appreciate it by working."

"But Mr. Olson said—"

"Never you mind what Mr. Olson said. I know different. We're here to work on our powers and stop the King of Crows, and then we're gone. I don't want you playing with her all the time. Tomorrow, you'll help Bill and me paint the barn." Memphis hated that it had to be said, but he needed to protect his brother in a world that wasn't going to do it for him.

Isaiah crawled into his bed. He turned away from Memphis, facing the wall.

"Hey. Ice Man. You want me to tell you a story?" Memphis asked.

"No," Isaiah said angrily. "Too old for bedtime stories."

And that cut Memphis the most.

＊

Jericho dreamed of Lupe. She was standing in a beautiful garden with the sea behind her. The wind lifted her dark hair, and in his sleep, Jericho moved his fingers as if they might stroke that hair. She carried a bouquet of flowers. She walked past a Ferris wheel turning slowly. Evie sat in one of the Ferris wheel seats. She opened the little door to welcome Jericho, but he let the chair take Evie up and away. Lupe was ahead on the path, and he would follow her wherever she was leading.

Jericho woke panting. Seeing Lupe, even in a dream, really got his heart beating. It was racing, in fact. He sat up to try to get it to calm down. His hands were shaking, too. Why were they shaking? Out of habit, he tried to make a fist. Only his pinkie and ring finger curled in. With his other hand, he forced the fingers down, and after a moment he was making a fist just fine. He was tired was all. He hadn't done farmwork in a long time. All that milking and roping and plowing. Anybody's hands would ache. Some fresh air was what he needed. He tiptoed out of the farmhands' quarters and into the cool, clear night. The stars were extra shiny. He spied Taurus and Canis Major making a show of it. He made another fist. A little stiff, but fine. In a few weeks, he'd meet up with Lupe. They'd made a plan to go to Coney Island and stroll the boardwalk. She was going to make him mofongo, which was a dish that had plantains, which were like bananas, she'd said, but sweeter and better.

"Hey, kid. Mind if I join you?" Sergeant Leonard was there in the grass. His dark-ringed eyes shone out from his dead face, and he was smiling.

"You're not here."

"Okay. Have it your way." Sergeant Leonard's smile disappeared. "Go on. Make a fist."

Jericho looked down at his hand as if it were a snake ready to bite. "I'm going to beat it," he said. He dropped to the cold ground and did fifty pushups without stopping, and when he stood again, the apparition was gone.

446

PUT THE WORD OUT

Missouri

Roy Stoughton rolled down his sleeves as he left the Fitter Families tent.

"That Diviner know anything?"

"A little. He got a feeling. He saw her somewhere in Nebraska, on a farm."

"Nebraska is lousy with farms, Roy."

"He said this farm had a girl on it. Another Diviner. Sarah Beth something-or-other. He thought it might be near a town with a B."

"That all we got to go on?"

"That's all he could say before he passed out."

"We know the klaverns in Nebraska. Let me call the Grand Dragon, put the word out we're looking for a farm and a girl named Sarah Beth. We'll find her. Hey, Roy? You got blood on your cheek."

Roy checked his face in the rearview mirror. Two flecks of fresh blood had settled in the lightly scarred flesh along his jaw. Theta had given him that scar. With the back of his hand, he wiped till his face was clean.

"Start the car," Roy said. "Make sure we got enough gas to get to Nebraska."

SACRIFICE

T. S. "Woody" Woodhouse had come up from nothing. From a cold-water tenement with six siblings, and an Irish father too sick with tuberculosis to work. Woody had shaved the lilt from his Bronx-Irish brogue and remade himself into the sort of fellow who might get invited to fancy Manhattan parties. Except that none of those fellows ever did invite him. Woody was too ambitious. Too Street. Too Irish. The smell of Bronx tenement hung on his suits like the wrong aftershave. The idea that America didn't have a class system was a lie. Woody had liked the idea of journalism. Of sticking it to those stuffed shirts by telling the truth and ratting them out in the pages of the *Daily News*. But somewhere along the way, after all he'd learned about Diviners, Project Buffalo, the lies, and the walking dead, he'd become a real journalist, committed to telling the truth no matter the personal consequences.

He'd done as Margaret Walker instructed. Deep in the bowels of some musty forgotten archives, he'd removed box after box until he found what he was after. The file, the proof, was tucked inside his jacket now. Woody had pursued the truth for personal glory. Now that he'd finally found it, he felt hollowed out. Truth had a way of doing that. It had a way of making you question everything.

Woody stood before the Lincoln Memorial in the rain. He'd needed comfort, and that need had brought him here. He tried to imagine the president's pain as the nation had come apart. Abraham Lincoln, like anyone, had been a complicated man who had done both harm and good. He wasn't the easy hero the history books made him out to be. Nevertheless, eventually he'd taken the words *all men are created equal* to heart and had been willing to shoulder the hatred and scorn of half the country in order to try to make it come true. Along the way, he had buried a beloved son and lost his wife to a melancholy that turned to madness. Still, he carried on. For an idea of freedom, true justice, and equality. To steward the nation toward its stated ideals. In the end, he'd taken a bullet for it.

Sacrifice.

Woody's Irish grandparents had left behind the potato famine to try their luck in America. They'd sacrificed everything to get here. What they'd found were NO IRISH NEED APPLY signs. It was always somebody's turn. The Irish, the Italians, the Jews, the Negroes or Chinese or Mexicans. A great wheel of bigotry, ever turning. Who got to decide what made somebody an American? America, the ideal of it at least, was its own form of elusive magic.

Overwhelmed by the vastness of the emotion inside him, Woody sat at the marble feet of Abraham Lincoln. Thomas Seamus Woodhouse knew that he was not a great man. Possibly not even a good one. But he was a darned good reporter. He'd changed over the past several months. It was no longer just about seeing his byline in print. About becoming famous. It was about telling the truth. It was about making sure that Jake Marlowe and the members of the Founders Club had to answer for their crimes, and about preventing them from creating an even greater catastrophe. It was about fighting back against Evil, yes, but also against all the small evils, too. It was about saving the nation that, Woody was surprised to discover, he believed in so fervently. And Woody knew that if somebody like him could change for the better, anything really was possible in America.

"'We are not enemies, but friends. We must not be enemies. Though passion may have strained, it must not break our bonds of affection. The mystic chords of memory, stretching from every battlefield and patriot grave to every living heart and hearthstone all over this broad land, will yet swell the chorus of the Union, when again touched, as surely they will be, by the better angels of our nature,'" Woody murmured, a quote he'd had to memorize in school. Why had it come to him now? The better angels of our nature... the better angels of our nature...

"Woodhouse..."

With a rabbit jump, Woody leaped up. "Hello?"

He was alone. Just him and the monument of a dead president in the rain. Still, he was sure he'd heard his name whispered.

"Hello?" he said again into the rain.

The hour was late, far later than he'd realized. He should be getting back to Union Station. He'd catch the next train back to New York. He'd stay up all night to write this story if necessary, because it needed to be told.

"Woody..."

"Wh-who's there? Show yourself!" T. S. Woodhouse gripped his umbrella tightly, ready to use it as a weapon if need be. Down at the base of the steps, the ghost of Will Fitzgerald glimmered in the rain. His mouth opened and closed frantically, as if he were trying to shout a warning in a dream. And then, finally, as he faded from sight, he managed two words: "Go. *Quickly.*"

Under the steady rain, Woody heard the even cadence of footsteps coming closer. Two pairs of footsteps, just slightly out of time, but deliberate. *Careful in the rain. On the marble.* Woody could practically feel Mr. Peterson gripping his hand and delivering his warning.

Woody hurried down the steps and walked quickly away from the monument, breaking nearly into a run. The footsteps followed. Frantically, he hailed a taxi, exhaling in relief as they pulled away from the curb. "Gotcha, you bastards," he muttered. The traffic was murder. By the time the taxi reached Union Station, Woody was sure he'd missed his train. The station was mostly deserted at this hour. The ticket windows were closed. A few bums walked through, looking for scraps or a place to sleep. It was another hour before the next train to New York City. Woody took a seat inside an empty telephone booth and shut the door. The adrenaline left his body, and Woody nodded off from the sudden fatigue. He dreamed of his ancestors on the boat to America, pale and hungry and hopeful. "Seamus," his grandmother said. "Wake up, boy."

Woody woke with a start. He didn't see the Shadow Men, but he felt them. They were here inside the train station, he knew. Some prickling on the back of his neck told him it was so. Woody left the phone booth. He patted the file beneath his suit jacket. If the men caught up to him, he needed to make sure he had no "seditious materials" on him.

A station maid swept the vast sea of floor. On her small wooden cart lay her coat. Woody took out his pencil and scrawled "Attention: New York *Daily News*—URGENT!" across the folder containing the files, and then stuffed the folder into that coat, marveling at the notion that the fate of this particular piece of truth now rested in the pocket of a cleaning woman in Union Station. He hoped she would get it to the paper. All he could do was trust.

The Shadow Men entered the waiting room, but they didn't seem to see Woody. Where could he hide? The men's washroom? If they followed him in there, he'd have no way out. Keeping his head down, he slipped out and hurried to the track to wait for the train.

They were coming. Of course they were. But Woody was a Bronx street kid. He hopped onto the tracks and into the dark stretch of tunnel. He'd find a spot to flatten himself, hide, wait it out. Behind him, the Shadow Men hopped onto the tracks, too. And Woody began to feel real fear. Carefully, he stepped over the rails, moving deeper into the darkness. He stopped short when he saw the ghost of Will Fitzgerald once more. He shook his sorrowful head, and it put Woody in mind of the murdered president whose memorial he'd just seen.

"Good evening, Mr. Woodhouse."

Woody turned around slowly, thinking of his grandparents who'd come to America to escape the troubles back home.

The Shadow Man's razor flicked open with an echoing crack. Far down the tunnel, too far, the headlamp glow of the last train to New York began to brighten the gloom. It caught on the razor's sharp edge—*in the dark . . . so sharp!*

It gleamed like a thing you've been expecting your whole life.

Sacrifice.

THE STORYLESS GIRL

Theta Knight did not know where she came from. There were no baby pictures of her, no memories shared by relatives, no funny nicknames that could be explained with, "Well, you remember the time…" She had been born, she felt, without a story. There wasn't even a house; Mrs. Bowers had kept them on the road, performing in vaudeville, for most of Theta's life. When she'd been young, she'd sometimes run a finger longingly over newspaper illustrations of happy families sitting around a dinner table. They were advertisements for something she couldn't recall—canned peas or dining room tables. But what it felt to Theta was that they were advertisements for a family and a happiness she'd never be able to buy.

It was why she'd fallen so hard for Roy. Yes, he was handsome. And yes, when he looked at her with those big brown eyes, she swooned. But mostly, she had felt seen and wanted. Chosen. And that was hard to give up, even after the hitting started. If Roy didn't love her, Theta had thought, then it meant that what she'd secretly suspected about herself—that she was unlovable—was true. When she thought about that, the hole inside her opened wider till she feared it would swallow her, and she tried harder to please Roy so that he would love her again. It seemed better than drowning in the emptiness. That was the trouble with having no story of your own. You tended to believe in whatever story somebody told you about yourself.

Adelaide Proctor, on the other hand, had a story. It was all right there in her diary. Her family. Her love for Elijah. A line of ancestors going back to Salem and, before that, England and burning witches. Like Theta, Miss Addie was also from fire.

One line from Addie's diary stuck out to Theta. Addie had gotten into an argument with her father, about what, the diary didn't say.

I was so very cross with Father today, and
I told him so. For this offense, he took away my

Anger made a girl not just unlovable, but unlikable. It got her punished. It could even get a girl killed. If Theta had ever smarted off to Roy, well, she was pretty sure she wouldn't be around worrying about ghosts and lost witches. Addie had been angry enough at the King of Crows to try to best him at his awful games. And she had, for a while. But just as when her father had taken away Addie's books, the King of Crows had the upper hand.

"What is it with these creepy fellas who think they can own a girl?"

For months now, Adelaide Proctor had been telling Theta to look into her heart. To know herself. Theta had mistakenly thought the old woman was telling Theta to let go of her anger. Theta's own shame had misled her. Miss Addie wasn't telling her to stop being angry. She was telling her to let herself get good and mad.

"When you free yourself, you free me," Theta repeated, feeling the itch of pent-up fire in her palms.

In Theta's dreams, a white clapboard church loomed. Miss Addie stood at the top of the church steps. The wind whipped her long white hair around her face. The church doors opened, and in the dark behind Miss Addie were trees with trunks like dried snakes.

"Theta, it's not a sickness. He has me. Break the spell."

"How do I do that?"

"Look into your heart, Theta, and you will know what to do. When you free yourself, you free me."

The tree limbs uncurled themselves from the base of the dead tree and coiled themselves around Miss Addie's frail body, crisscrossing her chest like the lacing of a corset, and yanked her back inside. The church doors slammed shut.

Theta woke with her heart racing. She blinked against the shadowy room. Nothing seemed amiss. It was the dream; that was all. The door was shut, just as it had been when she went to bed. Unsettled, Theta left the room she shared with Ling and walked through the dark kitchen and dining room, coming at last into the front parlor. Moonlight seeped in through the windows. Looking out, she could see the dim silhouette of acres of corn. All calm. Why was she so frightened? All she wanted was to be safe in bed. But what if her bed wasn't safe?

Theta stood on the rug in the parlor, listening. Wind. The soft rustling of corn. The small creaks and groans of an old house. And something else. A faint hiss, like gas slowly escaping a tire. What *was* that?

A night fog was rising in the cornfield, making it hard to see. Theta tiptoed out onto the porch. *This is nothing, Theta. Don't be such a baby.* Her heart hammered anyway. The hiss grew louder. Crickets? Bees? The smell hit her first. The unmistakable stench of decay. And then she saw Elijah coming through the corn.

Theta stumbled backward. *I got rid of you. I got rid of you in Gideon.*

She ran back into the house, straight for the kitchen, riffling through the cupboards till she found the salt. Then she raced back to the porch. Elijah had cleared the corn and was in the yard by the swing. Quickly, Theta began pouring the salt along the edge of the porch to keep him out.

"No," she pleaded as the salt ran out. "No, no." She bent down and scooped up what she could, tossing it in front of the door. Theta burst into desperate tears; there simply wasn't enough to protect her. Elijah kept coming. The heat that could be a weapon hid like a frightened child. She needed to stop him somehow.

"Where is Miss Addie?" Theta said. "What have you done with her?"

Elijah stopped. "He has Adelaide. Her heart is weak. He may take her at any time. She'll become part of our world. A many-eyed tree that watches all but cannot speak. A lowly toad covered in sores. A crow who can travel between worlds but never rest. Or he will let her rot, but her mind will be awake. Voiceless for eternity."

"Why can't you let her alone—or better yet, fight for her?" Theta said, horrified. "You loved her once. You *loved* her."

"She is owed to me."

"Nobody's owed to anybody," Theta said.

"She brought me back."

"She made a mistake! She tried to fix it."

"She and I are bound together for all time. And now you have bound yourself to me as well. We are coming for you. For all of you. You cannot win against us."

Elijah, coming for her, like she was his to claim. Just like Roy.

The anger that had been timid a moment ago slithered inside her now, a dragon begging to be let out. Theta had started this life in a fire, and the fire had become a part of her. The fire was awake, and she was ready to let it roar.

"Leave now," she commanded.

Elijah stepped forward. The flames overtook Theta. "I'm going to light you up like a goddamned Christmas tree, you backwoods son-of-a-bitch."

Theta would not remember how it started. Rage has a way of blotting out reason and memory. It was as if she were transported to another fire, the one that swept through her village when she was only a baby. She was vaguely aware that she had run screeching toward Elijah and grabbed him by the throat. The fire caught on the dried kindling of his Confederate shroud. Somewhere in the part of the brain where memories are stored, she noted that when he screamed, it sounded for all the world like a murder of crows shrieking into the night. Theta was there, setting Elijah alight, but she was also standing on the edge of her village in the snow, watching the cabins burn orange, watching her people running out only to be shot by wicked men with secrets to cover up, watching the snow bloom red with blood. She was there as her frightened mother gathered Theta into a blanket and into her arms and tried to make a doomed run for it. Even after the men had shot her down, she'd crawled to a tree to spirit Theta inside. There was so much fire within Theta, she felt as if she could burn for the rest of her life and it wouldn't be enough.

"Theta! Theta!" Evie's voice brought Theta back into her body, which hurt as if she, herself, had been burned. Sweat ran down her back. She blinked. Elijah was gone, a pile of ash at her feet. All around her, the dried corn was on fire. The fire was spreading fast. And she was stuck in the middle of it. Through the burning corn going black, through the smoke, she saw Evie racing for the pump and bucket. Mr. Olson stumbled down the steps. Mrs. Olson came out just behind him and put a hand to her mouth.

Sam and Jericho and Bill had joined Evie at the pump. They raced toward the blazing corn, tossing bucket after bucket of water on the flames. She'd done this. She and her fire. She was out of control. Just like at the asylum. Just like at Sarah Snow's memorial. She couldn't be trusted. She couldn't trust herself.

Memphis was running toward her.

"No," Theta screamed. "Stay back!"

"Theta, hold on!" Memphis yelled. He tossed another bucket of water on the corn, putting out enough of the fire for her to make a run for it. "Come toward me, okay? Just don't look back!"

Theta cried out as her bare feet touched the smoldering corn silk. Smoke filled her lungs, making her cough, but at last she was through. Jericho worked the pump furiously, filling the buckets and handing them off, everyone working together to contain the blaze. Theta saw Bill Johnson step to the edge of the corn and put his hand on the ground while the others were running around. She saw him draw the oxygen from that fire to put it out. She knew it cost him to do that, and as she watched gray pebble his dark hair, she felt responsible for this, too.

"Thank you," she said.

"It'll be all right," he said and patted her back. "It's out," Bill announced to the exhausted, filthy crew.

"Once I let it go, I couldn't control it, Evil," Theta said quietly a few minutes later as Evie escorted her back to her room. "It was everything I was afraid of."

Evie sat on the edge of Theta's bed. "Well, maybe we need to lose control sometimes."

"Easy for you to say."

"All right, then. What if you thought of your fire less like this thing that has power over you and more like an object you can read?"

"Whaddaya mean?"

"What is it saying to you? What does it want you to know? At least, that's what I think about." Evie shrugged. "I don't know. I don't understand any of this, but maybe if you let it know you're in charge, you will be."

"I thought I was, until I wasn't."

"There has to be a middle ground between holding it in and setting fire to an acre of corn."

"Half an acre," Theta mumbled.

"What if we practiced together?" Evie suggested.

Theta thought about all that corn, now blackened to ash. "I don't know, Evil…."

"Who was it who went with me to rescue Sam?"

"Me."

"That's right. And now I'm going to help you. That's how it works."

"How what works?"

Evie kissed Theta on the cheek. "This crackers little thing called friendship."

PURPOSE

The next morning, after they'd gathered the eggs and put away all the breakfast dishes, Evie led Theta past the barn and out farther, into a pasture sweet with tall green prairie grass and cows that grazed and flicked their tails, disinterested in the two determined figures tromping past them.

"You think you should warn Clarabelle over there that she might end up a steak?" Theta joked and rubbed her palms against the sides of her dress.

Evie glanced over her shoulder at the cow. "Nah."

"What about you, Evil? Aren't you scared that I'll...?"

"Petrified." Evie held out her hands.

"But I could...you know."

"You won't. Remember: You're in charge of the fire. It's not in charge of you," Evie said.

"I'm in charge," Theta said. "I'm in charge here." She glanced over at Evie. "But just in case, you might wanna back up, Evil, and let me try one on my own."

I'm in charge, Theta thought. The fire boiled up inside her, a howl wrapped in rage, but then she grew afraid and it went away.

"Theta, darling. You can do this."

"It's so much," Theta said.

Evie waited for her to say more.

"I used to feel numb a lot. When you grow up like I did, having to perform onstage and then having to perform so people...so..." Theta swallowed. "So they'll love you. It's easier just to push it all down. But now, ever since we all got together and started moving our atoms around or whatever it is Ling says it is, well, I can't be numb anymore. I feel everything, Evil. I'm so"—Theta's mouth opened a little wider, like there was a scream prying its way out—"*angry* all the time. I don't know what to do with all these feelings coming up inside me. I don't know where to put 'em."

Evie often felt a sadness that had no borders, as if she'd been set adrift on a great sea of lonesome with no way back home. She would do anything not to feel lost in all that awful loneliness—drink, jump out of cakes, kiss boys, shop. "It's easier not to feel sometimes, but that just means when it comes back—"

"It'll come back threefold," Theta said.

"There's a lot to be angry about," Evie said.

"There's a lot to be sad about," Theta said.

And this, for some reason, made them both fall down laughing till tears came.

"We are pos-i-tutely perverse, Theta!"

"Completely crackers, Evil."

"Do you want to try again?" Evie asked.

"What the hell. Let's go."

This time, Evie held Theta's hands.

"Are you sure?" Theta asked.

"Pos-i-tutely," Evie answered.

When Theta Knight finally willed her fire to blossom, what she felt was alive. It was as if the scar tissue of her past was kindling for this new, cleansing fire. It burned away shame. This fire was fuel. Theta was fully awake in her body. She rejoiced in this fact, in this body, fully hers. She was letting the fire in slowly, listening to it like Evie had suggested. She could hear Evie asking, "What is it telling you?"

It's about time, Theta thought. Having Evie near gave her confidence. "I'm going to try to direct it," she said.

"All right. I'll hold your arm, instead of your hand, then. But I'm right here, by golly!"

Theta put up her hand and imagined sending the fire out in a straight line, as if it were a piece of fishing line. Her hand warmed, and in a moment, the fire shot forward toward a dying tree.

"Come back," Theta murmured. "Come back."

The fire sucked back up into her hand, which smoked slightly. The tree was barely singed.

"How was that?" Evie asked.

"Good," Theta said and burst out smiling. "Real good."

"All the cows are safe and accounted for."

"Well," Theta said. "I guess it's a start."

From the sunroom window, Ling watched Evie and Theta in the field.

Ling had judged Evie harshly before, but she was starting to have a complicated respect for Evie now. No, she and Evie would never be best friends, but Ling was starting to understand that you didn't have to be best friends with someone in order to work with them. The two of them shared a common purpose, and they could work together toward that purpose.

※

"I think we might do better if we had a common goal in mind," Ling said later, when they had gathered in the pasture once more. "I think we should try to enter the land of the dead."

Shortly after they'd arrived in Bountiful, Ling and Jericho had told everyone about the night they'd managed to make brief contact with that other world. She reminded everyone of that now.

"Why wait for him to find us? Why not surprise him at home?" she said.

"That's a bad idea," Sarah Beth said.

"Why?" Jericho asked.

"It's not a good place. Somebody could see us. He could see us. Right, Isaiah?"

"Right," Isaiah said, looking defiantly at Bill and Memphis.

"Waiting around isn't safe, either," Ling said. "I vote we try."

"All those in favor, raise your hands," Memphis said, raising his. One by one, the Diviners agreed. All except for Sarah Beth and Isaiah.

"I don't wanna go," Sarah Beth said. She seemed genuinely frightened, and Evie thought about the girl's near-death experience. She wanted to tell Sarah Beth that she understood. After all, it had happened to her, too.

"It will be all right," Evie said.

"How do you know that?" Sarah Beth said.

"I promised your mother I'd look after you, and I will," Evie said, hoping to make Sarah Beth feel better. "Here. Let's stand in a circle."

"If nothing else, we've really mastered facing one another in the round," Sam said.

Evie kicked him.

"Now what?" Isaiah asked.

"I have no idea. Oh, why couldn't Sister Walker and Will have managed to teach us something?" Evie said.

"I don't think they knew, either. They created a problem they couldn't solve," Ling said. "I think it's always been up to us. We're just going to have to take some chances. Accept the risks."

"That's easier to do when it's the stock market and not when you might, just possibly, blow up half of Nebraska," Henry said.

"Hands," Ling said with great irritation. "Think of a portal."

There was a tug. *Portal*, Ling thought. *Portal*. She had the slightest sense of Memphis beside her thinking the same thing. Energy was building between them, stretching into the others. It was like a wild horse, exciting and terrifying. Ling felt pressure rising inside her, and then, all at once, they were standing in the land of the dead. A sound like wind on the top of a mountain raged in her ears. She saw her friends in the circle looking like wispy ghosts of themselves, fighting to take more solid form, and then, in a whoosh, it was gone. They were back on the prairie again, looking at one another with wide eyes.

"Don't you see what this means?" Ling said later as they drank cold Coca-Colas on the porch.

"Why, yes!" Henry said excitedly. "Just as soon as you tell me!"

"That's how we heal the breach," she said.

"Still not on the trolley," Henry said.

Ling placed her empty Coca-Cola bottle on its side. "It's like a tunnel connecting the two dimensions. We are here." She placed a pebble at one end of the bottle. "And the land of the dead is here." At the other end, she placed another pebble. She removed the bottle. "Without our powers, the only way to punch a hole into the King of Crows's world is with the Eye. But using our powers, we"—she put the bottle down between the two pebbles again—"create a tunnel that connects the two dimensions."

"Okay. Then what happens?" Memphis asked.

"We go into the land of the dead, find the crack, and seal it up. Then we come back out and seal the hole we've created."

"But what about Marlowe's machine? Won't he just create another rip into that world?" Henry asked.

"If we destroy the Eye in that dimension, I don't think the one here will work anymore.

"What's to stop Jake Marlowe or anybody else from doing it again?" Theta asked.

"We can't guard against every act of malfeasance," Jericho said. "We have to do what we can when we can."

"*Malfeasance*," Sam sputtered. "Holy cow, Freddy, do you read the dictionary for fun?"

"I also know the words *nuisance* and *irritant.*"

"Let's go again," Ling said, rising from the porch and heading to the yard. The others followed suit.

"I don't think we should," Sarah Beth said, still sitting on the steps.

"Why not?"

"I don't know. I don't feel right. Isaiah? Do you feel it?"

Isaiah didn't want to admit that he didn't. "I . . ."

"Aw, c'mon, Sarah Beth, you're not chicken, are ya?" Sam goaded.

Sarah Beth narrowed her eyes at the insult. "Fine!" She stomped back to the circle and squeezed Evie's and Sam's hands tightly. It was like an electric current stinging. The insect drone was everywhere, along with the faces of the dead. They could feel the dead moving through them, thousands strong. Evie wanted to scream but she could scarcely breathe from the unholy pressure. And then, mercifully, it was gone.

"Wh-what was *that*?" Theta said, coughing.

"Sarah Beth? Sarah Beth!" Isaiah shouted.

Sarah Beth writhed on the ground, her body contorting with a violent seizure.

"She told you!" Isaiah shouted. "She told you!"

☀

"How is she?" Evie asked Mrs. Olson once she'd emerged from Sarah Beth's too-quiet room.

"Resting. She'll be all right," Mrs. Olson said tersely. "You promised to look after her. I reckon your promises don't count for much."

"I'm sorry," Evie said, but Mrs. Olson didn't want to hear.

LIFE AIN'T ALWAYS FAIR

The next morning, everybody was acting awfully glum because of Sarah Beth, and so Isaiah took it upon himself to see to the kittens. Then he would have something to tell her when he went to visit. But when Isaiah got to the kittens' sleeping spot under the porch, there was nothing there. He called and called for Mopsy.

Theta and Evie were gathering eggs in Theta's apron and talking quietly about something serious, it looked like. "You seen the kittens?" he asked them.

"No, honey," Theta said.

He asked Memphis and Bill and Sam and Jericho, but nobody had seen the kittens. Mr. Olson came through the field. Isaiah thought he'd ask him. Surely Mr. Olson would know.

"Mr. Olson, I can't find the kittens," Isaiah said, and some terrible feeling perched inside him, like when he thought he was going to throw up but hoped he wouldn't.

Mr. Olson looked down at the ground. "They're gone."

"Gone where?" Isaiah asked.

"I drowned 'em in the river."

Isaiah felt as if somebody had clean punched him in the chest. He could scarcely breathe. "Why?" he asked, careful not to sound rude, but it cost him to do it.

"Son, I've got nothing to feed a bunch of kittens. I can barely keep this farm together. It's better this way. They won't suffer," the farmer said and went into the house, letting the screen door snap behind him.

The mother cat crawled back under the porch. Isaiah could hear her mewling for her missing babies. Bill reached out and put a hand on Isaiah's shoulder. "I know what you're thinking."

"He killed 'em, Bill. They were living things, and he just coldhearted killed 'em."

"Sometimes folks think they're doing a kindness picking the lesser evil. Reckon he thought it was better to do it quick rather than let 'em starve slow."

"I would've fed 'em. I would've found a way," Isaiah said, inconsolable.

"You not gonna stay here to tend 'em. They wadn't yours." Bill crouched before Isaiah so he could look him in the eyes. Tears streamed down the boy's cheeks. "Life ain't always fair, and the choices we gotta make sometime ain't always clean, Little Man."

"I would've fed 'em! I would have!" Isaiah blubbered and fell into a full cry. He wiped an arm across his wet eyes and ran off toward the shelter of the cornfields.

"If I'd known, I'd've put those kittens down gentle," Bill said to Memphis as they worked side by side tilling the hard earth and planting more seed. It had gotten to him, seeing Isaiah all broken up like that. "You oughta go to the boy. He needs you."

"I need to see to the planting."

"Go on. I'll do this."

Memphis found Isaiah in the corn with his face buried against his arms, which were resting on his knees. Memphis sat down beside Isaiah. Every chance Memphis got, he was coming up with words. But now words failed him.

"I'm sorry, Ice Man." It was the best he had.

All Isaiah could do was cry "Why?" over and over until Memphis thought his heart would break. No matter how hard you tried to keep the unfairness of life from kids, it found them sooner or later.

"You did right by those kittens, Ice. I was real proud of you the way you took care of 'em."

"For what? So he could drown 'em!"

Memphis put a steadying hand on Isaiah's too-warm back. "We can't do nothin' about what other people do. We can only do right by what we believe. It's a hard path to be who you are and try to put your best self into a world that doesn't always show thanks for it. A world that can be unfair. Downright cruel at times. But otherwise…well, you might as well be one of those soulless dead." Memphis embraced his brother, sheltering him with his arms. "I love you, Little Man. I won't ever, ever, ever stop. Never."

"Promise?" Isaiah said. His voice was thick with snot.

"Promise. We're going to get our powers working and put things back to order."

Isaiah looked up. "Why?"

"Whatcha mean?"

"The order's all wrong."

Memphis's heart tightened. No matter how hard you tried, kids saw the world as it was.

"Then we're going to make a new one."

※

The day was coming on hot. The bath Evie had taken last night was for naught. She sweated through the cotton of her shapeless dress. "I want to try again."

"Yeah? You want to see all those dead faces again?" Theta said. "Because I don't think I can."

"And anyway, we can't. Sarah Beth is still feeling poorly," Isaiah protested.

"I know, but we can't afford to rest," Evie said. "The King of Crows certainly isn't. Neither is Jake Marlowe. And we might not have long here anyway."

The night before, the doctor had come to the house to see to Sarah Beth. The Diviners had made themselves scarce, but Evie and Memphis had accidentally run into him as they left their nightly broadcast in the barn. The doctor had looked from Evie to Memphis. "How do you do. I'm Virginia, Ada's cousin," Evie had said as Memphis slunk away to the farmhands' quarters, out of sight. But Evie could see the suspicion in the man's eyes. And Mrs. Olson was certainly not happy about what had happened to her daughter.

"Sarah Beth'll be sore," Isaiah grumbled. "She'll be sore at me."

"I'll take the blame," Evie promised, and Isaiah relented somewhat.

The Diviners came together once more.

"I'm scared." Evie hadn't meant to say it. It just crept out.

"You're telling the truth," Ling said.

Evie's laugh was brittle. "Is that so unusual?"

"Yes. You don't always trust us," Ling said.

"Oh," Evie said. "I'm sorry."

Ling took Evie's hand. "What's next?"

"Honestly? I don't know," Evie said. But wait—she did know something. Perhaps it was nothing, but sometimes the tiniest things moved mountains. "When I was attacked in Gideon"—she did not say, *When Mabel attacked me*—"there was a moment where I was just free. Like with Henry and Ling, trying to find each other in the dream world. Instead of trying to make something happen, let's just look for one another."

"When Theta created that disturbance in Times Square, she said 'stop' and then 'stop' was all I could think about," Memphis added.

"Just look for one another?" Henry said.

"Yes," Memphis said. "Feel for one another."

The moment they shut their eyes, Sam started thinking of the stargazer and zooming through all that space, but this time he wasn't afraid. It was as if he and his friends were floating up toward some great unknown all together. They were making a dimension. They *were* the dimension, and it, them. They were no longer bound by line and shape, by shame and fear. They simply were. A state of being so pure it was as if they had never been cut from the fabric of time and hurtled into physical bodies but existed in all time, all space at once. They were part of one another. It was beyond telepathy; they were transcendence. They could feel one another's heartbeats. It was as if they lived in one another's skins. Jericho's fingers wanted to move across the piano keys of Henry's memory and the face of a beautiful boy in New Orleans. Theta's anger and fear swirled inside Sam, but so did her joy at singing and dancing. Evie was Memphis on Lenox Avenue, a poem half-formed in his heart. Ling was Isaiah saying, "Listen. Listen!" while people talked around him, over him, ignoring him. Memphis felt a nagging pain in his legs and then the beauty of physics making sense as he became Ling and she him and they were all one being. Jericho could touch Theta's firepower, borrow it, make it his. Isaiah reached into his brother's healing with a mischievous joy—*so that's how it is!* Somehow, they had gotten past shame and pride and fear to vulnerability. They weren't just combining powers, they were connecting. Anticipating one another's moves. Beating with one heart. It was like the most beautiful voice surrounding them, looping through them, promising that no one is ever alone because aloneness does not exist. All are connected.

When they broke the circle at last, Memphis could still feel the others within him. It was fading, but he'd felt it nonetheless.

Ling smiled in wonder. "I think we've just discovered what we can do. We're not a weapon. At least, not the one they were counting on."

"So what, precisely, is the special Diviners power that's going to help us win the day?" Henry asked.

"I think..." Ling started. "I think it's trust."

THE WRONG SIDE OF HISTORY

The two Shadow Men drove into the night. Adams had been driving, but he was tired now, and so Jefferson took the wheel. For a long time, there was only the soft purr of tires on road.

"You're awful quiet," Jefferson said at last.

"You ever have bad dreams?" Adams asked. The wind swam past the half-open windows.

"Me? I sleep like a baby."

The brown sedan turned right at the crossroads. It, too, simply followed orders.

"This machine of Marlowe's. I had a bad dream about it."

"What dream was that?"

Adams frowned. "Don't wanna say. It got me thinking, though. About what he's doing. What we're doing."

Mr. Adams waited for Mr. Jefferson to say something. When he did not, Mr. Adams continued.

"Take Al Capone, for instance. You know he gives out food and toys to the families of the South Side? To them, he's not a gangster; he's a hero who looks out for them when no one else does. Doesn't matter he's the same character who orders another massacre and turns the streets bloody. Al Capone passes out some toys at an orphanage and makes himself the hero of his own story."

"Is there a point to this meandering little tale, Mr. Adams?"

"You ever wonder if maybe we're on the wrong side of history?"

The brown sedan bumped over rutted road. It scraped the car's undercarriage.

"Most people are sheep, Mr. Adams. They must be led by men unafraid of consequences, men unafraid of power. Would you agree?"

Adams shrugged.

"They don't want the responsibility of democracy. They'd rather shop the sales at Gimbels or see what's playing down at the picture palace.

They would prefer to think of democracy as a machine built by demigods, shrouded in heroic myth, controlled by forces beyond them, but always humming along, productive and inexhaustible, looking out for their interests."

"We the people…" Adams muttered.

"Are. Mostly. Sheep."

"Apes," Adams said after a pause.

"What's that?"

"If we evolved from apes, like that Scopes fella taught, that means there is no God. We're alone out here."

The moon was a fat circle. It sat above the land pregnant with some unnamed dread.

"Everyone's alone out here," Jefferson said.

"Not me. I'm in the car with you."

"I'm not here. You just think I am."

Jefferson was joking, Adams knew, but it didn't sit right. In his bad dream, Adams was stranded in the desert. The clang of the Eye was everywhere. Blood seeped up from the soft dirt and Adams saw that he balanced on the bony back of some long-dead animal. A wolf appeared in the darkness. It had a man's face. It attacked Adams, gnawing through his stomach. No one could hear his cries, and when Adams looked up, he was the wolf.

Jefferson was talking. "You should try warm milk before bed. Puts me right out. Like I said, I sleep like a baby." The brown sedan shuddered to a stop at the edge of the fairgrounds. Jefferson pulled on his black gloves. "Come on. Time to go to work."

Jefferson cut the headlights and let himself out of the car. He walked purposefully toward the silent circus and did not look back. Adams stared down at his hands resting on his knees, at the bandage wrapped around his right hand. Blood seeped through in the spot where the last Diviner they'd forced into Marlowe's Eye had bit him.

"Babies don't sleep so well," he said.

He got out of the car.

SARAH BETH

It was Saturday when Mr. Olson announced he was headed into town for some feed and groceries. "Happy to take anybody who wants to go," he said.

"Oh, I would adore going into town! Any town," Evie said.

"You suppose it's safe?" Jericho asked.

"I don't care," Evie said. "I can't stay on the farm one more minute. Besides, we might be able to get news about Marlowe." There had been nothing further in the papers about Marlowe testing the Eye in the desert. It had gone very quiet all of a sudden, and that worried Evie.

It was decided that Jericho, Evie, Theta, Henry, Sarah Beth, and Isaiah would accompany Mr. Olson into town. Memphis and Sam were concerned about being seen. Bill wanted to finish painting the barn. Ling's body hurt, and she didn't think she could bear walking. "Bring me back something to eat, please?" she begged Henry. "Nothing with mayonnaise."

Bountiful was a sweet little town, but Evie was longing for New York. Every night, she whispered to Sam, "I hope you don't think you're getting out of taking me to Goldberg's Deli for that pastrami sandwich." What she was really saying was, *There's a future. There's always a future.* She needed to believe in that just now.

"I need to bring a few things home for Mrs. Olson," Mr. Olson said and stepped into the dry-goods store. It was clear from his tone that they were not to follow.

"I suppose we'll wait out here and soak up all that Bountiful has to offer," Henry said.

"Don't be snide," Theta said, grinning.

"Who's being snide? It's got fresh air. I'm breathing, aren't I?"

Theta arched one eyebrow. "Yes. Snidely."

"How do, Bert," Mr. Olson said, nodding at the shopkeeper behind the counter inside the dry-goods store.

"Afternoon, Jim. I see you brought company with you today." The shopkeeper looked out the window to where the Diviners strolled along the sidewalks. "Family of yours or Ada's?"

"Mmm," Mr. Olson said, ignoring the man's nosy questions. "I'll take a sack of flour, another of sugar, fifty pounds of feed...."

The shopkeeper didn't budge. "I heard from Maryellen that they've been staying on your farm and helping out."

"Don't even know why anybody has a telephone when they can just get the news from Maryellen," Mr. Olson said. He tried to make the comment sound lighthearted, but that wasn't his specialty.

"She got the news from Dr. Wilson. Heard Sarah Beth had another fit."

Mr. Olson only nodded.

"Where do these folks come from? Who are their people?" the shopkeeper persisted.

"They're helping 'round the farm. They're hard workers. The rest ain't my business."

"It ain't? They're strangers staying on your farm. You got a wife and daughter to think of, Jim."

"Then I'd best get my goods and get back to 'em. Uh, just put this on my bill, Bert."

"You're out of credit." The man behind the register leaned forward. He lowered his voice. "Now, you know I don't want to see your farm go under, Jim. The boys have heard about this."

The boys. The Klan.

"Word spread from some of the other klaverns. Seems like those folks match up with these Diviners that are wanted. There's reward money they'd split with you, Jim. Big money. You could get Sarah Beth a good doctor in Omaha. You could pay off what you owe, with money left over for a new tractor and plow. Fix up the house with electricity! The boys just want those Diviners. That's all."

Mr. Olson was a decent man. Or he'd always tried to be. What was a decent man supposed to do when times were so hard? The muscles along his jaw tightened. He said nothing. The shopkeeper took it as consent. "Just leave it to us. We'll take care of it. Go on, take the feed, Jim. Seems your credit's good after all."

"No, thank you. I don't believe I will." Mr. Olson left the goods on the counter and pushed out of the store.

"Best be getting back," he announced as he emerged from the store empty-handed.

"Oh, but Mr. Olson, didn't Mrs. Olson need sugar?" Evie asked.

"They was out," he growled.

The Diviners hoisted themselves into the back of the truck. Evie sat down gingerly and waved away the dust with a sigh. "I will be so happy never to ride in a chicken truck again."

Isaiah passed by Mr. Olson. The farmer was just sitting there behind the wheel with his hands in his lap, staring out through the glass at the dry-goods store. Isaiah hadn't forgiven Mr. Olson for the kittens. He wasn't sure he ever could. But he could tell Mr. Olson was sadder than usual. He was worried it had something to do with Sarah Beth.

"Everything all right, Mr. Olson?" Isaiah asked.

Mr. Olson didn't answer for what felt like a very long time. "Fine. Go on and get in the back, son," he said at last and started the engine.

※

When they got back to the farm, it was afternoon. The sun was strong and high. The outdoor thermometer affixed to the back porch of the farmhouse read nearly eighty-five degrees. The day had bloomed into a true late-spring beauty.

The phone rang in the parlor. Mr. Olson answered. "Uh-huh. All right. About three o'clock. Right," he said and hung up. "Ada and I got to go to town again. Forgot something," he announced.

"Lands' sakes, Jim. I'm not decent."

"You look fine, Ada."

"Sarah Beth? You want to go to town, honey?"

"No. I'm feeling poorly," Sarah Beth said in such a perfect sigh that Evie had to admire the craft of it. Hadn't Evie used that same sighing voice to get out of going to school when she was bored?

"Well. All right, then." Mrs. Olson fixed Evie with a stare. "Can I trust you to look after my daughter?"

"Yes. Of course," Evie said, feeling guilty.

Mrs. Olson smiled at her daughter and gave her cheek a kiss. "Now, don't be any trouble."

"Don't be any trouble," Sarah Beth singsonged in reply, too low for her mother to hear her.

Mrs. Olson grabbed her hat and joined her husband. In a moment, the truck was backing down the dirt drive toward the road into town.

Sarah Beth tossed off her blanket and crossed the room, helping herself to some of the bridge mix Mrs. Olson kept in a bowl on an end table.

Nicely done, Evie thought.

"You want to practice our powers again?" Sarah Beth asked.

"I don't believe we should. You heard your mother—you should rest," Evie said.

Sarah Beth's lips tightened like she might spit or bite. It was a frightening transformation.

"You practiced without me, didn't you?" Sarah Beth demanded.

"I . . . I don't know what you mean." Evie felt quite off balance suddenly.

Sarah Beth narrowed her eyes. They were such an unnerving shade of gray. "You said I was one of you. And then you went and did that. You don't care about me at all!"

"That isn't true, Sarah Beth. We didn't want to hurt you. That's all."

"You're lying," Sarah Beth said. "You're a liar. Nobody likes liars."

The girl ran off into the yard toward Isaiah, who was painting the fence. Evie sank into the chair, shaking. *What just happened?*

"Look what I found," Sarah Beth said, startling Isaiah. She had a way of sneaking up on a fella.

"Hey-o, Sarah Beth," Isaiah said, laying the paintbrush in the grass and wiping his brow with his wrist.

From behind her back, Sarah Beth produced a mason jar. Inside, a tiny frog hopped, desperate to be let out.

"It's a chorus frog. They come out in the spring and sing. That's how the lady frogs know it's time to mate."

Isaiah blushed at the word *mate*. He put his face up to the jar. The frog's huge eyes blinked. It pressed webbed fingers against the glass like it was begging.

"We should put him in the river," Isaiah said.

Sarah Beth yanked the jar away. "He's mine. I caught him."

"He's scared. I can feel it. Maybe he's got a family that's missing him."

The kittens. He still ached for them.

Sarah Beth thought it over. "Okay. Come on. Let's go to the river together. I have a surprise."

✳

Evie couldn't shake the unsettled feeling in her gut about Sarah Beth. Yes, she was immature—she lived on a farm, isolated from others her age. But there was a cunning about the girl that Evie had seen in girls back in Zenith. The way they'd snipe or pinch when they thought no one important was looking their way. How they'd spread all manner of spiteful gossip, then go big-eyed and innocent, even blubbery, if they thought it would get them out of some trouble they'd caused. The truth was, Evie hadn't been able to warm to Sarah Beth. She kept trying to talk herself out of that feeling. After all, the Olsons were so nice to let them stay, and Mrs. Olson had brought Evie soup and tea while she was recuperating—had treated her like a daughter. Sarah Beth's birth had been difficult, and Jake Marlowe's serum had clearly damaged her. She was lonely and strange, and that needy, petulant oddness isolated the girl further. But no matter how much Evie's heart and head tried to strong-arm her gut, her gut got the last word: *There's something not right about this girl. There's a reason you feel uncomfortable in her presence.*

Of course, there was a way to know. Evie knew that to read an object without a person's permission was considered a violation of privacy. It *was* a violation; Evie couldn't deny that. But she remembered her third-grade teacher saying once that if keeping a secret was harmful, then it was right to tell it. Evie needed to know. From her bedroom window, Evie had seen Sarah Beth loping across the yard toward Isaiah. Evie stole into Sarah Beth's room. What to read? It needed to be something Sarah Beth used every day. The dolls. They sat in the rocking chair, staring back at Evie. She lifted them into her arms and pressed into their history—into Sarah Beth Olson's secrets.

She could feel the girl's loneliness first, and that struck a chord with Evie. Her anger was in there, too. Sarah Beth wanted more than this small life on a dying farm in the middle of Nebraska, and Evie understood that viscerally. It was the first time she'd felt a true kinship with the girl. She had half a mind to stop right then. This was terrible, what she was doing now.

Then something pricked.

Evie could feel it scratching inside her, begging to be let in.

Something about the night Sarah Beth died.

"No. Oh, no, no, no," Evie moaned as the hidden life of Sarah Beth Olson began to scream its horrors.

※

The rains had swelled the river to the very edges of its banks. The water rippled and swirled across nearly submerged rocks that two days earlier could easily be seen. Where it sprayed up and caught Isaiah's arm, the water was still very cold.

Sarah Beth marched right up to the bank, though, unafraid. Isaiah hung back. The frog was starting to tire in the jar.

"Let him go now," Isaiah said.

Sarah Beth clamped a hand on top of the lid. "I will under one condition. You got to share some of your moon glow with me first."

Isaiah didn't want to do that. Every time he did, he ended up feeling kind of sick, and really tired. "Just let him go, Sarah Beth."

She bunched up her lips and narrowed her eyes. "Moon glow first."

Isaiah looked at the frog, so desperate to be let out. He couldn't bear it. Not after the kittens. "Fine," he growled. He let her take what she wanted, but it felt like a lot this time. More than the other times. When he surfaced, he was tired. A deep throb troubled his muscles; a touch of fever haunted his blood, as if his power had not been shared with Sarah Beth so much as it had been drawn from his body.

True to her word, Sarah Beth let the frog out of the jar. It plopped into the mud, unsure, and then hopped away into the grass.

"So long, Froggy," Isaiah said. He was a little wobbly, and sick to his stomach. All to save a little frog who might get eaten by something in the tall grass anyhow. But the frog needed saving. Isaiah could sense its misery and fear as it gasped for breath in that jar. And if he hadn't saved the frog, well, then, who would?

Crows had taken up residence in the trees. It was like they were watching. They started in on their cawing, and Isaiah got that bad feeling in his stomach like he sometimes did before a vision came on. But ever since he and Sarah Beth had been sharing moon glow, he'd been having a harder and

475

harder time seeing those visions. It was like a dream he half remembered but couldn't quite get back to sleep to finish.

The current was swift. Rapids foamed across the smooth black rocks near the bank. Isaiah could only think of the kittens. *His* kittens. It was unbearable. He wanted to go back and join the others.

"Aren't you coming?" Sarah Beth called.

Seeing her there at the edge of the river, Isaiah remembered the vision he'd had weeks earlier of Sarah Beth's discarded socks and shoes near the fast water, and there'd been blood on the rocks. He couldn't leave her. What if something happened to her?

"Let's go back, Sarah Beth. I'll push you on the tire swing!"

"I don't want to go back yet." Sarah Beth unlaced her shoes and laid them in the grass along with her socks. Just like in the vision.

Isaiah watched the water slipping over the rocks. "I can't swim," he said.

"Oh, is that all? Isaiah, this li'l ol' river can't hurt you. You and me, we're special. Come on," Sarah Beth beckoned. "I won't let anything happen to you."

He couldn't leave her here.

Isaiah took off his own shoes and followed Sarah Beth out across the slippery jetty. The water was knife-prick cold, and the rocks were slick under Isaiah's bare feet. If they lost their balance, they could be swept up in the current. At last, they made it to the big rocks. Isaiah sat down. That made him feel less wobbly. The river roared around them. The spray hit Isaiah's cheeks, and it felt good enough to make him laugh.

"See? Don't you feel brave?"

He did. They were here with the river around them and everything was fine.

※

Evie came out of her trance. She tossed the dolls away, no longer caring if anyone knew she'd read them. She hobbled down the stairs and out the front door, screaming Isaiah's name. Theta came running up, Ling making her way behind.

"What is it? What's the matter?" Theta asked.

"Where's Isaiah?" Evie said, twirling around, hoping to see him coming out of the barn wearing his goofy grin.

"He was painting the fence earlier," Ling said. The paint bucket and brush sat in the grass near the unfinished fence.

"It's…Sarah Beth," Evie panted.

"What about Sarah Beth?" Theta asked.

"I think they went down to the river together," Henry said. He dipped a ladle in a bucket of water and drank it.

Evie's gut was screaming at her. "I read her dolls. I know I shouldn't have, but I had a bad feeling."

"Spare us the monologue. Skip to the end," Theta said.

"I saw glimpses of the King of Crows. She knows him. She *admires* him. The night she died, she met him. He whispered in her ear, and I couldn't hear what he said, but she's been talking to him this whole time! I think *that's* her power—it isn't visions like Isaiah's. It's talking to the King of Crows."

"She never said what she saw while we were under. She'd always get Isaiah to say it first," Ling said, piecing it together.

"I think…I think the King of Crows put her up to this. It was part of his plan all along, to get us to come to Bountiful. To keep us distracted so we couldn't work on our powers. Even Gideon and my injury." *Even Mabel*, Evie thought. "Sarah Beth's been his accomplice this whole time. I think that's why we couldn't make our powers work before. She was keeping us from it!"

"The gentleman caller," Theta said, her eyes widening. "It was right under our noses. She was practically flaunting it."

"If Isaiah's alone with Sarah Beth…" Henry said.

"We need to find him," Evie said.

But suddenly, Jericho was shouting their names. He sounded alarmed. A huge cloud of dust was barreling up the road.

"Something's coming," Henry said.

"The King of Crows?" Ling asked.

They raced to join the others.

"What is it?" Ling asked.

"Don't know. Stay here," Bill said and marched toward the road to get a better look. He tented his hands over his eyes to cut the glare. "It ain't the

King of Crows," Bill called back. He counted a truck and two cars. Bill kept his eyes trained on the wall of dust and the glimpses of white inside. He had a bad feeling in his gut. Something with the feel of inevitability. He could see the men in those cars and trucks. Even from where he stood, Bill could see their white sheets and white hoods.

Sam had come to stand beside him. "What is it?"

Bill felt the world fall away. "Ghosts on the road."

GHOSTS ON THE ROAD

Bill and Sam hurried back to the others just as the caravan pulled up the dirt road and parked down the drive from the old farmhouse. The men stepped out of their cars with a mean confidence. There were ten, Sam counted, and two carried rifles.

One man marched forward and perched on the front of one of the cars, resting his foot on the grille. Another man with a rifle slung over his shoulder stood beside him.

"We're looking for Mrs. Roy Stoughton," the man with the rifle said.

"There's nobody here by that name," Evie said. She wished Mr. Olson were there now to tell these men to leave his property. And Isaiah. Oh, where was Isaiah?

"That farmer turned us in," Ling whispered to Henry.

"We don't know that," Henry said. He hoped it wasn't true.

"That's not what we heard," the man shouted. "See, we heard y'all are all Diviners. The ones they've been looking for. You're worth a lot of money. But first, there's a little lady needs to be returned to her husband."

"He's not my husband anymore," Theta yelled back. "And nobody's returning me. I'm not a bad Christmas present."

The man sitting on the car rose. He climbed the steps with swagger, coming right up to her. Memphis came forward, but Theta waved him back. The man in front of Theta removed his hood. The scar on his face was particularly red today.

"Hello, Betty Sue," Roy said. "Get in the truck."

"No," Theta said. Memphis was beside her. All of them were beside her.

"You know what I can do, Betty Sue," Roy said with a sneering smile.

"And you know what I can do, Roy. And I don't need nine other fellas in bedsheets to do it."

The two men with rifles trained their guns on Memphis and Sam.

"I don't think you better do it, Betty." Whip-quick, Roy snaked a chain around Theta's neck. "Mr. Marlowe's fellas told me this was the way to keep you cool. You won't be doing any of your magic today."

Jericho yanked the screen door free of its hinges. "I can do worse."

Roy laughed. "Not against two guns."

On cue, the Klansmen fired. The bullets nicked the tree.

"Roy, you don't know what you're doing," Theta said.

"Sure I do. Collecting my wife and a reward at the same time. I'll be a hero. We'll all be heroes."

"You're not heroes, pal," Sam said.

One of the Klansmen shot his rifle, narrowly missing Sam's feet.

"Next time I'll shoot straight," the man called, and the others laughed.

Men with guns. Shooting in the village. Her mother bleeding in the snow. Fire spreading from house to house until her entire past had been erased. No. Not completely. Theta was from fire. She had swallowed it down her entire life, until it had become as much a part of her as her heart and lungs. She'd tried for so long to be rid of it. Now she knew that no one could take it from her.

"You know what goes up real quick in a fire?" Theta said, staring down the men. The familiar heat slithered through her veins like gasoline. The iron at her neck was no match for it. She did not try to stop it.

"What, Betty?"

"Sheets," Theta answered.

"What's she going on about, Roy?"

"Shut up, Betty Sue," Roy said. "Shut up and get in that truck."

"Evie," Theta said, and Evie knew. They all knew.

"I'm here. We're all here," Evie said. Theta could feel them in her, with her. She moaned, welcoming her rage like a lover. And then she blazed like a phoenix.

"Your chains don't work on me, Roy," Theta said in a voice that crackled with new heat. She walked forward, forcing Roy back down the porch steps. The chain slipped from her neck. The ground was unharmed by Theta's heat. Like Miss Addie had said, Theta knew her own heart. She knew her intent. Theta was in charge. Her friends were with her, helping her, keeping her safe. She didn't know just how much fire was inside her this time, but she knew she was no longer afraid of her power.

Theta lifted her hands. Flames shot from her palms, trapping the Klansmen in a perfect ring of fire.

"Are you going to behave?" she asked the men.

"Lady, you're crazy!" one of the Klansmen said.

"Wrong answer," Theta said. She inched the fire closer, and then a little closer still.

"Roy, I've got a family at home to think about!" one of the Klansmen shouted. "Lady, I'm sorry. Let me out! Please!"

"I'll only get stronger, Roy," Theta said. "And when I do, I promise you, you will never have a peaceful night's rest again. I will come for you. And everyone will know the truth. Truth is like a fire, Roy."

"It's true," Sam said. "You really don't wanna be on her bad side, Roy."

"If you leave and promise never to bother me ever again, I'll stop."

Closer by a hair.

"Okay!" Roy screamed. "Okay."

"Okay, what?"

"I promise."

Theta retracted her fire, sucking it back into her palms, where it was just a simmer. Roy didn't need to know that she had precious little of it left, nor how much it had cost her to use it.

"Evie," she whispered, and Evie understood.

"Get in your cars and go, gentlemen," Evie said, taking over.

"I wouldn't call them gentlemen," Henry said.

The Klansmen raced to their cars and truck. For good measure, the Diviners made their engines run, startling the men with their show of combined energy.

As the Klansmen disappeared down the road, Theta collapsed against Memphis. She was sweating and exhausted.

"Hey, Princess. Nice show."

"Thanks, Poet."

"Never mind that. We have to find Isaiah!" Evie said.

※

The river sprayed past the jetty where Isaiah sat with Sarah Beth.

"What's the surprise?" Isaiah asked.

Sarah Beth grinned. "I wanted you to be the first to know. My gentleman caller's coming to take me away."

This again. Isaiah couldn't believe he'd risked getting in trouble with Memphis over something so dumb. "You brought me down here to tell me that?"

Sarah Beth frowned. "I can't marry you, Isaiah. I thought you understood that."

Isaiah blinked in astonishment. She thought he wanted to marry her? Before he could think of what to say back, Sarah Beth continued. "Anyway, I thought you'd be happy for me. After all, if it weren't for sharing our moon glow, my gentleman wouldn't be able to come for me."

"What do you mean?"

"I was supposed to keep you here, and I did." Sarah Beth smiled her little gray-toothed smile. "You know."

Isaiah was bored and mad. "Can you just tell me?"

"I've only ever had one power—I could talk to my special gentleman. The man in the stovepipe hat. The King of Crows."

The wheat bent in the wind like a parade of mourners. Isaiah blinked, trying to keep it in focus. "But..." was as much as he could manage.

"I know I told you I was working against him, but I'm not." She let out a little giggle. "Oh, Isaiah! It's so pretty where he is, didn't you think? Not like this." She growled and gestured angrily at the fading farm that he and his friends had been slowly bringing back to life. "I'll be his queen. I'll have everything. I won't have fits ever again. Nobody will make fun of me anymore," she said on a near-whisper. Her jaw jutted forward, quivering. "Nobody."

Beneath his growing horror, Isaiah also felt sorry for this girl. She was what his mama would call "pitiful" with a shake of her head.

Sarah Beth's strange silvery eyes took on a new fire. The sad whisper was gone. "'Cause if they do, my gentleman'll break 'em apart like twigs. His army will eat up their souls. They're coming, you know. This world's as good as gone."

"What did you do to me?" Isaiah asked.

"He needed some of your power. He needed to see the future so he could shape that future. So he used me to get it from you," Sarah Beth said, and Isaiah felt so dizzy he was afraid he'd slip right off the rocks and into the current. "Because you're my friend, he's going to let me keep you. I told him, 'You can't hurt Isaiah. He's very dear to me.'"

"What about the others? What about Memphis?"

"They don't understand you. They don't treat you proper. Only I do."

Sarah Beth snuggled closer to Isaiah, as if he were her very best friend and she had the best secret in the world to share with him and only him.

Fear buzzed with a cicada whine in Isaiah's head. The way the light fell on the rippling water. The crows in a line, screaming and screaming at him, and he'd just been too caught up to hear their warnings. Hadn't he seen this very moment weeks ago in a vision? He hadn't understood what it was, then, only that it was very bad. He'd thought it was about keeping Sarah Beth safe. He had to get back to his brother. He had to tell Memphis and Uncle Bill. Had to warn the Diviners. His friends were in trouble. That had been the vision's message, he knew now.

"W-we...we oughta, oughta get back. Th-they'll be looking for us." Isaiah took a step backward. His ankles wobbled. The ground was slippery with mud. The river roared behind them.

Sarah Beth's face clouded over. She set her teeth in a line. "You're gonna tell."

Isaiah shook his head. He couldn't speak.

"Yes, you are."

"I just wanna get back." She stood between him and the bank. Why had he let her talk him into coming out on the rocks? He hadn't wanted to, but he was afraid to stand up to her and say no. He moved to the left and so did Sarah Beth. But she was sure-footed where he was wobbly. The wet rocks were algae-covered and very slippery. He needed to keep one eye on where to put his feet and another on Sarah Beth, because he was frightened of her. She wasn't the Sarah Beth he had known. She was someone who'd been siphoning his power, he realized; someone who'd been playing with the King of Crows all along.

"My gentleman told me something else. He said if you made me mad, I could make your power mine." Sarah Beth picked up a rock and threw it at Isaiah.

He ducked, nearly losing his balance. The rock sailed over his shoulder and crashed into the current and was borne quickly downstream. Isaiah's heart pounded. Sarah Beth grabbed another rock. This one clipped Isaiah in the arm. He grabbed at the place where it stung, slipped on the rock, and fell. A precarious tangle of roots stopped his slide into the surging water.

"I want what you got. Give it to me."

She wasn't content with sharing moon glow anymore. She wanted it all to herself, would do anything to get it. Isaiah could see it in her steely eyes, in the set of her teeth peeking out from underneath her curled lip.

The swollen river pushed at Isaiah's legs, throwing him off-balance. Gasping, he managed to right himself by pushing off from a rock. No helpful tree limbs extended out over the river at this point. The water was up to his thighs, but when it surged, it hit his chest like an icy fist.

"I want it. I want all of it. Give it to me, and I'll help you out of the river."

Isaiah slipped, and in his panic, he grabbed at Sarah Beth's hand. The vision came on, bucking like the river. He saw dust kicking up on the road, the flickers of white behind it. Ghosts on the road. Bill. He had to warn Bill.

He counted: Memphis, Theta, Evie, Sam, Jericho, Henry, Ling, Bill.

Memphis. Theta. Evie. Sam. Jericho. Henry. Ling. Bill.

Isaiah searched for his face among them.

The rock came down on his head. The vision vanished. Isaiah looked up through dripping blood to see Sarah Beth's face. Her mouth was set in a grim, determined line. She gripped the rock tightly in her good hand.

"Wh-why?" was all Isaiah could ask.

She hit him again, and he slipped into the water up to his chest. Sarah Beth put her other hand on him. She was trying to pull what power he had right out of his body anyway, trying to make it hers. Isaiah fought back, but the blows had left him dizzy. Sarah Beth was only grabbing straws of magic from Isaiah, and it was making her very angry; he could feel her inside him, all that anger coiling around him like a snake waiting to strike.

Sarah Beth broke away, panting, and for a second, Isaiah thought it was over. He was awfully woozy from the pain in his head. Nevertheless, he'd crawl over the bank and run as hard as he could to Memphis and the others. He'd do whatever it took to get away from this girl and warn the people he loved.

Sarah Beth was looking down at him through narrowed eyes. "This world will be ours."

All she had to do then was push. With a scream, Isaiah was pulled into the churning water.

"Hurry, oh hurry," Evie said. She couldn't say why she was so panicked. There was no reason to think that Sarah Beth would hurt Isaiah—that she *could* hurt Isaiah. But reading the girl's dolls had filled her with terror. She had seen Sarah Beth writing her name inside the King of Crows's coat. She had felt the girl's adoration of him, her willingness to follow him blindly into chaos if that's where he was leading. Her deep need to feel important—not just important, but superior. Evie realized that they had let a fox into their henhouse.

She could hear the river before she saw it. There on the bank was Sarah Beth, sitting in the grass.

"Where's Isaiah?" Evie demanded.

"He's not here," Sarah Beth said.

The others were just coming up now.

"Isaiah!" Memphis called.

"Isaiah! Little Man!" Bill joined in.

"You've been in league with the King of Crows this whole time, haven't you?" Evie said.

Sarah Beth looked up at Evie coolly. "He's going to make me his queen."

"He's not going to do any such thing. He's a liar and a trickster. His promises are empty. And you are a very foolish girl," Evie said.

"You're jealous that he chose me and not you," Sarah Beth said.

Sam looked down and saw the bloodstained rock in the grass. "Evie," he said under his breath.

"I can't find him," Memphis said, panicked.

Evie could feel the world slipping off its axis and spinning toward the cold, dark unknown. With a trembling hand, she reached down and touched the rock.

"No, no, no!"

She ran along the riverbank. Memphis chased after, calling, "Evie? What is it? Evie, tell me!"

The river had carried Isaiah to an inlet. His shirt collar had caught on a branch near a barn swallow nest. It held him there, letting him float out a ways, then tugging him back in. He looked as if he were simply taking a nap, but the bloody wound on his head told another story.

"Isaiah! Isaiah!" Memphis cried and waded into the river after him. Sam stripped off his shirt and jumped in after Memphis.

"Not the boy," Bill prayed. "Please, Lord, not the boy."

Jericho waded in to lend a hand. "Sam," he said and shook his head.

"Isaiah," Memphis said, hollowed out. "Isaiah?" he said again, as if he couldn't quite trust what the world was showing him. The water was not water. The grass just a cruel imitation of grass.

Sam unhooked Isaiah's shirt from where it had caught on the branch. Jericho lifted Isaiah from the river and carried his lifeless body back to the farm. The Diviners and Sarah Beth followed in a procession. Theta spread a blanket on the ground, and Jericho laid Isaiah down gently. Memphis fell to his knees beside his brother, weeping. He looked up at Sarah Beth with murder in his eyes.

"You killed my brother! All this time, I tried to keep him safe. All this time, it was you he should've been afraid of!"

"Stay with him," Bill advised the others, and they surrounded Memphis like a shield.

Bill lifted his face, but the sun had gone sour. Everything seemed to tilt sideways. The wind was southerly. It brought the smell of the rotting corn. This land was cursed and nobody knew how to make it right. There were ghosts on the road and ghosts in his heart and he could scarcely breathe.

There were moments in a man's life, Bill believed, when he could see the shape of his future as if he'd carved it himself from a piece of wood. Ghosts on the road, ghosts on the road. Isaiah had warned him all those months ago. Isaiah. Isaiah was dead.

Memphis was on his knees in the dust, broken, eyes red, seeing nothing. He was hot pain trapped inside skin clawing to get out, and when it did, god help him and everyone else. Theta and Sam were trying to help him up, holding him back. It was too much, too much. No. It was enough. Bill had had enough.

Under the sheltering oak, Sarah Beth swayed back and forth on the tire swing. She rubbed her fingers down the sides of her pink cheeks as if they were brand-new to her. A half smile played at her lips. All that power. She was punch-drunk on it. Bill watched the girl for as long as he could stand.

He motioned Jericho over to his side. He spoke calmly, firmly. "You need to get them all in the truck, you hear? Start it up. *Throw* Memphis into the back if you gotta. But get him in."

"Then what?"

"Then you drive, and you keep driving. Go west. All the way to Death Valley. You got to stop this thing. Understand?"

Jericho nodded. By the fledgling willow tree, Memphis had crumpled next to his brother's lifeless body. From the corner of his eye, Bill saw the girl still swinging, not a care in the world.

"You'll meet us at the truck?" Jericho asked.

"Ain't goin' with you."

"We'll see you in Death Valley, then?"

Yes, sometimes a man just knew the shape of his future.

"Go on," he said, shooing Jericho toward his friends. "Git."

He watched as Jericho hurried back to the others. When Theta tried to coax Memphis toward the truck, he cried out and refused to leave Isaiah's body there, so Jericho carried the boy in his arms and placed him in the back of the covered truck. Ling looked dazed and lost. Evie, Theta, Sam, and Henry supported Memphis, half dragging him to the truck. Bill watched all of this. He watched as Jericho hopped behind the wheel and put the truck into gear. He watched as the truck drove across the dry field, wheels kicking up dust. He watched the ashen, expressionless faces of the Diviners peering out at where they'd been, what they'd seen by the river. They were ghosts on the road.

Bill watched and waited until they were safely down that road, a spot vanishing to a speck making a left past the railroad tracks. Coming up the other end of the road was the Olsons' truck. It would be at the farm soon enough. When Bill could no longer see the Diviners, he walked toward the old oak, rolling up his sleeves as he went. The wind had shifted. It no longer blew from the south but from the east. That was the wind for you, constantly changing course. His shadow fell over Sarah Beth as she swung disinterestedly on the old tire.

"Where'd they go?" she asked.

"Never you mind."

"Doesn't matter. I can see everything if I have a mind to."

"Can you now? Can you see everything?" Bill asked. He was very calm. He could hear the Olsons' truck getting closer.

"I can see into the land of the dead. I can talk to him. He'll want me more now, I'm so powerful." She pushed off with sudden force, kicking dirt onto the tips of Bill's shoes. He did not take a step back.

Bill grabbed hold of the rope. The swing stopped midair.

A tiny bit of fear flickered in Sarah Beth's steely eyes, but only for a second. "I'll scream for my pa. I'll tell him you tried to rape me."

"No, you won't, neither." Quick as the old days, Bill took Sarah Beth by the neck with both hands as if she were a goose ready for a Thanksgiving feast. "You cain't have his power or yours no more. I won't let you."

"What are you doing?" she asked in a strained whisper. Her eyes were wild, but mean, too.

"And here I thought you could see everything."

After Memphis had healed his eyesight, Bill had made a promise to whatever god he still believed in that he would do right. He wouldn't take Diviner energy anymore. He was a man redeemed. But now Isaiah was going cold, with his skull bashed in, and the sun was dead, dead, dead in the sky, and who could say what was right in such a world? He wouldn't kill the girl. But Bill Johnson would take justice for Isaiah Campbell. And he would make sure Sarah Beth Olson no longer had the means to hurt anybody else.

"No," Sarah Beth whispered once she realized what Bill was about.

As Bill drained the Diviner energy from Sarah Beth's veins, he could feel Isaiah in there, what she had stolen from him, and he could feel Sarah Beth's gift for prophecy as well. It was all leaving her, flowing into Bill. His hair was graying at the temples and his pulse galloped under the strain of the sudden aging. That was the price. So be it. Sarah Beth pounded her fists against Bill's strong hands, but his hold was firm. Almost there.

"You let her go or I'll kill you where you stand."

From just behind him, Bill heard the click of Mr. Olson's rifle. Bill loosened his grip just a little, stopping the flow of magic. How close was the man's gun? Was it aimed at his head? His legs? His stomach? A stomach wound was a nasty way to go.

Bill tightened his clutch on Sarah Beth once more. "You ain't never gonna take what ain't yours ever again." With that, he sucked up the last of the magic.

When her father's shot rang out two seconds later, clean and clear, tearing a straight path through Bill's heart, he thought of Samson, the gentle horse he had loved and cared for, the horse he had needed to put down with a merciful touch of these same hands. His damaged heart slowed to a blues tempo. Six-eight time at the end of the night with a bad drummer. Blood drowned the breath in Bill's lungs. His vision was going hazy. He tried to draw another breath and could not. His eyelids fluttered. His knees softened. This was the shape, then: He was going down hard onto the barren dirt of Bountiful, another ghost on the road. As Bill lost control of his limbs and the air died to a last wheeze in his throat, it was Samson he thought he saw. Samson running fast and free, showing Bill the way home.

BARGAIN

Jericho kept his foot on the gas as they bumped over dirt roads. They'd been driving for hours. An orange sun wounded the clouds into a bruising dusk. The flat farmland of Nebraska had given way to the stark, red-rocked beauty and rolling hills of Wyoming, and if this weren't the end of the world, Jericho might have loved the chance to stand by the side of the road and enjoy the wonder of it all.

"Where are we going?" Ling asked.

"I don't know," Jericho said in a monotone. Then: "West. To Death Valley. We're going to stop them."

"Bill's not meeting us, is he?" Ling didn't really want the answer.

"No," Jericho said, and neither of them spoke again.

"You're gonna have to do something, kid." Jericho slid his eyes sideways. He did not see Ling sitting there, but the ghost of Sergeant Leonard. "How are you feeling these days?"

I'm fine, Jericho thought.

"You know that ain't true, kid. The Daedalus program. You had a good run, but it comes for all of us in the end."

"I'm fine," Jericho said firmly.

"Jericho?" Ling was looking at him strangely. "Are you all right? You look kind of funny."

"I'm…it's nothing," Jericho said and gripped the wheel with trembling hands.

In the back of the truck, Memphis cradled Isaiah's body and wouldn't let anyone else near. "Gonna be okay, Ice Man. Gonna be okay," he murmured until Theta thought her heart might break. They were all numb with horror.

"Hey. Hey, Memphis…" Sam tried at one point.

Memphis shrugged off his touch and cupped himself over his dead brother like a shield that was too late in arriving.

"Theta?" Sam pleaded.

She shook her head and tried not to cry.

"We're going to stop them," Evie said through her teeth. "If it's the last thing we ever do."

Jericho pulled over by the side of the road. The Diviners piled out of the truck, except for Memphis, who wouldn't leave Isaiah's body. Their collective gaze was drawn to the sight of a magnificent natural formation that jutted up from the soft green and scrub. It reminded Ling of a New York skyscraper made completely of rugged rock. It quite took her breath away. "What is that?" she asked.

"Devils Tower," Jericho said. "It's a national monument. I've seen pictures in a book, but…"

Ling stared at it. It made her feel small and vast at the same time. There was so much in the country she hadn't seen. She hoped she'd still have that chance. Ling allowed herself to imagine coming west with her parents and Uncle Eddie, posing for a photograph against all that sky. Her mind was trying desperately to distract her from the sorrow in the back of the truck, the danger ahead.

Sam came around the side of the truck. "Why'd you stop driving, Freddy? We need to get to California."

Jericho turned away from the breathtaking view. "We have to help Memphis."

"Help him how?" Henry asked. "His brother's been murdered."

"I don't know how to say this. But Isaiah's…" Jericho paused, fumbling for words. "*Corpse*… could attract more dead. He's a Diviner. They… might want him. He could become one of them."

"No," Theta said, steely-eyed. "He would never."

"Mabel did," Evie said quietly.

"Not Isaiah."

"We need to bury him," Sam said, nodding at Jericho. "We need to give him a proper grave."

"You mean *here*?" Theta said, incredulous.

"It's gotta be done, Theta," Sam said.

Theta felt a pull toward this starkly beautiful land, but it was far from New York and all Memphis knew. How would Memphis ever visit his brother's grave out here?

"Theta, you have Miss Addie's spell book. Surely there's something in there for making sure the dead don't come back," Evie said gently.

"You'll never get Memphis to leave Isaiah here. I know him," Theta said.

They fell into arguing. The light was fading, the last of the sun bleeding out over Devils Tower.

"Wait! Wait!" Jericho held up a hand and everyone stopped. "Where'd Memphis go?"

※

Memphis staggered up the rocky incline leading to Devils Tower carrying his fallen brother in his arms. "Just hold on, Ice Man. I'll fix this."

Behind him, his friends were shouting his name. Coming after him. Memphis kept going. Just a little farther. He stumbled and fell to his knees, barely registering the pain of it. Isaiah lay in the sweet grass of Wyoming. Memphis had hoped they'd see the West someday. Maybe ride the palominos, or watch the elk come down from the Tetons. All things he'd read about in books back at the 135th Street Library in Harlem. "I'm gonna fix this," he said again. He screamed at the sky. "You're not taking him! You hear me, you greedy son-of-a-bitch? You take and you take and you take! Well, you can't have him—I won't let you!"

"Memphis! *Memphis!*" Theta jogged after Memphis and got down on her knees beside him. She tried to take his hand, but he wouldn't let her. "Don't do this, Memphis. You can't. It's unnatural."

"Nothing about this is natural," Memphis murmured. "It's an unnatural world."

"You remember what your mother told you? You can't bring back something once it's gone. Think about Miss Addie and Elijah."

"You all want to bury him. Well, you can't."

Theta looked down at Isaiah. His lips were as pale as the night's last hour of moonlight. When she spoke, her voice was thick with tears she was doing her best to hold back. "Hey. *Hey.* You remember that day you and Isaiah snuck in to see Babe Ruth hit a home run? Or when we helped paint the barn on the farm? We'll always have that. We'll always have Isaiah that way, and we'll carry him around with us forever."

"No." Memphis's voice was a croak. His lips quivered. Tears coursed down his cheeks. "No."

"He deserves a grave, Memphis," Henry said, joining them.

"No, no, *no*!" Memphis's eyes narrowed. "I'm not letting him die. I'm gonna heal him. I can do it. I know I can."

His mother had told him that this, above all things, was forbidden. *You can't bring back what's gone,* she'd warned. He would see about that. Memphis laid his hands on top of Isaiah's cold, stiff body. Jericho made to stop him, but Memphis was too quick. He pressed his palms to Isaiah's still chest, right above the no-longer-beating heart. He opened himself up, willing the healing magic to come down. His fingers twitched and smoked. He would do it. Nobody could stop him.

"You give me back my brother. *Give me back my brother!*" Memphis gathered Isaiah in his arms, hugging him close. A roar filled his ears. The earth around him swept up into columns of dust. Lightning shot from the sky and electrified the top of Devils Tower, and then leaped down the side of the butte, where it reached into Memphis's body. Memphis felt as if he were being pulled into that electrified sky, through the clouds, and drawn into darkness.

It was suddenly quiet and still. Memphis no longer held Isaiah. He was surrounded by a circle of the dead. They didn't advance. It was almost as if they were asleep standing up, eyes open, seeing nothing. Behind them was an endless forest of dead trees and walls made of skulls. An ossuary fit for a King of Crows.

"Will you make a bargain with me at last?" the King said. Lightning strobed across his face. He was shadow and light.

"Give me back my brother," Memphis said.

In his right hand, the man in the hat held the crow, silencing it, silencing Memphis's mother. She was warning him, Memphis knew. He didn't care. He would do whatever it took to have his brother back.

The King of Crows tilted his head in his strange, jerking fashion. "What will you give me for him?"

"What do you want?"

"Your healing power. All of it."

The ash trees were diseased. The bark peeled down like loose skin, exposing the mangy, pustule-ridden sapwood underneath. Mushrooms popped up from the ground. A worm nibbled at one, then curled up and convulsed, helpless. There were no stars above, only a fat, jaundiced moon and strands of wispy clouds. The place felt airless and fetid and lost.

"If I give you this power, you'll give me back Isaiah?"

"You have my word. Look into my coat. What do you see?"

Memphis saw the true history of the nation. Blood and blood and blood. Blood shed and bloodlines revered. He saw the Cherokee marched out of Georgia until they dropped. He saw the pioneers lost on the Oregon Trail, eating one another down to the bones to survive. He saw the white-wigged men of ideas signing declarations, then going home to whip their slaves. The history reached down Memphis's throat. He wanted to speak but found he couldn't. The force of all that history at once curdled his voice. The insect-like hum of the dead filled his ears. A war cry mingled with the noise of an approaching swarm. All that history trying to be screamed at once.

"No one really wants to see, hmm? No one wants to know. Better to create a story we like to tell ourselves about ourselves. For we are the mythmakers."

Memphis felt as if he were falling into the coat's vast lining, into the morass of all those stories. He was being overwhelmed by facts and myth intertwined, a tangle of slippery roots that had no beginning and no end. He felt he might drown in it. He tried to tear at the threads, but they would simply shift and become some other narrative over which he could not gain control. He grabbed for a loose thread and gasped at the bloody cut it left in the skin of his palm. Finally, he threw himself against the lining. Like an enormous gut, the coat began to devour Memphis. He was being swallowed up and absorbed into the coat's history. The chorus of the dead grew louder. Memphis felt as if he were being buried alive inside the King of Crows's blinding coat.

"Where is my brother? You promised to give me my brother!" Memphis yelled. "Stop! Can you please *just stop*?"

In a snap, the noise was gone. And so was the King of Crows. Memphis was on his knees, alone, in the land of the dead. Skeletal trees arched toward one another, forming a long corridor. Pale fog spilled out between their haggard limbs. Memphis pulled himself up and staggered over. Something was coming. He was afraid but he did not run. The figure moved closer. Closer still. And then tears streamed down Memphis's cheeks.

Isaiah smiled at his brother. "Hey, Memphis."

Imprisoned in the chair connected to Jake Marlowe's Golden Eye, Miriam Lubovitch squirmed and moaned. "No…" If Marlowe and his thugs hadn't put her through so much already, she'd have been able to contain what she knew. But they'd weakened her with so much exposure to the machine. Already, she could feel the Eye's radiation twisting the cells in her body, shortening her life.

"Turn it on again!" Jake Marlowe said. "Where are they, Miriam? Tell us where they are and this ends."

"It will end," Miriam whispered. "But not the way you think."

As the current coursed through her damaged cells, Miriam felt her connection to Memphis and to her son and to all the Diviners. "D-Devils T-T-Tower," she croaked.

Jake turned down the dials and whipped off his goggles. "Ready my plane."

Sam's voice reached Memphis from far, far away. Memphis opened his eyes. He was on his hands and knees on the ground, vomiting into the spindly grass. Grave dirt and a tiny splat of blood came up in his bile, along with two wriggly baby frogs, each no bigger than a fingernail. With a startled shout, he rubbed feverishly at his mouth with the back of his hand, leaving a bloody smear on his knuckles. His stomach clenched again, but he swallowed against the urge to vomit. The tang of blood sharpened the usual softness of his mouth. The point of his tongue pressed against a loose lower tooth that wiggled in its swollen socket. His hands. Cuts appeared on his arms, as if he'd been clawed by an angry beast. He felt as if he'd been gone for several generations, as if he'd swallowed down the history of the nation all at once. But they were here in the fabled west of Wyoming, with the night of fixed stars a hard shell above them. The others were gathered in a line, staring at him. Theta edged nearer. Her voice was a faraway train of sound rushing closer: "Memphis, what did you DO?"

Memphis's head ached something powerful. And his hands…they no longer seemed like his hands. They were cold and wrong, somehow.

"Memphis?" Theta again. She sounded frightened, as if *he* were the monster, and not this rotten world.

His friends crept forward. He could tell they were newly afraid of him, too, now that he'd done this. Now that he'd shown what a man could be pushed to do. Memphis looked down at the ground. His brother's body was gone.

Memphis laughed. "He's coming back."

"What's he talking about?" Sam whispered to the others.

"Memphis, oh, Memphis," Theta said, holding him.

Memphis took Theta's face in his cold hands. "Did you hear that?"

"Hear what?" Evie asked, wary.

Memphis staggered to his feet and took a step into the brush. "He's here."

"What is he talking about?" Ling asked.

Memphis waved his arms. Out in the grass, near where the bison had roamed, Isaiah glowed like a promise. He smiled at Memphis and waved back. Memphis smiled, too. His mouth still tasted of blood. When he blinked, he saw the terrible history inside the coat. He wanted to claw his eyes out to make it stop, but every time he blinked, there it was. It had crawled inside him. He'd never be rid of it now. No matter, because there was his brother. There was Isaiah. Returned to him, for a price.

"Isaiah," Memphis said, scratching at his arms. They erupted in long red streaks. "He's here. He came back. I told you I'd do it."

Memphis kept his eyes trained on the field. He could hear the thumping of Isaiah's heart inside his head. "You're gonna be fine now. I promise. Let's get back to the truck. It's cold. Don't want you to be cold."

"Do you see anything?" Sam asked the others. They shook their heads.

"Gonna be right as rain soon enough," Memphis said to the air.

Theta shook her head. "No. No, this isn't right."

Memphis snatched a horse blanket from the back of the truck and wrapped it around nothing. The blanket fell to the earth, but Memphis didn't seem to notice.

"I don't know who that is, Memphis, but it isn't your brother," Jericho said, not without gentleness.

"Talking nonsense. 'Course it's him! He's come back. Hey. Hey, Ice Man."

"Memphis." Theta now. Warning. Afraid.

Doubters. Unbelievers. His brother had been dead and was returned to him, just like that resurrection thousands of years ago. But why wasn't he talking? Isaiah used to talk a mile a minute. He was tired, was all. He needed to get his feet under him.

"It's all right, Little Man. You're back. You're here. I won't let anything hurt you, I promise," Memphis said, looking over at the brother only he could see. Isaiah glowed faintly. A fly landed on Isaiah's lips and Memphis brushed it away. "Shoo!"

"Where did Isaiah's body go?" Henry asked quietly.

"Pal, I don't know. I don't know anything about what's happening right now," Sam said under his breath.

"Memphis, what happened in the land of the dead?" Ling asked, because she was beginning to understand something she did not want to know.

Tears blurred Memphis's vision. He felt cold. Why did he feel so cold and yet feverish at the same time? His teeth chattered as he spoke: "I m-made a b-bargain."

"What kind of bargain?" Ling asked.

"I c-couldn't let my b-brother d-die."

"What kind of bargain, Memphis?" Ling pressed.

"My h-healing power f-for Isaiah," Memphis said.

"Oh, that's just terrific. That's swell," Sam said, angry.

Theta glared. "Stop it, Sam."

"What are we supposed to do now? How are we supposed to heal the breach without a healer?"

"He just lost his brother!" Theta shouted, and a little fire erupted at the ends of her fingers. She blew it out.

"I'll be f-fine. I just…n-need to r-rest is all," Memphis said, falling to his knees. It was hard to walk. He looked over at Isaiah, who smiled again. He still wasn't talking, but in time, he would. They'd talk about everything well into the evening, the way they used to do back at Aunt Octavia's house.

Theta put the blanket across Memphis's shoulders and helped him stand again. He was shivering and his lips were pale. "Hey, Shrimpy. You 'member that time after church when the Elks had a parade, came down Lenox Avenue in their sashes, and Papa Charles was out in front carrying the banner? Mr. Reggie gave you a root beer float for free, wouldn't even take your nickel," Memphis said to the air. "Yeah. And we bought penny candy after church, too."

Evie wanted to cry but she was too horrified. There were no tears for what was happening to them. It was beyond crying. Losing Isaiah had been heartbreaking. Now they were losing Memphis, too. He was getting weaker. She could see it. Sweat beaded along his upper lip and forehead. His eyes were bloodshot.

"What does he see?" Henry asked.

"The King of Crows played a trick on him," Theta said through gritted teeth. Her hands were warm all the time now. She would burn everything down if she could. She might still. "Just like he did Miss Addie."

"You cold? Don't worry. I'll share my blanket," Memphis said. He lifted one edge to let an imaginary Isaiah in next to him.

The night sky with its beautiful stars was an affront. Nothing should ever shine on such a night. There were whip-poor-wills calling into the darkness, reminding Evie that even the night had layers. The ghosts watched from the prairie edges. She could see them out there, winking in the dark. When the wind whipped up, it carried their whispers: *This is the history*, they said. *Blood.*

"Jericho," Evie said.

"I see."

"Do you think they'll come after us?" Evie asked. "How're we going to protect ourselves?"

"Something's coming from the other way," Theta said, pointing into the dark distance, which was alive with the incandescent eyes of some rumbling monster. Instinctually, the Diviners moved closer to one another.

"If it comes to it, we can use our powers," Sam said, reaching for Evie's hand. She, in turn, reached for Henry's.

"Memphis is in no shape for it," Theta warned.

"It's okay, Little Man. It's okay," Memphis said to an imaginary Isaiah.

The glow grew wider, more distinct. Headlights. Lots of them. A convoy of military trucks and, out front, a brown sedan. The Shadow Men had arrived.

Mr. Adams and Mr. Jefferson exited the car. Jefferson buttoned his gray suit jacket. "Time to go, chickadees. You have a date with destiny."

The trucks rumbled over an arbitrary state line into the Utah desert. Memphis dreamed. Or at least he thought he did. He could no longer be sure what was dream and what was real. Sometimes he was in the back of a canvas-paneled truck with his friends. Sometimes he was alone, and there would be Isaiah, smiling that same smile, unchanged. Other times, though, the King of Crows would be sitting across from Memphis. Saying nothing. Just a smug expression that would've rankled Memphis if he didn't feel quite so sick. The King of Crows held up an hourglass with all the sand in the bottom. Quickly, he flipped it over, and the sand began pouring in a slow stream into the empty glass bell. When Memphis stared at it, he saw that on each grain of sand was the image of a town. Memphis could hear screaming as the towns squeezed through the narrow strait and became smoke drifting down into a steadily growing pile of ash. In these moments, he thought he saw the squawking mouths of so many birds coming alive on the King's coat. This made him uneasy. His body strained with the urge to fight. But just as quickly, the King of Crows would open his strange coat, and Memphis would be mesmerized by the horrors and delights within.

The truck carried the Diviners to an airfield. The thwacking *whirr* of an airplane's propellers drowned out any chance of the Diviners speaking to one another, but who could speak anyway? Jake Marlowe walked across the landing strip flanked by a pair of generals.

"Welcome aboard, Diviners," he said. "Let's go make history."

DEATH VALLEY

Jericho had never been on an airplane before. The roar of the engines was loud, but the view was spectacular.

"Everything is so small," he said, gazing down at the twinkling lights of America below.

"Where are you taking us?" Sam demanded.

"Death Valley," Marlowe responded.

"I think I played that club once," Henry said, glaring at Marlowe. "No one tips."

"What's wrong with Memphis?" Marlowe asked.

In his seat, a shivering Memphis stared out the window, occasionally murmuring to Isaiah. Theta sat beside him, keeping watch. Evie could see the pale red glow of Theta's palms as she kept them near Memphis to warm him.

"He's sick. So we shouldn't do this," Evie said.

"What's the matter with him?"

"Grief," Evie said.

Marlowe hung his head for a moment. "The loss of Isaiah is unfortunate. But we'll still be able to carry on without him. The serum and the modifications I've made to the Eye should see to that," he said.

"You're a real son-of-a-bitch," Sam said.

"I'm not the one who killed Isaiah Campbell."

"You're part of the reason he's dead," Henry said.

"He's not dead. He's not. Just...lost..." Memphis murmured.

Evie glared at Marlowe. "I thought we were Public Enemy Number One. How will you explain our participation in this little event?"

"Once we've conducted the experiment and stabilized our connection to the land of the dead, you'll be fully exonerated. We'll change the story to suit. Why, there'll be a ticker tape parade for our new heroes."

Evie snorted at that.

"Americans have short memories," Marlowe said. "Revolutionaries become Founding Fathers. Outlaws become legends. It's who we are."

"You don't think we'll survive anyway," Ling said. "There's a lot of radiation coming off your machine."

"All perfectly safe, I assure you," Marlowe said.

"What's to keep us from just destroying the Eye once you strap us in?" Jericho asked.

Marlowe smiled. "I thought about that, believe me. There's iron in each of your helmets to recalibrate your poles. You won't be able to use your powers to affect it."

"Each of our…?" Jericho's eyes widened. "You really are a monster."

Marlowe glowered. "All great men are denigrated by people who don't understand them in their time. By people who fear greatness."

Theta blew a Bronx cheer, startling Marlowe. Her heat moved through her with nowhere to go. The iron in the handcuffs kept her power on an invisible leash. "When have you been denigrated?" she said. "Looks to me like you've been given everything you ever wanted, pal." She wanted to light up Marlowe, and all the men like him, and watch them burn.

"I've had to make terrible sacrifices for progress," Marlowe answered.

Henry clucked sympathetically. "I, too, hate it when my tea gets cold while I'm plotting destruction. Such a sacrifice."

Marlowe stared at Henry. "How would you like it if the whole world knew about you and those degenerate clubs you haunt in Greenwich Village?"

"How would you like it if I used you for kindling?" Theta shot back.

"Your village didn't like it much," Mr. Jefferson interjected with a snort.

Jefferson's comment, a confirmation, was like another slap to Theta. Tears sprang to her eyes. These men had robbed her of so much. One terrible moment that lit a fuse leading to so many others. These men never thought about the consequences of their actions. They never thought about the people on the other end of an order.

Evie jumped up from her seat and kicked Jefferson in the shins, hard. "That's for Theta." She kicked him again, higher up. "And…and…that's for Theta, too."

"You still got a good kick on you, Baby Vamp," Sam said admiringly.

Mr. Adams picked Evie up and forced her back into her seat.

"Thanks, Evil," Theta said, and it seemed to her that she had never been so grateful for a friend.

"You and me," Evie said back to her. "If they come for one of us, they come for all of us."

"How sentimental," Jefferson said in a strained voice. He'd gotten back to his feet with murder in his eyes. He moved toward Evie.

Marlowe held him back with his hand. "Your department can take over once we've secured the land of the dead."

Jefferson eyed Evie. "You're mine."

And Evie mouthed back a phrase for which she was certain her mother would still wash her mouth out with soap. Beside her, Sam grinned. "Oh, Baby Vamp. Let's get married tomorrow. Promise?"

Evie softened. "Promise."

Marlowe peered out the window at the barren landscape below the clouds. "Looks like we're here."

The plane pitched left to right on its approach. It sailed down and screeched to a stop in the desert, and Evie thought that she might have enjoyed her first airplane ride had it not been this one.

There were several fighter airplanes lined up across the desert floor. Men in aviator suits stood at attention beside them.

"What are they for?" Evie asked.

"We'll send them into the breach once you've stabilized it," a general explained.

"You're sending in a battalion?" Henry said, incredulous.

"We have to secure our new territory," the general said.

"I told you we've taken every precaution." Marlowe, smug as usual.

"In addition to being a lousy fella, you're also a goddamned idiot," Sam said.

Adams moved forward to hit Sam, but Marlowe stopped him. "We need him to function. He'll quiet when he sees her."

Mr. Jefferson brought forth Miriam from the sedan. She was still in irons. She looked much worse than she had a few weeks earlier. Her skin was mottled and she limped.

"Mama," Sam said.

She looked his way. He heard his mother's voice in his head. She sounded weak but determined. *You must close the breach. Even if it means we are trapped inside. You understand, Sergei?*

There'll be another way, Mama, Sam answered.

Promise me.

Yes, Mama. I promise.

The Shadow Men and generals gathered by the fighter planes to confer with Jake Marlowe. The Diviners still stood near Marlowe's plane, with an armed guard nearby. The desert heat was a shock after the cold of Wyoming, and Ling marveled that two such different climates could exist in the same country. It was so many countries in one, she knew. Back home, her parents would be resting, getting ready for another day at the Tea House. The dawn would rise over the Lower East Side. The streets would respond with a symphony of smells, a daily re-creation carried over from the villages of Russia and the towns of Sicily, the fields of Ireland and the winding streets of Poland and Germany. Somewhere out there, maybe Mississippi or Oklahoma, Alma and the Harlem Haymakers were finishing up a night's work in some vaudeville dance hall. Ling wished she could see Alma and her parents one last time. In Kansas and Nebraska, Oregon and West Virginia and Washington, D.C., people had gone to sleep thinking about all they'd left unfinished today and all they'd need to do tomorrow, thinking that there would be a tomorrow.

The Shadow Men marched the Diviners forward into the desert. Heat lightning crackled above. The heat sucked the life right out of the Diviners. Fear sucked up the rest. Evie felt sleepy and a little light-headed. She was worried mostly about Memphis, though. Anybody could see that he was getting sicker. And his healing power was gone. He'd given it up in a bad bargain, just as his mother had made her bargain to try to save her boys. Isaiah was dead and Memphis was the living dead.

What would happen to him when they were hooked up to the Eye? A Diviner's power could fend off its relentless energy pull for a while, but what about a Diviner whose power had been stolen by the King of Crows? Without Memphis, they might not be able to heal the breach. He might die. They all might.

"What is that?" Theta asked as they neared a giant canyon of striped rock.

"The Ubehebe Crater," Mr. Jefferson informed them.

"*I got them Ubehebe Jeebie bluuuues*," Henry sang. Ling shot him a contemptuous look. "Sorry. I couldn't let that one go. It might be my very last joke."

Down at the crater's bottom, the army men set up generator-fed klieg lights around the perimeter of Marlowe's latest iteration of the Eye, and for one brief moment, Ling was completely taken by its beauty. The Eye was a true marvel of ingenuity and, yes, science. Jake Marlowe had managed to open a doorway between dimensions. How many other dimensions existed in the universe? How many universes? An ax could be used to till the earth. An ax could be used to kill. Tool or weapon. It was all in the intent. The knowledge that had gone into constructing the Eye was knowledge that could have been used to advance humankind, and Ling hated that the beauty of physics was being used to create an imperial death machine.

Evie stared at the golden sphere of the Eye, sitting in the middle of the desert crater. It was also built from death, and it would bring more pain and suffering than it already had. Once they were hooked up to its immense power, they'd have no protection from it. The Eye would drain and break them like the others. Unless . . .

"Sam!" Evie said. "Can you tell the Eye not to see us?"

Sam was beginning to understand what Evie meant. "Not with this iron on us."

"But the iron is part of the machine . . ." Ling said, a hint of a smile showing. "Isn't it?"

"Worth a try," Sam said. "But you know I can't do it forever. How long will Megalomaniac Marlowe have us on that thing for?"

"It might last longer if we're inside a dream state," Henry suggested.

Evie looked confused, but Ling was nodding. "If Sam can keep the Eye from seeing us long enough for us to go to sleep—"

"You're just gonna go to sleep with that Eye thing on you?" Theta said.

"I was talking," Ling said, narrowing her eyes at Theta, who put up her shackled hands in a *Pardon me* gesture. "Don't you see? We'll be connected through the Eye. Whatever one of us feels or experiences, the others will, too. Isn't that right, Jericho?"

"Yes. The Eye will connect us all," Jericho said.

"For the record, I also know this. Because I also got to ride on

Marlowe's not-so-merry-go-round," Sam complained. "It hurt. A lot. I did not enjoy it. I would just like some recognition of my troubles."

"I will make you a swell little medal if we survive," Evie said with a generous roll of her eyes.

Sam nodded approvingly. "I like medals. I accept."

"Evie, I don't suppose you still have that feather Isaiah gave you?" Henry asked.

"It's in my pocket. Why?"

"I don't know. But Ling often needs an object to find the dead in a dream."

"It might lead us to the King of Crows," Evie said, thinking aloud.

Henry gave a wan smile. "See? We don't even need to be hooked up to that big gold spider for all of us to be on the trolley."

"Here," Evie said, handing the feather to Ling, who cupped it tightly in her hand, out of sight.

"Where's Isaiah?" Memphis asked. "Where'd he go?"

"Poet, he's not here," Theta said gently.

"The King of Crows did something to me. I can f-feel it. Like p-poison ins-side me," Memphis said. "Get it out. I want it out."

Theta touched Memphis's shoulder. "Memphis? Can you do this?"

"We're going to have to give him as much of our strength as we can," Ling said. "He's the one who can actually close the breach."

"My power, my healing power..." Memphis said, examining his hands as if they were not his hands at all. His eyes filled with tears. "He's not here, is he? He was never here. It was just a trick."

Theta slipped her arm through his. Memphis shut his eyes tightly. When he opened them again, he looked to his friends and nodded. "Heal the breach," he said with renewed determination, echoing his mother's long-ago warning. "Somehow. Somehow."

"Here they come," Sam said. "Look innocent."

"Good luck with that, Sam Lloyd," Evie muttered.

"Baby Vamp?" Sam was looking at her with such tender affection it nearly broke her. *"Ikh hob dikh lib."*

"I love you, too, Sam," Evie whispered.

The Shadow Men and the soldiers marched the Diviners down into the mouth of the crater. Evie was afraid she'd turn an ankle on the steep slope of rock and sand. "I wish I'd worn different shoes," she grumbled. She wished so many things. That Isaiah were still alive. Mabel and James, too. Wishing wasn't enough.

"Sam, you see what I see?" Jericho asked on their descent.

"Yeah," Sam said, trying to keep his footing.

There were no longer two helmets attached to the Eye; there were eight. One for each of them. The chairs were arranged in a circle around the Eye, with their backs to the belly of the machine. They wouldn't even have the comfort of looking at one another.

They'd reached the bottom of the crater. Nearby, the golden machine hummed and glowed. Jericho nodded to the eighth spot. "You know about Isaiah," Jericho said carefully, with a quick glance at Memphis. "What are you going to do about that, Jake?"

"Miriam can fill in. It will be enough," Marlowe said, busying himself with examining the paper scrolling out from the side of the machine, a communication with the other world.

"We're all completely interchangeable to you, aren't we?" Evie said. She wanted to spit in Jake Marlowe's eye. Given the chance, she would.

"You'll be making history."

"If we live through it. And then who would know? Your sort gets rid of any inconvenient history," Evie said.

"Gentlemen, looks like we're ready at last," Jake said, dropping the paper. "Strap them in."

The Shadow Men and soldiers did as they were told. Each Diviner was forced into a chair. The golden helmets were secured. Evie could feel the weight on her skull as they tightened it. What if they ended up like her brother and the One-Forty-Four, living out this terrible day for the rest of time, for as long as there *was* time? What if they were banished to different dimensions, chasing one another through doorways that never led them where they needed to go, never home? She glanced to her left at Sam, and she knew he was trying to figure a sneaky way out of those restraints; she was overcome with a crazy love for him. He was a fighter to the very end. To her right, she saw the tufts of the feather sticking out from between Ling's fingers. The others she couldn't see, but she knew they were there. They were all there together, no matter what the future held. She had to trust in that.

Little Fox. Sam's mother, in their heads. *I will free you from the iron's constraints. I have been working against it for some time, figuring out a way. But they are too stupid to know.*

Sam smiled. "Thanks, Ma."

Don't talk out loud, Miriam scolded.

"Thanks, Ma," Sam said, a little sarcastically.

Marlowe flipped his switches. Cones of striped white light shot down over the Diviners. Evie's breathing came faster. She was quite scared. This was a voyage into the unknown. It felt like an execution.

"Ling!" Henry's voice, somewhere behind her, on the other side of the machine.

"I-I can't fall asleep!" Ling answered in a high-pitched voice.

Blue lightning struck the ground of the crater. The Eye whirred louder, faster. Whatever was going to happen would happen soon.

"Listen to the hum of the machine," Henry shouted back. "Hold on to that feather."

"You c-can d-do it," Evie said through chattering teeth. The pressure had increased. Above them, the ominous clouds were tearing each other apart like a pack of wild gray dogs.

"Sleep, sleep, sleep," Ling intoned. "Dream."

"Dream," Evie echoed.

"Dream," Theta said.

They were all thinking it now, with purpose.

Spears of light shot through the dark clouds. With a mighty groan, the sky opened its huge dark mouth, ready to devour them. A jolt passed through Evie. It was as if the electric hand of god had reached in and thrown apart her atoms like marbles.

"S-Sam," Evie managed.

Sam writhed in his seat. "Don't. See. Us. Don't…"

Beside her, Evie heard Ling crying out in pain—or maybe it was her own voice she heard. They were joined now; all their pain was shared. It was a tight squeezing, like a birth.

"…See…US—aaahhhh!" Sam cried out.

Evie felt herself being sucked up into that giant tear in the sky and the unknowable dark beyond, into the wicked soul of the Eye. Into the land of the dead.

Evie looked at her hands. They were her hands, she knew, but they were not quite the same. They belonged to a slightly altered Evie. She was existing in two places at once, in Death Valley and the land of the dead, connected via the Eye.

Memphis was beside her, examining his own hands.

"Memphis," Evie said. "Do you feel...?"

"Yes," Memphis answered, intuiting her thought. "I'm me, but a different me." He raised his head. "Where are the others?"

"I don't know," Evie said, taking in their surroundings.

The land of the dead was a desolate, miserable place. Cadaverous vultures settled their bony forms in the blighted branches of monstrous yew trees. The ground was hard and cracked, punctuated here and there by foul, oily ponds thick with flies and sulfurous fumes. Everywhere, an ashy snow fell. It smelled of grave dirt and the sickly sweetness of rotting flowers, of old blood, and tainted meat. The discordant whine of the Eye hung in the stultifying air, like the thin, high scream of the factory whistle. As with Gideon and the other towns devoured by the King of Crows, everything here was dead, diseased, or dying. And Evie wondered what Jake Marlowe possibly thought he could claim in this world. What here was worth owning?

"Sam?" Evie called. "Theta? Ling!"

"Here," Theta said. "Memphis?"

"H-here, Princess," Memphis said, throwing his arms around Theta.

Evie let out a sigh of relief. Everyone had made it. She did not see Sam's mother, and she hoped Miriam was all right.

"She's okay," Sam said, glancing at Evie. "I know she's okay somehow."

"How do you feel?" Evie asked the others. The extreme pain had ebbed to a dull tension, like a headache trying to come on.

"Better," Jericho said. "A little odd."

The others nodded. Ling did not have her crutches here, and Evie supposed it was because she and Henry had created a bubble of a dream for them to inhabit. Hadn't Henry said that Ling could walk unaided in dreams?

The dead were everywhere, standing in the broken fields, not moving or thinking, staring off into nothing, a story without an end. There were thousands of them, too many for the land of the dead to house for long.

Theta held her breath as a listless ghost woman, face eaten by rot, shuffled past in search of something that could not be named. Theta felt a touch of the woman's restlessness inside her own soul. The dead woman stopped and sniffed but, seeing nothing, moved on.

Theta exhaled. "Sam. Your power seems to be working."

"For now," Sam said. "Whatever we're gonna do, we'd better do it fast, before Marlowe and the generals start invading—or those dead get wise to us."

"Look!" Ling pointed to a long rift on the horizon. The giant, breathing wound stretched wider with each groan on its way to permanence.

"The breach . . ." Memphis said.

Henry's eyes widened. "*That's* what we have to heal?"

"Don't be a baby," Ling grumbled.

"How is it possible for you to insult me in two worlds?"

"Practice."

The rift was a wonder to behold, though, like being present at the creation of a new universe, and Ling marveled that so much death and such new life could exist in the same place at the same moment.

"This is a lot of atomic energy," Ling said. "If you could harness all that, the power it generated would be enormous."

"So we're existing in two universes at the same time?" Evie asked. She wanted to be sure she understood.

"Yes," Ling said.

"And they're connected?"

"Yes," Ling said in an annoyed voice. "I don't have time to teach a science class."

"So if we destroy the Eye in this universe . . ."

"It should destroy it in our world," Ling confirmed.

"And what happens if we die in this world?" Sam asked.

Ling swallowed hard. "As I said, it's all connected."

A palpable current ran from the Eye through the Diviners' bodies and back into the land of the dead. Every second they spent here empowered the King of Crows and fed the widening breach. The longer they stayed, the more they were being threaded into this world. If they stayed too long, they might not have the power to get out again.

"Why aren't we burning up, like the other Diviners did?" Theta asked.

"I imagine the dream state Henry and I created is keeping us protected for now, like being inside a womb. That along with Sam's 'don't see me' act."

Henry gestured to the swirling, expanding breach. "At least it's a womb with a view."

"You want me to kill him for you?" Theta asked Ling. "I got firepower."

But Ling's thoughts were on solutions. "I don't know how long we can keep it up. I don't know how long our bodies can withstand the damage the Eye inflicts. Pretty soon, we're going to end up like the others," she warned.

Memphis wiggled his fingers. They itched and prickled with something new. He touched his right hand to one of the dead trees, concentrating very hard. Two tiny green shoots poked out from the end of the branch.

"It's coming back!" Theta said excitedly.

"Why is it doing that?" Ling asked.

"I don't know," Memphis said, staring at his hand, which felt strange but not unwelcome. Something was happening to him. Something he could not explain. But then, as fast as they'd sprouted, the new green vines shriveled in on themselves and turned the same gray as everything else.

"Not enough," Ling said. "We need all his strength."

"But that's a good sign, isn't it?" Evie asked.

"Probably another one of the King of Crows's little tricks," Sam said.

"We don't know that. We don't know anything about this world or how it works," Jericho said.

"There's a memory to everything. You just have to listen." Evie put her hand to the cracked ground, but its story was as barren as the trees, just the slightest residue of history being sucked up and devoured by the King of Crows. But something did catch. She could read small bits of a life still beating here, and it belonged to Adelaide Proctor.

"Theta, Miss Addie is here."

"Where? Can you find her?"

"You know who's great at finding people?" Henry jerked his thumb at Ling.

"If I have an object of theirs," Ling said in apology.

"What about the memory of an object?" Evie asked.

"As a good man once said, 'There are more things in heaven and earth, Horatio—'"

An irritated Ling interrupted Jericho. "Who is Horatio? Why are we talking about Horatio? We're trying to solve a problem here." Ling turned to Evie. "All right. Let's try."

Evie stooped and put a hand to the ground. Ling went to touch Evie.

"I don't think you'll have to," Evie said. "We're all connected. Remember?"

Ling nodded. She shut her eyes, concentrating. Evie felt Ling's power joining to hers as well as Theta's loving attachment to Miss Addie, and in a few seconds Evie saw a white clapboard church nestled deep in the dark wood. Miss Addie was inside that church, she knew.

"Somewhere over there," Ling said, opening her eyes. She pointed to a gnarled forest under a yellow moon.

"Yes," Evie and Theta both said.

"We don't have much time," Sam reminded them.

Memphis sagged against Jericho, who held him up. It was clear that Memphis was still deeply unwell. The show with the vines had been promising, but it might mean nothing.

"I want to take him down," Memphis said and coughed.

"Marlowe?" Jericho asked.

"The King of Crows. For all he's done."

"I understand, Memphis," Jericho said. "But we can't do everything. We need your strength. We have to heal the rift."

"And destroy the Eye," Evie said. "I won't have my brother trapped for eternity."

"Baby Vamp—" Sam started. Evie cut him off.

"I won't!"

"The King of Crows took my mother and my brother from me," Memphis said.

"Are we going to argue about whose mission is most important?" Henry asked. "Either we do all of it or none of it."

"I vote for only fixing the breach," Jericho said.

"I won't leave my brother to suffer," Evie said.

"I won't leave my mother at the mercy of the King," Memphis said.

"Looks like we do all of it," Theta said.

"We have to wait for Memphis's power to regenerate," Ling said.

"If it does," Sam said.

Memphis touched the tree again. This time, only one vine emerged, and then, as before, it died.

"Stop doing that!" Ling reprimanded him. "You have to save your energy."

Nearby, several of the dead sniffed again and growled low.

"Miss Addie. Now," Theta said.

"I'm going with you," Evie said.

"Be quick about it, Baby Vamp," Sam said and kissed her.

Evie and Theta set off in pursuit of Miss Addie.

"Careful," Theta whispered as she and Evie passed among the many dead. Their rotting bodies were so close. Theta had to stifle the urge to scream. She was relieved when they came out on the other side of the sniffing, grunting horde.

The grating, mechanical noise of the Eye grew louder. Their journey was bringing them closer to it. There, suddenly, was the clearing Evie had seen so many times in her dreams, a version of it, at least, with the missing Unit 144 going about their looping existence. And there was her brother. There was James. Alive.

"James? James, it's me. It's Evie." She left Theta's side and ran toward the field.

"Say, what's this mission the department's got us on, anyway?" James asked another soldier.

"Beats me. S'posed to help us win the war and show those Germans who's boss," another soldier answered. "Say, O'Neill, what card am I holding?"

Without looking, James answered, "The eight of hearts."

"Son-of-a-bitch! Right every time!"

"James," Evie said. For years, she had longed to see him again, to hug him, talk with him. He was so close. She could reach out and touch him. But she would only be holding a memory, she realized now, with great sadness. She would only be touching a ghost.

"Evil," Theta said gently.

"I know," Evie said. She took Theta's hand instead, and side by side, they marched toward the skeletal forest.

Evie and Theta crawled over thick brambles that poked and tore at them. Theta's foot came down on something that gave with a squish.

"When we get back, I'm gonna scream for a whole day," she said.

"Just keep going," Evie said, trying to ignore the red-eyed vultures perched on the tops of gnarled trees.

Theta pushed aside a cluster of thorny twigs, and there it was: the white clapboard church under a yellow moon.

"I think this is from Miss Addie's memory," Theta said. "She wrote about this church in her diary. It's where they buried Elijah. Where they were supposed to marry."

Thick branches encased the church like a cage. Its walls bowed in, splintering from the trees' tightening grasp.

"We have to hurry," Evie said.

Evie and Theta climbed the church steps and let themselves inside. The place had the feel of memory, too. Its existence was unreliable. One minute, there were ten pews; the next, there was only one. The pew had three blue hymnals stacked at the end, then they were all gone. Evie feared that if Addie stopped dreaming of this church, it would go up in smoke, and Evie and Theta with it.

An enormous oak had pierced the front of the church. Its muscular branches embraced Adelaide Proctor, holding her fast. They could see the pointed end of one poised above Miss Addie's heart, ready to impale her if she moved.

"Miss Addie?" Theta said into the dark. At the sound of Theta's voice, sun began to filter along the sides of the church through long, tall windows that had not been there before.

"Theta?" Miss Addie said on a thinning rasp.

"It's me, Miss Addie. I'm here."

"Theta, you...you must defeat him."

"We're trying, but we don't have much time. We need your help."

"If you destroy him, you destroy it all. He is the key," Miss Addie said with great effort.

"So Sarah Beth wasn't lying about that part," Evie whispered to Theta.

"Theta!" Miss Addie cried. "You must release me."

"That's why we're here. Just tell us how."

"You must perform a spell."

"No, Miss Addie. I told you, I'm not a witch. I tried to bind Elijah and just made it worse."

"But you are!"

"You're the witch, Miss Addie. I'm a dancer who sometimes catches things on fire. We all have our gifts. I gotta learn to use mine. Okay?"

The trees roared. The church walls buckled from the pressure. The branch tip pressed against Miss Addie's chest and she cried out.

"Memory, memory, memory," Evie murmured, thinking. Her head snapped up. "What was this church to you, Miss Addie? What is its significance?"

"It was the place where we buried our dead," Miss Addie said after a moment. "Elijah. My mother and two brothers. It was here that I realized fully what I had done. And now it is where he has me trapped. If I try to move away from it, it will come for me, and I shall be pierced through the heart."

"She's trapped herself here," Evie said to Theta. "She's built a prison from her guilt."

Theta thought of Miss Addie wandering the halls of the Bennington, spreading salt in the hopes that she could protect everyone from some unnamed evil. But she'd also been trying to protect herself from her own regret and loss.

"Miss Addie. You can leave this place. You don't have to stay," Theta said to the older woman.

"But Elijah…"

"Elijah's gone. He's not coming back. And I'm pretty sure the Elijah you loved wouldn't want you to keep suffering forever for what you did."

"I never should've done it."

"Time to let it go," Theta said.

"How?"

Theta's hands glowed orange. "Sometimes you just gotta burn something down so you can build something else in its place."

The trees groaned in protest and squeezed, refusing to let go. A rafter fell and smashed a pew. The church would be crushed and Evie and Theta with it. But Theta Knight did not waver.

"Go on. Make yourself a new story, Miss Addie," she said as her hands filled with cleansing fire.

Miss Addie nodded. "Burn it down, my dear."

Theta put her hand to the side of the crumbling church, and instead of fire, light poured in through the windows, filling the room. The trees vanished. No cage held Miss Addie any longer. Instead, she was in her bed at the Bennington, sleeping peacefully, Miss Lillian beside her. Miss Addie's final dream and memory was of the lifelong bond she'd shared with her sister and the home where she had chosen to make her life. The light grew so bright that Evie and Theta had to shut their eyes, and when they opened them again, the church, the bed, and Miss Addie were gone. Only the light remained, and even it was fading until there was nothing but forest again.

Evie hugged Theta. "You did it, Theta. You did Miss Addie proud."

Theta sniffled. "Yeah? Then why do I feel so lousy?" She wiped her eyes. "C'mon. Let's get back to the others. I just wanna finish this and get outta here."

But when they turned to flee, the woods were filled with the dead, and at the front of the feral pack was Mabel Rose. She stared straight ahead at Evie. And Evie realized how foolish she'd been to think that Sam's power could shield her from this. Just as in life, her friend saw right through her.

Mabel sniffed. Her lips curled back from sharp teeth. "Evie."

Theta readied her hands, but Evie waved her off. "Please, Theta."

Atop thinning, red-gold hair, Mabel wore Evie's rhinestone headband, its luster dulled by grave dirt. Worms had made a home in the beautiful yellow dress, which was now dotted with holes. This was Mabel. Not the illusion conjured in Gideon. And Evie understood: Mabel Rose was really gone. She was dead and deserved rest, and Evie had to let go.

"Yes, it's me, Mabesie," Evie called. She felt the ache in her side. Would always feel the ache.

"You brought me back," Mabel snarled. "It's your fault."

"Yes, I did. It's my fault. And I'm so, so sorry, Mabesie. Truly I am."

"Why did you bring me back?" Mabel whimpered.

"I was wrong to do it. But you are not this person, Mabel Rose." Evie walked toward Mabel. "Remember how selfish you thought I was?"

Mabel's eyes were deep and dark. Evie could lose herself in them. She sensed Theta following behind her, those hands ready, if it came to it. Evie glanced back and shook her head, and Theta nodded.

"You *were* selfish. You *are* selfish," Mabel said in her dead voice.

"Yes. I am selfish. I'm a selfish, attention-seeking, pigheaded, lonely girl. But not all the time. You were good. But not all the time. You were also jealous and secretive, and boy, could you hold a grudge. You expected people to notice you, and when they didn't, you got mad. And you wanted to be important. Who doesn't? I should have let you be all those things instead of just the ones I wanted you to be. The ones that made you fit more easily into my life." *We are so many stories*, Evie thought.

Mabel's nostrils flared. She was inhaling Evie's scent. "I hunger, Evie."

Evie stood right in front of her dead friend and willed herself not to run. "Everybody does, Mabesie. But did you, do you, know how much I love you?"

"I…" Mabel faltered. Her eyes shimmered from black to brown, back and forth. "I tried to stop Arthur from planting the bomb. I tried to stop it."

"Of course you did." Evie smiled through tears.

"I died trying."

"I knew. Somehow, I knew. Mabel, you can still do good. Do you want to help us stop *this* explosion?"

Mabel's struggle showed in her eyes, now brown but always on the verge of turning. "How?"

"We need to get through those trees and back to the others. To our friends. *Your* friends. Sam and Memphis and Ling and Henry and Jericho."

"Jericho…" Mabel said. "He did not love me like I loved him."

"Well, he never was terribly bright, was he?" Evie said, managing a laugh. She saw the faintest hint of a smile on Mabel's lips, before it disappeared.

Mabel looked toward the trees. "I will go with you."

"What does that mean?" Theta asked.

When Mabel turned, the dead did as well. One mind. All connected. She led Evie and Theta through the dark wood, past the snakes and lizards and two-headed frogs and diseased vines choking the life out of anything that tried to grow from the blighted land.

As they neared the edge of the wood, when the way was nearly clear, Evie felt newly afraid. Mabel and her retinue of the dead stood between Theta and Evie and the way out. What if Mabel changed her mind? What if she couldn't let go of her fury at Evie after all? What if this hope that Evie was clinging to, that there was still a spark of humanity left in Mabel's heart, was but one more illusion?

They'd reached the end of the woods. Mabel stepped to the side to let them pass. The dead followed suit, and as much as Evie wanted to run back to Sam, she was also sad to say good-bye.

"Evie?" Mabel said, almost sweetly.

"Yes, Pie Face?"

"I'm so tired. I want to rest now. Can you help me rest?"

Mabel and James had been Evie's ghosts in more ways than one. It was time to let Mabel Rose, all of her, rest in peace.

"Do you remember how we used to lie in your bed and talk half the night until we finally fell asleep, Mabesie?"

Mabel nodded slowly. Evie could see that she was trying to remember.

"It's just like that."

"Okay."

"We'll just...talk."

"Okay." Mabel nodded. "Okay."

"Do you remember the time we sneaked out through the window to go see Theta in the Follies and you got so drunk, Mabel? Pos-i-tutely blotto. I had to help peel that terrible boy off of you, and you threw up all over Washington Square Park! Your mother had absolute kittens. She forbade you from seeing me. But we got around her. We always did."

A tiny smile played at Mabel's lips. "Yes. Yes, I remember...."

"We remember," the dead echoed.

"How about when you almost bobbed your hair? Theta and I made a bet about it. You sat in the barber's chair, and oh, I could feel your terror when he brought out those scissors and you said, 'Nope!' and ran out to us on the sidewalk and we laughed and laughed about it afterward. I lost that bet, by the way. I really thought you'd go through with it."

Mabel was growing fainter by degrees. "So many stories."

"Yes." Evie swallowed hard. "And do you remember when I went to Naughty John's house? Who went with me? You. You were so brave. I never would've been able to do that without you, Mabesie."

"That's all we are in the end. Stories." Fainter and fainter. "Will you remember me fondly?"

"Always."

"Evie. I'm tired." Fainter still.

"Then rest, Mabel Rose."

And then, like a firefly realizing morning has come, Mabel Rose winked out of existence and became a memory.

ONE CHANGE

"Sam!" Evie shouted, running toward him with Theta just behind.

"Did you find her?"

"Yes, and Mabel, too," Evie said.

"Miss Addie said if we can take out the King of Crows, we can get rid of his dead. Seems Sarah Beth was right about that," Theta said.

On the horizon, the breach gave another birthing moan.

"It's getting bigger," Memphis said with alarm. How could he possibly close such a wound?

"Don't look now, but we got company," Sam said.

Through the broken trees, across the salted land, the King of Crows strode toward the rest of the Diviners. Behind him the dead followed blindly, sniffing, always hungry. In the multitude was Gabe, Memphis saw.

"What a surprise. I don't usually get visitors here. Well, live ones, at least," he said. "But I'm not here for you. Yet."

The King of Crows turned his attention toward the breach. There was a high-pitched mechanical whine, different from the noise the Eye emitted. The whine grew louder as the first battalion of fighter planes approached the threshold of the breach. The King of Crows watched, unconcerned, as the first dozen planes sailed through the breach and skittered to a stop in the clearing. A second wave was nearing the breach.

"That's quite enough," the King of Crows said. He lifted an arm, shooting lightning into an edge of the rift. The dead stiffened from the energy being sucked from their ravaged bodies. The Diviners, too, felt some of the same pull, as if they'd all bitten down on a fork at once.

The breach burned with an unearthly glow. As the planes crossed the barrier, they burned to ash, leaving dark shadow impressions across the landscape.

The planes on the ground unloaded their soldiers, who marched across the land of the dead, guns at the ready.

"Company, halt!" a general commanded and the troops knelt, guns

"What is that?" Sam asked. He couldn't look away from its devastation. Couldn't even blink.

"Some of your Diviner kin's borrowed talents allow me to glimpse possible futures. Or to help fashion them. Mr. Marlowe was only too happy to build toward one of those futures. All that uranium, wonderfully enhanced by more than a decade of Diviner power, further manipulated by industry into serum and joined to some rather impressive machinery—helped along by me, naturally." He closed his coat. "That is what you will unleash if you destroy the core of the Eye."

"It'll be like a bomb beyond any bomb you could imagine," Ling said to the others, as the full scope began to take shape in her mind. "The explosion would be devastating. The radiation would poison everything—people, livestock, crops. The consequences would be catastrophic."

"We'll stop it somehow," Evie said, but her voice sounded small to her ears. She was out of ideas.

"Ticktock, ticktock. Forgive me, but I've an army to ready and a world to invade." The King of Crows turned and walked away.

Out on the clearing, the Eye was sitting right there, but the soldiers didn't see it. Wouldn't see it until it was too late. There they were simply going about their everyday business. Shaving. Dancing to a record. Laughing. And all the while, it was there, watching. Ready to devour them. Somehow, they had to break the cycle.

"I'm going to help James, even if it means I'll be trapped here," Evie said.

"Whither thou goest, I will go," Sam said, taking Evie's hand.

Evie kissed Sam's cheek. "Leave it to you to quote Shakespeare at a time like this."

Sam looked to Memphis. "Don't tell her."

※

Evie stared up at the Eye. It ran on pain and suffering and stolen life. Evie watched, helpless, as James and the other soldiers took their positions to play out the same awful moment. Again, the explosion. Again, the men—her brother—screaming in agony, being ripped apart as they were sucked up toward the sky and into the heart of the Eye, to become its fuel. She knew that despite what Marlowe had promised about this horror show ending once they'd stabilized the breach, it would never end. It would only get worse. She put a hand over her ears to block their screams echoing through all time, creating new universes. Everything went quiet. The world wobbled, went sideways for several seconds. The Eye stopped clanging, and then, like a watch that's been wound, started up again. The One-Forty-Four blinked back into existence, ready to go through the same terrible motions.

"Say, what's this mission the department's got us on, anyway?" James asked. Same inflection. Same bemused smile.

"I won't let this happen to you again." Evie marched over to the tree stump. "I hate that song," she growled, and lifted the needle from the record on the Victrola. But the soldier kept dancing beside it. Even without the record, he sang along, "*Smile, smile, smile!*"

The field phone rang. The sergeant answered. "The time is now!" he yelled.

"How can I get him to stop?" Evie pleaded.

"I don't think we can," Henry said. "I think...they're the only ones who can stop it."

"James, you've got to listen to me," Evie pleaded. "We've got to stop this madness, all right? You're all caught in a terrible loop of time and trauma. We want to free you. But I need you to listen to me. Just do one thing differently. One thing. You'll muck up the Eye's works and give old Jake Marlowe, the Founders Club with their lousy eugenics nonsense, and those awful Shadow Men a stick in the eye! Just make one change. That's all it takes. Just one change."

"Say, O'Neill, what card am I holding?" the soldier asked.

"Eight of hearts," Sam answered.

"The eight of hearts," James said.

Evie wanted to scream. This was it—their last chance to save James. How could she get him to listen? How could she...

"Henry," Evie said. "You talk to people in dreams all the time. You make suggestions. Get him to listen. Please? Please, try?"

All this time, Henry had thought his dream walking wasn't terribly useful, not compared to the others' powers. But he'd always been able to talk to people.

"James," he said now. "The phone is going to ring. You mustn't pick it up. Don't pick up that phone."

On cue, the field phone trilled. The soldiers reacted exactly as they had every time since that fateful day during the war.

"Doll, if this is the last cycle, we gotta heal that breach and get outta here," Sam said. "I'm sorry."

"Hey, Sarge," James said suddenly. "Don't pick up that phone."

The sergeant's hand stopped mid-reach. He looked at James. "What's that, O'Neill?"

"I said: Don't pick up that phone."

It rang again.

"We have our orders, soldier," the sergeant said.

"The orders are bad. Don't pick up the phone."

The phone rang and rang and rang. The record sped up, slowed down. And then, all at once, the Eye's clanging heart skipped a beat. It began to wheeze. One tiny piece of golden machinery came loose and spun to the ground. Just one thing. A chain reaction of change set in motion.

The soldiers were gathering, looking up at the Eye, having just noticed it for the first time. The dancing soldier had stopped. He cupped a hand over his eyes and stared at the Eye, beginning to change. "Say, what is that thing?" he asked.

Luther Clayton was coming toward them.

"There you are!" James said, and Evie could hear the love in it, could see her brother's eyes shining. This was a moment that had happened, was happening, but what had happened before would not happen in the same way again. No longer were they tied to Marlowe's machine. They were free of the agonizing wheel. They were free.

"Hey!" The sergeant held up a glimmering hand.

Evie gasped. James was silhouetted by a fiery glow. Released at last from his pain, her beautiful brother shone.

"It's over," James said, smiling.

Behind him, the unit stood at ease. She and her friends had freed them. But Evie knew her supernatural connection to her brother was over as well. He was letting her know that it was time to let him go for good. It was past time to bury the dead. Poppies sprang from the barren field. They leaned their sweet red petals toward the radiance of the soldiers and threaded themselves around their ankles and trouser cuffs, which began to soften with rot.

James raised a hand in farewell. Already the edges of him had begun to fuzz into pale gold. He turned toward his waiting unit. The field was a riot of color now. A bright red sea of poppies. The golden brilliance brightened and brightened again until it consumed James, until he was the light itself and the light was everywhere.

A loud boom shook the ground, pitching the Diviners sideways. Steam shot up from the top of Jake Marlowe's golden machine. Rivets popped loose, sailing down like bullets. The Eye was wildly unstable.

"Something has to contain it," Ling said.

"We've got to go," Sam said.

"We can't leave it like that," Ling insisted. "There's no telling what it could do."

They were connected. That was the one true beauty of Jake Marlowe's awful machine, and Marlowe never even saw it. They were connected, and so Evie knew what was in Jericho's heart before he said a word.

"Jericho, no."

"Someone has to, Evie." Jericho held out his hand. He squeezed his fingers, but try as he might, they would not close. "I can't make a fist."

"No. Jericho. We'll find another way."

"This *is* the way, Evie." He looked down at his trembling hand. "Look at that. I'm scared. Guess I'm mostly human after all."

"You don't have to do this," Evie kept insisting.

"Ling," Jericho said. "Ling, will you tell Lupe..." He swallowed hard. "Will you..."

Ling nodded. "I will."

"Evie," Jericho said.

"Yes?" She was crying.

"Don't waste it. Make a good life."

"Jericho!" Evie grabbed for him, but already he was running toward the Eye.

The land of the dead had fused with Ling and Henry's dreamscape. It was changing rapidly, atoms realigning and realities folding in on themselves.

"Hen! Make it stop!" Theta screamed.

"I can't! It has a will of its own now. We're connected to it. We've got to get out of here!"

"Memphis. The time is now," Theta said.

Memphis faced the great wound between worlds. It was so big. How could he possibly hope to heal such a rift? The King of Crows's words played in Memphis's head, stealing away his hope: *You gave away your power.*

And suddenly, Memphis realized: He *had* given away his power. *Willingly.* But not to the King of Crows. He'd given his power to Bessie Timmons to cure her typhoid, and to the Widow DeVille for her bad arm. To the Washingtons' baby with the croup, and to John Booker's broken leg. To Dutch Schultz's men and to his mother. And to Evie and Bill and Theta and Isaiah and all those hopeful faces showing up at the storefront church years before when he was the Harlem Healer. The King of Crows hoarded power; Memphis had shared it, and now, when he had need of it, that harvest had come up strong and fine inside him. This was his strength. All those people were within him—their atoms had become his atoms, a whole community carried forward, coming together now to heal the healer. He had not come here alone, and he had not come unarmed. He felt something new stirring within, rising up. Like standing in that wheat field the day the rains came, or in the wings of the Hotsy Totsy when the band was on fire. The healing power was coming on strong—stronger than before. Memphis was incandescent with energy. He burned as brightly as the Eye itself. Like the King of Crows, electrical sparks played at his fingertips, golden, bright, alive.

He placed his hands on the edge of the portal and felt it soften under his touch. Then he stood back and watched as his work took hold, spreading.

Healing.

THE ETERNAL RECURRENCE

As Jericho ran toward the rapidly devolving Eye, he heard whispers. It was like an ancestral memory playing out. As if all the stories collected here feared being obliterated, too. They were rising up around him, talking to him. Letting him know they were there.

How many times had Jericho read Nietzsche's passage on the eternal recurrence?

> *What, if some day or night a demon were to steal after you into your loneliest loneliness and say to you: "This life as you now live it and have lived it, you will have to live once more and innumerable times more; and there will be nothing new in it, but every pain and every joy and every thought and sigh and everything unutterably small or great in your life will have to return to you, all in the same succession and sequence—even this spider and this moonlight between the trees, and even this moment and I myself. The eternal hourglass of existence is turned upside down again and again, and you with it, speck of dust!"*
>
> *Would you not throw yourself down and gnash your teeth and curse the demon who spoke thus? Or have you once experienced a tremendous moment when you would have answered him: "You are a god and never have I heard anything more divine." If this thought gained possession of you, it would change you as you are or perhaps crush you. The question in each and every thing, "Do you desire this once more and innumerable times more?" would lie upon your actions as the greatest weight. Or how well disposed would you have to become to yourself and to life to crave*

> *nothing more fervently than this ultimate eternal confir-*
> *mation and seal?*

Jericho had reflected on that passage so many times. It had seemed to him a rebuke to any religious notion of living not for this world, but for the idea of the one after, a paradise that rejected all that was human: no strife or greed or want. No discovery or sudden joy. But if you abandoned the idea that such a paradise awaited you, and believed that you would live this life over and over again, would you not live the life you had more thoughtfully? Would you not think carefully about your choices? Would you not love with abandon—love and love and love some more?

Sergeant Leonard fell into step beside Jericho. He grinned. "Let's see how far we can take this ride, kid."

What makes a man? His choices. That was at the heart of an argument Jericho had been having with himself for many years.

The soldiers were gone, but the record still spun around and around on the Victrola, endless revolutions. It spun so fast that the song was lost to a whine. The Eye was breaking open, releasing all it held. Around Jericho, beautiful chaos unfolded. Atoms splitting, absorbing and releasing, throwing off particles. Jericho was in the middle of it. The machine had split apart and was re-forming around him. Jericho was inside the Eye and he was the Eye and he and the Eye were in decay, transforming, becoming energy.

Light punctured his hands.

His skin glowed like a Blake painting.

Jericho saw the land. And he saw the dead underneath the land. He saw them decomposing, their flesh sinking into the ground. The dead became the land. Nutrients for crops, which the living harvested and ate. The dead became the living until the living became the dead. An eternal recurrence. A circle. This was the oldest and most important story humankind told itself: that it could transcend death. All religion, all stories boiled down to this: We are born. We live. We struggle. We love. We search for meaning. We die. Again and again and again.

Sergeant Leonard took hold of Jericho's dissolving hand until they, too, were joined. Even at this last moment, Jericho was not alone.

There had been Sam and Will. Memphis and Isaiah, Ling and Henry and Theta. Lupe and Evie. There had been someone named Jericho, but none of that mattered now.

"Ready, kid?" Sergeant Leonard asked. He was coming apart and blowing into the wind.

Jericho opened his mouth, laughing, and the light came pouring out.

ANOTHER WAY

Under the moonless sky, Isaiah stirred in his mother's winged arms. "Mama, did you hear that?"

Viola hadn't heard anything but the constant murmurations of the dead. The night-song of the desiccated cicadas still chirped in the tall, brittle reeds sheltering Viola and her son.

"What did you hear, baby?"

"I heard somebody calling my name, Mama. I heard Memphis calling me." Isaiah pulled away and lifted his head, listening.

Viola tensed, listening, hearing nothing. What if it was some new trick cooked up by the King of Crows to hurt her baby all over again? With him here in her arms, maybe she had a chance to protect him. To ease him into this world of the dead with as little harm as possible. She would keep him hidden for as long as possible.

"Come here, baby. Rest," she said.

"Okay," Isaiah said, and lay back down in his mother's soft arms, just like a baby bird in a nest.

He was getting sleepy lying here. And it was getting harder to remember things from before. One by one, the memories were being plucked from inside him and carried away. Isaiah didn't like not remembering. He wanted to fight it. So he tried to fix just one memory hard in his head. He was thinking about the kittens under Sarah Beth's porch. There had been...how many? Isaiah thought and thought. Seven. There had been seven. He had a favorite among them. Ma...Mo...Mopsy! All at once, he saw Mopsy's sleepy little furred head. With that detail came the pain. Mr. Olson had drowned them. He had drowned them because he couldn't see another way.

"But there's always another way," Isaiah murmured, an idea fighting to come alive inside him.

"Shhh, baby," his mother soothed. "Rest."

"There's always another way," Isaiah said, a little louder.

Something else was coming back to him now. It traveled along his nerve endings and made his eyes roll back in their sockets.

"Isaiah!" his mother whispered urgently. "You can't use your power here. They'll find you if you do. Isaiah, please!"

Isaiah barely heard his mother's voice. The vision had also found another way. It had him now. For one brief moment, he could see his own future: Isaiah saw himself speaking from a great height, his voice echoing through a microphone to massive crowds. There was change in the air. And song. And the people lifted that song and carried it into the streets, arm in arm, and it was all possible. This future rippled through Isaiah's body, warm and hopeful, like bright sun on the longest day of summer. It felt like a beginning, of what, he could not say. But he saw it. He *saw* it. He had a future, and it needed him.

"I have to go back. I *want* to go back. I'm not done yet, Mama."

His mother looked sad. "Baby. There are some things you just can't change. You can't go back. *Those are the rules, son.*"

Isaiah looked down at his hand in his mother's. How he'd missed her. How he'd missed that hand on his back, that arm around his shoulders. Missed her nightly tuck-ins and glasses of water and gentle scoldings to *Get to sleep and I better not hear a peep from this room*. He was not asleep but awake now. Truth was shining through the windows of his soul, keeping him up.

Isaiah let go of his mother's hand. "Then I'm gonna change the rules, Mama. Watch me."

Isaiah began by walking, but soon enough, he was running. When the dead saw him moving among them like some new hope they had not been able to imagine, they parted to let him pass.

"Thank you," Isaiah said to them. Because he could feel them.

Some among them began to weep. *When we go, will we go to nothing? Will we become nothing forever?* they asked. And Isaiah knew that this frightened them. It had frightened him sometimes, too.

"My friend Ling says there's no such thing as nothing," Isaiah answered. *What will become of us, then?*

"You'll become stories we tell," Isaiah said. He looked behind him, over his shoulder. At the end of the row was his mother, and for one moment, he faltered. More than anything, he wanted to run back to the safety and warmth of her arms. She was the story he did not want to leave.

"Go, Isaiah," she said. "Change the future. I will be with you."

The whisper became a noise and then a chant, echoing through the land of the dead: *Isaiah. Isaiah. Isaiah.*

He ran forward.

❋

Isaiah knew where to find the King of Crows, because he'd seen it before, with Sarah Beth. The King sat sprawled across his throne of skulls with one long, skinny leg hitched over the bony arm the way Isaiah's mother would've fussed at him for doing, along with an admonishment to *Sit up straight and act right.* The King of Crows watched a patch of gray sky above his throne, where events of the nation's past played out like at a picture show. They were scary pictures of people doing terrible things to one another. Blood seeped into the land. Isaiah could feel it dripping down, being sucked up into the crops that the people ate, over and over. *There has to be another way,* Isaiah thought. He wanted to see his friends and his brother. He wanted that future he saw in his vision. The one that showed another way.

The King closed his hand into a fist, sat up straight at last, and faced Isaiah. "Ah. The little visionary come to visit. Our own Diviner Cassandra. Tell me. Have you come to make a bargain?"

Isaiah didn't know what the King of Crows meant by that, but he knew that the man in the hat wasn't to be trusted, so he said only, "I'm going back."

The King of Crows clapped his hands together and laughed as if Isaiah had told a good joke. He laughed the way his aunt Octavia used to do when she said she was "delighted." But Isaiah didn't think the King of Crows was delighted. Just a liar.

"I see," the King of Crows said in a tone of voice that made Isaiah mad. "And why should I let you live?"

"Because my story's not finished yet," Isaiah said.

"Is that so? Very well, then. But first, we'll need to play a game. Do you like games, Isaiah?"

"Some games."

"If you want to leave, you'll need to play a game with me. You'll need to make a bargain."

Isaiah was uncomfortable. He didn't know what the King of Crows was up to, but he also knew there was no chance of leaving without agreeing to his game. He was going to have to be brave. He was going to have to be smart. "Okay," Isaiah said. "I accept."

The King of Crows smiled and rose from his throne. His shadow fell across Isaiah as he strode toward him. The moon was yellow and leaking drips of sickly light. The diseased trees bore no fruit. Isaiah was afraid.

The King of Crows opened one side of his coat, and Isaiah saw that it was a blank gray slate of the sort they had in school. With his other hand, he gave Isaiah a piece of chalk. "Go on, then. Write yourself a new ending, and I'll let you go."

Isaiah bit his lip and stared at the slate. He did not trust the man in the hat.

"Wait! I want a condition of my own," Isaiah said.

"My. Making conditions now, are we? We *are* feeling our oats."

"You don't get to make all the rules," Isaiah shot back.

The King of Crows put his face right up to Isaiah's so that Isaiah could see the hatred swirling in those enormous dark pupils. And for a moment, Isaiah forgot everything except his fear. Because those were eyes that said, *Struggle, but you will never win*, and it made Isaiah feel so tired. "I made myself king. Never forget."

The King stepped back. From behind his throne he produced an hourglass. In one swift motion, he turned it over. Isaiah watched the sand pour down. It was going fast.

"Your time is now," the King of Crows said and opened his coat once more.

Isaiah tried to write on the slate, but no sooner would he get a few words down than the slate would erase them. New words would appear in their place. Words he had not written.

"That's no fair. You're cheating!" Isaiah yelled. He kept trying. Again and again, his words were erased and replaced. The sand rushed through. He was running out of time, and that made him panicky. But then he saw the look on the King of Crows's mottled face. Smug. Angry. He expected to win. It pricked at Isaiah. He couldn't beat him by these rules.

There's always another way.

Isaiah stared at the moving lining of the King's coat. Always moving. It was all happening inside the coat. That's what the man did; he would rewrite it until you couldn't find a way out. Until you were trapped in the story he wanted to tell. How did you unravel such a story? The same way you did a coat. You picked it apart, thread by thread.

Look inside. See what's really there.

"That's it. Look inside. What do you see? Do you see yourself in there, Little Man?"

Sarah Beth had said that the King of Crows's story was in there, too. And if you knew it, you could reveal the truth of him. But you had to be able to see through it all to what was really there. Isaiah frowned and touched his head. Sarah Beth had been a big liar. She'd stolen his magic.

Look beyond it. See what's really there. But the inside of the coat was so bright and blinding. And the sound! Like a million voices talking at once, with no space to think. It made him weak. He wanted to lie down and go to sleep for a long, long time. Fierce blue electricity sparked in an arc around the King of Crows, and Isaiah knew that Jake Marlowe's machine was working to join the worlds. They were connected, each side thinking it was winning. The King of Crows grew taller. Wider. He opened the other side of his coat, and it took on the appearance of a demon's wings, spreading out like a night that would never end. Isaiah had to think! What was it that Theta told them Miss Addie had said? The King of Crows could only take. He could not create. *See beyond to what's really there.* A memory fought against Isaiah's fear. He had plucked a feather from the King's fantastical coat once. Yes, he remembered that now! He'd given it to Evie to read. But she'd found nothing. No memories. No history. No family or friends. Just emptiness. Isaiah's heart sank at another dead end.

"Isaiah. My patience is growing short." The King of Crows's voice had deepened. It was everywhere. How could you fight against something that was everywhere? The coat was whispering to him, wrapping its lies around his neck like a heavy weight. It would not let him in. Isaiah's knees buckled. He wanted to lie down. Just lie down. Mama had said she would keep him safe. But that was as much of a lie as the song on the Victrola the soldiers had been listening to. No mama could keep you safe from this.

The sand was down to a thin coating of grains. He was losing. He would be trapped here forever, and the King of Crows would continue to bring misery and strife to the world.

See what's really there.

The King of Crows's voice boomed like cannon fire. It whistled past

Isaiah's ears and made him tremble. "Tell me, Isaiah Campbell, Seer of Visions, Teller of Truths, Diviner. What do you see written here? If you can truly see it, you're free to go."

Isaiah squinted against the glare and stared into the great abyss of the ever-changing coat. The feather he'd taken. The reading. The strange feeling he'd gotten from his visions about the man in the hat. As the last few grains slipped through the hourglass, it came to Isaiah. He stood tall and tilted his head back, looking up at the King of Crows looming over him like an eternal predator.

"Nothing," Isaiah said firmly. "There's nothing there but what you steal and make your own. You're just an empty coat."

The King of Crows's rictus smile twitched. His soulless eyes blinked. A single feather loosened itself from the outstretched wings. It drifted slowly down, and when it hit the ground, it shriveled into itself and blew away like dust. All the feathers fell then, like a rain of ash. Inside, the vein-like threads unstitched themselves. The coat was unraveling, thread by thread, feather by feather, lie by lie. The lining fell away, gone in a puff of smoke.

"No!" the King of Crows screamed. He tried desperately to hold the coat together, but it was hopeless. It was unwinding, twisting and tangling him up in its threads. The King of Crows screamed and cursed and cawed as his lies consumed him, until he was a scrabble of lines and squawking. Until, at last, he dissolved into nothingness. All that remained was a pile of feathers and, on the throne of skulls, the blank gray slate.

Isaiah stepped over the pile of feathers and approached the slate. He raised his chalk, scraping out the sentence he'd tried to write:

"Hello. My name is Isaiah Campbell."

The sentence remained. It thrilled Isaiah to see his words recorded there, like they were looking back at him, waiting for more.

"Isaiah."

Isaiah's mother stood among the dead. She wasn't covered in feathers anymore. Instead, she wore her favorite dress, the one she used to wear out dancing with his daddy. It was a royal purple, and it made her look like a queen.

"Mama?"

She waved to him. "Time to go, baby."

"Time to go!" This time, it was Memphis's clear, strong voice Isaiah heard.

Up ahead, Isaiah saw the breach between the worlds. But it was closing. Memphis had managed to heal it, just as he'd promised he would! This made Isaiah happy—until he realized he still had to get out of the land of the dead. Something else was happening, too. The trees were changing. The land was moving. Isaiah felt Jericho's presence. He was holding something back for Isaiah, but he couldn't hold it for long. There was a light getting brighter, like a star being born.

"Wait!" Isaiah called. He started moving toward the portal.

Around him, the dead called: "Go quickly. Don't look back."

Isaiah started running. As he ran, he felt within him the stirrings of his ancestors. As if he had drunk a powerful potion stirred with generations of dreams. He was bare-chested and barefooted, running across a fertile land, feet slapping against the rich earth of another continent. His soles hitting the ground with the same rhythm: *Free. Free. Free. Free.*

His feet showed him the way.

The stories his mother had carried here, the music of his father, they lived inside him.

They showed him the way.

The grandmothers were singing. The grandfathers, too.

They showed him the way.

He was from princes and kings.

They showed him the way.

He was from François Mackandal and his Maroons.

They showed him the way.

He was from the slaves who survived.

They showed him the way.

He was from Harlem. He was from Floyd's barbershop and the old men arguing. He was from Mother AME Zion Church on hot summer-Sunday mornings and the soft, cool breeze from Aunt Octavia's round straw fan. He was from his parents, Viola and Marvin, and a house that had been filled once upon a time with laughter and love. He was from the numbers runners taking dimes near the 125th Street subway stop. From jazz burbling out along Lenox Avenue with all the swells. From baseball played in the streets and the double-Dutch girls chanting over the rhythm of their one-two feet and neighbors on their stoops talking late into summer nights. He was from Harlem's great heart.

It showed him the way.

He was from his brother, Memphis, whom he missed more than anybody, and he was from the Diviners, the family he'd made along the way. He, Isaiah Campbell, was from the future that needed him. He was tomorrow.

He would show them the way.

Up ahead, at the edge of the nightmare, the portal between worlds was shrinking to a narrow doorway of blue. Within seconds, it would close, trapping him here in the land of the dead forever. But Isaiah was no longer afraid. He was carried by the hands of so many spirits, so many stories pushing him forward. He could hear their voices like a song getting louder and louder, letting him know there was a story and a song and a way. He opened his mouth and swallowed it down. It pierced the broken shell of his body. Came out in swords of light shining everywhere.

Isaiah smiled.

And then he leaped.

Silence.

Shadow.

And light.

HOPE ON THE ROAD

Where am I?
Am I alive?

Silence.
Then:

"Evil, that you?"
Theta! Yes, yes, it's me!
"Hiya."
Hiya.
"Princess, you okay?" Memphis's voice. Stronger than it had sounded before.
"Oh, Poet, I am now."
Sam? Where's Sam?

Silence.
Evie saw nothing yet. It was as if her atoms were still forming. Becoming something new.

"Henry, you better not have done something stupid like die." Ling being Ling.
And Henry's answer: "Miss Chan, looks like you're stuck with me for a while longer."

Sam. Where are you?

Evie's eyes fluttered open. The pale light hurt, and she had to blink several times. With each blink, a strange, alien landscape greeted her. It had no form she could discern just yet.
"Am I...are we...alive?" She'd said that out loud. She had a mouth.
"Yeah. I think so. My ribs hurt something fierce." Memphis.

Evie blinked. *Sam?* Ahead of her, the landscape took shape. The side of the crater. Death Valley. They'd made it back. Evie pushed herself onto her hands and knees. The upended helmet lay next to her, its wires mangled.

"Theta? Memphis?" she called.

So much smoke all around. It was hard to see, but she could make out the splintered debris of the Eye scattered all around a wide ring of scorched earth. A few remaining pieces still smoldered. Henry emerged from the haze. He was shuffling toward her, a dazed expression on his face.

"Henry! Over here," Evie said, staggering to her feet.

"A little help?" Ling. She was sprawled near the ruins of a chair. "Has anyone seen my crutches?"

Henry and Evie helped Ling up and shouldered her weight.

Evie looked up. The sky was no longer bothered by angry clouds. There was no trace of the breach, not even a scar to mark the spot. The day was beginning, a purplish pink hinting at blue.

Theta came out of the fog hoisting one of Ling's crutches. It was a bit bent, but still functional. "Sorry. I only found one," she said, handing it over. Evie moved and let Ling balance. "Anybody seen Memphis?" Theta asked.

Evie shook her head. It made her a little dizzy. "Anybody seen Sam?"

"Theta!"

"Memphis!"

Memphis ran to Theta, and they wrapped their arms around each other, holding tightly.

Evie felt a tiny surge of panic. "Sam? Sam Lloyd? Please, please, please answer me—"

"I'm here, Lamb Chop."

Tears sprang to Evie's eyes. "Sam?"

And then, there he was, just as he'd said he would be. He was smudged and his hair stood up in funny cowlicks, but he was there, and he was limping toward her. "Didn't I promise you I'd be here?"

Evie ran the best she could, and it seemed to her that their kiss would be the kiss she would remember for the rest of her days.

Evie wiped her eyes but it didn't seem to matter. "I was afraid I'd lose you."

Sam brushed his lips softly across her forehead and nuzzled her neck. "You'd never let me die when I owed you twenty bucks."

"Sam?"

"Let me guess—shut up?"

"No. No, talk to me. Keep talking to me."

"There'll be time," he said and kissed her again.

"We did it," Evie whispered.

"Little Fox!" Miriam called. She limped toward Sam. Freed from the Eye, she held her son tightly for the first time in nearly a decade. Evie stepped back, but Miriam pulled her close. "So you are the one my Sergei loves?" she said.

"*Ma*," Sam said, embarrassed.

The military men were already talking about what they'd witnessed. "Did you see? The energy was unlike any I'd ever seen before. Bright white light, and then that cloud came up from the ground like...like a giant mushroom! Mr. Marlowe—did you see that? Mr. Marlowe? Mr. Marlowe!"

Jake Marlowe lay on his back beside the ruins of his golden machine. His eyes were open, unseeing. In his hand was the shattered heart of the Eye. It was empty. Miriam Lubovitch looked down into Jake's lifeless eyes. She spat in his face.

"Jericho?" Evie said suddenly. She waited, hoping for an answer. The smoke was clearing, blown away by a morning breeze that reached down into the crater.

Jericho's chair remained.

He was no longer there.

Evie brushed her fingers across the chair's battered arms.

Two tears streamed down her face. "Oh, Jericho, Jericho."

"*Memphis?*"

Memphis thought he'd heard his name, but he couldn't be sure. Exhausted, half-delirious, grief-stricken, he was no longer sure of anything. But then he thought he heard it a second time. "*Memphis? Where are you?*"

He looked around wildly. "Isaiah? Isaiah?"

"Memphis! Memphis!"

The sound carried down into the crater and bounced off the sides, echoing, overlapping until it sounded like the call of seagulls. Memphis ran to the steep incline. "Isaiah?"

Memphis reached the top. Isaiah stood on the dusty road, blinking against the first rays of sun. He'd returned. He was alive and standing in the middle of the desert like hope.

Slowly, he smiled. "Hi, Memphis."

THE DEAD

The dead do not rest. Not really.

They hum in the air above the empty seat at the table.

They perch at the window, drawn to the light.

They make their peace with regret and wish that it, too, could be buried deep in the earth.

They walk across the battlefields of Antietam, Gettysburg, Fort McHenry, Wounded Knee. They watch as the people struggle to form a more perfect union and secure the blessings of liberty.

Sometimes their sins stretch like a shadow over those they have wronged.

Sometimes the kindnesses they planted bloom in the next generation.

And so on.

And so on.

And so…

We go on.

We are remembered, for a time.

All is ephemeral.

All is eternal.

The dead come to us however they can.

They are with us. Always.

Hear what they have to say:

You are the stories.

Make a better history.

EPILOGUE / PROLOGUE

The parade carried the great aviator up Fifth Avenue under a fusillade of paper streamers and ticker tape so thick it looked like snow in summer. American flags had been hung from high windows and balconies; they fluttered against the sides of buildings, a patriotic drapery. And why not? The aviator, Charles Augustus Lindbergh, was the nation's new favorite golden boy, a certified American hero. He'd done something remarkable, and for a moment, the people forgot all that had come before. Forgetting was a pastime as popular as baseball.

Through the windows of Goldberg's Delicatessen, over plates of the world's best pastrami-on-rye, Sam and Evie watched over the heads of the shouting, streamer-throwing crowd. They were hopeful they could catch at least a glimpse of the motorcade.

Evie grabbed for the binoculars on the table and took a look.

"Anything yet?" Sam asked. He seized the opportunity to steal three bites of her unattended coleslaw.

"No, just a lot of police on horses and old men in top hats," Evie said. She put the binoculars down and frowned. "Didn't I have more coleslaw than that?"

"Was I telling the truth about that sandwich?" Sam asked, wiggling his eyebrows.

"You were pos-i-tutely on the money. I could eat this every day for a week," Evie said and tucked into another generous bite.

The diner wasn't very crowded. Most people were outside on the streets, eager to cheer on the aviator, to feel like they were part of his triumph. Mrs. Goldberg fiddled with the radio on the diner's sparkling countertop so that the regulars who were there could hear the announcer's play-by-play of the parade.

"I used to be big on the radio, you know," Evie said to Sam nonchalantly.

"You don't say! Let me guess: the farm reports." Sam grinned and winked, and Evie burst into giggles.

"You should hear me read in cow," she said.

"You might not want to say that in front of the pastrami," Sam whispered.

A smiling Mrs. Goldberg stopped by their table. She was a soft, round woman with large brown eyes. "More coffee?" Her English still carried a faintly German accent. Sam had told Evie that Mr. and Mrs. Goldberg had emigrated to New York from Berlin. The rest of their family—aunts and uncles, parents, sisters and brothers—still lived in Germany, but, as Mrs. Goldberg had said, "New York is for me."

"Thanks, Mrs. Goldberg," Sam said.

"Maxie!" Mrs. Goldberg called across the cafe. "We have fresh coffee?"

"In a minute, in a minute, Fanny," Mr. Goldberg called back.

Mrs. Goldberg shook her head. "That man. We have been married twenty-five years last Tuesday. So. When is the big day?"

"As soon as she'll let me," Sam said and kissed Evie's hand, and it made Evie so happy she was afraid her happiness was a bird that might fly away.

"You'll come to see me after, right?" Mrs. Goldberg said.

"Yes. You can make us special wedding pastrami," Sam said.

"With extra coleslaw," Mrs. Goldberg said with a wink as she walked away.

Mrs. Sam Lloyd, Evie thought. And then, *Evie Lloyd*. And then, *Mrs. Evie O'Neill-Lloyd*, like British royalty. It would look very dignified on her calling cards. She'd mail a bunch of them back to the girls in Zenith. The pettiness of this warmed her.

"What are you smiling about?" Sam asked.

"Oh, nothing."

"Now I'm worried."

Through the diner's windows, Evie watched the parade and day-dreamed about a wedding at City Hall downtown, with Theta and Ling by her side. She thought of Mabel and felt the twinge in her heart. *I'm getting married, Mabesie*, she thought, and she wished that she could share the day with her best friend. She thought of James and Will, Woody, Bill, and Jericho. She could do nothing but face the future. She would live every day fully. She was not the same girl she'd been nearly a year ago. She would never see things so blithely again. Even now, as Evie watched the parade and the people alight with pride and joy, she knew how easily that same crowd could become angry. The things that divided them. The things that brought them together, too. They couldn't afford to become complacent.

Sam swiped the pickle from Evie's plate and took a big bite.

"I saw that!"

He offered her the bitten end. "You want I should give it back?"

Evie waved it away. "Go ahead. I don't want to smell like pickle juice anyway."

"Me? I've always liked your perfume, Baby Vamp. Well, look what the cat dragged in!" Sam got up to welcome Henry and Ling. Theta, Memphis, and Isaiah were right behind them. They made room at the table, and then room again, until everybody had a place and nobody was too squished.

"Mrs. Goldberg! I think we're gonna need more pastrami!" Sam called.

"Coming right up!"

It had been a few weeks since they'd been together in Death Valley. In that time, Woody's stories had been found, mysteriously, by a cleaning woman in Union Station in D.C. and printed in the *Daily News*. The whole ugly business of Project Buffalo and the Shadow Men had come to light. Sister Walker had been exonerated. So had the Diviners. A full pardon from President Coolidge himself. For some Americans, the late Jake Marlowe's reputation had been tarnished beyond repair. Others still clung to him as an icon. Nothing had happened to the wealthy men of the Founders Club. Their names stayed out of the press. They had enough money to make sure of it. There were even some people who were discrediting eugenics. People had begun fighting to have racial hygiene laws overturned.

There were still people who didn't trust the Diviners. It would always be that way, they knew. Debates had sprung up at town halls and school auditoriums across the country about what made somebody an American. Was it simply being born here? Was it an allegiance to a flag? Or was it something deeper and more fluid—finding common purpose, a commitment to democratic principles that said all were created equal, that great shared story?

"So. Are we going to be bridesmaids?" Theta asked.

"Of course! I couldn't get married without you and Ling by my side," Evie said.

"I've never been a bridesmaid," Ling said, and she seemed genuinely happy.

"I believe the phrase is 'always a bridesmaid, never a bride,'" Henry quipped.

Ling scowled. "What does that mean?"

"Ling, when does Alma get home?" Sam asked and sipped his coffee.

Ling smiled. "Day after tomorrow. She said she brought me a souvenir. I'm afraid it will be something with mayonnaise."

"Did...she talk to Lupe?" Evie asked gently.

Ling nodded, and for a moment everyone fell silent.

"I'm moving up to Harlem," Theta said, breaking the tension. She smiled at Memphis and Isaiah. "And I'm going to open a dance studio with Alma."

"That is pos-i-tutely the cat's meow!" Evie cheered.

"So long to the Bennington," Henry said.

"Hen. Tell 'em," Theta prompted.

"Paul Whiteman's orchestra wants to record one of my songs," Henry said.

"Why, Hen, that's wonderful!" Evie said.

"Apparently, he heard me playing at a little club on Fifty-second Street and he liked what he heard. David and I have already penned three more! Before long, we'll have our own catalog. Take that, Tin Pan Alley!"

"My parents are letting me enroll at Hunter College," Ling said. "I'll still work at the restaurant. But I'll be in college."

"Ling Chan, coed," Henry said.

"Professor Ling Chan," Ling said a little dreamily. "One day. One day. Oh, Henry, my mother wants to know when you're coming to our house for dinner," Ling said. "If I tell her you've got a song to be recorded, she'll be marrying us off."

"If it means your father's dumplings, I accept," Henry said.

They rejoiced in one another's good news.

They would be there for the bad as well.

"Memphis?" Evie asked. "What about you?"

Memphis was thoughtful. What had happened inside the rift and in the days before had dismantled him utterly. The Memphis who left the land of the dead was a different Memphis, the atoms Ling spoke of so often with reverence rearranged. They had not settled. He was vibrating at a new frequency. His Diviner power as he'd known it had left him after he'd healed the rift. But it was not gone so much as it had changed. He felt it now when he laid his hands upon the page. A healing of words and ideas. Every day, he went to the 135th Street Library to write until Mrs. Andrews teased that she might have to give him a job there. Memphis felt life all around him now. From the secretaries hurrying to their jobs in the big office buildings, humming with busyness, to the old men buying their cigars on the corner of

Lenox Avenue and 135th Street. The street sweepers and the beat cops, the shoeshine boys and the chorus girls. The cheerful drunks searching for god in the gutters, the little girls playing dress-up in newspapers but seeing them as silk gowns. The searchers. The strivers. The lost. The lonely. The hurting. The hopeful. He felt them all. And every dreamer who stepped outside to look up past the neon haze into the souls of stars watching them below. They were with him. They were all with him. Connected. On the way to see his friends, as the bus jostled its way downtown, Memphis had noticed a small sign propped against the window of a building on the West Side. Hand-painted, it read, simply: I BELIEVE IN THE VOICE OF TOMORROW.

"Memphis?" Evie prompted again, breaking his reverie.

"I don't know," Memphis said. He was no longer so easily defined. He was possibility. He was *becoming*. He smiled. "I don't know…yet."

"Yet," Evie echoed in sympathy.

"I'm gonna play baseball!" Isaiah said, nudging the conversation toward a kind of loose joy, a shifting of atoms again.

"So, uh, how are your powers?" Sam whispered.

Memphis shook his head slowly. "Just a little left. Enough to fix your bruise, maybe."

"I said *Don't see me* to a fella the other day and he looked right at me and said, 'What do you mean, don't see you?' I guess my pickpocketing days are truly behind me," Sam said.

"I picked up this saltshaker, and do you know what it told me?" Evie said.

Ling swallowed a bite of sandwich. "What?"

Evie put the shaker back down. "Pos-i-tutely nothing."

No more dream walking. No bursting into flames. No more ghosts.

"I don't see so much anymore. Just little things here and there," Isaiah said with a shrug.

That was about all the future anybody should probably see, Evie thought.

The powers that Project Buffalo had forced on them were fading away. What remained was all they had been through together. They could still feel one another, still sense one another's moods and hurts. What remained was friendship. What remained was love. It was, they knew, their greatest power.

Mrs. Goldberg fiddled with the radio until a flood of German poured out.

"Whatcha listening to, Mrs. G?" Sam asked.

"A political rally in Nuremberg," she answered tightly.

It was astonishing that a wire was picking up this sound in Germany and carrying it via a transatlantic cable all the way to this deli in New York City, as if the world were so easily connected, all one big ball. It didn't hurt that Sam and Evie had used some of the last dregs of their Diviner power to soup up the Goldbergs' radio so they could listen to news and music from back home.

The man on the radio was shouting. He sounded very angry. When he paused, the crowd responded with chants. Mr. Goldberg had stepped out from the kitchen. He was listening to the angry, shouting man. Listening to the people clamoring for him. He came to Mrs. Goldberg's side. Evie watched as the couple clasped hands. They did this without a word, almost without thought, she could see. It was instinctual, animal. They were frightened, and they each sought comfort from the other.

"Do you know what he's saying?" Evie asked her friends.

"Beats me. I don't speak German," Theta said.

Behind the counter, the Goldbergs stood perfectly still. Outside, there were ripples of excitement. The noise began to swell. The aviator was approaching. The Diviners kept their eyes on the Goldbergs, who, in turn, watched the radio as if it needed watching, as if it might become a monster they could not stop. Evie listened closely to the German chants coming through the radio speakers. That crowd was getting louder, too. And though she didn't know German, it made her uneasy all the same. She sensed the fury underneath it. Seeds of evil. Growing. Metastasizing. The chant repeated several times, and she began to pick out the words being shouted over and over again: *"Heil Hitler. Heil Hitler. Heil Hitler."*

Mrs. Goldberg looked into her husband's eyes. "Max?" she said, worried.

Out on the street, the motorcade drove by at last, below balconies draped in red, white, and blue. The hero lifted his arm in acknowledgment of the crowd. The citizens screamed, and the cheer became a roar.

Author's Note

This is a work of fiction, and as such, certain liberties have been taken in order to "make it work" (thank you, Tim Gunn), starting with the fact that, as far as I know, there are no supernatural entities roaming the streets of New York. Well, other than the subway rats. But that's another story. Timelines have been conflated here and there. For example, Charles Lindbergh's New York City ticker tape parade happened in June of 1927, but Hitler's Nuremberg rally—arguably the beginning of the rise of the Nazi Party—happened in August of 1927. But while this is a work of fiction, it incorporates aspects of our very real history: the KKK, the American eugenics movement, Fitter Families tents, Jim Crow laws, xenophobia, the racial injustice and government-sanctioned abuse enacted upon African Americans caught up in the tragedy of the Great Mississippi Flood—abuses of power that victimized them twice. All of that is true. It continues to haunt us today.

It has taken me nearly ten years to write this series. When I started, all I knew was that I wanted to tell an American ghost story. I had no idea where that story would take me, or that the writing of it would coincide with such a tumultuous and divisive period in America, one containing within it the echoes of our unresolved, often unacknowledged past. I believe that with every book we write, we are changed, but nothing I've written has so fundamentally challenged and changed me as the Diviners has. The necessary research involved in the writing of this series forced me into an unavoidable, often uncomfortable dialogue with my identity as a white American. It forced me to understand how hundreds of years of white supremacy in this country have created a distorted lens on race and actively suppressed narratives from the marginalized whenever those stories proved inconvenient for this hegemonic viewpoint. It forced me to understand how every time there was a push toward greater equality for all Americans, especially Americans of color, there was a power play by white America not only to impede that progress but to reassert dominance and reestablish oppression through everything from perception-shaping to laws—and the criminal justice system entrusted to enforce those laws—to acts of inhuman violence. It has forced me to grapple with how easy it is to be complicit if we don't interrogate ourselves about our false inheritance.

It has made me think about the mythmaking we do, both as a country and as individuals going about our daily lives. The way the narratives we create can be used to obfuscate facts, to manipulate a populace, or to allow ourselves deniability of wrongs; the way narrative—especially the stories of those who have lived these injustices firsthand—can be used to bring truth into the open. Story is powerful. I believe we can write a better one together going forward. But only if we are willing to truly see and reckon with our ghosts. And we are surrounded by them. They are there on the prairies where the buffalo once roamed, where the subdivisions and chain stores now spread out against the frayed horizon. They are there in the ports where the auction blocks stood and on the hills where the "witches" were hanged. They are there on the Trail of Tears and on the edges of the reservations. They are there in the shadows, trying to move into the light. They are with us always. They are talking to us.

It's up to us to listen.